Also by Leonardo Padura

Heretics

HERETICS

Leonardo Padura

Translated from the Spanish by Anna Kushner

Farrar, Straus and Giroux   New York

Farrar, Straus and Giroux
18 West 18th Street, New York 10011

Library of Congress Cataloging-in-Publication Data
Names: Padura, Leonardo, author. | Kushner, Anna, translator.
Title: Heretics / Leonardo Padura.
Other titles: Herejes. English
Description: First American edition. | New York : Farrar, Straus and Giroux, 2017. |
    Translated by Anna Kushner.
Identifiers: LCCN 2016025617 | ISBN 9780374168858 (hardback) |
    ISBN 9780374714284 (e-book)
Subjects: LCSH: Jewish refugees—Germany—Fiction. | Art thefts—Investigation—
    Fiction. | Conde, Mario—Fiction. | Private investigators—Cuba—Havana—
    Fiction. | BISAC: FICTION / Literary. | FICTION / Historical. | GSAFD:
    Detective and mystery stories, Cuban. | Historical fiction.
Classification: LCC PQ7390.P32 H4713 2017 | DDC 863/.64—dc23
LC record available at https://lccn.loc.gov/2016025617dfd

APR 2 6 2017Designed by Jonathan D. Lippincott

www.fsgbooks.com
www.twitter.com/fsgbooks • www.facebook.com/fsgbooks

1 3 5 7 9 10 8 6 4 2

Once again for Lucía, the leader of the tribe

There are artists who only feel safe when they are free, but there are also such as can breathe freely only when they are secure.

—Arnold Hauser

Everything is in the hands of God, except the fear of God.

—The Talmud

Whoever has reflected on these four things would have done better not coming into the world: What is above us? What is below us? What came before? What will come after? —Rabbinical maxim

HERETIC. From the Greek αἱρετικός—hairetikós—adjective derived from the noun αἵρεσις—haíresis, "division, choice," coming from the verb αἱρεῖσθαι—haireísthai, **"to choose, to divide, to prefer,"** originally to define people belonging to other schools of thought, in other words, who have certain "preferences" in that area. The term comes to be associated for the first time with those dissident Christians in the early Church in the treatise of Irenaeus of Lyon, *Adversus haereses* (*Against Heresies*, end of second century), especially against Gnostics. It probably derives from the Indo-European root *ser* with the meaning "to seize." In Hittite, the word *šaru* is found, and in Welsh *herw*, both with the meaning "booty."

According to the *Diccionario de la Real Academia de la Lengua Española*: HERETIC. (From the Provençal *eretge*). 1. Common. A person who denies any of the dogmas established by a religion. ╢2. A person who dissents or moves away from the official line of opinion followed by an institution, an organization, an academy, etc. . . . . Colloquial. *Cuba*. **To describe a situation: [To be a heretic] To be very difficult, especially in political or economic aspects.**

Contents

Author's Note

Many of the episodes narrated in this book are based on exhaustive historical research and were even derived from primary sources, including *Abyss of Despair* (*Le fond de l'abîme*) by N. N. Hanover, a shocking and vivid testimony of the horrors of the slaughter of Jews in Poland between 1648 and 1653, written with such a capacity to unsettle the reader that, with the necessary cuts and edits, I decided to incorporate it into the novel, rounding it out with fictional characters. Ever since reading that text, I knew I would not be able to better describe the same explosion of horror and, less still, to imagine the depths of sadism and perversion reached in the reality that the chronicler witnessed and described shortly after.

But since this is a novel, some of the historical events have been submitted to the demands of plot development in the interest of, I repeat, their novelistic use. Perhaps the passage in which I carry out this exercise most vehemently is the one with events taking place in the 1640s, which in reality constitutes a sum of events relating to the moment, mixed with incidents from the following decade, like the excommunication of Baruch Spinoza, the pilgrimage by the supposed Messiah Sabbatai Zevi, or Menasseh ben Israel's voyage to London in which he achieved, in 1655, Cromwell and English parliament's tacit approval of the presence of Jews in England, who soon began to settle there . . .

In later passages there is a strict respect for historical chronology, with minor alterations in the biographies of some characters taken from real life. Because history, reality, and novels run on different engines.

Book of Daniel

1

Havana, 1939

It would take Daniel Kaminsky many years to grow accustomed to the exuberant sounds of a city built on the most unwieldy commotion. He had quickly discovered that everything there began and ended with yelling, everything sputtered with rust and humidity, cars moved forward amid the wheezing and banging of engines or the long beeping of horns, dogs barked with and without reason and roosters even crowed at midnight, while each vendor made himself known with a toot, a bell, a trumpet, a whistle, a rattle, a flageolet, a melody in perfect pitch, or, simply, a shriek. He had run aground in a city in which, on top of it all, each night, at nine on the dot, cannon fire roared without any declaration of war or city gates to close, and where, in good times and bad, you always, always heard music, and not just that, singing.

At the beginning of his Havana life, the boy would often try to evoke, as much as his scarcely-filled-with-memories mind would allow, the thick silences of the Jewish bourgeois neighborhood in Kraków where he had been born and lived his early days. He pursued that cold, rose-colored land of the past intuitively from the depths of his rootlessness; but when his memories, real or imagined, touched down on the firm ground of reality, he immediately reacted and tried to escape it. In the dark, silent Kraków of his infancy, too much noise could mean only two things: it was either market day or there was some imminent danger. In the final years of his Polish existence, danger grew to be more common than merchants. So fear became a constant companion.

As expected, when Daniel Kaminsky landed in the raucous city, for a long time he would process the pounding of that explosive, resounding environment, one alarm bell after another, until, with the passing of years, he managed to understand that, in this new world, silence tended to herald only the most dangerous things. Once he overcame that phase, when he finally came to live amid the noise without hearing the noise, the way one breathes without consciousness of each breath, young Daniel discovered that he had lost his ability to appreciate the beneficent qualities of silence. But he would boast, above all, of having managed to make peace with Havana's racket, since, at the same time, he'd attained the stubborn goal of feeling like he belonged to that turbulent city where, lucky for him, he had been spit out by the wave of a curse of history or of the divine—and until the end of his days he would wonder which of these was more accurate.

The day on which Daniel Kaminsky began to experience the worst nightmare of his life, and simultaneously to get the first hint of his privileged fate, an overwhelming ocean smell and an ungodly, almost physical silence hung over Havana in the wee hours of the morning. His uncle Joseph had woken him earlier than he usually did to send him to Hebrew school at the Israelite Center, where the boy was receiving academic and religious instruction in addition to the essential Spanish language lessons that would allow for his integration into the motley and diverse world where he would live only God knew for how long. But the day revealed itself as different when, after having imparted the Sabbath blessing and expressed his best wishes for Shavuot, his uncle broke with his usual restraint and kissed the boy on the forehead.

Uncle Joseph, also a Kaminsky and, of course, also Polish, had by then taken to being called Pepe the Purseman—thanks to the masterful way he carried out his work as a maker of bags, billfolds, and purses, among other leather goods—and was always, and would be until his death, a strict follower of the precepts of the Jewish religion. As such, before letting him taste the awaited breakfast already laid out on the table, he reminded the boy that they should not merely do the customary ablutions and prayers of a very special morning, since it was God's will, blessed be, that Shavuot—the great ancient festival commemorating the giving of the Ten Commandments to the patriarch Moses, and the joyous acceptance of the Torah by the nation's founders—fell on the Sabbath. They should also offer up prayers to their God that morning, as his uncle reminded him in his speech, asking for His divine intervention in helping them resolve in the best possible way something that seemed to have become complicated in the worst way. Although the complications may not apply to them, he added, smiling mischievously.

After almost an hour of prayers, during which Daniel thought he would faint from hunger and fatigue, Joseph Kaminsky finally signaled that his nephew could help himself to the abundant breakfast featuring warm goat's milk (which, since it was Saturday, the Roman and apostolic María Perupatto, an Italian woman chosen by his uncle as the "Sabbath goy," had left on the burning coals of their portable cooker), the square crackers called *matzot*, fruit jams, and even a fair amount of baklava dripping in honey. The feast would make the boy ask himself where his uncle found the money for such luxuries, since what Daniel Kaminsky would always remember of those days, for the rest of his long years on earth—besides the torment caused by the surrounding noise and the horrible week that followed—was the insatiable and unending hunger that nagged at him like the most loyal dog.

Filled with such a sumptuous and unusual breakfast, the boy took advantage of his constipated uncle's delayed trip to the communal bathroom of the phalanstery where they lived to go up to the building's rooftop. The tile was still wet with dew in those hours prior to sunrise and, defying all prohibitions, he dared to lean over the eaves to con-template the panorama of Compostela and Acosta Streets, the heart of Havana's growing Jewish population. The unkempt Ministry of the Inte-rior building, an old Catholic convent from the colonial era, remained closed under lock and key as if it were dead. Under the contiguous ar-cade, the so-called Arco de Belén below which Calle Acosta ran, not a single being walked. Ideal Movie Theater, the German bakery, the Polish hardware store, Moshé Pipik's restaurant (which the boy's appetite con-sidered the world's greatest temptation)—all had their curtains drawn and darkened windows. Although many Jews lived around there, and as such, the majority of the businesses were Jewish-run and in some cases remained closed every Saturday, the reigning calm was not only due to the hour or to the fact that it was the Sabbath, Shavuot day, synagogue day, but also because at that instant, while Cubans slept the day away, the majority of the area's Ashkenazi and Sephardic Jews were picking out their best clothes and getting ready to go out with the same purpose as the Kaminskys.

The silence of the wee hours, his uncle's kiss, the unexpected break-fast, and even the happy coincidence that Shavuot fell on Saturday had really only come to confirm Daniel Kaminsky's childish expectation of the day ahead. Because the reason for his early start was that, at Havana's port, at some point around sunrise, the arrival was expected of the passenger ship the S.S. *Saint Louis*, which had set sail from Hamburg fifteen days prior and aboard which traveled 937 Jews authorized to emigrate by the German National Socialist government. And amid the *Saint Louis*'s passengers were Dr. Isaiah Kaminsky, his wife, Esther Kellerstein, and their small daughter, Judith—in other words, little Daniel Kaminsky's father, mother, and sister.

2

Havana, 2007

From the moment he opened his eyes, even before he managed to re-cover his dilapidated consciousness, still soaked in the cheap rum that marked his night with Tamara—because it was Tamara, who else would it be, sleeping beside him—a treacherous feeling of defeat stabbed Mario Conde as it had been doing for far too long already. Why get up? *What could he do with his day?* the nagging feeling asked him. Conde didn't know what to say in response. Overwhelmed by the inability to answer himself, he left the bed, careful not to disturb the woman's placid dreams, as a silvery thread of drool escaped from her half-open mouth along with an almost musical snore, higher-pitched perhaps because of the secre-tion itself.

At the kitchen table, after drinking a cup of freshly made coffee and lighting the first of the day's cigarettes that helped him so much to re-gain the dubious condition of rationality, the man looked through the back door, where the first light shone of what threatened to be another hot September day. His lack of prospects was so glaring that at that moment he decided to face it the best way he knew and the only way he could: full-on and in fighting mode.

An hour and a half later, sweat pouring out of his pores, the very same Mario Conde was running around the streets of the Cerro neighbor-hood announcing his desperate aim like a medieval merchant. "I buy old books! Come on and sell your old books!"

Ever since he had left the police force, almost twenty years before, and as a saving grace taken up the very touchy but profitable exercise of buying and selling used books, Conde had played all the roles he could in that business: from the old-fashioned method of a street vendor announcing his wares (which for a time hurt his pride so) to specifically seeking out libraries a former client or some informant noted, or even to that of knocking door-to-door on houses in el Vedado and Miramar, which, due to some characteristic that passed unremarked by others (an unkempt garden, windows with broken glass), suggested the possible existence of books and, above all, the need to sell them. Lucky for him, when he met Yoyi the Pigeon, that young man with an enormous knack for business, a while later, and started to work with him in search of only select bibliographies for which Yoyi always had so many specific buyers, Conde started to experience a period of financial prosperity that lasted several years and allowed him to pursue, almost without constraint, activities that gave him the most satisfaction in life: reading good books and eating, drinking, listening to music, and philosophizing (talking shit, really) with his oldest and closest friends.

But his commercial activities didn't have infinite potential. For the last three or four years since stumbling upon the Montes de Oca family's fabulous library, sealed and protected by siblings Dionisio and Amalia Ferrero, he had not found another collection that extraordinary, and each request made by Yoyi's demanding buyers required a great effort to meet. The terrain, increasingly mined, had become cracked, like the earth after a long drought, and Conde had begun to live through times in which the lows were much more frequent than the highs, thus forcing him to hit the streets more frequently in this sweaty, poor man's way.

Another hour and a half later, when he had crossed part of the Cerro neighborhood and taken his shouts to the neighboring Palatino, without any result whatsoever, fatigue, laziness, and the harsh September sun forced him to shut down for the day and climb aboard a bus that came from God knew where and that miraculously stopped in front of him and carried him close to his business partner's house.

Yoyi the Pigeon, in contrast to Conde, was an entrepreneur with vision and had diversified his activities. Rare, expensive books were just one of his hobbies, he maintained, since his real interest was in more lucrative matters: the buying and selling of houses, cars, jewels, valuable objects. That young engineer who had never touched a screw or entered any job sites had long ago discovered, with a clairvoyance that always surprised Conde, that the country where they lived was far from the

paradise painted by newspapers and official speeches, and he had decided, as the most adept do, to turn misery to his advantage. His skills
and intelligence enabled him to establish himself on many fronts, on
the borders of what was legal, although not too far from the limits, in
businesses that made him enough money to live like a prince, restaurant-
hopping in designer clothing and gold jewelry, always in the company of
beautiful women as they traveled in his 1957 convertible Chevy Bel
Air, the car that anyone in the know considered to be the most perfect,
enduring, comfortable, and elegant ride ever to come out of an American
factory—and for which the young man had paid a fortune, at least in Cuban terms. Yoyi was, in effect, the prototype taken from the catalog of the
New Man eked out by the reality of the moment: aloof from politics, addicted to the ostentatious enjoyment of life, bearer of a utilitarian morality.

"Son of a bitch, man, you look like shit," the young man said when
Conde showed up, sweaty and with a face described so aptly semanti-
cally and scatologically.

The recent arrival merely said, "Thanks," and fell onto the springy
sofa, where Yoyi, freshly showered after having spent two hours at a
private gym, was whiling the time away watching a Major League Baseball game on his fifty-two-inch plasma TV.

As usual, Yoyi invited him to have lunch. The cook who worked for
the young man had made cod à la Biscay, black beans and rice, plantains
en tentación, and a salad full of several vegetables that Conde devoured
hungrily and avidly, with the aid of a bottle of reserve Pesquera that Yoyi
brought out of the special refrigerator where he kept his wines at the
right temperature as required by the heat of the tropics.

As they drank their coffee on the terrace, Conde again felt the stab
of the overwhelming frustration hounding him.

"There's no more to be had, Yoyi. People don't even have old newspapers around anymore . . ."

"Something always turns up, man. You can't lose hope," Yoyi said as he
sucked, as he usually did, on the huge gold medallion with the Virgin
Mary that hung on the thick chain made of the same metal over his
puffed-out pectorals, like the pigeon's breast that gave him his nickname.

"So if I don't lose hope, what in the hell do I do?"

"I can sense in the air that something big is coming down," Yoyi said,
and even sniffed at the warm September air. "And your pockets will fill
up with pesos . . ."

Conde was aware of where those sensory premonitions of Yoyi's would lead and was ashamed of knowing that he had stopped by the young man's house to prompt them. But there was so little of his former pride left standing that, when he felt too pinched for cash, he went there with his complaints. At fifty-four years old, Conde knew he was a paradigmatic member of what years before he and his friends had deemed to be the hidden generation, those aging and defeated beings who, unable to leave their lairs, had evolved (involved, actually) into the most disappointed and fucked-up generation within the new country that was taking shape. Without the energy or the youth to recycle themselves as art vendors or the managers of foreign corporations, or at least as plumbers or bakers, their only recourse was to resist as survivors. Thus, while some subsisted on the dollars sent by their children who had gone off to anywhere in the world but there, others tried to do what they could to avoid falling into absolute poverty or jail: work as private tutors, drivers who rented out their battered cars, self-employed veterinarians or masseuses, whatever came up. But the option to make a living clawing at the walls wasn't easy and caused that stellar exhaustion, the feeling of constant uncertainty and irreversible defeat that frequently gripped the former policeman and drove him, with one rough push, against his will and desires to hit the streets looking for old books that would earn him, at least, a few pesos to survive.

After drinking coffee, smoking a couple of cigarettes, and talking about life, Yoyi emitted a yawn that could have shaken the whole building and told Conde that the time had arrived for a siesta, the only decent activity that any Havana man who was proud of being so could engage in at that hour and in that heat.

"Don't worry, I'm leaving . . ."

"You're not going anywhere, *man*," he said, emphasizing this pet word of his in particular. "Grab the cot that's in the garage and take it to the bedroom. I had the air conditioner turned on a while ago . . . Naps are sacred . . . I have to go out later, I'll take you home."

Conde, who had nothing better to do, obeyed the Pigeon. Although he was about twenty years older than the young man, he tended to trust Yoyi's wisdom on life. It was true that after that cod and the Pesquera he had drunk, a nap imposed itself like a command dictated by the tropical geographic fatalism and its best Iberian legacy.

Three hours later, in the shining Chevy convertible that Yoyi proudly drove down Havana's potholed streets, the two men were headed to Conde's neighborhood. Shortly before arriving at the former policeman's house, Conde asked Yoyi to stop.

"Drop me off at the corner, there's something I need to deal with there . . ."

Yoyi the Pigeon smiled and started to pull the car over to the curb.

"In front of Bar of the Hopeless?" Yoyi asked, knowing the needs and weaknesses of Conde and his soul.

"Around there."

"Do you still have money?"

"More or less. The funds for book purchasing." Conde repeated the formula and, to take his leave, held out his hand to the young man, who firmly shook it. "Thanks for lunch, the nap, and the boost."

"Look, man, take this anyway, so you can get a leg up." From behind the Chevy's wheel, the young man counted several bills from the stack he had taken out of his pocket and handed some to Conde. "A little advance on the good business deal I'm sensing."

Conde looked at Yoyi and, without too much thought, took the money. It wasn't the first time that something similar had happened, and ever since the young man had started to talk about sensing a good business opportunity, Conde had known that would mark their goodbye. And he also knew that, even though the relationship between them had been born from a commercial connection to which each brought his own skills, Yoyi truly valued him. Because of this, his pride didn't feel any more damaged than it already was by accepting some bills that would give him some breathing room.

"You know something, Yoyi? You are the nicest son of a bitch in Cuba."

Yoyi smiled as he stroked the enormous gold medal on his breastbone.

"Don't go around saying that, man . . . If they find out I'm also a nice guy, it will ruin my reputation. See you!" And he drove off in the silent Bel Air. The car moved forward as if it were king of the road. Or the world.

Mario Conde looked at the heartbreaking scene before him and noticed sharply how what he saw painfully brought down his pitiful mood. That corner had been part of the heart of his neighborhood and now it looked like an oozing pimple. Overcome by perverse nostalgia, he remembered when he was a boy and his grandfather Rufino taught him the art of training fighting cocks and tried to impart a sentimental education adequate for surviving in a world that looked very much like a cockfighting arena. He found himself this afternoon at that exact spot where his education had taken place, and from there he could see the constant to-and-fro of the neighborhood's well-known bus terminal where his father had worked for years. But, with the bus lines now out of service, the building was rotting like a battered parking lot in its death throes. Meanwhile, Conchita's food joint, Porfirio's sugarcane-juice counter, Pancho Mentira and the Albino's *frita* stands, Nenita's hardware store, Wildo and Chilo's barbershops, the bus stop cafeteria, Miguel's chicken place, Nardo and Manolo's bodega, Lefty's cafeteria, the Chinese shop, the furniture store, the shoe store, the two auto body shops with their tires and car-washing areas, the billiards hall, La Ceiba bakery with the way it smelled like life itself . . . all of that had also disappeared, as if swallowed whole by a tsunami or something even worse, and the image of it all survived by only a small margin in the stubborn minds of guys like Conde. Now, flanked by streets full of holes and broken sidewalks, one of the service station buildings had started operating as a cafeteria where junk was sold in CUCs, the dodgy Cuban national currency. There was nothing at the other service station, and in the place that used to be Nardo and Manolo's bodega—made over so many times that the original had been both diminished and given a new life—protected from possible robbery by pirates and corsairs by a fence of corrugated steel screws, there was a tiny bar facing Calzada that served as the local alcohol and nicotine dispensing center, baptized by Conde as the Bar of the Hopeless. It was there, and not at the CUC-charging cafeteria, where the neighborhood's drunks drank their cheap rum any time of day or night, without so much as an ice cube, while standing or sitting on the sticky floor, fighting with stray dogs for their spots.

Conde edged his way around some dark puddles and crossed Calzada. He approached the prison fence erected over the new bar. His thirst for alcohol that afternoon wasn't the worst he'd felt, but he needed to quench it. And Gandinga the bartender, "Gandi" to the regulars, was there to receive him.

Two stiff drinks and two long hours later, after showering and even applying German cologne that had been a gift from Aymara, Tamara's twin sister, Conde went back out. In a small bowl next to the kitchen's open trapdoor, he had left food for Garbage II, who, despite having turned ten already, persisted in his inherited predilection for living like a stray dog, one never renounced by his father, the noble and deceased

Garbage I. For himself, however, he hadn't prepared a thing: like almost every night, Josefina, his friend Carlos's mother, had invited him over for dinner and, in that case, it was best to have the maximum amount of space available in his stomach. With the two bottles of rum that, thanks to Yoyi's generosity, he had been able to buy at the Bar of the Hopeless, he boarded the bus and, despite the heat, the promiscuous behavior, the auditory and moral violence of reggaeton, and the reigning feeling of suffocation, the prospect of a better night led him to realize that he was again feeling acceptably calm, almost outside the world in which he found so much dissatisfaction and received so many blows.

Spending the night with his old friends at the house of Skinny Carlos, who had long since ceased to be skinny, was, for Mario Conde, the best way to end the day. The second best way was when, by mutual agreement, he and Tamara decided to spend the night together, watching some of Conde's favorite movies—something like *Chinatown, Cinema Paradiso,* or *The Maltese Falcon,* or Ettore Scola's ever squalid and moving *We All Loved Each Other So Much,* with that Stefania Sandrelli, who could awaken your cannibal instincts—and then ending the day with a roll in the hay that was slower and less feverish each time, but always deeply satisfying. Those small revelations amounted to the best he had to show for a life that, with all the years and blows accumulated, had lost all ambitions except those related to mere survival in its basest form. Because he had given up, he had even shed the dream of one day writing a novel in which he told a story—squalid and moving, naturally—like the ones written by Salinger, that son of a bitch who had to be about to die already, surely without publishing even one more miserable little story.

It was only in the realm of those worlds stubbornly maintained at the margins of real time, and around the borders of which Conde and his friends had raised the highest walls to keep out invading barbarians, where friendly and permanent universes existed that none of them, despite how much they changed physically or mentally, wanted to or attempted to renounce: the worlds with which they identified and where they felt like wax statues, nearly immune to the disasters and ills of their environment.

Skinny Carlos, Rabbit, and Candito the Red were already talking on the porch. For a few months already, Carlos had had a new electric wheelchair that was battery-operated. The device had been brought from the

Great Beyond by the ever faithful and attentive Dulcita, Skinny's most loyal ex-girlfriend, exceedingly loyal since she became a widow a year earlier and started doubling the frequency of her trips from Miami and lengthening her stays on the island for an obvious reason, although she wouldn't publicly say so.

"Have you seen what time it is, you animal?" was Skinny's greeting as he set his automatic chair in motion to approach Conde and grab the bag where, he well knew, was the necessary fuel to get the evening going.

"Don't fuck with me, you brute, it's eight thirty . . . What's up, Rabbit? How's it going, Red?" he said, shaking his other friends' hands.

"Fucked-up, but happy," Rabbit replied.

"Same as this guy," Candito said, using his chin to point at Rabbit, "but no complaints. Because when I think of complaining, I pray a little."

Conde smiled. Ever since Candito had abandoned the frenetic activities to which he devoted himself for years—head of a clandestine bar, maker of shoes with stolen materials, administrator of an illegal gas depot—and had converted to Protestantism (Conde never really knew which denomination), that *mulato* of once saffron-colored hair now turned white with the snows of time, as the saying goes, tended to solve his problems by handing them over to God.

"One of these days, I'm going to ask you to baptize me, Red," Conde said. "The problem is that I'm so fucked that I'm going to have to spend all day praying after."

Carlos returned to the porch with his automatic chair and a tray on his inert legs where three glasses full of rum and one of lemonade clinked. As he distributed the drinks—the lemonade, of course, was Candito's—he explained, "My old lady is finishing up with the food."

"So what's Josefina going to hit us with today?" Rabbit wanted to know.

"She says things are bad and that she was lacking inspiration."

"Get ready!" Conde warned, imagining what was coming.

"Since it's so hot," Carlos began, "she's going to start with a chickpea soup, with chorizo, blood sausage, some chunks of pork and potatoes . . . The main dish she's making is baked snapper, but it's not that big, about ten pounds. And, of course, rice, but with vegetables, for easy digestion, she says. She already prepared the avocado salad, beans, turnips, and tomatoes."

"So what's for dessert?" Rabbit was drooling like a rabid dog.

"The same as usual: guava peels with white cheese. You see how she lacked inspiration?"

"Dammit, Skinny, is that woman a magician?" asked Candito, whose great capacity for belief, even in the intangible, appeared to have been exceeded.

"Didn't you know?" Conde cried out and lowered his glass of rum. "Don't play dumb, Candito, don't play dumb!"

———

"Mario Conde?"

As soon as the question came from the behemoth with a ponytail, Conde started to do the count in his head: it had been years since he had cheated on anyone, his book business had always been as clean as business could be, he only owed Yoyi money . . . and it had been too long since he'd stopped being a policeman for someone to come after him now in revenge. When he added the hopeful as opposed to aggressive tone of the question to his calculations, along with the man's facial expression, he was a little more confident that the stranger, at least, didn't seem to have come with the intention to kill him or beat him up.

"Yes . . ."

The man had risen from one of the old and poorly painted chairs that Conde had on the porch of his house and that, despite their sorry state, the former policeman had chained together and to a column in order to make difficult any attempt to move them from their place. In the shadows, only broken by a streetlight—the last lightbulb Conde placed on his porch had been switched to some other lamp one night when, too drunk to think about lightbulbs, he had forgotten to change it back—he was able to form his first impression of the stranger's appearance. He was a tall man, maybe six foot two, over forty years old, and of a weight that was proportional to his height. His hair, thinning in the front, was pulled back at the nape of his neck in an overcompensating ponytail that also balanced out his large nose. When Conde was closer to him and managed to notice the pink paleness of his skin and the quality of his clothing, business casual, he was able to assume this was someone who had come from an ocean away. Any of the seven seas.

"Pleased to meet you. Elias Kaminsky," the foreigner said. He tried to smile and held out his right hand to Conde.

Convinced by the heat and softness of that huge hand wrapped around his that this was not a possible aggressor, the former policeman set his rusty mental computer going to try to imagine the reason that, at almost midnight, the foreigner was waiting for him on the dark porch of his house. Was Yoyi right and now here he was in front of him, a rare-book seeker? He looked like it, he concluded, and made his best not-interested-in-business face, as the Pigeon's commercial wisdom advised.

"You said your name was . . . ?" Conde tried to clear his mind; fortunately for him it was not too clouded by alcohol, thanks to the culinary shock old Josefina delivered.

"Elias, Elias Kaminsky . . . Listen, I'm sorry I was waiting for you here . . . and at this late hour . . . Look . . ." The man, who spoke a very neutral Spanish, tried to smile, apparently embarrassed by the situation, and decided the smartest thing was to throw his best card on the table. "I'm a friend of your friend Andrés, the doctor, the one who lives in Miami . . ."

With those words, any of Conde's remaining tension disappeared as if by magic. He had to be an old-book seeker sent by his friend. Did Yoyi know something and that was why he was saying he had a feeling?

"Yes, of course, he said something . . ." Conde lied, as he hadn't heard anything from Andrés in two or three months.

"Oh good. Well, your friend sends his best and"—he searched in the pocket of his also business casual shirt (by Guess, Conde managed to see)—"and he wrote you this letter."

Conde took the envelope. It had been years since he'd received a letter from Andrés and he was impatient to read it. Some extraordinary reason must have pushed his friend to sit down and write, since, as a prophylactic against the artful creeping of nostalgia, once established in Miami, the doctor had decided to maintain a careful relationship with a past that was too stirring and thus a danger to his present health. Only twice per year did he break his silence and indulge in homesickness: on the night of Carlos's birthday and on December 31, when he called Skinny's house, knowing that his friends would be gathered there, drinking rum and counting losses, including his own, which had happened twenty years before when, as the bolero warns, Andrés left to never return. Although he did say goodbye.

"Your friend Andrés worked in the geriatric home where my parents spent many years, until they died," the man spoke again when he saw how Conde was bending the envelope and putting it away in his small pocket. "He had a special relationship with them. My mother, who died a few months ago . . ."

"I'm sorry."

"Thank you . . . My mother was Cuban and my father was Polish, but he lived in Cuba for twenty years, until they left in 1958." Something in Elias Kaminsky's emotional memory made him smile vaguely. "Although he only lived in Cuba for those twenty years, he said he was Jewish in origin, Polish-German by birth, and because of his parents, legally an American citizen, and that the rest of him was Cuban. Because in truth he was more Cuban than anything else. On the black-bean-and-yucca-with-*mojo*-eating team, he always said . . ."

"Then, he was my kind of guy . . . Shall we sit?" Conde pointed at the chairs and, with one of his keys, unlocked the chains that united the seats like a marriage that forced them to live together, and then tried to arrange the chairs in a way that was more conducive to a conversation. His curiosity to know the reason for which the man sought him out had erased another part of the slump that had been dogging him for weeks.

"Thank you," Elias Kaminsky said as he got comfortable. "But I'm not going to bother you much. Look at the time . . ."

"So why did you come to see me?"

Kaminsky took out a packet of Camels and offered one to Conde, who politely turned it down. Only in the event of a nuclear catastrophe or under threat of death would he smoke one of those perfumed, sweetish pieces of shit. Conde, besides being a member of the Black Bean Eating Party, was also a nicotine patriot and he demonstrated this by lighting up one of his catastrophic, black-tobacco, filterless Criollos.

"I suppose Andrés explains in his letter . . . I'm a painter, I was born in Miami, and now I live in New York. My parents couldn't stand the cold so I had to leave them in Florida. They had an apartment in the nursing home where they met Andrés. Despite their origins, this is the first time I've been to Cuba and . . . Look, the story is a little long. Would you let me invite you to breakfast at my hotel tomorrow so we can discuss things? Andrés told me that you were the best possible person to help me learn something about a story that has to do with my parents . . . Of course, I would pay you for your work, as if I wouldn't . . ."

As Elias Kaminsky talked, Conde felt his internal alarms, dimmed until recently, start to light up one by one. If Andrés had dared to send him that man, who didn't seem to be seeking rare books, there must be a serious reason. But before having coffee with that stranger, and well before telling him he didn't have the time or energy to get involved in his story, there were things he had to know. But . . . the guy had said he would pay him, right? How much? The financial penury hounding him the last few months made him take in the information gluttonously. In any case, the best thing, as always, was to start from the beginning.

"Would you excuse me if I read this letter?"

"Of course. I would be dying to read it."

Conde smiled. He opened the door to his house and the first thing he saw was Garbage II lying on the sofa, in the precise spot left open by various piles of books. The dog, rude and sleeping, didn't even move his tail when Conde turned on the light and tore open the envelope.

Miami, September 2, 2007

Condemned:

The end of year phone call is a long way away, but this couldn't wait. I heard from Dulcita, who came back from Cuba a few days ago, that you're all well, with less hair and more fat. The bearer of this letter IS NOT my friend. His parents ALMOST were, two super-cool old folks, especially the father, the Polish Cuban. This gentleman is a painter; he sells pretty well by the looks of it and inherited some things ($) from his parents. I THINK he's a good guy. Not like you or me, but more or less.

What he's going to ask of you is complicated, I don't think that even you can solve it, but try, because even I am intrigued by this story. Besides, it's the kind that you like, you'll see.

Incidentally, I told him that you charge one hundred dollars per day for your work, plus expenses. I learned that from a Chandler novel you lent me a shitload of years ago. The one that had a guy who talked like Hemingway's characters, you know the one?

Sending hugs for ALL OF YOU. I know that next week is Rabbit's birthday. Please wish him a happy one on my behalf. Elias also has a gift for him from me and some medicines that Jose should take, besides.

With love and squalor, your brother ALWAYS,
Andrés.

P.S. Oh, tell Elias that he must tell you the story of the Orestes Miñoso photo . . .

Conde could not help his eyes getting misty. He lied to himself im-modestly that with all the fatigue and frustration logged, plus the heat and surrounding humidity, his eyes got irritated. In that letter, which hardly said anything, Andrés said it all, with those silences and empha-ses of his, typed out in all caps. The fact that he remembered Rabbit's birthday several days beforehand betrayed him: if he didn't write, it was because he didn't want to or couldn't, since he preferred not to run the risk of falling apart. Andrés, across the physical distance, was still too close and, by the looks of it, would always be so. The tribe to which he be-longed for many years was inalienable, *PER SAECULA SAECULORUM*, all caps.

Conde left the letter on the defunct Russian TV set that he hadn't made up his mind to throw out and, feeling the weight of nostalgia that added to his most exposed and dogged frustrations, he told himself that the best way to bear that unexpected conversation was to soak it in alcohol. From the bottle of cheap rum he had in reserve, he poured two good doses in two glasses. Only then did he gain full consciousness of his situation: That man would pay him one hundred dollars per day to find out something? He almost felt woozy. In the falling-apart, poor world in which Conde lived, one hundred dollars was a fortune. What if he worked five days? The wooziness got stronger, and to keep it at bay he took a swig directly from the bottle. With the glasses in hand and his mind overflowing with financial plans, he went back to the porch.

"Do you dare?" he asked Elias Kaminsky, holding out the glass, which the man accepted while murmuring his thanks. "It's cheap rum . . . the kind I drink."

"It's not bad," the foreigner said after cautiously tasting it. "Is it Haitian?" he asked, as if he were a taster, and immediately took out another Camel and lit it.

Conde took a long drink and acted as if he were savoring that cata-strophic crap.

"Yes, it must be Haitian . . . Well, if you want, we can talk tomorrow at your hotel and you'll tell me all the details . . ." Conde began, trying to hide his anxiousness to know. "But tell me now what it is that you think I can help you find out."

"I already told you, it's a long story. It has a lot to do with the life of my father, Daniel Kaminsky . . . For starters, let's say that I'm on the trail of a painting, according to all information, a Rembrandt."

Conde couldn't help but smile. A Rembrandt, in Cuba? Years ago, when he was a policeman, the existence of a Matisse had led him to get caught up in a painful story of passion and hate. And the Matisse had ended up being more false than a hooker's promise . . . or that of a policeman. But the mention of a possible painting by the Dutch master was something too compelling for Conde's curiosity, which was all the more amped up, perhaps because of the chemical reaction between that horrific rum that appeared to be Haitian and the promise of a solid payment.

"So, a Rembrandt . . . What's that whole story and what does it have to do with your father?" he egged on the foreigner, and added statements to convince him: "At this hour there's barely any heat . . . and I have the rest of the bottle of rum."

Kaminsky emptied his drink and held the glass out to Conde.

"Count the rum in your expenses . . ."

"What I'm going to count is a lightbulb for the lamp. It's better if we can see each other's faces well, don't you think?"

While he looked for the lightbulb, searched for a chair to climb up on, placed the bulb in the socket, and at last turned on the light, Conde was thinking that, in reality, he was hopeless. Why in the hell was he pushing that man to tell him his father's story if he probably wouldn't be able to help him find anything? *Is this what you've come to, Mario Conde?* he asked himself. He preferred, for now, not to make any attempt to respond to that question.

When Conde returned to his chair, Elias Kaminsky took a photograph out of the extraordinary pocket of his business casual shirt and held it out to him.

"The key to everything could be this photo."

It was a recent copy of an old print. The photograph's initial sepia had turned gray and you could see the irregular borders of the original photo. In the frame was a woman, between twenty and thirty years old, clothed in a dark dress and seated in an armchair with brocade cloth and a high back. Next to the woman, a boy, about five years old, standing, with one hand on the woman's lap, was looking at the camera. By the clothing and hairstyles, Conde assumed that the image had been taken sometime in the 1920s or '30s. Already alerted to the subject, after observing the people, Conde concentrated on the small painting hung behind them, above a small table where a vase with white flowers rested. The painting was, perhaps, fifteen by ten inches, based on its relation to the woman's head. Conde moved the photo, trying to shine better light on it so he could study the framed print: it was the bust of a man, with his hair flowing over his scalp and down to his shoulders, and a sparse, unkempt beard. Something indefinable was transmitted from that image, especially from the gaze, halfway between lost and melancholic, coming from the subject's eyes, and Conde asked himself if it was a portrait of a man or a representation of the Christ figure, quite close to one he must have seen in one or more books with reproductions of Rembrandt's paintings . . . A Rembrandt Christ in the home of Jews?

"Is this portrait by Rembrandt?" he asked, still looking at the photo.

"The woman is my grandmother, the boy is my father. They're in the house where they lived in Kraków . . . and the painting has been authenticated as a Rembrandt. You can see it better with a magnifying glass . . ."

From the pocket of his button-down shirt now came the magnifying glass, and Conde looked at the reproduction with it as he asked, "And what does that Rembrandt have to do with Cuba?"

"It was in Cuba. Later, it left here. And four months ago, it appeared in a London auction house to be sold . . . It came out on the market with an initial price of one million two hundred thousand dollars, since rather than being a finished work, it appears to have been something like a study, one of the many Rembrandt made for his great Christ figures when he was working on a version of *Pilgrims at Emmaus*, the 1648 one. Do you know anything about the subject?"

Conde finished his rum and looked at the photo again through the magnifying glass, and couldn't help but ask himself how many problems Rembrandt—whose life was pretty fucked-up according to what he had read—could have taken care of with that million dollars.

"I know very little," he admitted. "I've seen prints of this painting . . . but if memory serves me, in *Pilgrims*, Christ is looking up, isn't he?"

"That's right . . . The thing is that this Christ figure appears to have come into my father's family in 1648. But my grandparents, Jews who were fleeing the Nazis, brought it to Cuba in 1939 . . . It was like their insurance policy. And the painting remained in Cuba. But they didn't. Somebody made off with the Rembrandt . . . And a few months ago someone else, perhaps believing the time was right, began to try to sell it. That seller gets in touch with the auction house through an e-mail address based in Los Angeles. They have a certificate of authenticity dated in Berlin, 1928, and another certificate of purchase, authenticated by a notary here in Havana, dated 1940 . . . at the exact moment my grandparents and aunt were in a concentration camp in Holland. But thanks to this photo, which my father kept his entire life, I've stopped the auction, since the whole subject of artwork stolen from Jews before and after the war is a very sensitive one. I'll be honest with you when I tell you that I'm not interested in recovering the painting because of whatever value it could have, although that's not negligible . . . What I do want to know, and the reason I'm here, talking to you, is what happened to that painting—which was a family heirloom—and to the person who had it here in Cuba. Where was it hiding until now? . . . I don't know if at this point it would be possible to find out anything, but I want to try . . . and for that, I need your help."

Conde had stopped looking at the photo and was watching his visitor, intrigued by his words. Had he misheard or did he say that he wasn't too interested in the million-something that the piece was worth? His mind, already on overdrive, had started seeking the ways to jump into this seemingly extraordinary story that had crossed his path. But, at that moment, he hadn't the foggiest idea: he only knew that he needed to find out more.

"So what did your father tell you about that painting's arrival in Cuba?"

"He didn't tell me much about that because the only thing he knew was that his parents were bringing it on the *Saint Louis*."

"The famous ship that arrived in Havana full of Jews?"

"That one . . . Regarding the painting, my father did tell me a lot. About the person who had it here in Cuba, less so . . ."

Conde smiled. Were the fatigue, the rum, and his bad mood making him more stupid, or was this his natural state?

"The truth is that I don't understand very much . . . or understand anything," he admitted as he returned the magnifying glass to his interlocutor.

"What I want is for you to help me find out the truth, so that I can also understand . . . Look, right now I'm exhausted, and I'd like to have a clear head to talk about this story. But to convince you to listen to me tomorrow, if we can, in fact, see each other tomorrow, I just want to share a secret with you . . . My parents left Cuba in 1958. Not in '59 or in '60, when almost all the Jews and people with money left here, fleeing from what they knew would be a communist government. I am certain that my parents' departure in 1958, which was quite sudden, had something to do with that Rembrandt. And since the painting showed up again for the auction, I'm convinced that the relationship between my father and the painting and his departure from Cuba have a connection that could have been very complicated . . ."

"Why very complicated?" Conde asked, already convinced of his mental anemia.

"Because if what I think happened, happened, my father may have done something very serious."

Conde felt he was about to explode. Elias Kaminsky was either the worst storyteller who ever existed or he was a certified moron. Despite his painting, his one hundred dollars per day, and his business casual clothing.

"Are you going to tell me once and for all what happened and the truth that is worrying you?"

The behemoth took up his glass again and knocked back the rum Conde had served him . . . He looked at his interrogator and finally said, "It's not that easy to say you think your father, whom you always saw that way, as a father . . . could have been the same person who slit someone's neck."

3

Kraków, 1648—Havana, 1939

Two years before that dramatically silent morning on which Daniel Kaminsky and his uncle Joseph were getting ready to go down to Havana's port and witness the awaited docking of the *Saint Louis*, the increasingly tense situation for European Jews had become more complicated at an accelerating rate with the promised arrival of new, great misfortunes. It was then that Daniel's parents decided that the best thing would be to place themselves at the center of the storm and take advantage of the speed of its winds to propel themselves to salvation. Because of that, making use of the fact that Esther Kellerstein had been born in Germany and that her parents still lived there, Isaiah Kaminsky, his wife, and his children, Daniel and Judith, after buying a government permit, managed to abandon Kraków and travel to Leipzig. There, the doctor hoped to find a satisfactory departure, along with the other members of the Kellerstein clan, one of the city's most prominent families, known manufacturers of delicate wood and string musical instruments that had given soul and sound to countless German symphonies from the times of Bach and Handel.

Once established in Leipzig, supported by the Kellersteins' money and contacts, Isaiah Kaminsky had started to evacuate his family members with the very complicated purchase of an exit permit and tourist visa for his son, who had just turned seven. The boy's initial destination would be the remote island of Cuba, where he would have to wait for a change in his visa status to travel to the United States and for the departure of his parents and sister, who trusted they would emigrate with a certain quickness, if possible, directly to North America. The choice of Havana as the route for Daniel was due to how complicated it was to immigrate to the United States, and to the positive fact that, for a few years already, there lived Joseph, Isaiah's older brother, who had already been converted by Cuban chutzpah into Pepe the Purseman and was willing to show up before the island's authorities as the boy's financial provider.

For the other three members of the family stranded in Leipzig, things ended up being more complicated: for one, there were the German authorities' restrictions against resident Jews emigrating anywhere, unless they had capital and handed every last cent to the state; and then there was the increasing difficulty that getting a visa entailed, especially to the United States, where Isaiah had set his sights, since he considered it the ideal country for a man of his profession, culture, and aspirations; and, finally, there was the stubborn belief among the Kellerstein family's patriarchs that they would always enjoy a certain consideration and respect thanks to their financial position, which should facilitate, at least, a satisfactory sale of their business, an act capable of allowing them to open a perhaps more modest one in another part of the world. It must have been that sum of dreams and desires, along with what Daniel Kaminsky would later deem a deep spirit of submission and a paralyzing inability to understand what was happening, that would rob them of precious months to try any of the means of escape that had already been carried out by other Leipzig Jews who, less romantic and less integrated than the Kellersteins, had convinced themselves that not only their businesses, houses, and relationships were at risk but, above all, their lives, by the fact of their being Jews in a country that had become sick with the most aggressive case of nationalism.

Their deep trust in the German kindness and courtesy with which they had coexisted and advanced for generations did not save the Kellersteins from ruin and death. While by that time German Jews had already lost all of their rights and were civil pariahs, another turn of the screw came then that turned their religious and racial condition into a crime. From the night of November ninth into the tenth of 1938, six months after Daniel's departure to Cuba, the Kellersteins lost practically everything during the blackness of Kristallnacht.

Inclined to seek out a visa to any part of the world where they wouldn't be in the same danger, Daniel's parents and sister went to Berlin, taken in by a Gentile doctor, a former classmate of Isaiah Kaminsky's from his university years. There, Isaiah, as he ran from one consulate to another, witnessed large Nazi marches and was able to gain a definitive notion of what was in store for Europe. In one of the letters he wrote to his brother Joseph at the time, Isaiah tried to explain, or perhaps explain to himself, what he felt in those moments. The missive, which years later Uncle Pepe would give to Daniel and, several more years later, Daniel would put in the hands of his son Elias, constituted a vivid confirmation of how fear invades an individual when the forces unleashed and manipulated by society choose him as an enemy and take away all recourse, in this case simply for professing certain ideas that others—the majority manipulated by a totalitarian power—have deemed a danger to the public good. The desire to escape from himself, to lose his uniqueness in the homogeneous vulgarity of the masses, was offered as an alternative against fear and the most irrational manifestations of a hate repackaged as patriotic duty and internalized by a society altered by a messianic belief in its fate. In one of the missive's last paragraphs Isaiah declared, "I dream of being invisible." That sentence, the summary of his dramatic will for a submissive evasion, would be the inspiration capable of changing many of his son's attitudes and would push him, more than the desire of acquiring invisibility, to the search to turn himself into someone else.

It was in the tensest moment of those difficulties, feeling on the edge of suffocating due to Nazi pressure, when Dr. Isaiah Kaminsky received a cable sent from Havana in which Joseph announced the opening of an unexpected chance for salvation: a Cuban government agency would establish an office inside the Berlin embassy to carry out the sale of visas to sons of Israel who wanted to travel to the island as tourists. The same day the agency started running, Isaiah Kaminsky went to the embassy and managed to buy three visas. Immediately, with the help of the Kellersteins and his doctor friend, he paid the sum the German government demanded to grant the exit permit for Jews and, finally, for the first-class tickets for a passenger ship authorized by the immigration authorities to set sail from Hamburg toward Havana: the S.S. *Saint Louis*, which took to sea on May 13, 1939, with an anticipated arrival in Cuba exactly two weeks later to deposit its human cargo of 937 Jews overjoyed by their good fortune.

When Joseph Kaminsky and his nephew Daniel arrived at the port the morning of May 27, 1939, the sun had not yet risen. But, thanks to the reflectors placed on the Alameda de Paula and the Caballería dock, they joyfully discovered that the luxurious passenger ship had already dropped anchor in the bay, since it had come in several hours ahead of schedule, pressured by the presence of other vessels loaded with Jewish passengers also seeking an American port willing to accept them. The first thing that caught the attention of Pepe the Purseman was that the ship had had to drop anchor far from the points where passenger boats tended to dock: the Casablanca dock, where the immigration department was, or that of the Hapag Line, the Hamburg-Amerika Linie, to which the *Saint Louis* belonged and by which the tourists passing through Havana would disembark.

Around the port there were already hundreds of people gathered, mostly Jews but also many, many curious onlookers, journalists, policemen. And just at six thirty in the morning, when the deck lights came on and the horn commanded by the ship's captain to signal the opening of the breakfast rooms blared, many of those gathered on the dock leapt with joy, causing a prolonged ruckus that was joined by the passengers, since one after another they assumed it was a sign of imminent disembarkment.

With the passing of the years and thanks to information he picked up, Daniel Kaminsky came to understand that that adventure, destined to mark his family's fate, had been born twisted in a macabre fashion. In reality, while the *Saint Louis* was sailing toward Havana, each step was already outlined of the tragedy that episode would become, one of the most miserable and shameful in all of twentieth-century politics. Because, crossed in the fate of the Jews aboard the *Saint Louis*, as if to give shape to the loops of a dead man's noose, were the political and propaganda interests of the Nazis, stubbornly trying to show that they allowed Jews to emigrate; the strict migratory policies claimed by different factions of the United States government; and the decisive weight that that government's pressures exercised over Cuban leaders. To top it off, the ballast of those realities and political machinations was rounded out by the worst sickness besetting Cuba in those years: corruption.

The indispensable travel permits granted by the Cuban agency established in Berlin were a key piece in the perverse game that would envelop Daniel's parents and sister and the vast majority of the other 937 Jews aboard the passenger ship. Very soon it would be known that their sale was part of a business put together by the senator and former army colonel Manuel Benítez González, who, thanks to his son's close relationship with the powerful General Batista, then unlawfully held the post of director of immigration . . . Through his travel agency, Benítez came to sell about four thousand Cuban entry permits, at $150 apiece, which generated the fabulous earnings of $600,000 at the time, cash that must have been shared by many people, perhaps even Batista himself, whose hands held all the strings moving the country from his Revolt of the Sergeants in 1933 until his shameful escape before the first dawn of 1959.

Of course, when he found out about those movements, then president of Cuba Federico Laredo Brú decided that the time had come to jump into the game. Pressured by some of his ministers, he tried to show his might before Batista's power, but also, as was the national custom, set out to obtain a slice of the pie. His first presidential gesture was to approve a decree by which each refugee who intended to arrive in Cuba should bring $500 to demonstrate he would not be a burden on the state. And when Benítez's permits and the *Saint Louis*'s tickets were already sold, he decreed another law by which he invalidated previously issued tourist visas and through which he demanded a payment of almost half a million dollars by the passengers to the Cuban government to allow their entry on the island with refugee status.

Those aboard the passenger ship couldn't come up with those sums, of course. Upon leaving German territory, the supposed tourists were allowed to leave with only one suitcase of clothing and ten marks, the equivalent of four dollars. But, as a part of the game, Goebbels, the head of German propaganda and demiurge of that episode, had started the rumor that the refugees were traveling with money, diamonds, and other jewels amounting to a great fortune. And the Cuban president and his advisors gave the Nazi leader much more than the benefit of the doubt.

When the sun rose, the multitudes clustered around the port were already more than five or six thousand people. Little Daniel Kaminsky didn't understand anything, since the comments around him were continuous and contradictory: some led to hope and others to despair. People were even running bets—whether they'd disembark or not disembark—

and they supported their decisions with a variety of reasons. To the passengers and their relatives' relief, someone reported that the deboarding process had been postponed due to it being a weekend and the majority of the Cuban bureaucrats being off. But the greatest trust among that group of relatives was placed in the certainty that everything could be bought or sold in Cuba, and, as such, soon some envoys from the Joint Distribution Committee would arrive in Havana, willing to negotiate the prices set by the Cuban government . . .

In reality, Joseph Kaminsky and his nephew Daniel would have a very powerful reason to be more optimistic than the rest of the relatives of the travelers piled up in Havana's port. Uncle Pepe the Purseman had already confided to the boy, with the greatest discretion, that Daniel's parents and sister had in their hands something much more prized than some visas: they possessed the key that could burst open the doors to the island for the three Kaminskys aboard the *Saint Louis*. Because with them, somehow saved from the Nazi requisitions, traveled the small canvas of an old painting that for years had hung on some wall of the family home. That work, signed by a famous and highly valued Dutch painter, was capable of reaching a sum that, Joseph assumed, would surpass the demands by a mile of any police bureaucrat or Cuban Immigration secretary, whose goodwill, the man assured him, tended to be bought for far less money.

───

For almost three centuries the painting that represented the face of a classically Jewish man, who simultaneously looked like the classically iconic Christian image of Jesus, had gone through various statuses in its relationship with the Kaminsky family: a secret, a family heirloom, and, in the end, a jewel on which the last Kaminskys to enjoy owning it would place their greatest hopes for salvation.

In the house in Kraków where Daniel was born in 1930, the Kaminskys, although no longer as financially comfortable as a few decades before, lived with all the comforts of a typical petit bourgeois Jewish family. Some photos saved from the disaster prove it. Expensive wooden furniture, German mirrors, and antique Delft porcelain vases could be seen in those sepia-stained photographs. And that exact photo of Daniel at four or five years old, with his mother, Esther, beside him—a snapshot taken in the light-filled living room that sometimes served as a dining room—revealed it especially. In that image one could see, just behind the boy and above a table decorated with a vase overflowing with flowers, the carved ebony frame in which Isaiah had placed, as if it were the clan's blazon, the painting that represented a transcendental man with Jewish features and a gaze lost in the infinite.

Forty years before, the fur trader Benjamin Kaminsky—father to Joseph, the deceased Israel, and Isaiah—had managed to amass a generous fortune and, resolved to guarantee his sons' futures, had insisted on leaving them something no one would be able to take away from them: education. Before the war of 1914 began, he had sent his firstborn, Joseph, to Bohemia so that he could develop his notable skills there, training with the best leather craftsmen, renowned in that region of the world. In this way, the day he inherited the family business, he would do so with a background sure to guarantee him quick progress. Later, Benjamin sent the deceased Israel to study engineering in Paris, where the young man quickly decided to establish himself, dazzled by the city and French culture. To his misfortune, in his process of becoming French, Israel would end up enrolling in the French army, to end his days in a trench overflowing with mud, blood, and shit just outside Verdun. After the Great War, even in the middle of the crisis that did away with so many fortunes and the political instability the family lived in, the fur dealer invested his remaining money in sending his youngest, Isaiah, to become a doctor at the University of Leipzig. It was at that time the young man met Esther Kellerstein, the daughter of one of the city's wealthy and reputable families, the beautiful young woman he married, and in 1928 he established himself in Kraków, ancestral home to the Kaminskys.

With Israel dead in the war and Joseph's professed intention to leave and seek his fortunes in the New World, where he wouldn't live in constant fear of a pogrom, Isaiah's father gave his youngest son custody of that old painting that, for generations, had always been handed over to the oldest son in the line. For the first time, the future ownership of the work, of whose value they had more trustworthy information, would be divided between two brothers, although from the beginning Joseph, always frugal, with a certain hermit's vocation and lacking in great ambitions, preferred to leave it in the care of his "intellectual" brother, as he called the doctor, since, besides, due to his orthodox religious leanings, he had never liked that portrait much. Quite the contrary. Thanks to all of these conditions, years later, when Joseph learned of the financial difficulties Isaiah had while trying to find a way out of Germany for himself and his family, it was easy to make a decision. That man, who tended to count his pennies, who kept his nephew Daniel—and himself— always at the brink of starvation to avoid excess spending on food that, after all, he would say, turned into shit (due to his chronic constipation, he lived until his dying day obsessed with shit and worried about the traumatic act of evacuating it), had written to his brother confirming that he had free rein to make use of the painting if its sale guaranteed his survival. Perhaps this was the manifest destiny of that controversial and heretical, ornate jewel obtained by the family almost three hundred years before.

No one knew for sure how that painting, a rather small canvas, had come into the hands of some distant Kaminskys, by all accounts in the middle of the seventeenth century, shortly after having been painted. That precise time period had been the most terrible era Poland's Jewish community had lived through until then, although its cruelty and death toll would soon be surpassed. Despite the amount of time that had passed, all of the world's Jews knew very well the story of the persecution, martyrdom, and death of thousands of Jews at the hands of the masses of Cossacks and Tartars drunk with sadism and hate, a slaughter carried out to the extreme between 1648 and 1653.

The family story regarding the painting that the Kaminskys possessed from those turbulent times forward was based on a fabulous, romantic, and, for many of the Kaminskys, false story of a rabbi who, fleeing the advance of the Cossacks, had escaped almost miraculously from the siege of the city of Nemirov, first, and of Zamość, later. The mythical rabbi, they said, had managed to arrive in Kraków, where, to his disgrace, an enemy just as implacable as the Cossacks had trapped him: the plague epidemic that in one summer wiped away the lives of twenty thousand Jews in that city alone. From generation to generation, the members of the clan would tell each other that Dr. Moshe Kaminsky had treated the rabbi on his deathbed, and since that wise man (whose family had been massacred by the Cossacks under the famous Chmiel the Wicked, a murderer in the eyes of the Jews and a tough hero in the eyes of the Ukrainians) understood how things would end, he handed over some letters and three small canvases to the doctor. The paintings were of that man's head, which appeared Jewish by all indications, and in a very naturalistic way sought to be a representation of the Christian Jesus, although with the obvious intention to make him more human and earthly than the figure that had been established by Catholic iconography at the time; a small landscape of the Dutch countryside; and the portrait of a young woman dressed in the Dutch style of that period. No one ever knew what the letters said, since they were written in a language that was incomprehensible for Eastern European Jews and Poles, and at some point they followed an unknown path, at least for the doctor's descendants, who maintained and transmitted the story of the rabbi and the paintings.

According to that family legend, the rabbi had told Dr. Moshe Kaminsky that he had received the canvases from a Sephardic man who said he was a painter. The Sephardic man had assured him that the portrait of the young woman was his, that the landscape had been painted by a friend, while the head of Jesus—or of a young Jewish man who looked like the Christian Jesus—was actually a portrait of himself, the young Sephardic man, and had come from the hands of his maestro, the greatest portrait painter in all the known world . . . a Dutchman named Rembrandt van Rijn, whose initials could be read on the bottom edge of the canvas, along with its date of execution: 1647.

Ever since then, the Kaminsky family, who had also only miraculously escaped the slaughters and illnesses of those dark years, had kept the canvases and the somewhat unbelievable story that, as far as they knew, the distant doctor had heard from the lips of the delirious rabbi who had survived the Cossacks' attacks. What member of the Polish Jewish community of the mid-seventeenth century, with the bloodshed and horror of the genocidal violence that decimated it, could believe that story about a Sephardic Jew, a painter, no less, lost in those parts? Which of those sons of Israel, fanatics in those times to the point of desperation over the wanderings in Palestine of a certain Sabbatai Zevi who had proclaimed himself the true Messiah capable of redeeming them, which of those Jews would believe that in the fields of Little Russia there could be wandering a Sephardic Jew who came to Amsterdam and who, to top off the nonsense, proclaimed himself a painter? Because, really, who had ever seen a Jewish painter? And how could that incredible Jewish painter dare to and actually wander around those lands with three oil paintings, a portrait of himself too similar to Christ among them? Wasn't it more possible that, during one of the Cossack and Tartar attacks, the supposed rabbi appropriated, God knows how, those paintings? Or that the thief was Dr. Moshe Kaminsky himself—the creator of that clumsy fable about the Sephardic painter and the dead rabbi in order to hide behind those characters some dark act carried out during the years of plague and slaughter? Whether the story was true or not, the case was that the doctor came to own the works and kept them until the end of his life without showing them to anyone, out of fear of being considered idolatrous. Unfortunately, said the descendants who passed along the story and the inheritance for centuries, the small landscape of the Dutch countryside had reached Moshe Kaminsky's hands in a deteriorated state, while, with the passing of years, the painting that copied the young Jewess's face, perhaps due to the poor quality of the pigments or the canvas, started to fade and crack until it disappeared, flake by flake. But not the painting of the young Jewish man. As one could expect, several generations of the Kaminskys kept that piece, perhaps even valuable, hidden from public view, especially from the view of other Polish Jews, who were increasingly orthodox and radical, since the act of displaying it could be considered an egregious violation of Jewish Law, since not only was it a human image but the image of a Jew who embodied the alleged Messiah.

It was Benjamin's father and Daniel Kaminsky's great-grandfather who became the first in the clan to dare to hang that painting visibly in his home. There was a reason: he was something of an atheist, like any good socialist, and he even became a somewhat important labor leader in mid-nineteenth-century Kraków. Since then, the family story about the painting acquired new dramatic flourishes, because one of those socialist Jews, a comrade-in-arms of Daniel Kaminsky's great-grandfather, turned out to be a French trade unionist, and, according to what he himself said, a close friend of Camille Pissarro, who was a painter and a Jew, and boasted of his knowledge of European painting. From the first time the Frenchman saw the head of the young Jewish man in the house, he assured his comrade Kaminsky that he had on his wall nothing less than a piece by the Dutchman Rembrandt, one of the artists most admired by Parisian painters at the time, including his friend Pissarro.

It was Benjamin Kaminsky, Daniel's grandfather, who was not a socialist but a man very interested in making money however he could, who one day took the painting off to Warsaw's best specialist. The expert certified that it was, in fact, a Dutch painting from the seventeenth century, but couldn't guarantee that it was a work by Rembrandt—although

it did have many elements of his style. The main problem for its authen-
tication was due to there having been many heads like that painted in
Rembrandt's studio, more or less finished, and there was great confusion
among catalogers regarding which ones were the maestro's works and
which were those of his students, whom he often had paint pieces with
him or after him. On occasion, if he was satisfied with the result, the
maestro would even sign them and sell them as his own . . . As such, the
Polish specialist, relying on the ease of its possibility as an unfinished
work, was inclined to think that it was a work painted by one of Rembrandt's students, in Rembrandt's workshop, and he mentioned various
possible authors. Nevertheless, said the man, it was without a doubt an
important canvas (although not very valuable in monetary terms since it
was not a Rembrandt), but he warned that his opinion should not be
taken as definitive. Perhaps Dutch specialists or punctilious German
catalogers . . .

The fact that he was a little disappointed by the probable author of
the painting being a student and not the increasingly valued Dutch master
made Benjamin Kaminsky give no other fate for the work but for it to
be placed in a modest frame on the wall of the family home. Otherwise,
had he been certain of its value, he would have surely exchanged the
heirloom for money—money that, also surely, would have become thin
air during any of the crises of those terrible years before and after the
world war.

It would be Dr. Isaiah Kaminsky himself who finally decided to submit the painting to rigorous analysis. A man more curious and spiritual
than his father, he wanted to erase all doubt and took it with him to Berlin
when he traveled to Germany to marry the beautiful Esther Kellerstein
in 1928. He made appointments with two specialists in the city, true
connoisseurs of Dutch painting of the classic period, and he showed
them the portrait of the young Jew similar to the Jesus of Christian
iconography . . . Both certified that, although it looked more like a study
than a finished work, without a doubt it was a canvas from the series of
the *tronies* (as the Dutch called bust portraits) painted in the 1640s in
Rembrandt's workshop, with the image of a very human Christ. But,
they added, this canvas specifically, almost certainly, had been painted . . .
by Rembrandt!

When he was sure of the work's origin and value, Isaiah Kaminsky
ordered its cleaning and restoration, at the same time writing a long

letter to his brother Joseph, already living in Havana and in the process of turning into Pepe the Purseman, narrating the details of the fabulous confirmation. Thanks to the specialists' opinion, Isaiah now thought there must have been a lot of truth in what that mythical Sephardic Jewish Dutchman, *supposedly* a painter, *supposedly* said when he *supposedly* handed the canvas over to the rabbi—Why? Why give it to someone if it was already valuable around that time—who, after escaping the Cossacks' swords and horses so many times, ended up trapped by the Black Plague devastating the city of Kraków and went to die in the arms of Dr. Moshe Kaminsky? The generous rabbi who, before dying, *supposedly* had given the doctor three oil paintings, a handful of letters, and that extraordinary tale about the existence of a Dutch Sephardic Jew in love with painting, lost in Little Russia's enormous meadows. A story in which, the painting's origins confirmed, the Kaminskys now had more reasons to believe.

———

The port would soon become a sort of grotesque carnival. From the very morning of Saturday, May 27, the day the *Saint Louis* arrived, the thousands of Jews living in Havana, whether they had relatives or not on the boat, had camped out on the docks, surrounded by countless curious onlookers, journalists, prostitutes, and lifelong seamen, as well as some policemen who wanted to do their job and exercise repression. On the sidewalks and porches, businesses and stands had gone up selling food and drinks, umbrellas and binoculars, hats and fold-up chairs, Catholic prayers and Afro-Cuban symbols, fans and flip-flops, remedies for sunburn and newspapers with day-old news about transactions that would determine whether the passengers would stay or take their music elsewhere, as one of the announcers would say. The most lucrative business, without a doubt, was the rental of boats aboard which people with relatives on the passenger ship could get as close to the vessel as the rope made up by police and navy launches would allow, to see their family members there and, if their voices reached them, to convey some message of encouragement.

In those days, Daniel Kaminsky soon noticed how his senses were dulled by the accumulation of experiences and discoveries that seemed amazing to him. If the months he had already lived in the city had allowed him to admire its vitality and ease, the fact that he had spent the majority of his time among Jews like himself and his inability to understand the quick slang spoken by Cubans had barely offered him the possibility of peering at the country's surface. But that human whirlwind unleashed by the ship crammed with refugees whom the people insisted on calling "Poles" would end up being a storm of passions and interests that somehow involved a poor immigrant like himself and the president of the Republic. For Daniel, the dramatic episode would function like a push in the direction of the belly of a bubbling world that was already magnetic to him: that Cuban capacity for living each situation as if it were a party seemed to him, even from the perspective of his ignorance and desperation, a much more pleasant way to spend time on earth and to obtain from that ephemeral passage the best that could be had. There everyone laughed, smoked, drank beer, even at wakes; women, married, single, or widowed, black and white, walked with a perverse cadence and stopped in the middle of the street to talk to friends or strangers; blacks gesticulated as if they were dancing, and whites dressed like pimps. People, men and women, looked into each other's eyes. And even when people moved frenetically, in reality no one seemed to be in a rush for anything. With the passing of years and an increase in his comprehension skills, Daniel came to understand that not all of his impressions from those times had a basis, since Cubans also dealt with their own dramas, their misery and pain; although, at the same time, he would learn that they did so with a levity and pragmatism that he would love for the rest of his life with the same intensity that would sustain his romance with black bean soups.

The tense week that the ship was grounded in Havana was a crazy time during which, from day to day and even within the same day—and at times in the space of a few minutes—euphoric moments were followed by disappointment and frustration, which was then relieved by the arrival of some hope that would later disappear and increase the quantity of accumulated suffering for the refugees' relatives.

Their dreams from the first moments were always maintained by the possibility of some financial negotiation with the Cuban government and, above all, in the pressure that Jews, established in the United States, exercised or tried to exercise on President Roosevelt so that he would dramatically alter the quota of admissible refugees in the Union. But as the days passed without any settled agreements in Havana or policy changes in Washington, any remaining dreams were deflated.

What most affected Daniel was seeing how, in that same lighthearted and festive Cuba, a country that was generally so open, anti-Semitic propaganda had reached unsuspected levels. Encouraged by Spanish fascists, by the anti-immigrant and anti-Semitic editorials in the *Diario de la Marina*, by the vocal members of Cuba's Nazi Party, by the money and pressures of German agents established on the island, that expression of hate invaded too many consciousnesses. The boy Daniel Kaminsky, who had the opportunity to see a Berlin march that brought together forty thousand people dedicated to yelling insults against the Jews and foreigners in general, came to feel that he had imagined his return to a lost world so many times that that world had come to find him in the distant, musical, and colorful capital of the island of Cuba.

The campaign against the refugees' possible disembarkment was an explosion of nastiness and opportunism. Small in number yet very vocal, the Cuban Nazis—who were opposed to any immigrants who were not Catholic and white—demanded not only barring the current voyagers but also the expulsion of the other Jews who were already living on the island. And, as long as they were at it, since they needed to whiten the nation, the expulsion of the Jamaican and Haitian laborers. The communists, on their end, saw their hands tied because of their battle to withhold jobs from foreigners, and admitting the recently arrived passengers could be counter to that policy. Meanwhile, several leaders from the community of the richest Spanish businesspeople, men who nearly all leaned toward Falangism, rejected the Jews on the basis of their scattered Republican compatriots, many of whom also sought to establish themselves in Cuba. The most painful thing, nonetheless, was seeing how regular people, usually so open, often repeated what had been ingrained in them—they said Jews were dirty, criminal, tricky, greedy communists . . . What Daniel Kaminsky, overwhelmed by so many discoveries, would never fully understand was how that could happen in a country where, before and after, Jews had peacefully integrated themselves, without suffering any particular discrimination or violence. It was clear, abundantly clear, as he would later come to understand it, that Nazi money and propaganda had succeeded in its goal, with the anticipated collaboration of the U.S. government and its immigrant quota policy. And, at the same time, that the Cuban political game had taken the refugees as hostages, or that the available sum for the Jewish organizations to purchase the disembarkation of the voyagers would not be enough for the politicians'

limitless ambitions. He also learned, forever, that the process of manip-
ulating the masses and bringing out their worst instincts would be easier
to exploit than one would believe. Even among the kind and educated
Germans. Even among the open and happy Cubans.

Very soon, the people on the island would know that President Brú,
pressured by the U.S. State Department, was not willing to risk the ire of
his powerful neighbor over $250,000, the sum that he had managed
to raise in his negotiations with the Joint Distribution Committee envoys,
the amount they were willing to pay for the disembarkation of the *Saint
Louis*'s passengers. Brú, hopeful that he would emerge from that mis-
step with very full pockets, at the least, insisted on fixing the demanded
sum at half a million dollars. But when he didn't achieve that sum and
was overcome by U.S. pressure, he would end up taking the least convenient option for him and the passengers; shutting down all conversations
with the committee's lawyers with the order that on June 1, the sixth day
since the *Saint Louis*'s arrival in Havana, the boat should leave Cuban
jurisdictional waters.

It was precisely the day before that Pepe the Purseman, giving in to his
nephew's many pleas and pushed by the alarming buzz in the air, agreed
to pay the two pesos, up from twenty-five cents per person the first day,
for the boat ride over to the passenger ship. In front of the Caballería
dock, Joseph and Daniel boarded the small launch and, when they were
at the closest allowable distance, the uncle started to yell in Yiddish until
a few minutes later Isaiah, Esther, and Judith, pushing and shoving,
were able to come to the railing of the lower deck. Daniel would always
remember, without ever being able to forgive himself, how at that moment
he was incapable of saying anything to his parents and sister: a suffocating desire to cry robbed him of his voice. But when it came down to
it, the trip had been worth much more than the exorbitant price they
paid, since Uncle Joseph was able to receive an encrypted, but definitive,
message from his brother: "Only the spoon knows what's in the pot." In
other words, the sale of the Sephardic man's legacy was already arranged.

Over the course of those five days, while the fate of the passengers
was negotiated, only about two dozen Jews whose tourist visas had been
switched to those of refugees before leaving Hamburg had been able to
leave the boat. Later, a few others, who for some reason had managed to
achieve a similar change in status, had generated a wave of hope. Mean-
spirited rumors spread that an old couple favored with a long-term visa

were the parents of the madame of a brothel specialized in relieving the urges of local magnates, all of whom, it appeared, she had by the balls . . . Thus, the confirmation that Isaiah was using the painting to buy a change in his status from tourist to refugee was a comfort that alleviated Joseph and Daniel Kaminsky's tensions for the next forty-eight hours.

As soon as they got back to shore, the uncle and his nephew walked over to the Adath Israel synagogue, on Calle Jesús María, since the one closest to the dock, Chevet Ahim, on Calle del Inquisidor, was Sephardic territory and Pepe the Purseman didn't compromise when it came to certain articles of faith or in cases of extreme emergency. Once they were at the temple, in front of the Torah roll and the menorah with all its candles lit since the previous Saturday, they did the best they could: ask God for the salvation of their own, including praying for his divine intervention to tempt the ambitions of a Cuban government worker, putting all of the faith in their hearts and minds into their pleas.

When they left the synagogue, Uncle Pepe the Purseman almost ran right into his then boss, who would again be so years later, the very rich American Jew Jacob Brandon, owner of, among other businesses, the leather workshop where the Polish man worked, in addition to being the president of the Joint Distribution Committee in Cuba. At that moment, Joseph Kaminsky put into practice the essence of Jewish wisdom and, while he was at it, gave his nephew a very important lesson: when someone suffers some kind of misfortune, he should pray as if help can only come from divine providence, but at the same time should act as if only he can find a solution to his misfortune. Thus, Joseph, treating his boss with the utmost respect, explained to him that among the *Saint Louis*'s passengers were three of his relatives, and any interest Mr. Brandon could demonstrate would be greatly appreciated. Jacob Brandon, who had already put on his kippah, about to enter the synagogue, took a small notebook out of his elegant woven jacket and, without saying a word, made some notes and said goodbye to Joseph, patting his shoulders before ruffling young Daniel's curls.

Their spirits raised, the Kaminskys went back to the dock. Their mission, from that moment on, was to look at every single one of the immigration workers and policemen who frequently boarded one of the official launches and went onto the passenger ship. Which one of these would be the one to take residency permits to Isaiah, Esther, and Judith? Uncle Joseph was betting on each and every one, although he preferred the ones who were dressed as civilians and wearing straw hats. Those workers, direct government agents, had been selected among the most removed from the now dismissed director of immigration, Manuel Benítez, who himself had been forbidden to come anywhere near the dock. But, like the rest of them, these would also have their own price, and if anyone among the more than nine hundred passengers on the *Saint Louis* could pay it tenfold, it was Isaiah Kaminsky, thanks to the legacy left by the supposed Sephardic painter who had appeared for God knew what reason on the plains of Little Russia with a portrait of the Christian Jesus in his saddlebags.

It was precisely that night from May 31 into June 1 that the presidential decision not to make any deals with the Joint Distribution Committee was announced, giving the passenger ship twenty-four hours to leave Cuban waters. The source of the information must have been all too reliable, since it was relayed to relatives by Louis Clasing himself—the Havana representative of the Hapag Line to which the S.S. *Saint Louis* belonged and, according to rumor, a partner of Manuel Benítez in the sale of the repealed visas and a close friend of General Batista.

Nonetheless, Daniel and Joseph Kaminsky, still buoyed by the hope represented by the old Dutch painting's persuasive powers and in Mr. Brandon's possible influence, decided to stay right around the port. Their anxiety had reached its climax, and every time a vessel passed through the line of police launches, they ran to the dock and, pushing and shoving, made their way through the crowd that, with the same hopes and purpose, was gathered to see who was traveling to the land of salvation, although not promised. Daniel's mind was never able to free itself of the memory of that tense and depressing display: the police launches surrounding the passenger ship had been outfitted with reflective lights meant to prevent the desperate escape of passengers or suicide attempts, and its halo of warning created a darkness so dense in the rest of the bay that, until they reached the shore, it was impossible to know who was disembarking, which increased the uneasiness of people already shaken up by the drawn-out hopes and the imminence of the government-ordered departure.

On one of those launches, a journalist came back from the *Saint Louis* with two pieces of hair-raising news: the first was that the police had had to intervene in a mutiny of women who, upon learning the presidential decision, had announced their intent to throw themselves overboard if they didn't receive a satisfactory answer to their demand for asylum; the second piece of news was that a doctor had tried to kill himself, along with his family, by swallowing some pills. When he heard the latter, Uncle Pepe the Purseman felt so weak he almost fell apart. Fortunately, Daniel didn't manage to understand the journalist, since he was still incapable of following speeches by rushed and babbling Cubans. But when, at the request of those standing closest to him, the journalist looked in his notes and read the last name of the attempted suicide, Joseph Kaminsky felt his soul rush back into his body, and it was another of the few times in his life that he was explicitly affectionate with his nephew: he pulled him into his arms and hugged him with such force that Daniel felt his relative's quickly beating heart against his cheek.

Despite the heat assaulting all who gathered around the port in those days, Uncle Joseph always went to the dock wearing the sports coat he used only for major events, and that night, when he decided to remain all night, he used it so that his nephew could set himself up in the doorway of a business located on the other side of the Alameda de Paula. As soon as he wrapped himself up, fatigue overcame the boy. That night, which would end up being too brief, Daniel dreamed the only thing his mind longed to dream: he saw his parents and his sister getting out of a launch at the Hapag dock. When Daniel woke up, alarmed by shouting in what were still the wee hours of the morning, it took him a few minutes to regain consciousness of the situation, and that was when his heart broke: he was lying on the floor, and next to him a man was either snoring or in agony. With no idea of where he was, no idea of where his uncle would be, and no idea who that being reeking of vomit and alcohol could be, the boy felt like screaming and crying. In that precise moment, a small lapse in what would be the length of his entire life, Daniel Kaminsky learned the meaning of the word "fear" in all its dimensions. His previous experiences had been too vague, caused more by the fears felt and demonstrated by others than by any he had sensed himself, born of his own instinctual awareness. Fortunately, that sudden stab of terror ended up paralyzing him, and thus he remained curled up against the step of the colonnade, covered in his uncle's sports coat and some of the previous day's newspapers, looking at the ants that transported the remains of vomit clinging to the fallen man's mouth. A few minutes later he breathed a sigh of relief when he saw his tutor, who had come back, besides, with encouraging news: six Jews had just arrived on land thanks to some visas granted by the Cuban consulate in New York. As always, money was still able to solve many things, even the most seemingly difficult. Hugging his uncle, unable to control himself, Daniel started to cry out of fear and out of joy.

Around noon on June 1, the last eighteen hours began to tick by, which—per the passenger ship captain's request—President Brú had extended the *Saint Louis*'s stay in the port, a time period granted with the goal of restocking the ship for a trip to Europe. For all of the Jews confined on the ship and for those hunkered down on land, it was clear that there would be no more delays. As a reaffirmation of this terrible fact, they were able to watch the arrival of new military launches coming from the ports of Matanzas, Mariel, and Bahía Honda, determined to stop escape attempts by the passengers and to force the ship's departure if the captain didn't comply with orders. That same afternoon, Louis Clasing, the man from Hapag, again sent around the communiqué in which he informed that, given Cuba's and the United States' refusal to take in the refugees, the vessel would return to Hamburg. And at sunset the real bomb dropped: the Joint Distribution Committee representatives were leaving the island with their tails between their legs.

The macabre displays of joy by the many proponents of the expulsion of the would-be refugees drowned out all cries of protest, the tears, shrieks, and pleas of thousands of Jews who, with relatives or not aboard the vessel, had hoped for a happy ending to that dark story, one that was nearly incredible in the sum of its cruelty. Neither the ones who felt victorious nor the ones who felt defeated were able to ignore what that round-trip could really mean for the passengers of the *Saint Louis*. Daniel Kaminsky, although he was too young to understand the seriousness of the problem in all its details, felt an uncontrollable urge to throw himself into the sea and swim to the ship where his loved ones were and climb the boat to join them and share in their fate. But at that moment, he also asked himself why his parents and hundreds of other Jews didn't do the opposite and throw themselves into the sea to play their last card with this action. Because they were afraid of dying? No, it wasn't fear of death, since everyone said that death almost certainly awaited them in Hamburg with open arms. What was stopping them, then? What improbable hope? The boy wouldn't have a satisfactory answer until several years later, but it was perhaps on that very day, when he was just nine years old, that Daniel Kaminsky ceased to be a boy: he still had a ways to go to become a man, to acquire the judgment and capacity for decision making that come with years, but that day he was robbed of the naïveté and willingness to believe that constitute the innocence of youth. And, in his case, also of the naïveté of faith.

———

At eleven in the morning on June 2, machines put the passenger ship's floating mass in motion. Silent, defeated, it moved forward slowly toward the narrow mouth of the bay, always watched over by the old colonial forts and surrounded by all of those army and police launches. From the decks, the passengers were yelling, waving handkerchiefs, saying a pathetic goodbye. Behind the official launches, several boats with relatives were following the ship's wake, to be as close as possible to their loved ones until the last minute, as if it were the final moment. On the dock and along the port's avenue, there remained relatives, friends, curious onlookers, and the expulsion's proponents. More than fifty thousand people. The scene was of such dramatic proportions that even those who had demanded the rejection of the ship and its load set themselves apart and maintained an embarrassed silence.

Daniel and his uncle, beaten down by the fatigue of a week on high alert, uncertainty, and unease, didn't even throw themselves behind the pursuit of the helpless, like other Jews did along the avenue lining the harbor. Seated on one of the benches on the Alameda de Paula—the old Havana promenade that Daniel Kaminsky would never again step foot on for the rest of the years he lived in Cuba—they let defeat flatten even the last of their bodies' cells. The boy was crying silently and the man was scratching the beard that had grown in those days, as if he wanted to pull the skin off of his cheeks. When the *Saint Louis* crossed the mouth of the bay, it turned to the north and became lost behind the rocks and walls of El Morro Castle. Daniel and Joseph Kaminsky stood up and, holding hands, went in search of the start of Calle Acosta, to return to the phalanstery where they lived. On the way, they passed close by the synagogue, but neither nephew nor uncle demonstrated any intention to get any closer to it.

Not one of the two Kaminskys stranded in Cuba, safe perhaps from Nazi threats, harbored any hope for future solutions. The following days would prove them right. On June 4, the United States issued an ultimatum: it wouldn't accept the refugees who begged for a disembarkment order just off Miami's coast. The next day, Canada, their last hope, also announced its refusal. Then the *Saint Louis* would head toward the Europe from whence it came, loaded with Jews and trust, just three weeks before.

When they learned that news, coming down like the confirmation of a death sentence, Daniel Kaminsky, mired in the depths of pain, made the drastic decision that he, of his own will and from the bottom of his heart, would from then on disown his condition as a Jew.

4

Havana, 2007

He felt a physical tightness in his chest and a strange unease in his soul. Mechanically, Conde dug around in his pack of cigarettes to make sure he had smoked them all. He gestured at the box of Camels resting on the table between him and Elias Kaminsky, who nodded. He needed a cigarette so badly that he was willing to give up one of the most sacred principles of his nicotine faith. That story about the ship weighed down with Jews, in which he was previously interested enough only to learn the most general outline, but that he had now seen from the inside, had shaken him to his very core and chased away any remaining sleepiness. He felt wrecked, but out of an exhaustion more harmful than physical or even mental exhaustion: it had to do with a shameful, visceral wooziness, born in the deepest recesses of his being. Like Daniel Kaminsky's decision to leave his tribe. Because at that moment, Mario Conde was ashamed of being Cuban. While he didn't have anything to do with what had happened during those ominous days, the fact that some of his compatriots were won over by political or economic interests to somehow facilitate the commission of a part—minimal but a part nonetheless—of Nazi crimes left him feeling disgusted, exhausted, and with a sour taste in his mouth, a feeling that the Camel, with its yellowish fibers, only enhanced.

"I warned you that it was a long story," Elias Kaminsky said, rubbing his hands together vehemently, as if he wanted to rid himself of something abrasive. "Long and terrible."

"I'm sorry." Conde emitted this apology because he truly felt sorry.

He couldn't imagine whether the outsider could infer the reasons for his unease.

"And that's just the beginning. Let's call it the prologue . . . Look, it's already too late for us to have breakfast in a little while . . . I need to sleep for a few hours. The preparations, the trip . . . this story. I'm exhausted. But we could have lunch. Shall I expect you at one at my hotel and we can find somewhere to eat?"

Conde noticed that, at that moment, his dog was coming out of the door of the house. Garbage II, with his pompous gait, was walking and taking each step as a chance to stretch and unwind, ready, perhaps to set out on his nocturnal rounds as a hardened dog of the streets. Conde remembered that he had brought a bag of leftovers from Skinny Carlos's house but that he still hadn't fed the animal; he felt guilty.

"Hey, you, don't leave," he said to Garbage II and patted him on the back. Then he turned his attention back to his visitor. "Okay, we'll meet at one. I had things to do, but . . ."

"I don't want to keep you, sir . . ."

"Can we be less formal?"

"We can."

"That's better for both of us. How are you getting back at this hour? It's almost three in the morning."

"I have the car I rented parked here on the corner. Or, at least, that's what I hope . . ."

"I have a thousand questions for you. The truth is, I don't know if I'm going to be able to sleep," Conde said, and stood up. "But before you leave, I need to tell you something . . . What some Cubans did to those nine hundred people fills me with shame and . . ."

"My father understood what had happened and was able to do something that helped him live: he didn't fill up with resentment. On the contrary, I already told you: he preferred to be Cuban and forget about that pettiness that can show up anywhere. There was a lot of political pressure, from the Americans, from Batista. I myself think that those factors had more influence than the issues of money and corruption. I don't know . . ."

"That makes me happy for your father," Conde said, because he really felt that way. "But there's something else that . . ."

Elias Kaminsky smiled.

"You want to know what happened to the Rembrandt?"

"Yep," Conde admitted. "I'm dying to know how it got to an auction house in London," he added, and prepared himself to hear any story, no matter how sad or crazy it was.

"Well, I don't know. That's another reason I'm here. There are still a lot of gaps in this story. But if my father did what I think he did, I can't understand why he didn't take the painting. Until it showed up in London, I didn't know where it had ended up. What I am almost sure of now is that that Rembrandt was never again in my father's possession . . ."

"Hmmm, now I don't understand a thing . . . Are you telling me that your father tried to get it back?"

"Can you wait a bit? If I don't tell you the whole story, you're not going to be able to help me . . . At one o'clock?"

"At one," Conde agreed when he understood he had no choice, and he shook Elias Kaminsky's outstretched hand.

From his corner, Garbage II looked at them as if he understood what that goodbye meant for him.

———

Almost every trace of the memories built by words had become so twisted that they showed their crudest insides. To highlight the losses and absences, some places seemed to have taken on the task of saving themselves by stepping aside and allowing disaster to take over. But the majority of references had gone up in smoke, some without leaving the faintest trail that could evoke them, as if the old Jewish neighborhood and the area where it had established itself had been mercilessly crushed up in a grinding machine wound by a universal time accelerated by history and the nation's apathy. Fortunately, there it remained, challenging, like the last hope of ill-conserved memories, the unprecedented Arco de Belén, carved out of the bona fide cement of the convent through the path of Calle Acosta, which dragged itself, dirty and agonizingly, under the old arcade; there were the unrecognizable ruins of what was once La Flor de Berlín pastry shop and the remains of the hardware store belonging to Poles by the name of Weiss. But, above all, the noise that had so unnerved Daniel Kaminsky was still there. Recognizable, whole, argumentative, exultant, Havanese, the noise ran down the streets as if it had always been expecting the unpredictable arrival of an Elias Kaminsky to

hand over the key that could open the gates of time to his father's youth
and adolescence and, with it, the possibility of finding the path of understanding that the foreigner was seeking.

Like a blind man who needs to cautiously and exactly measure each
step, the sweaty, ponytailed behemoth started up the sordid steps of the
large nineteenth-century house on Calle Compostela, the former property of apocryphal counts, where the recently arrived Joseph Kaminsky
had put a bed, a table, a sewing machine, and his leatherworking tools,
and where, for almost fourteen years, his nephew Daniel had lived. The
mansion, abandoned at the start of the twentieth century by the descendants of its original owners and very soon turned into a multifamily
dwelling with a common kitchen and collective bathrooms, showed the
marks of growing apathy and the effects of excessive use over too long a
period of time. On the second floor, where once had lived *la mulata*
Caridad Sotolongo—the sweet woman who, over time, would turn into
Joseph Kaminsky's final and forever lover—life had seemed to stop in
the persistent and painful poverty of those who are crammed together
without any hope. By contrast, the third floor, the building's most noble
back in its day, where the original inhabitants' bedrooms were and later
the Poles' room and those of six other families of black and white Cubans, besides one belonging to some Catalan Republicans, had lost the
ceiling and part of the balconies and warned of the irreversible fate awaiting the rest of the structure. Making the most herculean effort, the
foreigner tried to imagine the Jewish boy going up the steps he had just
conquered; he forced himself to see him leaning over the no-longer-
existent wall of the third floor to watch, in the interior courtyard of that
hive, in front of the common kitchen, another blow of the mythical fight
between black Petronila Pinilla and Sicilian María Perupatto, in which
there was always the appetizing prospect of seeing a tit or two or even
four on the days of the rowdiest confrontations, and later he insisted on
seeing him go up to the rooftop with the twins Pedro and Pablo, black as
embers, and Eloína the tomboy, a freckly blonde, to hold up kites or
simpler constructions made with old newspaper sheets. Or to do other
things. But he couldn't.

Elias Kaminsky, seconded by Conde, asked several neighbors if they
remembered the Pole Pepe the Purseman, Caridad *la mulata*, and her
son, Ricardito, who had the gift of making up rhymes, but the memory

of the drawn-out stay of those tenants also appeared to have disappeared, like the structure's top floor.

They went down to the street and saw that the movie theater that had operated on the opposite sidewalk, where Daniel Kaminsky had acquired his incurable addiction to Westerns and gangster movies, was no longer a theater, or anything at all. And the famous Moshé Pipik, the city's most splendid and most visited kosher restaurant, looked like anything but a palace of ancestral aromas and flavors: it had been reduced to a brick shell darkened by mildew, urine, and shit, where four young men with prison-worthy faces and undoubtedly atrophied senses of smell were playing dominoes dispassionately while they drank from their bottles of rum, waiting perhaps for the inevitable building collapse that would end it all, leveling the interminable game in process. There, in that place, lively and well-lit in their memories, was where, after a dinner that was, for her, extravagant, and for him, the one he had dreamed of since his arrival to the island, Marta Arnáez and Daniel Kaminsky, Elias's future parents, had begun a courtship so pure that it would only end on the afternoon of April 2006 when she, with a shaking and wrinkled hand, closed Daniel's eyes.

"They met at the Havana Secondary Learning Institute, when my father was seventeen years old and my mother, the daughter of Galicians, but Cuban herself, had just turned sixteen. It wasn't easy for him to resolve to confront his uncle's reservations, since, of course, Joseph had expected him to marry some young Jewish girl in order to preserve blood and tradition. It was even harder for him to dare to stand up to the opposition of my Galician grandparents, who were doing quite well for themselves and were not in the least pleased that their daughter was interested in a Jewish Pole who was practically starving to death. But when she fell in love with him, nothing could be done. Marta Arnáez was sweetness itself, but she was also capable of withstanding anything when she set a goal for herself, desired something, or was keeping a secret. Almost a Galician at heart, don't you think?"

5

Havana, 1940–1953

Once the *Saint Louis* set sail from Havana, it would take Daniel Kaminsky nineteen years to again hear about that portrait of a young Jew made by the greatest Dutch master, the work on which his parents had pinned their hopes of salvation. By then he barely remembered the painting's existence and, above all, the presumed existence of a god.

Each time that Daniel recalled the seemingly valuable portrait that didn't end up bringing any benefit to the Kaminsky family, he felt frustration overtaking him. He tried to imagine when it could have changed hands, or, even better, he thought, it had been destroyed by his parents, a drastic and terrible solution that seemed more just, given his pained memory.

From what he was able to learn, the *Saint Louis*, turned away by the governments of Cuba, the United States, and Canada, was authorized to drop anchor in Antwerp, Belgium. Several European governments, less small-minded, decided to distribute the refugees among themselves: some would go to France, others to England, some would stay in Belgium, and the rest, around 190, were sent to Holland. Years later, Daniel Kaminsky would learn that his family had been part of that last group. The majority of them had been confined to the Westerbork refugee camp, a swamp surrounded by barbed-wire fences and guard dogs, where they were caught by the unchallenged German occupation of the Low Countries. The invaders immediately began to clear the territory of Jews and the solution was to send them to work and death camps in the eastern territories. It appeared that the Kaminskys, after almost two years spent in a camp in Czechoslovakia—had Judith, the little girl, survived hunger, illness, fear?—were sent in 1941 or 1942 to Auschwitz, on the outskirts of Kraków, precisely from where they had left a few years before in search of salvation from the terror on the horizon. It was a leap to the beginning of everything, the macabre tying-up of the journey through hell of a family and a portrait of a nameless Jew, the round-trip that would lead some of the Kaminskys to the crematories where they would turn into wind-scattered ashes. Many times, Daniel would ask himself if that portrait of a Jew who looked too much like the Catholic West's popular image of Christ had ended up in the hands of a Standartenführer or some other top leader in the SS, or if his parents, aware of that possible fate, had destroyed it as the useless canvas it had become.

That unfortunate story, the climax of which occurred in Havana's port just three months before the fascist invasion of Poland, in addition to the successive news of events coming from Germany and German-occupied countries regarding the European Jewish community, led adolescent Daniel Kaminsky to take the path that would turn him into an unbelieving skeptic. If certain stories about God's relationship with His chosen people had seemed excessive to him as a child (especially the one about Yahweh demanding the sacrifice of Isaac, the son of his favorite, Abraham), from that moment on, he would also dare to ask himself, obsessively, why the fact of believing in one God and following His commandments to not kill, not steal, not covet could make the history of Jews become nothing but a series of agonies. The end result of that sentence had been, undoubtedly, the suffering of the most horrifying of the holocausts, in which, even without the certainty he later had, he was sure that his parents and sweet sister Judith, from whom they hadn't heard another word, had perished.

So it was that young Daniel, disoriented, began to question his very identity and the suffocating weight it represented. What did he, Daniel Kaminsky, have to do with everything that was said about those born as Jews? Because their foreskin was cut, they ate certain foods and not others, prayed to God in an ancestral language, did they, he, his sister Judith, deserve that fate? How was it possible that some Jewish thinker came to say that that suffering constituted another test imposed on God's people because of their condition and earthly mission as the flock chosen by the Holiest? Since the answers eluded him while the questions wouldn't disappear, Daniel Kaminsky would decide (long before his uncle Joseph would present him at the synagogue to carry out the initiation ceremony of the bar mitzvah that would turn him into a responsible adult) that, due to dozens of historical lessons and practical reasons, and although he would remain so to everyone else, he didn't want to keep living as a Jew. Above all, he didn't want to take on that cultural belonging because he had lost faith in the God associated with it. And in all gods. Floating above men, there were just clouds, air, stars, the young man had concluded, because nowhere in any cosmic and divine plan could there be written or ordered the persistence of so much agony and pain as payment for the necessary transit through a bitter earthly life, plagued besides by prohibitions, a life of sorrows that wouldn't be redeemed until the arrival of the Messiah. No, it couldn't be. He couldn't believe in the existence of a God capable of allowing such excesses. And if He had ever existed, it was clear that He was too cruel a God. Or, further still, that that God didn't exist or had died . . . And, the young man asked himself many times: Without the oppression of that God and without His tyranny, what was Judaism?

———

Those were hard years that were simultaneously full of revelations for Daniel Kaminsky. The stabbing feeling of uncertainty came to join the hunger always beating at his door and the city noises determined to besiege him. When the *Saint Louis* returned to Europe and it became known that Great Britain, France, Holland, and Belgium would accept the refugees, hope was reborn in his heart and that of his uncle Joseph. But with the start of the war, they began to live with that anxiety determined to embitter the lives of all Jews with relatives in Europe, and also those who didn't have any family there, since no one knew the reach of that avalanche of hate moving and growing like a dark snowball that nobody seemed able to stop.

They spent all their time hunting down news, always unclear, increasingly more terrible, reading any and every report that fell into their hands with the fear of finding the last name Kaminsky on some list of detainees, transfers, or victims, with the piercing anxiety of not knowing more perverse than even the certainty of knowing. The first devastating blow had come with the news of the easy Nazi occupation of Holland and the confinement and transfer of Jews living there. Later, when the initial news came out of mass executions of people and entire communities in Poland, Ukraine, Turkey, and the Balkans, the details of what was to many the incredible horror of the death camps, in conjunction with the unbelievable addition of those trains loaded with emaciated men, women, and children and of the trucks designed to use their own exhaust pipes as a gas to suffocate the prisoners, a curious and explainable phenomenon occurred in that small family: while Joseph Kaminsky became a fanatic, going to the synagogue more often, dedicating more hours to prayers and clamors for the arrival of the Messiah and the end of time, Daniel, increasingly better equipped to analyze and understand what was happening and what his life had been and could be, became more of a skeptic, an unbeliever, irreverent, a rebel before a suspicious divine plan overflowing with cruelty. Simultaneously, he was becoming more Cuban and less Jewish.

Daniel knew that, to proclaim his freedom and achieve anything, he would need time and support, and the only person in the world capable of offering these to him was his uncle Joseph. So, at ten, twelve years of age, the boy learned the art of wearing a mask, something that would serve him well throughout his life. The mask he wore at home and in everything relating to his uncle was a caricature painted with the necessary features to satisfy (or at least not irritate) Pepe the Purseman. By contrast, the side he started to develop on Havana's streets was pragmatic, mundane, essentially streetwise, and Cuban. Using their economic difficulties as an excuse, he managed to convince his uncle to enroll him in a Cuban public school and leave his religious education to lessons taken through Adath Israel synagogue's free services teaching the Torah Vaddat. The option freed him from the Israelite Center school, allowed him to socialize more closely with Cubans and to start establishing friendships with kids his age, like the twins Pedro and Pablo and Eloína the tomboy, and even with some who didn't live in the tenement. The ones who would end up being two of his closest friends from that time period were his classmates from public school: *un mulato lavado*, as they called light-skinned blacks who passed for white, named Antonio Rico, who had amazing eyes that all the girls fell for, and a hyperactive redhead, the most out-of-control and most intelligent in their class, named José Manuel Bermúdez, nickname "Scatterbrain," because of permanent restlessness.

With Pedro and Pablo the twins, at age eleven, Daniel learned the pleasure of rubbing his dick. The site where he was initiated in masturbation and where so much of it occurred was a pigeon loft made by the twins on the tenement's rooftop. From up there, while they melted under the sun, it was possible to watch, through the open window, the pink ass, extraordinary tits, and long, wiry pubic hair belonging to Russian Katerina, who, always overwhelmed by the heat, fearlessly paraded the plump nudity of her thirty-five years around the room where she lived, on the other side of Calle Acosta. Shortly after, Pedro, Pablo, and Daniel went up a notch in their sexual explorations when Eloína the tomboy, who had grown pointy and exciting tits overnight, showed them that, even though she was better than most boys at playing baseball, her feminine sexual inclinations were very well-defined. Thanks to this, as if it were just another outing to send off kites, in the best spirit of camaraderie, the former tomboy initiated them (and initiated herself) in partnered sex, although under the condition that penetration only happen through the rear door, since her Red Diamond (that's what she called her freckly pussy with its saffron-colored curls) had to reach the marriage to which she aspired without any fissures, since, she said of herself, she was "poor, but honest."

Thanks to those hardened street dwellers, Daniel also learned how to speak Havanese (he called his friends *negüe*, buses were *guaguas*, food was *jama*, and the sexual act was *singar*), to spit out of one side of his mouth, to dance *danzón* and later mambo and cha-cha-cha, to flirt with girls, and the treacherously, deeply enjoyed freedom of eating pork cracklings, ground-pork spiked *fritas*, and almost anything that would satisfy his hunger, without caring whether it was kosher or *treyf*, only that it was delicious, abundant, cheap.

Antonio and Scatterbrain, for their part, facilitated the greatest and most defining revelations of Havana, which would always remain in Daniel's memory as transcendental discoveries, capable of marking him for the rest of his days. With them, both members of the school team, he learned the infinite secrets of the incredible sport known as "ball" by the Cubans, and acquired the incurable virus of a passion for that game when he became a fan of the Marianao club team, in the Cuban professional league, perhaps motivated by the fact that that club was always losing. With those friends, he learned to fish and swim in the bay's warm waters. With them, on many nights, he crossed the imaginary border of his neighborhood, marked by Calle Ejido and Calle Monserrate—the path where the wall encircling the old city had once run—to peek into the entrances brimming with lights, announcements, music, and passersby of the Paseo del Prado, where the city exploded, overflowed, came off as rich and prevailing, and where it was possible to enjoy from any corner the acts of female orchestras charged with animating cafés and restaurants on the central avenue, places that never closed their doors, if in fact doors existed. (In a voice that he always lowered, Daniel would later confess to his son that those musical acts led by women had left him forever with the magnetic attraction he felt when he saw a female blowing on a flute or a saxophone, playing an upright bass or some metal drums. A downright feverish attraction if she was *una mulata*.) With those friends, he took refuge hundreds of times in the Ideal Movie Theater, built with the columns worthy of the dreamlike palace that it actually was, to take in their favorite movies, almost always thanks to Scatterbrain's congenial generosity, since his father was a driver on Route 4 and earned a fixed salary: Scatterbrain tended to pay for Daniel's and Antonio's tickets, at five cents a head, to enjoy a banquet of two movies, a documentary, a cartoon, and a newsreel.

As he opened the doors of a noisy city in which there were no physical or mental dark corners reminiscent of Kraków and Berlin, Daniel Kaminsky felt like he was leaving himself and living inside another Daniel Kaminsky who would live without a thought to prayers, restrictions, and thousand-year-old laws, but above all, without feeling the pernicious fear that he had learned from his parents (although he was always tangibly afraid of Lazarito *el mulato*, the neighborhood's typical tough guy, who owned a mythical switchblade with which, they said, he had sliced up a bunch of asses). The boy was living it up and was able to shout obscenities with the crowd at baseball games, swim like a dolphin in the Malecón's reefs, sympathize with Hollywood heroes, and live with his love for the ass of a *mulata* flute player with promising lips while he masturbated gazing at the straight hairs hanging from a Russian woman's crotch: the perfect combination.

If that had been his entire life, if that had been the only Daniel Kaminsky, perhaps he would have been able to say, years later, that, despite the poverty, malnutrition, and absence of his parents that marked those years, he had had a happy, almost full, adolescence. But the other Daniel, who lived in anxiety over the war and in desperation to receive any news regarding his parents and his sister, was moving within a lie that made him feel as if he were suffocating. His goal, at that time, was to reach a sufficient age to declare his independence, although he knew he had to do so in a way that wouldn't hurt the sensibilities of his uncle Joseph, to whom he owed so much and whom, without expressing it physically or verbally, he loved like a father. He would buy his freedom with time and money.

Daniel the Pole, as his classmates and Havana street friends called him, was able to enroll at the Havana Secondary Learning Institute only one year behind students his age, specifically his future girlfriend Marta Arnáez and his pal in street wanderings José Manuel "Scatterbrain." By then, he had already been through his bar mitzvah, the war was over, and he had suffered the painful and liberating experience of having read, among the lists of Holocaust victims provided by the Israelite Center of Cuba, the names of his father and mother amid the Jews who, throughout those awful years, had been sent to Nazi camps and crematories, the horrors of which had finally come to light in full and were publicly condemned in the Nuremberg trials. The name of his sister Judith, on the contrary, never appeared, as if the girl had never existed, and for many years Daniel held on to the slight but persistent hope that Judith, by some miracle, had stayed alive: maybe adopted by some Soviet officer, perhaps rescued by some partisans, maybe hidden in the woods and taken in by some country folk . . . but alive. In his imaginings, Daniel had come to identify his sister with the heroine to which she owed her name and who, according to the books considered apocryphal by biblical compilers, had slit the throat of General Holofernes, who was sent by the powerful Nebuchadnezzar to subdue the unruly Israelites. Thanks to his recollection of one of the many books that existed at his Kellerstein grandparents' house, Daniel could see his sister Judith transfigured into that beautiful and rebellious woman, painted by Artemisia Gentileschi, dagger in hand, in the act of decapitating a Babylonian general, who in his mind appeared as an officer of the terrible Hitlerite SS from whose claws she was escaping . . .

If the end of Daniel's childhood could be marked by the morning on which he saw the *Saint Louis* set sail from Havana's port, the beginning of his adulthood happened in October 1945, at the age of fifteen, as the feeling of absolute loneliness fell on his shoulders when he confirmed that his parents had been killed by the most rational and intellectualized hate. He would make his first decision as an adult a few days later when he refused to please his good uncle Pepe the Purseman by continuing his studies at the Yavne Institute, known for its Orthodox leanings.

Daniel Kaminsky would always remember that time, so full of difficulties, as one of the most complicated in his life both before and after. In the span of those six dark wartime years, Uncle Joseph had shown Daniel, upon taking him in, his limitless goodness in spades by protecting him, feeding him (more or less), and supporting him as a student, something that was a luxury for the majority of Cuban young people, many of whom barely finished elementary school, as had happened with his friend Antonio Rico. Although in the Kaminskys' daily life things hadn't changed too much, Pepe the Purseman's finances had to be (Daniel would assume, and gratefully confirm it years later) much less tight since he was promoted to main leather cutter and turned into the heart and soul of Jacob Brandon's increasingly prosperous leather workshop. That American Jew's businesses had taken off in the years of war and shortage, thanks to the improvements he had introduced to all of them, including the leather goods shop, by reinvesting the earnings gained with the very productive lard contraband. Joseph's decision to send Daniel to the Jewish high school, nonetheless, had been assumed as an investment, and constituted common practice even among the most impoverished Jews in the community, who were aware that only with higher education could doors be opened in a country where, since the United States' entry into the war as an enemy of Germany, the relationship with Jews had again come to be cordial.

Conscious of his obvious inability to support himself, the young man tried to be as delicate as possible when he communicated his decision to his mentor to continue his studies like any other Cuban and to limit his relationship with the family religion to a minimum, since he could no longer spend time faking something he didn't feel, particularly when it came to a matter so serious for the Jewish people.

Joseph Kaminsky's reaction turned out to be violent and visceral, as expected: resorting to Yiddish to best express his disappointment, he called Daniel a heretic, an ingrate, senseless, and demanded that he leave his house. With a small leather satchel that fit his belongings—a few clothes, two or three books, the photos of his parents that he'd had with him since leaving Kraków—Daniel went out to Calle Compostela to go up Acosta and cross through the Arco de Belén, which, without his willing it, introduced itself in his mind as the exit from a rowdy Jewish paradise established in Havana's oldest neighborhood. But still a paradise at the end of the day.

His dreams of being able to continue his studies with some normalcy now undone, Daniel was lucky that his friend Scatterbrain got his parents' permission so that, for a few days, he could sleep on some blankets thrown on the floor of the small living room in the Calle Ejido apartment where the family lived. A big question mark hung over the young man, who had neither a profession nor any skill, since he knew that even if he managed to get any kind of gig, he would never earn enough to find a room and pay for a meal every day.

One week later, a stopgap appeared, at least for his sustenance, both nutritional and, in part, physical, when Sozna the Jew, the owner of the bread and pastry shop La Flor de Berlín, provisionally offered him the arduous night cleaning shift. The German Jew put him in charge of cleanup at the back of the work- and salesrooms, washing trays and utensils and even lugging tons of vegetable oil and sacks of sugar and flour back and forth, to leave it all pristine and in the exact order in which the master baker and his helpers should find it at the start of their first shift, at one a.m. Thanks to the backbreaking work he meticulously carried out (at times, with help from Scatterbrain, Antonio Rico, and Pedro the twin, since Pablo, convicted of several robberies, had been sent to Torrens, a famous and dark reform school), he not only received twenty-five cents per day but could also eat all of the scraps and rejects that the bakers (and the owner himself, who wasn't Jewish for nothing) hadn't made off with themselves, scrape the bottoms of the jelly jars, and, removed from the workshop's own noises, sleep for a few hours atop the mountains of Castilla-brand flour sacks. Although he forced himself each morning to overcome his exhaustion and to attend his classes at the Havana Secondary Learning Institute, the worst part of his situation was the absolute darkness in which his future had fallen, since, while he still didn't know what path he would take, he had never seen himself as a baker's helper.

The morning when he was leaving La Flor de Berlín and found his uncle Joseph sitting on the curb across the street, along with a cardboard box, he knew immediately that the light was returning. No, his uncle couldn't be bringing bad news, because the quota for that type had already been exceeded. And he wasn't wrong . . . Pepe the Purseman was

coming to look for Daniel so he would live with him again in his room in
the Calle Compostela tenement and so Daniel could attend the school
of his choice as a normal student. The man had given a lot of thought
to it and made the decision to allow his nephew to come back since he
believed he understood the reasons behind his decision: he himself,
he then confessed, his eyes teary with a good dose of fear or pain over the
losses he had suffered, more than once had felt, like the boy, an uncontrollable urge to tell it all to go to hell, tired of shouldering an ancestral
stigma that persisted when he hadn't done a thing, in any regard. The
price paid by that family was already too high to increase it with separa-
tions and punishment, he said, and Daniel was old enough to exercise
the free will that the Holy One had given him along with his life. Besides, his uncle added, the truth was that he missed him and felt alone.
So alone that he had done something excessive, the man said, pointing
at the cardboard box and then asking Daniel to open it. Then the young
man almost fell over in shock in the middle of the street. His uncle had
gone nuts and bought him a radio!

His tutor's timely reconsideration and the freedom from the weight
of a double life turned young Daniel Kaminsky, at the age of sixteen, into
a real man, who then enjoyed the best years of his life, enhanced by
the enjoyment of musical programs, the play-by-play of baseball games,
and the adventures of the Chinese detective Chan Li Po, which he could
now enjoy as much as he wanted with that brilliant radio device. The
peace and kinship existing in Cuba, where being Jewish or not didn't
seem to matter much to anyone, where Poles, Germans, Chinese, Italians, Galicians, Lebanese, Catalans, Haitians, people from all corners
of the world came together, allowed him a fullness that no Jew had
imagined even in his dreams since the distant times in which the Sephardic people had been allowed into Amsterdam. Among Cuba's Jews,
besides, there were devouts and skeptics, communists and Zionists, rich
and poor, Ashkenazim and Sephardim, some days at war with each other,
other days living in harmony, but nearly all of them were almost always
willing to pursue two aspirations in those propitious lands: money and
tranquillity. What most annoyed Daniel about the efforts made by that
community to which he belonged less and less, from whose orthodoxies
he increasingly distanced himself, was how it sought to isolate and close
itself off precisely in the places where they were welcomed and had
doors opened to them. The ghetto spirit had left a mark on their souls

after centuries of experience and persisted in hounding them, even in freedom. The sustained attempt to live and progress as a closed, inbred group, with businesses among Jews, marriage between Jews, ceremonies between Jews, food for Jews (although always differentiating between Sephardim and Ashkenazim, rich and poor) seemed absurd to Daniel and was something that his liberal, open spirit rejected, despite knowing that his attitude was considered integrationist by rabbis and by any believer in the significant fate chosen by divine plan as the mission of the sons of Israel. Luckily for Daniel and his happiness, despite that stubbornness, there were increasingly more Jews established in Cuba who thought like him and, further still, who lived according to their own wills.

It was true that in those years the country's prosperity and its Republican democracy, which allowed the Jews' progress, had to endure the rise of one of the worst social scourges: corruption. The quest to get rich in the shortest amount of time possible was so visceral that it overtook politicians, business owners, investors, military leaders and policemen, and more or less public figures so that even violent wars between factions occurred with a certain frequency, as exemplified by the so-called Cuban gangsters. But when it came to a student without two pennies to rub together like Daniel, those dealings barely touched him, or so he thought in his naïveté at the time as he enjoyed the pleasant feeling of living fearlessly (completely fearlessly, since Lazarito was locked away at the Castillo del Príncipe jail for his excessive use of a switchblade). As his years and experiences as a Cuban added up, the young Jew would rectify many of his first impressions about the Cuban character, cheerfulness, and levity. He would learn that, as part of the human condition, on that sun-blessed island, with all the physical benefits to generate wealth, where cultures and races mixed and everyone sang or danced, hate and cruelty could also flourish, even the most sadistic kind; social climbing and the ever sordid social and racial differences could spring up; and, especially, an evil could appear that seemed to have invaded the hearts of many in the country: envy. Was this permanent and petty envy an inherited quality or, on the contrary, was it a patentable and specific result, like all the mixtures that made up a Cuban? Many years later, a friend would offer him a plausible answer . . .

Despite his improved situation, Daniel Kaminsky decided to continue working on the cleaning crew at La Flor de Berlín while going to high school so that he could have some money to cover his growing needs for clothing, school supplies, the luxury of a snack, or the possibility of spending an afternoon at the Grand Stadium of Havana when his favorite team, los Tigres de Marianao, played. During his second year and after several weeks of saving, that salary was even enough to take the little *gallega* Marta Arnáez, with whom he had fallen desperately in love, to dinner at Moshé Pipik. At the restaurant of his dreams, besides impressing the young girl who still hadn't accepted him but always listened to his declarations of love, Daniel wanted to satisfy the persistent and old desire to sit at one of the red-and-white-checked-tablecloth-covered tables, at the center of which reigned a blue bottle of seltzer water, and to enjoy those foods that, had he not been spellbound with the vision of his almost-girlfriend (as he thought of her), perhaps they would have transported him to his Polish childhood down the path between his taste buds and his so-called emotional memory. Especially if that path is taken after a plate of *kneidlach* in which the balls of egg and flour floated in chicken stock and, upon entering the mouth, crumbled with their pleasant softness, drowning everything with their taste of heaven.

———

It took Daniel Kaminsky a year of persistence, initiated with looks, smiles, and any creative ploy he could think of, followed up by declarations of love, both verbal and written, to win a yes from Marta Arnáez. And it wasn't because the young girl didn't like, from the start, that Pole with the unruly curls, whose eyes were more stunned than large, and who was thin as a rod but muscular. As he told his son Elias many times, seated below a canopy of bougainvillea in the yard of their Miami Beach house, or on a white-painted bench under the shade of the leafy acacias belonging to the exclusive Coral Gables nursing home, from the beginning she felt a certain sympathy for, and soon after, a definite attraction to Daniel. But she felt forced to respond to his amorous pretensions with a phrase that neither rejected him nor accepted him: "I need to think about it," she would repeat to her stubborn would-be boyfriend. "That's how it was back then," she would explain to her son Elias Kaminsky years later, always with a smile on her face.

They became a couple at the end of the spring of 1947, when they were finishing up their second year of high school, and from that moment on they began to wander around the city holding hands, at least until they approached the young girl's house on the corner of Virtudes and San Nicolás, close to busy Calle Galiano. Then they would separate, without even a kiss on the cheek, and she would go on to her house without turning around and he would return to Old Havana, very pleased with himself, with the hope that Russian Katerina, with the help of vodka, rum, or gin, would have one of her hottest days and, as had been happening for a year already, would motion to him with her finger, implying an invitation to come up to her apartment, where she would offer the young man another lesson in her free, hands-on course on Slavic abandon.

A few weeks later, it was summer vacation, and Marta, along with her parents, went to spend it in the remote and supposedly flourishing town of Antilla, in the northeast of the island, where a brother of her mother's lived and worked. Although old man Arnáez returned after a week to man his store, which specialized in liquor and provisions, mother and daughter remained for an outrageous eight weeks in that part of the world—the longest eight weeks in the life of Daniel Kaminsky, who felt he was about to go crazy as he counted the days and, at times, even the hours separating him from a reunion, when he imagined himself going out to Antilla and kidnapping his beloved to then take her to another of the island's remote spots. He was so desperate that he didn't even seek out another invitation from the Russian woman, and, out of sheer lack of alternatives, he even returned to the synagogue to numb himself with prayers and the reading of the Torah's passages. He also put in more hours working at the German Sozna's bakery so he could save up enough money to buy himself the suit with which he would, at some point, appear before his future in-laws to formalize the courtship by asking for his girlfriend's hand.

While neither Daniel nor Marta knew it, the women's prolonged stay in the east was part of a strategy meant to cause their separation and encourage them to forget each other, since neither Manolo Arnáez nor Adela Martínez found the discovery that their daughter was going out with a scruffy Polish Jew to be a pleasant one. But both parents, already familiar with the young girl's ways, chose to use subtle methods before a full-on confrontation from which, they predicted, they would emerge defeated. Because Martica was more stubborn than a mule, according to her own father, an expert mule raiser in the finest Galician style.

The solution her parents sought had the opposite effect to what they had hoped for. When she returned to Havana and dove into her studies, Marta Arnáez, who was already seventeen, decided to allow her boyfriend to move forward one more step in their courtship and they at last kissed for the first time. Although passion was coming out of their respective pores, from that point on, despite the desire filling their heads with naughty thoughts, they had enough restraint to limit themselves to kissing and light caresses. "Of course, again, those were the times," Marta would occasionally say to her son. "And to let off steam, your bastard of a father had Katerina, free for the taking, the whore of all whores, but from me . . . nothing more than innocent kisses."

Unwillingly, the young girl's parents accepted the formalization of the courtship when Daniel and Marta were about to finish their third year of high school. Daniel had arrived wearing the cheap fake muslin checked suit that he had bought from the Lebanese vendors on Calle Monte and the blue-striped tie, a gift from the owner of La Flor de Berlín. Sitting for the first time in the living room of the Calle Virtudes house, after telling his presumed in-laws about his serious intentions, Manolo and Adela asked him to come back the following day for their verdict. Once they were alone with Marta, her parents asked the girl what she thought of that declaration. She answered with the phrase that would mark her life, and with such a tone that made it clear to her parents it was best to give her freedom in that respect. "Daniel is the man of my life" were the girl's words, and she remained true to them until the end.

———

Just when he was trying to, and succeeding at, finally formalizing his courtship, Daniel Kaminsky had a deep identity crisis that shook all of his deep-rooted beliefs. At the end of that year, 1947, in the land of Palestine, the new state of Israel had been born and its entry into the world had been chaotic and painful, but full of hope. Like almost all Jews spread around the world, Havana's Jews greeted the development joyfully, even when, as seemed to occur in every important or unimportant case, they processed it from the perspective of different factions, running from militant Zionism to outright apathy toward a set of events so removed from their daily lives. But between one extreme and another, there were numerous positions, encouraged by communists, Zionists, socialists, Orthodox, reformists, moderates, liberals, militarists, pacifists, Sephardim, Ashkenazim, atheists, or believers of a messianic bent, and as many mixtures of positions or identifying subtleties as one could imagine.

Daniel, who thought he was so removed from those debates, then felt the ungovernable call of tradition deeper and more dramatic than he could have imagined. After several years of dogged and beneficent distance from Judaism, now the fate of Eretz Israel and its ongoing earthly and heavenly problems had come back to shake him. The much-anticipated and necessary birth of the Jewish state came with the conviction that merely by having their own country, precisely in the lands that their God had promised them, the Jews would be able to avoid the horror of another Holocaust like the one they had just suffered, the dimensions of which they learned more with each terrible revelation. To obtain that refuge, the Jews channeled all of their passion, their peaceful and violent tricks, and their talent into exerting economic and moral pressure. They came to count on the support of the same North Americans who nine years prior had prohibited the docking of the *Saint Louis*, and even of the powerful Soviet Union, which was interested in a strategic friendship with the Jewish state. Even though the Cuban government refused to recognize Israel, the entire process, which focused international attention, reached Daniel Kaminsky in mysterious ways, as if to remind him that, in the end, he had more than a cut foreskin in common with those people. He was also tied to them by blood, and, further still, by death. That feeling of kinship besieged him so that, a few months later, when the fate of the recently born state was jeopardized by the military response of several Arab armies, he, like other young people in the community—mainly the children of Turkish Sephardim, hardened proletarians—came to wonder whether he shouldn't also volunteer to go defend the resurrected country of the Israelites, lost so many centuries before.

The Saturday morning on which, after a long absence, he went with his uncle Joseph to the Adath Israel synagogue to catch up on the serious events occurring on the opposite side of the world, the rabbi's words set off remote fibers of his consciousness that Daniel Kaminsky had thought had disappeared. "God gave every nation its place, and to the Jews he gave Palestine," the officiant said, standing among the rolls of the Torah. "The Galut, the exile in which we have lived for so many centuries, meant that we Jews had lost our natural place. And everything which leaves its natural place loses what sustains it until it returns. We know that well. Since the Jews have shown national unity since the time of the patriarchs to a degree that is higher than that of other nations, since it was the will of the Holiest one, blessed may He be, it's necessary for us Jews to return to our real state of unity, which we can only obtain in contact with the sacred land of Eretz Israel, there where it all began, a land whose ownership is confirmed by the sacred book and divine word."

Perhaps it was the vital perspective that the formalization of his courtship offered that most influenced his final decision to distance himself from the temptation circling him and in which some of his neighbors and former classmates from the Israelite Center and many of the young men enrolled at the Yavne Institute had fallen. Or, at least, that was what he told his uncle Joseph when they discussed the issue. Because, in reality, after the initial feelings brought up by his ancestral instincts, Daniel Kaminsky felt that he found himself too far from that world of Jews in search of a fatherland to risk his own life in a military conflict of unpredictable proportions. Beyond egoism, he would say, what was at play in his case was an absolute lack of faith, of commitment to a cause dressed up as messianism and rebellion against old and limiting religious precepts rescued by the newborn country. All of it resting on a very rational stubbornness: his dramatic and nearly puerile purpose, in principle, of leaving Judaism, and his decision, stronger now, to share his life with a Cuban woman who—Daniel was horrified when he found out—could never be his legal wife in a country that, before it was born, had proclaimed the exclusion of Gentiles and, in the name of God's laws, had forbidden so-called mixed marriages. Without his noticing how deep the process went, that defensive feeling of cultural and definitively rebellious distancing had grown more than he himself believed and left a generous space for his decision to be nothing but Cuban, living and thinking like a Cuban, a desire that became an obsession capable of dominating him consciously and subconsciously, so much so that it didn't seem to have left too much room for any Jewish fanaticism to reach greater proportions.

Many years later Daniel Kaminsky would revisit the dilemma of that defining decision of his life in a letter sent to his son Elias, who by then was established in New York, where the young man was trying to start his career as an artist. It happened in the late 1980s, a few months after Daniel had undergone a successful operation for prostate cancer. Pushed by that mortal warning, as soon as he recovered, he surprised his family with the decision to return to the city of Kraków, to which he had never previously wanted to return. In addition, against all logic, Daniel Kaminsky chose to carry out that journey to his roots, as Ashkenazi Jews the world over called it, alone, without his wife or his son. When he returned from Poland, where he spent twenty days, the man, who was generally loquacious, barely made a few banal remarks regarding the trip to the place of his birth: the beauty of the city's medieval plaza and the strikingly vivid memory of the horror embodied by Auschwitz-Birkenau, the visit to the ghetto to which the Jews had been confined and the impossibility of finding what could have been his house in the Kazimierz neighborhood, the visit to the New Synagogue, with its candle-less candelabras, gloomy in the solitude of a country that was still uninhabited by Jews and sick with anti-Semitism. But the emotion over his encounter with the cradle of his past that he had tried to cover up for years, from which he had even seemed to free himself a long time before, had touched on the darkest corners of Daniel Kaminsky's consciousness. So, months later, he finally carried out that unforeseen confession.

In the letter, he told his son that, ever since his return, he hadn't been able to stop thinking about the certainty that, as in all Jewish history, the most regrettable thing, which he would never be able to abide, was related to what he considered a deep sense of obedience, which times had devolved into the acceptance of submission as a survival strategy. He was speaking, of course, of his always problematic relationship with the God of Abraham, but, especially, about what occurred during the Holocaust, in which so many Jews assumed their fate as unchallengeable, considering it a divine curse or a heavenly decision. He couldn't fathom that, their fate decreed, many of them even collaborated with their victimizers, or prepared themselves almost religiously to receive their punishment; that they went to the pits where they would be executed on their own two feet without any attempt at rebellion; that they boarded the trains where they would die of hunger and dysentery; that they would organize themselves to live in the camps where they would end up gassed. And he spoke of the way in which the hope of surviving contributed to the submission. The combination of the totalitarian powers of one God and one state had crushed the wills of thousands of people, strengthened their submission, and even snuffed out the desire for freedom that, to him, was the essential condition of a human being. Many people—millions—had accepted their fate like a divine mandate so that, in the end, among a few thousand of them, there would be explosions of rebellion, partisans in antifascist guerrillas, and rebellions in ghettos like the one in Warsaw. "Although," he said at one point in his letter, "you should also keep in mind that so many of those submissive men and women came to view death almost with joy, in comparison to the life of pain and fear they were living. If you look at it that way, perhaps you can see many of their attitudes through a different perspective. You can even, Goddamn it, you can even justify the submission and I refuse to justify it . . . Or is what they repeated to us at the Israelite Center classes a lie, what the rabbis, Zionists, pro-independence activists declared when they told us that today's Jews were descendants of Joshua the Conqueror and his indomitable Jewish peasants, of King David, the victorious general, of the warrior Hasmonaean princes . . . ? How was it possible that, in the end, submission would overcome us?" Perhaps that conviction, which in 1948 was just a shapeless shadow in his consciousness, was the one that, with its dark weight, had kept him from the idea of getting on a ship to Israel and leaving with his friends to participate in the war for independence, he confessed to his son. The mark of that resigned behavior, which his grandparents and Kellerstein uncles and perhaps even his parents participated in, was impressed so deeply upon him that he had lost not only his faith in politics and in God but even in the spirit of men, and as such he preferred to remain at the margins of that delayed rebellion, hunkering down in his more comfortable self as a Cuban. Living with his choices and at ease at the margins of the tribe, in that corner where he had found freedom.

———

As could be expected, Polish Daniel's dearest friends at the time were all Cuban and Catholic—in the unorthodox way practiced on the island. He was still very close to his old mate José Manuel Bermúdez, whom no one called Scatterbrain anymore, but rather Pepe Manuel. That boy had grown and become strong, while the saffron color of his hair was now limited to some highlights, and even his freckles had disappeared. His natural intelligence, all the more developed, had turned him into one of the best students at the Secondary Learning Institute and, because of his magnanimous character and his habitual loquaciousness, into one of the student leaders. Another of his friends was called Roberto Fariñas and was the black sheep of one of Havana's bourgeois families, the coproprietors of a small rum factory and of apartments on the outskirts. Roberto had refused to study at a private school and, less still, with priests, whom he detested, and as such had enrolled at the public school where the least privileged went. Thanks to his unlimited budget, Roberto tended to be that friend who more often than not paid for ice creams, shakes, sandwiches, and burgers at the area's eateries, especially at the sophisticated one that had just opened on the ground level of the new Payret Cinema building. Pepe Manuel's girlfriend—Rita María Alcántara— and Roberto's—Isabel Kindelán—had also become friends with Marta Arnáez, and the six young people had made up a sort of informal club, despite their differing origins, economic circumstances, and family relationships. They had more important things in common: their passion for dancing, their connoisseurship of baseball, their love for the sea, and the comfort that they didn't keep too many secrets from each other—those clear waters on which true friendship floated. And, further down the road, they would also share an interest in, or at least (in Daniel's case) politics or political sympathies.

When Roberto Fariñas turned eighteen and could finally get his driver's license, one of his older brothers put at his disposal a 1944 Studebaker, which became his friends' daily wheels. With the permission of the girls' families, they were able to start going to the beach at Guanabo and they even went to Varadero for the first time to see the superfine sand in that practically deserted haven. Of the three couples, only Roberto and Isabel had crossed the complicated border of premarital sexual relations. Pepe Manuel, who was so revolutionary in everything, ended up being conservative on that specific issue, while Daniel, although he was dying to take things to the next level (especially since Katerina's decision to go live in the far-off neighborhood of La Lisa as the concubine of a black trucker), didn't dare ask Marta, who years later confessed that, had he asked, she would have said yes, since she was seething with envy when she knew Roberto and Isabel were doing it.

"Five years of courtship with no sex, how scandalous!" Marta would once tell her son Elias.

Living in that pleasant universe of girlfriends, friends, schoolwork, outings, and work, to earn something of his own, Daniel Kaminsky made his way through life, distancing himself from his ancestors and their worries, to the point that he removed himself so much from whence he came from that one day he even believed he had forgotten that part of his identity existed. It was then that the head of a young Jew painted by Rembrandt crossed his path, determined to complicate his life and warn him that some things are hard to give up.

———

What had happened to his parents aboard the *Saint Louis* during the six days that the passenger ship had been berthed in Havana Bay? How badly did they dream of going on land thanks to the negotiations based on those few inches of canvas stained with oils three hundred years before? To whom had they given that painting? And how? From the moment that he again had the unexpected and moving certainty that the family relic had remained on the island ever since that bitter May week in 1939, those and other questions knocked around in his head so much and so violently that Daniel Kaminsky felt he was on the edge of delirium.

When Daniel finished his studies at Havana's Secondary Learning Institute, his future was already decided. While his in-laws agreed to support Marta in her stubbornness to study education at Havana's Normal School, he would look for a more appropriate and better-paying job than that of cleaning crew at a pastry shop, and, at the same time, would enroll in courses at the business school to become an accountant. The plan included a wedding celebration, set for a year later, and an agreement with the *gallego* Arnáez that they could live in his own house until Daniel graduated and the couple was in a position to proclaim their independence. That whole project was being forged in a country where, again, they were living amid sharp tensions, ever since, in March of that year, 1952, General Fulgencio Batista brought soldiers out onto the streets and took power in order to prevent an election being held in which, with all certainty and despite the death of its leader—Eddy Chibás—the increasingly more numerous militants and sympathizers of the Cuban

People's Orthodox Party would have won, under its slogan and program of "Shame against money."

The military coup polarized Cuban society and a substantial majority of young students, including Pepe Manuel Bermúdez and Roberto Fariñas, Orthodox Party militants for several years already, and Daniel himself, who sympathized with the party under the influence of his friends. Due to the charismatic attraction of its founder—the already deceased Eduardo Chibás—they believed in the dream of a political renewal in the country. The three friends, like so many Cubans, took Batista's actions as an assault against a defective democracy, but still a democracy when all was said and done and which the Orthodox Party could have improved with important social changes and the full-on struggle against corruption that the deceased Chibás had championed with his promising program for a civic and political housecleaning.

While Pepe Manuel and Roberto became more involved with the opposition movement, Daniel, as was his tendency in life, concentrated on himself. During the first two years of his studies to become an accountant, at the exact time set for his wedding, his life entered another phase. Thanks to his uncle Pepe the Purseman's friendship with the increasingly powerful Jacob Brandon, now co-owner of the nascent and revolutionary supermarkets named Minimax, the young man had obtained a part-time job as a clerk in the very modern establishment opened in El Vedado, where he was also in charge of daily accounting and managing requests to the suppliers. Daniel was already earning thirty pesos per week, a more than worthy sum in a country where a pound of meat cost ten cents.

That saving gesture by Uncle Joseph Kaminsky, who was in a position to receive favors from one of Cuba's richest Jews, never ceased to be a mystery to Daniel. The young man wouldn't understand the relationship uniting the furrier and the magnate until a few years later when, under very delicate circumstances, his uncle would again save him with a surprising gift. Pepe the Purseman, who until his revolutionary intervention in 1960 served as the cutter and maestro of Brandon's leather workshop, had also turned into the maker of the special shoes that the businessman's bunions required; into the crafter of belts that, like saddle straps, circled his belly; and into the designer of fine purses, luggage, cigar cases, and even gloves for trips to New York and Paris—always made with the best and most appropriate leathers for each item and the most exquisite cuts and seams, learned by Joseph years before from Bohemia's artisans.

Without a doubt—as his nephew thought and would say—Joseph Kaminsky must have been earning a salary with which any man could have left the increasingly dark rooming house at Compostela and Acosta and moved to an apartment or even a small stand-alone house in any Havana neighborhood. But Pepe the Purseman remained surrounded by Jews, hunkered down in the motley phalanstery and living as parsimoniously as always. Daniel thought he found the main reason for his uncle's insistence on remaining in the tenement when he discovered that that fifty-something-year-old conservative Pole had found an outlet for his loneliness in *la mulata* Caridad Sotolongo, who some time before had become a tenant in that ruinous building. Thirty-something, a widowed concubine, and very shapely, Caridad was also the mother of Ricardo, a fairly mischievous young *mulato* for whom Uncle Joseph always showed a certain weakness, perhaps born from the boy's innate capacity for inventing poetry and reciting it as if he were a machine.

Caridad's story was soon known by all of the neighbors. Her lover, a white man, Ricardito's never legally recognized father, had been one of the revolutionaries from the 1930s who, frustrated and disappointed by the small political and economic gains obtained from his often violent struggles, strayed with some of his other mates toward the groups of gangsters who, with increasingly less political sheen, used the barrel of a gun for the political and economic rewards they said they deserved. That man had died in 1947 during a confrontation between gangsters and policemen who were no less gangsters, and, immediately, Caridad's life, which had been comfortable to a degree, evaporated, since she had never been more than a gunman's lover. She was thirty-six years old, nearly illiterate, but still very beautiful, and, together with Ricardo, who was seven years old at the time, they had to leave the little house in Palatino, where they couldn't pay the rent, and ended up in the tenement at Compostela and Acosta, so that she could dedicate herself to the poorly remunerated job of washing and ironing for others.

In contrast to the rest of those crammed into those quarters, Caridad was discreet and silent, for which she was quickly deemed a proud and haughty *mulata*, and even a *capirra*, as people in Havana called blacks and *mulatos* who preferred to marry whites. At some point, thanks to some favors they exchanged, a certain friendship grew between that woman and Joseph Kaminsky, who had just crossed the threshold of his fifties. Daniel had a flash of intuition of what was going on the day that Caridad brought them a clay pot of thick black beans—*dormidos*, as they called them in Cuba—redolent of cumin and bay leaf, those legumes that Joseph Kaminsky had never seen in his Polish days but that in his Cuban stay had become his favorite dish . . . and his nephew Daniel's weakness. The look the Pole and *la mulata* exchanged at that instant was more revealing than a million words. Words that Uncle Pepe wouldn't say to his nephew until years later. The words acknowledging Caridad's existence and the feelings she had awoken in the furrier that so influenced Daniel Kaminsky's fate.

Thanks to his salary at Brandon and Company's market, Daniel threw himself into the preparations for the wedding, which occurred in the summer of 1953 and ended up being much more magnificent than the young man could have afforded and even desired due to his natural discretion. But Marta's parents, resigned at first and later taken with the young Polish man who was climbing the social and economic ladders, and content to see their only and dearest daughter's exultant joy, spared no expense. The most difficult demand on Daniel came when it was time to discuss the type of ceremony they would have. For his betrothed's parents, it was practically a matter of honor that the marriage, after being notarized, would take place before God and be consecrated in a Catholic church. Daniel invested weeks in discussing the options with Marta, coming from a position that seemed fair and clear to him: since he himself was not capable of asking her to marry before a rabbi, she shouldn't demand that he should do so before a priest. His reason was simple: he didn't believe in the rabbi of his ancestors or in the Catholic parish priest. It wasn't that hard to convince Marta, since the young woman could do without the religious ceremony, although she found its pomp and circumstance attractive—among her reasons was the fact that even Pepe Manuel Bermúdez himself, who was turning more red by the minute, as everyone remarked, had agreed to marry Rita María in the falsely Gothic church on Calle Reina, to the beat of a wedding march composed by a German Jew . . . Marta understood her groom's reasons. The ones who wouldn't understand were Manolo Arnáez and Adela Martínez, without whose support the marriage could not happen, or would happen under different circumstances, she said to him.

Daniel Kaminsky thought a lot about his options. The easiest and simultaneously most complicated would be to take Marta, get married before a notary, and forget about the Arnáezes. For someone who had lived in an old Havana tenement for so many years without ever being able to fully satiate his appetite and with just a couple of cheap shirts to his name, that to-do with ball gowns and crowded parties seemed optional and unnecessary. But it seemed cruel to the girl, and even to her parents, to deny them the dream with which they crowned a climactic moment in their socially successful lives. The most difficult, though simultaneously perhaps less disruptive, of his options was to accept the formality of a required Catholic baptism and a marriage officiated by a priest, since neither of the two acts held any meaning for him. Many practicing and believing Jews throughout the centuries had had to accept Catholic sacraments in varying life circumstances, even while knowing they would never be able to later save themselves from selling out like that, since their God ordered them to die venerating His name. Why had it always been so complicated to be a Jew? He had asked himself this many times before sitting down to discuss this excruciating conflict with his uncle Pepe the Purseman. Around that time, as if in anticipation of what would happen soon after, Daniel thought several times of the portrait of the young Jew who looked like the image of the Catholic Christ under whose watch he had lived out his earliest years, without it meaning—for him or for his parents—anything more than that: a beautiful portrait of a young Jew with his gaze lost somewhere on some corner of the painting.

As he would always remember, for weeks Daniel put off the time to have the conversation that he imagined would be the thorniest one of his life, since it implied not only a break with his origins and the religion of his ancestors, but also because it might gain the understanding of or cause the most heartbreaking disgust of the good man who—without expressing his affection with a single gesture or word—had allowed him to have a worthy life in its poverty and served as the steady support from which Daniel Kaminsky would soon obtain the benefits of economic mobility and even of social respectability. For many years before, Uncle Pepe would talk to him, for as long as he could and always in passing, about some of the young Jewish girls in the neighborhood, trying expressly to push the boy's interest, although with the greatest discretion, toward a woman of his own background, to perpetuate with a union of that kind what they themselves were and what their children should be for many more centuries.

"You know I am an atheist, Uncle Joseph," the conversation began. Daniel had preferred to hold the dialogue in Spanish, since he was no longer confident in the depth of his Polish nor of his Yiddish for matters of great subtlety. Since the spring afternoon was brisk, thanks to a dense covering of clouds, he had chosen to speak to his uncle on the section of the rooftop of that crumbling little palace where he had lived since the day in 1938 when he had ended up in Havana and felt alarmed by the ruckus that he hadn't noticed now for a long time.

"I don't understand how someone can be an atheist, but if you say so . . . God is greater than your disbelief."

"Well, I stopped believing a long time ago. You know why. What's important is that I am incapable of believing."

"You're not the first to think that way. It will pass . . ."

"Perhaps, Uncle. Although, I don't believe so."

Daniel had paused after that statement with which, he knew, he was attacking some of the principles his uncle Joseph had clung to in his solitude as a poor emigrant man with no other living family in the world but Daniel himself. "And I have to make a decision that is not important to me, but is to other people. A decision that has a lot to do with faith. With yours and with theirs," Daniel added, to be more explicit.

Pepe the Purseman, looking into the young man's eyes, had allowed himself the slightest smile. A sad one, more than happy, in reality. It would have been difficult for the Polish furrier, who had gone through so many difficult moments and known the most immense horrors, to feel surprised or overcome by anything. Or, at least, that was what he believed, as he used to say to his nephew. "I can imagine where you're going . . . And I'm going to make things easier for you. I will only tell you that every man has to resolve his questions with God on his own. For worldly problems, some help is always welcome. I have given you what I could give you. Do you know why Sozna gave you a job and lodging at La Flor de Berlín? I couldn't let you starve out there. Taking care of you was my moral obligation—more still, an obligation with my faith and tradition. And the result hasn't been all bad: you are an honorable man and you have a good job, studies that can help you very much, a good life that is going to be even better. Perhaps one day you'll even be a rich man . . . Of course, I regret your distance from God and our customs, but even I am capable of understanding them. You wouldn't be the first Jew to turn his back on his faith . . . My son, do what you have to do and don't worry about me, or about anyone. At the end of the day, we're all free due to divine will, even to not believe in that will."

As he listened to him, Daniel started feeling an indefinable sensation washing over him in which gratitude for his uncle's understanding, handed over like true freedom, mixed with a jabbing impression of his weakness, capable of bringing him to the edge of a convenient acceptance of something his spirit denied. Like never before in his life, at that moment he felt miserable and petty, devoid of soul, identity, the will to fight. If Uncle Joseph had shouted and insisted on his damnation, like the day that the boy had refused to enroll at the Jewish school, perhaps everything would have seemed less humiliating, since he could also have yelled his reasons, become stubborn, and chosen even to act rebellious and offended. But when his uncle revealed that even during Daniel's rebellion he had been protecting him and taking him away from the possibility of a confrontation, Joseph had surprised him, leaving him alone with his soul, with the void that his life and his own insistence had created in the space where other men, like his uncle or his future father-in-law, housed the consolation of feeling the company of a God, his God, any God. "The same God?" he would sometimes ask the offspring of that painful conflict.

"I appreciate your understanding, Uncle. To me, that's the most important thing," Daniel could barely say. Joseph Kaminsky removed the round-rimmed glasses he had been using for a few years and wiped them off with the edge of his shirt. "You should appreciate Cuba. Here is where I have worked, lived in poverty, suffered disappointments, but I've gotten to know another life, and in many ways that changes one . . . I am no longer the same skittish and fanatical Pole who arrived more than twenty years ago. I have lived here without fearing the next pogrom, which is already enough, and no one cares much which language I use to pray. Despite whatever you may have heard, you cannot have any idea what that means, because you haven't lived it . . . Wanting to be invisible, as your father came to think . . ."

"So, you're not upset with me?"

Pepe the Purseman looked into his eyes, without answering, as if his mind were elsewhere. "Incidentally," he said at last, "do you know why I haven't married Caridad?"

Daniel was surprised by the abrupt change to a subject that had never been brought up by his uncle, at least not with him, and to which Daniel, out of respect, had never referred.

"Because she has her beliefs and I have mine. And I am not capable of asking her to give hers up. I don't have the right, it wouldn't be fair, because that faith is one of the few things that truly belongs to her and that has most helped her to live. And I am not going to give up mine. She is uneducated, but she's a good and intelligent woman, and she has understood me. For the two of us, the important thing now is that we feel good when we're together, and that helps us live. Above all, we no longer feel alone. And that is a gift from God. I don't know if from mine or hers, but a divine gift . . . In sum, do what you want. You have my blessing. Well, it's a saying, you don't believe in blessings . . ."

The sky, besieged by dark clouds coming from the south, opened up at that moment in a torrent of water flecked with the flashes of electric discharge that, according to the Pole Pepe the Purseman, were never as resounding in his far-off country. When the men returned to the tenement room, Joseph Kaminsky went in search of the small wooden chest that had accompanied him since he left Kraków and where he kept his now obsolete passport, a few photos, and the tallith that his father had given him for his bar mitzvah, which was held in the city's great synagogue. He opened it with the key that he always wore around his neck, and from inside took an envelope that he handed to his nephew.

"What's this, Uncle?"

"My wedding present."

"You don't have to . . ."

"Yes, I have to. Dignity requires it. If your in-laws are going to help you, you have to contribute. That contribution will make you freer."

Daniel, without understanding his relative's intentions too well, opened the envelope and found the check. He read it. He couldn't believe it. He reread it. His uncle was making him the owner of four thousand pesos.

"But, Uncle . . ."

"That is almost all of my savings from these years. You need it much more than I do now . . . For that especially you need money, to buy your freedom."

Daniel was shaking his head. "But you could move out of here with this, live with Caridad, help Ricardito with school . . ."

"From this moment on, you're not financially dependent on me, or on anyone, I hope. With what I earn, I believe that Caridad and I can soon move. And I already set aside an amount for Ricardito's needs. You know, with a plate of rice, black beans, and some kosher meatballs, I have more than I need. And now I'm a better furrier than ever, so don't worry, I'm not in want of work, thanks to the Most Holy."

Daniel Kaminsky couldn't take his eyes off the paper, which was worth much more than the fortune of four thousand pesos. That money was the product of infinite refusals, privations, and the impoverished situation in which he and his uncle had lived for years. It also represented the valid passport with which Pepe the Purseman could bring joy to his nephew's life. And, Daniel knew, had been saved to congratulate him on the day he, in a synagogue and before a rabbi, sealed his matrimony according to Jewish Law.

Overwhelmed by the invasive tide of his heresy, Daniel Kaminsky had begun to cry: while his uncle Joseph handed him understanding and money, Daniel was stealing from him the dream of seeing him break the crystal glasses with the stomping of his foot, to recall with that action the destruction of the temple and the beginning of the interminable Diaspora of the Israelites, and the need to remain united in the tradition and Law written in the Book as the only mode for survival of a landless nation. Unable to contain his sobs, that afternoon, for the first time in many years, Daniel hugged his uncle and kissed his cheeks, always in need of a closer shave, several times.

Perhaps due to Joseph Kaminsky's liberating attitude, two months later, when Daniel went to the small Church of Espíritu Santo to be baptized and receive the decree certifying his conversion, allowing him to pronounce his marriage vows before a priest, the young man couldn't help feeling that he was carrying out a shameless abandonment for which, despite his convictions and denials, he was not really prepared. In the company of his betrothed, his future in-laws, and his godparents for the occasion, Antonio Rico and Freckly Eloína, the still-Jewish young man entered a Catholic temple for the first time in his life with the intention of doing something besides satisfying his curiosity. Although he already knew what he would find there—childish images of martyrs and supposed saints, crosses of all sizes, including the necessary one with the bleeding Christ nailed to the wood, that whole exulted imagery—he couldn't avoid the emotion and visceral, more than rational, desire to run right out of there. This was not his world. But that escape, if it happened, would be fleeing from the earthly paradise that he wanted to enter, that he deserved to enter. Later, he would think that what most helped him to contain his impulses was the unexpected sight of Caridad Sotolongo's figure, seated humbly in one of the last pews of that small temple, wearing a white dress, doubtless the finest in her closet, and with a handkerchief covering her head.

Standing before the priest responsible for officiating the ceremony destined to change his religion, Daniel Kaminsky managed to escape his regrettable reality by concentrating on evoking the fable that, many times as a child, his father had told him, in the still-pleasant days in Kraków and, later, in the tense ones in Leipzig and in the desperate ones in Berlin. The young man was able to remember how, just the night before he left for Havana, during the last occasion on which Dr. Isaiah Kaminsky would dress him before bed, his father again narrated that mythical story of Judah Abravanel, the outstanding descendant of the predestined branch of King David's house, the line charged with the responsibility of bearing the true and awaited Messiah . . . According to what his father said, and as Daniel would later tell his son on steamy evenings in Miami Beach, the real or fictitious character of Judah Abravanel, already thrown out of Spain like all Sephardim who didn't accept Catholic baptism, had taken refuge in Portugal, where, soon after, he again found himself in the terrible circumstance of choosing between baptism and the death of his children, his wife, his coreligionists, and of himself. In that Lisbon cathedral where a wicked king had confined the Jews and placed them before the quandary of Christ or the bonfires, the Sephardic wise man, doctor, philosopher, poet, and financial genius decided to set an example and accept conversion, condemning his soul but preserving not only his body but the lives of many of his own and, especially, the fruits of his line that were fated to bring salvation to his people. Perhaps Judah Abravanel—Isaiah Kaminsky used to say—at the moment he felt holy water fall on his head, had thought he was submerging himself in the Jordan to purify his body before going to the resurrected Temple of Solomon to lie down before the Ark of the Covenant. Now, while the water poured by a priest fell on his head, Daniel Kaminsky took refuge in evoking his father. In that protective notion he was again surprised by the vision of a familiar image of the face of a young Jew too similar to that of Jesus of Nazareth and, he was thinking it for the first time, also like the Judah Abravanel of his imagination. Marta's hug and kiss, overflowing with joy over the gift that her beloved had given her, brought the heretic out of his inner labyrinth and returned him to the reality of the Catholic temple, which, even after the completed conversion, did not cease to appear to him as a scene for fanatical children.

Daniel, still stunned but feeling free, accepted his father-in-law's invitation without hesitation for all of them to go out to lunch at the nearby restaurant Puerto de Sagua, where, it was said, they served the best and freshest fish one could eat in Havana. Only when he searched for her as he was leaving the temple did Daniel discover that Caridad Sotolongo had disappeared. Had she been there or had he imagined it? he asked himself. How influential was that woman, the devotee of boisterous black gods, in preventing the recently completed ceremony from turning into a dramatic event that would distance Daniel forever from his uncle Joseph, the mild-mannered and stingy furrier who, for better or for worse, had turned him into the man he was? Daniel would never dare to ask that, but, sensing the answer, he professed a gratitude to the woman that remained steady throughout the years and the distance. Until death.

6

Havana, 2007

Since all that remained of Moshé Pipik were just some foul-smelling ruins incapable of evoking the kosher restaurant that had once shone there, destined for years to satisfy Daniel Kaminsky's hunger, Elias suggested to Conde that they try their luck at the Puerto de Sagua, where, his father used to say, the fish was always excellent.

"*Was*, in this case, could strictly be *was*," Conde warned him. "Past tense, imperfect, but past. Like the time of Moshé Pipik and other things you've wanted to see . . . By the way, did you say *cuqueado*?"

"Yes," Elias Kaminsky confirmed, wrinkling his brow. "Did I say it wrong?"

"No, not that I know of . . ."

"My mother used that word. For years, I've lived speaking English, but when I speak Spanish, I subconsciously connect with the way she spoke. They're like old gems. You clean them a bit and they shine again. Let's see, what do you have to say about the word *zarrapastroso*? My father was a thin and *zarrapastroso* Jew . . . Perhaps no one says that anymore."

"He was what we call an *habitante*. An *habitantón*." Conde clinched it. Elias smiled.

"Damn! It's been years since I heard that. My father also said, when he talked to other Cubans over there: 'Don't be an *habitante*, Papito!' He would say that to a Cuban with whom he became friends in Miami . . ."

As they wandered through the places hinting at the life, memory, and lost words belonging to Daniel Kaminsky the Pole and his wife,

Mario Conde had the pleasant feeling of peeking into a world that was nearby yet distant, faded ever since he was old enough to notice. The lives of those Jews in Havana were of a bygone era, of which only a few traces remained and very little will to evoke them. The massive stampede of the Jews, Ashkenazim as well as Sephardim (in agreement for once), had occurred first with the suspicion and then, soon after, with the confirmation that the rebels' revolution would choose a socialist system. The change had pushed eighty percent of the community to a new exodus, to which many saw themselves forced to depart as they had arrived: with just a suitcase full of clothing. From what those men knew of the fate of the Jews in the vast Soviet territories, few of their customs, beliefs, and businesses would emerge unscathed from the confrontation, and despite their cherished experiences on the island, the Jews left, taking their suitcases, their prayers, their food, and music elsewhere. For the majority, even the converted Daniel Kaminsky and his wife Marta Arnáez, who got a head start by a few months, it was Miami Beach, where other Jews in the United States already lived, the place in which they engaged in the uphill battle of making new lives and, with thousands of years of experience under their belts, established a community that was once again like the sticky ghetto culture. The disquieting difference in dates that encouraged the painter's doubts lay in the fact that, while the largest part of the community left the island between 1959 and 1961, Daniel Kaminsky and his wife had left in April of 1958, long before others and with a quickness destined to reveal pressing needs.

They found the restaurant's spacious salon to be nearly empty. When Conde read the menu's prices, he confirmed the reason for such desolation. A plate of lobster cost what the average Cuban earned in one month. That place was another ghetto: for foreigners like Elias Kaminsky, for homegrown tigers like Yoyi the Pigeon, and, these days, for a lucky one such as himself, hired with all expenses paid seemingly just to hear the life story of a Jew who insisted on renouncing Judaism and who, at some point, as far as Conde knew, seemed to have killed a man.

The restaurant's refrigerator-like atmosphere smelled like beer and the sea. The dimmed lights were a relief to the pupils of the newly arrived, burnt by the September sun. The waiters, a true squadron, took advantage of the room's calm to chat while leaning against the long, polished-wood bar, perhaps the same bar on which, fifty-five years before, the newly converted Daniel, his girlfriend, friends, and relatives had huddled together to toast to the lack of obstacles to a Catholic wedding.

Elias chose the lobster with chili sauce. Conde selected a hogfish stew. To drink, they asked for the coldest beers in the place.

"My father could never have been a lone wolf. He needed to belong, to be part of something. That's why his friends were so important in his life. When he lost the closest ones, it was like he lost his compass . . . It's also because of that that he became Jewish again. Although he couldn't believe in God." Elias smiled.

"Now that you mention it, there's something I haven't asked you . . ."

To the painter's surprise, Conde lit up a cigarette, colossally and Cubanly telling the supposed prohibition announced by the sign with a red circle to go fuck itself. "Are you a practicing Jew?"

Elias Kaminsky shrugged his shoulders and imitated Conde, lighting up his Camel after drinking more than half of his tall glass of Bucanero beer in one swig.

"Strictly speaking, Judaism is transmitted through one's mother, and my mother was not a Jew by birth. But when my parents arrived in Miami, things went in a different direction, and as part of that direction, my mother ended up converting and it turns out that that automatically made me a Jew—although I'm one of those who only goes to synagogue on Yom Kippur, because it's a beautiful holiday, and I eat barbecued pork ribs. But let's say that, yes, I am."

"So what does that mean to you?"

"It's rather complicated . . . My father was right when he said that being Jewish is something tricky. For example, the condition of Jews was a problem even for the Germans who killed six million of us, including my grandparents and aunt . . . Recently, I read a book that explains it in a way that really left an impression on me. The writer explained how the decision to annihilate the Jews was, above all, a form of necessary self-annihilation on the part of the Germans themselves, or at least, a part of their own image that they wanted to get rid of in order to be the superior race . . . Although they didn't acknowledge it, and in fact, they never acknowledged it—what the Germans essayed with the elimination of the Jewish attitudes that they called greed, cowardice, and ambition was in reality an attempt to erase those qualities in themselves, in the Germans. The fucked-up thing about it is that when the Jews were doing these things in the German way, it was because they dreamt of seeming like the Germans, because many of them wanted to be more German than the Germans themselves, since they considered the men among whom they lived to be the perfect image of everything that is good and beautiful in the world of the illustrious bourgeois, the civility to which many of them aspired to belong in order to cease being different and to be better . . . Something like that had already happened in Greece when many Jews hellenized themselves, and later in seventeenth-century Holland . . .

"Or, it is also possible that the Jews wanted to seem like the Germans in order to leave behind the image of the stout-bellied business owner, miserly, petty, who counts each coin, thus achieving acceptance by the Germans . . . It's not a coincidence that many German Jews totally assimilated, or nearly, and some even abominated Judaism, such as Marx, a Jew who even hated other Jews . . . The terrible thing, says the man with such disquieting opinions, is that, nevertheless, the German dream was quite the opposite: like the Jews in key things, in other words, being pure of blood and spirit as the Jews said they were; feeling superior, like the Jews, due to their condition as God's people; being loyal to Laws that were thousands of years old; being a people, a *Volk*, like the national socialists said; and, thanks to all of those marvelous possessions, they became indestructible, like the Jews, who, despite not having a country and having been threatened with destruction thousands of times, had always survived. In short: being different, unique, special, thanks to God's protection."

"I don't really understand," Conde admitted, "but it sounds logical. With a perverse logic, given what happened in Germany and in Europe . . ."

"But there's more . . . What led to the disaster and the Holocaust was that they were all wrong: the Jews, in wanting to be German without ceasing to be Jews, and the Germans in their aspiration to take the example of Jewish predestination and singularity. Something like that, although luckily not ending in tragedy, had already happened in Amsterdam when the Dutch Calvinists and Puritans found in the Jewish book the basis for enshrining their national singularity in myth, to explain the history of their national mystique as a chosen and prosperous people. In the Jews, they found a glorious parallel to their exodus and the foundation of a country . . . even the justification for becoming rich without moral or religious prejudice. Thus, they accepted the Sephardim expelled from Spain and Portugal and even let them practice their religion and build something as majestic and impressive as the Portuguese Synagogue, which is a futuristic variation of Solomon's Temple, placed in the middle of Amsterdam. Why do you think Rembrandt and the rest of the painters of that time preferred to find themselves in Old Testament scenes . . . ? Look, if being Jewish has come to mean something, it is precisely being the other, a way of being the other that, despite not having worked many times for the Jews, has survived three millennia of attacks. And that's what the German national socialists most wanted: to be other and eternal, to have a feeling of belonging as strong as that of the Jews . . . And to achieve it, they had to make them disappear off the face of the earth."

"Things are getting sinister."

"Could be, in fact, they are," Elias Kaminsky admitted. "Everything I've told you could fit together pretty well if you stop to think about it for a while, right? Look, my advantage lies in my being a peripheral Jew, in all senses, and although I belong, I don't belong, although I know the Law, I don't practice, and that gives me a certain distance and perspective to see certain things. What the Germans did with six million Jews, including what must have been my grandparents, my great-grandparents, my aunt, can't be forgiven. But at the same time it requires an explanation, and the hate for other races or the death of Jesus Christ on the cross can't cover it all in a process that ended up being so deep and so radical that it encompassed an entire continent. That's why I like that explanation. I almost believe it . . ."

The food put a pause to that conversation, which had veered off on paths too thorny for Mario Conde's mental exhaustion. According to Elias, the chili sauce was excellent; Conde found the hogfish sauce to be a mediocre copy of one he tasted some time before at a modest eatery in Caibarién or of the one Josefina prepared with the stark simplicity implicit in the improvised but simultaneously fabulous combination of basic ingredients available to the poor fishermen who set a pot of water over a flame while cleaning the scales of a hogfish. To make it better, the former policeman had drizzled some hot sauce on it that was making him sweat, despite the restaurant's freezing temperature.

"When I told you about the *Saint Louis*"—Elias poured a new beer into his glass—"and you told me that you were ashamed to hear that story . . . well, a few years ago, the United States offered an apology to the Jews, but Cuba did not."

"Naturally," Conde said, and reflected on the rest of his comments for a second. "We're too proud to apologize. Besides, the past is in the past and no one today would ever think to apologize for something other people did, even if they were also Cuban . . . I'm ashamed of that story because I'm a first-rate moron."

Elias Kaminsky smiled, making the moment less dramatic.

"By the way, something I can't leave without doing is visiting the cemetery where Uncle Joseph is buried," Elias said.

"It must be one of the ones in Guanabacoa. Since there are two."

"Yes, one for the Ashkenazim and the other for the Sephardim."

"I've never visited them," Conde admitted.

"Are you on board?" Elias Kaminsky asked, relying on his mother's lexicon again.

"I'm on board," Conde said. "But after dessert and coffee. That's also part of my expenses," he added, and lifted his arm to get any of the blasé waiters to actually deem them worthy of their attention.

———

Misinformed by a passerby for whom all Jews and all dead people were one and the same, Conde and Elias Kaminsky went to the Sephardic cemetery first. What they found was not encouraging in the least. Dusty tombstones, some of them broken, weeds growing everywhere, a crumbled wall, tombs cannibalized by the seekers of Jewish bones to round out the symbols in the ritual pots belonging to Cuban followers of Palo. Because, Conde knew all too well from his time with the police, the bone of a Chinese person or a Jew strengthened the power of the religious "accessories" of the *paleros*, even more so if it was for doing evil. But he didn't comment on this to Elias Kaminsky.

Fortunately, the Ashkenazi cemetery was a few blocks away, and since they chose to cover the distance by foot, Conde took advantage of the walk to keep satiating his unbridled curiosity.

"Your parents left, but Uncle Pepe stayed. How did that happen?"

"After the wedding, my father moved to my grandparents' house, until they bought a little house in Santos Suárez. But his uncle stayed in the tenement for three or four more years. Until he got married before a notary and went to live with Caridad and Ricardito in a neighborhood called . . . I can't remember now. When my father established himself in Miami, he asked Uncle Joseph if he, Caridad, and her son wanted to go live with them. But he said no, at his age, he didn't have the will anymore to start over. He didn't want to go anywhere, and less still to a country where a black woman couldn't live like a normal person. He would stay in Luyanó. Could it be Luyanó?"

"Uh-huh, yes, Luyanó."

"Well, he rented a little house with two bedrooms, one for him and Caridad, and another for Ricardito. He put his sewing machine and his tools in a shed at the back of the house, but he almost exclusively worked in Brandon's workshop by then, until communism came and the workshop, Brandon, and nearly all the Jews disappeared . . . Uncle died here, in 1965, before turning seventy years old. In the end, he was earning a living by fixing shoes . . ."

"What about Caridad?"

"My parents kept in touch with her until she died, in 1980 or so, around then. Whenever he could, my father sent her a package of clothing, medicine, something to eat. It was very complicated at the time."

"What about Ricardito?"

"As far as I know, he became a doctor. He was able to finish high school before 1959, thanks to Uncle Joseph. Later, it was easier for him and he went on to the university. But since my father left here, he was never in direct contact with Ricardito, he only received news of him through Caridad. She explained to my father that for Ricardito, especially as a doctor, it wouldn't help him to have a relationship with people who lived in Miami."

"I know that story well," Conde confirmed.

"Me too. Your friend Andrés told me about that. He spent years without a word from his father because he lived in Cuba and his father was in the United States. That made them practically enemies. What nonsense!"

"The New Man can only have fraternal relations with those who share his ideology. A father in the United States was an infectious contamination. You had to kill all memory of the father, the mother, and siblings if they weren't in Cuba. It was much more than nonsense . . . What do you know about Ricardito?"

"Nothing . . . I suppose he is still here, don't you think?"

When they arrived at the Ashkenazi cemetery, the gatekeeper-gravedigger was about to shut the gates, but a five-dollar bill kept them open and guaranteed his services as a guide and, had they requested and had the man been capable, even some funeral prayers in ancient Hebrew or Aramaic. Just barely over the threshold—*Abandon all hope, ye who enter here*—Conde noted that the distance between one hallowed ground and the other was imposed not by doctrinal differences but by an economic abyss. Although the state of abandon was similar to the one that reigned over the Sephardic cemetery, the surviving tombstones, marbles, and mortuary symbols announced that these dead Ashkenazim had been living people who reached their ends with much more money than their Sephardic counterparts.

Like the other necropolis, some of the tombs were crowned with small stones placed there by some relative or friend. But the effects of time and neglect had eroded almost everything. Those final dwelling places expressed their fate better than any other testimony of a community that, in its heyday, had been active and thriving. Even their sepulchres were dead.

Conde noted the differences in the existing last names between one cemetery and the other, imprints of the parallel paths that those Jews had followed for centuries, some in Spain, the prosperous Sepharad, and some in the exodus and the dispersion through the vast regions of Eastern Europe, the territories where each one of the branches of the chosen people had arrived just to forge their own languages and to shape their own last names capable of announcing their belonging to the two cultures united by the Book. But the prosperity of the Ashkenazim who came to Cuba from Poland, Austria, and Germany contrasted with the humble origins of the Turkish Sephardim, even after death.

The gravedigger-guide led them to Joseph Kaminsky's tomb, covered with a cheap granite slab on which, with difficulty, could be read: KRAKÓW 1898–HAVANA 1965, and in backward Hebrew letters that, most possibly, the uncle himself had ordered as a message to posterity, so that, if anyone was still interested, they would know who he had been in his life. The efficient gravedigger rubbed his damp handkerchief over the dew on the granite plaque, until Elias was able to read: JOSEPH KAMINSKY. BELIEVED IN THE SACRED. VIOLATED THE LAW. DIED WITHOUT FEELING ANY REMORSE.

7

Havana, 1953–1957

It was during the winter baseball season of 1953–54 that the great Orestes Miñoso, "the Cuban Comet," the very spirit of the island's professional Marianao team and, during the summers, also of the American Chicago White Sox, made the longest home run ever in the Grand Stadium of Havana, built just a few years before. The opposing team's pitcher was the American Glenn Elliott, who was at the service of the powerful Almendares club that season, and what Miñoso delivered was an out-of-this-world *lineazo* that went far over the central garden fences, an inhumanly good hit in which that five-foot-ten, compact black man had invested all of his energy and his incredible talent for hitting the ball with the beauty and perfection of his terrifying swings. When the league's inspectors tried to take the measurements of that connection, they tired of counting once they went past the distance of five hundred feet from home plate. As a souvenir of that great feat, a sign was hung announcing: MIÑOSO WAS HERE. Starting with the next season, when Marianao's star approached the batter's box, the megaphone of the greatest sanctuary in Cuban baseball played the cha-cha-cha recorded in his honor by Orquesta América and whose most popular refrain said, "When Miñoso swings the bat, the ball goes cha-cha-cha like that."

On that historic day, about which baseball fans would talk for years and years, Daniel Kaminsky the Pole and his friends Pepe Manuel and Roberto were three of the 18,236 fans occupying the Grand Stadium's stands to enjoy the game between the destructive Alacranes de Almendares and the humble but seasoned Tigres de Marianao. And, like almost all those other fortunate fans, Daniel and his friends would remember for the rest of their days—many days for some; very few, in reality, for another—the home run by that black Matanzas-born angel descended from slaves brought all the way from Calabar, Nigeria.

On the streets, Daniel had been infected with the incurable virus of passion for baseball that ruled over Cubans. And, by that absurd logic which love sometimes follows, from the beginning he proclaimed his preference for the humble Marianao team, a team that in fifty years of history had barely risen up on four occasions with the Winter League champion crown. Two years before Daniel arrived in Cuba, the Tigres had achieved glory for the second time. And they wouldn't do that again until the fabulous seasons of 1956–57 and of 1957–58, when, led by Miñoso's unsparing bat and the joy with which that man went on to the playing field, they would do so in a crushing manner. Daniel Kaminsky would always think that his choice to love a losing team was part of a complicated plan of recompense, since after a long period of frustrations it was precisely in the last two years that he would live in Cuba, wrapped up already in the definitive tensions destined to change his life, that the Marianao team won those championships and Orestes Miñoso, the most loved hero in his entire life, would achieve the climax of his glory, show-ing, as never before, that "When Miñoso swings the bat, the ball goes cha-cha-cha like that."

Despite Marianao losing season after season during almost all of Daniel Kaminsky's Cuban stay, the young man who that 1953 afternoon had gone to Havana's stadium had many other reasons to consider himself a happy man. "What is happiness?" he once asked his son Elias, many years later, when he was already a guest at the exclusive Coral Gables geriatric home and, on his night table, occupying the most visi-ble spot, was an enormous photo in which the Polish Jew and the black Cuban baseball player were shaking hands, smiling, although the Jew was already bald and the Cuban was already going gray. The painter thought about the possible response, tallied up proofs, but preferred to remain silent.

"You tell me."

"Happiness is a fragile state, sometimes instantaneous, a flash," Daniel started to tell his offspring while he directed his gaze at the photo where he appeared with the great Miñoso, and later, to the face of Marta Arnáez, covered with wrinkles and far removed from the beauty she had displayed for years. "But if you're lucky, it can last. I had that luck. At the time you make your lifelong friends, I found those friends. And ever since I met your mother I was, in life's main areas, a happy man. But when I think of things like the privilege of being one of the eighteen thousand people on earth who was at the stadium that afternoon and could enjoy Miñoso's super home run, I know that for a few moments, I was very happy . . . For years, even, I was able to bury the pains of my past and live looking toward the future, only toward the future. The screwed-up thing is that, when you least expect it, even those pains that you believed to have conquered come out of the shadows one day and tap you on the shoulder. Then everything can go to hell, including happiness, and it's not easy at all to get it back later."

The Santos Suárez house that the newlyweds had managed to buy in 1954 with the combination of their own savings and the generous contribution of their Galician in-laws and their Jewish uncle was modest and comfortable. It had two bedrooms, a living room, dining room, kitchen, and, of course, its own bathroom with all the amenities, a brilliant little black-tiled corner where you could take a shit privately when you liked and as often as you liked. In addition, the house had a small yard and the luxury of a covered porch through which a breeze blew, even on the steamiest days of summer. It had been built in the 1940s by the owners of the ostentatious, modern, and roomy neighboring house, whose head of household had experienced a quick financial ascent ever since his friend Fulgencio Batista came to power and turned him into one of the heads of the Havana police and could allow himself, thanks to the many bribes he received due to his position in the police, the immediate construction of that mansion that made the Kaminsky house look so puny.

Once he had graduated and became the accountant for Brandon's luxurious Minimax, Daniel's salary had gone up to two hundred pesos monthly, which went further, given the discounts with which he was able to acquire the market's magnificent products. Marta, meanwhile, even though she didn't need to for them to get by, had insisted on working in her professional field, and, always thanks to Brandon's influence, had gotten a spot at the recently opened Edison Institute, in the neighboring area of La Víbora. By 1955 the couple could allow themselves the luxury of acquiring a same-year Chevy model and, for Christmas, spent their vacation in Mexico City, where they saw Dámaso Pérez Prado's orchestra perform and danced to María Antonieta Pons just when there was a world furor over mambo and Cuban *rumberas*. Life smiled upon them. To top off their dreamed-of perfection, all they needed was for nature to award them the arrival of the son or daughter they both desired, and for whose gestation they had been trying with determination, frequency, and love.

Uncle Pepe the Purseman had also introduced changes able to improve his daily life. While remaining the man he always was, he had chosen to move to a modest little house on Calle Zapotes, in Luyanó, a single-family house with its own bathroom and kitchen where, as a housewarming gift, the luxury of a brilliant white Frigidaire was awaiting them, purchased by Daniel and Marta. Since long before the marriage and move took place, the furrier had allowed his amorous relationship with Caridad Sotolongo to become public knowledge—although, for reasons of space, they had continued to live in their separate quarters in the tenement on Acosta and Compostela. The fifty-something Pole had valiantly taken on the brunt of the deep racial prejudices existing in Cuba, and as such, as soon as his relationship with Caridad began, he never allowed himself to be bullied by the indiscreet and even disdainful stares that placed them both under the same scorn as they walked hand in hand, the pale Jew and the fleshy *mulata*, going to the movies, to the Martí theater, or, to the surprise of everyone who knew the Pole and his relationship with money, to the kosher restaurants in Pepe the Purseman's old neighborhood.

The greatest cause for concern hounding Daniel Kaminsky's life was related to his friends Pepe Manuel Bermúdez and Roberto Fariñas. Pepe Manuel had enrolled at the University of Havana, where he was studying Law—What else? Daniel always said—and had followed his vocation as a student leader. By 1955, from the ranks of the Directorio Universitario, he was actively participating in the opposition to Batista that was growing by the day throughout the country. Roberto, meanwhile, who had decided to return to the fold and was working in the family business, was active in a clandestine group of Orthodox Party sympathizers, who became radicalized after the attack on the Moncada Barracks and were insistent on removing the general and his band of violent accomplices from power, even by force. Nonetheless, Pepe Manuel and Roberto's political activism never came up against Daniel's permanent and pragmatic apolitical stance, and the complicity between the friends and their girlfriends (Pepe Manuel had surprised the others with the news that he was breaking up with Rita María, while trying to incorporate into the tight-knit group his new girlfriend, Olguita Salgado, who came to them with the reputation of being a communist) continued to be as close as it was during high school, and each one of them enjoyed the other's company, the trips to the beach, the dances at the social clubs with the many and very good orchestras of the time, and the evening or night outings to the Grand Stadium of Havana.

Based on his conversations with his friends and what he managed to hear on the street, Daniel started to feel how the mean shadow of fear, increasingly tangible and damaging, was quickly changing with a macabre force that state of grace he enjoyed so much. To the naked eye, the political situation in the country had gotten tense, and more and more forces, one way or another, with peaceful or violent means, were opposed to General Batista's de facto government. But that man who in the shadowy days of 1933 had leapt from sergeant to general and ruled Cuba's fate publicly or from the shadows, and even from afar, was trying to keep that juicy position at any cost. Although, to do so, he had to resort to extreme methods of repression and violence: like all men addicted to power and its many benefits, financial or spiritual. Batista, of course, had amassed an extraordinary fortune and simultaneously created a network of financial commitments that a group of American Mafia leaders had joined, among them the Polish Jew Meyer Lansky, who became a regular presence in Havana, although, as Uncle Joseph used to say, luckily that embarrassment to the Jews spent his time in casinos, cabarets, and secret meetings with Batista and his secretaries and not in the synagogue.

For the first time since he arrived in Cuba, Daniel Kaminsky felt too many silences. And not only because he moved away from working-class and raucous Old Havana to the more bourgeois and residential Santos Suárez. Perhaps it was some sort of innate capacity, as he would one day explain to his son, a genetic predisposition, the historic experience accumulated over centuries by his line to sense danger and terror, thanks to the most unusual or subtle signs. In this case, it was silence. Because of it, although his life had developed as best as it could and he remained removed from politics as much as he could reasonably stay at the margins of something so ubiquitous, he had the sense that the surrounding environment was charged with danger. And events, which were isolated at first and then began to occur daily, would prove him right. That explosion of fear would happen just around the time that, thanks to Miñoso, the Tigres de Marianao had their greatest moment of glory. In a not-so-unpredictable way, the expansive wave of fear reached Daniel's life, led by the actions and needs of his friend Pepe Manuel and by the hand of his friend Roberto Fariñas as well. The perfect ruse of fate was that those complicated and dangerous political games would be the ones to again place Daniel Kaminsky before the portrait of the young Jew too similar to the image of Christian iconography's Jesus, the same portrait engraved in the pleasant family photo that had crossed the Atlantic with him almost twenty years before.

8

Havana, 1958–2007

Once he showered to remove from his skin the uncomfortable feeling of proximity to death that cemeteries provoked, Conde decided that, with the last pesos tucked into his pockets, the least he could do was buy half a bottle of rum at the Bar of the Hopeless before stopping by Skinny Carlos's house on his way to see Tamara. But not even the prospect of relaxing as much as possible and having a couple of drinks, or talking to his friend and seeing the girlfriend who had put up with him for so many years, managed to erase the malaise that had started to take hold of the former policeman with the latest installments of the story that Daniel Kaminsky's son had so carefully delivered in bite-size portions. That afternoon, when they left the Ashkenazi hallowed ground and Conde felt that the story was headed toward comprehensibility, when at last the circumstances hidden by time—for whose supposed revelation he had been hired—would appear, the painter decided to return to his hotel under the pretext that perhaps the lobster he'd eaten for lunch had upset his stomach. Conde then had the certainty that the visit to the necropolis had had a much deeper effect on the foreigner than the mere rejection of death and its rites from which he himself suffered. And the feeling of malaise had invaded him.

Keeping with his habit from the prehistoric times when he was a policeman, when he arrived at Carlos's house, after the first round of the aberration that was as raw as it was Haitian was served, Conde told his disabled friend the known details of the story in which, for one hundred dollars per day, Andrés had gotten him involved. All of the exasperation that he felt incapable of expressing to Elias Kaminsky, for subjecting him to a delayed entrance into the matter, came to the surface in that dialogue through which he sought to unburden himself.

"I don't know what the hell it could have been . . . But something happened when that man read the tombstone belonging to his father's uncle."

"What did you tell me it said?" Carlos asked, immersed in the story.

"'Joseph Kaminsky. Believed in the sacred. Violated the Law. Died without feeling any remorse.' Yes, that was it . . .'"

"Which law did he violate? The Jewish one or civil law?"

Conde thought for a few seconds before responding.

"The Jews are so complicated that they've made a mess of all of that, and many times the two laws coincide. Remember: 'You shall not kill. You shall not steal . . .' Religion as ethics and law, right? But I swear to you by Yahweh that I don't know what the hell that man could have done or what law he violated. Was it because he let his nephew convert and marry a non-Jew? I'm not very sure, either, of what Elias's father did, whether he ended up slitting some guy's throat or not, if that's just a suspicion or what . . . And less still of why in the hell Elias wants me. For me to listen to his story?"

His friend thought it over for a few moments.

"Yeah, it's all really screwed-up . . . But be philosophical about it, *salvaje*. Think like a Jew and do the math: if the painter wants to come across as interesting and tell you the story little by little, but is paying you a hundred bucks in the meantime . . . it's good business . . . With how screwed-up everything is around us . . . But surely he wants something else. No one goes around giving away money . . . and less still, a Jew . . . In my opinion, what he's trying to find out has to do with something that's going to help him recover that painting worth about two million . . . Shit!" Skinny pressed his temples. "I can't even imagine what a million would be like, or half, or a quarter . . . But, two!"

Conde nodded: yes, in the background of everything was the painting, its fate in Cuba, and, of course, its recovery, so, as Carlos suggested to him, he should be "philosophical" about it. But which philosophy? Marxism? It was all the same. At the end of the day, there was nothing better to do, since he didn't have the energy or the desire to go back to kicking around the city in search of some old books from which he could earn, in the best-case scenario, two or three hundred Cuban pesos. In that September heat, it wasn't profitable at all to waste hours and wear out shoes on chancy searches. He definitely had to start considering a change in profession. But how in the hell could someone as useless as him earn a living in a more or less decent way, refusing as he did to invest eight hours each day just to earn the four or five hundred pesos at the end of the month that wouldn't be enough to support him? Conde's individual outlook was as grim as the country's collective outlook and he felt more and more worried. The foreigner sent by Andrés, with his offer of well-paid work, had arrived just when he was about to start making SOS signs. Forget it, he was going to accept all of that as a materialistic philosopher. So Marx the Jew resented Jews?

"I'm going to have a problem on my hands when he tells me everything and demands that I find a response to something that he's been obsessed with for years. Something to do with the painting, his father, or both. And also something to do with that uncle who violated the Law yet still died more at peace than anyone. Truthfully, I'm not sure that what the painter wants to know has anything to do with recovering the two-million-dollar painting. I think it's something else . . ."

"You've always been a believer . . . and a bit of a dumb-ass . . . It's two million!"

"There's something besides the money. I'm sure of it . . ."

"So forget it. You keep listening and when whatever is going to come up comes up, let it come up, and fuck it . . . Have a drink and go with the flow . . ."

Conde shook his head. He had discovered that he didn't even really have any desire to anesthetize himself with shot after shot. He felt so strange. In the face of Conde's lukewarm enthusiasm for alcohol, Carlos claimed the rest of the rum, poured it in his glass, and drank it down in one gulp.

"Conde, you're unbearable . . . Listen, take the Jew wherever he wants to go, tell him whatever he wants to hear, and grab your money. After all, he seems to have too much of it, while you—"

"Dammit, Skinny, stop playing the same old song. That's not the way it is, *salvaje* . . . That man needs to know something that has really fucked him up. Look, maybe I should get the hell out of here. Yesterday I didn't go to Tamara's and she's really got to be mad . . ."

To relax, Conde decided not to think about the Kaminskys anymore as he covered the eight blocks to Tamara's house on foot. When he arrived, he found the woman sitting in the TV room, seemingly calm, concentrated on enjoying an episode of *House*, an abominable and repulsive show to Conde. In his opinion, that doctor was the biggest, most petulant asshole, an imbecile and a son of a bitch who had emerged from a script-writer's head, and just hearing his voice brought down his spirits again.

When she saw him arrive, the woman stopped the show and, after receiving the most affectionate kiss Conde had in his repertoire of guilty kisses, she was silent, watching him.

"Oh, come on, Tamara," Conde protested. "You take out wisdom teeth, I buy and sell books or go in search of a lost past. Now I'm dealing with one out there . . . Look, it doesn't matter. You know I was working."

"Okay, okay, don't get like that, I haven't said a word," she said, as if she were apologizing, although Conde could feel her words dripping with the thickest irony. "But the Cuban detective with rum on his breath can't even pick up the phone?"

"Yesterday, the Cuban detective got home feeling like shit and with smoke coming out of his ears. Today, before coming here, I went to see Skinny. And you know how I am . . ."

"Sometimes I do, sometimes I don't. Let's see. Are you going to stay the night tonight?"

Shamelessly and quickly, Conde replied, "Of course I am."

The woman's face relaxed. She took up the remote control again and turned off the VCR and the TV. Conde started to feel better when House's face disappeared from the screen.

"Have you eaten yet?"

"I had a late lunch and Josefina gave me some malangas with olive oil and garlic that she had saved for me. I'm full," he said, patting his stomach. "I just need to brush my teeth before I eat anything else. But something delicious that doesn't raise my cholesterol . . ."

Half an hour later, Conde and Tamara were enjoying their sexual banquet. That was just the medicine he needed, and he slept like a babe. Before sunrise, like a furtive hunter, the man left the bed. He brewed the coffee and left the house, but not before writing a goodbye note. He had hunting to do that morning.

———

Despite his professed atheism at the time and—although once again hidden—for the rest of his life, the sum of unforeseen circumstances that led Daniel Kaminsky to again meet up with the canvas painted by the Dutch master always seemed to him like the true manifestation of a cosmic plan.

Perhaps that whole path had begun to take shape on March 13, 1957, just a month after the Marianao team's grandiose victory. That had been the day set by a group of Pepe Manuel's political comrades-in-arms who banded together in the Directorio Estudiantil Universitario to attack and seize the Presidential Palace and resolve the Cuban political problems by revolutionarily executing—as they themselves declared—the dictator Fulgencio Batista. The plan's failure, nearly due to bad luck (or the tyrant's good luck), led to a real witch hunt that turned into a massacre. Pepe Manuel, convalescing from an emergency appendicitis operation due to the suffocation of his useless gut, didn't directly participate in the action. But the young man knew the plan and its masterminds. Later, Daniel and Roberto would know that, if not for his physical condition, Pepe Manuel would have actively participated in the attacks on the palace and the Radio Reloj station, where the students read their statement to the people. And, they thought, it was very possible that he would have also ended up massacred by the police, like many of the members of the Directorio Estudiantil Universitario enmeshed in the tyrannicidal attempt.

The persecution that began then of all the known figures of the university political group was systematic, brutal, bloody. Fortunately, Pepe Manuel had managed to escape his house and hide at a location unknown even to his closest and most trustworthy friends: a small farm in the area of Las Guásimas, on the outskirts of Havana, where he was taken in by his godfather, a fighting-cock breeder from the Canary Islands named Pedro Pérez. Pepe Manuel's only option, in those initial months, was to remain in hiding, and at the time, no one, not even his girlfriend Olguita Salgado or his two best friends, Daniel and Roberto, knew where he had ended up. That ignorance, they knew, guaranteed that Pepe Manuel would not be discovered. But at the same time it posed the greatest danger to Olguita, Daniel, and especially to Roberto, since his political sympathies with the fugitive were public knowledge and, if the police decided to interrogate them, they would surely be the ones to suffer the worse consequences, even more so without even having the terrible option of betrayal. As such, from that day, Daniel Kaminsky started to live in fear: his own tangible fear, dormant for years, that now became unbearable on certain nights when, tossing and turning in his insomnia, he heard the sound of silence and his heart leapt when he thought he heard steps on the porch of the little Santos Suárez house and sweat poured over him as he waited to hear the knocks and the fateful cry of "Police! Open the door!"

The passing of nine months after the failed attack on the palace, when time had gone by without the police looking for him, had helped Daniel to manage his fears. Roberto Fariñas invited him to see a baseball match in the just-kicked-off season and swung by the Santos Suárez house to pick him up. As usual, already, on the corner where now stood a luxurious mansion belonging to the former owners of Daniel's house, was a patrol car full of cops permanently guarding the police chief's safety. When he passed the patrol car, Roberto, as always, greeted them and pointed at the neighboring house, where he stopped the car to pick up his friend. But instead of going to the stadium, the men headed to El Vedado and sat down at a table in the restaurant/diner Potin, a place frequented by young people from bourgeois families. Roberto and Daniel considered it the place that was safest and most removed from suspicions to hold a delicate conversation in which their wives should not participate.

Roberto explained Pepe Manuel's situation to the Pole and even revealed his hiding spot. Following the massacre of the Presidential Palace attackers who were caught in a surprise raid on the Calle Humboldt apartment, at that moment their fugitive friend had two options: go to the mountains to join one of the guerrilla groups in action or, keeping in mind his nonexistent military abilities, leave the country for the United States, Mexico, or Venezuela, where other fugitives from the opposition were dedicated to raising moral and economic support for the combatants or waiting for the much-discussed landing in Cuba. Then Daniel asked him why he was telling him all of that, and Roberto responded, "Because I think that it's best for Pepe to leave Cuba, and for that he needs money."

A friend of Roberto's older brother was the son of a certain Román Mejías, a high-ranking immigration official who, for many years, felt strongly hostile to Batista. With enough money, that official could certainly draw up documents that were as close as possible to legal ones that would, of course, allow Pepe Manuel to board the ferry to Miami as calmly as possible. The price? With things as they were, according to Roberto's brother, it would never be less than the outrageous sum of ten thousand pesos. Could they each put in five thousand? Roberto asked him then, and without thinking about it for an instant, Daniel said yes. At the end of the day, he would tell himself afterward, although he was clueless about the bloodletting, he owed Pepe Manuel all of the tickets, at five cents each, that he had gifted him in the far-off times in which they went to that palace of dreams, the Ideal Movie Theater, to feast on films, documentaries, newsreels, and even some comics.

————

Conde didn't want to smile, but he had to. Once more, he confirmed how history and life are a spider's web in which you never know where certain threads cross and even become knotted together to form the fates of people and even of a country's history. When Elias Kaminsky mentioned the name of Pedro Pérez to him, the Canary Islands–born fighting-cock breeder in Las Guásimas, the image of the man everyone knew as Perico Pérez appeared in his memory fully shaped. That character, showing up as a figure in a story so removed from him, had been one of his grandfather Rufino's best friends, thanks to their shared love for fighting cocks. Conde clearly remembered Perico Pérez's farm, at the end of an unpaved alley at the town's entrance. Access to the property was through a simple wire gate, and the path to the house was flanked by the very dark, wrinkled trunks of the sweetest tamarinds Conde had ever tasted in his life. Beyond the house, with its brick walls and Cuban-made shingled roof, were the cow stalls, the simple livery, and a long hallway-shaped shed with a guano roof, under which ran the rows of cages where were housed the magnificent birds for which the fighting-cock breeder charged breeders and fighting fans a small fortune, among them—as Conde knew well—Ernest Hemingway himself. At the back of the property, beyond the well with the mechanical water pump, rose the ring where the Canary Islands–born man trained his cocks and, to the right, before the malanga, yucca, and corn plants, a low dirt-floored hut, a hurricane-proof building of trunks nailed to the ground at a forty-five-degree angle, tied together at the top and covered with palm leaves that simultaneously served as walls and a roof: the dirt hut that Conde remembered well and where José Manuel Bermúdez had been hidden for eleven months, until his friends Daniel Kaminsky and Roberto Fariñas obtained for him the passport that would take him out of Cuba and, at the time, save his life.

When Conde told Elias Kaminsky about that extraordinary coincidence, the man took it as a favorable omen.

"If you already discovered where Pepe Manuel was hidden, you're going to discover what happened to my father and to the Rembrandt painting."

"Are you superstitious?"

"No, it's a premonition," Elias said.

"I'm the one with the premonitions around here," Conde protested. "And I'm still not getting any of the good ones, the ones that hurt right here." He touched the left side of his chest.

Conde had waited for Elias Kaminsky on the porch of his house, with the percolator ready on the stove. Sitting on the iron chairs, they had drunk the recently brewed coffee while they enjoyed the brisk September morning that would soon be a memory.

"But what I do have is a bunch of questions."

"I imagine," the painter said, and Conde discovered how Elias, every time he was being evasive or feeling overwhelmed, pulled slowly, but persistently, at the ponytail gathered at his neck. "But I prefer that you let me finish the whole story, try to understand it better than I do myself, and that you have it as close to complete as possible."

"We've been doing this for three days . . . For now, answer just one question."

"First you ask and then I decide," the painter said, determined in his strategy.

"Why were you so moved when you read Joseph Kaminsky's tombstone? To which law does the epitaph refer? Of what remorse is he speaking?"

Elias smiled.

"You're like a machine gun. You must be desperate."

"Yes, I am."

"I'm going to try to answer you . . . Let's see, the easiest part. Being as Pepe the Purseman was, surely he was talking about Jewish Law. I'm not sure what the thing about remorse means, at least not yet, although I have some suspicions. And I felt moved because I suddenly felt the solitude in which that man, who, as far as I know, was someone good and decent, must have lived. Luckily, he had Caridad with him until the end . . . But in every other respect, he was alone, and I know well what the abandonment of being uprooted is. I myself feel at times that I don't belong to any place, or that I belong to many; I'm like a puzzle that can always be taken apart. I suppose I am North American, the son of a Polish Jew who commanded himself to be Cuban among other things while here so that he wouldn't suffer from being uprooted and other pains, and of a Catholic Cuban, the daughter of immigrants from Galicia, Spain, who at decisive moments took on her husband's pragmatism when he decided that the best thing was to be Jewish again, and so she converted. I was born in Miami when Miami was nothing: because, if anything, what it most looked like was a bad copy of a Cuba that no longer existed. But I wasn't raised among those Cuban-Cubans, but rather among Cuban Jews and Jews from a thousand other parts of the world, a community in which we were all Jews but not equal"—he made the sign for money with his fingers—"and we didn't even feel equal. At least my parents always felt Cuban. So I am very familiar with what I am talking about. Uncle Joseph, as opposed to my father, wanted to continue being what he had once been, but everything around him had changed: the country where he lived, the family he had once had, the way of practicing his religion . . . In the end, not a single rabbi was left in Cuba, almost no Jews were left. Well, even black beans became scarce . . . So he must have felt like a shipwrecked man. Not like the sailor my father imagined when he went back to Kraków in his dreams . . . but like a real shipwrecked man, without a compass or any hope of touching on dry land, because that land had disappeared centuries before, as all Jews know well. Can you imagine what it is like to live like that, forever, until the end? Not only could my father not be with him when he died, he only found out a month after he had been buried. Well, luckily Caridad was there . . ."

"I can imagine that feeling you're talking about and almost understand it," Conde said with a certain hint of remorse for having forced Elias Kaminsky to voice that diatribe. "With all of that, you still want to see the house where your father once thought he was happy?"

The painter lit another of his Camels and became lost in a long silence.

"I have to do it," he said at last. "I came to Cuba to understand something, as my father went back to Kraków once to find himself and, in the end, to discover the worst in himself . . . And although it may be the worst, I also need to know, I have to know."

—————

Following Conde's instructions, the car Elias was driving left the ever hostile Calzada del 10 de Octubre in order to enter the heart of Santos Suárez via the more pleasant Avenida de Santa Catalina. As they moved forward on the blooming flamboyant tree–flanked street, Conde was explaining to the foreigner that that area was one of the realms of his life and his nostalgia. Very nearby lived many of his oldest and closest friends (also Andrés's friends: before leaving, Elias should meet them, he told him) and the woman who had been something like his girlfriend for the last twenty years.

When he got to Calle Mayía Rodríguez, Conde indicated that Elias should turn to the right and, two blocks down, take a left and stop before the house that was, according to the address written down, where Daniel and Marta Kaminsky lived until April 1958. Conde, who had relaxed talking about his friends and lovers, felt at that moment how something deeply hidden started to stir in that search.

"That was my parents' house?" Elias Kaminsky asked, halfway between stunned and overwhelmed, but Conde answered him with a question. "Who did you say lived in the big house on the corner?"

"A police chief under Batista."

"But who?"

"I can't remember the name," the painter said, almost apologizing, without understanding Conde's interest in the detail.

"It's just that . . . Pull the car over here and lend me your phone!" Conde said.

When he moved the car and got close to the curb, beneath the cool cover of an *ocuje* tree with a gnarled trunk, the painter held out his phone to Conde. Without offering any other explanation, the former policeman dialed several keys until he had composed a number and hit the green button, trusting that that was the necessary step to work that apparatus with which he neither had nor pretended to have the least familiarity.

"Rabbit?" he asked, and got right to it. "Yes, it's me . . . Okay, but shut up now and tell me something . . . Whose was the pretty house on the corner of Mayía and Buenavista that you like so much? The old owner . . ." Conde listened for a few seconds. "Uh-huh, Tomás Sanabria . . . And he was what?" He listened again. "Uh-huh, uh-huh. And before that?" He paused again and almost yelled, "I knew it, of course I knew it! Well, I'll call you later to explain," he said, and, however he could, ended the call and returned the phone to Elias, who, behind the wheel, hadn't stopped looking at him with his eyes practically out of their sockets, trying to piece together what was intelligible.

"But what happened?"

"The one who lived next door there was Tomás Sanabria, Havana's second chief of police. That was your parents' neighbor who always had a patrol car in the street to protect him."

Elias Kaminsky was listening and trying to process the information. But he seemed incapable of following Conde's logic.

"That man, Tomás Sanabria, was a son-of-a-bitch murderer and a sadist . . . Do you know if he had anything to do with your father or with your father's painting?"

The painter lit a cigarette. He was thinking.

"No, not that I know of. He told me about the policeman who lived next door to them, but right now, I don't think he even told me his name."

"That Sanabria was very close with the son of Manuel Benítez, who was named after his father, Manuel Benítez, and according to some, was Batista's best friend . . . You already know, Benítez the elder was the one who sold the fake visas to the passengers of the *Saint Louis*."

Elias Kaminsky's surprise was obvious and resounding.

"Could it all be a coincidence?" Conde asked out loud, but talking to himself. "A chief of police who was friends with Benítez's son, living next door to the son of some Jews that Benítez conned with some fake visas? Couldn't all of those people, or at least some of them, have something to do with that Rembrandt painting?"

"Well, I don't know," Elias said, and seemed sincere, in addition to stunned.

Not even that response managed to stop the accelerated growth of a premonition that was taking over Mario Conde's entire body and consciousness. Several paths could cross at the heart of that story.

———

The mansion that Tomás Sanabria had built for himself, now in the hands of someone with enough political or economic power to have taken it over, had survived the passing of decades triumphantly and in good shape. By contrast, the more modest neighboring building, where Daniel Kaminsky and his wife, Marta Arnáez, had spent four years of their lives, had not had the same luck. At first glance, it was not due to problems with the quality of the building, since the columns, architraves, and roof still looked solid despite their age. It had to do with the effects of the scourge: doors and windows had been subject to multiple indignities, the walls seemed to have been bitten by giant ants and painted for the last time when the Marianao club still existed as the team of the socialistically exterminated Cuban professional league, and several of the porch's tiles had been broken, while the low wall separating it from the street had lost all of its whitewash, part of the fence, and even some bricks. What had once been a garden, meanwhile, had devolved to the point of being mere brush with serious aspirations of becoming a garbage dump. Even the trunk of the *ocuje* tree in the flower bed appeared eaten away by hate and malice.

"Are you sure that this was my parents' house?" Elias Kaminsky had to ask, leaning on the car so that he wouldn't fall backward before the contrast between the bitter reality of the present and the mental image of some photos and his father's evocations of a happy past suddenly sullied.

"It must be." Conde had no choice but to pour salt in the wound.

"I wanted to go inside . . ." Elias Kaminsky began to say, and Conde took advantage of his pause.

"It would be better not to even try. What you're looking for isn't in there. Those ruins are no longer your parents' house."

"At least they never came back," the man consoled himself.

"It would have been like returning to Kraków just after World War Two, I'd say . . . No, it can't be a coincidence that just next door lived Tomás Sanabria."

The painter didn't seem very interested in the original owner of the neighboring house, moved instead by the one having to do with his past—in reality, his parents' past.

"What happened when they left in 1958?" Conde tried to lead the conversation down a path that interested him.

"My Galician grandparents were able to sell the house shortly after. My father, who was short of funds after handing over five thousand pesos to buy Pepe Manuel's passport, used that money as a down payment on the little house they bought in Miami Beach and to leave his uncle Joseph some cash. The university was closed, but Uncle Pepe was saving money for his stepson's studies, Caridad's son . . . That's how he was. Since he saved his money under the mattress, he later lost nearly all of it when they decreed the change of money here and would only agree to change two hundred pesos per person . . ."

Conde nodded; he knew the story. A landmark in the process of generalized poverty.

"From what you tell me, your parents didn't even have time to sell the house. Can I think that, because of José Manuel Bermúdez's problem, they also had to flee?"

"No, it wasn't because of Pepe Manuel. Although it had a lot to do with that story. As I told you, while trying to arrange his friend's departure, my father ran into the Rembrandt painting again."

"How is it that he came across the painting again?"

"Because he was at the home of that immigration official, that Mejías, the one whom Roberto and my father went to see to buy Pepe Manuel's passport."

"And Mejías didn't have anything to do with Sanabria?"

"Not that I know of . . . or as far as my father told me . . ."

Conde felt at that moment how the crossing of worlds that had been parallel until then, but unknown to each other, inhabited by fighting-cock breeders who turned out to be one and the same, chiefs of police, and revolutionaries chased by those police, in addition to renegade and non-renegade Jews, formed a whirlwind that crashed in his mind to create a spark. The same as, or at least very similar to, the ones that, in his days as a police investigator, had so helped him get out of jams.

"Tell me something before we continue with this interminable story and so that I can understand something . . ." He started to speak to Elias as pleasantly as possible, but couldn't help the leap to a stricter demand. "Is what you want to know going to help you get back the Rembrandt painting?"

Elias pulled on his ponytail a bit. He was thinking.

"Perhaps, but not especially. I think."

"We're talking about more than a million dollars . . . So what in the hell is it that you want me to help you find out? Is it what I imagine?"

Elias Kaminsky remained calm. Now, with barely a thought, he answered with obvious prior knowledge of the answer.

"Yes, I think you can imagine it. Although it's difficult to know, I want to be positive whether it was my father who killed Román Mejías. The man showed up dead in March of 1958, killed in a rather horrible way, and my parents took off barely a month later . . . But above all, I want to know why my father didn't recover the painting that belonged to him, especially if he did what he seems to have done. And where in hell that painting has been all these years . . ."

9

Havana, 1958

Daniel Kaminsky was able to feel how the world stopped turning, with a spectacular planetary full-stop brake that could throw everything out of its place and send it reeling, flying through the air, taking each thing out of the corners in which they had settled or taken refuge. But once inertia was conquered, the globe had started to move, even though the young man had the dizzying perception that it was doing so in the opposite direction, undoing the last nineteen years of his movements, as if searching for that exact week in the past, forgotten by many, painfully lived by him, in the last days of May 1939, when they forced him to acquire the acute conviction that he had ceased to be a child. The point of that return was the Genesis-like moment in which that canvas—on which appeared the face of a young Jewish man too similar to the image of the Jesus of Christian iconography, the same canvas that for three centuries had accompanied the Kaminsky family—had been separated from his parents' custody so that, with that desperate gesture, it could attempt to facilitate the supreme act of granting life to three Jewish refugees: the same three Jews who, rejected by the Cuban and American governments, would soon after be devoured by the Holocaust, but always, always, always after the painting had come out of its hiding spot and passed into hands that, in some way, had taken it to the place where it now hung, with the greatest pride and impunity.

Roberto Fariñas couldn't help but notice that something deeper than resentment and even the fear with which they arrived at that place was running through his friend. In a whisper, he asked if something was wrong, but Daniel Kaminsky barely shook his head, saying no, incapable of talking, of thinking, of knowing.

The housekeeper at the luxurious building on Miramar's Séptima Avenida had offered them a seat on the soft sofas covered in blue velvet, harmoniously in line with the living room's sumptuous décor, the most refined part of which was due to the paintings hanging on the walls, reproductions of famous works from the golden age of Dutch art. Among the paintings, placed on the room's best wall to highlight the role of its certain authenticity and its overwhelming beauty, that young Jewish man's head, signed with the initials of Rembrandt van Rijn, yelled out its presence to a stunned Daniel Kaminsky. The obsessive contemplation of the work in which the young man had thrown himself caught Roberto's attention. "There's something strange about that painting, isn't there? Is it a portrait of a man or an image of Jesus Christ?" Daniel didn't respond.

Román Mejías appeared a few minutes later. He was a man of about sixty years of age, wearing a shiny linen suit made of *dril cien*, as if he were about to go out. Daniel did the math: that man would have been about forty at the time of the *Saint Louis* incident, so he could well have been one of the ones going on and off the boat due to his job as an immigration official.

The Polish man barely listened to the conversation between Mejías and Roberto. He was trying to look, without making his interest too obvious, at the small painted canvas and only came back to reality when his friend asked him for the money that Daniel was carrying in the inside pocket of his jacket. He handed the envelope to Mejías as the first part of the deal: five thousand pesos to start, another five thousand when they received the passport. Mejías put away the envelope without counting the money while he explained to them that from the minute he gave them the fake document the beneficiary had to leave Cuba within a week, maximum. He committed to having it ready in ten days. Roberto extended the photos of Pepe Manuel to him, now with a mustache and Coke-bottle glasses, and Mejías asked if they had any preference regarding the name. Roberto looked at Daniel, and from some corner of the Polish man's memory came the name: "Antonio Rico Mangual," he said, since a few months before he had received the news that his old buddy Antonio, the *mulato lavado* with the beautiful eyes who was by his side in his first adventures in Old Havana, had died of tuberculosis in a sanatorium on the outskirts of the city. But a light in his mind made him add, to Roberto's surprise, "That's my name. I don't have a passport nor do I have any plans to travel, so you can use it, no problem."

"That's fine by me. I'll take care of getting the birth certificate," the man said and concluded, "Done deal."

Mejías held out his hand to his visitors. Roberto shook it, but Daniel acted like he didn't notice so as to avoid contact.

"We'll see each other here in ten days," the man added. "And discretion will guarantee your friend's life, yours, and mine. Batista swore he would kill all of those guys. And he won't stop until he does so."

When Daniel and Roberto were about to leave, a force that was stronger than all of his precautions pushed the former Jew. "Mr. Mejías, that painting over there"—he pointed out the head painted on canvas—"is it by a well-known painter?"

Mejías turned around to contemplate the work, like a father who is proud of his daughter's beauty. "The others, of course, are reproductions. But that one, although you may not believe it," he said, "is an authentic painting by Rembrandt, a famous painter, beyond well-known."

———

Daniel Kaminsky's life, already wounded by the fear surrounding him and by his own tensions, fell from that moment into a dark labyrinth. Without even discussing his terrible discovery with Marta or with his uncle Joseph, he devoted several days to thinking about his options. In his mind, nonetheless, the conviction had taken root: that man, or someone connected to him, had conned his parents. Mejías or whatever person had given him or sold him that painting held a lot of responsibility for the death of his family. And, in any event, he had the obligation to recover the painting, property of the Kaminskys since the far-off days when the dying rabbi had handed it over to Dr. Moshe Kaminsky in a distant Kraków devastated by violence and plague.

With all the discretion required by the matter, Daniel started to investigate the life of Román Mejías. All of his precautions would be too little, he thought, and that is what he would tell his son Elias: although he wasn't dealing with a man in Batista's inner circle of friends and favorites, he was a government official and, as such, a regime man, and like all of those people, Mejías lived in a state of permanent alert. Besides, the man was involved in the preparation of Pepe Manuel's passport and that was the priority at the moment.

By using trivial reasons to ask any question and reading old newspapers, Daniel was able to piece together that man's life. The necessary data point was that Mejías had been, in fact, one of the officials picked by President Laredo Brú's minister of the interior to substitute for Colonel Manuel Benítez's acolytes in the immigration administration following the battle over the visas sold in Berlin. The possibility that he was one of the ones overseeing the *Saint Louis* incident was more than probable, and a copy of *El País* from May 31, 1939, which published a photo in which Mejías appeared, twenty years younger, proved it. In the image, he was in the company of two other officials at the moment in which, recently disembarked after a stay on the passenger ship, they refused to give the press any information regarding the rumor that the government was asking double the amount of money offered by the Joint Distribution Committee. But couldn't it have been another colleague of his who made away with the painting and, for some reason, then handed it over to Mejías? Although far-fetched, there existed that explanation that could even exonerate Mejías.

The first person to whom Daniel owed an explanation was Roberto Fariñas. Four days after they began their dealings with Mejías, when they again saw each other, Roberto asked him why he said his name was Antonio Rico Mangual, and about his strange attitude during their whole negotiation with that individual and his interest in that painting that he refused to believe was a real Rembrandt, no matter what, just like the others hanging there weren't real Vermeers or Ruysdaels. Based on what he knew of art—not much, but something—Roberto expounded that the face was missing something of the mastery transmitted by all Rembrandts, the greater and lesser works, even the overlooked ones, he concluded. Then Daniel Kaminsky, who already felt like he was suffocating under the weight of the revelation and the suspicions that went along with it, chose to unburden himself and tell his friend the story and that he had decided to recover what belonged to him. Because that painting, despite Roberto's opinion, despite being just a study, was a true Rembrandt, the real deal—and he knew it well, he said, and showed his friend the photo of the family living room in Kraków. As he listened to him, Roberto almost didn't put much stock in the story and even had the childish idea that, as soon as they got the passport, someone, perhaps Uncle Joseph Kaminsky himself with the support of powerful Brandon, would denounce the corrupt official. The young man immediately realized the improbable success of his idea, since in practice guys like Mejías always managed to hide the body from the justice system of a country that had turned into nothing but a gigantic lair of competing self-interests. But, as could be expected, he put himself at his friend's disposal to do whatever was necessary—*whatever*, he emphasized. That's how Roberto Fariñas was and always would be, Daniel Kaminsky would tell his son Elias. That's how he was, even in the times when politics had taken care of creating the largest distances imaginable between old buddies and filling in the differences with resentment. At that moment Daniel only asked Roberto for the greatest discretion, at least until they could get Pepe Manuel out of Cuba. Afterward, they would see.

A brilliant idea then came to his aid. The afternoon prior to the agreed-upon day for the passport's delivery, Daniel left the market, got into his Chevy, and headed toward his old neighborhood, in Havana's Jewish quarter. On Calle Bernaza, between Obispo and Obrapía, one of the city's most renowned photography studios, Fotografía Rembrandt, had been in operation since the 1920s. Its original proprietor, very old, but still lucid, was a Jew, Aladar Hajdú, who was such a fan of the Dutch master's work that his notoriety as such led his clients and those who knew him to call him "Rembrandt." It wasn't a mere coincidence that he had chosen the artist's name when he christened his prosperous business, in which he displayed not only photos of famous customers but also some works by Cuban painters and several Rembrandt reproductions, the leading one being *Belshazzar's Feast*, placed in such a way that the biblical character, with the dramatic gesture that distinguished him in all of art history, was pointing at the interior room where the backdrop was set up for studio photos.

Daniel asked to see Hajdú and introduced himself. The old man, luckily, knew Pepe the Purseman and even knew about his close relationship with the powerful Brandon. It wasn't hard for Daniel to get the old Jewish man, in between whose lips there was always a cigarette burning, to accept his offer to have a beer at the corner bar, since he needed to discuss something with him. When they were already sitting at a table, surrounded by all of the possible sounds generated at that vital and overwhelming place in the city, Daniel asked that the conversation they were about to have remain secret, for reasons that he perhaps could explain. Hajdú, part curious and part alarmed, wouldn't promise anything until he knew what it was about, he said.

"I need to know something, perhaps very easy to find out for someone like you," Daniel began, putting it all at risk. "Does someone in Cuba have a Rembrandt?"

Hajdú smiled and blew out smoke, as if he were burning inside. "Why do you want to know?"

"I am the one who can't tell you. I just need to confirm that I saw one."

The old Jew took the bait. "Román Mejías. Years ago, that man came to see me to find out if the Christ figure he had was an authentic Rembrandt. As far as I know, it seemed that it was. One of the various Christ figures that Rembrandt painted."

"So when did he consult you about that?"

"Hmmm, about twenty years ago," Hajdú said as he lit a new cigarette, and added, "He told me it was a family legacy. Then he showed me some of the work's certificates of authenticity, but they were written in German, and I don't speak German. What I do remember is that they were dated in Berlin, in 1928."

That was the confirmation sought by Daniel: those were the documents obtained by his father, and the painting that Mejías had was his family's. "So now can you keep this conversation a secret?"

Hajdú looked at him with an intensity that Daniel felt could strip him down. "Yes . . . but with a tip that I'll give you for free, kid: Román Mejías is a dangerous guy . . . Be careful, whatever it is that you have going on. By the way, I don't know you and I've never spoken with you. Thanks for the beer," he said, blew out smoke, and stood up to head back toward his photo studio.

That same afternoon the young man drove out to the neighborhood of Luyanó, since the time had come to talk to Uncle Joseph, to whom this story also belonged. Caridad greeted him with the same affability as always, offered him a seat, and told him that his uncle had been in the bathroom for half an hour. "Doing you-know-what. He should be about to come out." Daniel withstood how he could the banal, to him, conversation with the woman, who was very worried about her son's future, given the indefinite closure of the university he planned to attend. When his uncle left the bathroom with the look of disgust with which he always finished his difficult bowel movements, Caridad left to make the coffee and Daniel asked Joseph to step outside the house for a moment. They headed to the nearby park on Calle Reyes, and on the way the nephew began to recount the dramatic discovery made a few days prior. When they were sitting on a bench, benefiting from the recently lit streetlamp, Daniel finished the story. During his entire narration, Uncle Joseph had remained silent, without asking so much as one question, but he looked as if he were waking from a dream when the young man revealed Mejías's unquestionable connection with the painting since the days of the arrival of the *Saint Louis,* confirmed by Hajdú's contribution regarding the certificates dated in Berlin.

"What are you going to do?" was Pepe the Purseman's first question.

"For now, get Pepe Manuel out of Cuba. Then I don't know."

"That guy is a son of a bitch," the man said, and added, with a determination capable of convincing Daniel of everything that painful discovery had awoken in Uncle Joseph, "and like the son of a bitch that he is, he has to pay for what he did."

———

On the morning of the tenth day, the end of the time period requested by Román Mejías, Daniel went to the terminal for the ferries that covered the Miami–Havana–Miami route and bought a ticket for the one leaving two days later, in the morning. Since the dock was close to the Hapag dock by which the passengers of the *Saint Louis* should have disembarked, for the first time in eighteen years Daniel Kaminsky dared to return to the site where, along with his uncle Joseph, he had joined the crowd to see who was on the launches coming back from the passenger ship. He remembered how his uncle had bet on how an official who was covered by a hat would be the one chosen by fate to carry out the deal with his brother Isaiah. The saving Sephardic legacy, *the spoon that knew what secrets were hidden in the pot* . . . Daniel tried to recover the intensity of those moments, to recover from deep within his childhood memory the faces of the men who, amid that frenzy, he identified as the visible part of the powers capable of decreeing his family's salvation. But Román Mejías's actual face insisted on occupying the space of the figures his imagination evoked or created.

That night, Daniel and Roberto appeared at Mejías's house and entered to conclude their business. This time, the official was waiting for them in the living room, where there was also a woman of about fifty, sitting in a wheelchair, who discreetly slipped away when the visitors arrived. "My sister, she's trustworthy," Mejías clarified as soon as they had exchanged greetings. He went over to a small cabinet from which he removed the passport and handed it to Roberto. The young man reviewed it and it looked authentic to him. "It's authentic," Mejías confirmed. "Well, as authentic as you need."

Daniel remained silent, trying to concentrate on studying that place, the possible ways in and out, what could be seen through the windows. When Roberto elbowed him, he took out the envelope and handed it over to the man, who received it with a smile. When he put the money in the interior pocket of his jacket, Daniel could see, in his holster, the weapon he was carrying.

"The last packet was twenty dollars short," Mejías said, "but don't worry."

Daniel, without saying a word, put his hands in his pocket and took out two twenty-dollar bills and handed them to the man. "This is for what was missing from the first delivery and in case we made another mistake," he said.

Mejías smiled and took the bills. At that moment, Daniel Kaminsky was absolutely certain that it was that miserable man, and no other official, who had conned his parents and put them on the path to the most horrifying of deaths. Román Mejías deserved to be punished.

The preparations for Pepe Manuel's escape were quick and concrete. The following morning, Roberto and Daniel went with Olguita to Las Guásimas. The reunion, after almost a year, was as happy and full of hope as could be expected among those shaken-up beings and given the situation at hand. But it was also brief. Roberto and Daniel agreed to come back the following morning at six, since Pepe Manuel had to board the ferry at nine, and they left Olguita with a suitcase of clothing for the traveler. The couple had one day's time and a rustic hut as the space for their farewell.

The following morning, while they traveled to the city center in Daniel's Chevy, dawn's light reached Havana. On the way, Pepe Manuel demanded that, to avoid the greatest risks, they leave him just around Parque Central, where he would take a taxi to the ferry docks. Once and again, Roberto and Daniel repeated to their friend to take all precautions, even knowing that Pepe Manuel, ever since he had ceased to be the fidgety Scatterbrain of old times, was a man with a deep sense of responsibility. Daniel was driving with tense shoulders because of the situation they were all in, but, above all, due to the excitement of the request he had to make to his friend before they separated. Daniel had to be grateful to Pepe Manuel for being the one to relieve a little of the weight of his anxiety when he congratulated the Pole for the new victory recently achieved by the Tigres de Marianao, Cuban Professional League champions for the second year in a row. "And that was with Miñoso at fifty percent." He would always remember saying to his friend the same words that, exactly thirty years later, he would say to his son Elias when they attended the gala honoring the Cuban Comet in Miami, and the Jewish man was at last able to achieve one of his life's dreams: shake the hand of that mythical black man, the one responsible for some of his best memories, and take with him a ball signed by the enormous Miñoso, although dedicated to "my friend Jose Manuel Bermudez," just like that, without accent marks.

Shortly before they arrived at their planned destination, Daniel, from behind the steering wheel, looked at his old and dear friend through the rearview mirror. "Pepe Manuel," he said to him at last, overcoming all of his fear, "I need your gun." The young man's words resounded inside the car and took all the attention of the other three, forgotten at that moment by the other worries. Daniel insisted, "Do you have it with you?"

"Of course not, *polaco*, I'm not crazy."

"To whom did you give it?"

Pepe Manuel looked at Roberto, and Daniel didn't need an answer.

Daniel stopped the car at the intersection of Prado and Neptuno, Havana's busiest corner, and where everyone assumed a man would easily disappear into the masses. Inside the car, over the seats, Pepe Manuel hugged his friends and reiterated his thanks for their loyalty. Then he turned to kiss Olguita's lips, perhaps too shyly because of the others' presence. Then he put on his translucent tortoiseshell glasses, squeezed Daniel's shoulder, and said, "Don't do anything crazy, *polaco*."

Dressed in a light gray suit, with a small piece of hand luggage, the man with a mustache and glasses who had turned into the ruddy Scatterbrain got out of the car and, without turning around, crossed Prado toward the taxi stand in Parque Central. From the Chevy, Olguita, Roberto, and Daniel saw him get into one of those black and orange cars, which immediately went down Prado toward the sea. Although the three knew how uncertain that journey would be, they trusted in the passport's quality and in Pepe Manuel's stoicism as the pillars of his success in overcoming that difficulty. As such, despite the existing risks, none of them was capable of imagining at that moment that they were seeing Pepe Manuel Bermúdez for the last time—the best of men whom, in their long lives, the believer Roberto Fariñas and the disbeliever Daniel Kaminsky had met and would ever meet.

———

That day in the month of February 1958 on which he said goodbye to José Manuel Bermúdez, Daniel Kaminsky began to live another of the phases of his life that he would have liked to erase from his persistent memory. But it was not one of the recollections that easily fade away. To make it worse, he didn't know nor would he learn how to fix it save for letting time pass and allowing for the arrival of new concerns that would suddenly take precedence over the evocations and seek to placate them but never serve as a definitive cure. If at another time, the drastic and complicated decision to forcefully remove Judaism from his soul had offered him a strategy to distance himself from a story that was too piercing and, simultaneously, allowed him to feel as if he were reaching a strange but palpable feeling of freedom that facilitated the act of breathing and looking at the sky and seeing clouds and stars as clouds and stars, certain that beyond them was only infinity, from the moment that he said goodbye to his friend, Daniel Kaminsky wed himself to something that he never thought he would possess and which would turn out to be like an indelible stain. The new determination didn't come from anyone else or many other people's actions but from his own sovereign will. Because at that moment, he confirmed to himself his decision to kill a man who had robbed him of what he held most dear in his life. He had to kill, no, in reality, he *wanted* to kill that man.

At twenty-seven years of age, that young man who was born Polish and Jewish, a convert to Catholicism, essentially and legally Cuban, already had a traumatic connection with death. But the concrete faces having to do with that wound were only the more pleasant ones: those of his parents and his sister, those of his grandparents and his Kellerstein aunts and uncles, that of Monsieur Sarusky, his first piano teacher over in Kraków, and of the maestro's beautiful wife, Madame Ruth, with whom Daniel fell in love to the point of feeling his child's heart bursting. All were devoured by the Holocaust. The killers, by contrast, tended to be shapeless shadows, demon-like specters, for whom it wasn't even worth trying to put a face to one of the Nazi leaders, guilty in the first

degree of his losses. Because, in the images brought up by his consciousness, and even by his subconscious, it was impossible for him to connect
the known features of the major ones responsible for the massacre with
the face of the actual man devoted to threatening, beating, spitting at,
and dishonoring the Jews, enjoying his great power to cause fear: the
man without specific features who, too many times in his evocations,
was pulling the trigger of a gun at the back of his head. But now, to fuel
his abomination and pains, he had been handed a real face, a flesh-and-
blood look, the petty smile of an individual as he took two twenty-dollar
bills after having pocketed ten thousand. He also had, besides and above
all, the image of his own face as he fired two, three bullets at the man's
chest, at his head. Didn't the gangsters in the movies say that lead in the
stomach caused a longer and more painful death? All of that represented
a new and unexpected connection to violence, vigilante justice, and
death for which he had never been prepared, for which, he believed, he
hadn't been born. It constituted a drastic application of the barbarous
law of an eye for an eye dictated by that same ruthless God who demanded
from Abraham the atrocious sacrifice of his son and later decreed from
the heavens, "Then thou shalt give life for life, eye for eye, tooth for
tooth, hand for hand, foot for foot, burning for burning, wound for
wound, stripe for stripe." "Life for life," Daniel would repeat.

That night, when he showed up at Roberto Fariñas's house, his friend
tried to bring him back down to earth. For a few years already, Roberto
had known some parts of the story of the Sephardic legacy and, after having witnessed the discovery of the Rembrandt painting at Mejías's house,
it was easy for him to make the mental connections allowing him to
imagine Daniel Kaminsky's purpose. First of all, Fariñas reasoned, the
mere fact of walking around Havana with a gun on him could guarantee
the Pole a ticket to a police station cell. And if that happened, the fact that
he was Tomás Sanabria's neighbor would put him on the pillory: if they
thought—and they would think it—that he was armed because he was
going to try to hurt that dictatorship official, and if they connected
him with José Manuel Bermúdez—and they would connect him—he
wouldn't escape with his life. But even if they didn't make any of those
connections, given the times in which they were living, he would surely
endure the violent and even cowardly reactions of some policemen who
were becoming increasingly bloodthirsty, perhaps because they already
foresaw the proximity of the end of their reign of terror and the possible

revenge that would follow. Last of all, Roberto didn't know anyone more ill-prepared than Daniel Kaminsky to confront a shark like Román Mejías, and, besides, to charge him what was due (Roberto chose to use the euphemism). But the Pole was determined. It had to do with a mandate that was stronger than his own powers of reason, he said, with a deep call for primary justice that had come in search of him and had found him when he least expected it, to place him before the proof that sometimes the guilty, faceless or not, had to pay, he had said that night, according to what he told Elias, years later. Because, Daniel thought, and he would tell his son this as well, at that moment he was only capable of feeling how in his deepest soul, the gears were moving of a walled-up primitive origin, that of the unrepentant Jew rebelling against submission— the desert nomad, vengeful, immune to containment—and less still to the absurd claim to turn the other cheek, a principle that his millennial line was unaware of. No, not for something like that: Daniel felt closer to the Jewess Judith, dagger in hand, ruthlessly slitting Holofernes's throat. And Román Mejías had turned into his Holofernes.

Daniel Kaminsky had an exact idea of the challenge he was facing when that same night he returned to his Santos Suárez house with Pepe Manuel's Smith & Wesson .45 hidden under the driver's seat of his Chevy. When he got close to the angle where he had to turn to go to his house, he saw two patrol cars instead of the lone, although habitual, official car stopped in front of the police chief's mansion, and Daniel almost lost control of his vehicle. His muscles had gone stiff with fear and the only thing that saved him from a barrage of machine-gun shots was that the sergeant in command of the group of guards that day recognized his car and identified him as Tomás Sanabria's neighbor, preventing the soldier from carrying out his intention. "Careful with the Bacardi," the sergeant yelled at him, and, from the steering wheel Daniel made a gesture that tried to make him seem apologetic.

The fear that invaded him was something so petty and visceral that, as soon as he entered his house, Daniel had to run to the bathroom with diarrhea. As he recovered and wiped off the sweat drenching him, he thought about when would be the best time to tell his wife about the decision he had made and didn't find any that seemed propitious. That was his problem and he had to resolve it on his own. What about the consequences? Couldn't his acts lead to tragedy that could even affect Marta? He understood that he didn't have the right to make his wife face that possibility without even giving her the slightest reason, and at last he thought he found an answer.

While he drank his café con leche in the morning, in which he dipped strips of crispy bread smeared with butter, he dared to tell his wife what he had thought to tell her. Marta Arnáez knew the story of the painting and what that piece had meant as the dream of salvation of her husband's parents and sister during the *Saint Louis*'s stay in Havana. Because of that, Daniel found it easier to only tell her that he had discovered that the painting hadn't returned to Europe with his parents; it had been in Havana since then. And now he knew whose hands it was in. In reality, he thought it would be complicated, he said, but he was going to do whatever he could to recover it, since it belonged to his family who was massacred by the most perverse hate. Marta, stunned by the news, asked the questions she couldn't keep from asking, but he barely responded, asking her not to worry. Although it was going to be complicated, as he had already told her, it wouldn't be anything dangerous, he lied. He took great care, of course, not to mention where he had seen the painting and less still the name of the person who had it. Nonetheless, the woman insisted, moved by a hunch and by her knowledge of the existing environment, "Daniel, for God's sake, be careful. We have a good life, it's getting better all the time . . . We don't need that painting to be happier . . . Why don't you forget about that darned piece?"

"It's not because of the money we could get from the painting, Marta. If I had it, I could never sell it, because it belongs more to my uncle Joseph than to me. It's for justice, only for justice," he said, and the woman didn't need to hear another word: from that moment on, she knew what her husband was thinking about doing. And she prayed to her God to dissuade him with His powers. Or at least protect him.

———

Daniel tried to prepare a plan. "That's what you usually do, isn't it?" his father would always ask Elias at this point as he retold the story of the hurricane that would change the Kaminskys' lives.

Ever since his father became a participant in that story, Elias Kaminsky would ask himself if in reality their fates would or would not have been different had the reunion between his father and the painting of the young Dutch Sephardic Jew not occurred. Because the concrete fact that Marta and Daniel left for the United States in April of 1958 was perhaps just an acceleration of what was going to happen anyway. One way or another, it was the path marked for his family: since eight out of every ten Jews living in Cuba ended up leaving the island in 1959 or 1960, or, like his Galician in-laws and many of the members of the middle class, would do so in 1961, when they became convinced that their interests and way of life were not only in danger but sentenced to death. Or would Daniel the nonbeliever have stayed in Havana like his uncle Joseph Kaminsky, a believer in his God who was, at the same time, sympathetic to the concepts of Jewish socialism? Or, like his friend Roberto, would he have handed himself over to revolutionary work with the task of building the new society they had dreamed of since the days in which they listened to steamrolling Eddy Chibás's radio speeches and public talks? Given his father's aspirations to economic prosperity, those possibilities seemed less probable to Elias.

After the clumsy, frightening, and brief surveillance that they conducted on Román Mejías, Daniel Kaminsky decided that the best occasion to carry out his purpose was to wait for him very early in the morning in front of his home and approach him just as he was leaving the house to enter his car, always sitting in the carport, since it was within the closed garage that his wife's brilliant Aston Martin—probably acquired on the basis of fake passports—usually rested. In the house lived, besides Mejías and his wife, his two daughters—still unwed—and the maid. His sister, who had been left disabled by a car accident that killed her husband, lived in El Vedado with her three children—two daughters and a son—and although she visited frequently, she never spent the night at Mejías's house.

The young man felt ready to act when he was able to picture his actions as if he were watching a movie screen. Mejías, with his inveterate cynic's face, his briefcase in one hand and the car keys in the other, was opening the door. The streetlights would have just recently shut off, but the March sun still wouldn't be up. Besides the maid and Mejías himself, the rest of the house's residents would still be sleeping. Daniel, after stopping his car a block away, would be waiting for him from behind a flamboyant tree planted in the flower bed of the house across the street. Then he would cross the avenue, protected by the half-light, just as he saw, through the frosted glass of the door, the man's figure, sheathed in his dark suit, ready to leave. Seconds later, Mejías would be outside the house, with the door still ajar, and he would open the gate, about twenty feet from him. Silently, he would approach Mejías, who, upon seeing him, and, in all probability, recognizing him, would wait for him by the door, thinking that he was seeking him out on some new matter. Daniel would walk toward him and, when only a few feet separated them, would remove his gun and perhaps tell him the reason for his visit. At that moment he would fire (he still had his doubts about where to aim, wanting him to suffer and at the same time to be efficient in his goal, without giving that vermin any chances), and lifting the handkerchief tied around his neck over his face, he would enter the house, stepping over the corpse, take the painting, and run back out, without any risk of being recognized by the maid if she happened to be in the living room, alarmed by the shots. At that early hour—6:45—in that residential and sparsely populated neighborhood, there wouldn't be anyone on the street. In any event, to avoid the possibility of being recognized, upon leaving the house he would lower the handkerchief but would pull his Marianao baseball cap down to his eyebrows. If he needed to run, he would run, get into his car, and immediately escape. In case things got too complicated, he would take his passport with him, since he could always take the picture out of its frame and hide it. He would buy a plane ticket and leave on the first flight headed anywhere: Miami, Caracas, Mexico City, Madrid, Panama City . . . The natural end to that movie hastily and unskillfully put together had him watching himself sitting on the plane at the moment at which, in flight already, he left the island of Cuba and started to float over the sea toward freedom and peace of mind.

———

Eight days after having received his friend Pepe Manuel's gun, Daniel Kaminsky left his bed at 4:06 in the morning and turned off his alarm clock, programmed to go off an hour later. It was March 16, 1958. As he had imagined, he had barely been able to sleep, feeling the stress of tension, anxiety, and fear. He left the bed trying to not wake Marta and went to the kitchen to make himself coffee. The early morning was brisk, although not cold, and he went out to the house's small yard to have his hot beverage and to wait.

Forty minutes later, well ahead of the planned time, he started to get dressed, trying not to forget any detail. He had bought a pair of blue jean overalls, with a shirt made of the same material and color. Behind the bib, he placed the gun and again tested whether he could remove it easily enough. With those clothes, he was trying to look like a painter or mechanic, just with brand-new clothes. He made more coffee and went back to the yard, where he closed his eyes to watch for the umpteenth time that movie he put together in his head, and he didn't feel like he needed to correct anything, only change the end: he couldn't escape on a plane, saving his life, and leave Marta behind at the mercy of any repercussions. He should face, with all of its consequences, the act he was going to carry out and, if necessary and possible, escape, but taking his wife with him.

At six on the dot, as he had planned, he peeked into the room and looked for a few minutes at the young woman who was sleeping. Despite his goal, not for a single instant did he consider the possibility that he was perhaps seeing her for the last time. Nor did he ponder what his life could be after the execution of the infamous Mejías. He took the paper bag in which he had a suit, a tie, and a white shirt, his work clothes for the Minimax, and went out to the street to get into the Chevy.

He drove carefully, respecting all lights and signals. At 6:32, he turned off the car, which he had parked on the nearly deserted Quinta D, about five hundred feet from Mejías's house. He had eight minutes to get to Séptima Avenida and take up his post behind the flamboyant tree. Then everything had to happen in just ten minutes. At that moment, skipping over the most complicated part of his actions, he didn't focus on anything but getting back to the car with the painting. From there the script had several variants that, in many cases, didn't depend on him. But he always got to the Chevy with the Rembrandt in his hands after having brought to justice the son of a bitch who had conned his family and sentenced them to return to Europe and die, in any of the horrible ways in which they must have died: starved, afraid, heads full of lice, eyes cloudy with gunk, and legs smeared in shit. "He will pay life for life," he repeated to himself, to give himself more reasons, and for the first time in years he invoked the Sacred. "The Lord is my strength," he whispered.

The thought that it was best not to lock the car made him turn back. He unlocked it and breathed several times to relax. He confirmed once more that he had the black cap in his pocket and that he could easily lift the handkerchief tied around his neck and cover his face. Finally, he walked down the sidewalk, quickly, and when he turned the corner to go to Román Mejías's house, the reflection of some red and blue lights coming from Séptima Avenida made him freeze. Those round flashes couldn't be coming from anything but a patrol car. Daniel Kaminsky then felt the deepest and most painful fear that would ever seize him in his life: a paralyzing fear, mean, full-bodied. He couldn't and didn't know what to do but return to the Chevy and, after hiding the gun under the seat, he managed to put it in motion and make it go in fits and starts, until he stabilized the gears and went along Calle Quinta D to reach Avenida 70 and distance himself from the place.

The mixture of fear and frustration clouded his vision. Daniel Kaminsky had not cried since the afternoon of May 31, 1939, on which, aboard a launch, he saw his parents and sister Judith for the last time, leaning over the deck of the *Saint Louis*. That terrible day he was still a boy and tears prevented him from saying anything to his parents, to his little sister, but since then he carried that verbal incapacity with guilt. Now he cried because his fear was in reality stronger than all of his desires for justice and because he felt relieved, since on that day some event had occurred that prevented him from killing the one man he knew had contributed to the deaths of his loved ones. Crying and fleeing danger were the only things Daniel Kaminsky could do at that moment.

10

Havana, 2007

Elias Kaminsky also cried. A pair of unstoppable tears ran down his cheeks before the behemoth with the ponytail had time to cut them off and prevent others from following. To help him in that goal, he took in a deep breath of nicotine-heavy smoke.

Mario Conde was able to contain his anxiety and kept a polite silence. That Santos Suárez park, halfway between Tamara's house and the one that Marta Arnáez and Daniel Kaminsky occupied for a few years, was miraculously well lit for this city of shady parks and shadowy streets. Conde had chosen that park as the ideal place for the conversation, since at one corner was the building of the school where Marta Arnáez had done her student teaching while working to get her education degree, but also because he liked the place and it evoked for him many pleasant stories from the past, a remote time in which, sometimes sitting on this same bench in this same park, he journeyed through years marked by loves and breakups, parties and baseball games, dreams of writing and traumatic disappointments, always in the company of his former companions, including the absent Andrés, who from the geographic great beyond had sent him this man who was trying not to cry while he evoked the roughest moments of his father's Cuban life—the former Jewish Pole Daniel Kaminsky, who felt driven to kill a man.

When Elias seemed to regain his composure, Conde didn't wait any longer and launched his attack.

"As you can imagine, I don't understand a damned thing . . . In the end, did he kill him or not?"

Now Elias even tried to smile.

"I'm sorry, I'm a real crybaby . . . And this shitty story . . . Well, that's why I'm here."

"There's nothing to be sorry for."

The painter tried to catch his breath. When he thought it possible, he spoke.

"He told me that, no, he hadn't killed him. When he escaped from there, without knowing yet what had happened, he was so afraid that he threw Pepe Manuel's gun in a river . . . Of course, the Almendares River, just like the name of the baseball team. He already knew he could never kill that guy, he told me. He hated himself for feeling like a coward . . ."

"But what happened to Mejías?"

Elias looked straight at Conde but kept silent for a few prolonged seconds.

"He was killed that morning . . ." he said at last. "The lights my father saw really were from a patrol car, because an hour before, the maid had discovered Román Mejías's corpse in the living room . . ."

Conde shook his head, denying something hidden but obvious that he had to put into words.

"No, it can't be . . ."

"I'm thinking the same thing . . . or I thought it," Elias corrected himself. "Roberto Fariñas thought the same thing. And my mother . . . Who would believe that the same day he decided to kill that son of a bitch, someone else would come, beating him by an hour, to kill Mejías and steal the Rembrandt. It's tough to swallow, isn't it?"

"Yes, that's hard . . ."

"There's something that doesn't fit and that has always made me doubtful . . ." Elias began. "The thing about Pepe Manuel's gun is true. My mother saw it. He had it . . . If you have a gun or a revolver, isn't it easier to kill a guy with a couple of shots instead of wrestling with him, immobilizing him, and then slitting his throat with a knife? A guy who, besides, could already be armed?"

The questions hit Conde like blows just as he was settling into the story's logic, after having seen the movie that Daniel Kaminsky's mind was projecting through the words of his son.

"They slit his throat?"

"That's how they killed him. They slit his throat in such a way that they ripped his head off . . . There was blood everywhere . . ."

"Like Judith and Holofernes?"

Elias looked around before answering.

"Yes, the way my father imagined Judith's Hebrew revolt, just like in his imagination he saw himself saving his sister, also Judith . . ."

Conde shook his head vehemently.

"Now I really don't understand a fucking thing, or many fucking things." Conde added the plural to convey how incapable he was of following any of it. He understood, of course, that a son would put up the most illogical defenses so as not to believe that his father had killed a man, even for the most justifiable reasons. What didn't make sense at all was that that same son would come to the ends of the earth, of his own free will, to roll around in shit before the eyes of a stranger, merely in search of some support that, by all accounts, he didn't need, since he believed or wanted to believe his father. And he was even paying for that unnecessary support. No, the list and the money weren't players in that game that, however ardently, was placing biblical myths and baroque painting on the stage of reality, in addition to the supposed lack of interest in the two million dollars that the recovery of the painting of discord was worth.

"Hmmm, explain to me what happened . . . My brain must be freezing."

"They tied Mejías's hands behind his back, put a handkerchief in his mouth, and stripped him of his clothes. Then they killed him with an enormous slit of the throat. But before that, they had cut him in several places, his arms, his stomach, lower down . . . It seems it was something terrible, very bloody . . . At the beginning, they said it was some revolutionaries, because Mejías was a government official. But that way of killing him . . . it looked more like a burglar who was caught by surprise and tied him up first, tortured him to find out something, like where he kept his money, and killed him in the end to escape or out of fear that Mejías would recognize him. Many burglars have no intention of killing anyone and only do so when they have no choice. But what happened to Mejías was too much . . . even his penis . . . Of course, for the government and the police, it was more convenient for it to look like political vengeance. That showed what those revolutionaries were capable of in their desperation and that they lacked scruples. And since, for some reason, the stolen painting was barely mentioned, this was the theory that had the most currency."

"I have to ask Rabbit if he knew that story. I had never heard it . . ."

"If my father is the one who killed Mejías," Elias continued, "at least he knew that it didn't have anything to do with the clandestine fighters who were in the city. If they were going to kill people, there were many others to kill before Mejías, who had even helped them in matters like Pepe Manuel's. Unless he tricked someone, right? The fact is that they didn't find any prints or other clues and they never found out who killed Mejías. My father told me that, in his opinion, the killer had been a burglar caught by surprise by Mejías . . ."

"Yes, that's all very well and good. But, for now, I don't believe it, to be honest."

"It seems that Roberto Fariñas never believed it, either. I already told you, he also knew it hadn't been the revolutionaries. Because he was one of them, right? Two months later, he would join a cell of clandestine fighters, the kinds who did 'action and sabotage,' as they said."

"Yes, I know . . . What about your mother?"

"What was she going to say? She said she was convinced it had been some burglars. She had to act convinced, even if she really wasn't deep down."

"And what do you think? Please, tell me the truth." Conde needed to get to the bottom of this, to find a point to latch onto so he could keep going.

"I don't have the clarity I need to judge this matter. All I know is this story, the one he told me . . . Ever since I was a kid, I started to suspect that there was something dark in my father's past, here in Cuba, but I had no idea what it could be. Until one day, about twenty years ago, he at last told me this story. And he told me because he wanted to. Or because he was scared due to the prostate cancer . . . Although there was always something strange about that story regarding my parents leaving Cuba in '58, the truth is that it wouldn't have even crossed my mind to come here and ask Roberto Fariñas if he knew something about my father's past that . . . For years I thought he had left Cuba because of something to do with Pepe Manuel."

"So what happened to Pepe Manuel?"

The painter looked at Conde as if he wanted to prepare him for the response.

"The same day they killed Mejías, Pepe Manuel killed himself in Miami."

Conde felt his mind going two steps backward to take the blow.

"He killed himself? A suicide?"

"No, no, it was an accident while loading a gun. Or that's what they assume happened. He shot himself in the neck."

"The same day?"

"The same day," Elias Kaminsky confirmed. "At dawn, nearly at the same hour."

Conde, who had forgotten to smoke, lit up one of his cigarettes. The accumulation of coincidences, incongruities, lucky or forced solutions in that story was too much for him. He even nearly felt the juices of his reflections running over the edges of his poor, watery old brain.

"So what about the damned painting?" Conde asked with his last sparks of lucidity.

"Well, I don't know, and that's the biggest mystery in this whole mess. Let's see: If my father had killed Mejías and taken the painting . . . where in the hell was it stuck until now? How is it that other people took it to London to sell it? How did those people have the certificates my grandfather asked for in Berlin in 1928 and that must have come with him on the *Saint Louis*?"

"You say that they never mentioned the theft of the painting? So that it would look like political vengeance?"

"My father told me that they barely mentioned the theft. Perhaps to feed the theory of political vengeance. I looked at the newspapers from 1958 that reported Mejías's killing, and it's true: on the first day they mention a stolen painting, but they don't say it was a Rembrandt. And a stolen Rembrandt has always been a serious thing . . ."

"So they don't know if the one who killed him stole the painting or not?"

"I'd say no . . . That he didn't steal the Rembrandt."

Conde smiled, overcome by the mess of contradictions.

"Elias, this is the moment where we get in your car, you drop me off at home, and you go, so I can think. Do you realize how tangled up this story of your father's is? How I can't make heads or tails of anything you tell me?"

"Remember that, for better or for worse, I'm Jewish. I'm not going to just give you one hundred dollars per day to listen to me speaking nonsense. It's because it's so complicated that I need your help."

"Of course . . . But, again, I ask you, what is it exactly that you want to know? And forgive me for insisting on this, is what you want to know going to help you recover the painting that is now worth more than 1.2 million dollars?"

Elias Kaminsky looked across the park, through the wrinkled trunks of the casuarina trees and the Mexican bay leaves. Even in that place, the September heat felt like a steam bath, and Conde noticed that the painter's forehead was damp with sweat.

"I want to know if my father tricked me and told me he didn't kill that man but really did, something I would understand. I already know that it's not easy to confess that you killed someone, even if he was a son of a bitch like that Mejías. But I know that my mother died thinking that, yes, he had killed that man. At the end, she herself told me so, at my father's funeral . . . And, as far as I know, his friend Roberto Fariñas thought the same thing. But I want to doubt. No, better yet, I want to believe him. Especially since that painting appeared in London. Because if my father killed that man, with all the reasons he had to do so, he had to have taken the painting. He couldn't have not done so. It was the family's legacy, wasn't it? It was justice . . . But somebody who was not him kept the painting, and right now I don't think that Mejías's killer, whoever that was, would have taken the original Rembrandt that day . . . Although after thinking about it a lot, I'm on the verge of believing that they did take the painting that was in the living room . . ."

"Did they take it or did they not take it?" Conde yelled, only to immediately regret the outburst.

"I mean to say that, yes, they took it, but it wasn't the original, as Roberto suspected. All of the paintings in Mejías's living room were very good copies, and whoever took the one of the Jew's head thought it was an original. But the authentic one must have been left behind at Mejías's house, hidden. If this is what happened, for Mejías's family it was best not to even talk about the theft, not to mention the Rembrandt and let the police insist that it was a political murder. Besides, that would explain what may have happened to the authentic Rembrandt: that one of Mejías's daughters, or who knows what other person close to the family, got it out of Cuba at some point, with my grandfather's documents of authenticity. Then, the person who got the painting out of Cuba sold it to someone, perhaps the same seller who is now trying to auction it off in London. Is it too much of a coincidence that it's coming to auction after the death of my parents? Two months ago, when I went to London, I saw the copies of that certificate. There is no doubt that it is the one my grandfather Isaiah obtained in Berlin in 1928, the same paper that Mejías showed to Hajdú the Jew, the guy from Fotografía Rembrandt . . . In short, Conde, what I want to know is the truth about my father, whatever that truth may be. I want to know who kept the painting that could have saved my family and made money from it, or tried to make money from it. And if it's possible, I also want to do justice and recover the painting that for three hundred years belonged to the Kaminskys. I have no doubt that it is here in Cuba, where the keys to that story lie. And I have only you to count on to help me get them . . . As you can see, what I want to know is not going to help me get back the Rembrandt. But it could help me get back my father's memory, perhaps do justice . . ."

Conde crushed his cigarette butt on the cement. He took a deep breath and looked at the edge of the park, where the most impenetrable darkness began. At that moment, he had the feeling that, in reality, he was looking inside his mind and seeing only a chaos of unconnected fragments dancing in the shadows.

"Why hadn't you ever come to Cuba before if you're part Cuban?"

Elias smiled for the first time in a long time.

"It's precisely because of that . . . I'm made up of too many things to explore them all. Since traveling to Cuba has always been a little complicated, it was the easiest thing to put off," he said. Without smiling, he added, "And because, until now, I preferred not to poke around in that story my father told me. But with the auction . . ."

"I understand that," Conde said. "Now help me see if I understand some other things. Let's say your father didn't kill Mejías . . . okay? So, then why did he run away from Cuba a month later?"

"Out of fear . . . the same fear that made him throw away the gun. He told me that when he found out about Mejías's death, he went crazy. From fear. He felt like a coward . . . Then he started to think about things he hadn't thought about. For example, that old Hajdú would say something about his questions regarding the painting. Or that his friend Roberto, knowing what he knew, would rat him out . . . These things were so absurd that my mother came to believe that they fled because he really had killed that man."

"I would have thought the same . . ."

"Then why didn't he take the painting?"

A light went off in Conde's head and he took off after it.

"And what if he killed Mejías, took the fake painting and got rid of it when he realized it was a trick?"

"I've also given a lot of thought to that possibility . . . Then why wouldn't he use the gun instead of killing him with a knife?"

"Eye for an eye, right? To make him suffer . . . To do what Judith did." Conde threw out possibilities.

"Then why would he tell me a story he didn't have to tell me, just to lie to me? No, he had no obligation to tell me anything."

Even though he was between a rock and a hard place, Elias Kaminsky wouldn't give up. Conde chose to get right to it.

"Elias, do you want someone to dig around a little and tell you, for your peace of spirit, that your father didn't mutilate and kill a man?"

The painter shook his head emphatically.

"No, Conde, you're wrong. I think—I'm sure—that he didn't kill Mejías. But I'd like absolute certainty and I'd like to know what happened to the Rembrandt painting. I can't stand by with my arms crossed while someone becomes a millionaire with what cost three of my family members their lives . . . And if in search of that truth it comes up that my father committed a crime, then that also helps my peace of spirit, as you say. Because I would understand what he did. And for whatever he could have done, I will always forgive him, as terrible as it was. What I wouldn't forgive is that he deceived us, my mother and me."

Conde sighed.

"You yourself told me that there are things it's better not to dig around in . . ."

"Or that we should dig around in. If they don't come up, all the better. And if they do come up, then fuck it . . . What I want—what I need—is the truth. Because of everything I've told you."

"The truth? Well, the truth is that right now I don't know how to help you . . . But if we find something out and with that something you can recover the Rembrandt, what are you going to do with that painting?"

Elias Kaminsky looked at his interlocutor.

"If I recover the painting, I think I am going to donate it to some museum, I don't know which; perhaps a Jewish one that's in Berlin. In memory of my grandparents and my aunt. Or to the Rembrandt House, or better still, to the Jewish Museum in Amsterdam, in memory of the Sephardic Jew who took the painting to Poland and no one knows who he was or what the hell he was doing in the middle of those pogroms . . . I still don't know what I would do, because it's rather improbable that I will recover it. But that is what I would do. I don't want that painting for myself, no matter how much of a Rembrandt it is, and less still the money that could come from it, as tempting as it might be . . ."

"That sounds good," Conde said, so susceptible to romantic and useless solutions, after weighing for a few moments the painter's dreams and considering the possible fates proposed for that painting of a young Jew who looked too much like the Christian image of the Messiah. "Let's see what we can do . . ."

"So you'll help me?"

"You want to know the truth?"

"About my father?"

"Yes, of course, there's the truth about your father . . . But now I'm referring to my own truth."

"If you'll tell me . . ."

"Well, half of my truth," Conde began, "is that I don't have anything better to do than waste my time, and trying to find out the why's of a story like this one is something I like to do. The other half is that you're going to pay me a lot for doing so and, given my own state and that of this country, you can't turn your nose up at money like that. And the third half of the truth is that I like you. With all of those halves, you can put together a pretty good and large truth. And it gets even better with the feeling that we're going to get somewhere . . . Even if we have to walk a lot before we do, right? By the way, since we're going to keep going on with this . . . could you advance me some of my pay? I'm really in the *fuácata*."

"*Fuácata?*"

"Broke, in poverty, penury . . . Yes, in the *fuácata*. Like Rembrandt when they took his house away with everything inside of it . . ."

———

The morning of June 14, 1642, Amsterdam enjoyed one of the most splendid days of its brief and barely temperate summers. That silver light, always pursued by its painters, tinged by the sun's reflection on the sea and the canals that cut across and surround the city, delighted in its encounter with the gardens, flower beds, and flowerpots where, encouraged by the heat and light, the highly coveted tulips, which, since their arrival to the world's richest city, unfolded proudly and competed with each other to achieve the most unbelievable tones on the chromatic scale.

But that day, Rembrandt van Rijn, a native of Leiden, painter and renowned member of Amsterdam's Guild of Saint Luke since 1634, didn't have the heart to appreciate that extraordinary show of light and color. Wearing a black suit, high boots, and a hat that was also dark, he had made the trip from his house, number 4 of Jodenbreestraat—Jewish Broad Street—to the Gothic Oude Kerk, beyond the little plaza and the De Waag market. Rembrandt was following the funeral procession of a humble carriage in which traveled the remains of what had once been his wife and most relied-upon muse, Saskia van Uylenburgh. Along with the painter, as if those accompanying him revealed the essence of his unconventional character, at the front of the procession were three of his best friends: one was Cornelis Anslo, a Calvinist preacher of the Mennonite sect; another was Menasseh ben Israel, a former Jewish rabbi and a Kabbalah expert; and the third was the Catholic Philips Vingboons, the city's most sought-after and successful architect.

Following the recitation of the funeral prayers, as the grave diggers deposited the body of Saskia van Uylenburgh in Oude Kerk's ossuary, Rembrandt van Rijn cried out his grief. The young woman's illness had been drawn out, devastating, and even though Rembrandt knew that her consumptive state was irreversible, for many months he had trusted that something close to a miracle would occur: perhaps between God and Saskia's youth they could achieve an unexpected recovery. But two days before, it had all ended, putting an end as well to all of his dreams and faith in miracles, and the man couldn't do anything but cry.

That same afternoon, while in the solitude of his study looking at the gigantic and incredible group portrait of *The Militia Company of Captain Cocq*, which was just awaiting some final touches before going out to the luxurious salons of Kloveniersdoelen, headquarters of the exclusive society of arquebusiers, the painter swore to himself that he would never again cry. For any reason. Because there was only one thing that could make him cry: the death of Titus, the only one of his four children with Saskia to survive. And Titus would not die, at least not before him, as the laws of life demanded. And if life forced him to see Titus die, instead of crying, he would curse God.

That man bestowed with genius, awarded the spirit of eternal nonconformity, the tireless pursuer of human and artistic freedom, although beaten by more failures and frustrations than his journey through this world deserved, was able to maintain this promise for years, until life shook him once again, with a mean force bent on knocking him down. Then Rembrandt van Rijn, so worn-out, no longer had the energy to fulfill the oath he had made to himself. Before he died, Rembrandt would have to cry four more times.

Because Rembrandt cried on the afternoon in 1656 on which, beaten by the pressures of his creditors, he had to declare bankruptcy and leave his dear house at number 4 Jodenbreestraat, while the members of the Court for Patrimonial Insolvencies drew up an inventory of all of his belongings, works, objects, and souvenirs accumulated for years, to be sold at public auction and the proceeds given to the creditors.

He would cry again on the night in 1661 when the leaders of Amsterdam's city government, without paying a cent for the work they requested, rejected, on the basis of considering it inappropriate, rough, even unfinished, his work *The Conspiracy of the Batavians Under Claudius Civilis*, that masterpiece devoted to celebrating the mythical birth of the country in the times of the Roman Empire and capable, in and of itself, of revolutionizing and moving forward seventeenth-century painting by two centuries. Such was the drought in commissions to which they had sentenced him, by considering him an out-of-fashion artist whose style was rough, that in the last five years he had received only two commissions: *The Anatomy Lesson of Dr. Deijman* (a bad copy of the one he dedicated to Dr. Tulp) and *Syndics of the Drapers' Guild*. Because of that, pushed to get some money out of the rejected work, the painter made the terrible decision of cutting that marvelous canvas to try to sell at least the fragment including three phantasmagoric figures with dark eye sockets, as if they were empty, appearing behind a glass cup: the only fragment of the piece that would survive, and which would be sufficient to immortalize the painter. Any painter.

The man would cry again on July 24, 1663, when he put in a tomb at Westerkerk the corpse of Hendrickje Stoffels, the woman who had been by his side for almost twenty years, who had given him love, a daughter, and was the model for some of his most beautiful and daring works, and, above all, who had orchestrated the miracle of making him laugh again and done so more times than he ever thought possible.

And, when he no longer had the strength to curse God, he would have to cry on September 7, 1668, when, against nature, he saw his son Titus die; just fifteen days shy of turning twenty-seven. He cried over that death so much that, just one year later, he would die, too, regretting the Creator's macabre delay. Since, if divine justice existed, He should have taken him a few years earlier to at least avoid the last two reasons for his tears.

If the most devastating events that would cause him tears after having made that promise in 1642 were the deaths of the kind Hendrickje and his beloved Titus, the most dramatic must have been the mutilation of what appears to have been the most explosive and daring of his creations—more, much more even, than *The Militia Company of Captain Cocq*, which would turn into one of the most famous works of global art history with the unlikely name of *The Night Watch*. Because on that day, Rembrandt had also cried for the death of his freedom.

By contrast, the most vulgar, meanest, most aggressive and regrettable of the reasons for his tears was him being thrown out of his house for nonpayment and the amputation of his memory due to the loss of the small and multiple treasures that had accompanied him throughout his life: exotic objects coming from every corner of the known world—stones, shells, maps, and souvenirs for which only he knew the reasons they had arrived at his home and remained there. He also had to hand over to the sale the collection of engravings and watercolors by Andrea Mantegna, the Carraccis, Guido Reni, and José de Ribera, engravings and xylographs by Martin Schongauer, Lucas Cranach the Elder, Albrecht Dürer, Lucas van Leyden, Hendrick Goltzius, Maerten van Heemskerck, and Flemish and contemporaries like Rubens, Anthony van Dyck, and Jacob Jordaens; he lost the xylographs made based on Titian and three books printed by Raphael as well as the various albums with etchings by the most well-known Nordic engravers. Rembrandt even had to hand over his own *tafelet*—those notebooks of pictorial notes that had become so popular and so common among the country's artists—to those vultures from the Court of Insolvencies.

"His biographers say that Rembrandt, using a hood so he wouldn't be recognized, went to the first of the public auctions of his belongings. They claim that from a corner of the main salon of the Keizerskroon Hotel, in the Kalverstraat, while he watched the disheartened bidding for the objects that were part of his life, although he had more than enough reasons to cry, that time Rembrandt managed to hold it together . . . The poor man was broke, in the *fuácata* . . . The fucked-up thing is that, with the price of his *tafelet* alone, today he would have been able to buy five houses like the one he lost." Elias Kaminsky pulled his ponytail a few times and at last began his tour, moving forward along the dark streets of Havana, the city in which his father had been happier and luckier.

———

The last time they had sat down to drink whiskey at the former office of Dr. Valdemira they had bottomed out, among other things, a bottle of reserve Ballantine's that, without their knowing it yet, was a legacy left by the already deceased Rafael Morín, whom they had thought was still alive until that moment and, consequently, still Tamara's official husband. Those drinks, redolent of wood and of an intense gold color, had helped them melt her last inhibitions and his policeman's precautions to act on their overflowing human anxieties and their most animalistic desires. With the taste of Ballantine's in their mouths they had gone to bed so that he could fulfill his oldest and most persistent erotic dream and she could purge herself of a burdensome marital dependence that was suffocating her. Both had felt how the act of coupling, so nervous despite the alcohol, implied much more than a physical resolution. It entailed a complete spiritual freedom that the revelation of her husband's death would end up sealing.

The country where they lived had also changed since that time period, and a lot. The illusion of stability and of the future went up in smoke after the fall of walls, and even of friendly and brotherly states, and those dark and sordid years at the beginning of the 1990s came immediately after, when all aspirations were reduced to the mere achievement of common subsistence. They were collectively broke, the national *fuácata* . . . With the uneven recovery that followed, the country would never again be what it had wanted to be. Just like they couldn't, either. The country was realer and harder, and the people became more disillusioned and cynical. But, above all, two perceptions had shifted: that which the country held of them and the one they held of the country. They learned of the many ways that the protecting heavens in which they'd been made to believe, for which they had worked and suffered privations and prohibitions for the altar of a better future, had been reduced to something that couldn't even protect them in the way they had been promised, and then they looked from afar at a land that was broken and inadequate and they devoted themselves to caring for (it's a manner of speech) their own lives and fates, and that of those closest to them. That process, at first glance traumatic and painful, was, in reality and essentially, liberating, through and through. They came to know the certainty that, at the end of the day, they were much more alone but were also introduced to the benefit of feeling that they were both freer and masters of themselves. And of their poverty. And of their lack of expectations of a future that, to make it all the more bleak, they knew to be worse.

The struggle to survive on which they had insisted all of those years, almost twenty, had been so visceral that on many occasions they only aspired to glide through the murky foam of their days in the best possible way. And get to the next day. And start again, always at zero. In that war for life or death, they became hardened and had to forget codes, niceties, rituals. There was no time, space, or possibility for the exquisiteness of nostalgia, only to ride out the Crisis, which Conde always evoked, thus, with a capital C. But when oblivion thought it was the victor, many times, memory, with its inconceivable capacity for resistance, had come out waving a white flag.

Before getting to Tamara's house, Conde made an important stop, with the very dear purpose of celebrating memory's capacity for resistance and of repeating a founding ritual. With the money he had earned, he bought a bottle of whiskey, square, with a serious and black label. With that bottle in one hand and a tray with its finest glasses and ice in the other, Conde started walking to the former office of Tamara's father, where the air conditioner was already going at full blast, with its pleasant purring, satisfied with its victory over the heat of the September night.

Sitting in the deep leather seats worn with use, next to a fireplace that had never seen a fire burn, Mario Conde and Tamara Valdemira tasted their drinks as if it hadn't been almost twenty years since the last time they had done that in that place and with whiskey, but conscious of the length of time that had passed since that liberating night. And they recognized their luck, since, despite all of their misfortunes, they were still there and in each other's company.

Outside, rain began to pour, crossed with lightning. Safe from all inclement weather, they drank in silence, as if they had nothing to say to each other, although, in reality, they didn't need to speak, since they had already said everything to each other. The years and the blows had taught them to fully enjoy the moments in which enjoyment was possible, so that, greedy, they could later draw on that ephemeral feeling of a life enjoyed from the warehouse of indelible earnings, a translucent container of memories that could always be broken if bad times approached, in which there would be even more reasons to cry. And they also knew that that was a possibility permanently lying in wait. But now they were there, tenacious and drinking, locked away of their own will between walls raised to protect the best parts of their lives, their only inalienable belongings.

Their second drink finished, they looked into each other's eyes as if they wanted to see something crouching there beyond the other's pupils, in some remote fold of their consciousness. As if everything they meant to each other was in their eyes. Leaving aside their mountains of frustrations, seas of disappointments, deserts of abandonment, Conde found behind those eyes the pleasant and protective oasis of a love that had been offered up to him without any demand of commitment. Tamara, perhaps, discovered the man's gratitude, with its invincible surprise before the certainty that something invaluable belonged to him and completed him.

Hand in hand, like nearly two decades before, they went up the stairs, entered the room, and, with less haste and more pauses than before, they took refuge in the security of love.

Outside, the world was coming undone under the rain and electric discharges, the chaos and uncertainty, that always foretell the Apocalypse. Or perhaps a Messiah.

11

Miami, 1958–1989

Daniel Kaminsky had to wait until the month of April 1988 to turn the longest-lasting and dearest dream of his life into reality, immortalized in a photo.

Strictly speaking, Daniel had never been the kind of guy you could consider a dreamer. His own son, Elias, had always considered him the opposite: a basic pragmatist willing to make the concrete decisions required of him by each situation, owner of a proverbial capacity to adapt to his environment, an ability that had allowed him to live in Cuba as a regular old Cuban, and to regain his condition as a Jew in Miami, without ever giving up that of being Cuban, thus saving the two sides of his soul, always in dispute, from the shipwrecked feeling of alienation, although since then he had been steeped in insurmountable regret over the noisy world he had lost.

Nonetheless, that same man capable of programming himself with equal measures of coldness and passion had lived for almost forty years with that romantic dream residing in his mind, and he kept it alive all that time, giving it color, shape, words; very convinced, besides, that that dream would come true before death—*la pelona*, as he called it when he spoke to his son in Cuban Spanish—came for him and he told Elias, before and after the photo was taken, and always as if it were the first time, the image of an old dream kept in the best corner of his proverbial hope chest. As such, on the April afternoon in 1988 when he could finally celebrate the fulfillment of that desire, Daniel Kaminsky got ready with the care that he bestowed upon an experience he had practiced numerous times in his imaginings. On his head he placed the old black cap, rather faded already, with the fraying yellow *M*, the same one he had purchased in 1949 at a stand in the then just-opened Grand Stadium of Havana. In the upper pocket of his white guayabera he placed the printed card he had saved in a plastic case. And lastly, after caressing for a moment the ball with its time-worn leather, he placed it in the right pocket of his wide, striped muslin pants, from where he was able to remove it with the same quickness and skill with which, in the movies seen at the palace of illusions that Old Havana's Ideal Movie Theater was to him, cowboys took out their Colt .45s in the dusty prairies of the Old West.

His excitement was such that he hurried on his son Elias and his wife Marta several times. Twenty minutes before their agreed-upon departure time, he was even sitting in the passenger seat of the 1986 Ford that he had gifted his son two years earlier when he finished his graphic design degree at Florida International University. From his position in the car, parked on one side of the garden, he looked at the two-story house, its portal with Spanish arches and art deco friezes always standing out in white against the darker background, a building with a certain air of being related to the house in the Havana neighborhood of Santos Suárez where he had lived what he always considered to be the best years of his life. Daniel Kaminsky had lived in that same house on Fourteenth Street and West Avenue since leaving Cuba in April of 1958 and deciding to establish himself in Miami Beach, led by his premonitions and sensibilities in the footsteps of the old Jews who came, especially, from the northern states of the Union in search of Florida's sunshine and lower rents and home prices. That was the house where his son was born in 1963 and the place in which he had suffered all of the anxieties plaguing him as he rebuilt his life after he had been so inopportunely taken out of his world. From that house, many times he had left for walks along the promenade of the nearby and, at the time, nearly deserted West Avenue, dragging along the certainty of his solitude and feeling more bereft than ever, to ponder the possible ways he could place himself in a city that seemed like a makeshift settlement, and where his gregarious spirit couldn't, for months, even count on the consolation of a single friend. And never again on the warmth and complicity of friends like the ones he had in Cuba. It had also been inside that house, seated in front of Marta Arnáez, that he had weighed his limited options and

made the third most transcendental decision of his life: that of returning
to the fold and living again as a Jew, seeking to return to that which he
had given up twenty years prior: a way of finding a solution not to the
conflicts of his soul but to the pressing needs of his body. Daniel Kaminsky needed to guarantee his family and himself a roof over their
heads, a bed in which to rest, and two meals per day to keep going. And
the proximity to his tribe seemed like the most cunning, but natural
and best, of his options.

Of course, it had also been in that house, built in 1950 with many of
the attributes of the style appropriated by the architecture of Miami
Beach, where he had most immersed himself in the invincible dream
born in Cuba more than thirty years before and that would finally turn
into reality that afternoon: that of shaking the hand of the great Orestes
"Minnie" Miñoso and asking him to sign a baseball card with his photo,
printed by the Chicago White Sox for what would be the fabulous 1957
season for the Cuban Comet (twenty-one home runs, eighty-eight runs
batted in), and the ball that in its younger days, when its leather was
smooth and shiny, had soared beyond the limits of the Grand Stadium
of Havana by one of the baseball player's hits during a game between
the Marianao club and the Leones de la Habana in the winter of 1958:
the ball that Daniel had the luck of being able to buy that very same day
for two pesos from the kid with the most determination who had chased
it and managed to catch it.

Young Elias Kaminsky, who had decided to try his luck as a student
at an art school in New York where he would complete his technical and
intellectual education, felt rewarded by the twist of fate that would allow
him to witness that memorable event. Ever since he heard of the tribute
to Orestes Miñoso—who had announced the end of his long sports
career, begun so illustriously in Cuba, continued in the United States,
and closed out in Mexico at an age that was beyond reasonable—which
would take place in Miami, the young man had decided that it would be
the best occasion for his father to live the dream that he had talked to him
about so many times. Immediately, Elias purchased three tickets that
guaranteed them a place at the tribute dinner and ran to tell his father
the good news.

When the Kaminskys arrived at the restaurant hall of the Big Five
Club, the preferred place of Miami's increasingly successful Cubans for
their social events, the mythical Miñoso still hadn't made his appear-

ance. "Good," Daniel murmured, and posted himself by the door after making sure for the nth time that his black Marianao cap was on right, that the baseball card was in his guayabera, and that the valuable ball was in his pants pocket.

To add to the sought-after, but obvious, air of nostalgia, over the hall's speakers blared an extraordinary selection of cha-cha-chas, mambos, *sons*, boleros, and *danzóns* that were popular in Cuba in the 1950s. Occasionally, Miñoso's cha-cha-cha came on ("When Miñoso swings the bat, the ball goes cha-cha-cha like that"), sung since the beginning of time by the Orquesta América, but each new piece he heard was immediately identified by the aggressive longing of Daniel Kaminsky, who whispered the name of each artist to his son: Benny Moré and his band, Pérez Prado, Arcaño y sus Maravillas, el Conjunto de Arsenio, Barbarito Díez, la Aragón, the old La Sonora Matancera, the real one, with Daniel Santos or Celia Cruz at the mic . . .

Fifteen minutes after the event's appointed start time, the unstoppable black 1959 Impala in which the baseball player traveled stopped in front of the place full of old Cubans brimming over with memories, both pleasant and cruel, of a lost life that seemed better to all (despite many of the émigrés' economic success) and had never stopped stirring up their longings or fueling their bitterness. Without thinking twice about it, Daniel Kaminsky put on his black cap again, took the baseball card out with one hand, the ball out with the other, and, as it later seemed, with a third hand took out a silver Paper Mate pen and went head-on into his dream come true.

Mere days later, the picture taken by Elias Kaminsky's Minolta was printed on an eight-by-ten sheet and framed. The image selected captured that moment at which Orestes Miñoso, with a smile displaying the very white teeth he inherited from his African ancestors, was shaking the hand of a nearly bald Polish Jew with quite a belly and a hooked nose, while the latter swore he was his oldest and most fervent admirer. Just like the signed card and the baseball, which Daniel had asked him to dedicate to José Manuel Bermúdez, both kept in small glass cases made especially for that purpose, the photo would remain on Daniel Kaminsky's night table from then on. First, next to his bed at the Miami Beach house, later in the apartment of the Coral Gables geriatric home, always keeping him company, making his guilt and nostalgia and his fear of death more bearable until the day in the spring of 2006 on which the old man left this world on a direct flight to hell. Because, he well knew and would say as much to his son several times: even though he had not carried out the execution of a man whom he had been ready to kill, for his heretic's soul, there wasn't even the consolation of spending some time in Sheol, where, they said, the spirits of pious Jews, observant of the Law, went.

———

It couldn't have been any other way: when they got to Miami, after moving into a modest little hotel on the beach, the first visit Daniel Kaminsky and Marta, who was still named Arnáez, made was to the Catholic cemetery on Flagler and Fifty-third Street, where just one month before, the corpse of his friend José Manuel Bermúdez had been buried.

On the journey to Miami's northwest, Marta had asked their Venezuelan taxi driver to make a stop at a florist, where she bought a large bouquet of red roses. At the burial grounds, the couple found that, behind the walls, there were only marble and granite slabs placed directly over the holes dug in the ground, identified by name and sometimes a cross. When they found the parcel where their friend rested, the scarcity of funds of Pepe Manuel's comrades-in-arms, who were charged with paying for the plot where the young man was buried, became clear to them. They must have had only enough to buy the space and a small, almost vulgar slab of molten granite with his name, birth and death dates, and a Christian cross drawn in black paint. The tomb of a forgotten man in a foreign land. Marta, who couldn't contain her tears, placed the red roses over the slab and stepped back a few feet, as if fleeing the perverse absurdity of that inconceivable death. Daniel Kaminsky, alone before the sandy earth that still showed the marks of his recent movements, was then hit with the most overwhelming feeling of helplessness he'd experienced in his complicated existence. The void left by that good man's death had fallen on the state of disorientation and the heavy sadness accompanying him and revealed to him the exact measure of all the losses he'd accumulated at that moment and in that place, and also of the effort required to redesign his life. In José Manuel Bermúdez, or Pepe Manuel, or Scatterbrain, the re-exiled Pole had lost not just a friend: that premature death served as a lobotomy of the best part of his memories since the witness and co-narrator of thousands of shared memories had disappeared, twists of recollections in common going up in smoke. Or, in the best of cases, they would never again be the same memories if he couldn't ask Pepe Manuel if he remembered some detail so that, with an affirmative answer, he could once again enter the pleasant domain of complicity and shared experience. Because of that, without knowing how or when he would do so, at that moment he promised the renewed image of his dead friend to buy him a decent tombstone, under which he could await the resurrection of the just, which, without a doubt, that upright man deserved.

In the initial days spent at the little Miami Beach hotel where they had taken a room, Marta and Daniel went over their prospects many times. The money they had, almost all of it extended by old Arnáez, would be enough to pay for a few months' rent and to support them while they looked for work, or until their Santos Suárez house and the Chevy were sold. The biggest problem, however, lay in the possible ways to relate to that world that was unknown to them, and as such, they started to reach out for the closest points of visible support on their horizon: Cubans and, due to Daniel's genetic predisposition, the numerous Jews established in Miami.

They soon discovered, much to their chagrin, that neither of those paths offered promising prospects. The small community of Cubans that had ended up in that young, scattered city was mainly made up of people who had preferred to or seen themselves forced to leave the island due to the police repression unleashed by Batista and his front men. Many of those pariahs lived in a precarious state of transiency, simply waiting for some regime change that they, from exile, supported and desired. The Jewish community, meanwhile, made up a kind of geriatric home of retired seniors on a beach vacation. They came from northern states, attracted by the heat and low real estate prices in that remote city, and had dressed themselves up in shirts in tropical colors and vegetable fiber hats, since all they aspired to was to peacefully live out, away from the cold and without too many expenses, the last years of their lives. Nonetheless, to get a better idea of the landscape, Daniel and Marta started to frequent the social places where Jews and Cubans got together, despite the scarce hope that those people inspired in them with their concerns governed only by politics or by the state of their bank accounts.

Working against a quick and satisfying relocation was, besides the financial precariousness and the lack of useful connections, the limited knowledge each had of the English language, which made it impossible to find a job in their respective professions of accountant and teacher. But Daniel Kaminsky was a stubborn fighter and knew all the survival strategies. And the first of these lay in the ability and willingness to adapt to one's surroundings, to study them to then find a way in. As such, following the weeks of initial stupor, he decided that both of them would enroll in a class to deepen and perfect their command of English. At the same time, when they received the money from the sale of the Chevy, they left the hotel and rented a house at Fourteenth Street and West Avenue, the property of a New York Jew who, he said, was even willing to sell the building if they paid fifty percent of the going price off the bat.

It was during an act of remembrance for Holocaust victims and thanks to the opportune invocation of the last name Brandon, mentioned to the old Ukrainian Jew Bronstein, owner of the beach's biggest grocery store, that Daniel and Marta would get the first jobs either of them would have in the city: Marta bagging groceries while Daniel worked as an assistant at the warehouse. For Daniel, that work, almost the same as what he did twenty years prior in Sozna's Havana pastry shop, signified a dramatic step back; for Marta Arnáez, born with a silver spoon in her mouth, thanks to the nearly backbreaking work of her Galician father, that option constituted a painful degradation that she faced head-on, determined to bear it, but with her dignity damaged. The worst part wasn't the fact of seeing themselves forced to resort to basic, poorly paid jobs to make a living. They were convinced that that first step would be temporary and that they would overcome it at some point, especially in that country, which was growing and so full of possibilities. The drama, especially for Marta, was processing that, from one day to another, she had become a second- or third-class citizen because of her tangible and never-before-imagined condition as an immigrant, a Latina, a poor and Catholic worker. She saw herself forced to feel like a servant, under orders, sentenced to spend many of her hours at the behest of some bourgeois Jews who enjoyed highlighting the beautiful Cuban woman's social and economic inferiority. For Daniel, meanwhile, the main difficulty was trying to find himself in a hostile land in which it was impossible to find an outlet for his gregarious spirit, shaped and fed by the air of Havana. In Miami, the people lived locked up in their houses, everyone traveled in cars; they thought only about work or their lawns, and there wasn't a stadium like the one in Havana where he could go have a good time and yell; there was no street overflowing with lights, people, music, and lust like the Paseo del Prado; there weren't even buses circulating on the streets. And the most painful thing was that he didn't have a single friend there. It was, besides, a city where a silence reigned devoid of connotations and where fear came from the terrible circumstance of not having money to pay the bills.

That deep change in their lives would prompt a searing feeling of guilt in Daniel. The mere fact of seeing Marta arrive home around midnight, exhausted by a day of work and several hours devoted to studying English, forced him to remember the unforeseeable meetings and decisions that had led them to this suffocating circumstance. Then, according to what his son Elias would later think, with almost all certainty, Daniel Kaminsky must have felt that his story was even more regrettable because of the absurdity underlying it: he was fleeing something he had meant to do, not even something he had done.

In the long workdays at the warehouse, as he carried sacks that reminded him so much of the flour bags he had heaved in La Flor de Berlín, Daniel Kaminsky devoted days and weeks to thinking about the paths by which he could come to build a new life. It took so much for him to get used to the idea of having to live in a city and a country that revealed themselves as much more distant and foreign than warm Havana had been in his dramatic years as a recently arrived boy, when he felt how the absence—perhaps permanent—of his family had left him in sidereal solitude. The blows received and Havana's own atmosphere had pushed him at that moment to make the decision to cease being Jewish and free himself of the weight of this condition and its laws. Now, as he thought and weighed the arduous possibilities for ascent and belonging, he started to seriously consider the previously unimaginable eventuality of going back to the fold: just like the mythical Judah Abravanel had done in his time, after allowing himself to be baptized to save his life and that of his people, he had reassumed the Law of Moses when he found it safe and convenient. At the end of the day, he, Daniel Kaminsky, had given up his religion of his own will: now, again, thanks to that will, he would choose to return. That was what man's free will was for.

In January 1959, when General Batista was just barely defeated and set on the run by the revolutionaries fighting him in the mountains and in the island's cities, Miami's small Cuban community experienced a drastic transformation that complicated the Kaminskys' adaptation even more. While the political exiles established there were returning to the country, the most nefarious characters from Batista's inner circle were arriving at that South Florida city, almost all of them linked to acts of corruption, repression, torture, and death. Daniel and Marta, who had once had a cordial though not particularly close relationship with the Cuban exiles, didn't make the slightest attempt to get close to the new refugees. On the contrary, they decided to keep a distance from them, even trusting that the country's government would kick out some of those murderers, who, it was said, came to Miami for a spell, since before year's end, they would take the rebels out of power and go back to the island.

The push Daniel Kaminsky needed to accelerate his rapprochement with the city's Jews came from how radically the character of the Cuban exile had changed. In July 1959, before the rabbi who had traveled from Tampa to officiate in a Miami Beach hall improvising as a synagogue, Daniel Kaminsky recovered his kippah, his tallith, and, at least formally and publicly, the principles of his religion. Also, as he himself had done at a decisive moment in his life in which he accepted Christian baptism, he convinced the Catholic Marta Arnáez, now Kaminsky, to convert to Judaism. The November 1960 afternoon on which Daniel and Marta together crushed, with the stomping of their heels, the glass cups before a roll of the Torah, the reconverted man thought of how much his uncle Joseph Kaminsky would have liked to attend that ceremony. Would it have mattered too much to him that Marta was a Gentile and not one of the young, pureblood Jewesses with whom, had he married one, he would have conserved whole, in body and soul, the condition of his possible offspring? Or would it all be the same already to the old and beloved Pepe the Purseman, legally joined with a black Cuban woman and the legal father as well of a little Havana-born *mulato* who improvised poetry? Were they, all of them, heretics beyond salvation?

For Daniel, and even for Marta Kaminsky, it was a breath of fresh air to find the tumultuous arrival to Miami Beach of dozens, hundreds, and soon thousands of Jews leaving Cuba, pushed by the fear of the communist regime that the trained noses of those men neatly sniffed out in the Havana air. While the second half of 1959 saw the appearance of some of the richest members of Havana's Jewish community (Brandon, who was a bigwig, moved directly to New York, where he already had businesses), between 1960 and 1961, the rest came, the majority of them poor or suddenly poor due to the losses they suffered upon leaving the island. While Jewish, more or less observant, almost none of them were too Orthodox, the recently arrived were above all Cubans, fortunately of a different kind than the first wave of those characters who were close to Batista, those shadowy men who, to the Kaminskys' relief, had settled down in the Southwest and in Coral Gables.

Although the couple started to toy with the idea of going back to Cuba, due to the old Galician Arnáez's growing fears over a yet-to-be clarified future and the silence of Roberto Fariñas—at one time or another, in those initial times, he used the long list of work and responsibilities undertaken in the process of rebuilding the country's structures as an excuse for distancing himself—they pushed it aside out of caution. At the end of the day, there would always be time to go back, they thought.

The Kaminskys had already begun to pay for the purchase of the little house on Fourteenth Street and West Avenue by the end of 1958 with the money from the sale of their Santos Suárez property and a new loan from old Galician Arnáez. At the same time, Daniel had become the one in charge of negotiating with the grocery's suppliers and quickly moved on to being the business's accountant and Bronstein's right-hand man. It was then that fate came to his aid. In mid-1959, the old Ukrainian man died of a heart attack, and his only son, who worked for the Democratic Party in Washington and had thought of the possibility of selling the business, agreed with Daniel to carry out an experiment in which the heir could only stand to gain with minimal effort: in the face of the continuous arrival of Jews from the North, and the massive arrival of Cuban Jews expanding the population of Miami Beach, it seemed like the best time to turn the modest grocery store on Washington Avenue into a market in the style of Havana's Minimax, whose operations the former accountant knew so well. To increase their space, they rented the neighboring store, looking over the more visible and advantageous corner of Lincoln Road, and, as a change over the original in Havana, they would devote a notable part of the market to kosher foods. Thanks to the money remaining from the sale of the Santos Suárez house, Daniel would go into the business with twenty percent of the capital (which would be used to modernize the property) and the younger Bronstein would put in the rest solely by investing what he inherited from his father. Meanwhile, the Cuban Jew would be in charge of managing the establishment, for which he would receive an additional fifteen percent of the earnings.

As for Marta, she had made great progress in perfecting her English and was hired as a Spanish and English teacher at the recently founded Jewish-Cuban academy on the beach, of which she would become the assistant director and a shareholder just two years later.

While the doors of financial well-being were opening up, Cuban politics had become radical, and American hostility toward the island was turning tangible, the idea of going back was fading away, despite neither Marta nor Daniel recovering—they would never recover—from the feeling of loss calling them from their Havana pasts. Then, the arrival of old Galician Arnáez and his wife were a relief to their feeling of alienation, while Uncle Joseph Kaminsky's refusal to go anywhere was taken as the natural reaction of a stubborn man who, in any event, was still living and would continue to live the best time of his life, which, to his disgrace, ended up being all too brief.

In his recovered role as a Jew, Daniel decided to take several steps forward in search of solidifying his position and, as he would tell his son many times, a sense of belonging that would allow him to calm his spiritual deviation. As such, sensing that he would thus strengthen his increasingly more prosperous business, located at the very spot that was turning into the heart of the neighborhood, he linked himself to a group of Jews from Cuba who were determined in the realization of a dream: to create a Cuban-Jewish community or society in Miami with which to face the future and preserve their identity formed in the past. In reality, that aspiration of those who called themselves Cuban Jews—many of them born in Poland, Germany, Austria, or Turkey, but Cuban to the core—was a response to the invisible but rather impenetrable wall raised by American Jews—many of them natives of, or children of natives of, the same places from which the Cuban Jews came—who were richer, with property and supposed seniority rights, and with an attitude that at times bordered on disdain regarding the recently arrived newcomers with their two suitcases in hand and their lack of English and their parties in Flamingo Park, in the middle of Miami Beach, where they danced to the rhythm of music played by Cuban orchestras with a surprising ability to imbue the movement of their waists and shoulders with African cadences, like any *mulato* from Havana.

Daniel was one of the thirteen Jews who, on September 22, 1961, founded the Cuban-Jewish Association of Miami in a hall at the Lucerne Hotel. Under the flags of Israel, the United States, and Cuba, the founders discussed the first project of rules for the nascent society. Daniel Kaminsky, who preferred to keep silent before the logorrhea of the other founders, almost all of them specialists in the creation of brotherhoods and more familiar with the thought patterns and the religious demands of their colleagues, thought then about how life's paths can lead men to circumstances never before imagined, even at their most delirious. But, he told himself, and would later tell his son, if the price of economic success and the need to feel like part of something were passing through that hotel ballroom, there he was to buy one and catch the other. Although in his heart, he continued to be the same renegade who, twenty-two years prior, had rejected a God who was too cruel in his designs. The truly sacred thing was life, and there he was fighting for it, to make it better. Because, at the age of thirty-one, Daniel Kaminsky could consider himself an expert on losses: he had lost not one but two countries, the one he had been born in and the one he had adopted; a family; the Polish language and Yiddish; a God and, with Him, a faith and militancy in a tradition built on that faith and its Law; he had forfeited a life that he liked and a culture he had acquired; he had lost his best and even his worst friends, some on earth, and others, like Pepe Manuel and Antonio Rico, already in heaven; and he had even failed in trying to carry out justice, although he was paying the price as if he had succeeded, without even gaining the relief of lifting that burden or the satisfaction of having carried out the warranted punishment. Daniel Kaminsky was sick of losses and, through the only path within his reach, he was now ready to receive gains. As long as his conscience could remain free.

———

For many years, Daniel Kaminsky would keep the habit of wandering alone along West Avenue's promenade, less favored and utilized by others than that of Ocean Drive, which ran along the beach. Thanks to those walks by the so-called intercoastal, which he could only make on Saturdays after temple in certain seasons, thanks to the many duties of his job, Daniel was able to witness the changes over the years to that part of Miami Beach and to the keys located on the other side of the canal, like the so-called Star Island, where mansions started springing up in the 1980s—a time when drugs flooded the city—that were more numerous, lavish, and almost unreal in their competition for the luxury and shine that easy money brings along with it. To Daniel, who was on his way to becoming a rich man and would eventually become one, that whole display seemed grotesque, since he was still living in the same little art deco house with two stories and two bedrooms where he lived at the beginning, and not even the mean-spirited people who accused him of being very Jewish would make him change his mind just to satisfy others' expectations through ostentatiousness.

Daniel liked to sit on the small pier at Sixteenth Street, from which you could make out the old bridges uniting the beach with firm ground, the islet with the obelisk raised in memory of Joseph Flagler, and, in the distance, the port of Miami, where, he couldn't help thinking of it, the *Saint Louis* had waited for forty-eight hours before receiving the final no. When he wasn't in a good mood, he took off for a solitary walk along the intercoastal to feel like he was trying to find himself and not get completely lost, since he was starting to sense that he was getting too far removed from what he had once been. Ever since deciding to return to the fold of Judaism, that man would always feel that he was living an apocryphal life, with his conscience and soul subject to a clandestine state. In his first years in Havana, when he chose to distance himself from ancestral beliefs and traditions, Daniel the adolescent had seen himself forced to go through the world with two faces: one to please his uncle and another to satisfy himself and get lost in the crowd. He had to undertake that painful dichotomy, to which his economic and emotional dependence on Joseph Kaminsky obliged him, as the only path toward the chosen path of freedom.

But his reconversion, which transfigured him again into wearing a mask, presented itself, by contrast, as a loss of many of the gains of a freedom that he had enjoyed so much in his Cuban life. Although the community in which he had inserted himself was much less restrictive than that of his country of origin or of the faction of New York Orthodox Jews, in which the Law and the rabbi's word were powerful and oppressive, a tangible social compulsion forced the Jews of Miami to be respectful of most social precepts if they wanted to be accepted. In contrast to the diffuse religiosity with which many Jews lived in Cuba, in Miami the need for social reaffirmation fell like an added weight on his daily life. Daniel knew that among them there were many who, like him, barely kept any vestiges of religious faith. Nonetheless, almost all of them publicly followed the regulations to maintain their belonging and to not seem too different, since the greatest risk was exclusion, marginalization. It could even be considered revolutionary, a bad word that summarized the status just below "heretic."

When he wandered alone, breathing in the canal's pleasant breeze, the man leapt over the border of his nostalgia for a lost world. He looked at his past and saw a Daniel who was fulfilled and satisfied, free as only a man who acts, lives, and thinks according to his conscience. The hypocritical submission he subjected himself to now seemed even more petty and cowardly, although he knew well that it was necessary to obtain the respect and even the impunity that power allows. And in his case, power was money.

What would he do with the money with which he didn't plan to buy himself a mansion or an ostentatious car, or jewelry he would never wear or even a sailboat, since, to top it all off, he was prone to seasickness? Daniel Kaminsky smiled, satisfied with his options: he would buy freedom. First, the most valuable one: the freedom of his son Elias; later, if he still had the energy and the desire, his own.

With those prospects in mind, Daniel was raising his son with a moderation that on occasion seemed exaggerated even by his wife's standards as a Cuban mother and old Arnáez's standards as a softy of a grandfather. But he was convinced that the boy had to learn that everything in life had a price and that when one pays for himself out of his own effort, he values his gains much more. Nonetheless, in contrast to what had happened to him, his son would have the advantage in life's challenges, since he would be able to study and gain the wealth of knowledge, which is not transferrable and constitutes a tangible wealth, as his Polish grandfather would have said. And, in possession of those advantages, Elias would be able to choose. Daniel would guarantee him the supreme freedom of choice, and for that, he was preparing Elias through moderation.

Daniel, who in his American life had discovered traditional Jewish literature and had become intimately familiar with the most rationalist thinkers, tried to pass on to his son the instruments that would allow him to make the best choices. From his readings, he had imbued his

paternal advice with the notion that human decisions are the result of a
balance (or lack of balance) between your conscience and arrogance, a
relationship in which one's conscience should be the driver toward the
best results and decisions. And he backed up that notion with the extraordinary assertions of that Sephardic scholar who had so dazzled
him, Menasseh ben Israel, a nonconformist dreamer, author of many
books, but above all, a treatise called *De Termino Vitae*, a curious text in
which the Dutch-Jewish sage, although Portuguese-born (and by the
way, a friend of Rembrandt's, as many confirmed), reflected about something as transcendental as the importance of knowing how to live life
and learning how to deal with death. Elias Kaminsky the painter, who
years later would also read Ben Israel and, through him, Maimonides
and even the arduous Spinoza, would always remember his father citing
the Sephardic philosopher in his conceptualization of death as a process
of loss of expectations and yearnings suffered by men throughout their
lives. Death, his father used to say to him, is just the exhaustion in life
of our yearnings, hopes, aspirations, and desires for freedom. And from
the other death, the physical one, one could only return if it was arrived
at with a life adequately used, with a fullness, consciousness, and dignity with which we led our lives, seemingly so small, but in reality, so
transcendental and as unique as . . . as a plate of black beans, the man
would say.

———

Two months after the glorious meeting with Orestes Miñoso, which
occurred in the spring of 1988, it was discovered that Daniel Kaminsky
had prostate cancer. He was fifty-eight years old, in robust health—
perhaps a bit overweight—the main shareholder of three markets, located in Miami Beach, the Southwest, and Hialeah, father of a son with
a university degree and already defined artistic aspirations, and, despite
his public dissensions, considered one of the pillars of the Cuban Jewish community in South Florida. A winner who now had the worst, irreversible defeat sneak up on him, but against which he would fight, as
he always did in life.

The revelation of the illness, the operation he underwent, the anti-
cancer treatment that followed, and the adaptation to a nuclear device
in the affected area (which he would always refer to as an atomic war-
head up his ass) prompted him to see life differently. In all his years in

the United States, the Jewish-Cuban Pole had silently and regretfully carried the weight of someone else's guilt that he could not shake. But before the more-than-possible prospect of death, he decided at last to share it with his son.

According to what he would tell Elias, Daniel Kaminsky was sure that his good uncle Joseph, dead more than twenty years before in his little Havana house in the neighborhood of Luyanó, had left this world convinced that his nephew had killed the man who cheated his parents and sent them back to the European inferno of 1939. He knew that his old friend Roberto Fariñas had distanced himself from him, not for non-existent political differences or because of the stellar distance created by geopolitics over the Florida Straits, but because of the conviction that he was a ruthless murderer. Even his beloved Marta, despite deciding, accepting, and wanting to believe him, at heart had never believed him. And because of that, faced with the oncologist's diagnosis, he had launched himself into confessing before his son, to relieve himself of the burden and, incidentally, to remove the possibility, improbable, but not impossible, that the young man would have to receive that same burden someday, through a less propitious route.

"In the hospital, as he recovered from the operation, he told me this whole story . . . My mother would spend the day with him. I was there nights. Since he couldn't sit, he lay on his side, with his face very close to mine, while I sat in an armchair. He spoke for five, six nights, I don't remember very well. He would talk until he fell dead asleep. He started from the beginning, enjoying that talk, and I remember how an image started taking shape in my head of my father's life that I had not had until that moment. Like a painting that starts taking on colors and the edges become outlines that attain shape. Before those conversations, sometimes due to lack of time, other times due to my lack of interest or because of his fears, or for years because of our being out of communication with each other, I didn't really know the details of his life and I wasn't too interested in knowing anything about Cuba. I think like the majority of children, right? He started telling me what his family life had been like in Kraków and in Berlin, before the war, in the time of pogroms and fear chilling the blood in your veins . . . His obsession with the subject of obedience and submission, the choice of free will. Later, he went into the discovery of Havana and his miserable life in the tenement on Acosta and Compostela, the friends he started making, the faith he started losing. All of that for me was a void, sometimes pages from some history book, and suddenly it became a life very close to my own. The story of the *Saint Louis* and my father's first years in Cuba, which went from tragedy and pain to joy and discovery. The reasons for his renouncing Judaism and even his condition as a Jew . . . His discovery of sex and his erotic obsessions with saxophone-playing *mulatas* from El Prado's cafés . . . All of that, he started handing to me. And finally, he told me the story of the plan and what happened the day he went to kill Román Mejías. Everything I've told you in the past few days," Elias Kaminsky said without ceasing to gently, but repeatedly, pull on his ponytail, as he always did when he got into thorny subjects. The painter left his hair alone for a moment and lit up one of his Camels, of which he seemed to have brought an abundant supply, and added, "You have the right not to believe him. In fact, you have reasons not to, as Roberto Fariñas did, as my mother did, as my uncle Joseph could have. But I have a greater reason to accept what he told me: if it was possible for the cancer to kill him, and if, of his own volition, he had told me the good and the bad of his life, his fears and his decisions to deny everything he had been and free his soul from something that was oppressing him and the rather hypocritical decision to return to the fold without handing over his conscience . . . why in the hell was he going to lie to me about Mejías if, for what that son of a bitch did to his family and God knows how many other people, he deserved to be killed a thousand times?"

12

Havana, 2007

From that vertiginous height, the view encompassed an exaggerated part of a tempting sea, crossed with incredibly precise swaths of color and shades invented by the ruthless scourge of the summer sun. The gray snake of the Malecón, spread at the foot of the improvised lookouts, marked, in dramatic contrast, a precise, oppressive arc, as if it were joyously fulfilling the mission of serving as the wall between what is contained and what is open, between what is known and what is possible, between what is crowded and what is deserted. Along that entire generous portion of ocean handed over by the mound of steel and cement, not a single boat was visible, which added to the desolate feeling of looking over a hostile or forbidden expanse. On the seaside, he saw some submerged reefs, in all probability placed there by a man, since they made some dark crosses, definitively gloomy; on the city side, he contemplated rooftops, antennas, ramshackle pigeon coops, sputtering cars trapped under clouds of fatal exhaust, trees eroded by the salt spray, and slow people made miniature by virtue of the distance capable of erasing even the joys and tragedies moving them. Lives flattened by perspective and perhaps by more painful and permanent reasons that Conde didn't even dare guess. People like him, he thought.

A woman of about thirty—one with perfectly sculpted flesh in its most splendorous state, almond-shaped eyes with a come-hither gaze, and smelling of liberally applied Chanel No. 5—had opened the door for them. After telling them that *Papi*—that was what she called him—was taking a quick shower but would be right out, she left Conde and

Elias Kaminsky with the smell of her perfume, the echoes of her local speak, and the magnetism of the memory of her in the living room that opened onto a terrace overlooking the sea, which they leaned out to look at. The former policeman, always suspicious due to his years in that profession, would ask himself what kind of *Papi* of that edible woman Roberto Fariñas could be: her biological father or the lucky *Papi* of more out-of-the-way and penetrable possessions?

Although he had prepared himself mentally for all the emotions, before that exultant landscape that the terrace offered and the lingering presence of that woman's image in his mind, Mario Conde understood how smug his aspiration had been: a fleeting vision of desire and the contemplation of how unfathomable what was waiting for them in Roberto Fariñas's apartment had shaken him, to the point that he felt his supposed abilities as a truth revealer were overcome by the continuous flow of surprises.

Conde had psychologically prepared himself, since he knew that, in all certainty, he would be witnessing the provocation of a mortal leap into the past, perhaps embellished with some unforeseen pirouettes. And he supposed that, with the effects of that fall, the most unanticipated revelations could come to light, implicating several beings, revelations capable of filling the dark parentheses of one or more lives. Spaces that, sometimes, it is best to leave empty.

The spectacular penthouse where Roberto Fariñas lived was located on the tenth floor of a building on Calle Línea, just 250 feet from the Malecón. In his preparation for that meeting, which Conde had set up without any great delay and in which Elias Kaminsky insisted on participating, the former policeman had managed to find out, with Rabbit's indispensable help, that the apartment's ownership dated back to 1958, when the building was constructed and Fariñas's father had gifted it to his unruly and rebellious offspring as the brass ring with which he could remove him from the turbulent sea of political activities. But, while one hand received the keys to the futuristic penthouse, with the other the young man continued to pull the trigger in his actions as a clandestine combatant. Had Fariñas been one of the participants in the attacks of that time period? That was another historical void, sealed under lock and key.

After the triumph of the revolution, while his whole family was going into exile, Roberto Fariñas handed himself over to his political loyalties and started working in different areas, redesigning the country that would soon go to another social system. His merits in the hard years of struggle kept him close to the decision makers, especially in the economic and production sectors, but after the 1970 sugar harvest debacle, in which the country set out with the intention of harvesting ten thousand tons of sugar (the tons themselves capable of promoting the island's great economic leap), the man's star, perhaps due to some cosmic collision related to that fiasco and kept secret even from Rabbit's inquiries and contacts who specialized in historic gossip, started to fade, until it was extinguished in obsolescence behind the desk of some ministry, from which he had retired several years before. Since then, Roberto Fariñas was invited, every now and again, to a remembrance act in honor of the martyred heroes and nothing more.

While they contemplated the sea's deceptive calmness, Conde came out with a question he'd been putting off for several days.

"Was Fariñas the friend who talked to your father about envy as a Cuban trait?"

Elias smiled as he lit up a Camel.

"No, no. That was a guy he met in Miami Beach. Perhaps the only friend he made there, although never like the ones he had here. In Miami, things weren't even the same with Olguita, Pepe Manuel's old girlfriend . . ."

"The communist?"

"My father asked her that every time he saw her. 'Hey, Olguita . . . weren't you a communist?' Well, that guy was a Cuban who went by Papito. Leopoldo Rosado Arruebarruena. The classic Cuban macho with a gold chain and two-toned shoes until he died of old age about three years ago. Papito left here in 1961; he said it was because of the law that closed Havana's brothels . . . A country without whores is like a dog without fleas: the most boring thing in the world, he would say . . . A nice guy, loquacious, he made a living by whatever came up and didn't care about politics . . . My father loved talking to him, and every once in a while he would invite him over to our house, him and whatever woman he was with at the moment, to have arroz con pollo . . . Papito was the one who told him about envy being like a Cuban national pastime."

"What did he tell him?"

"Papito thought that Cubans can put up with anything, even hunger, but not the success of another Cuban. Since they all think they're the best in the world—and I'm saying what he used to say, the most amazing, intelligent, the most clever, and the best dancers—every Cuban has a winner inside of him, a superior being. But since not everyone wins, the compensation they have is envy. According to Papito, if the successful one is American, French, or German, no problem, Cubans fall over with admiration. But if it's someone like them, a Latin American, a Chinese person, a Spaniard, they think it's some lucky asshole and don't pay much attention . . . Now, if it's another Cuban, they are overwhelmed by a *carcomilla*—yes, Papito would say *carcomilla*—an itch in their asses that they can't stand . . . and envy comes out of their pores, and they start to shit all over the winner. I don't know if it's true, but . . ."

"It's true," confirmed Conde, who in his time had seen many outbreaks of Cuban envy directed at other Cubans.

"I assumed that . . . Papito would say it so humorously that—"

"Living with this curse of being completely surrounded by water is to blame . . ." They were interrupted by a voice quoting the poet Virgilio Piñera and forcing the men, taken with the panorama and lost in the digression about the Cuban national character, to turn around toward their recently arrived host, who smiled as he looked at Elias. "Holy shit, kid, you are the very likeness of your Galician grandfather."

Faster than Elias could keep up with, the man squeezed him in a hug. At seventy-eight, Roberto Fariñas exhibited an appearance that was too young but looked good on him. His arm muscles looked compact and worked on, his chest was solid, and his face, carefully shaven, was so lacking in wrinkles that Conde dared to assess two possible deals he had made: either with the devil or with the plastic surgeon.

Their host shook Conde's hand forcefully, as if he wanted to prove his physical power (perhaps to make tangible his ability to be the Chanel lady's *Papi*), and, with a smile, enjoyed the reaction of surprise and pain he caused in his visitor. Back in the living room with the wide hurricane-proof windowpanes, they found the table set with coffee cups, glasses of water, a bucket of ice, and a bottle of Irish Jameson Limited Reserve.

"You have to try this whiskey. It's the best of the best . . . Do you know how much this bottle cost me? I'm embarrassed to say . . ."

Despite the propaganda, Elias Kaminsky chose only the coffee. Conde also accepted the coffee and turned down the drink, a superhuman effort on his part, especially given the prospect of having only one opportunity to drink it. If he was going to be left wanting, it was better to not even try it at all.

"You're missing out," their host warned them. "You don't know how happy I am to see you . . . Oh, you are the spitting image of your grandfather . . ."

Roberto Fariñas focused on Elias Kaminsky, and for several minutes he ignored Conde in the most colossal way, while Conde, almost with pleasure, accepted his role as an invisible guest in that meeting between two strangers who had actually known each other since long before one of them had come into the world. Because of that, without ceasing to listen, he was able to focus on observing the concentration of valuable objects on display in the living room: a forty-eight-inch (he guessed) flatscreen TV with a whole home movie theater system, a living room set made of real leather, a bar with more bottles with shiny labels, in addition to candelabras, vases, and other illustrious and refined objects. Where did the retired Fariñas get the money for all of that?

"I don't know why, but I was always sure that one day this would happen," Fariñas began, talking to Elias. "Just like I knew from a certain point on that I would never again see your father, I knew that someday I would see you . . . And I even knew why I would see you . . ."

A light went off in Conde's head at that moment. Now he suddenly understood why Elias Kaminsky had requested his services and demanded that he be present at that meeting: out of fear. The painter, Conde thought, wouldn't have really needed him to get to that Havana summit where surely some of the answers to his questions—perhaps more definitive answers—lay. A telephone call would have sufficed to deposit him there, in front of the man his father had confirmed he could rely upon for whatever was needed, fully conscious of what that offer could mean. But Elias's fear of hearing a revelation he didn't want to hear, although he needed to know, had forced him to seek out neutral assistance, a presence on which he could lean if everything came down. The price of several hundred dollars, which represented a fortune to Conde, was, to Elias—the inheritor of three supermarkets opportunely sold to large American chains, a moderately successful painter, and the presumed inheritor of a Rembrandt—nothing more than the down payment on a larger gain: not having to face the truth by himself, whatever that truth might be.

"My father spoke of you and Pepe Manuel a lot. He never had friends like you again. How is it possible that, in over forty years, you never spoke again, never even wrote each other a letter?"

"Because life is a real *barca* . . . as Calderón de Shit once said," the old-young man said, and laughed at his own joke, as archaic as it was, but more worn from use. He seemed to be a fan of destroying literary references. "But I was up to speed on your lives. I always was."

"How so, if you didn't talk to each other?"

"No, I didn't talk to your father. But I was in touch with Marta . . . When they told us that having a relationship, that any contact with those who lived outside the country was practically a crime of treason to the homeland, we discovered a system to stay in touch. My godmother, who stayed in Cuba and could care less what others said about her, wrote letters to Marta that I dictated and sent with her own return address. And your mother replied to her. That's how I knew you had been born, for example. That's how I got the photo of the bronze-inlaid marble tombstone that your father bought for Pepe Manuel at that horrible Miami cemetery. I also found out about the cancer, the operation, and the atomic missile that they put up the Pole's ass. And she found out things about me. That I became a widower in 1974. Marta and Isabel, my wife, loved each other very much . . . Well, it was a close relationship behind your father's back and that of the political Taliban around here."

Elias tried to smile and looked at Conde. The revelations were starting, with their accompanying surprises. Where had his mother put those letters? How had she received them to avoid his father finding out about that sustained yet pleasant infidelity? Or had Daniel been aware of that connection and hidden it from him?

"The last letter, she wrote when the Pole died. By the silence that followed, I was able to guess what had happened to her and then a friend confirmed it. I'm not going to give you the other letters, but I want to give you this last one as a present. It's one of the best love letters ever written. When I read it, I knew that Marta's life was over. Because her life was Daniel Kaminsky. Her love for you, excuse me for saying so, was more a consequence of her love for the Pole than because she gave birth to you . . ."

Now the painter did not smile. As he pulled on his ponytail, the approaching tears dampened his pupils. Roberto's words didn't reveal anything to him: he knew what that relationship had meant to his parents, the struggles they endured to make it happen, the sacrifices and the things they gave up in order to sanctify and preserve it, the silences they kept to not sully it. But, coming from a surviving witness from the time in which it had all began as puppy love, they added the devastating connotation brought by sixty years of persistence, a time period in which so much had changed, but not the decision that had most had an impact on the lives of the scruffy Pole Daniel Kaminsky and the little Galician, nearly rich, Marta Arnáez. And on his own life.

From the backpack he had brought, Elias then removed a small wooden box. He opened it and, like a magician, removed a glass cube within which rested a baseball, yellowed with age and marked with blue letters.

"Although I didn't know if I was going to see you or not," Elias said, "I brought this, because it is more yours than mine. You see? It's dedicated to Pepe Manuel, signed by Miñoso . . ."

The foreigner held out the glass cube, which Roberto Fariñas took delicately, as if he feared destroying it.

"Shit, kid," he muttered, moved. "What a time that was, dammit! How we lived, at what speed, what things we did, and how we enjoyed it all . . . And suddenly, everything changed. Your father was away, Pepe Manuel was dead in the most absurd way, I was a socialist leader without ever having wanted to be a socialist or a communist . . . It was never the same again . . . A while ago, I read a book by a Spaniard, who's not a bad writer, incidentally, in which a character quotes Stendhal with some words that are the honest-to-God truth. The Spaniard says that Stendhal wrote, 'No one who has not lived before the revolution can say that he has lived . . .' Did you hear that? Well, I can put my seal of approval on that phrase. I'm telling you, since I'm a survivor . . ." he said, and concentrated on his memories, perhaps the happiest ones, as he looked at the ball placed on the glass urn. "I was with Daniel the day Miñoso hit this ball out."

"That story I know. There are others I don't . . ."

"Sometimes you don't need to know everything."

"But the thing is that my father lived until the end with one regret," Elias began, but Roberto, after placing the glass cube on the coffee table, rushed to stop him with a flash of his hand.

"You really want me to talk to you about your father? That I tell you the things I would have wanted to say to him for the last fifty years?"

Elias dared to think about it. Even though he had no choice. Conde noticed that the painter wanted to look at him, but didn't dare.

"Yes, as if I were him."

"Then I should start at the beginning . . . Your father lived with that regret you mention because he was a sacrosanct moron. A pigheaded Pole who was lucky not to meet up with me again, because I would have kicked his ass . . . Not for what he did or didn't do, that doesn't matter, but because he didn't trust me. I never forgave him for that."

Stoically, Elias received that diatribe without ceasing to pull on his ponytail, so much so that Conde feared it would be ripped out of his scalp at any moment. From the witness stand, Conde saw that Roberto Fariñas's threats and insults came enveloped in a cover of affection resistant to all storms, the pre- and post-revolutionary years, the lack of understanding and the forced and sought-out distances. They sounded like learned, perhaps even practiced, sound bites.

"One of his problems was that I could think that he had killed the son of a bitch who conned . . . yeah, your grandparents and your aunt. But ever since I learned how they killed Mejías, I realized your father didn't do it. And it was easy to know why he hadn't killed him: Daniel would have never killed a man like that. Not even that colossal son of a bitch. What complicated everything was that when they found out Pepe Manuel had escaped them, they put me in jail for almost three weeks, interrogated me twice every day, and gave me several blows, despite my last name and my father's connections . . . And since I was in jail, I couldn't talk to the Pole again. When they let me out, he had already left. Lucky for him, since he could have been the next one to go to jail."

Roberto Fariñas, so exultant from the start, started losing vehemence in his speech. Conde knew that process and prepared himself for the true revelation.

"The other problem," he said, getting back on track after a pause during which he anxiously caressed the elegant gold watch soldered to his wrist, "the real problem, is that he thought that while I was in prison I could rat him out as Mejías's possible killer . . . That's why he left Cuba, not out of fear over Pepe Manuel's whole story. And that's also why he never wrote to me later. Shame wouldn't let him. He thought something of me that he had no right to think . . . That was the real weight that moron carried until the end, and since he could never relieve himself of it, his body dragged it into the tomb."

Elias stayed silent, trapped by the shame genetically handed down to him, but at the same time relieved by Roberto Fariñas's conviction that his father had not killed Mejías. Conde, in his role as silent witness, shifted uncomfortably, needled by the questions that had him in agony and the ones that, in his condition as a listener, he had to keep under control. He increasingly had the feeling that something in Fariñas's tale didn't match up.

"I understand why Daniel thought that way," Roberto continued his monologue. "At the time, many people who thought they could withstand it all broke. Fear and torture have survived for centuries because they've proven their effectiveness. And he had the right to feel fear, even fear of my ability to resist . . . Because sometimes, when the only thing you want is to stop feeling pain, to have the hope of surviving, you're capable of saying anything to put an end to the suffering. But if I'm proud of anything in my life, it's that I was able to resist that time. I was afraid, very afraid. Luckily, they didn't really torture me . . . They hit me a few times, but I immediately realized that they were doing it with the brakes on. The sons of bitches didn't want to leave any marks on me. And I figured that if they only left me standing or seated for hours, without letting me sleep, I was going to fall apart physically but I could resist psychologically. So I didn't say a word: nothing about how Daniel and I had gotten Pepe Manuel out, and far less still, of course, about what your father had considered doing and what I knew he hadn't done."

"I'm really sorry." Elias finally managed to express his apology and made an attempt to change the direction of the conversation. "So, if it wasn't my father, who could have killed Mejías?"

"Anyone," Roberto Fariñas let out his conclusion. "Mejías had spent twenty years fucking over and conning people. He could have even been killed by one of Batista's men if they found out what he was doing with the passports and the revolutionaries."

"But you don't have any idea?"

"I do, but it's just a suspicion. What I am sure of is that your father didn't do it."

Conde felt the gears in his mind speeding up, and he supposed the same was happening in Elias Kaminsky's brain. A "suspicion," as Fariñas would call it, would logically have a name. That of a person who, in almost all certainty, must already be dead, like nearly all of those involved in that story. Why wouldn't Fariñas provide Elias that relief?

At the back of his storehouse of policeman's intuition, dusty but still there, Conde felt another light going on, with greater intensity. What didn't make sense about Fariñas's speech, he thought, had to be the lie on which he had placed the truth on display: the man said he had a suspicion but didn't want to say it, which was either petty or false.

"Do you know that the Rembrandt painting that was at Mejías's house came up for auction in London?" Elias asked him.

Roberto Fariñas reacted with genuine surprise.

"The Golden Painting of Discord . . ." he murmured as if disappointed. "No, I didn't know."

"And, based on what I know, my father didn't take it out of Cuba. He never got it back because he didn't kill Mejías, as you yourself say, and, of course, he never again entered that man's house. Almost all of Mejías's family left Cuba in 1959 . . . Did they take it out of here?"

"When they killed Mejías, there was a stolen painting. From the beginning, I thought that the Rembrandt we saw at Mejías's house could be fake, and I was convinced that was so when I saw that they didn't talk much about the robbery. Mejías's people, his wife, and I think two or three daughters, left at the very beginning of the revolution, so it could be that they took the authentic painting, the one that your grandparents brought." Fariñas was trying to find alternatives, and Conde, forced to remain silent, was convinced that something was screeching all the more forcefully. But he was still unable to make out what link in that story was causing the friction, until the implosion in his mind started to prove stronger than his agreed-upon nonintervention policy. The key was to peel off the truths from the trunk of a lie. He was going to earn his salary.

"It wasn't easy for those people to get that painting out of Cuba," Conde suddenly interrupted, trying to contain his vehemence. "You know that. They would search them head to toe . . . Couldn't they have left it with someone? Couldn't it have been confiscated and then stolen by someone here?"

Roberto Fariñas was listening to Conde but looking at Elias.

"Did you have to bring this guy along?" he asked Kaminsky, pointing at the former policeman as if he were a repellent bug.

"He's helping me . . ."

"Here in Cuba, to make a buck, they'll sell you the nails from the cross and a couple of Rembrandt paintings . . . Helping you what, kid?"

Even though he knew he was going over the line, Conde decided to rise to the attack, since he sensed that it could lead him to a path by which he could arrive at the truth and because he felt his dignity was wounded. He thought about it for a moment: he knew Fariñas would be hard to break, but he had to do it.

"You were one of the ones who knew that that painting, the real one, was worth a lot of money, weren't you?"

"Yes, of course . . . But what in the hell are you insinuating?"

"I'm not insinuating anything. Just confirming something. You knew it . . . and who else?"

"What do I know?! Mejías was a charlatan. Anyone could have known it. He strutted around, showing off that he had an authentic Rembrandt, and the painting was in the living room of his house, for all to see . . ."

"Not as far as we can surmise. What was there had to have been a copy, as you yourself say. Like the other paintings. Because while it's true that Mejías was a charlatan, he wasn't a moron. So the mystery as to why no one talked about the stolen painting can be explained because it wasn't authentic and the family wasn't interested in the painting being mentioned, not the fake one or the real one, because they had the real one . . ."

"Yeah, okay, so what?"

"What do you mean 'So what?'?" Conde thought about it again. Did he have the right to keep going? He told himself, yes: the right was conferred by the need to get at the truth. "That you've been retired for twenty years. That you were removed from power a long time ago. But keeping up this house, buying all the shit you have, being the *Papi* of that woman who could be your granddaughter . . . With what money, Fariñas? What connections did your family have so that you emerged perfectly alive and wagging your tail from a place where other revolutionaries emerged without eyes, without fingernails . . . or dead? Was Mejías really the friend of one of your brothers? Or might he not be your buddy in things like the sale of passports and other matters like that? And now, and right now . . . what connections do you have to be able to buy yourself all of these things?"

The owner of the spectacular apartment and beneficiary of the kindness of the overwhelming Chanel lady seemed to have lost his ability to speak before that ruthless barrage. Conde took advantage of the mute-

ness that overtook Fariñas to launch into his petty demolition. Elias
Kaminsky, on his part, looked like a modern version of Lot's damned wife.

"Daniel had reasons to be afraid of you. He knew you could rat him
out. That's why he left and never wrote to you again. That's why Daniel
never returned to Cuba, not even when Batista and his people left. If he
never told Elias his suspicions, it's because he preferred to blame himself before revealing any doubts he had about you and your friendship.
That's why I wouldn't be surprised if you and the original painting had
some kind of connection . . ."

Roberto Fariñas managed to get a second wind, only to protest.

"What in the hell is this idiot talking about?" he said, referring to
Conde but addressing Elias.

Conde looked at Fariñas's seventy-eight-year-old biceps, inches more
muscular than his own, and decided to take the risk.

"I'm talking about you having some connection with the Rembrandt
painting, perhaps with that painting having appeared in London for auction just after Daniel and Marta died, and, perhaps, about you having
some connection with Mejías's death . . . Because not even Marta knew
what day Daniel was going to kill him, and she always suspected that
he could have killed him. But you did know everything, so much, that
you're convinced that it wasn't Daniel who killed Mejías . . . And at the
same time you let Marta live with her doubts until the end . . . So what
about the date of José Manuel's death? Did he really kill himself acci-
dentally the same day that they killed Mejías or was the thing about the
date some kind of cover-up all of you put together? Wasn't it that José
Manuel took the lead and killed Mejías and then took the ferry? Or was
it you, who was running around with a gun, who was interested in the
Rembrandt painting, and who had the balls to slit the throat and cut the
dick off of some guy, or fire two shots at him, as you almost surely did in
1958? Besides, didn't you yourself tell Daniel that you were willing to do
whatever had to be done?"

Fariñas had been going red in the face as his blood pressure went up.
Conde, throwing punches in all directions, had managed to take him to
the edge of the ring where he needed him. If Roberto Fariñas had anything left, it was his love for his own self-image, both physical and moral.
So now he couldn't do anything but defend it in front of the man who
was the son of one of his best friends, the witness by proxy to his past.

"Enough already, dammit!" he exclaimed. "I don't know a fucking thing about that shitty painting! What I have here, including the woman inside, I have and I keep thanks to the jewels my family left me that I've been selling for years. I wasn't one of those morons who handed over his jewelry to the government because they were saying it was the revolutionary thing to do. I had already given enough, I risked my own skin, yes, with a gun in my hand, and I killed a couple of son-of-a-bitch torturers and laid down bombs right under the police . . . And I'm selling those jewels because, before I die, I am going to spend it all on eating well and fucking well, until Viagra makes me explode like a glutton . . . All of this shit you're saying about Pepe Manuel is just that . . . shit, shit, shit." Roberto Fariñas's diatribe seemed to get stuck in shit and, to extract it, he looked to Elias, leaving Conde out of his range of focus and more or less in that pile of feces. "Kid, I would have never ratted out your father. And he knew that. He left Cuba because he was afraid, that's why. But he wasn't afraid of what would happen to him; rather, he was afraid of what he was capable of doing . . ." Roberto Fariñas paused and expanded the range of his gaze to include Conde, who got ready to listen to the end of the true story, hidden for fifty years, which could finally provide Elias Kaminsky with relief. "His fear in some way was connected to Mejías, that they would put him in jail and force him to confess. Because he did know who had killed that man. And, of course, he knew it hadn't been Pepe Manuel, as this imbecile says, because he himself helped him leave a few days before and even kept his gun . . . I myself gave it to him. And he also knew that it hadn't been me, because when he left Mejías's house, he went to get me and found me still sleeping . . ."

Now it was Elias Kaminsky's robust face that went red. He left his ponytail alone. The clarity of an ancient, repressed suspicion had begun to take shape, to be tangible. The behemoth needed to clear his throat to ask Fariñas, "My father lied to me?"

"I don't know . . . but he surely didn't tell you the whole truth."

"He told you he knew who had killed Mejías?"

"He told me that," Fariñas confirmed. "A few days before they put me in jail, he talked to me. He felt really fucked up; he blamed himself for not being the one to snuff out that son of a bitch. And he was afraid that if he was connected with that man and put in jail, he wouldn't be able to resist. It was a terrible time . . . and your father was a real coward . . . So

I myself gave him an idea: if anything happened, we were going to blame Pepe Manuel, who had already escaped them . . . forever."

Conde listened and confirmed a simple conviction to himself: sometimes you don't need to exhume buried truths. The epitaph read three days prior was finally making sense in his mind: "Joseph Kaminsky. Believed in the Sacred. Violated the Law. Died without feeling any remorse."

"The only time I wrote to your father"—Roberto Fariñas concentrated on Elias Kaminsky once again—"was to tell him that old Pepe the Purseman had died. And he asked me to do him the favor of having a tombstone made for him. He told me what I had to put on it. He wrote it in Hebrew . . . I can show you that letter . . ."

"So why did my father tell me that whole story and not say that he knew Uncle Joseph had killed Mejías? Why didn't he ever tell my mother?"

"That, I don't know, Elias. I think to save his uncle's name even if he was fucking up his own . . . Or because he should have been the one to kill Mejías. I don't know, your father was always a complicated guy. Like all Jews, no?"

———

Elias Kaminsky confessed to Conde that he didn't know if he felt better or worse, relieved or weighed down with a bad conscience, regarding what he had come to think about his father and of the secrets and fears that the man had never confessed to him, to protect himself and others from his feelings of guilt and blame. What he did know, he told Conde, was that he wanted to finish with that plunge into the past, and even forget the painting that, at least to Daniel Kaminsky, hadn't brought any satisfaction and had only served to twist his life again and again. To hell with it if others got rich because of it.

"So you don't care if the heirs of those guilty of what happened to your grandparents keep the painting or the money from the painting? Your father did care. Your uncle cared . . ."

"Well, I don't care," he said, as if raising a white flag.

"And it doesn't interest you, either, to see your almost-cousin Ricardo Kaminsky?"

When they left Roberto Fariñas's house, Conde had invited Elias to have some beers at a ramshackle bar from which they could see the Malecón. The painter needed a break to digest the revelations, and his first reaction had been that of complete rejection. But Conde, who felt invested, was anxious to learn the remaining truths, and was taking him to the edge of the ring, letting him get fresh air and pushing him to go on. When he heard that question, Elias reacted.

"What can that kid know, Conde?"

"Well, I don't know. But I'm sure he knows something. Ever since I heard Fariñas, I can feel it here, right here . . ." He patted the area just below his right nipple. "I have a smarting premonition: he knows something important about this whole story."

"What does he know?"

"Well, I don't know. But we could go see him this afternoon. And he's not a kid. Remember, he's older than you."

The previous night, after making the appointment with Roberto Fariñas, Conde had tracked down Ricardo Kaminsky's telephone number in the most basic way: by looking in the telephone book. The phone book had only one person with that last name, he lived on Calle Zapotes, in Luyanó, and, of course, couldn't be anyone but the offspring of Caridad *la mulata* who had gone on from being Joseph Kaminsky's stepson to become his legally recognized son, with the Polish Jew's name and everything. From Skinny Carlos's house, Conde had called, explained to him that the son of his adopted father's nephew—yes, the son of Daniel Kaminsky, Elias—was in Cuba and was interested in seeing him. Dr. Ricardo Kaminsky, once he overcame his surprise, had agreed to a rendezvous that had been entirely unexpected for him.

"Did you arrange a meeting?" The behemoth seemed halfway between alarmed and annoyed. Conde chalked it up to the conversation with Fariñas.

"Yes, of course. That's what you're paying me for, isn't it?"

"Why did you think I would want to speak with him?"

"Before, because he knew your father here in Cuba and because he was one of the last people who must have seen your uncle Joseph alive. Now, because I am convinced that he can tell you things that would interest you . . . Unless you really want to say the hell with all of it and get on the first flight out of here without learning everything you wanted to know."

Elias took a long sip of beer and sought out his handkerchief to wipe off his mouth and, incidentally, the sweat from his brow. Even in that open shack, just by the sea, the heat pulled all the moisture out of bodies. Elias shook his head, denying something only he knew the nature of. For now.

"Did I tell you I have two kids?"

"No. This whole time, you've been looking back at the past . . ."

Elias nodded.

"A boy who is fourteen and a girl who is eleven. I don't see them as much as I'd like to now. I divorced their mother three years ago and they went to live in Oregon. She got a position at the university. Don't act surprised: my ex became an expert on Northern European Baroque painting. At the beginning of last year, when my father started to get worse, I took my kids to Miami. We lived there for three months, until the old man died. The strange thing is, they weren't months of mourning. Rather, of sympathetic discovery. My father was fully conscious until the end. In his final days, he even refused to be drugged, he didn't complain, he asked that they bring him black beans . . . Your friend Andrés helped him a lot. The fact is that my children had only known their grandparents through the summer vacations we spent in Miami. My son was thirteen years old and was a New York kid, which means everything and nothing. No one is from New York and everyone could be from New York, I don't know. My father then told him, whenever he could, a lot of things about his life. He taught my son about Jewish Kraków before World War Two, Nazi Berlin, the persecution that is fear, the story of his great-grandparents and the *Saint Louis* . . . Some of those things were already the subjects of movies for him, things out of *Indiana Jones*, and thanks to my father he was able to understand that the reality was very macabre . . . But he especially told him about his life in Cuba and about how and why he had decided to stop practicing Judaism and even tried to stop being Jewish. And he spoke to him a lot about freedom. Of man's right to choose independently. Whether to believe or not in God; whether to be Jewish or anything else; whether to be honest or a bastard. He repeated the story of Judah Abravanel, which is a Jewish story to me . . . I think he spoke to him about the things you are and can't stop being, and how you can never be freed of them . . . But do you know what he most spoke to him about?"

Conde thought. He hazarded a guess.

"The Rembrandt painting?"

"No . . . Well, he talked about the painting because, without that, you wouldn't be able to understand some important things about all of our lives. But what he talked about the most was his relationship with Uncle Joseph. He would tell my son how important to him that man had been, he who seemed so cheap and reserved, who in the most fucked-up moments of his life had been at his side and had guaranteed him the possibility of choosing his options freely . . . And he told Sammy—well, my son's name is Samuel—he told him something he had never said to me: that he could never have paid back his uncle Joseph the debt of gratitude that he owed him, not because he had taken him in or because of the money that he gave him, but because his uncle had been capable of pawning even the peace in his own soul in order to save him, his nephew. When I heard him say that to Sammy, I thought the old man was talking about something religious—complicated Jewish things, as Roberto says. But now I know he was talking about more important problems. He was speaking of damnation and salvation. Of life and death. My father was referring to his own life and to the death of a man.

———

Ricardo Kaminsky could introduce himself as the most unlikely and yet simultaneously most faithful heir of a tradition that went back to Dr. Moshe Kaminsky, a Jew from Kraków. Like that distant Ashkenazi Pole whose blood he didn't carry but whose surname had been handed over to him, the Havana-born *mulato* practiced medicine, had achieved a second-degree specialization in nephrology, and was a tenured professor in that field. But, to Elias Kaminsky's complete surprise, this other Kaminsky, the Cuban one, who was white-haired and sixty-six years old, despite his scientific merits and achievements, still lived in the more than modest little house, built in the 1930s, in the neighborhood of Luyanó, that he had inherited from his parents, Caridad *la mulata* and Polish Pepe the Purseman.

In the car, as they closed in on the address Conde had indicated to Elias Kaminsky, the continuous squalor and unstoppable decay of that Havana neighborhood became patent, more still, insulting. The houses, the majority of them without the benefit of any kind of porch, had dirty doors right on top of grimy sidewalks. The streets, full of potholes of historic dimensions, where all kinds of water pooled up, looked like they were the product of a carefully planned bombing. The buildings, many of them made from less-than-noble materials, had outlived the time span for which they were made and gracelessly exhaled their last breath. Meanwhile, the houses that sought to impose a distance in class and size from their poorer neighbors had met the fate of fragmentation in many cases: decades before, they had been turned into tenements, where families crammed themselves together into tight spaces, and, even in the twenty-first century, still had those collective bathrooms that brought such agony to Pepe the Purseman in his day. On the streets, the sidewalks, the corners, people without any hope and at the margins of time, or, worse still, flattened by it, saw the shiny Audi pass by with looks that went from indifference to indignation: indifference to a possible life that never, not even in their dreams (since they didn't dream anymore), would be theirs, and indignation (their last resort) caused by the visceral reflux from what had been denied to them for generations, despite so many promises and speeches. They were beings for whom, regardless of their sacrifices and obedience, their lives had served as a transition between nothing and a void, between oblivion and frustration.

"Look," Conde said. "This is Parque de Reyes. That's where your father and your uncle had a talk when Daniel discovered the Rembrandt painting at Mejías's house."

What Conde called a park was an undefined territory. Several bins overflowing with trash; piles of litter, old, new, and ancient; the remains of what one could, with plenty of imagination, make out were once benches and playground rides for children; damaged trees with the patent desire to die. A compendium of disaster.

"Uncle Joseph left the tenement on Compostela to live here?" Elias Kaminsky didn't understand.

"It was a working-class neighborhood. But remove fifty years of apathy and abuse and ten million tons of shit . . . and at least it was a single-family house with its own bathroom to give him time to deal with his constipation, right?"

"He gave my father a fortune and kept living in shit" was the terrified foreigner's painful and astonished conclusion.

Conde gave the final directions for Elias to take Calle Zapotes. They followed the numbers in descending order until they reached number 61. To their relief, the numbered plaque, instead of hanging over the sidewalk, was adhered to the wall of the only house on the block with a porch. A small porch, but a porch nonetheless. In front of the house, a car in its death throes was parked, a Soviet car that, the newly arrived guests would soon learn, Dr. Ricardo Kaminsky had been allowed to purchase, thanks to his profession, almost twenty-five years before.

From the Audi, they saw the doctor. The man was waiting for them on the porch, dressed up as if for some occasion: cream-colored pants and a shirt with the visible marks of a fresh ironing. The expectations of the person who had once been Ricardito, the little light-skinned *mulato* who could make up verses and, holding on to his mother's hand, had stolen the heart of Joseph Kaminsky, were palpable. When the newly arrived guests got out of the shiny vehicle that cruelly highlighted the decrepitude of the car belonging to the nephrologist, the man's eyes immediately dismissed Conde's figure—it was so secondary in their search—and concentrated on the ponytailed behemoth. That face spoke to him of his own past. And it did so quite loudly, as Conde and Elias would soon confirm.

After greetings and initial introductions, the doctor, somewhat nervously, insisted on introducing his family to the son of Daniel Kaminsky, that painter who had come with no prior warning from the mists of the past. His wife, two daughters, respective sons-in-law, and three grandchildren—two boys, one girl—emerged from inside the house, where those beings of various skin colors seemed to have been crouched, awaiting to be summoned. The last figure to peek out stirred Mario Conde's curiosity, but not Elias's, who was surely used to those kinds of faces: the girl, who turned out to be the doctor's oldest granddaughter, a young woman, newly out of adolescence and paler than the rest of her relatives, was wearing an outlandish outfit, full of rivets and metallic pieces, and had her lips, nails, and the corners of her eyes painted black; a kind of striped-fabric tube covered one arm while a silver ring shone in her nose, and she had a collection of rings in the only ear that could be seen, given the piece of hair that, like a dark veil, covered half of her face. The girl stood out in that environment like a dog in the middle of a clowder of cats.

The introductions were an act that Ricardo Kaminsky carried out with an old-fashioned formality, as if he were placing the members of his clan in front of a shaman or someone of similarly transcendent status. The women, even the young goth, kissed Elias's cheek and the men shook his hand, all repeating the same phrase, "*Mucho gusto, es un placer . . .*" As such, after saying the names and relationship of each of his family members and their pleasure expressed, he addressed them, pointing at Elias. "As you already know, this man is the great-nephew of Pipo Pepe. The son of my cousin Daniel. This gentleman, if he allows me to say so, is my family, my cousin, the only one I have, and, as far as I know, I am the only Kaminsky cousin that he has, since his paternal family was killed by the Nazis. But the most important thing, and you all know it: if Grandmother Caridad was a happy woman and I am the man who I am and you are the people you are, it is because that Pole, this gentleman's great-uncle, my father, gave my mother and me the three most important things that a human being can have: love, respect, and dignity."

Joseph Kaminsky was Pipo Pepe? Daniel Kaminsky, Cousin Daniel? Cuban, white, black, *mulato* Kaminskys, proud of that outlandish last name that had taken them out of misery? Elias Kaminsky had been attacked again and again, from behind, by surprise. He went mute, and tears started falling down his face, unstoppable. He had come in search of a truth and, as recompense, discoveries were raining down on him that could loosen the tap of his tear ducts.

"If you would be so kind," Dr. Kaminsky continued, now addressing the visitors, "we'd like to invite you to have a meal here at the house. It's nothing special, remember that I'm just a doctor, but for us it would be an honor. I mean, it would bring us great joy if you'd accept the invitation. Since I don't know if you are a practicing Jew," he continued, addressing Elias, "we've only made kosher dishes, nothing is *treyf* . . . I cooked them myself, like my mother used to prepare them for Pipo Pepe . . ."

The stabs of emotion wouldn't let Elias Kaminsky speak; he merely nodded.

"Great . . . but, please, sit down. It's cooler here on the porch. Mirtica . . ." Ricardo addressed one of his daughters. "The lemonade, please."

The doctor's family asked permission to withdraw and returned to their secret refuge. Elias and Conde settled into their chairs and Ricardo finally took his seat. A minute later, the goth girl (Yadine, Yamile, Yadira? Conde tried to remember the name that began with "Ya") and her aunt, whose skin was lighter than her sister's but who had an African ass that Conde couldn't help but admire, served them from a pitcher frosted over by the cold liquid inside, and handed them some tall, elegant crystal glasses.

"You know something? These glasses were a gift from Mr. Brandon to Pipo Pepe and my mother when they married. We only take them out on very special occasions."

For several minutes, the two Kaminskys spoke of their respective lives, each one giving the other an overview. Elias told Ricardo of his profession, his family, his parents' final fate. Ricardo spoke of his work as a nephrology expert at the hospital, of the joy that this unexpected meeting brought him, also of his family, who lived with him.

"Do you all live together?" the visitor asked, perhaps keeping in mind the information that the Luyanó house only had two bedrooms.

"Yes, all together; what else can we do? And we're grateful to have inherited this house. Now my daughter Mirtica, who is a teacher, lives with her husband and her two children in the first bedroom. My daughter Adelaida, who studied economics, lives with her husband and her daughter, Yadine, in the second bedroom. My wife and I set up a bed in the living room at night . . . The problem is the line for the bathroom . . . especially when Yadine goes in there to dress up . . ." he said, and smiled.

"Can't you do anything?" The painter still didn't understand.

"No. The house you get is the one your family left you, the one you had built if you had a lot of money, or the one that, one way or another, the government gave you. I devoted myself to doing my job and only earned a salary . . . They didn't give me anything . . ." Ricardo Kaminsky pondered for a moment whether to continue or not and decided to go on. "The problem is that I'm very Catholic. And when they were going to give something out at the hospital, they always left me out, because I was devout and that was perceived very negatively . . . It was a miracle that they sold me that Moskovich. It's funny: now that they don't give any- thing out, it doesn't matter what you believe. When they did, it did. But what I couldn't do was hide my beliefs. And I paid the price, without regret. After all, I love having my family close by . . ."

As he listened to a story he knew well, given how common it was, of the nephrologist Ricardo Kaminsky's overcrowded dwelling, Conde thought about the immense distance between the doctor's world and that of Roberto Fariñas. It was the same, more insulting perhaps, as Daniel Kaminsky had found between his own poverty and the possibili- ties afforded to rich Jews in the Havana of 1940 and the Miami of 1958. And he estimated that, even with five years of college under his belt, the painter Elias Kaminsky wasn't going to understand the twists and turns of that panorama that needed to be lived to be understood—more or less. The lives of those two men, legally cousins, had gone down paths so divergent that they seemed to be the inhabitants of two different galaxies. But, with mathematical fatality, Conde would prove that in a distant corner of the infinite, even parallel lines could find their meeting point.

———

"I will never forget, I can't forget, that your father was the person who took me for the first time to see a baseball game at Cerro Stadium. I was about eight, nine years old and was a die-hard Almendares fan, and I would spend all day playing ball at any of Old Havana's little plazas. Daniel still hadn't gotten married or moved, but he was already Martica's boyfriend, and one Saturday morning, when I was coming down the tenement's stairs to go play ball, he called me over and asked me if I had ever seen the Almendares play. I told him no, of course. And he told me that that afternoon I was going to see them: that I should go take a bath and tell my mother to get me ready to go to the stadium at two o'clock . . . Although Daniel's Marianao beat the Almendares, I think that was the happiest afternoon of my whole childhood. And I owe it to a Kaminsky. You can't imagine how proud I was when I came back from the stadium with that blue Almendares cap that Daniel bought me . . .

"My mother and I were very lucky to meet your uncle and father at the tenement. Especially your uncle, of course, who began a relationship with my mother that gave her something she had never known before: respect. And he offered me something that, according to him, would make me rich: the possibility of continuing my studies. With the passing of years, my mother and Joseph even married, and I ceased to be called Ricardo Sotolongo. I went from being what they called at the time an *hijo natural* to having two last names, as it should have been: Kaminsky Sotolongo. But before he became my legal father, I was already calling him Pipo Pepe. And your father, when he saw me, would always call me cousin. They made me feel like I was part of a family, something I'd never had . . .

"When Daniel left Cuba, Pipo Pepe refused to leave because of us. He didn't want to leave in 1960, either, when Brandon offered to open a workshop with him in New York as partners. He knew how fucked-up life could be for blacks in the United States, and that's why he stayed here with us. Although he also stayed because he didn't have the will to start over. When he got sick and died, in 1965, my mother and I felt that we had lost the most important person in our lives. Then your father, Daniel, told my mother that, if we wanted, he could claim us as the widow and son of a Polish Jew and take us to live with him and Martica. But I was finishing up at the university; things were very difficult here, but we were still living with a lot of hope that everything was going to be better and neither she nor I wanted to go anywhere. In any event, we were grateful that Daniel remembered us, as if we were his family . . . That's why I always fault myself for not having had more contact with your father and with Martica, for having been stupid enough to accept what they told us, all of that about how those who left were enemies with whom we shouldn't have a relationship . . . In sum, the things they force you to do. And that you accept . . . until you shake yourself and decide not to take anymore, at the risk of being separated from your tribe.

"A few years later, it was my mother who got sick. She, who had never even had a beer, was diagnosed with a sudden and raging case of cirrhosis of the liver. One night, almost at the end, when she knew the end was coming, she told me that she had to tell me a story that, she emphasized, I had to know . . . And from what you've told me, now I think that you also deserve to know . . . Because it's a story that shows the kind of person that Joseph Kaminsky was and what his nephew Daniel meant to him."

The doctor took a deep breath in and rubbed the palms of his hands on the tops of his cream-colored pants, as if he needed to clean them. Conde noticed that his eyes were moist and shiny, as if in the grip of great agony. Elias Kaminsky, meanwhile, was moving his mouth, anxious and pained.

"Pipo Pepe killed that man, Román Mejías. He did it so that your father, his nephew, wouldn't do it, wouldn't have to do it. He killed him with his fixed-blade leather knife . . . He ran the risk of being executed, of rotting in jail, of Mejías killing him, of Batista's men hacking him to pieces. But above all, he killed him to save Daniel from all of those dangers. The old man well knew what he was doing, my mother told me, because not only was he tempting justice and the fury of men but also losing the forgiveness of his God, who, despite having deified revenge, places an inviolable commandment: You shall not kill. I, who knew him, and knew his generosity, can't imagine how he could have entered the house of that man, delivered several slashes across his whole body, and then slit his neck, practically beheading him. But I can understand his reasons. More than the hate he could have felt toward that man who conned his family and sent them back to Europe, to torture and death, he was pushed by his love for his nephew. Only a man who is very, very upright is capable of making that sacrifice, and losing the most sacred part of his spiritual life, when that life matters to him—and very much at that. That's why, I think, despite everything, he lived in peace until the end. He knew his soul would have no salvation, but he died satisfied that he had fulfilled his word to his brother, Daniel's father: to take care of his son in all circumstances, as if he were his own son. And he did so."

Elias Kaminsky had listened to the doctor with his gaze fixed on the porch's ceramics, worn by the rain and sun. The definitive confirmation of his father's innocence came with the clamor of that epiphany that revealed the capacity for sacrifice of a man who, out of love and duty, had turned into a ruthless killer and condemned himself with complete consciousness and of his own volition. Mario Conde, observing the attitudes of those two beings from different worlds, interconnected through the infinite kindness of Pepe the Purseman, decided to risk being impertinent enough to try to reach the remaining far corner of an exemplary story.

"Doctor," he said, pausing and then jumping in, "your mother, Caridad, did she ever talk about the painting that Mejías had conned out of Joseph's brother?"

Ricardo Kaminsky nodded but remained silent for a few seconds.

"Pipo Pepe took it out of Mejías's house. It was in a frame and, with the same fixed-blade knife he had used to kill the man, he cut out the canvas and put it inside his shirt. Since at that moment he was the owner of that work, and since that work was the only thing that could connect the Kaminskys to Mejías, he decided that he didn't want it and burned it in the yard. He didn't care that that painting could be worth a lot of money. He didn't want the money that, when it could have done so, had done nothing to save his family . . . My mother didn't dare tell him that burning something so valuable was crazy, because it was his property and his decision, and she thought she should show respect. She knew that through that act, Pipo Pepe was giving his soul some peace . . ."

As Ricardo Kaminsky was explaining the extreme actions of his adoptive father, Elias had started lifting up his head, and then, compulsively pulling at his ponytail. He turned his gaze toward Conde. The former policeman, meanwhile, felt his heart speeding up with the doctor's revelation.

"So he burned the Rembrandt painting?"

"Yes, that's what my mother told me."

"Knowing that it was a Rembrandt and that it was worth a lot?"

"It was a Rembrandt and it was worth a lot," the doctor confirmed, incapable of understanding the ins and outs of those questions or thinking that his present interrogator was experiencing a cerebral cortex spasm caused by a serious urinary tract infection.

"How did he know?" Conde insisted.

"He knew it because he knew it, I'm telling you! It was a portrait of a Jew who looked like Christ. He had seen it many times at his house, in Kraków."

"And of course, before he burned it, he didn't show it to any expert?"

Ricardo Kaminsky felt the effects of the panic overtaking Conde.

"Of course not. I don't know. How would he . . . But, what's going on?"

Conde looked at Elias Kaminsky and the painter understood that it was up to him to explain.

"Well, that original Rembrandt is now in London and they want to sell it. It has been proven and authenticated, of course . . . Uncle Joseph thought he took the original and that he had burned it, but it was a copy."

Ricardo was shaking his head, having reached the limits of his capacity for understanding and surprise.

"The terrible thing is," Elias continued, "my uncle thought he was destroying the original, a painting that was worth a lot of money that he didn't mind losing. He only wanted to protect his family."

———

The beer and the wine that Elias Kaminsky brought contributed greatly to softening the formality of his Cuban relatives, all crammed around the dining room table of the Luyanó house. To the painter's surprise, the dishes they served were Cubanized re-creations of old Jewish and Polish recipes, although they included the indispensable black beans that all of the Kaminskys gathered there, by blood or by name, considered their favorite dish.

In one corner of the dining room, solid though lackluster, still hummed the Frigidaire that Daniel and Marta had given Joseph Kaminsky in 1955 when he rented the house. Alongside the appliance was the glass cabinet where they kept the plates and elegant Bohemian crystal glasses that were a gift from Brandon the magnate. Over that piece of furniture, Elias found a wooden cross and the menorah, the eight-armed candelabra brought from Kraków by Joseph Kaminsky and with which, according to his father, their uncle celebrated Hanukkah every year, lighting one candle each evening in memory of the Maccabean victory at the Temple. While regarding that candelabra and crucifix, Conde listened to the conversation and learned that, through his dialogues with his grandfather, Elias's son Samuel had decided to become Jewish through the ceremony of ritual circumcision and the celebration of his bar mitzvah at a New York synagogue. A return to the flock carried out by his own free will by the grandson of a man who, persuaded by blows, had never again believed in the existence of God. Any god.

"So what do you have to do to become Jewish?" Yadine—her name was Yadine—wanted to know. Apparently, she was intrigued by differences.

"That's very complicated, leave that alone," her grandfather interjected.

"What about being a private detective in Cuba?" the young goth kept asking as she looked at Conde.

"That's harder than becoming Jewish," her target replied and the others, with the exception of Yadine, laughed at his response, making Conde clarify, "I'm not a detective. I was a policeman . . . Now I am nothing."

The goodbyes, around midnight, after all of those hours of increasingly relaxed company, had been happy and emotional, with promises to keep in touch and even Elias's promise to return to the island with his children, Samuel and Esther, so they could meet their Cuban relatives and all go to enjoy a baseball game together at the Havana stadium where many years before Orestes Miñoso had shone so brightly.

In the painter's rental car, as they traveled toward Tamara's house, Elias Kaminsky relayed his decision to Conde to return to the United States the following day.

"I'm going to hire some lawyers to do whatever is necessary to re-cover the Rembrandt painting. Now I am determined: I can't allow those people to get rich off that painting. People who fucked up the lives of my family . . ."

"So if you get it back, are you going to donate it to the Jewish Museum or any of the others that you told me about?"

"Of course. Now more than ever," Elias said, emphatic, seemingly wound up by everything he had had to drink.

"That seems beautiful . . . even glorious and worthy of your family name. But can I say something?"

With one hand, Elias removed a Camel from the pack he carried in the pocket of his Guess button-down shirt. How many packs of ciga-rettes fit in that damned pocket? Was it the same shirt he'd worn on the first day or did he have several that were alike? He looked for his lighter and lit it up. The smoke went out the open window into the steamy night.

"Well, tell me," he said at last.

"Who was it who said that when someone experiences misfortune, he should pray, as if help can only come from divine providence; but at the same time, should act as if only he himself can find the solution?"

"Uncle Joseph used to say that to my father . . ."

"Uncle Joseph, the most Jewish of all of you, was a damned pragma-tist! Elias, doesn't it seem like that noble, symbolic act of donating the painting is what we in Cuba would call a great old *comedera de mierda*? In that museum it would do well and would keep alive the memory of a Jewish family massacred in the Holocaust. But come on, man, what about the living? Can you imagine what the lives of those people we just saw would be like with just a fraction of that money? Yes, you can imag-ine . . . but . . . May I continue?"

"Go on, go on," the other man said as he drove with his gaze fixed on the road.

"That painting belongs to Ricardo Kaminsky as much as to you. Legally, he is the son of Joseph Kaminsky. What's more, in fact, I think it belongs to him more than to you, although it would never occur to him to ask you for anything, because he is a decent man and because the gratitude he feels for you wouldn't allow him to . . . But do you think that because you are a natural-born Kaminsky you're the only one who can decide? After what you heard today, would you have the balls to be so egotistical?"

Elias threw the half-smoked cigarette out to the street. He shook his head defiantly.

"Does everyone in this country have to beat up on me?"

"Maybe that was your destiny . . . To come back here and leave all beaten up, but more intact."

"Yes . . . And Ricardito's destiny is being more of a moron, as you say, than Uncle Joseph. Do you think he would accept money from the painting if he wouldn't even accept the two hundred dollars I offered him?"

"The thing is, there's a big difference between charity and having a right to something. All Ricardo Kaminsky has is his dignity and his pride."

"So you think . . . ?"

"I already told you what I think. The rest, and what really matters, is what you think."

———

On the hotel terrace, they ordered two coffees and aged rum to toast their goodbyes. Mario Conde, who had spent so many days immersed in those tangled-up stories, full of the guilt and atonement of a Jewish family, was already starting to feel how finding the truth was only good for putting six hundred dollars in his pocket and a void in his soul.

"I brought this letter," he told Elias Kaminsky, and held out the envelope. "It's for Andrés."

"You don't write to him via e-mail?"

"What's that?" Conde asked. Elias smiled at his supposed joke, which, in fact, it was not. Definitively, Elias Kaminsky was still a foreigner.

"I'll take it to him as soon as I get there . . . Besides, I have to thank him for his help, for your help."

"I didn't do anything. Just listened to you and helped you get things straight in your mind. Incidentally, I know almost everything about you, but not the most important thing."

"The most important thing?"

"Yes. You haven't told me about your own painting. What the hell is it that you paint? Don't tell me it's like Rembrandt . . ."

Elias Kaminsky smiled.

"No . . . I paint urban landscapes. Buildings, streets, walls, stairs, corners . . . Always without any human figures. They're like cities after a total holocaust."

"You don't paint people because it's forbidden by Jewish Law?"

"No, no, that doesn't matter much to anyone anymore . . . What I wanted was to represent the solitude of the contemporary world. In reality, there are people in those landscapes, but they're invisible; they've become invisible. The city itself has swallowed them up, has taken away their individuality and even their corporeal nature. The city is the jail of the modern individual, isn't it?"

Conde nodded as he tasted his rum.

"So where do the invisible people find freedom?"

"Inside themselves. In that place you can't see but that exists. In each one's soul."

"Interesting," Conde said, intrigued but not persuaded. Sparked by that conversation, a concern he had put off then came to mind. "What about the Sephardic Jew who was going around Poland saying he was a painter. Do you know what he painted? What in the hell was he doing in Poland when they were killing Jews there?"

"No idea . . . I don't even know his name. But . . . do you read French?"

"I read a lot when I was in Paris. I always had breakfast at the Café de Flore, bought *Le Figaro*, swam in the Seine, and went everywhere with Sartre and Camus, one arm around each of them . . ."

"Go to hell," Elias said when he realized the nonsense the other man was telling him. "Well, there's a book written in Hebrew but translated into French called *Le fond de l'abîme*. It's the memoir of a rabbi, a certain Hannover, who witnessed the massacres of Jews in Poland between 1648 and 1653 . . . Earth-shattering, as you say here. If you read it, you can guess where that Sephardic Jew lost in Poland ended up. I'll send you the book . . ."

"And what did the Sephardic Jew paint?"

"If he really studied with Rembrandt and left Moshe Kaminsky a portrait of a Jewish girl, I can imagine what he painted and how he painted it."

"Let's see . . ."

"Rembrandt was magnetic," Elias began. "And a bit of a dictator with his students. He forced them to paint according to his ideas, which sometimes seemed quite clear, but other times were rough, according to what you see in his work. Rembrandt was a seeker; he spent his life searching, until the end, when he was in the *fuácata* and dared to paint the eyeless men of *The Conspiracy of the Batavians Under Claudius Civilis* . . . What he did have quite clear was the relationship between human beings and their representation in a painting. He saw it as a dialogue between the artist, the subject, and the model. And also as the capture of a moment that was already fleeing into the past and demanded to be fixed in the present. The power of his portraits resides in their eyes, in their gaze. But sometimes, it went beyond that . . . and he even came to paint them without eyes, and that made the painting even more powerful. But the gaze is what makes that study of the portrait of a young Jew—who was perhaps his student—stand out. That small piece of canvas is a masterpiece. Beyond the eyes, in that portrait—just like in that of his friend Jan Six and in some self-portraits—Rembrandt was searching for the man's soul, the permanent thing, and he found it . . . Perhaps that is what that heretical Jew learned from his master and tried to do with his own painting . . . In my opinion."

"By painting, he was a heretic?" Conde wanted to clarify.

"Yes, that man violated a rigid law of the time . . . Although, perhaps, like my uncle, he died without feeling remorse. No one can force you to paint. So if he did so, it's clear that he was acting of his own free will. And he had done so at Rembrandt's side, no less. Or so I imagine . . ."

Conde nodded, drank his coffee, and lit his cigarette.

"That Jew could have been condemned for painting people. While you, who are, practically speaking, not Jewish and could give a shit about being condemned, are not interested in painting people. That's really crazy . . ."

"No one knows why he is a painter or why he isn't. Nor why you end up painting in one way and not another, no matter how much you try to explain the matter . . . My mother liked my painting. My father didn't. For him, people were always the most important thing."

"Your father was one of my kind. People, noise, friends, baseball, black beans, women with flutes or saxophones . . ."

"You're not Jewish, are you?" Elias smiled.

"Maybe . . . And my Jewish spirit asks you, What are you going to do, finally, if you recover the painting?"

Elias Kaminsky looking into the eyes of the seller of old books. He raised his drink and emptied it in one go.

"There's still a ways to go to get to that point. But I promise you something: whatever I do, you'll be the first to know."

"Good," Conde said. "Here's hoping you don't do something idiotic . . ."

———

The idea had been circling Skinny Carlos for days; he was just waiting for the right time to focus on making it happen. When he found out that Conde had finished his Jewish job, wanting to be brought up to speed on the search's most recent turn of events, he channeled his skills as an organizer and, at five in the afternoon, the friends were arriving at the beach of Santa María del Mar in Yoyi the Pigeon's spacious Chevrolet Bel Air and in the car rented by Dulcita, Skinny's long-ago ex-girlfriend, who had just arrived from Miami.

For Carlos, the act of spending the afternoon's final hours facing the sea on that beach, where one could watch a spectacular sinking of the sun into the marine horizon, represented much more than caprice or desire: it was a way of communicating with the young man he had once been, the man with two useful legs, like the majority of men, capable of playing squash on the nearby courts, of running on the sand, of swimming in the sea. That is why all of his friends agreed to his proposal and threw themselves into the afternoon at the beach, after having made the indispensable collection of necessary beverages.

The September sun was still beating down when they arrived. Between Conde, Rabbit, Candito, and Yoyi, they carried the now-obese Skinny on his obligatory throne to the edge of the sea, where they arrived faint and sweaty. Tamara and Dulcita took care of transporting the drinks placed in plastic thermoses, then laid out some sheets on the sand.

While Conde relayed the grand conclusions of his search, the sun began the final phase of its daily descent and the few other people still on the beach made their departures, giving the friends exclusive use of the area. In the solitude of that place, and caught up in a story of death and love, once again that feeling of time stopping (even being inverted) took over the tribe's spirit. Those gatherings of the fundamentalist followers of friendship, nostalgia, and complicity had the beneficial effect of erasing the pains, losses, and frustrations of the present and relegating them to the impregnable territory of their most emotional and beloved memories.

The alcohol was fulfilling its mission of catalyzing the process. To

Conde's frustration, neither Dulcita, with her conscience befitting an American driver; nor Yoyi, who knew he was the owner of a diamond on wheels; nor Candito, because of his dealings with the great beyond; nor Tamara, who wasn't up to facing those nearly Haitian rums, allowed themselves to be carried away by the ethylic temptation, to which Conde, Skinny, and Rabbit had submitted with abandon, until they reached the perfect state: that of enjoying talking shit. As was inevitable that afternoon, the subject came to the possibilities that would open up for them if they owned and sold a Rembrandt painting. Worth how much? Two million?

"If they sell it for five, it would be good, but seven would be better," Carlos said.

"Seven? Why so much money?" Rabbit asked.

"It's never so much, man, never," interjected Yoyi, the most financially savvy of the group.

"Seven, because then we'd each get a million, right?"

"Seven, okay, seven million," Conde granted. "But not a penny more, dammit. These rich guys are insatiable . . ."

"Conde," Candito wanted to know, "did you really tell the painter that his idea of donating the painting to the Jewish Museum was moronic?"

"Of course I told him that, Red. How in the hell wasn't I going to tell him that?! After everything his family had gone through for that painting, and is still going through, someone has to get something good out of it, don't they?"

"It seems to me like it would be nice if he gave a fair amount of that money to the doctor and his family," Tamara jumped in with her trade unionist's spirit.

"Cuban millionaires! With half of that money, they could buy all of Luyanó," Yoyi said, but corrected himself. "No, it's better not to buy shit . . ."

"What I still don't get," Dulcita commented, "is where that painting was all these years . . ."

"One of the Mejíases," Conde supposed.

"It would be good to know," Tamara opined.

"All that is well and good, but . . . getting back to the money. I, just me, wouldn't share any of it," Rabbit said, shaking the sand from his hands. "I would keep it all, would buy myself an island, would build a castle, would buy a yacht, and . . . I'd take all of you there . . . and the doctor's family. With Dr. Kaminsky and with Tamara, there would be free public health care; with the daughter who is a teacher, free university, and Conde would be the librarian; with the Kaminsky who is an economist, there would be central planning, and we'd put Yoyi in as a manager . . . Skinny would be the prince of the island, Dulcita, the princess, Candito, the bishop, and I'd be the king . . . And whoever misbehaves gets thrown the hell out."

"There's a tyrant born every minute," Dulcita declared. "But I like my job on Treasure Island."

"What about you, Conde? What would you do with seven million?" Tamara wanted to know.

Conde looked at her intensely. He stood up and stumbled. As theatrically as he could, he looked over his captive audience.

"How in the hell do you expect me to know that? Look . . ." He stuck his hand in his pocket and took out the six hundred dollars he earned for the job. "I don't even know what I'm going to do with this."

He immediately started giving a hundred-dollar bill to each of his friends.

"A little end-of-year gift," he said.

"In September?" Dulcita tried to impose logic on the nonsense.

"Well, for Rabbit's birthday, which is coming up in a few days . . ."

"Forget it, girl, he's completely crazy," Yoyi said.

"No, the thing is that he's more of a moron than the painter," Carlos— who, in the midst of his alcoholic haze, with a hundred-dollar bill in his hand, had a sudden spark of lucidity—corrected him. "Shit, look over there, the sun is leaving."

On the horizon, the sun was about to touch the polished surface of the sea.

"Listen, asshole," Conde yelled at the sun. "We came to see you and you're leaving with no notice?"

Using one foot and then another, Conde managed to take off his shoes and, balancing more than precariously, leaned his ass on Carlos's body and took off his socks. Then he unbuttoned his shirt and let it fall on the sand. The rest watched him do it, intrigued. Candito's wisdom, nonetheless, advised them of Conde's intentions.

"Listen, Conde, you're a little old already for one of those . . ." Candito began, but Conde, as he lowered his pants and displayed his briefs, kept going, without paying attention to Candito, and undid his watch, which fell alongside his shirt. He took a few steps toward the coast and started to lower his briefs, showing the audience his skinny butt cheeks, barely lighter skinned than the rest of his body.

"What an ugly ass!" Rabbit said.

"You wait there," Conde then yelled toward the sun, and after taking off his last item of clothing, took up his march again toward the golden star that, from the planet's last visible curvature, was spreading over the ocean in order to die at the edge of the beach of dreams, memories, and nostalgia. From the vortex of the alcoholic storm devastating his mind—at just that moment and through unforeseeable mental paths—came the words of a dying man from the future: "I've seen things you people wouldn't believe. Attack ships on fire off the shoulder of Orion; I watched c-beams glitter in the dark near the Tannhauser Gate. All those moments will be lost in time, like tears in the rain."

The naked man entered the sea without ceasing to look at the sun, determined to interrupt its descent, the end of the day, the arrival of shadows. Insistent on stopping time and preventing all losses from destroying them.

Book of Elias

1

New Jerusalem,
Year 5403 Since the Creation,
1643 of the Common Era

Elias Ambrosius Montalbo de Ávila withstood the blades of damp air
that, in their search for the North Sea, ran freely over the Zwanenburgwal and cut across his cheeks and lips, the only parts of his anatomy
exposed to the city's aggressive weather. Up to his ankles in snow and
cramps seizing his fingers, the young man maintained his determined
watch for the fifth morning in a row as he sought relief by calling to
mind his grandfather Benjamin's dramatic life story and what he had
learned from him, as well as the lessons from his turbulent teacher,
Hakham ben Israel. Because, like never before in his life, Elias Ambrosius
needed that support to dare make the leap obsessing him and, as such,
to undertake the struggle for the life he wanted to live, willing to accept
the consequences of an irresistible exercise of his free will. An exercise
that, if he went through with it, would with all certainty change his life
and, perhaps, even his death.

The young man had heard the story so many times of his grandfather
Benjamin's escape and his joy at arriving in Amsterdam that he thought
himself capable of imagining every detail of the adventure lived out alongside his grandmother Sara (who had been disguised as a man, despite
being six months pregnant with what would be his aunt Ana) and his
father, Abraham, who was then seven years old (he'd been wrapped up
as if he were some kind of merchandise). The escape had occurred forty
years prior, in the filthy hold of an English ship ("It stank of tar and
salted fish, of sweat, shit, and the pain of Africans turned into slaves"),
which had reached port at a Lisbon estuary en route to New Jerusalem,

where the fugitives aimed to recover the ancestral faith of their fore-bearers. That episode, which took place at a time in which old Benjamin Montalbo didn't even dream of becoming anyone's grandfather, was the landmark in the creation of the fate of a family who, in that world, knew how to get what they wanted as they overcame adversity and understood that God more gladly helps those who fight than those who do nothing.

But, above all, the young man owed Benjamin Montalbo de Ávila what he considered to be the most valuable of life's guiding principles. The old man, a learned person despite his wandering existence, a man given to pronouncing statements, had repeated to him several times that the human being can be Creation's best-made and most resistant tool if one has enough faith in the Holiest, but, above all, also has a sustained belief in oneself and the necessary ambition to achieve the loftiest or most arduous goals. Because, as his grandfather tended to highlight in the long monologues to which he so enjoyed handing himself over every Friday night, in the familial and joyous wait for his majesty the Sabbath—"*Shabbat shalom!*"—man can do very little without his God, and the Creator can do nothing, in earthly matters, without the will and reasoning of his most indomitable creation . . . The seasoned Benjamin maintained that, thanks to that belief, three generations of the Montalbo de Ávila line had been able to withstand the humiliations perpetrated by the most overwhelming earthly powers, determined to divest them of their faith and even of their own selves ("But first of our riches, don't forget, my son, and then, only then, of our beliefs"). Only through the force of his own perseverance, he remarked, was it that he, born and bap-tized in the Christian faith as João Monte, that he—and he patted his chest to avoid any ambiguities—had managed to leap over the very high barriers raised by intolerance and throw himself into the search for freedom, a freedom that included his God and the existence that, in communion with the Holiest, he wanted to live. Then, at the age of thirty-three, he had been reborn as Benjamin Montalbo de Ávila, whom he always should have been.

In contrast, thanks to his tutor, Hakham Menasseh ben Israel, the wisest of the many Jews who were then settled in Amsterdam, Elias Ambrosius accepted the notion that each action in the life of an individ-ual has cosmic connotations. "What about eating some bread, Hakham?" Elias, who was still a small boy, once dared to ask when he heard him talking about the matter in his classes. "Yes, also eating some bread . . .

Just think of the infinity of causes and consequences that there are before and after that action: for you and for the piece of bread," the wise man had responded. But besides, he had acquired from the Hakham the pleasant conviction that life's days were like an extraordinary gift, which he had to enjoy drop by drop, since the death of the physical matter, as he tended to declare from the bimah, means only the extinction of the hopes that already died in life. "Death does not equal the end," the teacher said. "What leads to death are the exhaustion of our desires and unease. And that death ends up being definitive, because whoever dies that way cannot aspire to return on the Day of Judgment . . . The next life is built in this world. Between one state and another, there exists but one connection: the fullness, consciousness, and dignity with which we have lived our lives, seemingly so small, although in reality so transcendental and unique as . . . as a piece of bread."

But it wasn't just to forget the cold and spur himself on that Elias Ambrosius had in those days succumbed to thinking again and again of his paternal grandfather's convictions and of the teachings of his ever-unconventional professor: in reality, he did so because, despite his determination, Elias Ambrosius was afraid.

As he sought the shelter offered by the eaves and walls of the lock house, withstanding the rank odors brought up from the dark canal waters by the wind, the young man, stubbornly enumerating reasons to sustain him, didn't stop looking at the house rising up on the other side of the street for a single moment. He focused on the green wooden door and on the barely visible movements behind the leaded-glass windows, steamed up by the difference in temperature. Elias watched and calculated that, if the Maestro hadn't left the dwelling in the last five days, then he should be leaving this morning, or the following. If it was true that he was working again ("He's fulfilling some orders and also painting another portrait of his deceased wife"), according to what Hakham ben Israel told him, the provisions of oil and pigments that he used in great quantities would run out, and, as was his habit, he would go to his providers on the neighboring Meijerplein and around the De Waag market in search of supplies. On one of those stops, if the situation seemed propitious, Elias Ambrosius would at last approach him and, with a speech he had already memorized, would present dreams and desires that, with no other options, would have to pass through the Maestro's hands.

For several months already, the young man had devoted himself to practicing those secret pursuits to which he would subject the owner of the house with the green door. At the beginning, it was like the game of a bedazzled child who curiously follows an idol or a magnetic mystery. But, as the weeks and months passed, his surveillance turned into a frequent—and, recently, daily—practice, since it included even his free hours on Saturday, the sacred day. His growing obsession had been rewarded, in spades, with the pleasant coincidence of having been the witness to the exit of the enormous canvas (protected by old, stained rags, an operation the Maestro directed himself, all while yelling at and insulting the students chosen as stevedores), a work that was destined to move the young man, like an earthquake, the afternoon on which, at last, he had been able to contemplate it in the main room of the Society of Arquebusiers, Crossbowmen, and Archers of Kloveniersburgwal. But his standing watch had also received the retribution of the tragic circumstance of being a spectator (this time amid a group of the curious, attracted by the spectacle of death) of the beginning of the funeral procession that was taking the remains of the Maestro's still-young wife to Oude Kerk. From the small square made by Sint Antoniesbreestraat as it crossed the lock bridge where the canal branched out in search of the sea, just at the point where the street changed names ever since everyone had started to call it Jodenbreestraat, Jewish Broad Street, Elias had followed the carriage on which rested the corpse, covered only with a simple shroud, as the precepts of Calvin's humility ordered. Behind the deceased, he had seen pass by his Hakham, the former Rabbi ben Israel, as well as Cornelis Anslo the preacher, Vingboons the famous architect, the affluent Isaac Pinto, and, of course, the Maestro, dressed for the occasion in a rigorous display of mourning. And he had discerned—or so he thought—the dampness of tears on that man's pupils, that man who was as loved by success and fortune as he was frequented by Death, who had already torn away three of his children.

Also thanks to that vigilance, which had led to long walks when Elias was in luck, the young man had received what he considered to be some valuable lessons for his intellectual property, since he had learned of the Maestro's obstinacy in not delegating the purchase of mounted canvases to any of his students. He had learned of his preference for linens that had already been treated with the first priming of dead color, capable of giving them a precise and malleable tone of matte brown on which he would continue the preparation work or, even, directly apply the paint.

He already knew, besides, that for his engravings and etchings, the Maestro usually bought the delicate papers imported from the remote country of the Japanese and, even, that he didn't trust anyone with the punctilious selection (bargaining included) of the necessary powders, stones, and emulsions to obtain the mixtures capable of achieving the colors and tones his imagination clamored for at every moment. Furtively listening to his conversations with Mr. Daniel Rulandts, owner of the most sought-out painting supply store in the city; with the German who had arrived a few months prior and was devoted to the importation of powerful mineral pigments brought from German, Saxon, and Magyar mines; and with the redheaded Frieslander, the seller of the most varied treasures from the Orient (among them, the coveted black oil known as Bitumen of Judea, the paper from Japan, and the valuable locks of camel hair that his students would turn into paintbrushes of different calibers), Elias had begun to penetrate the interstices of the practice of that art, forbidden by the second commandment of the sacred Law to those of his race and religion, that universe of images, colors, textures, and feelings for which the young man suffered the out-of-control and irresistible attraction of one who is predestined. The reason for which he was now stiff, from cold and fear, on the Zwanenburgwal.

———

Ever since his school days, as he took courses in the basement of the synagogue opened by the members of the Nação, attached to the house where the Montalbo de Ávilas lived around that time, Elias had felt that empathy, at first diffuse and then increasingly decisive, and finally overwhelming. Perhaps the attraction had been born in his handling of the illustrated and illuminated books that were the only material possessions that traveled with his grandfather Benjamin, his pregnant wife, and the oldest of his offspring from the lands of idolatry toward the land of freedom. Or perhaps the seduction had been forged by the very graphic histories of pilgrimages and travels to distant worlds taken by his most remote ancestors, the stories that the loquacious Hakham ben Israel would tell his students, journeys that were capable of firing up the imagination and feeding the soul. Many afternoons, for many years, instead of going with his classmates and his brother Amos to play in the fields or in between the wood posts on which they would erect the magnificent buildings that were being constructed at a frenetic pace on the borders of the new canals, Elias had spent his time running around the many markets of a city riddled with them—Dam Square, the Flower Market, the Spui Square, the De Waag Esplanade, and the New Market, the Botermarkt—where, between market stalls, scales, and bundles of recently arrived merchandise, the aroma of Oriental spices and tobacco from the Indies, the stench of herring, Nordic cod, and barrels of whale oil, amid very expensive furs from Muscovy, delicate pieces of ceramic from nearby Delft or remote China, and those hairy onions, the chrysalis of future tulips of unpredictable colors, there were always for sale the works of the countless painters living in the city and gathered together in the Guild of Saint Luke. Night would come out to surprise him on some of those outings with the shouting of closing sales of etchings and drawings, the putting away of canvases and breaking down of exhibition easels, after having gotten lost for hours in the contemplation of landscapes that were always adorned by a windmill or by a current of water, of still lives that lent to one another their figures and abundances, of typical scenes at home and in the street, of dark biblical re-creations inspired by the warm Italian current in vogue throughout the world, images sketched or imprinted on linen, wood, and cards by some men gifted with the marvelous capacity of capturing on white space a piece of real or imagined life. And of pausing it forever through the conscious act of creating beauty.

Stealthily, with charcoals and paper taken from the trash pile of the printshop where his father worked and where Elias had apprenticed ever since he was ten years old, the young man had handed himself over to the practice of his forbidden hobby. He had drawn (as he supposed the painters who sold their work at the market did) his cats and dogs, or the burning flame whose light cast shadows at whim around the edges of the apple he would later eat, or his grandfather, observed through the minimal separation of the door, more worn every day, pensive and biblical. He tried to reproduce the delicacy of the tulips of the neighboring balcony, the panorama of the canal with and without barges, the street viewed from the windows of the attic of the family house on Bethanienstraat. He had even given form, a face, and a background to the imaginings forged by his teacher's stories and by accounts of the conquest of fabulous worlds that narrated the existence of Eden and El Dorado in volumes that, in recent years, his grandfather sent for from Spain. Of course, he had also been encouraged by readings of the Torah, the sacred book in which, in a precise and unmistakable manner, that very practice of representing men, animals, and objects from the sky, sea, or earth was anathema, according to the message transmitted by Moses to the tribes gathered in the desert, by virtue of the Maximum Creator of All Forms considering it improper of his chosen people, due to promoting idolatry. Because of that biblical reason, Elias Ambrosius Montalbo, grandson of Benjamin Montalbo de Ávila, the secret Jew who had arrived in the lands of freedom in 1606 clamoring to be circumcised and to return to the faith of his ancestors, saw himself forced to carry out his passion in secret, even from his brother Amos, and, before lying down on his cot, devoted himself to the meticulous and upsetting destruction of the sheets marked with his charcoal.

Perhaps due to the very weight of those impediments, Elias's love for colors and forms became increasingly more feverish: it was the source from which flowed the energy that allowed him to withstand, like a condemned man, and during all of the time he could take from his obligations, the surveillance carried out on the square over the canal of Sint Antoniesbreestraat. The tremendous choice, which violated a mitzvah, and that, if made public, could cost him a *niddui*, even the greatest sentence of a *cherem* from the increasingly strict rabbinical council (a punishment capable of excluding him from his family and community and their benefits through excommunication) had so brutally but predictably turned into an irrevocable decision the afternoon of the previous fall when, the Sukkot celebrations barely finished and work at the printshop recommenced, his father, affected by pains in his waist that forced him to move as if he had sunk into his pants, had transferred to him the responsibility of handing over reams of flyers, still smelling of ink, at the Kloveniersdoelen, the new and imposing headquarters of the city's militia society.

At the mere mention of the nature of the task, as he felt a barely contained explosion of joy, Elias Ambrosius thought of how inscrutable the paths of life outlined by the Creator are: those flyers would be the letters of safe passage that would allow him, the poorest of all of the city's Jews, to enter Amsterdam's most elegant and exclusive building and, however he could, observe the Maestro's work destined to adorn the large reunion hall, the gigantic piece that some months before he had seen come out of the house on Jewish Broad Street, covered with some dirty rags and of which was spoken of (ill or well, but talk all the same) by all who, in the world's city where the most painters lived and where the most paintings were made and sold, had some relation, interest, fondness, or vocation for that art.

Carrying that heavy load, the young man had flown through the streets that led to the headquarters of the arquebusiers' society. He didn't have eyes or ears to process what was around him, imagining only what the painting must be like in reality that had caused so much conversation and debate, to the point that it was discussed in churches, taverns, and plazas, and almost as much as business, money, merchandise. The building's custodian, advised of the delivery of the flyers, pointed out access to the second floor, after shouting out to the caretaker tasked with receiving the printed copies and of leading the boy to the treasurer responsible for paying for them. Elias Ambrosius greedily took in the Carrara marble steps of the imposing staircase and found open before him the doors to the *grote zaal*, the great hall where the city's most important meetings and celebrations were held. Then, favored by the light of the high windows overlooking the dikes of the Amstel River, he saw the canvas, shiny with varnish, still leaning against the wall where it would be hung at some point. Elias Ambrosius, already capable of identifying with just one glance the works by the city's most important artists, but especially all of those coming from the Maestro's paintbrush (although on more than one occasion, he had to recognize, he had confused his work with that of some outstanding student, like the now famous Ferdinand Bol), didn't need to ask in order to know whether that outsized linen, more than thirteen feet long and almost six feet high, was the work that had the whole city in an uproar.

Before the young man, more than twenty figures, led by the very well-known and beyond opulent Frans Banning Cocq, gentlemen of Purmerland and captain of the city's society of arquebusiers, and his second lieutenant, Mr. de Vaardingen, were preparing themselves to carry out their morning round toward immortality, which appeared to begin at that precise moment, when Mr. Cocq took his first steps and placed his left foot on top of the checkerboard tiles of the *grote zaal* over which the painting still rested and, without too much ado, asked Elias Ambrosius to step out of the way . . . Shaken from his stupor by the caretaker's voice, the young man executed the handing over of the flyers and received, from the hands of the treasurer, the two florins and ten placke warranted by the work. Without even worrying about counting the money in front of the payer, as his father had indicated, he asked the treasurer for his authorization to look at the painting again, without immediately understanding the reaction of contempt that his request caused in the man.

Facing the enormous collective portrait, which still smelled of linseed oil and varnish, as he perceived a tremendous excitement overcoming him, Elias Ambrosius had taken delight in observing the details. He was determined to search for the imprecise but flashing sources of light and followed the dizzying feeling of movement that came from the painting, thanks to gestures like Captain Cocq's, in the front, whose half-raised arm and slightly open mouth indicated that his marching orders were the spark destined to make the action dynamic. The captain's proclamation seemed to surprise the standardbearer in the act of taking the flagpole, and alerted the other figures, several of them in the middle of conversations. One of those portrayed (wasn't it Mr. Van der Velt, a contractor and also a customer of the printshop?) was raising his arm in the direction of the path indicated by the captain and, with that gesture, he covered more than half of the face of a character whom Elias managed to identify as the treasurer with whom he had just closed the deal, and he was easily able to understand the man's reaction when he asked for permission to see the work. To his left, toward where Mr. Frans Banning Cocq proposed the march of the militia, the action sped up as a boy (or was it one of those midget buffoons?) raced by, carrying a drum of gunpowder and covered by a helmet that was too big for his stature; but, walking in the opposite direction, like an explosion of light, a golden girl (what was she doing there with the hen tied to the waist of her skirt?) was enjoying a privileged space and, with the unmistakable cunning of an adult, was watching the scene—or perhaps the painting's viewer—as if mocking the pantomime set up around her with her daring presence. Meanwhile, in the center of the space, behind the white feather of the hat worn by the second lieutenant to whom the captain's order was directed, there came from an arquebus a luminous flash, instantaneous, more than daring. The second lieutenant, on whose Naples-yellow uniform was projected the shadow of the captain's raised hand, had not, however, transmitted to the rest of the men Mr. Banning Cocq's order: Elias then understood that that entire representation constituted the beginning of something, alive and resounding like that escaped flash, a mystery about the future that was beyond the stone bridge on which the commanders were getting ready to march, a chaotic mobility prepared to break inertia. Something that exploded in several directions, but always pointing toward the future.

Alarmed by the vivid potency of that image of unleashed forces, insistent on challenging all logic and the most basic learned precepts (how was it possible that Captain Cocq, dressed in black, although wearing the exultant red-orange band across his chest, gave the impression of climbing on top of the spectator, in front of the second lieutenant who was outfitted in shining yellow, when everyone knew that light colors advanced and dark ones gave the impression of depth?), Elias Ambrosius barely had eyes to see the remaining six paintings charged with adorning the *groote sael*, all already placed in their spaces. The other pieces were group portraits (was the Maestro's painting one?), respectful of the established laws, perfect in their way. But next to that spectacular whirlwind, full of implausible optical effects that, nevertheless, managed a patent feeling of reality and life, the young man felt that the other works seemed like mere playing cards from a deck: figures that, in their desired and perfect uniformity, were made to look rigid, basic, empty of life compared to the Maestro's painting . . .

The caretaker's voice, reminding him of the need to close the hall, was barely able to remove Elias Ambrosius from the enchantment into which he had fallen, the storm of disquiet in which he would live from that day on, when his decision to become a painter became irreversible and, with his sovereign or inevitable choice (only God would know the precise adjective), he placed his fate in the eye of the storm that would mark the greatest joys and sorrows in his life.

———

It didn't happen that morning. Or on either of the following two days. Just when the young man was starting to think of taking a break from his chilly surveillance for a while, of waiting for less crude temperatures, his expectations turned out to be compensated with the sound of the locks on the green door being opened to allow the cloaked Maestro out. At the mere sight of him, Elias Ambrosius felt a wave of satisfaction embrace him, capable of making him forget the cold, his fears, and even the hunger pangs.

An hour before, a little earlier than usual, Elias had seen young

Samuel von Hoogstraten enter the building and, shortly after, his neighbor from Bethanienstraat, the Danish Bernhard Keil, in the company of the Fabritius brothers, all of them lucky students of the Maestro, and he congratulated himself, since he had the hope that on that morning they were coming earlier because they would surely go out shopping and he, at last, would break the frozen monotony of his waiting.

From Keil the Dane himself, who was lodging in an attic close to his house and was in possession of an exacerbated loquaciousness that multiplied when treated to a beer, Elias Ambrosius had learned of (besides the house's and the studio's routines) the Maestro's discouraging demands when it came time to accepting new students and assistants. Although the apprentices guaranteed him a notable source of income (enrollment alone reached a hundred florins, before accounting for the other practical and commercial utilities they represented to him), the Maestro demanded that candidates come to his workshop with prior preparation and something beyond enthusiasm or basic knowledge of the art of painting. His job, he repeated, was not to teach them how to paint, rather to force them to paint well. ("'My studio is not an academy, it is a workshop,'" the Dane said, citing the Maestro, and even made the attempt to appropriate the surly expression of the face that the painter must put on when speaking of the matter.) That demand, in and of itself, closed to Elias the green door that gave access to his aims: first, because of his condition as a Jew, it would be impossible to share his concerns with his parents such that they would even consider the possibility of breaking with convention to send him to train with any maestro of that art. And secondly—but of no less importance—because at that moment, due to his very tight finances, it was almost impossible for him to find another instructor who would also be discreet, cheap, and skilled, capable of showing him the basics so that he could aspire to a spot in the workshop of his dreams. But the Maestro's favorable affinity with his neighbors in the Jewish quarter and Elias's highly personalized knowledge of his methods (for months, Elias had memorized all of the Maestro's pieces placed in public sites and even in various private ones throughout the city) turned out to be a magnetic pole toward which all of the young man's expectations pointed, expectations that multiplied and burned into him on the afternoon on which he contemplated the march of Captain Cocq's company. If he risked so much for his love, if he lived and should live part of his life in a kind of secrecy, he would do so in the best possible way. And for Elias Ambrosius, the path toward that obsession had just one name, and there was just one way of understanding the art of drawing figures: that of the Maestro. He would have the Maestro, or he would have no one. Which, the young man knew well, may be the most probable, in truth . . .

For all of those insurmountable reasons, as he waited for a way to fulfill his aspirations, the young man had had to resign himself to listening to his grandfather Benjamin's digressions about the importance of a direct relationship between man and his Creator, and to dreaming of the works to come from his hands as he spent his nights drawing on humble pieces of paper. But he was also insistent on enjoying the discreet physical proximity with the Maestro obtained via pursuits through the streets and markets as he sought to pick up any of his words, carrying out his apprenticeship—thinking it would be useful at some moment—by learning the painter's preferences regarding pigments, oils, cards, and canvases, about his obsessive enjoyment in purchasing ordinary or extraordinary objects (from a shell to African spears), and of the ecstatic contemplations to which the man handed himself over at times: of buildings, streets, common or singular men and women from the overflowing city in which there was a confluence of every race and culture.

Although it seemed strange to Elias to see that the Maestro was going out alone, adjusting his calfskin gloves, it surprised him more to see him cross the street, as if he were headed to the exact spot where he was standing. His heart leapt and he began to imagine possible responses to any of the man's questions regarding his insistent presence before his dwelling, and in an instant he decided on just one: the truth. The Maestro, however, skirted a pile of snow and a muddy puddle, trying not to sully his outfit, and, without paying the least bit of attention to the smooth-faced young man, directed himself to the house of Isaías Montalto, the affluent Sephardic Jew who, like all who have reason for that type of pride, liked to announce his family's noble and Spanish lineage, crowned by his father, Dr. Josué Montalto, a doctor in the court of Marie de Médicis, the Queen Mother of France. That Isaías Montalto, who had acquired the first and one of the most luxurious homes of the so-called—by people like him—Jewish Broad Street, had made such a considerable fortune since his arrival in Amsterdam that he had already ordered the construction of a wider dwelling in the area of the new canals, where a yard of land taken from the swamps reached dizzying prices. As everyone knew, the Jew had maintained a close relationship for years with the man who, after ringing the little bell, entered the dwelling's interior from which he emerged just five minutes later, carrying around his neck one of the small, fragrant bags, weighed down with aromatic herbs and made of green linen, specially designed by Isaías Montalto, and in his hands another bag, this time made of brown paper, in which were wrapped the city's penultimate whim: the tobacco leaves arrived from the New World, which Montalto was supplied with by Federico Ginebra the *converso*, who had them brought from the meadows of the Cibao, on the remote island of Hispaniola.

Instead of getting together with his students and going toward the Meijerplein, where he usually started his shopping, the Maestro went in the opposite direction, passing nearly in front of Elias (whose nose received a fleeting note of lavender and juniper emanating from the small scented bag), crossed the lock bridge and, after spitting a piece of hard candy over the rail, advanced along Sint Antoniesbreestraat, as if he were going to the city center. He left behind him the luxurious house of his friend Isaac Pinto and the warehouse containing the dwelling and art business that belonged to the merchant Hendrick van Uylenburgh, a relative of the Maestro's deceased wife, the place where the latter had lived upon settling in the city. But when he arrived at the arch decorated with two skulls that opened onto the esplanade of the Zuiderkerk, the man stopped and uncovered himself, despite the cold. Elias knew that in the atrium of the old church rested the remains of his first three children, all dead just weeks after being born, and only at that moment did he asked himself why the man had decided to bury the children's mother in the Oude Kerk and not at that site, which was already marked by his pain.

The Maestro took up his walk again and, after passing in front of the house where his instructor, the now deceased Pieter Lastman (Amsterdam's best professor at the time, the maestro who turned him into the Maestro), had lived for years, he entered the New Market on the always noisy esplanade of De Waag, where just a century and a half before was Sint Anthonispoort, the door that marked off the now overflowing metropolis on the West. The frenetic activity of the traders and importers who certified the weight of their merchandise via municipal scales, the yells of the auctioneers and purchasers of existing and not-yet-existing products, brought from all confines of the universe, was joined at that moment by the metallic sound of the shovels with which the city government-employed work crew picked up the snow to then deposit it in the carts that would take it to be dumped into the closest canal. The cleaning was due, perhaps, to the circumstance that before noon, one of the executions so frequently carried out in the Plaza could take place there, a sentence that, as usual, would occur as quickly as possible so as not to take precious minutes from the market. When he passed the corner where some paintings for sale were on display, made to the specifications of the most common taste, the Maestro barely glanced at them, and Elias thought that he was writing them off. And nearly all of them deserved it, the young man told himself, assuming the man's supposed criteria.

The Maestro took Monnikenstraat to cross over the Archerburg canal and Elias wondered if his steps were not headed toward the now nearby Oude Kerk, the temple erected by the Christians, converted a few decades before by the Calvinists. But when he reached Oudezijds Voorburgwal, he turned to the left, distancing himself from the building with Gothic towers where he had buried his wife a few months prior, and entered the first tavern of the many that sat on the banks of the canal. The young man, although familiar with the Maestro's fondness for fermented beverages, found it strange due to the early hour at which he sought it out.

Increasing his precautions, Elias approached the place, surely full of mercenaries arrived from England, France, and even the kingdoms from the East to fight against Spain for the good salaries the Republic paid. The door of the place, in recent fashion, had been outfitted with an enormous transparent glass, through which the young man looked inside. He didn't need to search around too much, but he did have to withdraw his face quickly: the Maestro, his back to the street, was already settling into a table where, on the opposite side, sat Elias Ambrosius's former teacher, Hakham Menasseh ben Israel. At that moment, the former rabbi, always a glutton for earthly pleasures, was sticking his nose in the brown paper bag weighed down with the aromatic American leaf to breathe in its warm perfume of far-off lands.

———

For months, the reckless idea had been circling around in Elias Ambrosius's head to approach his old teacher and confess his aims. But that day, as he saw him drink, smoke, and pat the Maestro's shoulder several times, he made the decision. Weighing his possibilities, he concluded that that man was his best and worst option, but, clearly, the only one within his reach.

Hakham ben Israel lived in a wooden house, more ramshackle than modest, in Nieuwe Houtmarkt, on the so-called island of Vlooienburg, on the banks of the Binnen Amstel, very close to where the Maestro and his now-deceased wife had lived a few years before. Perhaps Elias had visited the dwelling of his religion, rhetoric, and Hebrew language instructor more frequently than could have been prompted by mere nostalgia for his school days, because there he could breathe in the most genuine atmosphere of Amsterdam's Jewish quarter: a mix of messianism and reality, of divine predestination and mundane behaviors, of culture that was open to the world and renewing ideas but also carried centuries-old Hebrew pragmatism. And also because in that house he could be in contact with the Maestro's spirit.

The physical conditions of the Hakham's dwelling obviously contrasted with the circumstance that his wife, the mother of his three children, was a member of the Abravanel family, once rich and powerful in Spain and Portugal, and now again rich and powerful in Venice, Alexandria, and also in Amsterdam. The Abravanels had arrived in the city even after Elias's grandfather Montalbo, but as opposed to him, as the passengers of a merchant ship, weighed down with bags of gold coins and chests of diamonds, and with political, social, family, and commercial contacts worth several more thousands of florins. A line of advisors, bankers, and royal civil servants to the Iberian crown before the fateful year of 1492, the propagators of businessmen, doctors, and even poets of renown throughout the West, the Abravanels appeared to be predestined for wealth, power, and intelligence. But the Hakham's house had nothing to do with the first two of those virtues; on the contrary, the place announced that commercial skills were not its inhabitants' forte. (He was the founder of several businesses, among them the city's first Jewish printshop, which was soon defeated by the competition and sold to another Sephardic Jew.) Above all, the building's precariousness and rotting wood evidenced that his relationship with the affluent Abravanels was none too cordial. Nonetheless, perhaps the best proof of the existing distance between the savant and his relatives was the one that cut short Ben Israel's career as a rabbi: if he had the support of the powerful clan, he would not have failed in his efforts for that coveted role.

That bitter dispute had occurred a few years before, when the Sephardic Jews, increasingly more numerous and prosperous, decided to breathe life into the Talmud Torah, the religious and community assembly in which they founded the city's three existing congregations, and, as part of the fusion, they decided to do away with some rabbis, whose salaries were paid by the community. And among those cast aside was the embarrassing Menasseh ben Israel. Despite his fame as a writer, Kabbalist, and disseminator of Jewish thought, the scholar had to resign himself from then on to the poorly compensated condition of Hakham, professor of rhetoric and religion, although he was allowed to keep a seat on the city's rabbinical council. Despite that fiasco, the learned man took public pride in his blood ties with the famous line, since, as several members of the family and he himself had been responsible for proclaiming, there was reliable proof that the Abranavels were directly descended from the house of King David and, consequently, the Messiah to come (whose arrival, according to well-versed Kabbalists in the West and mystics in the East, appeared to be closer every day) would bear that last name . . . And thus the Awaited One could well be one of the former rabbi's children, conceived in an Abravanel womb.

Despite having to live counting the dusty centimes in his pockets, the scandalous rabbinical humiliation, and his Portuguese and sustained fondness for wine, Menasseh ben Israel continued to be one of the most influential men in the community and, incidentally, for three years had been the director of Nossa Academia, the school founded by the powerful Abraham and Moshe Pereira. In his youth, in order to print and circulate his writings, he had founded that first Jewish printshop in Amsterdam, and, as much as the business ended up being a fiasco, it was an enlightened decision as a platform for his ideas and for disseminating knowledge of many classics of Jewish literature. His own books, written in Spanish, Hebrew, Latin, Portuguese, and English (he could, besides, express himself in five other languages, including, of course, Dutch), moved around half the world and had readers not only among the Jews of the West and the East (his *Nishmat Hayim* was already considered one of the most substantial Kabbalistic commentaries), but also among Catholics and other Christians. He had found this last audience through his works such as *The Conciliator*, a curious Hebrew view on the sacred scriptures, an inclusive perspective that marked the coincidences between the Catholic and Protestant readings of the text and those that had been made over three thousand years by the sons of Israel. All of his works were read by his former student—who was encouraged by his grandfather—but, among them, Elias Ambrosius continued to prefer the booklet *De Termino Vitae* (whose original, which rapidly became a scandalous success, the printshop had put together), since it communicated to the young man that notion of life and its demands, of death and its anticipations, that pleased him so much as a conceptualization of human existence, here and now.

Perhaps because he was such a peculiar nonconformist, landed in the middle of a newly formed and turbulent community, that, to strengthen itself, had to rely on the most ironclad orthodoxy, Ben Israel's career was as full of successes as of setbacks. But, without a doubt, because he was an iconoclast capable of revealing the riskiest ideas (either due to their novelty or to how conservative they were) and living a public life at the limits of what was accepted by Judaic precepts, his links with the rest of Amsterdam's Protestant society came to be closer and more fluid. And if visible proof was necessary of how deeply those ties ran, in the small living room of his very humble dwelling was the testimony: there, defiant, hung the portrait that, a few years before, the Maestro had done of him, when he was already the Maestro and the most well-known and sought-after painter in the city. That drawing, in which the then rabbi displayed a wide-brim hat, a trimmed beard, and a mustache, in the style of the villa's burghers, emanated life thanks to an impressive job on the eyes, from which shone the intelligent vulture gaze that characterized the model and that the Maestro knew how to reflect so well. The work served as a magnet that, on each visit to the house, Elias Ambrosius Montalbo de Ávila contemplated until he nearly wore it out, and turned out to be another one of the reasons that fed the young man's growing desire to approach the Maestro and imitate him.

The friendship and trust between a painter who was critical of dogmatic Calvinism (although a member of his friend Cornelis Anslo's Mennonite sect) and a controversial Jewish scholar became stronger perhaps because neither of the two professed the exclusion of others and less still did they resign themselves to the intellectual possibilities offered by their time. Both men, thwarted in their aspirations to social ascent, had ended up proving to be incapable of following accepted norms for a successful Dutch painter and for a preeminent Jew, those canons and preferences established in time by ancestral traditions or maintained out of convenience by those wielding money and power; those men upon whose capital, whether they liked it or not, the painter and the student of sacred texts had to rely.

Through his former tutor, Elias knew of the long talks held in the artist's studio, at the Hakham's house or in Amsterdam's beer halls where the two men loved meeting up and handing themselves over to libations, dialogues in which those opposing yet kindred spirits usually referred to their disagreements and notions. Their often insolent ways of behaving in public had also contributed to garnering them the attention of an ebullient community for whom the enjoyment of freedom of ideas and creeds had been established as the most valued good to which all who lived there had the right, including the sons of Israel: there was a reason that the Jews did not just consider it a New Jerusalem but also called it *Makom*, "the good place," where they had found the acceptance of their customs and faith and, with it, the peace to live their lives, lost in almost all other places in the known world.

That morning, when Raquel Abravanel, poorly coiffed and sour-faced (as always), received Elias, she immediately spit out that her husband was still sleeping off the ethylic excesses of the previous night and closed the door in his face. Leaning against the doorway of the house, just under the mezuzah, the cylinder with a fragment of the Torah devoted to reminding those who entered or left the dwelling that God is everywhere, the young man decided to wait out his teacher's recovery, since he was determined to have the difficult conversation with the man most capable of helping him or sinking him. An hour later, far too underdressed for that morning's cold, sporting the dirty trousers and threadbare cape with which he usually walked around the city to make more patent his nonexistent interest in material goods and in his neighbors' opinions, his host settled down on the step with the young man and offered him a mug of warm, watered-down wine, sweetened with honey and flavored with cinnamon, similar to the one he himself was drinking.

Elias asked him how he felt. "Alive" was the response of the Hakham, who, strangely, did not seem to have any desire to digress. What did Elias want to see him about? Why so rushed? Wasn't he cold? And what had become of that ingrate Amos? The young man decided to start with what was easiest for him, even though it wasn't in reality, because his brother Amos, also a former student of Ben Israel's, had had a spiritual crisis and had become one of the followers of Breslau, the Polish rabbi, the most recalcitrant local defender of Judaism's religious purity and, as could be expected, a public enemy of Ben Israel and his ways of thinking. Because of that, he gave the most polite and simultaneously explicit response that popped into his head:

"Amos must be reading the Torah at the German synagogue," he said. He took a sip of the already cold wine and, without further hesitation, dove into what really interested him. "My dear Hakham, I would like for your friend the Maestro to accept me in his workshop. I want to learn how to paint. But I want to learn with him." The professor continued drinking from his mug, as if the words of his former student were an intranscendental commentary about the state of the weather or the price of wheat. Elias knew, nonetheless, that the learned man's mind must be digesting those words weighed down with complications and placing them on the balance against the counterweights of what was logical, possible, admissible, and intolerable.

Few men in Amsterdam knew more than Menasseh about the reality of living with secrets and hiding behind a mask: in his Portuguese childhood, when he was still called Manoel Dias Soeiro, he had been ripped from his home and hidden in a monastery where, for several years, some Franciscan Friars, without much mercy, had educated him as a Christian, teaching him (rod in hand) the reasons for which he should spurn and repress the practitioners of the religion of his ancestors, who were directly responsible for the death of Christ, practitioners of ritual sacrifices of children, stinking of sulfur and greedy by nature, among many other sins and stigmas. His stomach, forced to digest pig meat, blood sausage, and as much *treyf* food as it could occur to the priests to serve, became weak to the point of developing a chronic illness that still plagued him and produced painful vomiting. But, he had also learned to survive in an adverse environment, to keep silent and know how to hide himself in the masses, to be neither seen nor heard and, above all, to take from that hostile environment the lessons that could be useful in the most diverse circumstances. He had come to the conclusion, thanks to his theological repressors, that the human being is a creature too complex for someone ("Apart from God, of course," he would tell his students, as Elias always recalled) to think himself capable of knowing him and judging him, while freedom of choice should be man's first right, since it had been given to him by the Creator: since the beginning of the world, for his salvation or perdition, but always for his use.

When he talked about this matter to his students, Ben Israel would repeat his favorite quote from Deuteronomy, "I, God, have set before you life and death; blessings and curses: *choose* life," highlighting the possibility of choice more than the final choice itself, and many times, as the climax, he would narrate the extraordinary story of one of his distant in-laws, Don Judah Abravanel, the man who, for the salvation of his life and that of his lineage, had chosen to publicly hand over his faith and deny all of his convictions. According to the story (Elias always believed it to be fiction on the Hakham's part to emphasize the family's messianic destiny even more), that man was the son of the powerful Isaac Abravanel, who gave so much support and so much money so that the Genovese Columbus could set sail with his vessels and bring power and glory to the Spanish Crown. Nonetheless, he also had to flee the country where for many centuries his ancestors had lived and prospered in order to seek refuge in Lisbon, like many other Jews pursued by the bishops of that same Spanish Crown (which, before expelling them, had confiscated their very considerable goods, as Grandfather Benjamin always recalled whenever he spoke of this and other persecutions). But, according to the teacher's story, it was in the year 1497 that Judah Abravanel lived the greatest moment of his existence: he, his wife, and his children, along with dozens of other Sephardic families, ended up confined in the cathedral in Lisbon and, by royal decree, were placed before the terrible choice to which Christians reduced the options of practitioners of the Law of Moses. Either they accepted Catholic baptism or they were taken to torture and death on the bonfire. (At this point—Elias remembered well—Hakham ben Israel would usually make a dramatic pause, destined to feed the awe of his pupils, although he saved the best silence for later on.) Many of the Jews trapped in the cathedral, hundreds of them, in order to not see themselves humiliated by the act of baptism, decided to die for their faith sanctifying the name of God. They chose sacrifice, as ordered by the Scripture, and began to kill their children and wives, and then killed themselves: if they had weapons, they slit their own throats, they cut their own veins, they wounded themselves in the heart, and if they were unarmed, then they strangled themselves with their belts and even with their own hands, and later sacrificed themselves by beating their own skulls against the temple's columns, which, it was said, still dripped with the great amount of blood absorbed by its stones. But not Judah Abravanel, the Hakham would say at this point of the story. That denial fell like a wave of relief over the adolescents, who were terrified by the story of other Jews' suffering in a way that they, the fortunate inhabitants of Amsterdam, the New Jerusalem where the doors had been opened to the sons of Israel, could not imagine enduring.

Judah Abravanel, whose line—as was well-known—went back to the very house of King David, was a doctor by profession and would be the poet who, under the name Léon Hebreo, would write the famous *Dialoghi d'amore*, read several times by Ben Israel to his students. A learned man, pious and rich, he had been trapped by the most painful circumstance and made his choice: Don Judah had taken his wife and children by the hand and, slipping about in the Jewish blood spilled in the Christian temple, had advanced toward the altar, clamoring for baptism (and here the Hakham made his longest silence). Choosing life. Even as his heart wept, conscious that his decision broke one of the inviolable precepts ("Do you know what those precepts are?"), Don Judah Abravanel walked willing to throw it all to the fire, to lose the salvation of his soul, but conscious of what his life and the lives of his children meant or could mean for the history of the world according to the cosmic proportions of a rigorous divine plan: they were the open channel on the path of the Messiah . . . Besides, with the example given by that man, considered a stalwart of the community, Don Judah saved the lives of many of the Jews enclosed in the church, who, knowing his prestige, influenced by his lineage, decided to imitate him . . .

Thanks to that act, incidentally, the Hakham would say—more relaxed, perhaps even with a hint of irony—Judah Abravanel was alive enough to flee Portugal with his people, settle in Italy, and, in the most favorable circumstances, again acquire wealth and return to the faith in which he had been born and where he was meant to be. In any event, Don Judah, perhaps forgiven by the infinite understanding of the Holiest, blessed may He be, had left behind a moving lesson (and here, the skillful narrator would usually allow a last silence to fall): at each moment, the wise man should act in the best way his intelligence deems, because the Creator has given humans that capacity for a reason. The Holiest had taught His people that no power, no humiliation, not even the most heated repression or conglomeration of pain and fear, could blow out the flame of desire for freedom burning in the heart of a man willing to fight for it, willing even to humiliate himself to reach that freedom, and He had taught them, after life was over, to trust in the Final Judgment. Because the desire for freedom is inseparable from the individuality of man, that intricate divine creation.

As dramatic as those silences in his stories was the silence that the Hakham now imposed that morning, after hearing Elias Ambrosius's confession. And it ended up being so long that the young man wondered if he would die of cold and desperation. Ben Israel, too absorbed, had taken out the barley cracker hidden in the pocket of his shirt to dip it in the rest of the wine and chew it unhurriedly before at last deciding to speak.

"I'm not going to ask you if you understand what you're requesting of me, since I assume you must understand it. I also assume that you know what my duty is supposed to be, right now."

"Yes, sir, try to convince me that it's crazy. Or denounce me to the Mahamad. Don't try the former: I am decided. The latter is up to you, as a member of that council."

Ben Israel left his already empty cup directly below the mezuzah, wiped his mouth and rubbed his hands together to get rid of the remaining crumbs, and, while he was at it, bring heat back into his fingers.

"I spent thirty years living here and I still long for the sun of Portugal . . . I wouldn't find it strange that there are Jews who refuse to leave there and others here who are desperate to return."

Without any further explanation, the teacher entered the house and came back out with a blanket over his shoulders. He took up his seat again, noisily sucked in his snot, and looked at the young man: "Why are you asking me to help you in something so serious? Why do you come to me?"

"Because you, Hakham, are the only one who can help me . . . And because I know that you would be able to."

The man smiled, perhaps made proud by Elias's opinion.

"You're asking my support to violate a mitzvah, nothing less than the second commandment written in the tablets."

"A mitzvah that we Jews have been violating for two thousand years. Or was it not the Jews, according to what I learned in your classes, who painted the panels with biblical scenes in a synagogue on the banks of the Euphrates? What about the mosaics with human and animal images in the synagogue of Hamat Tiberias, on Lake Galilee? You say they didn't just fall from the sky. What about the illustrated Sacred Scriptures? And don't the tombstones in the cemetery of Beth Haim, right here, in Amsterdam, have images of animals on them . . . ? And what about the angels in the Ark of the Covenant? King Solomon's fountain raised over four sculpted elephants . . . ? Excuse me, Hakham, but what I'm going to say to you is pertinent . . . Isn't having images on the walls of your house a violation of the Law?"

"Yes, there are bad precedents and others . . ." The wise man smiled again, wounded by his former student's jab that reminded him of the portrait that for years Ben Israel had exhibited, like a challenge, right there, in his house. "There are others that are confusing. The cherubs that adorn the Ark were requested by the Creator Himself, it's true. Although He never invoked anyone to adore them . . . The carved marble in our cemetery was entrusted to Gentile artisans . . . And I'm not the only Jew who has been painted by Mr. Van Rijn. There is also an excellent portrait by him of the notable Dr. Bueno . . . What I mean to say is that none of this exempts you from obedience and less still from the danger of punishment . . ."

Then Elias Ambrosius played the trump card he thought would guarantee his victory: "The Torah prohibits us from adoring false idols, that is even one of the three inviolable precepts, and that is where the condemnation of the act of representing images of men and animals comes from, or of adoring them in temples or in houses . . . But it does not speak of the fact of learning to do so, and I only want you to help me learn with the Maestro. What I do later is my conscious responsibility . . . Are you going to help me or are you going to inform against me?"

Ben Israel finally laughed openly.

"Every time that he had to battle with his people, Moses asked himself why the Holiest, blessed may He be, had chosen the Hebrews to follow His mandates on earth and foster the arrival of the Messiah. We are the most disobedient race in creation. And that has come at a price, you know that . . . The worst is not that we question everything but that we rationalize that questioning. You are right . . . No one is preventing you from studying. But you know something? I feel to blame for you having learned to think that way . . . Besides, the Law is clear regarding the representation of figures that could be idolized. The prohibition refers above all to building false idols or supposed images of the Holiest . . . Although, I say, it leaves space for the act of creating if that task does not lead to idolatry . . . And each new generation, you know well, is obligated to respect the Torah and its Laws, but it is also obligated to study it, because texts require being interpreted in the spirit of the times, which are changing . . . Now, independently of how we interpret the Law, I ask you: Would you be capable of stopping yourself at the limit? Studying and only learning, as you say, for the joy of doing so?" He made one of his pauses, again so long that Elias came to wonder whether he had finished his speech, when at last he stood up and added: "Come, I want to show you something."

The Hakham picked up his mug and climbed the two steps that led to the house. The young man imitated him, intrigued by what the man could show him. They crossed the living room in disarray, deserted at that moment, and entered the cubicle where the scholar usually read and wrote. Mountains of books and papers, seemingly placed any which way, surrounded the small table, where there rested several sheets written in Hebrew, some goose feathers, and a bottle of ink. Also a carafe of wine, the luxury that the teacher could not give up. Ben Israel turned around and looked into his former student's eyes—"Discretion is a virtue. I trust in you as you trust in me"—and, without waiting for his former student to make any comment, he leaned over the table and from a drawer took out a rolled piece of heavy paper that he handed over to the young man. "Open it."

At the mere feel of the texture of the paper, Elias Ambrosius knew that it was one of the engraving cards of the kind sold by Mr. Daniel Rulandts and, with utmost care, he began to unfold the roll until he opened it before his eyes. In fact, the surface was engraved with an etching, and the image represented was the bust of Ben Israel himself, dressed with forced elegance, his beard and mustache well trimmed, his head covered with his Jewish kippah. The young man said the first thing that occurred to him: "But this is not a work by the Maestro."

"I see how well you know him," the Hakham admitted. "That's what is interesting about this engraving . . ."

"So who is it . . . ? Salom Italia?" He read on the bottom corner, where the date of execution was engraved in Roman numerals: MDCXLII, 1642. "Who is Salom Italia . . . ? Don't tell me he's a Jew." Ben Israel allowed a small smile to spread across his lips.

"Elias, all you need to know, which is already a lot, is this: yes, he is a Jew, like you, like me."

"A Jew? And you knew he was doing this? Whoever this Salom Italia is, he's not an apprentice . . . He's an artist."

"You're on the right path . . ." Ben Israel threw some books to the floor and settled into his chair. "He's not an apprentice, although he received almost no lessons from any maestro. But he has a gift. And he couldn't avoid developing it . . . Of course, Salom Italia is not his real name . . ."

"And what are you going to do, Hakham? Are you going to denounce him?"

"After posing for him . . . ?"

Elias Ambrosius understood that he was facing something too serious, definitive, capable of pushing him forward in his aims but at the same time filling him with fears.

"So then, what are you going to do?"

"With this engraving, keep it. With Salom Italia's secret and his etching, the same thing. With you, help you . . . After all, it's your choice and you know the risks . . . As Salom Italia knew them. Besides, in this city, secrets multiply: there are several of them hidden by every Jew you see . . . Yes, I have an idea . . . And I hope that the Holiest, blessed may He be, will understand me and forgive me with His infinite grace."

Menasseh ben Israel stood up and rubbed his hands again: "We need firewood again and I am in ruins . . . Have you noticed that I don't even have enough to buy milk? When will this damned winter end? Go now, I have to pray . . . Although it's already a little late, isn't it? Did you do your morning prayers . . . ? And then I'm going to think. About you and about me."

———

When he was finally in front of the green door of number 4 Jodenbreestraat, Elias Ambrosius felt the desire to run away. It's not the same to make a decision as it is to carry out an act; and if he passed the threshold surveilled by him for months, always dreaming of that moment, he would be taking an irreversible step. Without wanting to, without thinking about it, he again reviewed his attire, the most presentable within his reach, but he comforted himself upon observing the careless aspect of his guide: the scholar Ben Israel looked like one of those crude and foul-smelling Jews who in recent years had migrated from the East to New Jerusalem and lived off of charity or meager municipal salaries earned for work such as removing grime and animal corpses from the canals, collecting snow in winter, and sweeping the dust from the streets the rest of the year.

Mme. Geertje Dircx opened the door for them and, with the muteness that was typical of her (Elias already knew it), led them to the receiving room. That soldier's widow, nearly a soldier herself, was the one charged with caring for Titus, the Maestro's small son, even before his mother's death, and following the passing of the mistress of the house, she had turned into a kind of housekeeper with all the power that entailed. They only waited a few minutes and from the stairs leading to the kitchen, out came the Maestro, still chewing a last bite and dressed in a smock that reached his ankles, stained in all possible colors and tightened at the waist with a hemp rope that was more appropriate for tying than for the function it was now deployed for.

"Good day, my friend," the Hakham greeted him, and the Maestro responded with the same words and a handshake. Elias, whom the host had not even looked at, felt his whole body tremble, shaken by the close presence of that man with the spout-shaped nose and eagle's gaze who had such a vulgar appearance that, even knowing who he was, it was difficult to accept that he was—and no one doubted it—the greatest Maestro in a city where painters swarmed. Ben Israel mentioned to him the reason for his visit and only then did the man seem to remember him and take a sideways glance at Elias.

"Ah, your young student . . . Let's go to the studio," he said, and after ordering Mme. Dircx to bring up a bottle of wine and two glasses, he started the ascent up the sinuous spiral staircase.

As they went up, the young man, without shedding his anxiety, was trying to piece together everything he saw in the images of that place that he had imagined based on descriptions by the Hakham, Keil the Dane, and the businessman Salvador Rodrigues, a neighbor of the painter's and friend of Elias's father. Without even daring to take a glance at the works hanging in the room, among which he recognized a landscape by Adriaen Brouwer and a bust of a Virgin (without a doubt from Italy) beside a pair of works by the host, he followed them to the floor where the Maestro had his studio and, through the semi-closed door of the annex of the antechamber, he managed to see the press on which the painter printed copies of his coveted etchings. When they reached the landing of the third level, he could make out in the room at the end, to his right, the warehouse of exotic objects that the Maestro so liked to acquire in auctions and small markets around the city and, to the left, the door that was already open and gave access to the workshop. It was at that moment, while the Maestro let the rabbi pass, that the man addressed Elias Ambrosius for the first time.

"Wait here. If you want, you can look at my collection. But don't steal anything," and, without another word, he closed the door to the studio behind him.

Elias, obedient, entered the chamber where, in chaos rather than order, were amassed the most inconceivable rarities. Although his state of mind was not propitious for concentrating on observations, he looked over that display of marbles in which *artificialia* cohabitated with *naturalia*, in an amazing or amazed variety and arrangement. Placed at an angle from which he could observe the studio door, the young man ran his eyes over the series of marble and plaster busts (Augustus? Marcus Aurelius? Homer?), the boxes of shells, the Asian and African spears clustered in a corner, the books (all in Dutch) placed on a bookshelf, the taxidermied exotic animals, the iron military helmets, the collection of minerals and coins, the jars imported from the Far East, two globes, various musical instruments of whose existence and sonority the Jew had no idea. On the table rested three enormous folders that, the young man already knew, capped engravings, etchings, and drawings by Michelangelo, Raphael, Titian, Rubens, Holbein, Lucas van Leyden, Mantegna! Cranach the Elder! Dürer! . . . Focused on looking at the albums, rubbing with the tips of his fingers the roughness of the impressions, all notion of time lost and removed unconsciously from his anxieties, the creaking of the door opening surprised him.

"Come, my son," the Hakham bid him and the trembling returned to the young man's body.

The Maestro's workshop occupied the entire front half of the floor. The two windows observed so many times from the square of Sint Antoniesbreestraat, on the banks of the Zwanenburgwal lock, had the cloth curtains drawn to diminish the light, but the young man could see on the easel prepared behind the Maestro, very close to a wrought-iron stove, a medium-format panel painting with the upper half darkened to a nearly cavernous depth where, nonetheless, it was possible to make out an enormous column, something like an altar weighed down by gold filigree, and a curtain that came down from the shadows on the left. On the panel's lower half, where the light was concentrated around a kneeling woman dressed in white, there was a group of several more figures, merely sketched over a gray background.

The Hakham took the other free bench and left Elias standing in the middle of the room, in an embarrassing position, since he could see his reflection face-on and in profile in the two great mirrors leaning against the workshop's front and side walls. The young man didn't know what to do with his hands or where to direct his gaze, eager to capture every detail of the sanctum sanctorum, although he was incapable of turning the processed images into thought.

"How old are you, kid?"

Elias was surprised by that question.

"Seventeen years old, sir. Just turned."

"You look younger."

Elias nodded.

"It's that I don't have a beard yet."

The Maestro nearly smiled and continued. "My friend Menasseh has spoken to me of your aims. And since I admire daring, I'm going to do something for you."

Elias felt that he could float with happiness, but he limited himself to nodding, his eyes fixed on the Maestro's hands, devoted to emphasizing his words.

"Since for my friend's sake, and yours, we should be discreet, and since my understanding is that you are an ambitious and headstrong young man without a pot to piss in, my only possible proposal is that, for everyone, you come to work in my workshop as a cleaning boy, for which I will reduce your tuition to fifty florins. Of course, for that price and so that everyone else thinks that you are cleaning, you really are going to clean, that's clear . . . First, you will learn by watching what the rest of the students do and what I do. You can ask, but not too much, and never address me when I am working . . . Never . . . When you know everything you should know about how to set out and mix the colors, grind the stones with the mortar, prepare the canvases and panels, make paintbrushes, and have an idea of how to paint a painting and why you paint one way and not another, then I will again ask you your willingness. And if you still insist, I will give you a paintbrush. If you take that paintbrush in your hands and if that act comes to be more or less public, then it will only depend on you, and you will assume the consequences. I have too many Jewish friends who are not as crazy as this friend of ours"—he pointed at Ben Israel with his chin—"to sully my relationship with them over a dreamer who aims to paint and perhaps isn't even good enough to prime the walls . . . Does that suit you?"

Elias, weighed down by that speech, finally looked at the Maestro's face, which remained awaiting a response, and then at that of his former instructor, who, with a beautiful half-drained glass of wine in hand, seemed tipsy and amused by the situation.

"Yes, I accept, sir . . . But I can only pay you thirty florins."

The Maestro looked at him as if he hadn't quite understood him and, with his eyes, interrogated Ben Israel.

"Please, sir, thirty florins is more than I have," the young man then added as he felt the world coming down at his feet when he saw the Maestro shaking his head again and again. Elias, like all who knew something about that man's life, knew that fame was not enough to meet the financial pressures to which his eccentricities led. Besides, his finances must have worsened considerably since the previous year, when various members of the arquebusiers' society commented freely that the work commissioned had turned out to be a scam, an impertinent painting in poor taste, since it did not resemble in any way the group portraits then in fashion. Some even commented that the painter was capricious, strong-willed, and bullheaded ("It would have been better to have commissioned Frans Hals," some of those portrayed had said, each one of whom had subscribed with the considerable sum of one hundred florins), and, almost as if it were a municipal decree, the Maestro ceased to receive that type of commission, the most profitable in Amsterdam's picture market. Because of that, the painter's response surprised the two Jews: "You may not have a beard, but you have guts . . . Well, there's a broom. Start by sweeping the stairs. I want to see them shine. When you finish, ask Mme. Dircx what other things you should do . . . I think we need peat for the stoves . . . Go now, I want to talk to my friend a little more. And dress like what you are, a servant. Come on, go and close the door."

———

He knew he was privileged. He surmised that he would witness some marvelous events and wanted to have the option of remembering them for the rest of the days of his life and, perhaps, in an unforeseen future, transmit them to others. Because of that, a few weeks after he started frequenting the Maestro's house and workshop, Elias Ambrosius decided to make a kind of book of impressions in which he would start writing down all of his emotions, discoveries, digressions, and acquisitions in the Maestro's shadow and light. And also his fears and doubts. He had to think a lot about where to hide that notebook, since, if it fell into anyone's hands—he thought, above all, of his brother Amos, who was, with each passing day, more intransigent in religious matters, insistent even on speaking the impenetrable jargon of those rustic Jews from the East—it would make all of his precautions and concealment unnecessary, and make any minimal attempt to defend himself impossible. In the end, he opted for an open trapdoor in the floorboards of the attic, hidden from view by an old wood-and-leather chest.

On the first page of the notebook, which he himself assembled and pasted together at the printshop according to the model of the *tafelet* in which the painters usually made their sketches, he wrote in Ladino, with large letters, putting great effort into the beauty of the Gothic calligraphy: *New Jerusalem, Year 5403 since the Creation, 1643 of the Common Era.* And to begin, he devoted himself to narrating what the possibility of sharing the Maestro's world meant to him, and later, in various entries loaded with adjectives and exclamation points, he tried to express the epiphany that was caused by witnessing the miraculous act through which that man touched by genius brought forth figures from the base of dead color primed on the oak board, how he dressed them, gave them faces and expressions with a touch of his brush. He tried to explain to himself how he managed to illuminate them with the fabulous, almost magical play of ocher colors, as he placed them in a semicircle around the kneeling woman dressed in white, to give definitive form to the Christian drama of Jesus pardoning the adulterer, condemned to be stoned to death. The work turned out to be a process of pure ex nihilo creation, in which, day to day, the young man had been able to contemplate a convocation of lines and colors that appeared and took shape often to be devoured by other lines, other colors capable of better outlining the silhouettes, the ornaments, the scenery, the shapes, and the lights (*How did he achieve that controversy of dark and light?* he would ask himself over and over again) until, after many hours of effort, he reached the most resounding perfection.

As they had agreed on the day of his first visit, Elias, once his daily work at the printshop concluded, worked at the Maestro's house every afternoon and evening, from Monday to Thursday, and even a few hours before sunset on Friday evening. ("When Friday ends, you must fulfill your commitments as a Jew. On Sundays, I sometimes go to my church and, if I can avoid it, I don't like to have anyone at home," the Maestro said to him.) Broom and cleaning rag in hand, following Mme. Dircx's instructions, the young man started to go all over the building where, at one time, happiness, celebrations, and chatter had filled the days and nights. But now the surrounding atmosphere was gloomy, forged by the presence of death, which had circled so much around it. The only things to bring signs of life and normality to the ambience were the running around, laughter, and tears of little Titus, the surviving son, and the presence of the students, some even younger than Elias, who oftentimes could not avoid an eruption of laughter capable of altering for a few moments the somber atmosphere enclosed within those walls.

Elias always carried out his tasks quickly, although conscientiously, desirous of going up as soon as possible to the attic where the students worked in their nooks. He even, if possible, tried to gain admission to the Maestro's studio before sunset, since, despite his preference for nocturnal scenes, he would discover that seldom would the man continue his work on a painting using the light of candles or a bonfire prepared by his assistants in a great copper pot designed for that purpose. But when spring arrived and the sun's disappearance became more delayed, Elias had more time at his disposal to wander, always in silence, broom and rag in hand, throughout the painter's studio; and when the latter was not working or when he had locked the door, on occasion he remained in the first-floor rooms, contemplating the Maestro's recent works (a delicate portrait of his deceased wife, adorned like a queen and showing her last smile; a magnificent image of David and Jonathan exuding tenderness, in which the Maestro had used his own face to create the second of these characters); paintings by his friends and most outstanding students (Jan Lievens, Gerrit Dou, Ferdinand Bol, Govaert Flinck); and pieces that he had acquired, some to keep, others to sell for some gain. Among those jewels, Elias found A Samaritan Woman by Giorgione, a re-creation of Hero and Leander by the exuberant Flemish Rubens, and that Virgin's bust he had seen on the day of his first visit to the house, which ended up being a work by the great Raphael. More often than not, of course, he directed himself to the stalls in the attic, set apart by mobile panels, where the apprentices worked, on some occasions guided by the Maestro, and others, working on their own pieces, according to the abilities they'd already acquired. With Keil the Dane, Samuel von Hoogstraten, the boyish Aert de Gelder, and, above all, with the very gifted Carel Fabritius (with reason, frequently invited by the Maestro to help him advance in some of his own works), he began his true learning of the mysteries of composition, light, and form, although with all of them, he took care not to reveal his actual intentions, even when he assumed that it would not be difficult for any of the students and apprentices to guess them, in addition to the fact that the possible aims of an insignificant Jewish servant could interest those offspring of businessmen and affluent bureaucrats very little.

In the initial weeks, the Maestro barely addressed a word to him, except for when he ordered him to clean somewhere or hand him a specific object. That treatment, bordering on contempt, motivated perhaps by how unprofitable his presence was, wounded the young man's pride but did not defeat it: in the end, he was where he wanted to be and learning what he had so desired to learn. And being invisible was his best shield, as much inside as outside that house.

Elias tended to pay particular attention to the jobs assigned to the students, since he knew well that these tasks had to do with the basic rules of the trade. Someday, with any luck, he, too, would receive those orders. With special attention, he followed the process delegated to the apprentices of applying second and third layers of primer to the canvases, over which, many times, they applied a thick, nearly ridge-like, mix of gray quartz colored with a bit of ocher brown, more or less reduced with white, all of it diluted in drying oil, to obtain the maximum roughness of texture and dead color demanded by the Maestro; he stopped to observe the art of preparing the colors, how the little mill pulverized the stones of pigment in the mortar, for the students to then mix them with precise quantities of linseed oil so that the paint would bind sufficiently, without being too thick; he studied the way of setting up the Maestro's palette (surprisingly limited in colors) according to the phase in which the work found itself or what piece of it the Maestro would be working on at that moment. All of those jobs were developed with precise mandates, and only on occasion did they come with any sort of a less didactic explanation of the artist's intentions. Elias discovered, besides, that the painter was generally the one who prepared the yellow, gold, copper, earth, and sienna colors (which he used profusely), as if he only trusted in his own ability to achieve the precise hue demanded by his mind. Nonetheless, it was while conversing with the pleasant Aert de Gelder—the student who could reproduce the Maestro's works with the greatest ease, as if the Maestro himself were inside him—when Elias Ambrosius had the first notion of how the colors had to combine to achieve those impressive effects of light and how to apply them to attain the gloomy shadows that gave such interior drama to the pieces coming out of the workshop.

One afternoon during the month of April—just barely after Pesach, the Jewish feast that, due to stipulated rituals, spaced out Elias's visits to the house—the young man found two occasions to be happy. The first was when, upon entering the studio, he saw the Maestro seated before a canvas that he had ordered Carel Fabritius to prepare a few days prior. During the days on which the student was working on linen that was six quarters high by one ell wide, Elias had witnessed the most remote origin of a work that at that moment was only in the mind of the Maestro, beating like desire. While Fabritius prepared the linen, the Maestro devoted himself to drawing on a tablet and watched the work of priming the canvas out of the corner of his eye. On two occasions, he requested "More," and Fabritius had had to add the dark Kasel earth powder paste, to give the surface an even deeper tone. At last, the Maestro drew some lustrous, white-lead lines across that nearly black surface that was tinged with a hint of brown, and Elias made out the shape of a head, covered perhaps by a bonnet . . . like the one that the painter was wearing at that moment. The position of the mirrors—placed near the easel in such a way that the artist could see himself full-on and at three-quarters profile and at an angle at which the sun's light, filtered by the windows, would highlight only one of the model's cheeks—revealed the work's subject matter.

As soon as Fabritius left the studio, Elias Ambrosius, moving as carefully as possible, placed in a bucket the dozen large, dirty paint-brushes picked up from the floor and recovered his friend the broom to depart: the first law he had learned upon arriving at the workshop was that when the Maestro was working on a self-portrait, he always had to be alone, unless he solicited someone's presence—either to use him as a clothing model or to retouch certain areas of the piece. That is why he was surprised when he heard the Maestro's voice speaking to Elias's image reflected in the mirror: "Stay."

Elias leaned the broom against the wall and lowered the bucket but did not move. The Maestro went silent again and looked his own face in the eye, as seen in the reflecting glass. That face had been, without a doubt, the most recurrent image in the Maestro's work. Several dozen of his self-portraits, including paintings, sketches, and engravings, had left his hands and found buyers in the market and space on the walls of Amsterdam's bourgeois houses, where they had nearly always arrived not for their beauty, but for having been considered a sure value by some daring buyers: the same as gold or diamonds, just like everything that came from the hands of that Maestro before his reputation was damaged by the piece in the great hall at Kloveniers. The search for expressions, feelings, real or feigned moods, had perhaps led the Maestro to consider himself the ideal model who was, of course, always available. Perhaps the search for images that could be used in the many other portraits he executed (with recognized skill) constituted another reason for that reliance. But, above all, Elias thought, after hearing commentaries on the subject from the students and apprentices, and after speaking about that obsession with his teacher Ben Israel, it appeared that the Maestro found in his features—none too noble, incidentally (his Roman nose, his rebellious and free curls—*cadenettes*, as the Dutch called them, using the word from the French—the expressive although harsh mouth, with his teeth increasingly darkened by cavities, and the always alert depth of his gaze)—the reflection of a well-known life, of whose gains and losses, happiness and disasters, he wanted or meant to leave testimony of, with the certainty (as he would one day, much later, tell Elias Ambrosius) that *one* man is *one* moment in time; and the life of a human, the consequence of many moments throughout the time, more or less extended, he was given to live. A face not as representation but as result: the man *is* like the emanation of the man who *has been*.

That skill so singular of the Maestro's was known to all: his capacity for reading consciences and reflecting them in the density of a gaze, which he later surrounded with a few meaningful attributes. In the city, the story was told that several years before, barely arrived in the metropolis from his native and more conservative Leiden, the young man's aptitudes underwent a scandalously definitive test: the rich businessman Nicolaes Ruts, the king of the leather business, the nearly exclusive seller of Siberian pine martens—more expensive than gold, even more than multicolored tulip bulbs—wanted a portrait made by that "kid" who was so talked about and who was even considered the new promise of Northern painting. That debut in the circle of the powerful, that God and the already visible talents of the young painter put in his path, turned out to be spectacular enough to leave the city's art merchants and connoisseurs with their mouths hanging open. Because the portrait of Ruts constituted, despite the few means utilized, the best possible representation of the businessman—powerful, sure of himself, but removed by ideology and faith from the siren song of ostentation. If the Nicolaes Ruts portrayed was covered in the fur of a pine marten drawn hair by hair, as pine marten had never been drawn, in an appropriation capable of carrying out the magic act of transmitting through the contemplation of the softness and warmth the pelt offered to the touch, it was because there was no one better than Nicolaes Ruts to wear one of those items. From there: the self-assured and calm gaze with which the businessman, covered by the coveted fur, looked at the spectators who were fortunate enough to see the canvas. And those who had seen it were other rich people in Amsterdam who socialized with Ruts and wore their expensive cloaks, those opulent ones who would take care of turning the portrait into a legend and into the work capable of fueling the trend so that, for ten years, those same rich people in Amsterdam would request the art of the young Maestro to immortalize themselves in the way that the city had determined to be the best possible one.

A few minutes after receiving the order to stay in the studio, Elias Ambrosius had the privilege of being able to observe how the Maestro, following a long contemplation, took the thin paintbrush and, without ceasing to look at himself in one of the mirrors, began to work on what would be his eyes.

"If you are capable of painting yourself and putting the expression you desire in your eyes, you are a painter," he said at last, without ceasing to move his paintbrush, without taking his eyes off of his work. "The rest is dressing up . . . Stains of colors, one next to the other . . . But painting is much more, kid . . . Or should be . . . The most revealing of all human stories is the one that is described on the face of a man . . . Tell me, what am I seeing?" he asked, and before the silence of his aspiring apprentice, he answered himself. "A man who ages, who has suffered too many losses and aspires to freedom that eludes him once and again, although he will not give in without a fight . . ." Only then did the Maestro move, to better accommodate his bottom. "Take a good look. There, along with the face, on the spectator's side, is where you should put the point of light. That way, you avoid a contour that is too neat on the other cheek. With that, you achieve breaking attention from the face as a whole. What matters are the features, especially the eyes, where you should find spirit and character. Starting with . . ."

The Maestro interrupted his monologue, as if he had forgotten he was speaking, because he was now working with gray and sienna in search of the form of the eyelid, rather thick, perhaps a bit fallen. Too fallen, he seemed to decide, and tried it again, after running his finger over the linen.

"The eyes are defined by shadows, not by light . . ." He took up his speech again and, for the first time, turned around to look at the young Jew. "The portrait is an event in time, a remembrance of the present that we visualize and eternalize. Tomorrow, I want to know what I'm like, or what I was like today, and that is why I am portraying myself . . . When you portray someone else, it becomes more complicated. It is no longer a dialogue between two people, but rather three: the painter, the customer, and the image of himself that that customer demands, weighed down with all of the social conventions that the person portrayed aims to satisfy . . . But when you paint yourself, only you are speaking to the spectator. It's like getting naked in public: what stands before you is what there is . . ."

The Maestro had again turned his back to Elias Ambrosius and focused on looking in the mirror that reflected his profile. "What about you, what are you looking for in painting?" he asked, and leaned his hand holding the paintbrush on his thigh as he moved his gaze in search of the mirror reflecting the young Jew, as if demanding a response this time.

"I don't know," Elias confessed, willing to say the truth, and for that reason, added: "I only know that I like it."

"That I already know: a man who is willing to be humiliated, mistreated, and even marginalized in order to achieve something; who pays thirty florins to sweep the house, do the errands, and throw out shit in the canal, because he hopes to learn something; who risks suffering the dogmatic fury of other men, which is, incidentally, the worst fury in the world . . . can only do so for something that he likes very much. But that thing about liking is fine for a lover, or a businessman, or even for a politician. Not for the minister in a church, like my friend Anslo, or for a fanatic of messianism, like my friend Menasseh . . . Nor is it sufficient for a painter, either. What else? Glory? Fame? Money?"

Elias Ambrosius thought that all of those things were appetizing and, of course, he desired them; but he also knew that they were not destined for him and that he would never achieve them with a paintbrush in his hand. If a maestro like Steen had to run a tavern where he sold beer, if Van Goyen was nearly a beggar, if Pieter Lastman had died forgotten, to what could he aspire?

"I want to be a good Jew," he said at last. "I'm not interested in bothering my people, or giving them any motive to become furious or to condemn me. I think that I want to paint only because I like it. I don't know if I have a gift, but if God has given me one, there is a reason. The rest is my will, which is also a gift from God the Holiest, who gave me the Law, but also intelligence and the option to choose."

"Think less about God and more about yourself and that will." The Maestro seemed to be interested in the subject. He left the paintbrush on the palette and turned around to look at the young man: "Here in Amsterdam, everyone talks about God, but very few count on Him to make their livings. And I think that's the best thing that could happen to us. We humans should resolve our human problems ourselves . . . Calvin, who read your Jewish Bible too much, also thought that doing what I do is a sin. But if I sin or not, that's my problem, not that of other Calvinists. Because, at the end of the day, I have to resolve it on my own with God, and in the end, neither the preachers nor the priests nor the rabbis are going to help me . . . For an artist, all commitments are a burden: with his church, with a political group, even with his country. They reduce your space for freedom, and without freedom there is no art . . ."

Elias was listening, and although he had his own judgment about that opinion, he preferred to remain in silence: he was there to listen, to see, perhaps to ask, and only to respond if it was demanded of him.

"Pour me a glass of wine," the Maestro requested, and when he received it, he took a loud sip. "Your people have suffered a lot for too long, and it is all the fault of the same God that some men see one way and others in a different way . . . If here in Amsterdam the people admit that each one believes in his God and interprets the same sacred words different ways, you should take advantage of that opportunity, which is unique in the history of man and, incidentally, I don't think it will last for too long or that it will again repeat itself for a long time, because it is not normal: there will always be some illuminated ones willing to appropriate the truth and try to impose that truth on everyone else . . . I am not enjoining you to do anything, just to think: freedom is the greatest good man has, and not practicing it, when it would be possible to practice it, is something that God cannot ask of us. Giving up freedom constitutes a terrible sin, practically an offense to God. But you should already know that everything comes with a price. And that of freedom tends to be very high. For aspiring to it, even where there is freedom, or where they say there is freedom—which ends up being more common—man can suffer a lot, because there are always other men who, just as it occurs with ideas about God, understand freedom in different ways, and these men reach the extreme of thinking that their way is the only right one, and with their power decide that everyone else has to practice it that same way . . . And that ends up being the end of liberty: because nobody can tell you how you should enjoy it . . ."

"The rabbis say we are lucky because we are in the land of freedom."

"And they are right. But I think that the word 'freedom' has lost a lot of currency . . . Those same rabbis are the ones who force you to fulfill the laws of God, but also the laws that they themselves have dictated, assuming that they are the interpreters of divine will. It is the rabbis, as they ponder freedom, who would mercilessly punish you if they knew you were here . . . Even if it's just because you like painting and not because you aim to be an idolater . . ." He left the glass on the auxiliary table where he placed the jars of paint. "Think, kid, there has to be something more than desire to dare to do what you are trying to do . . . Listen well: if there is no supreme goal, it's better to save yourself the thirty florins . . . Or spend them on one of those Indonesian whores who are rightly so coveted." The Maestro looked to the side and, as if he were surprised, noticed a figure in the mirror. "At your age, that's what I would recommend. Now go." He recovered his paintbrush, turned around, and studied the lines drawn on the cloth. "I'm going to continue with the eyes. Remember what I told you: everything is in the eyes."

"Thank you, Maestro," the young man whispered and left the studio.

———

Everything is in the eyes, he told himself, and he looked at them in the surface of the mirror he had bought and taken up to the attic. On the

improvised easel, where he had nailed a sheet of paper, the white surface was unsullied. Why was he going to attempt it? The Maestro was
right: he must have a reason, a deep and elusive basis, as difficult to
pinpoint as a convincing gaze on a virgin surface. Although that reason
lay somewhere within that hunt for what was out of reach for the majority of men, in what was possible only for the chosen. Elias Ambrosius,
looking at himself in the eyes through the polished surface of the cheap
mirror, was asking himself questions, since he knew that, just at that
moment, he was at the threshold and, if he crossed it, he had to do so
with a response in his consciousness. Until that moment, his exercises
with the charcoal on remains of paper had been part of a juvenile game,
the manifestation of an innocent whim, the riverbed of a small, pleasant
brook of a hobby without consequences. Not now: in his hands was
beating a reason, an intentional possibility that, at the end of the day,
did not care too much if it was made public or not. In reality, all that
mattered was whether something was carried out before the eyes of He
who Sees Everything. He would only transcend if he exercised that act
that implied his free will and, with it, the fate of his immortal soul: the
choice of obedience or disregard, of submission to the ancient letter of
the Law, or the election of a freedom to choose with which that same
Creator had gifted him. The submission could end up being comfortable
and certain, although bitter, and his people knew that well; freedom
could be risky and painful, but sweet; the peace of his soul, a blessing
but also a prison. Why did he want to do it if he knew everything he
would put in the balance? That Salom Italia who had engraved the image of Hakham ben Israel on a sheet, had he had the same doubts? And,
what responses had he given himself to dare to sully the sheet's purity
and turn it into the basis of an image of a torso, a face, human eyes? Had
he felt, like him, the crouching fear and so many, many doubts?

Elias always marveled at the series of circumstances and decisions
that had brought him to that attic in a city considered by those expelled from Sepharad as the New Jerusalem and where those of his race
were enjoying an unprecedented tolerance that allowed them to pray in
peace each Saturday, gather by the lights of the menorah, read the rolls
of the Torah at their ancestral feasts, and practice without greater fear
the right of Brit Milah—circumcision—or the bar mitzvahs that initiated one into adulthood. And, at the same time, they could enrich their
pockets and their minds and be respected for their wealth of gold and

ideas, since ideas and gold, simultaneously, made the welcoming city shine. The good place, *Makom*. Amsterdam, a metropolis that was growing by the hour, where one could always hear the friction of a handsaw, the beating of a hammer, the scraping of shovels, the same city that just two centuries before was little more than a swamp full of reeds and mosquitoes and now took pride in being the world capital of money and commerce and where, as such, making money was a virtue, never a sin . . . So that that could happen and Elias could pose these piercing questions, a war had to occur that was still ongoing between Catholics and Christians divorced from the Roman pontiff, between monarchists and Republicans, between Spaniards and the citizens of the United Provinces before that unexpected door was opened in Amsterdam to tolerance and to some Jews who, in the name of God, some monarchs had expelled from what those Jews had already considered their land. The suffering and humiliation also had to erupt, and the blood of many sons of Israel had to run. Many other Jews had to reject their faith, deny their customs, lose their cultures with the conversion to the adoration of Jesus or of Allah to save their lives (and properties), so that a man like Elias could be in that place, enjoying the freedom to ask himself whether he should carry out the act of crossing the threshold or not to which his spirit, his will, and that elusive reason, still imprecise, were leading him. His grandfather Benjamin Montalbo de Ávila, who was able to bring the family back to their faith, had to exist, and there had to exist the heart-breaking experience of that pious man who spent many years as a Christian without being so, tormented by the secret that each Friday, when the night's first star shone, his father would whisper in his ear *"Shabbat shalom!"* and who lived disguised in a hostile environment . . . All of this so that Elias Ambrosius could receive, nearly through his bloodline, the conviction that, more basic than the social demonstrations of belonging, attendance at a synagogue, or obedience to the precepts of the rabbis, was man's interior identification with his God: in other words, with himself and with his ideas . . .

But, above all, so that he could be there, fear had to exist. That permanent, oppressive, infinite fear, also inherited, a fear that even Elias, born in Amsterdam, knew very well. It was that invincible fear that what was his could end at any moment, and that repression, exterior or interior, could arrive once again. Or that there would be an expulsion and, any morning, the club would be used again or the bonfire would burn anew, as so many times had happened throughout the centuries. That petty and very real fear for him had to exist so that he, too, could be afraid of the extremes to which men could go, who, from the seats of power, proclaimed themselves pure, to be the shepherds of collective destinies, there, in Amsterdam, where all prided themselves on the existence of so much freedom.

Elias Ambrosius continued looking in the mirror, observing his eyes (light and shadow, life and mystery), and vowed that he would not allow himself to be conquered by fear. If he was there, if he was truly free, if all of the strength of seventeen years were with him, he should take advantage of that extraordinary privilege of having been born and still living in a city where a Jew could breathe in a freedom that for centuries was unimaginable for those of his line, and that, in his case, included the grace of the proximity of a rebellious man, a painter who was already predestined to be one of the great maestros, a giant on the altar of Apelles. Elias knew that, if he learned of his purposes, his grandfather Benjamin would not celebrate him but would not condemn him, either: the old man had lived in his own flesh all of the imaginable vexations for believing in something and, despite being a devout Jew, he was also a committed defender of freedom and of the respect for others' choices that this demanded. Elias also sensed that his father, Abraham Montalbo, would suffer, would be sorrowful, but would not repudiate him, since his open mind, thanks to the books he read (with much discretion, he and his grandfather sent for the literature they most enjoyed from Spain and Portugal), to the books they printed and distributed around half the world, permitted him to have a tolerant relationship with everyone else, since he himself was tolerated and knew something of intolerance. At the same time, he was convinced that his brother Amos, saved by the decisions and risks of his elders from having suffered repression or violent contempt, and who perhaps due to that circumstance had been infected with the most orthodox ideas, could be the source of his misfortune. Like those parrots arrived from Surinam, Amos tended to repeat the words of the men who advocated that only the strict fulfilling of sacred Law and full obedience of the illuminated Talmudic precepts could save the sons of Israel in a world that was still dominated by Gentiles: the words that those same men capable of condemning a son with a *niddui* because he maintained a relationship with his father who was living in Portugal or in Spain—again the feared lands of idolatry of which, despite everything, so many Jews still dreamt, with which many of those same supposed Orthodox Jews, capable of condemning others, engaged in commerce and enriched themselves. Elias knew it: his own brother was the one who could come to accuse him before the council of the Mahamad, become his pursuer, perhaps even his prosecutor, sure that with his action he was fulfilling his responsibility as a good representative of his people.

In the mind of the entire Jewish community of Amsterdam—and beating like a drum in Elias Ambrosius's mind each day—still floated the echoes of the process expelling Uriel da Costa, sentenced by the rabbinical council (including Hakham ben Israel!) to a lifelong *cherem* that implied the cutting off of all communication with the entire community, a true civil death. Da Costa had been sentenced for the sin of publicly proclaiming that the precepts of the rabbis gathered in the Talmud and the Mishnah, as far as men were concerned, were not the supreme truths that they proclaimed, since that privilege belonged only to God. Da Costa had demanded a separation of religious commandments from civil and legal ones, and had even dared to propose an individual relationship between the believer and his God (the same as was advocated in the heart of Elias's family by his grandfather Benjamin), a communication in which the religious authorities had only the role of facilitators and not of regulators. And for that he had been accused of disqualifying the Halakha, the ancient religious law, as such, a code dedicated not just to regulating religious conduct, but also private and public conduct.

Then that man who was so daring had reached the extremes of his naïveté when he proclaimed, during the summary of his excommunication, the hope that his brothers, the same rabbis whose ancestral power he was attacking, would have "an understanding heart" and be capable of "wisely meeting with firm judgments," as thinking beings, sons of a very different time to that of the primitive patriarchs and prophets, creatures who broke out of the darkness of the origins of civilization, nomads who adored idols and wandered through the deserts. The dramatic process, during which Da Costa was accused of being an agent of the Vatican's powers, in which the rabbinical tribunal humiliated him and vilified him, had ended with the pronouncement of that lifelong *cherem*, read by Rabbi Montera, who among other horrors declared that "with the judgment of the Angels and the sentence of the saints, we anathematize, execrate, curse, and expel Uriel da Costa, pronouncing against him the anathema with which Joshua condemned Jericho, the curse of Elijah and all of the curses written in the book of the Law. May he be cursed by day and cursed by night; cursed when he goes to bed, rises, goes out, and comes in. May the Lord never forgive him or recognize him! May the Lord's anger and disgust burn against that man from here on and rain down upon him all of the curses written in the book of the Law and erase his name beneath the sky . . . As such, we warn everyone that no one should address him by spoken word or communicate with him in writing, that no one should offer him any services, live under the same roof as him, or get any closer to him than four elbows' distance . . ."

Elias could well remember how, as Rabbi Montera read the inquisitorial excommunication, the synagogue where the members of the Nação squeezed together had been inundated by the prolonged moan of a great horn that could be heard here and there, each time more hoarse and duller. With those eyes that now looked in the mirror, the adolescent Elias Ambrosius, clinging to the hand of his grandfather and trembling in fear, had seen how the lights of the ritual candelabra, intense at the beginning of the ceremony, had extinguished themselves as the reading of the *cherem* progressed, until the last one went out when the horn fell mute: with the silence and the agony of the light the spiritual life of the sentenced heretic was also extinguished.

The bombastic process, directed against Uriel da Costa but in many ways against all of Amsterdam's disobedient and heterodox, had aimed to plant a seed of fear in those who could have the daring to think in a way that was not that decreed by the powerful community leaders, proclaimed by tradition as the owners of the only admissible interpretations of the Law. It was that pernicious and ubiquitous fear of suffering a similar fate, of course, that at that moment beat in the hand of young Elias Ambrosius, armed with charcoal, as he observed his eyes in the mirror and contemplated the formidable white paper spread out on a crude easel. Would he assume that risk merely because he liked painting? The Maestro knew it and now Elias Ambrosius, too, knew it: yes, something else had to exist, *there had to be* something else. Would Hakham ben Israel know what it could be? Salom Italia, who had gone through the mirror, had he discovered what that something else was? Elias Ambrosius had a hint of the mystery when his hand, obeying a mandate that seemed to come from a source placed well beyond his conscience and his fears, grafted on the empty surface the first line of what would be the eye. Because everything is in the eyes. The eyes of a man who weeps.

The mystery, he knew at that moment, was called power: the power of Creation, the impulse of transcendence, the force of beauty that no legal authority could conquer.

2

New Jerusalem,
Year 5405 Since the Creation,
1645 of the Common Era

Time moved quickly and, contrary to what he had imagined or pre-dicted, Elias Ambrosius was far from feeling happy. Sometimes the feel-ing of misfortune brushed against him enigmatically, like a stab of guilty conscience, and the young man again asked himself: Is it worth it? Other times, it did so with animosity, forcing him to do his accounting in practical terms: money, time, results, satisfactions, risks, accumulated fears . . . He counted on his fingers, although many times he tried to keep money out of the equation, so that no one, not even himself, could accuse him of reacting from a perspective that was too Jewish, although there was more than enough proof that in Amsterdam not only the Jews lived obsessed with money. A French writer living in that city had said it well, a certain René Descartes, who had also been considered a heretic by those of his faith, to whom was attributed the phrase that, except him, everyone in the metropolis was dedicated only to making money . . .

Elias experienced a few disastrous days, full of that sadness, as he added up his doubts and convictions; the young man even arrived at the decision: no matter how much of a maestro the Maestro was, no matter how famous he had been a few years before, and despite the fact that he, Elias Ambrosius, believed him to be the greatest painter in the city and even in the known world—two years mopping floors, gathering shit and carrying peat, receiving more orders and reprimands from the scowling Mme. Dircx than advice from the Maestro (with the not negligible pay-ment of thirty florins, because yes, it was pertinent to include money, which was firmly demanded when he fell behind on a payment), in contrast to the few conversations that the painter, when he was in a good mood, could gift to any visitor or buyer—made up more than enough reasons to consider the possibility of putting an end to that dangerous adventure.

Elias Ambrosius could not deny that proximity to the Maestro and his environment, that world where everything was thought and expressed, with a nearly sickening recurrence, in terms of painting (technically, physically, philosophically, and even financially), had already made him another man and, even if just to live humiliated by his own misfortune, he would never again be who he once was: he knew greatness, he had received the light and warmth of a genius and, above all, had learned that greatness and genius, when mixed with the propensity to challenge and the will to exercise freedom from criteria, could (or tended to? he hesitated) lead to disaster and frustration.

But what did that knowledge do for him? The young Jew was thinking about his situation and weighing his drastic decision with more determination on those nights on which, facing a piece of clumsily stained linen, he convinced himself that, no matter the effort dedicated to absorbing everything he saw or heard, and despite his enthusiasm and tenacity, there was still lacking between his brain and that challenging surface something of the undoubted emanation of divine grace that he, it seemed clear, would never possess: true talent. And if his whole life was going to be mediocre, it wasn't worth the expenses, the humiliations, and the weight of a secret that he couldn't trust even his best friends with. For a mediocre painter, he told himself, the affronts and fears he'd accumulated were already enough.

That cold afternoon on which his life would experience an unpredictable and encouraging jolt, the recurring idea of giving up had followed him like a tenacious dog while, sinking his feet into the recently fallen snow, he headed to the Maestro's house. But an imprecise agitation, as intangible as a premonition, prevented him from taking the step that, like others taken in his short life, he knew would be definitive.

The new maid in the house, the young Emely Kerk, was the one who opened the door, and Elias Ambrosius approached the stove of the neighboring room to try to rid himself of the cold he'd accumulated during the walk. In an almost automatic way, he thought, seeing flames flicker and the metallic container for the peat nearly empty, that that afternoon they would order him to go to Nieuwemarkt to advise the provider that he was required at number 4 Jodenbreestraat. Elias Ambrosius was preparing himself to go down to the kitchen to change his heavy clothing for the old work shirt and collect his daily weapons, the bucket and the broom, when the Maestro came out of his room and, after placing in one cheek one of those melted sugar sticks that had caused and would cause so many toothaches (those sticks which, he assured, he would not be able to give up), he looked at him and said, "Don't change your clothes, today *you* are coming with me."

At that moment, without being able to guess what still awaited him, Elias Ambrosius had the certainty that—whatever the possibility was—those magic words placed his relationship with the Maestro on another level of proximity in one fell swoop. And he immediately forgot about the well-worn decision, as if it had never existed.

Of all his habits, the Maestro's preference to go out in the morning to make his purchases was known. Always, around ten in the morning, he chose one or two students, according to his intentions, and took up going around to different stores that could best meet his peculiar demands. The adventure finished around twelve thirty, generally at the food stand that an Indonesian couple with lots of kids had set up in the port, and where, alongside black stevedores, English and Norwegian sailors, Magyar and German mercenaries, and other extraordinary characters (Indians from Surinam selling parrots or dark Jews from Ethiopia dressed in pre-Christian attire), one could observe faces, dress, and gestures, as he took delight in eating the dishes of meat with seasonal vegetables, overflowing with flavors and aromas evoking mysterious remote worlds, delicacies prepared by those two beings with ashy skin and bodies as flexible as swamp reeds. Depending on the Maestro's mood, the students accompanying him—ever since his favorite, Carel Fabritius, had left the workshop to try out his luck as an artist, he almost always chose his brother Barent, who was bad at painting but good at carrying, and sometimes he also took Keil the Dane, other times Samuel van Hoogstraten or the recently arrived Constantijn Renesse—followed him to the unpolished wood tables belonging to the Indonesians, or he ordered them to return with the acquired materials. In any case, participating in those excursions was considered a privilege among the apprentices, who, upon returning, displayed the new provisions to the others and narrated, if they had existed, the Maestro's chats with his providers or with the crowds at the port.

Without ceasing to keep in mind the difference in his situation and that of the other students who were admitted as such (the oldest of whom, having overcome certain prejudices, already considered him *nearly* an equal), Elias Ambrosius, while simultaneously obsessing about his doubts and fears, had begged his God for almost two years to one day (just one day!) hear the order that would individualize him, at least as a human being. The reason that the painter had not gone out in the morning, it was easy to surmise, was due to the fact that, from dawn until midday, a persistent snow had been falling. Although, the young man also knew, at the same time that he had started smiling again, the Maestro had spaced out his morning outings to the street, ever since, a few months before, around his house started to flutter the young figure of Emely Kerk, hired part-time as Titus's governess, an impossible responsibility for Mme. Dircx, given her scarce relationship to literacy. But the important thing was not the reason, but rather the choice, since with all certainty, in the attic's stalls there would still be working some of the students, who paid the required one hundred florins: like other times, the Maestro's order could have been that Elias himself go to the upper floor and tell one or some of the apprentices that he was ready, about to go. But this afternoon, he had chosen *him*.

When Elias's mood changed (and sometimes this happened easily, thanks to a talk the Maestro dedicated to him, or over the discovery of a new capacity to paint something that until then had eluded him or at the prospect of a meeting with Mariam Roca, the girl who for a few months had attracted him almost as much as painting), the young man placed in the balance the fact that throughout those two years—full, it was true, of surprises, fears, and disappointments—he had also come to know, for a more than modest price, the joys of learning in the most prestigious workshop in Amsterdam and in the Republic. Elias Ambrosius recognized in the entrance that he had crossed the rocky stretch of sidereal ignorance to that of knowing how much he had to learn if he aimed to turn his obsessions into works and prove, with the necessary instruments, the qualities of his possible talent (which had suddenly grown in his own opinion when those circumstances arose, more by virtue of the waves of euphoria that ran through his spirit than because of concrete work). The Maestro's conversations with his students that he had been witness to, the careful curiosity with which Elias approached them to interrogate them without appearing to, and the open voracity with which he devoured the occasions on which the painter addressed him, as well as the fact of having been witness to the birth, growth, and conclusion of several works by that genius (he had been fascinated by the portrait of Emely Kerk, whom he had placed in a pose as if she were looking out of a window; and on two occasions Elias had even prepared his palette for the piece he had been painting for months, a mundane domestic representation of the Christian Sacred Family at the moment of being visited by some angels), each propitious circumstance allowed him to further penetrate a world much more fabulous than he had imagined, and, for him, definitively magnetic, despite all of its sorrows . . . Because of that, from the charcoal and paper of the past, he had gone on to experiment on card stock with watercolors, sketching with the Maestro's characteristic large and simple lines and, for a few months already, to painting on linen, the cheapest ones, bought on occasion as scraps, to which he applied himself in an abandoned room, found out past Prinsengracht, the remote Prince's Canal, since he feared that the unmistakable smell of linseed oil would betray him if he worked with it in the attic.

Several times, he had had to lie when a friend or someone in the house asked him about his work in the Maestro's workshop: the pretext that he worked as a cleaning boy fulfilling the request of his former Hakham ben Israel, a great friend of the painter's, was sufficient to inform his grandfather (anything having to do with Ben Israel seemed appropriate to him), calm down his father (although he did not understand why his son, with two jobs, was always short on money), and, for the moment, trick Amos and his own friends, or, at least, aim to do so.

That joyous afternoon, when they went out, Jodenbreestraat looked like a white carpet rolled out to receive them. The snow collectors had still not begun their task and the path was only marked by the footprints of some passersby. When they went down to the street, the Maestro took a right, to go up to Meijerplein, and, immediately, Elias knew that something had happened, an event capable of putting the painter in a good mood: only thus could he explain to himself the loquaciousness with which the man surprised him in the first yards they covered. As they walked, sinking to the ankles of their boots in the still-soft snow, the Maestro devoted himself to telling Elias how he had met each one of his Jewish neighbors—Salvador Rodrigues, the Pereira brothers, Benito Osorio, Isaac Pinto, and, of course, Isaías Montalto, all favored for their opulence—in whom he admired the capacity to maintain their faith in the midst of greater adversities and, of course, to multiply florins. Without transition, he went on to reveal his theory, many times discussed with Ben Israel and some of those Sephardic neighbors, about why Amsterdam's citizens maintained that close relationship, more than tolerance, with the members of the Sephardic Nação: "It is not because your people and my people are enemies of Spain, nor because you help us become more wealthy. Spain has more than enough enemies and we don't need business partners. It's not because we are more understanding and tolerant, either, or even close to it: it's because the Dutch are as pragmatic as you are and we identify with the history of the Hebrews to improve and adorn our own, to give it a mystical dimension, as our friend Ben Israel says so well. In two words: Protestant pragmatism."

Elias Ambrosius knew that the Maestro had a difficult relationship with the creators of the myths about the history of the United Provinces and with the most active and radical Calvinist preachers. The fiasco in which, a few years before, the commission of a painting devoted to celebrating the union of the Republic (still involved in its infinite war against Spain) had devolved and had damaged the painter's relationship with the country's authorities. The work, which should have been on display in the royal palace of The Hague, was never finished, since the promoters of the commission, warned by the sketches, considered that the Maestro's interpretation did not meet with the demands or with the historic reality as they understood it and, much less, with the patriotic spirit that it should exalt. On the other hand, his friendship with the problematic preacher Cornelis Anslo was also public, as was his active participation in a Mennonite sect, propagators of a return to the simplifying and natural ways supported by the Scriptures. His new and capricious sympathy for the Arminianists, defenders of adhering to the original spirit of the Protestant reform and much more liberal than the pure Calvinists, was now very well-known. As if that bunch of heterodox or orthodox attitudes weren't enough, the Maestro prided himself on his dynamic and spiritual closeness with the Jews and even with Catholics: he was a friend of Steen the painter, who professed that faith; also of the city's most sought-after architect Philips Vingboons, a frequent visitor at the house on Jodenbreestraat. All of those challenges had made of him a man at the limits of what was tolerable by the ideological rectors of his society, who apprehensively looked at an artist always fighting against what was established, an artist who was too much of a transgressor of the accepted.

When they reached the Meijerplein, Elias Ambrosius would know where their first stop would be and, soon, the reason for the Maestro's euphoria. At one of the plaza's angles, in front of the terrain acquired by the Spanish and Portuguese Jews to carry out the dream of raising a synagogue, at last conceived as such and projected as a challenging modern version of Solomon's Temple, was the store of Herman Doomer, a German who specialized in the making of hard ebony frames, who also offered supports in other less noble woods and even blackened whalebone, a cheaper substitute. The relationship between business and painter was very close since, a few years prior, the Maestro had done a portrait of Doomer, while his son, Lambert, had spent some time as an apprentice in the workshop—seemingly without too much success. Because of their closeness, the German always gave the Maestro the best prices and the most beautiful woods he had.

His greeting of a friend and favorite client was as warm as could be expected from a man who was as Lutheran German as could be. He included not the usual invitation to beer or wine but rather a cup of the infusion that was beginning to become fashionable in the United provinces: coffee come from Ethiopia, a luxury that few could permit themselves. Standing at a prudent distance, savoring his cup of black liquid sweetened with molasses, Elias Ambrosius followed the two men's conversation and at last understood the reasons for the Maestro's euphoria: the stadtholder Frederik Hendrik de Nassau, supreme magistrate of the Republic, had commissioned two new works from the painter, and, of course, for that order, the frames had to be of the highest quality (regardless of the price, which, at the end of the day, would be charged to the powerful customer).

Like all in the know about the interstices in the country's art world, the young Jew was aware of the rumors that aimed to explain the end, seemingly turbulent, of the relationship of business and sympathy between the gentleman from The Hague and the Maestro from Amsterdam. Six years before, after concluding *Resurrection*, the third of the paintings commissioned by the stadtholder representing the Passion of Christ (he had before turned in *Ascension* and, nearly along with the last one, *Burial*), the Maestro had written to the prince humbly but in very clear terms, suggesting that, instead of the six hundred florins agreed to, he pay him a thousand for each one of the last two paintings—taking into account, according to the Maestro's thinking, that his prices in the market had gone up in the last two, three years, along with the complexity and quality of the works. The stadtholder's response came with a bill of exchange for the agreed-to sum and a reprimand for all the time, excessive in his opinion, that he had had to wait for the works . . . And it was marked with a pernicious silence as the only rebuttal to the new letters sent by the Maestro. With that affair and with the immediate rejection of his projected painting about the union of the Republic, the artist had seen his dreams crumbling of becoming, like that Rubens he envied, loved, and hated so much, a famous painter of the court, owner of estates and art collections.

Ever since his wife's death, which so affected his spirits, and since the confusion and alarm that the Maestro's work for the *grote zaal* at Kloveniersburgwal created among potential customers, but above all, since the scandalous judicial dispute to which Andries de Graeff, equally rich as he was stupid, subjected him for considering that the portrait he commissioned the painter, for which he had paid the enormous sum of five hundred florins, was far from seeming finished and even offering any likeness with his person, the levels of demand for the Maestro had visibly fallen. Amsterdam's powerful no longer lined up to be immortalized by that always problematic and strong-willed painter, and his commissions now went to the hands of more docile artists—of which there were dozens to choose from in the city—whose paintings were more polished and light-filled. Following those setbacks, the Maestro's momentum had lessened and, to anyone who knew him, it could seem evident that his most recent commissions (in which he had resorted more than usual to the help of Carel Fabritius and the young Aert de Gelder) were elegant works, well determined, but scarcely personalized and barely worthy of his genius. Although it was also true, as Elias Ambrosius could testify, that his work that was less committed to reigning tastes, less concerned with pleasing, had been turning deeper, more free and personal. And there was another portrait to prove it: that of Emely Kerk, young, unpretentious, and earthy, looking out a window from which she offered a palpable sensation of *truth*. With his thwarted dreams of reaching the court, the Maestro had freed himself at last of the most difficult burden he'd been dragging along for several years: that of the mundane example, the out-of-control pictorial drama, and the imagery that was overwhelming but always pleasing to the tastes of the Flemish Rubens's patrons. He had made himself more free.

Elias Ambrosius trembled when he heard the price of the ebony frames, almost six quarters high and one ell wide, but when he heard that the works would be sold for one thousand two hundred florins each, he had the sense that the money to pay for the most luxurious frames was not going to be a problem for that noble customer and that the Maestro, always capable of squandering on his whims more than he earned with his work, would be giving a rest to his turbulent finances, which prompted so much discussion over expenses with Mme. Dircx.

When they went back out to the street, the rushed winter twilight had fallen over the white square, but the Maestro's enthusiasm remained unaltered, or perhaps powered by two cups of the dark and reviving infusion offered by Mr. Doomer. The man looked around, as if only thinking about his next steps at that moment, and he seemed to make the decision: "We're going to drink a beer here around the corner . . . Then we'll visit Isaac Pinto. But before, I want to finish explaining what I was telling you."

Behind the Maestro, Elias, nearly strutting, entered the Meijerplein tavern, to his dismay much less crowded than the always overflowing ones in De Waag, the Dam, or the area around the port: *See, gentlemen, here I am drinking dark beer with the great Maestro,* he thought, looking at the patrons, the majority of them too inebriated at that point in the day to notice the recently arrived men. With the beer served in hammered tin pitchers and as he devoured a piece of salted herring, the Maestro sought to pick up the thread of his previous speech about the construction of his country's mystic destiny, and explained to his near-student: "As I was saying . . ." He swallowed the herring, drank half a pitcher of beer, and went on. "It's true that we have behind us a century of exodus from the Catholic South toward the Calvinist North and of wars with the greatest imperial power that has ever existed. We also have the relationship with a poor land that we have made flourish and, because it is a small but ambitious country, a very strong feeling of predestination. It is not strange then that we consider ourselves a chosen people . . . Perhaps by God or by history, perhaps by ourselves, but by someone. If not, how would you explain that this New Jerusalem, as your people call it, has been able to turn itself into the richest, most cosmopolitan, most powerful city in the world . . . ?" He drank the rest of his beer in one gulp and lifted the pitcher to order another. "Ever since we broke with Rome, our Calvinist mentality has preferred to understand the messianic predestination of our history through the account of your people, the Jews, a nation through which the All-Powerful has made His will on earth and in history . . . According to the book written by you yourselves . . . We turn our exodus into the same thing it was for biblical Jews: the legitimization of a great historical rupture, a break with the past that has made possible the retrospective building of a nation. An entire lesson in pragmatism . . . But the truth, the truth," the Maestro insisted, "is that this Republic constitutes the result of a combination of the incompetence and brutality of the Spanish crown with Calvinist pragmatism, but above all, the work of good business. And once the Republic that we like so much and enriches us so much was built, these conditions, the true ones, were hidden by us beneath the patriotic mythology according to which divine will was being carried out in these provinces . . . As will be carried out in Jerusalem . . ."

More calmly, he downed the second pitcher, while Elias drank his in small sips.

"Do you know why I'm telling you this whole story about well-manipulated mistakes . . . ? Well, it's to tell you the subject of the paintings that the stadtholder has commissioned . . . As you can imagine, they are two scenes related to your people and also to ours, that identify us and speak to each other: an adoration of the Messiah by the pastors, which, seen from history, can only be imagined as a Jewish picture, and a circumcision of Christ, who, at the end of the day—right?—was as Jewish and as circumcised as you are . . ."

The Maestro dug around in his pockets and placed on the table the three plackes with which he paid for what he had drunk, and looked at his companion. "Now let's go to the house of my friend Isaac Pinto. After what I have told you, what you're going to see there could help you a lot."

"Help me? To what, Maestro?" The young man wanted to know and found himself facing the other man's smile, ironic and stained by tobacco and cavities.

"To find yourself, perhaps. Or to understand why the Jewish people have survived for more than three thousand years. Let's go."

In his nineteen years of life, he had never set foot—and never would again set foot in the years he had left to live—in a house with as much brilliance, as much luxury, with such a display of silver, of shining wood multiplied by mirrors polished to perfection that could only have been made in Venice or Nuremberg, of floors shiny as only the white marble ones coming from Carrara could shine, with yellows extracted from Naples and black flecked with green of the neighboring Flanders. Everything shone brightly between the heavy curtains, without a doubt made by Persian wool and hands, as if the dwelling were on fire with prosperity and fortune. Had it not been for his own paintings and those of others that hung on the walls and provided their own shine, the house of the Maestro, in comparison with that of Isaac Pinto, would have looked like a military barracks (although it did have much in common with that).

That Jew, who had arrived to Amsterdam at more or less the same age as Elias's father Abraham Montalbo was when he disembarked in the city and with more or less the same poverty, was the living proof of the success of the Sephardic mercantile genius that the New Jerusalem had fostered. Despite the limitations imposed by the city's authorities so that the Israelites would not dedicate themselves to the traditional activities of the region and enter their most coveted guilds, Hebrew inventiveness had found unexplored spaces and, almost with a fury, exploited rubrics like the production of chocolate, the cutting of diamonds and glass, the incredibly prosperous industry of refining honey from the Americas. Soon, some of them, thanks to their centuries-old commercial wisdom and their intimate and efficient relationship with money, had begun to amass fortunes. That of Isaac Pinto, nonetheless, was of a more predictable origin: commerce with the past. Already possessing contacts and merchants on four continents—Europe, Africa, Asia, and the New World—in reality his great centers of operations were, above all, the lands of idolatry, Spain and Portugal, where he not only negotiated with relatives and friends of his family converted to Christianity and very well placed in the social registers of those territories, but also with very Catholic agents of the Iberian crowns, without other rectors from the community of Amsterdam, many of them also partners or beneficiaries of similar businesses, daring to anathematize him or even criticize him.

As a requirement of his social status, Isaac Pinto dressed, wore shoes, and cut his hair and mustache like the patricians of Amsterdam with whom he socialized as an equal. And, like them, he also decorated his house with the indispensable paintings by Dutch artists, among which Elias Ambrosius made out a landscape with cows by Aelbert Cuyp; a windmill that screamed out its belonging to Ruysdael; a still life with pheasants by Gerrit Dou, a former student of the Maestro's; and a delicate drawing by the Maestro himself, which looked more like a dream landscape than of a countryside of the real swampy Holland. At the end of the day, Isaac Pinto's success—like that of the Pereiras, or that of Isaías Montalto—turned out to be the best example of what Hebrew pragmatism could achieve in somewhat favorable conditions. Or the worst, although nobody, not even Rabbi Montera nor the recalcitrant Pole Breslau, would have dared say it thus when speaking of the powerful Isaac Pinto.

Moved by that panorama of pageantry and attracted by the smiling face of the owner of so much wealth, who, as he welcomed him in Ladino dared even to hug the famous painter, generally so standoffish, Elias Ambrosius Montalbo de Ávila better understood the speech that the Maestro had gifted him shortly before and, at the same time, explained why Isaac Pinto already felt closed in on the so-called Jewish Broad Street. As all of the members of the Nação commented in their little cliques, the businessman was having a bourgeois palace made for himself, designed by none other than the much sought-after Philips Vingboons, in the area of the new and aristocratic canals where, regardless of their particular relationships with the divine, the Jewish and Protestant owners of the world commercial routes were immigrating.

When the Maestro introduced him to his young companion, Isaac Pinto smiled and switched to Dutch. "How is Mr. Benjamin? I haven't seen him for ages," he said and shook the hand of Elias, who had barely begun to thank him for his interest in his grandfather when Pinto was already turning toward the Maestro and asking him: "It's not him, right?"

"Yes, it is him," the painter said.

Elias Ambrosius perceived Pinto's reaction of discomfort upon knowing that *he* was *him*. Surprise, opposition? Why did *he* doubt, the powerful Isaac Pinto? With the discovery of that attitude, it was the young man who perceived how a feeling of fear ran through him even when he thought that the Maestro would not be capable of placing him in a situation of danger after having covered for him for almost two years. It did not even calm him down to know that that man and his many commercial agents in Spain were the ones who devoted themselves, behind the rabbis' backs, to supplying suspicious literature, printed in the lands of idolatry, to people like his own grandfather Benjamin Montalbo.

"You have my personal guarantee, Isaac," the Maestro then said. And, without a small grimace of opposition abandoning his face, the magnate admitted, "If you say so, then it shall be," and he made a gesture, inviting them to make themselves comfortable in the armchairs covered in lustrous Chinese silk.

Elias Ambrosius knew that his role was to remain silent and wait, and he tried to fulfill this perfectly, despite the state of anxiety running through him. At that moment, a maid—a German Jew, by all appearances—came into that dazzling room, with a tray that was also dazzling because of its silver, on which was balanced a green glass bottle and three glass cups. She left the tray on the dark marble-topped table with ebony legs, and withdrew.

"You have to taste this," Isaac Pinto said to the Maestro.

"Spanish?"

"No, from Bordeaux. An exceptional harvest," the Jewish man clarified, and served the coveted drink in the three glasses. When the host went to give him his glass, Elias Ambrosius wiped his palms on his thighs, as if his hands were not worthy of receiving the Venetian cup.

"Cheers," the Maestro said, and the two men drank while the young man devoted himself to breathing in the delicate aroma, fruity but firm, of that beverage that made the Maestro exclaim, "I am not a connoisseur, but this is the best I've had in years."

"Then I have a bottle reserved for you."

Their cups emptied, Isaac Pinto stood up and looked at Elias Ambrosius, who felt diminished in the deep stuffing of his chair.

"My son, I already know your secret . . ." Pinto pointed at the Maestro. "My dear friend told me, to convince me to do what we are going to do now. But listen well, my son . . . In this Amsterdam that is so free, all of us live keeping one or several secrets. Yours is nothing in comparison to what I'm going to show you. As such, your silence is a condition that you cannot violate. If you mention it to anyone, perhaps that could force me to explain some things, but for you it would be the end of everything. And when I say everything, it's everything. Let's go. The Blessed One is with us."

Elias Ambrosius felt his fears rising before that presumed test of trust that came adorned with a clear threat. Already standing, he followed Pinto and the Maestro toward the stairs and they went up to the second floor, where a dark wooden door punctuated the room's wall. Pinto dug around in his pockets in search of the key capable of allowing entry into a room that, Elias assumed, was his office, the place from where he managed his countless and powerful businesses. The young man was not mistaken: a table with drawers, bookcases with a few books, armoires to store papers, all done by the city's best ebony workers and varnishers, occupied the space they entered. From the beginning, Elias's gaze discovered on the table a wooden ark crafted with care, fairly similar to the Aron Kodesh, the receptacle to keep the scrolls, but more luxurious than even the most luxurious one at the synagogue. The Maestro looked at Elias and then said to him:

"What you're going to see is going to make you feel better . . . Or worse, I don't know for sure, but ever since I saw it, I thought that you, too, should see it." While the Maestro spoke, Isaac Pinto, with another key, applied himself to opening that kind of ritual ark that had captured the young man's attention. To his first surprise, Elias saw that it contained, as could be expected, a roll of parchment gathered in the fashion in which the Torah was kept, although less bulky. Elias Ambrosius's mind turned into a whirlwind of speculations: if all of that mystery was related to a scroll inscribed with biblical passages, without a doubt it was because its text contained some revelation that was perhaps devastating; but the parchment, like everything in that mansion, appeared to be of the highest quality, brilliant, which eliminated the possibility of it being an antique weighed down with disturbing secrets. Moved by his expectations, the young man watched how Isaac Pinto took out the scroll with great care to place it on the table.

"Come, open it yourself," he told Elias, who, almost mechanically, obeyed the order. When he touched the parchment, he confirmed the high quality of the material. He took the wooden handle on which the book was rolled and, part of its surface barely uncovered, he knew at last that he was in for something more awe-inspiring and resounding than he could have speculated: above the image of a typical Dutch landscape, drawn in the Dutch manner, he could read, in Hebrew, that it was the book of Queen Esther. A biblical episode, designed like the scrolls of the Torah but illustrated like a Catholic Bible? He kept pulling the handle and uncovering the parchment, on which there were drawn animals, flowers, fruits, landscapes, and angels in profusion, and with a quality in the lines, perspectives, likenesses that took his breath away. At last, he raised his eyes toward those of the two men. The Maestro was smiling and commented:

"A marvel, don't you think?"

Isaac Pinto, with pride-filled seriousness, meanwhile, said, "You see why I demanded your discretion? Isn't it more than you could have imagined? Isn't it more than our rabbis would want to allow? A marvelous heresy."

As he agreed in silence, Elias Ambrosius studied several of the pictures illustrating the biblical passage and suddenly felt something like a new revelation forcefully.

"May I know who drew it?"

"No" was Isaac Pinto's response.

"He didn't sign it?"

"No," his host repeated.

"Because he's a Jew, right?"

"Perhaps. Well, let's say yes," Pinto admitted, and Elias heard a guffaw from the Maestro, who at last interjected, "You're so complicated, dammit."

Elias nodded: the Maestro was right. And then the young man said, "I know how this man calls himself," and he touched the parchment to say, "Salom Italia."

———

Facing the sea, breathing in the fetid dark waters brought by the drainage and the Norwegian smells of labored wood from the shipyard (firs of penetrating aromas for the masts, oaks and beeches for the vessels), Elias Ambrosius Montalbo de Ávila seemed to be studying the flight of the seagulls who were insistent on getting some food out of the spots of shrimp and crawfish carapaces and the heads of the herring devoured by the city and dragged by the currents of the canals to that rotting bank. But the young man's mind, in reality, was focusing great effort on the tenacious examination of possible (and even impossible) strategies to learn the true identity of that Salom Italia, who was determined to turn his life upside down.

Even knowing that he was violating the promise he had made, his first step, several weeks before, had led him to the house of Hakham ben Israel, with the weak hope of getting some information out of his teacher that was capable of placing him on the path to revealing that ubiquitous and elusive character who signed his works as Salom Italia. To Elias's surprise, the teacher's first reaction was that of feeling offended when he learned that the painter was dealing with the most affluent members of the Sephardic community without even deigning to give him the opportunity to buy the piece described with so much awe and admiration by his former student: sure, he said, that ingrate Italia had considered him incapable of affording his prices. Nonetheless, not for a moment did he seem concerned by the fact that that Jew drew a scroll—more still, as an illustration of a much-loved book of sacred history—but rather that the commercial operation was carried out behind his back, as if the object of discord were the work of one more of Amsterdam's many painters. But even so, he maintained his muteness and reiterated what he had said to Elias: Salom Italia was a *nom de plume* (or of a brush, in his case?) of a Jew whom, incidentally, he did not want to hear from at all again, ever again . . . And he concluded the conversation.

Sustained by tenuous hope, Elias turned to another front and dedicated many days to running around the city's markets where artworks were sold, in search of some piece that would fit the Jewish painter's style. On several afternoons, he carried out those pilgrimages in the company of the young Mariam Roca, with whom he was advancing little by little on the path of his amorous pretensions, but, he thought, with necessary and sure movements. Since he didn't dare confess to this beautiful young woman his true intentions during those rounds, Elias pretended that his insistence on visiting the art markets, beyond a mere lovers' outing, allowed them to enjoy the greatest exhibition of paintings, drawings, and engravings in the world. But, no matter how many landscapes and portraits he studied (he dazzled Mariam with his knowledge, fruit of an inherited fondness from his reconverted grandfather for the beautiful representations and literature of Gentiles, he told her), he was incapable of confirming whether any of those marked by unknown signatures could be, or not, the work of that Salom Italia. But, what if he sold his work under another name, or under the name of some maestro to whom he was linked, as was usual in the country's workshops? Dealing with a person who behaved with so much impudence, any alternative seemed possible, including the far-fetched one of living with two names: one for Jews (Luis Mercado, Miguel de los Ríos) and another (Louis van der Markt, Michel van der Riveren) for the Dutch society in which he had inserted himself.

Looking at the dark silver sea, Elias Ambrosius thought that, despite the failures he'd experienced, in reality he had made considerable advances in hunting down that elusive character. To his certain condition as a Jew, he could add the irrefutable fact that he was Sephardic, never a German or Polish Ashkenazi, such fanatics and retrogrades, since it was more plausible that someone of Spanish or Portuguese origin could have access to the cultural knowledge and the basic training that that artist displayed, which were, without a doubt, exquisite. He had to be, of course, a man of culture and healthy finances, with well-oiled links in order to manage moving in such complicated and simultaneously distant spheres (religious, social, economic) as those represented by Isaac Pinto and Menasseh ben Israel. But that refined Sephardic Jew, perhaps affluent and without a doubt well-connected, used his work and his name to leave other visible footprints, although these in turn were confusing: above all, the near-absolute certainty that he could not be one of the poor Jews—the majority of the community, many of them settled around Nieuwe Houtmarkt, on the island of Vlooienburg, where the Hakham lived—since his gifts, it was easy to tell, had been honed by a maestro and fed by the consumption of Italian art and by knowledge of the Dutch school. That reduced the number of possible candidates. Following that logic, the painter was either an Italian Sephardic Jew or had done his apprenticeship in Italy, because he wouldn't have chosen that peculiar pseudonym without a reason so appropriate for an artist of his style (or was the choice part of the concealment?), and he lived or had lived for years in Amsterdam or in some neighboring city. Although, the more Elias thought about it, he could also be a Marrano Jew, learned in painting during his past life as a presumed convert in Spain or Portugal. Or, he could even be a true convert, of the many who, upon arriving in Amsterdam in search of a less dangerous environment, recognized themselves as Jews, without the need any longer of hiding their Hebrew origins but who nonetheless opted to keep themselves at the margins of Judaism and its heavy social and private restrictions, bonds to which they did not

wish to return . . . He had to be, besides, a man of great personal courage, with enormous certainty in his beliefs in order not just to execute
those works exuding heresy but also to do so with such mastery and so
publicly as to gift and sell them to members of Amsterdam's richest Jewish and Calvinist households. How many men like that could there be in
the city? Elias Ambrosius understood that, with a little bit of dedication
and intelligence, perhaps he would manage to meet him, because, it was
obvious, there could not be many men like that ghost in the city, not even
in the world.

En route already to the Maestro's house, where the broom and bucket
awaited him, Elias Ambrosius crossed the Dam Square, where the fish-
mongers were fighting over the space with stone blocks, the sandbags,
and the wood destined to form the scaffolding that would be used to
grant the luster that, all said and admitted, the heart of the richest city
in the world deserved. Following the fire at the Nieuwe Kerk a few
months before, the Calvinists had decided to rebuild the temple, granting it crushing proportions, and the project included the erection of the
city's tallest bell tower, which should rise over the ostentatious cupola of
the Stadhuis, since religious power should be imposed over civil power,
at least in architectural proportions. Elias Ambrosius, always curious to
know about those city happenings, this time barely paid attention to the
movement of the master cathedral builders come from Lutecia—jealous
owners of the secrets of their profession (more secrets for that city)—
since his mind was still stubbornly focused on finding a possible path
toward that individual who was an enigma. Because the great question,
he had concluded, was not the man's identity but rather his individuality,
a concern that in one way or another obsessed all Jews. What agreement
had he come to with his soul, that Salom Italia, to decide to throw himself down that path? Did he think, like Elias himself, that his freedom
of choice was sacred for being, above all, a gift granted to him by the
Holiest? Despite that, did he attend, as Elias attended, synagogue, did
he pray accordingly and respect the Sabbath, as Elias did, and did he
follow all the laws, except one, as Elias did? That individual must have
already asked himself the questions that the young Elias still repeated,
concerning the law and his obedience, and, it was obvious, he had found
his own answers. Because while he hid behind an alias and worked clandestinely, his decision to make his work known was an open challenge

to the thousand-year-old precepts and a clear choice for his freedom of thought and action.

The afternoon on which Isaac Pinto showed him the marvelous illustrated scrolls of the book of Queen Esther, that man whose fortune and contributions to the community gave the privilege of seeming so liberal had reminded the young Elias that the origin of the decisions of man was centered in the relationship between his conscience and his arrogance, both inalienable essences of the individual. "The more you follow your conscience," Pinto had said, "the better the results you will obtain. But if you allow yourself to be guided by arrogance, the results will not be good. Following only arrogance," he then gave an example, "it's the same as the latent danger of falling in a ditch when you're walking in the dark, since you need the light of your conscience, which illuminates the way." Weren't those words a variation on the relationship between the fullness, conscience, and dignity with which we should live our lives, about which Hakham ben Israel would write upon referring to death and the intangible great beyond? Those men, so skilled at making money or speculating with ideas, were they pushing Elias in his pretensions as a creator of images?

The words of Isaac Pinto, related without a doubt to Salom Italia's artistic practice and with that of Elias Ambrosius Montalbo de Ávila himself, should point toward the concept of free will that had turned into the focus of discussion among the city's learned Jews. The fact that, in Amsterdam's permissive environment, more and more Hebrews were beginning to distinguish, or aiming to distinguish, between the terrains of religion and those of private life was—the Orthodox said—a gigantic sin tinged with the colors of heresy: yes, Judaism was a religion, although it was also a morality and an edict, and as such should govern each of man's acts, no matter how minimally or how removed from religious precepts it appeared to be, since all of those acts, in one way or another, were regulated by the Law. And a confessed heretic like Uriel da Costa and others of his ilk could say whatever they wanted, but human acts, in one way or another, have cosmic significance, since they became part of the universe of the created, gave shape to history, and carried the weight of serving to anticipate or delay the saving arrival of the Messiah, who had been awaited by the people of Israel for so long.

Elias Ambrosius would then ask himself if in reality it was possible that an insignificant being like him, by personally and privately violating the toughest interpretation of the law that in its distant time responded to the need to discipline some lost tribes, without a homeland or commandments, in the desert, was causing an imbalance in the universe with his decision and even delaying the coming of the Anointed. The young man thought it wasn't fair to make him carry that weight: he already had more than enough with the responsibility of playing with the destiny of his soul to then be forced to think about the fate of all Jews, even the fate of the created universe. Why did they associate his own freedom to decide the path of his individual life and his personal preferences with the collective destiny of an entire race, of a nation? What had been Salom Italia's response before that dilemma? Elias Ambrosius didn't know; perhaps he would never know. But he knew one thing: Salom Italia, whoever he was, had continued to paint. Clandestinely, under a mask, but he painted . . . Why shouldn't he do so? What was moving Elias to make his decision: conscience or arrogance? Or the biblical option of choosing life? Why, O Lord, why did everything have to be so difficult for a member of His chosen people?

———

The news fell like a thunderbolt in the heart of Amsterdam's Jewish community: Antonio Montesinos, barely disembarked from the brigantine that had brought him from the New World, appeared in the synagogue and, after asking that all members of the community gather there, made the devastating announcement. He, Antonio Montesinos, said before those congregated in assembly that he had reliable, irrefutable proof, confirmed with his own eyes, that the indigenous people of the lands of the Americas were the descendants, finally found, of the ten lost tribes. The businessman then narrated his journeys through the lands of Brazil, Surinam, and New Amsterdam in the north, displayed some sketches he had made, transcribed words, and, he declared, he had been able to prove that the misnamed *Indians*, by virtue of the confusion caused by Columbus, had to be the disappeared brothers from the distant days of the exile to Babylon. The fact that they would have crossed the Ocean Sea by a route that was unknown for centuries (as the Greeks conjectured, who well before had spoken of a land of Atlantis beyond the columns of Hercules) explained their disappearance. Their physical being, elegant and well built, confirmed a Semite origin. Their language, he said, and read isolated words from his notes, incomprehensible to all, was a corruption of ancient Aramaic. What other proof could be needed? The most important thing, the author of this colossal finding claimed, turned out to be that the presence of those brothers at the confines of the earth announced the most important condition necessary so that the awaited arrival of the Messiah would happen: the existence of Hebrews settled in all points of the universe, as predicted by the prophets, who considered planetary dispersion one of the inalienable demands for the Coming.

The sacred days of Passover that year were devoted to discussing the finding, qualified by some as a revelation, almost as marvelous as that received by Moses on Mount Sinai. Always divided into many factions, the community this time polarized itself in two groups: the Messianics, in reality less numerous, who supported Montesinos's conviction, and the skeptics, captained by Hakham ben Israel, who considered the voyager's presumed discovery a regrettable and even dangerous falsehood. The rabbinical council, gathered many times following the announcement, debated Montesinos's arguments, but without arriving at a definition.

For Elias Ambrosius, the commotion and war of factions, so typical of Jewish nature, became, above all, the revealing of a delicate reality: the extremes reached by the religious fanaticism of his brother Amos, who immediately had supported the group of the most apocalyptic Messianics, presided over by their spiritual guide, the Polish rabbi Breslau.

To the surprise of Grandfather Benjamin and Elias's father, Abraham Montalbo, more than skeptics, amused by what they considered to be an insane notion of that Montesinos, the young Amos appeared at the house one day announcing his enrollment in the party that, they said, would go meet the lost brothers to help them return to the faith, customs, and obedience of the Law. Elias, who was shaken as he listened to his brother's decision, was not surprised when his elders tried to dissuade Amos, but he was alarmed, and very much so, when he heard his brother's response, refusing to discuss the decision he had taken, as he regretted that his father and his grandfather maintained that heretical attitude before such a great event, a prelude to the revelation of the Messiah.

Elias, once again warned that he lived under the same roof as a fanatic so extreme as to dare to threaten his elders with divine condemnation, convinced himself of the reasons for which, even in a land of freedom, many Jews preferred to live under a mask, amid secrets, instead of living openly amid exposed truths. He understood, of course, the attitude of a man like Salom Italia and the decision to maintain his hobbies in the shadows. And, further still, he obtained the evidence of why he himself needed to cover his secret in the most hermetic way possible if he did not want to run a grave risk.

That same night, taking advantage of his brother's absence, Elias Ambrosius, as if he were carrying out a theft, removed from the house with the greatest care the notebook, the folder full of drawings, and the small linens stained with the ditherings and searches of an apprentice painter. Among the possible places to keep them well hidden, he chose at that moment the attic of Keil the Dane, in whom, he believed, he could trust. And although it was painful for him, he had to accept that he felt more protected by a man of another faith than by many of his own. More sheltered by a tolerant stranger than by his blood brother contaminated by fanaticism and intransigency and, there was no other way to qualify it, full of hate.

———

Spring was delivering itself like a gift from the Creator to the city of Amsterdam. Everything was alive again, shaking off the lethargy of ice and the aggressive winter winds that, for months, had beaten the city and oppressed its inhabitants, its animals, its flowers. While the temperatures rose without too much hurry and the rain came down frequently, the colors stretched out, divesting of their starring role the near-absolute white of snow on the rooftops and the brown of the quagmires that the streets had become where the legions of municipal collectors had still not passed. With the recovered hues, noises were also reborn and smells came back to life. To the markets returned the dog sellers, with their packs of noisy hounds and shepherds; out came the shouting vendors of spices and aromatic herbs (oregano, myrtle, cinnamon, cloves, nutmeg), as delicate to the touch and the sense of smell as they were incapable of withstanding winter temperatures without losing the perfumed warmth of their souls; the taverns opened their doors, gifting the fermented smell of malt beer and the laughter of their customers; and the purveyors of tulip bulbs returned to the city with shouts announcing promises of a flourishing of colors and later whispers of their over-the-top prices, as if they were ashamed—only as if they were ashamed—to exploit the fashion and ask exaggerated sums for a hairy onion that barely enclosed the promise of its future beauty. The voices of the traders, wagoners, barge drivers, and drunks clustered together on any corner (countless in the city where water was barely consumed, they said, to avoid certain dysentery), joined the penetrating noises of the weapon makers' workshops beating like drums, and the monotonous song of the sawmills, to form a steady racket that many times per day turned out to be covered by the quick pealing of the city's infinite church bells, which, loosened, seemed to ring more resoundingly in their mission of announcing any event. Solitary bells, towers with multiple bronze bells and musical chimes brought from Bern, announced the hours, half hours, quarter hours, the opening and closing of businesses, the arrivals or departures of boats and celebrations of Mass or burials, of baptisms and weddings delayed by the winter, and of some executions by drowning, to which the Dutch were so addicted, always as if the tolling of the metallic notification made real the fact that prompted it. In the Sint Antoniesbreestraat, on the way to the Maestro's house, in front of the building where Isaac Pinto lived, Elias Ambrosius Montalbo de Ávila stopped that midday and shared his springtime good mood with the sound (a harmonious one, indeed) of the thirty-five bells, lined up like birds on a fence, hanging from the top of the tower of Hendrick de Keyser, over the cross of the Zuiderkerk.

The young man's good mood had much to do with the season and the promising turn taken by his meetings with Mariam Roca, which had evolved from walks without any specific destination along streets and markets and from conversations that were increasingly full of deeper intentions, to the caressing of hands and whispering in ears, capable of provoking such ardor that it caused him to demand relief by rubbing himself, which led to a subsequent demand for understanding and forgiveness from the Holiest. But, more than spring and the throbbing of love and sex, the state of enthusiasm in which Elias Ambrosius lived was related to the tremendously special function that, for weeks, he had been serving in the Maestro's workshop: he was a model for the very Jewish mohel at the moment in which he was getting ready to carry out baby Jesus's circumcision, the Brit Milah ordered by Yahweh to distinguish all of the males of the chosen people.

Ever since the afternoon that the Maestro took Elias along to visit Isaac Pinto, the relationship between the painter and the apprentice had taken on a certain warmth—almost all of the warmth the Maestro's standoffish nature was capable of generating with those who were not his most intimate friends—and Elias Ambrosius, without having freed himself of the bucket and broom, had not only been promoted in the workshop's practical tasks, crushing the pigment stones with the heavy mortar and preparing colors with the precise proportions of linseed oil, but the Maestro had also devoted several conversations to him, monologues rather, in which, according to his mood, he sometimes became entangled as if losing all notion of time. Some days, he only talked about artistic subjects, such as (according to the notes of Elias Ambrosius, who was always insistent on writing down his lessons to later reread them and process them) his ideas about the need to break the established relationship between classical beauty and the feminine nude, which, in his opinion, did not need to be perfect to be feminine and beautiful, since the Maestro liked to capture wrinkled skin, cracked feet, flaccid muscles, in search of a tangible sense of authenticity that the rest of the city's artists did not approach. Other days, he dove into laying out the foundation of his peculiar understanding of harmony and elegance as qualities serving the work and not as values in and of themselves, which was the way in which the devotees of classic painting understood it, including the Flemish Rubens. No, no: that deeper sense of harmony pursued by him turned out to be the great lesson that, according to the Maestro, the painter Caravaggio had left the world; not the control over cavernous darkness upon which his followers had insisted, he asserted, incapable of seeing beyond what was apparent, but rather the revelation that truth and sincerity must be placed above canonized beauty, supposed symmetry, or the idealization of the world. "Christ, with dirty feet and open sores due to the desert sands, preached among the poor and hungry, and sat. Poverty, hunger, tears are not beautiful, but they are human." "There is no reason to shun ugliness," he would conclude, and he illustrated those digressions with the study of a *Christ Preaching*, drawn on paper, in which the speaker, curiously, lacked a defined face.

There were days, by contrast, on which the Maestro preferred to become immersed in more mundane matters, given his lack of interest in public life and, above all, politics, which he considered a dangerous temptation for the artist who seeks to appear involved. And days on which he got caught up in the obsessions of a man always in great need of money, speaking of the importance and at the same time the burden signified by the painters of the United Provinces who had become the first artists in history who didn't work for the court or the Church but rather for the type of customer who was completely different in his demands, tastes, and needs: rich men born of the benefits of commerce, speculation, large-scale manufacturing. Then he stated that those individuals, often of plebeian origins, always pragmatic and visionary, were increasingly less interested in history or mysticism. Their anxieties expressed themselves in their desire to see paintings in which their own material creations were represented: their country, their wealth, their customs, they themselves, with their jewels and clothing, satisfied at last with a fortune of which they were more proud every day. That reflection had to materialize itself on canvases of reasonable dimensions, conceived to adorn the wall of a welcoming family home instead of an overwhelming church or royal palace. And to adorn, they demanded what they considered beautiful, what they deemed to be theirs.

"We have created a different relationship for art," he had said on one of those afternoons on which, after ordering him to postpone cleaning the studio, he had demonstrated more loquaciousness with Elias Ambrosius who listened to him while nearly hypnotized by the ease with which the Maestro outlined the contours, volumes, spatial placement, and the areas of shadows of what would be the scene of the adoration of the shepherds of the baby Jesus requested by the stadtholder Frederik Hendrik de Nassau. "In the city where all are engaged in commerce, we are inventing something: the commerce of painting. We work to sell to new customers with new tastes. Do you know who the best buyer of Vermeer of Delft's is? In fact, a rich baker. A patron who sells pastries, not a bishop or a count! And chasing the money of those who call themselves burghers, be they bakers, bankers, shipbuilders, or tulip traders, painting has had to change, and has had to please the tastes of men who have never stepped inside a university. That is why specialization has appeared: for those who paint rural scenes and sell them well, then painting rural scenes it is; they could just as well paint battles, oceans, still lifes, or portraits . . . We have invented the commercial picture: each artist has to have his own and cultivate it to gather his fruits in the market, like any businessman. My problem, as you may know, is that I don't have that kind of brand, nor do I care if my painting is brilliant and harmonious, as they now want . . . I'm interested in interpreting nature, including that of man, including that of God, and not the canons; what matters to me is painting what I feel and how I feel it. As long as I can . . . Because I also have to make a living." And he pointed the end of his paintbrush toward the canvas where the Sacred Family and the shepherds requested by the gentleman in The Hague were already outlined. "I know I am no longer in fashion, that the rich are not begging me to portray them, because they are the ones to create fashion and the rich of today don't have the beliefs of their Calvinist fathers: now they want to display wealth, beauty, power . . . Since that is what they have obtained that wealth for. They build palaces in the new canals and pay us for our works, since, fortunately, they consider that we are a means of investing that wealth and, at the same time, a good way to adorn those palaces and show how refined they are."

However, the Maestro had not been communicative at all on the afternoon on which, without yet having revealed to him his purpose of using him as a model, he had ordered Elias Ambrosius to leave his cleaning utensils aside and come up to the studio, the place where, for the previous two weeks, an order had been established in which the only ones who could enter were the Maestro, his student Aert de Gelder, and the young Emely Kerk. Upon entering the workroom, Elias Ambrosius was surprised by the reason explaining its closure: on the back wall, there were two paintings, strangely alike but fundamentally different, of the hackneyed Christian scene of the adoration of the shepherds, that depiction on which the painter had been working for too long. Without giving him the opportunity to stop and contemplate the two canvases made enigmatic by their similarities, the Maestro had asked him to don a heavy brown nightshirt and placed him before a fragment of a Greek column that reached his chest. After looking at him from several angles, he began to ask him to assume different poses as, with loose strokes, he started reproducing the positions with charcoal over the rough pages of his *tafelet*. Something very remote and visceral had to be occupying the Maestro's mind in the process of looking at and sketching the young Jew, in a silence broken only by his indications to modify the positions. The Maestro, Elias thought, seemed focused on a hunt rather than a work of art. And he was sure that he was witnessing an invaluable lesson.

A few weeks before, when he began to work on one of those versions of *The Adoration of the Shepherds*, the painter had made the predictable decision of once again using the young Emely Kerk, his son Titus's governess, as the model for the figure of the Virgin Mary, as he had already done in the scene that he titled *Sacred Family with Angels*. The work, finished and handed in at the beginning of that year, and whose process of creation Elias Ambrosius had had the privilege of watching, had sparked a near-magnetic attraction in the young apprentice. He devoted long hours to its contemplation, trying to discover, since he found himself capable of it already, the effects by which that familiar and magical scene managed to transmit an emotion that, despite his Jewish education and beliefs, Elias could not help but feeling; and one day, he found that the key to the painting was not in its representation of a mystical event but in quite the opposite, in the manifestation of its earthly serenity. The Maestro seemed to be further and further away from the expression of obvious feelings of fear, pain, surprise, sorrow, and fury, to which he'd handed himself over, years before, in his paintings about the story of Samson, or in his works about Abraham's sacrifice for the so-called *Belshazzar's Feast,* all so dramatic and full of movement. Now, in contrast, he had opted for the internalization of feeling and, in that scene, had been capable of concentrating all of the emotion of the circumstances in the careful gesture of a hand. The hand of the young and beautiful Emely Kerk, turned into the Mother of God, summarized, as a last emission of her character, the perfection that began in the oval shape of her face, in the softness of her demeanor, and continued with the pleasant curve of her shoulders, to go on to the delicacy of that extremity that approached the boy to confirm if he was sleeping: it was just one gesture, easy and routine, almost vulgarly maternal and earthly, but it successfully conferred to the representation of the Virgin a sweetness capable of proclaiming, in its tenderness that was simultaneously human and cosmic, that this was not a normal mother, but rather, the Mother of a God. The Maestro had created an explosion of the magic of beauty and had been capable of turning his own carnal desires for the model into a universal and transcendental lesson in love. And Elias Ambrosius understood that only the most gifted maestros were capable of achieving so much with so little. Could he, someday, come anywhere close to that greatness?

In the work of the adoration of the shepherds to which the painter had devoted himself for the previous two months, there appeared the same Virgin, but as part of a group of characters. With the Christ child lying in a Moses basket—more so, a rather ordinary basket—placed on her lap, the Virgin is showing the foreign shepherds the recently born Son of God. Mother and child, ever since they were sketched, appeared to benefit from the painting's only light, the source of which one would say came from the divine beings themselves. Nonetheless, something in that work, destined for the stadtholder's palace, did not seem to please the Maestro, and its conclusion had been delayed for several weeks already, throughout which the man, without even dipping his paintbrush, devoted himself to look at what had already been painted or to wander the city, as if he had completely forgotten the piece. Pushed by that dissatisfaction with the work, as all in the workshop would later find out, the Maestro had made a strange decision: he had asked Aert de Gelder, the most gifted of his young students, to use a canvas of similar dimensions to the one he had chosen and reproduce the main body of that painting. De Gelder had to copy the scene with the greatest fidelity, although with the freedom to introduce any variations the young man thought necessary. Aert de Gelder, who was the most surprising pictorial imitator of the Maestro who ever existed, had accepted the challenge and, with delight, had focused on the work, knowing that it was not a matter of a simple exercise of copying but rather a more intricate experiment whose final goal he did not yet know. It was in those days that entering the studio had been forbidden to all of the house's workers and inhabitants. As such, it was only that afternoon, after receiving the Maestro's command to move until he was standing just before him, that Elias Ambrosius at last had the opportunity to stop and study the two works, still very much in need of touch-ups and concluding treatments. It surprised him to see how the paintings multiplied the feeling of symmetry, since they seemed to be looking at one another in a mirror, and the young Jew surmised that, in all certainty, de Gelder had decided to carry out the task of reproducing what already existed by relying on the optical instruments that the image made by the Maestro projected over the canvas on which the student had copied it. For that reason, the figures in the reproduction were inverted in regard to the original, with the characters somewhat more concentrated on the light source, although transmitting the same feeling of respectful introversion. But, for anyone who did not have the background that Elias and the rest of the students possessed, the question that would immediately arise from the contemplation of those twin works without a doubt would be: Which was the original and which was the copy?

"Do you want to know why I am doing this?" the Maestro asked at last without needing to confirm the object of Elias Ambrosius's hypnotized gaze.

"With all due respect," the young man said, and the painter then turned to stand facing the works, his back to his apprentice.

"It's the price of money," the Maestro said, and remained silent for a few moments, as Hakham ben Israel usually did when he was about to make a speech. "This time I cannot fail. I am counting on the stadtholder's money to settle the back payments for this house. In sum, I don't get commissions like this anymore; some say that my paintings look more abandoned than they do finished . . . A few years ago, this same stadtholder was my hope for becoming a rich, famous man and being able to live in a palace in The Hague . . ."

"Like the Flemish Rubens?" Elias dared to ask.

The Maestro nodded. "Like that damned Flemish Rubens . . . But I am not and have never been able to be like him, no matter how hard I work to achieve that, no matter if I steal his subjects, compositions, even his colors . . . My salvation was what at one point seemed to be my disgrace: that the stadtholder did not turn me into the court painter and that he dealt with me just as I am: a common man willing to sell his work . . . At that moment, I felt myself sinking, I had to give up wanting to live like Rubens, to paint like Rubens. But I also turned into a man who was a little more free. No, much more free . . . Although, listen well, freedom always has a price. And it tends to be too high. When I thought myself free and wanted to paint like a free artist, I broke with everything that was considered elegant and harmonious, I killed Rubens, and I conquered my demons to paint *The Night Watch* for Kloveniers's walls. And I received the punishment warranted by my heresy: no more commissions of collective portraits, since mine ended up being a shriek, a burp, spit . . . It was chaos and a provocation, they said. But I know, I know it well, that I achieved that unusual combination of desires and fulfillment that constitute a masterwork. And if I am mistaken and it contains nothing of mastery, then the important thing is that it was a work I wanted to make. In reality, the only one that I could make while I had before my eyes the evidence of where life leads us . . . Toward nothing. My wife was extinguishing, spitting her lungs out, she was dying more every day, and I was painting an explosion, a carnival of rich men who were disguised, playing at being soldiers, and I did so however I felt like . . . The dilemma was simple: either I pleased them or I pleased myself, either I remained a slave or I proclaimed my independence." The painter stopped his diatribe, as if he had suddenly lost his enthusiasm, but he immediately took up his digression again: "But the bitter truth is that, as long as I depend on the money of others, I will not be completely free. It doesn't

matter if the one paying is the stadtholder or the treasury of the Republic, the Church, a king, or a wealthy baker from Delft . . . In the end, it's
all the same. I can paint Emely Kerk as I want to paint her, or a sacred
family that looks like a Jewish family from your neighborhood while
receiving the visit of some angels as if it were the most normal thing in
the world. And then sit and wait for a generous buyer to show up . . . Or
not show up. But that which you see there"—he unnecessarily pointed at
his painting, the larger one—"that does not belong to me: it is the stadtholder's work. He requested it from me with what he wanted to see in
detail and he is paying me to fulfill that desire . . . And I already learned
my lesson. I know well that the stadtholder does not want to display in
his palace dirty feet or ragged shepherds recently emerged from the desert, how it must have been in reality. He does not want life; just an imitation of it that is beautiful. That is why I asked Aert to make his version
so that I could retouch mine with the solutions he finds . . . I chose Aert
because he is one of the best painters I know, but he will never be an
artist. And there is the proof: it looks like a work of mine, doesn't it?
Look at those lines, look at the depth of the chiaroscuro, enjoy the tech-
nique with which he works the light. Observe and learn . . . But, you
should also learn something more important: that picture of Aert's is
missing something . . . It's missing a soul, it has no mystery of true art . . .
It is just a commission. And I am copying Aert because you have to paint
that way if you want to fulfill the desires of power and earn the florins I
need so badly." He stopped, concentrating on the two paintings, and shook
his head, denying something, before saying: "Art is something else . . .
And that's enough for today. Now clean this studio thoroughly, it looks
like a pigsty . . . Starting tomorrow, I need you here with me. Tell Mme.
Dircx that you will not be helping her for the time being. You're going to
serve as my model for the mohel in the painting of the circumcision of
Jesus . . . And, when we finish with this commission, I will give you a
paintbrush. I am curious to see if, in addition to value, vocation, stubbornness, and perhaps even talent, you have the soul of an artist."

———

Once again, Emely Kerk was the Virgin who, in the foreground, watched
with devotion as her husband, Joseph, held in his arms the boy swaddled in
white sheets, while Elias Ambrosius, transfigured into a mohel dressed
like a character from Persian tales, his head covered in the style of the

primitive eastern Jews who increasingly swarmed about Amsterdam, prepared himself, his back nearly turned to the spectator, to perform the ritual surgery on the descendant of the house of David, arrived on earth to change the fate of the religion of the Hebrews and even the very history of the people of Israel, who did not recognize him as the Messiah. Behind those characters, over whom the light was concentrated, was a cavernous darkness in which figures could be made out, all of them dressed in dark vermilion tunics, and, in the background, a curtain with some gold reflections and the columns of the temple of Zorobabel and Herod the Great, the last great vestige of the glory of Judah that, shortly after, the Roman legions would destroy.

Several times, as the Maestro worked on that *Circumcision of Christ*, Hakham ben Israel came to the workshop to help him in the interpretation of a biblical scene referred to only by Luke so that he could accurately represent the thousands-year-old ceremony. Deeply familiar not only with the Torah and the books of the prophets, but also with the so-called New Testament written by the disciples of the man whom Christians considered to be the Messiah, Ben Israel possessed a deep mastery of Christology. Drinking the painter's wine, he again enjoyed that work as a consultant, which he had already carried out on several occasions, since, although the Maestro knew the Scriptures by heart—he read almost no other books—their deeper historic meaning and connections with the complicated Hebrew imagery could always escape him, something that he did not want to risk in that commissioned work. Several years before, fulfilling a similar mission, it had been the Hakham who, in a game of Kabbalistic meanings whose specifics the Maestro did not master, had written the message that, in a divine cloud, covers the wall of Balthazar's palace and announces to the Babylonian emperor the end of his corrupt reign. The Hebrew letters, arranged on vertical columns, instead of appearing arranged horizontally and from right to left, enclosed in the encrypted warning and esoteric meaning that only those familiar with the mysteries of the Kabbalah and its cosmic projections could understand, as was the case with Ben Israel.

In those talks, almost always dampened with more wine than was required to calm their thirst, of which Elias Ambrosius was the witness several times from his position as a model, the Maestro and the Hakham frequently talked about the messianism, which, from the precepts of their respective religions, they understood in different ways. Elias discovered that his former teacher differed from the conclusions of the schools of Kabbalist scholars settled in the Eastern Mediterranean—Thessaloníki, Constantinople, Jerusalem itself, places where those maestros or their immediate ancestors had arrived following their exit from Sepharad— which had propagated the lost theory of their esoteric interpretation of the writings that, in the nearby year of 1648, in other words, year 5408 since the Creation, was marked in the Book as that of the arrival of the Messiah. The great disgraces suffered by the Jews in recent centuries, the new exodus signified by being expelled from Sepharad, the hostility lurking everywhere ("This new Jerusalem is an island," Ben Israel would say, with words that he could have stolen from Grandfather Benjamin), the loss of faith by so many Israelites converted to Christianity, Islam or, worse still, handed over to disbelief (the excommunicated Uriel da Costa was not the only heretic who had grown among them, and he mentioned the controversial, nearly dangerous, ideas of a young man who was too intelligent and rebellious, called Baruch Spinoza, of whom Elias was hearing for the first time), constituted, according to the Kabbalists, the first of the great catastrophes. They were just a foreseeable prologue of the enormous disgraces to come, announced to precede the true arrival of the Anointed and to celebrate, at last, the judgment of the just and begin the era of the universal acknowledgment of the God of Abraham and Moses. But, besides, the Hakham disagreed with the reflections of the Eastern scholars over one specific point: the prophets Daniel and Zechariah, he said, clearly warn that the arrival of the Messiah would only occur when Jews lived on every corner of the earth. Never before.

On the same day that Ben Israel arrived at that crucial point of his messianic analysis, the Maestro asked a question capable of driving the expert crazy: "So what about what Antonio Montesinos is saying in the taverns and synagogues about having discovered the descendants of the ten lost tribes in the New World?"

"Nonsense! He's a fraud! A trick that greatly pleases Rabbi Montera because it serves to control the people, but that not even he himself believes!" the teacher yelled. "How can that Antonio Montesinos say that some ugly, ignorant indigenous people are the heirs of the ten lost tribes? Who's going to believe him that they speak a form of Aramaic if the Indians of one tribe can't even understand their neighbors?"

"But if it were true, that would mean that Jews live all over the world," the Maestro replied.

"Not even Rabbi Breslau believes Montesinos's tale . . . Because the problem is not the New World, where there are already Sephardic settlements and even some of those Ashkenazi mules, even in the territories of the Spanish king, incidentally . . . The problem is in England, from where we were expelled three and a half centuries ago. England is the key to the arrival of the Messiah to occur . . . And I am going to focus my strength on nothing short of opening the doors of Albion: if I achieve it, I will have made a great step so that the kingdom of the Holiest, blessed may He be, can extend across the whole earth and the world will be ready for the arrival of the true Messiah and the return to Jerusalem."

One afternoon on which the Maestro relieved Elias Ambrosius at the same time that Ben Israel was taking his leave, the young man took advantage of the occasion to accompany the Hakham on his journey toward the house on Nieuwe Houtmarkt. It was already dark, but the temperature remained pleasant, and they decided to walk along the left bank of the Zwanenburgwal, until the roving foulness of the waste barges forced them to seek out an alleyway that would take them closer to Binnen Amstel. Each night, that load of human and animal detritus went up the canals toward the Amstel's inner harbor, in the direction of Ij, to then sail to the strawberry fields of Aalsmeer and the carrot fields of Beverwijk, which in time would grace the city's markets with their brilliant colors.

Sitting in the Hakham's jumbled study, with the windows closed to prevent the smells drifting in, the scholar prepared his pipe in which he liked to smoke the tobacco leaves that his friends gave him as he handed himself over to reflection or reading. Elias Ambrosius, lowering his voice, then told him about the Maestro's decision to have him paint in the workshop. That marvelous opportunity of taking his apprenticeship to the next level signified, nonetheless, that his true relationship with the painter would become public, at least to the other students in the workshop and even the servants in the house. And that revelation could not help but cause justified fears in the young man. Although the Hakham was not the only one who could show his understanding as a Jew, he who was otherwise observant of his religion's laws and commandments, Elias Ambrosius felt fearful of radical reactions, which were more and more frequently occurring in the city. It did not console him too much to know that men like Isaac Pinto and surely others in his circle were devoted not only to buying paintings, but paintings made by a Jew who had settled among them. Because it was also obvious to all of the members of the

Nação that the rabbinical council, fearing the loss of control over the community, was becoming more inflexible every day regarding certain attitudes that were considered blasphemous. On each occasion when they were presented with a case of disobedience or laxity to be analyzed or judged, the rabbis repeated the harangue that the atmosphere of prosperity and tolerance was making the flock more licentious by the day. It was not a coincidence that, in recent times, the condemning *cherems* were coming down like rain for maintaining relations with converts living in the lands of idolatry and even visiting those lands, for keeping distance from the synagogue, for ignoring fasts or violating the prohibitions of the Sabbath as they met worldly needs or demands, or, in the worst of cases, for expressing ideas or carrying out acts considered to be heretical. What could he expect to happen if what constituted, for the majority of Jews, a flagrant violation of the Law was discovered? Didn't Salom Italia hide his identity to avoid the rabbis' punishment? How long could Elias keep living among painters, working in secret without his true intentions being discovered by his brother Amos, who, as fanatical as he was, would denounce him before the Mahamad?

The Hakham seemed more amused than concerned by the fears of his former student. A nearly imperceptible, but permanent, smile tilted the pipe toward the left corner of his mouth.

"But what do you really fear, Elias, God or your neighbors?" he asked at last, using the tongue of the Castilian Sephardic Jews, after leaving the pipe on his desk. Elias was surprised by the difficulty that responding to that simple question entailed.

"I know I can expect it from God . . . And from my neighbors as well" was what it occurred to him to say, in the same language used by the Hakham, who barely nodded, now without the hint of a smile on his face.

"To you, what is the sacred?" The interrogation continued.

"God, the Law, the Book . . ." The young man enumerated and immediately knew he had made an error, because he added: "Although the Law and the Book have a human component."

"Yes, they do . . . And isn't the human being, made by Him in His image and likeness, isn't he sacred . . . ? And what about love? Isn't love sacred?"

"What love?"

"Any love, all loves."

Elias thought for a moment. The teacher was not referring to the love of God, or not only this. But he responded, "Yes, I think so."

"We are in agreement," Ben Israel said after a pause, and added: "Perhaps you will remember this story, since I spoke of it at the school . . . As you know, on August 6 of year 70 of the Common Era, the armies of the Roman emperor Titus took Jerusalem and destroyed the Second Temple. Curiously, that same day of the year 586 before the Common Era, the First Temple had been destroyed—"

"Tishah-b'Ab, the saddest day of the year for Israel," Elias interrupted him as he asked himself why the Hakham was repeating that story that even the most ignorant Jews knew.

"If you do not want to listen to me, you can go."

"I'm sorry, Hakham. Continue."

"The point I want to get to is to remind you that, beginning with the destruction of the Second Temple and Emperor Hadrian's persecutions of any practitioner of Judaism, the history of Israel, as a nation, has continued for one thousand seven hundred years. But not built on a land whose last vestiges we lost at that time, but rather built on books written centuries before by the members of the people who never had great artisans, or painters or architects, but did have great narrators who made writing a sort of national obsession . . . Ours was the first race capable of finding words not just to define all of the complexity of the relationship between man and mystery but also to express the deepest human sentiments, including, of course, love . . . Shortly after the destruction of the Temple, amid Hadrian's various persecutions, a great assembly of rabbis and doctors took place and the basic rules for the survival of the fate of the Hebrews were established; two rules that are still valid today . . . The first is that to study is more important than to observe the prohibitions and the laws, since knowledge of the Torah leads to the obedience of its wise prescriptions, while pure observance, without reasoned understanding of the origin of the laws, does not guarantee true faith, that faith born of reason. The second rule you will remember from Judah Abravanel's story, which I told you so many times, has to do with life and death. When is it necessary to die before giving in? Those scholars asked themselves more than one thousand five hundred years ago, and responded to all of us that it was necessary only in three situations: if the Jew finds himself forced to adore false idols, forced to commit adultery, or forced to spill innocent blood. But all other laws can be transgressed under threat of death, since life is the most sacred thing," the teacher said, and moved his arm as if to recover his pipe, but he desisted. "I want to tell you just two things with this, Elias Ambrosius Montalbo de Ávila . . . One is that laws should be rationalized by man, because that is why he has intelligence, and faith should involve thought, not mere acceptance. The second is that if you do not violate any of the great laws, you are not offending God in an irreversible way. And if you do not offend the Blessed One, you can forget about your neighbors . . . Of course, if you are resolved to assume the risks of facing the fury of men, which, on occasion, can be more terrible than that of the gods."

———

So then, were life and love sacred? What exactly is *the sacred*? Does it only refer to the divine and its works or also to what is most revered by the human being? And were life and love a gift from God to His creatures, and thus sacred?

Elias Ambrosius could not help but ask himself these things as he looked at the blushing face of Mariam Roca, listened to the girl's deep breathing, and felt a joyous beating between his legs, as urgent as he had ever felt.

He did not have to insist too much, so that, instead of walking through the city, they went that day to wander through the pleasant fields extending beyond the new canals. It was a light-filled Sunday morning, with open skies like a flower in the summer heat, and they entertained themselves contemplating the Prince's Canal's palazzos, Amsterdam's newest and most luxurious.

"Would you like it if we lived in one like that?" the young man asked her as they passed before the nearly finished building where Isaac Pinto would soon live, and she blushed because of the connotation enclosed in that question. They later took the path that led to the solitude of the abandoned shed where Elias usually placed his easel and his linens to paint in oil. As they walked between locust trees and willows growing at the edges of the swamps, the young man asked himself how far he could go that day in his relationship with Mariam and thought of all the possibilities that his inexperienced mind was capable of offering him. But when he had sat down alongside her, their backs leaning against the worn walls of that shed in the shade, and almost by instinct begun an advance toward new territories, which she had not rejected (caresses on her neck with the back of his hand, a light touch of her lips with his finger), Elias did not hold back. He took the girl's face in his hands and placed his lips atop hers, thus prompting the vigorous response that was incapable of conquering the questions besieging his mind before the certainty that the magic of that instant, Mariam's beauty, and the beating, the hardening of his member, and the sensation of power that exalted it, were also the sacred. They had to be, since they led to the very essence of life, to the most sublime communication with the best thing God had given his creatures.

Ever since he saw her for the first time at Hakham ben Israel's house, almost a year before, Elias Ambrosius had had the feeling that that girl, barely sixteen years old, was predestined to enter his life. Mariam's parents and grandparents, former Portuguese *conversos*, for years had preferred to settle in Leiden, where her father, a doctor by profession who took his degree in Porto, had obtained a discreet post as a professor of medicine at the city's famous university. Later, when her father was called to work with the famous Dr. Efraín Bueno, they ended up in Amsterdam at last. The link with that doctor connected Mariam's father with the scholar Ben Israel (friend of any doctor existing in the city, whom he compulsively consulted regarding his real and imagined illnesses) and, due to the closeness of the elders, also connected the two young people. Elias and Mariam's outings, initiated under the pretext that the young man would show the recently arrived girl the city where she was now living, had placed Elias in the privileged circumstance of having the time and space to feed a sentimental relationship whose growth the girl's family seemed to accept with good humor, despite the fact that the Montalbo de Ávila clan did not figure among, or come even close to, Amsterdam's wealthiest, although they were among the most respected for their education and work ethic.

That unforgettable morning, when Elias was getting ready to kiss Mariam Roca for the second time, he rested his gaze for a few seconds on the young woman's eyes: clear eyes, honey-colored, through which he managed to contemplate the sources of desire and fear, of the decisions and the doubts of their owner. And also, without being able to help it, he thought that someday he should paint those eyes—since everything is in the eyes. And if his paintbrushes or charcoal managed to capture the beating life in that gaze, then he would have been capable of exercising the power of trapping a tangible glimpse of the sacred. Like a god. Like the Maestro.

————

The days, which tumbled forward in search of autumn, passed slowly over the scarce works to which the Maestro devoted himself around that time. In those months, two of the oldest students left the workshop, first Barent Fabritius and later Keil the Dane, who, before returning to his frozen lands, gave the Jew for whom he had bought so many beers a small canvas on which he had painted a marina, a work that, along with Elias's folders and notebooks, had to return to the hiding place in the attic of his house. Shortly after, to occupy the vacancies, other apprentices joined them, such as a certain Christoph Paudiss, come from Hamburg with the express pretension of turning into his country's greatest painter. In addition, week after week, Mme. Dircx's face became visibly more hostile due to the youthful presence and rising role of Emely Kerk in the home . . . Everything moved, turned, ascended, or descended, but the weeks passed and the promised paintbrush did not reach the hands of Elias Ambrosius, who was plagued by an anxiety that not even his well-requited love could manage to calm. An anxiety that had been on the rise, when, in the most unexpected way, he had discovered with certainty the true identity of Salom Italia.

For several months, on each occasion that arose and led by his obsession, Elias Ambrosius dedicated hours to again visiting the sellers of paintings in all of the city's markets, jumping from the contemplation of the works to an interrogation about possible knowledge of a certain Salom Italia, engraver and illustrator, almost certainly living in Amsterdam. The street merchants, so in the know of what moved (and what didn't move) in the city's painting market, always denied having ever heard that name that, by all accounts, must be that of a Jew. And they added: *A Jewish painter?*, accentuating their suspicion of the inconceivable.

At the synagogue, each Saturday, the young man devoted himself to observing the attendees, focusing on the sons of the affluent businessmen on one day and on the artists specializing in carving diamonds on another day; and on yet another, on the men who had arrived in recent years, as if the observation of their physical presence could open the door to the secret that was so well guarded by some of the Jews present there.

He was convinced, besides, that not only Isaac Pinto and Hakham ben Israel had dealt with that ghost who even dared to decorate Queen Esther's scroll. If the man was dedicated to making engravings, there must be several copies of each work, and someone must've bought them or, at least, received them. The work carried out on a roll of Scripture must not be, he thought, a unique effort, and there was no one better than another Jew to appreciate a work like the one Isaac Pinto treasured.

It was the last Saturday in August when Elias Ambrosius finally found, at the very moment in which he was not seeking it, the clue capable of leading him, as he immediately realized, to knowing the identity of Salom Italia. It happened right at the synagogue, during one of the last morning prayers (the *musaf*, with which Jews are reminded of the sacrifices carried out in the temple), when, deep in prayer, he lowered his gaze and what he saw made him lose the rhythm of the words. On the other side of the main aisle, in the same row where he was praying, there was a boot on which a yellow dot shone that could only be a drop of paint. Slowly, without ceasing to move his lips empty of words, he began to run his eyes over the physical presence of the man dressed in that boot and found, at last, the face that was unknown to him. The man, a few years older than him, had a trimmed beard and mustache, in the new fashion, and below his tallith was wearing a finely woven shirt, without a doubt expensive. That man could be anything but a poor house painter who owned just one pair of boots. That stain had to be a splash of pigment diluted in oil . . .

The close of the morning ceremony stunned him into a state of total excitement over what he sensed was the unquestionable discovery capable of leading him to the resolution of his doubts and fears. Without waiting for his parents and his grandfather (Amos had been attending a service for months that brought together the boring and very formal Germans in a small room turned synagogue), without looking toward the balcony occupied by the women where his beloved Mariam was, the young man left the temple, removing his kippah and tallith and, with the skill he had already acquired, posted himself behind the stall of some street vendors of fruits and vegetables in season to await the exit of the man with the stained boot. Who was that character? Why had he never seen him before?

Before the majority of the faithful had left the synagogue, the unknown man, after trading his ritual kippah for an elegant, cream-colored felt hat, went out onto the street and, with evident haste, began to cross the Visserplein in the direction of Meijer Square. At a distance that he considered prudent to not risk discovery but not lose his target, Elias Ambrosius followed him over the new and wide Blauwbrug Bridge, over the Amstel behind him, and, after crossing the Botermarkt, he was fairly surprised when he saw the pursued man digging around in his pockets until he extracted a key with which he opened the door to one of the houses on the Reguliersdwarsstraat, quite close to the north shore of the Herengracht, the Gentlemen's Canal.

Two days later, Elias Ambrosius had already accumulated all of the information necessary to and capable of confirming for him how a furtive drop of paint could reward the work of several months and revealed to him one of the best-kept secrets in the city of secrets. The dweller of the house around Herengracht was said to be called Davide da Mantova, and he was (as those who knew him proclaimed) a great-grandson of Spanish Sephardic Jews, although a native of that city in the north of Italy, to which he frequently traveled for long periods of time. In Mantova, the man maintained commercial contacts with the Venetian Jewish community, thanks to whom he imported to Amsterdam mirrors, glass, vases, and high-quality glass beads from the famous factories of the lagoon of Venice, with lucrative benefits that were possible to infer, and, further still, demonstrated by the clothing he wore and the door of the dwelling where he lived. Due to his financial position and the particularities of his business, Davide da Mantova—as young Elias already imagined him—when in Amsterdam, moved in the circle of wealthy Sephardic Jews and powerful local burghers whose doors were always open to that provider of exclusive marvels.

Elias Ambrosius did not doubt it any longer: that man had to be Salom Italia, and if he was not familiar with him before this, it was only due to the fact that his presence in the city tended to be sporadic, since he spent the majority of his time in Italy. But the identification solved only part of the problem, while the essential parts remained: how to access this man, would he reveal that he knew his secret, and, above all, how would he make him speak of his hidden vocation? The possible paths that he knew to approach Davide da Mantova had already revealed themselves to be impassable: neither Hakham ben Israel nor Isaac Pinto nor the Maestro were going to betray the man's trust, and, to be fair, it would be petty of him to ask them for that infidelity when he owed them the preservation of his own secret, so similar to that of Salom Italia.

The feeling that he was before an inaccessible mystery so necessary to penetrate in order to calm his own unease made Elias Ambrosius feel all the weight of his double life, loaded with silences, concealment, and even lies, a mask that he had been dragging along ever since he made the decision to see through the realization of his forbidden vocation. Several times, as he followed the presumed Jewish painter around the city, moving like an otherworldly shadow, he tried to imagine how that Davide da Mantova must manage his life, always worried about not taking people into his confidence more than was recommended, showing the world only half of his face, reducing his artistic accomplishments to a circle of accomplices committed to silence—perhaps the worst punishment for an artist. He asked himself if his parents, over in Italy, or his wife, here in Amsterdam, participated in the arrangement or if they were, like Grandfather Benjamin, his own parents, and his beloved Mariam, asking themselves about the fate and origins of strange attitudes of a being who was simultaneously close and unknown, a grandson, son, and boyfriend whom they did not even know was spending every minute of his existence besieged by the fear of man and the most transcendental doubts.

It was then that Elias Ambrosius came to ask himself if it was worth living under those conditions: if it was what was best for his loved ones and for himself, if a permanent double life represented the only option that his time, race, and vocation allowed him, or if there was some way out that did not lead to disaster. Perhaps the most advisable, he came to think, would be to forget about a flirtation that, at the end of the day, still had not led him to anything, and, while he still had time to avoid greater disgraces, he could hand himself over to building a normal life, without any distress, in which he could open himself up, body and, above all, soul to everyone else. In that way, he would live a life without fears (always that damned fear), but also without ambitions or dreams; he would glide through the clamor of days that were increasingly the same, without ever again feeling that exciting desire, born in the deepest part of his being, to take up a piece of charcoal or a paintbrush and face the supreme challenge of aiming to internalize the gaze of happiness of the young lover, the fragment of a pleasant landscape, the power of

Samson, or the faith of Tobit, just as his unrestrained imagination showed them, just as the Maestro had captured them. A normal man's normal life with room for being even better.

One night, when his sickening obsession to penetrate the world of the man he pursued made him stand watch in front of the house on Reguliersdwarsstraat until the last candle in the dwelling went out, the young man, as he weighed his excruciating options, discovered that the problem did not lie in knowing how Salom Italia or Davide da Mantova thought and lived: the problem lay in knowing how Elias Ambrosius Montalbo de Ávila wanted to or could act on his desire.

———

"Drop that damned broom. Take this square palette . . . Grab this bunch of paintbrushes . . . Come on, we're going to work!"

Elias Ambrosius felt his legs go weak, his voice falter, his breath escape his soul until he was left inert. But he also discovered the way in which an unknown, superhuman power came to his aid to help him obey the order for which he had been waiting for almost three years: the Maestro was inviting him to paint! His doubts and even his determination to end that juvenile flirtation that had pursued him in recent weeks as he followed the trail of Salom Italia's enigma, where did they go? He didn't even manage to ask himself, because the only possible response he could give at that moment, the only one he really wanted to give, was the one that finally came from his lips: "I am ready, Maestro."

The painter, covered with a white bonnet under which he restrained his curls when he worked, sat down on a bench in front of which there were two small primed canvases. From there, he looked at the young man, palette and brush in hand, and smiled. He left his own brush and palette on the bench, to remove an apron from a hook. "Let's see," he said, and Elias lowered his head so that the Maestro could place the protective fabric, stained in a thousand colors, over him with the gesture similar to that of awarding a military decoration.

"Put ocher, yellow, vermilion, white, and sienna on your palette. With those colors, Apelles was able to paint Alexander taking a thunderbolt in his hand in front of Artemis's temple. With those colors, you can paint everything," the Maestro said, and, after pointing out the porcelain jars with the already diluted pigments, he turned toward the linen and looked at it, as if questioning it. Elias, in silence, awaited a new order and only then had enough lucidity to overcome his emotions and ask himself what they were going to paint. He looked around and understood the Maestro's intention: by the placement of the mirrors, that of the easels, and the angle at which the painter had placed himself in relation to the light coming from the windows, the object to be worked on could be none other than the Maestro himself.

"I don't have an outstanding commission," the painter nearly whispered, without ceasing to look at the linen. "And today I have lost my best model . . . I had to throw Emely Kerk out of the house because I caught her fornicating with one of the students . . . You can guess who. And since I cannot do without the florins that the father of that apprentice pays me . . . That whore."

Elias Ambrosius finally had the answer to the unusual pleasantness with which, just a few minutes before, Mme. Dircx had received him, as she was playing with little Titus in the kitchen. In some way, the old lioness had arranged things to take the young claimant out of the game.

"Are you really ready?" the Maestro asked him, pointing with the end of his brush at the other bench, placed before the second canvas. Elias did not delay in responding this time:

"I believe that I have spent my whole life waiting for this moment, Maestro."

"So, do you now know why you are willing to risk everything and prove yourself as a painter?"

"Yes, I know now . . . Because . . ."

The Maestro lifted his paintbrush, asking him to stop. "That is important only to you . . . And do not worry if the answer seems too simple. Mine is extremely simple . . . Had I kept studying medicine at the university, perhaps I would be rich now and living calmly . . . Today, my life is riddled with problems. And I do not regret my response."

Elias Ambrosius nodded. Could there be anything more basic than wanting to paint because one feels the need to do so, an incorruptible need, capable of taking him to face all difficulties and risks?

"A few weeks ago, I discovered who the man is who painted the scroll of Queen Esther," he then said, also because he needed to. "I know the name of that Salom Italia, where he lives, what he does for living . . ."

"But you didn't do something as foolish as try to talk to him?"

"No, I didn't know how to do it . . . But, why foolish?"

The Maestro sighed and looked at the challenging canvas awaiting him.

"Because you have no right to violate his privacy, just as others have no right to violate yours. Besides, whatever he would have told you would have been his response, not yours."

"You are right . . . After following that man for several days, I thought about not going back to the workshop anymore, about forgetting all of this." He made a gesture with his paintbrush to indicate everything surrounding him: a gesture he had copied from the Maestro. "But I know that that is impossible . . . At least now. And less still, now."

The Maestro nodded, still looking at the linen primed in an earth color before him. "You don't know how much what happened with Emely hurts me . . . But, it's better for you: thanks to her, today you will paint with me."

"I am glad, Maestro," he said, and immediately felt the desire to bite his damn tongue. But the man seemed to have not heard him, absorbed perhaps in his thoughts.

"Before dipping your paintbrush, you should have an idea of where you want to go, although you may not know how you're going to do it . . . Today, I would like to get to the sadness that's in the soul of a forty-year-old man. I'd like to discover it, because it is a new sadness . . . Pain is not the same as sadness, did you know? I have a lot of experience with pain, as well as with fury, with disappointment, with frustration . . . And also with the enjoyment of success, even when others have not understood and have pushed me aside . . . Which is not strange, after all . . . But sadness is a deep feeling, too personal. Joy and pain, surprise and fury, are exultant, they change the face, the gaze . . . But sadness marks one inside. Where do you think I can find sadness?"

Elias Ambrosius responded immediately, satisfied with his wisdom: "In the eyes. Everything is in the eyes."

The Maestro shook his head no.

"Do you still think that you know something . . . ? No, not sadness. Sadness is beyond the eyes . . . You have to get inside his thoughts, inside the man's soul, to see it and speak with those depths to try to reflect them . . ." The Maestro dipped his brush in the yellow pigment and started to mark the lines of what soon started to be a head. "Because of that, very few men have managed to portray sadness . . . A sad man would never look at the spectator. He would search for something beyond the

person looking at him, a far-off point, lost in the distance and simultaneously inside himself. He would never look up, in search of hope; nor
down, as if he were ashamed or fearful. He should have his gaze fixed on
the unfathomable . . . His face lightly leaning inward, the light not shining too much on the cheek turned to the spectator, very visible lids . . .
To make that face stand out and so that you can concentrate all the strength
in it, it has always been best to use a dark brown background, but never
black: the depth of the atmosphere corresponds to the depth of feeling,
it would reiterate them and eliminate their mystery . . . Tell me, kid, do
you feel capable of painting my sadness?"

"I'm going to try it, with your permission . . ."

And Elias dipped his brush in the same matte yellow used by the
Maestro and placed the damp coarseness on the canvas to make it run
down, softly, marking the first contour of the face. Then he looked at
the mirror placed in front of him, in which were reflected, at a slight tilt,
the Maestro's head and torso. He looked at the well-known form of his
face, his distinctive features—the flattened nose, the nearly fleshy mouth,
the fleeting angles of the slightly leaning chin—he assessed the weights
of the white bonnet and of the reddish curls falling over his ears, and
stopped on his eyes, in that gaze of a man who touched the heavens so
many times, whose fame was known in capitals across Europe, before
whom The Hague's stadtholder, after having offended him, had given in
and agreed to pay him a fortune for two works that only that man was
capable of achieving with the dreamed of mastery, the same man who,
at that moment, had decided to make a self-portrait and offer himself to
a pupil so that, between both of them, they could try to hunt his sadness
over having lost something as mundane and, for someone of his position,
so easy to replace, as a young and beautiful lover. Through those eyes,
Elias Ambrosius Montalbo de Ávila was opening the path for himself
toward his paradise or his Inferno, but without a doubt toward the luminous place at which, with all of his soul and consciousness, he wanted to
arrive.

———

Yes, this is the sacred, he told himself when he felt, after briefly fighting
her hymen, how his body slid into the deepest parts of Mariam Roca.
Following the rupture, which caused her the annoyance of a pain she had
already been warned about, she opened her eyes and swallowed air as

she devoured in her deepest insides the circumcised penis now ambitiously occupying her favorable female space, giving her a greater sense of life. The unpredictable but visceral movement of the novice lovers' hips acquired a rhythm and made the fit decisive and later, moved by runaway, dizzying, devouring, and still more dizzying grinding that later became slow, slow, slow . . . Until, trained by his readings of the Bible, Elias Ambrosius had enough lucidity to execute Onan's strategy and disconnect himself, to ejaculate outside of the young girl's well. He knew that before giving in to complete enjoyment it would be necessary to break the glass with which the matrimonial ceremonies celebrated by their ancestors in the demolished Temple of Jerusalem were recalled. For now, he had to resign himself to enjoying that revelation of the sacred, without aiming to internalize it with the miracle of procreation.

3

New Jerusalem,
Year 5407 Since the Creation,
1647 of the Common Era

It is written: Immortality is the supreme privilege that only a select few will enjoy. Armed with the patience of incommensurate time, the souls of those fortunate ones had to wait in Sheol, an intangible territory, extended like a mass of water under the world inhabited by the living. There they would rest until the coming of the Messiah and the Day of Judgment, when the possible, only possible, resurrection of their bodies and souls would occur, decided at last by divine will. Of the many beings who would pass over the face of the earth, only select dwellers of Sheol would be chosen to participate in that last phase. Among them would be the men and women who in life were pious, children who died in their innocence, those fallen in combat defending the rights and the Law of the Holiest and of His chosen people. Elias Ambrosius treasured that personal image of the apotheosis that would come after the journey of souls through Sheol. His grandfather Benjamin Montalbo de Ávila had given him that on the day of his initiation into adult life and responsibility, celebrated in the synagogue and officiated by then still rabbi Menasseh ben Israel.

"I am happy for you," the old man had said to him, after adjusting the kippah on his skull and kissing him on both cheeks. "You are lucky to have been born in the most propitious and longed-for time and place for a Jew since we abandoned our land and went into exile. You are going to discover for yourself that living in this city is a privilege, that Amsterdam is *Makom*, the good place. But never forget it: there is a place that is much better. Only the Messiah can take us there when he gathers the living and the dead and opens the gates of Jerusalem to us. Because of that, with our thoughts and actions, we should foster the arrival of the Anointed, so that we can enjoy this marvelous world where there is always light, where it is never cold, where one never feels hunger or pain, much less fear, because in the end, there is nothing to fear. For that place where one is so at ease, the Eden that Adam knew before the Fall, we have to fight while we are in this other world, which, dealing with *Makom*, we must recognize, my son, is not bad at all."

Grandfather Benjamin's words and the sweet images they managed to evoke in Elias Ambrosius's imagination had come to the aid of his mind to ease the painful moment of seeing himself forced to watch how the old man's body—wrapped in the first tallith he used upon arriving in Amsterdam and initiated himself in the faith of his ancestors—was lost to the depths of the grave, in search of proximity to the dominions of Sheol, where that pious and steadfast man had every right to go. While Hakham ben Israel proclaimed the ritual prayers invoking resurrection, Elias Ambrosius could not help but wonder, worried about his grandfather's fate, whether the news that had arrived from the eastern reaches of the Mediterranean (which his skepticism had not allowed him to devote too much attention to until then) referring to the wanderings in those lands of a self-proclaimed Messiah, a maker of miracles, and who had awoken so much expectation among Jews around the world, had any basis in fact and would allow him, perhaps, the best meeting, in the best of places, with that man of such an understanding heart, the person whom he had most loved in his life until his virility was won over by Mariam Roca.

The death of Grandfather Benjamin surprised them, although they expected it. Seventy-eight years already celebrated, the old man had lived much longer than the majority of his contemporaries ("almost as much as a biblical patriarch," he himself would say, smiling, when he spoke of his extreme age), but in recent times, his frame had been diminishing at a visible rhythm, although without pain or loss of intelligence. The Friday afternoon on which he left them, he had even asked them to help shave him and seat him in the living room, to attend the ceremony of lighting the Sabbath candles and, as the true patriarch of that home, welcome the happy day, devoted to the Lord and to celebrating the freedom of man. But when the table was set, the candles lit, and the shadows of the night allowed them to see the shine of the first lights announcing the victorious arrival of the awaited day, the greeting that Benjamin Montalbo de Ávila was supposed to proclaim ("*Shabbat shalom!*") was not heard by his children and grandchildren. Just like a star in the heavenly orbit: thus had his grandfather's life gone out.

On the small table where the old man—from the time in which he was still far from becoming an old man—used to write, study the sacred texts, and read the books that cheered him so, his son Abraham Montalbo found the sealed paper where the man, in foresight, had a few weeks prior written his last wishes. No one in the house was surprised that he would order each detail of his funeral; he even wrote some well-reasoned advice for each member of the family, and that he would leave the only material goods of value accumulated throughout his long life to his grandson Elias Ambrosius: that desk and those books were meant for him. And only when he received the news of the inheritance could the young man finally cry some tears that had seemed to have dried out. Later, seated behind the beautiful desk, as he caressed the leather spines and covers of the prodigious volumes that now belonged to him, Elias discovered how several of them seemed more worn by the intense handling to which their owner must have subjected them. Among the more worn ones were, of course, two works by Maimonides, Benjamin Montalbo's favorite thinker, and Léon Hebreo's *Dialoghi d'Amore*, but also several modern authors, not related at all to faith or religion, such as that Miguel de Cervantes, author of a thick novel called *The Ingenious Hidalgo Don Quixote de la Mancha*, and the so-called Inca Garcilaso de la Vega (incidentally, the translator of the *Dialoghi* into Castilian Spanish), author of *La Florida del Inca*, a chronicle of the frustrated attempts at conquest of that territory in the New World where, it was said, the Fountain of Eternal Youth had been found. The physical contact with those books—destined to keep his grandfather in communication with the lands of idolatry from which he had escaped to recover his faith, but whose language and culture he loved as his own—made Elias understand the real dimension of the conflict in which that unfathomable human being had lived: the dispute maintained by his spirit between belonging to a centuries-old faith, culture, and traditions, which he felt linked to through his blood, and the proximity to a landscape, a language, a literature, among which several generations of his ancestors had lived— ancestors who had arrived on the Peninsula with Berbers from the desert in a remote time, and amid whom he had spent the first thirty-three years of his life and whose products he had never been able to or wanted to renounce (as he had never renounced chickpeas, rice, and, whenever he could, the luxury of dipping his bread in olive oil). No, he never was able to nor wanted to renounce that belonging, not even after having lived in *Makom* and having learned of the rabbis' precepts, aimed at cutting off all of those dangerous approximations to the past and what they considered to be hidden dangers of idolatry.

Throughout the seven days of observing shivah, confined with his parents and brother in the house as the ceremony stipulated, Elias Ambrosius came to convince himself that he had been terribly small-minded by not having made his grandfather privy to his disquiet and his decisions. More than anyone else in the world, Benjamin Montalbo would have been in a position to understand him: because he was his grandfather and loved him, because he knew many of his secrets, and because he had lived for so many years with a divided soul. Perhaps, even, the old man would have marveled at the young man's progress and asked him for one of the canvases that, rolled or folded, he now hid in a trunk at the Maestro's house. Perhaps his grandfather would have reached out to him there, in front of the table where he enjoyed writing with his pen, that corner from where he traveled with his books and where, upon feeling death's call, he had left his testament.

Many times in the last two years, lived by Elias in a vertigo of overwhelming feelings, a vertigo of lessons and of increasingly less clumsy works, the young man had thought about the possibility of opening the physical and mental closet of his secrets to the old man. Of course, he was the only one of his relatives to whom he would speak of the beauty that the Maestro was capable of generating and of the obtuse reaction of the buyers of his paintings, who considered him a violator of precepts instead of a forger of unexplored paths. His grandfather had also been the first to whom he communicated his decision to become formally engaged to Mariam Roca, and then Elias received the most logical and sincere response from the old man: "I am dying of envy, son." But, in contrast, he had never had the courage to cross the borders of his fears and tell him about his loves as a painter's apprentice and speak to him of the moments of joy lived with the paintbrush that the Maestro had given him: moments such as the one dedicated to painting a bust of the beloved old man on a canvas.

Because in those two years, Elias Ambrosius had had other opportunities to practice his presumed abilities following the Maestro's guidance and orders, given to him specifically or obtained as a collective benefit during the process of some joint work with the rest of the students. Besides receiving the responsibility of priming the linens so that he could familiarize himself with the creation of those earthy backgrounds that the artist used so much, Elias learned to paint some of the objects and works collected by the man—a conch shell with its spirals, a bust of a Roman emperor, a marble sculpted hand, besides copying sketches by other artists and themes—which had served, alongside several live models, including nude ones, as didactic exercises through which the Maestro's advice refined and confirmed the young man's doubtless abilities. Meanwhile, in the attic of the house and in the shed in the field, Elias Ambrosius had tried to put that knowledge into practice and carried out several self-portraits, outlined landscapes, copied objects (always hearing in his mind the words of the painter) and, in a fit of daring, would make the decision to tell Mariam Roca his burning secret, since he wanted, more than anything in the world, to do an *au naturel* portrait of his lover and betrothed.

The girl's surprise at hearing Elias's confession turned out to be as obvious as it should have been and had to be. They spent several days talking about the subject, and the young man had to dodge the abundant reasons accumulated in those years to justify an act that many could consider heretical. When the discussion stalled and the young man lost all hope of being able to convince Mariam that doing what he was doing was his right as an individual, and even feared that the young woman could inform on him, Elias consoled himself by thinking that, sooner or later, he would have needed to make that confession—and run all the implicit risks—to the person with whom he aimed to share the rest of his life. That was why, when Mariam, seemingly more used to the idea, had agreed to serve as his model, under the condition that her decision also be a secret, Elias knew that he had obtained an important victory and preferred not to ask the young woman if her acceptance was limited to her role as a model or if it also implied acceptance of the exercise of painting by her betrothed.

The first portrait of Mariam, leaning on the window of the shed and looking out at the spectator, was in reality a painful exercise of copying the marvelous portrait that, some years before, with a similar composition, the Maestro had carried out of the beautiful Emely Kerk. The difficulties that the lights, anatomy, or proportions could present were overcome fairly easily by the young man, who had already learned so much about those elements. The use of the colors to create the skin and the hair, cut out against a deep background, was almost easy for him, after having seen so much skin and so many backgrounds painted, after having painted them with two hands with his companions and even with the Maestro. It was more complicated for him to achieve a reasonable likeness, to fix the woman's beauty, although at one point, with much effort, he thought he had achieved it and Mariam, looking at herself in the mirror, confirmed it for him. But what he most pursued and what, nonetheless, remained evasive and uncapturable for his abilities as a portraitist, was the young woman's soul. If he had been able to enter into possession of each of the girl's feelings and thoughts, physically and through love, when he tried to bring her spirit to the small canvas, he discovered his inexperience and shortness of breath to reflect the expression of that face on which Elias could see vitality and unease, doubt and love, the enjoyment of risk and the fear that this caused. But he did not manage to capture them. Moved by his failure, Elias reconsidered his intentions. He then began to work on a second portrait, a work that was his in every way. He placed Mariam in a complicated profile in which her face was turning, making a delicate downward diagonal with the line of her neck, while her eyes, visible, remained focused on an imprecise spot in the direction of the canvas's lower corner. At that moment, he understood that—as the Maestro had said to him once, so it could not fail to be—all of the humanity in transposition lay in the challenge of the eyes. He thought that if he had failed in his purpose it was due to his determination to reflect the young woman with her gaze facing forward, with a direct, explicit, leading expression. When in reality what the best representation of Mariam required was a mystery. He then asked the girl to, without looking at him, speak to him with her eyes, as if she were whispering something in his ear . . . Carefully, in several work sessions, he went outlining the eyebrows, lids, pupils, and iris of that gaze as he avoided the obvious and sought out the unfathomable. And when he believed he had reflected the gaze, he let the paintbrush establish its own dialogue with the rest of the details of her face, to make believable the miracle of understanding a suggestion . . . The Sunday afternoon that he made that discovery and immersed himself in the struggle to express it was one of the fullest moments in the life of Elias Ambrosius Montalbo de Ávila, since he again had the feeling of discovering what the sacred was. Because there was, beating, on a small piece of canvas stained with pigments, a woman who, from her forced stillness, offered the illusion of life.

How had it been possible for his fears to prevent him from showing his grandfather Benjamin Montalbo that small portrait in which he had succeeded in capturing something evanescent and opening the powerful doors of creation? The old man—dead now that Elias had that conviction—would not only have understood but would have encouraged him: because that man had not been more sensitive to anything than to the desire and human will to reach a goal despite everything. And on that linen was the ambition of a man and the will to meet the objectives with which the Creator had gifted him . . .

Elias would end up consoling himself with the idea that if it was actually true that in the lands of the Turks, the Persians, and the Egyptians the Messiah was going around announcing his arrival (he seemed to wander through all of those regions at the same time, judging by the multiple echoes reaching Amsterdam of his wandering and even of his miracles), perhaps very soon he, Elias Ambrosius Montalbo de Ávila, would be able to approach his grandfather and, in the middle of the apotheosis of the Final Judgment, ask his forgiveness for his lack of trust. Because that was the true sin that he should be sorry for, in the eyes of God and in the face of the memory of the spirit of a pious man. And he hoped to obtain a pardon from both.

———

Amsterdam was a beehive, as was Elias Ambrosius's heart. A few weeks after Grandfather Benjamin's funeral, the news of the death, in The Hague, of the stadtholder Frederik Hendrik de Nassau, who would be succeeded in his dignity by his son William, increased the expectation in which the city's inhabitants were already living because of, they said, the until then imminent signing of a peace treaty between the deceased stadtholder and the Spanish crown. That peace, which could put an end to a century of wars and would consolidate the independence of the Republic of the United Provinces of the North, would arrive as the deserved prize for the heated resistance of the country's inhabitants but, above all, as a result of its economic success, such a contrast to the critical state of the Spanish empire's finances, which were already incapable, as everyone knew, of maintaining Spain's armies any longer in an encampment stranded at sea and unable to last for long in the swamps and winters of that inhospitable territory. But the joy inspired by the awaited political and military dénouement began to fade, dragged by the greater danger of William of Nassau's ascension to stadtholder, a man whose monarchic aspirations were well-known and, with them, his opposition to the republican and federative system to which citizens attributed the country's success in mercantile, political, social, and even military matters. Due to the economic bonanza, the Republic had been able to finance ground forces, made up in their majority not by Amsterdam's burghers, The Hague's noblemen, or Leiden's scholars, but rather, above all, by mercenaries and warlords who had come from all over Europe to fight for a fair quantity of healthy florins. Only the republican regiment, it was also thought and said, had allowed the economic ascent of a great mass of merchants in the country, generators of wealth, inspired in their efforts by the fact of having freed themselves from dragging along the burden of a court, a nobility, and a parasitic bureaucracy like the ones bleeding Spain. And now, when they seemed so close to military and political victory, William of Nassau could annihilate that social balance thanks to the fact that many citizens had found a better life, with the pleasant benefits of freedom—a freedom that could soon be, as the crowning decoration, political as well if the new stadtholder signed the peace with the Spanish.

If Elias Ambrosius was so up-to-date on the specifics of his country's public affairs, it was not due to his wisdom but rather the privileged situation of his ears and his mind, which, because of the responsibilities and abilities he now enjoyed in the Maestro's house and workshop, allowed him to be the witness (silent in his case) to some of the passionate conversations maintained between the painter and many of his friends, but especially the young burgher Jan Six.

Since the previous year, when he arrived at the Maestro's house to negotiate the making of a portrait, Jan Six had begun to establish a relationship with the painter that soon went beyond the fleeting and pragmatic limits of a pictorial commission. A current of mutual sympathy, which in Six's case was fueled by his artistic aspirations—since he thought himself to be a poet and playwright—and for the Maestro by his commercial vocation and his constant need for money, had drawn together those two men, who were ten years apart in age and separated by the fortune of one and the never-ending economic binds of the other.

Besides, the current of affinity had as its basis the fondness both shared for collecting, which would make of Six, who was a compulsive purchaser of art, a dazzled admirer of the paintings, books of engravings, and many incredible objects amassed by the Maestro.

Despite his youth, Jan Six already held the position of auxiliary *burgemeester*, and served as one of the city's magistrates, due to the circumstance of belonging to one of Amsterdam's most affluent families. The Sixes were the owners of a dwelling in the exclusive Kloveniersburgwal, the so-called Houses of the Blue Eagle, next to the famous Crystal House, the property of Floris Soop, the very rich maker of mirrors and glasses, and a stone's throw away from the citizen militia's luxurious building displaying the Maestro's great work that, like Elias Ambrosius, had also stirred great feelings in the young Six and generated a solid admiration for its creator.

Since the first attempts and studies for Jan Six's possible portrait, for a variety of reasons, the young Jew closely followed the Maestro's strange creative process, which, two years later, had still not produced the great portrait that Six had at one point sought to have to feed his ego and his collection, and that the Maestro wished to carry out, for obvious monetary reasons and for the revaluation of his work in the world of the city's great burghers. At times like one more disciple, at others as the painter's assistant, Elias had watched the elaboration of two marvelous drawings, made as sketches, with which the Maestro resolved to define his customer's tastes to fully satisfy them and avoid unpleasant episodes like the one with Andries de Graeff, which, should it repeat itself, would have been devastating for his prestige already in question as a portraitist.

The *burgemeester* had welcomed one of the sketches with absolute enthusiasm. Not the one that highlighted his condition as a politician and man of action, but rather the one in which he appeared as a young and beautiful writer, armed with a manuscript on which he concentrated his attention, his body leaning against a window through which light entered to illuminate his face, the manuscript, and part of the room, until falling over the armchair where other books rested. That drawing gave Jan Six the image of himself that he most desired to give others. It satisfied him so much that he would ask the Maestro for something unusual: that instead of painting it in oil, he do so on an etched plate, so that he could make several copies for different purposes. And he would pay the price for an etched plate equal to the value of an oil painting.

In that way, first as a generous customer, later as a pampered admirer and very soon as a friend, Jan Six became a habitual presence in the Maestro's house and workshop at a time in which the painter was living one of his ecstatic moments, since just a few months prior he had managed to hire as his son Titus's governess the young Hendrickje Stoffels—less beautiful, although by all appearances more intelligent than Emely Kerk—from a humble family like her predecessor, whom he had very quickly brought to his bed. And he had so enjoyed that awakening of his passions as a mature man, that he had made a beautiful and provocative painting on a panel that he titled simply *Hendrickje Stoffels in Bed*, in which the young girl, half-dressed, with no other adornment but a golden ribbon in her hair, is raising the bed's curtain with her left hand and peeking out at the observer, covering her breast with a sheet and lying on a soft pillow . . . In the Maestro's bed.

The beneficent presence of Jan Six and of Hendrickje Stoffels greatly improved the mood of the artist, who was again—in Elias's opinion—the man whom a few years prior, before the death of his wife, he must have been. Even more lively, perhaps, since, as he had declared, he now felt free from artistic and even social conventions, as demonstrated by that painting of Hendrickje in which he publicly aired, and with pride, his amorous relationship with a maid. The feeling of self-satisfaction radiated to everyone surrounding him—an exception made, of course, for Mme. Dircx, with whom he lived at war—including his students. The relationship with Elias Ambrosius had reached the point of being warm, and, thanks to it, the young man was able to sit in on the dialogues with Jan Six, through which he learned so much about the Republic's political situation. And, likewise, their relationship would lead him to become the main model for the great work that the Maestro was handing himself over to (favored by the fact that his beard had grown out at last, a bit patchy, but a beard at the end of the day) with all of his abilities and rebellions at the ready then: an image of a resurrected Christ having supper after his encounter with his disciples on the road to Emmaus.

His increasingly visible and important responsibilities in the Maestro's workshop (as at other times had occurred with Carel Fabritius, now it was Elias who always accompanied him on his shopping expeditions and also served as his most recurred to canvas primer), his own progress as a painter, the public proclamation of his marriage engagement to Mariam Roca, and his promotion to the position of operator in the printshop overseen by his father filled every second of the young man's life with brilliance while simultaneously leading him to the dangerous circumstance that his secret would be evermore exposed and could be revealed by people capable of complicating his existence, to an extreme degree.

Luckily for him, people's attention seemed to be focused on the great political conflicts of the moment, which could bring unpredictable consequences for the members of the Nação, and on more attractive events, such as the publication of a scandalous treatise on the relationship between Man and the Divine, written and distributed by the young Baruch, son of Miguel de Espinoza; or the material problems of placement posed by the arrival of an increasing number of poverty-stricken Jews from the East, a real plague; or the commentaries (loaded with commercial and familiar expectations, for many) on the possible opening of Spanish and Portuguese ports to commerce with Amsterdam. But, above all, the most active and militant part of the Hebrew community was spellbound by the news, increasingly disquieting, generated by the acts of the self-proclaimed Messiah, who now appeared to be wandering about Palestine, on the way to no other place than Jerusalem and announcing the arrival of the judgment in the nearby year of 1648. So one would be hard-pressed to find anyone who, in Amsterdam, would take special interest in the relationship between a painter and a Jew, and Elias Ambrosius was able to enjoy the benefit of some shadows amid which his heart enjoyed a peaceful space.

Young Elias had been living in a true state of ecstasy ever since the Maestro chose him to work with him on that piece that, before the first brushstroke, already had the only title it could have, the same one that on other occasions the painter had used, a title that was simultaneously so susceptible to and so complacent with the Maestro's obsessions: *Pilgrims at Emmaus*.

"I'm not interested in the mystical side of the story but rather in its human condition, which is inexhaustible. That is why I always come back to this passage until I manage to domesticate it, to feel it as definitively mine," the painter explained to him the afternoon on which, just after the apprentice's arrival, he communicated his decision to him. "I have been obsessed with the scene for almost twenty years. The first time I painted it, I made Christ a mysterious specter and of the disciple who recognized him, a shocked man . . . Now I want to paint some normal guys who have the privilege of seeing the Son of God resurrected as he carries out the most common and most symbolic of actions: breaking bread, *a simple piece of bread*, not the cosmic symbol that your Hakham ben Israel talks about," he emphasized. "Some common man, full of fear of the persecutions they are suffering, at the moment in which their faith is overcome by the greatest of miracles: the return from the world of the dead. But above all, I want to paint a flesh-and-blood Jesus, a Jesus who has returned from the great beyond and has walked like a living being with those disciples toward Emmaus, and should appear as human and tangible as no one has ever painted him. More alive than the one by the great Caravaggio . . . But at the same time, possessing power. And that Jesus that I am going to reproduce as a living man is going to have your face and your figure . . ."

Then the Maestro, to close in on his objective, proposed to the moved Elias that they carry out an experiment: he would paint a *tronie* of the young Jew in oil—those busts had been the Maestro's foremost specialty, back in his distant days of trial and error in his native Leiden—since what interested him most was achieving a recognizable expression of humanity on the divine face. But, and here came the unexpected twist: they would do so with two hands. While he worked on the portrait of Elias, Elias would work on his self-portrait, and between both of them, they would seek out the earthly depths of the man marked by the transcendent condition of having returned from the dominion of death and experiencing a brief earthly transit before taking up his place alongside his Father.

The greatest drawback that Elias immediately noticed about the tempting project that would put him to work side by side with the greatest painter in the city and perhaps the known world was the public resonance that that piece would achieve by being the Maestro's work, and the presumable reaction it would provoke among the community's religious leaders when they saw not that Elias had offered his services as a model for a painting but that he had done so for a painting of the greatest of heresies. And those patriarchs, who were increasingly more inflexible with the worldly reactions of a community over whom they could not lose control, seemed to have had enough already of real heresies or those assumed as such.

It was, as always, his former professor who became the man he chose to seek clarity in his reasoning. The night on which he appeared at his house, Raquel Abravanel, uncombed and complaining, as usual, told him that her husband was at a meeting of the Mahamad, the rabbinical council, and if he wanted to wait for him, to do so on the steps outside, beneath the mezuzah. And, as usual, she closed the door.

The spring evening was more temperate than usual for the season and Elias barely gave any thought to the rudeness of the woman, who long ago had ceased to repeat the old Sephardic sentence that summarized her dreams of greatness: *"Jajám i merkader, alegría de la muzer."* As both a teacher and a wealth-generating businessman, her husband had proven to be a most resounding failure, and Raquel Abravanel blamed him for all of her misery.

Although he was about to flee due to the stench of the excrement barges that, every evening, crossed the Binnen Amstel, the joy and fear amid which the young man was living since that afternoon were stronger. And with reason: he himself and his face, fortunately bearded already, would be the object of the Maestro's art, which would place him in the arena of the most sublime earthly immortality, a condition for which Amsterdam's richest citizens, including Jan Six, had to pay several hundred florins.

The Hakham arrived at nearly nine o'clock on a night that took just a few minutes to cool off. From their initial greeting and exchange, the young man understood that the scholar's mood was not the best. Sitting already in Ben Israel's chaotic workroom as the Hakham served the first glasses of wine, Elias received a summary of the circumstances that had irritated the man.

"To instill fear in people, those rabbis are capable of doing anything. Now they want the head of Baruch, the son of Miguel de Espinoza. And, on top of everything, several of them, like Breslau and Montera in the lead, say that they are convinced that the signs coming from Cairo and Jerusalem must be taken into account. That that crazy man wandering around out there could well be the Messiah!"

After his second glass of wine was in hand, Hakham ben Israel finally told him about the latest adventures of the enlightened one who introduced himself as the Messiah. Everything had begun in Smyrna, where that Sabbatai Zevi was born and, very precociously, had studied the books of the Kabbalah in depth. It was there that, drunk on mysticism or insanity—in Ben Israel's words—he had launched himself on the most dangerous path toward heresy, willing to challenge all precepts: before the ark of the synagogue, he had pronounced God's secret and forbidden name, the one that is written, but not said . . . The reaction of Smyrna's rabbis was logical and immediate: they excommunicated him, as he deserved. But Sabbatai had more tricks up his sleeve: he left his city and went to Thessaloníki, where he began preaching and, at a meeting of Kabbalists, imitated a marriage ceremony with a scroll of the Torah and proclaimed himself Messiah. He had also been kicked out of Thessaloníki, as could be expected . . . But that crazy man (they said he was a beautiful man, tall, honey-colored hair, eyes that changed colors like a lizard's skin, and the owner of an enveloping voice) had ended up in Cairo, where he was welcomed in the house of a rich businessman, the site where the city's Kabbalists met. There, with his speeches, he convinced— and only the holiest knows how he did it—the city's scholars and the powerful, who gave him their support and even money. Since then, he had wandered, preaching around Jerusalem, where he had arrived preceded by the fame of his acts, and he had devoted himself to distributing alms, practicing charity, and, they said, carrying out miracles. That entire circus, in the Hakham's opinion, was rather similar to that of other "messiahs" that we have suffered ("One of those who was quite successful, you already know who"), had entered its most dangerous phase when a certain Nathan of Gaza, a young Kabbalist, supposedly the possessor of prophetic gifts, announced that the enormous truth had been revealed to him: Sabbatai Zevi was the reincarnation of the eternally awaited prophet Elias, and his arrival, coinciding with all of the disgraces suffered by the sons of Israel in recent centuries ("As if suffering disgraces were something new for us"), constituted the definitive announcement of the coming final judgment, marked for the year 1648, when still unimaginable misfortunes for the sons of the Chosen People would occur, the final, apocalyptic ones, prior to the arrival of redemption.

"Right now, that fake is running around Palestine, followed by that Nathan of Gaza and hundreds of Jews so desperate that they are capable of believing in his sermons, and inviting everyone to 'scale the wall' and gather in Jerusalem," he said.

Elias Ambrosius, whose rebellion and rationality had never managed to stamp out the strong messianic feeling with which his grandfather Benjamin infected him, felt that there was something new, although difficult to pinpoint in Sabbatai's story—perhaps not only the insanity of an unhinged man. The rabbinical prohibition against "scaling the wall" and entering Jerusalem to gather anew the descendants of Abraham, Isaac, and Moses represented a real challenge to which no other enlightened one had dared. Since the days of the founding rabbinical councils that served to establish the precepts and laws gathered in the Talmud and the Mishnah, it was well-known by all Jews in the world that that act of aspiring to a massive return to the Holy Land was considered a precise way of tempting the arrival of salvation and, as such, was absolutely prohibited, since exile formed part of the destiny of that people until the determination of the true Messiah.

"With all due respect, Hakham . . . Why couldn't Sabbatai be the Messiah? So many indicators, so much daring . . ."

"He is not for the many reasons that I took care of reminding those fanatics with whom we live and who take advantage of everything to feed the people's fear and thus control them at their will," the scholar said, nearly yelling, losing his temper. "Because the prophet Elias himself warned that the Anointed would only come when Jews lived in every corner of the earth, and that still has not happened."

"Because the American indigenous people are not the descendants of the ten lost tribes?"

"For starters, that . . . And to continue, because in England, as you well know, as I have said thousands of times, there have been no Jews for three hundred and fifty years . . . Because the Messiah will be a warrior. Because his arrival will be preceded by great cataclysms . . . But think, kid, think: Where did this Sabbatai of Smyrna come from?"

With the revelation of that detail, Elias Ambrosius ended up understanding the Hakham's position: to accept even the possibility of Sabbatai's messianism would mean the loss of his signature struggle for the admission of Jews in England and, above all, the abandonment of the Abravanels' aspirations that he, part of the clan, took so much responsibility in predicating.

"It doesn't matter what other members of the council say, nor that some rich Sephardic Jews in Amsterdam—along with many of the city's poor—are throwing away their fortunes for a spot on the boats leaving toward Jerusalem, where they will all join the crazy man's retinue. I am only concerned with what will be my life's work from now on: opening the doors of England to the Jews, building the necessary bridge to open the path to the true Messiah and not to this new illuminated man who—you know something?—will only bring us more disgrace, as if we didn't have enough. You live and you learn . . ."

Elias, who had not managed to express the reason for his visit to his former teacher's house, took his leave around midnight, weighed down by marvelous disquiet and new doubts. The revelations of the history and wanderings of Sabbatai Zevi had managed to move him and make him think. The fact that some Jews believed him to be the Messiah and that others rejected him was not at all an unprecedented attitude in the chronicles of Israel, in which credulity and doubt always went hand in hand. From the times of Solomon, the greatest and most illustrious of the wise men of his race, a fertile time for profits and great events (the creation of the kingdoms of Judah and Israel, the construction of the Temple, the great wars and the decisive exile to Babylon of nearly the entire Hebrew population, including the ten tribes lost since then), Ecclesiastes had manifested a frank and free doubt over the Orthodox dogmas, as each of the chapters of his book reflected. Despite that, it was considered sacred because Ecclesiastes's skepticism was not a heresy but rather part of Jewish thinking, and it demonstrated how difficult it was to sufficiently show capable proof of satisfying the vocation for questioning everything on the part of a people with such an accentuated critical nature. In reality, Elias thought, a people more incredulous than given to believe. The people who, paradoxically, had created, through the holiest revelations, the foundation of a religious faith capable of igniting the souls of the entire civilized world.

So, in that environment that gave everyone a front-row seat to all kinds of anguish, struggles in which everything unnecessary would be tossed aside, was he going to rise to the challenge of posing as the supposed Messiah who introduced himself as Jesus, the Christ? That man had been the one who would cause the deepest divisions among the Jews, making dissidents out of those who would go on to become the forefathers of future oppressors of other Jews, the founders and practitioners of an anti-Semitism that, from the pulpits of the new religion proposed by Jesus, had brought so much suffering, pain, exploitation of goods, and, of course, so much death to their former confreres, solely for having remained true to the original faith and its laws. Elias felt his soul breaking as he pondered past and present stories of messianism, and each piece floated on its way without his being able to catch it and try to put it all back together. If Sabbatai Zevi was the Anointed and his invitation to "scale the wall" constituted a divine mandate, then there was nothing to do, only wait for the prodigious celebration of Judgment (and he again embraced the idea of a reunion with his grandfather). If he wasn't, as his beloved Hakham stated and as he himself, in the back of his mind, felt more tempted to think, then the world would go on its path plagued by sorrows until the real Coming of the Messiah and of salvation. Then, as Ben Israel himself would say, there would be no reason to hand over hopes, passions, and dreams to death, vegetating in life until the inevitable end of the flesh. Although his attitude entailed risks, and despite the fact that the usual Orthodox members could even accuse him of betraying those of his race and that fear would not leave him in peace, he would choose life . . . And he felt a hint of relief when he understood that, while each man could help the Coming with his actions, this essentially depended on the supreme will of the Holiest, whose decisions had already been made since eternity. His individual actions, as such, were part of a great cosmic balance but did not determine it. He, as a mortal being, had a territory that had been given him (by the Creator himself), and just one time: the space of his life. That space could be filled with his actions as a man, and he could do no better because his conscience, the most important source of decisions, advised him that with those actions, he himself was not violating the essence of a Law. His problem, he again felt, was with himself and not with his neighbors . . . The fate of the soul of the Maestro (who rejected any kind of interference by others in his personal life and, above all, in his religious life) was the Maestro's responsibility, and the Maestro well knew what he wanted to do with it. Elias's own, although tied to tradition and some rules, continued to be his own problem. His and his God's; in other words, his and his soul's.

When Elias Ambrosius entered the studio, he discovered that the Maestro, with his impulses unleashed already, had been laboring, perhaps with the help of some student, to achieve the work besieging his mind. Like the first time that they had painted together, he had set up two easels, with their respective stools, and placed the mirrors such that the stand and seat on the right, farthest from the window, would be reflected at three different angles on the silver surfaces. The looking glass placed just behind the easel would provide a frontal image and the other two, one placed on either side, a semi-profile and a full profile, the latter visible through the mirror that reflected the semi-profile. That was going to be, it seemed obvious, the place for the person drawing the self-portrait. The other stool and easel had been placed in such a manner that it would receive all of the light from the windows and at the same time would give a frontal view of whoever sat in the chair surrounded by mirrors. What surprised the young man was discovering that, on the small stands on which they would work, of unusual although similar dimensions (about three-quarters of an ell by a bit more than those three quarters high), were, nevertheless, different materials: that of the portraitist was a canvas; that of the self-portraitist was a panel, purchased a few months before by the Maestro, already primed in matte gray, and then, perhaps due to its seldom-seen size, forgotten in the studio.

Allowing time for the Maestro to finish his siesta—over the years, he had acquired that habit of having a rest to regain his strength, since, besides, he tended to suffer from insomnia because of the frequent toothaches that persisted after his visits to the surgeon—Elias Ambrosius decided to entertain his anxiety. With the professionalism he had already acquired, he began to prepare the colors with which they would work, previously chosen by the Maestro, without great surprise: white lead and earth colors. There were ocher red (for the shirt that he had asked Elias to wear for their work sessions), sienna, ocher yellow, and the red-orange, whose use and place in the work still intrigued the young man.

When he had prepared the required quantities for about three hours of work, Elias settled onto his stool and studied the images of his face he was receiving from the mirrors. Ever since he had begun to paint himself in the solitude of the attic, a few years before, his features had changed a lot, making the journey from the disproportion inherent to adolescence to the settling of the characteristics of adulthood of his confirmed twenty-one years. His hair, which he always wore parted down the middle, was loose over his shoulders and had darkened some, although it maintained a reddish sheen, and his mouth seemed firmer, perhaps harder. His beard, now extended over his cheeks and chin, and his mustache over his upper lip, were sparse with thick whiskers, and the hairs of his beard, darker than the hair on his head, were corkscrew curls. But his features also announced other, less perceptible, hidden changes, caused by the experiences lived in those years during which he

had discovered, enjoyed, or suffered the deep feelings of pain over the
death of a loved one, the joy of love and its physical consummation,
the weights of living with a secret and dragging along fear and, above
all, the certainty and uncertainty of an apprenticeship so weighed down
with responsibilities, stabbing tension, and fabulous finds. His face now
matched that of a man who has lived his indispensable trials and, even,
feels capable of turning them into material for the knowledge of others
through a marvelous exercise of art.

Elias felt the unrestrainable impulse and, without waiting for the
Maestro's arrival, dared to prepare his palette and returned to the stool
and to self-contemplation. Without knowing it, at that moment he was
at last discovering why he had decided to throw it all in the fire and
dive into painting: not for money, or for fame, or to satisfy his tastes. What
moved him and now sustained his hand as he drew the lines that would
hold his face was the certainty that, with the paintbrush, some pigments,
and the right surface, he could enjoy the power of creating life, a life un-
noticed by many people, which he was capable of seeing and, in possession of the weapons given to him by the Maestro, of reflecting, with
passion, emotion, and beauty. What the young man did know in that
precise moment, even when he was risking reprimand by the painter who
always had the first and last word in the workshop, was that, in that instant, he was a satisfied and happy man. Just like when he coupled with
Mariam; just like he had been on the day on which his grandfather took
him to initiate him in the synagogue and kissed him on the cheeks after
adjusting his kippah, leading him so he could become an adult; just
like in the best moments of his life, because he was doing that which
the Lord—he no longer had any doubts—had created him for. As he gave
shape to his face, seeking himself out through a direct, clean gaze, he
reached the elusive answer that for years before the Maestro had
demanded from him at that same place and that only now arose in an
overwhelming way. Elias Ambrosius wanted to be a painter to have that
precise power. The power of creating, the most beautiful and invincible
of the powers with which some men tended to govern and, almost always,
bully other men.

———

Summer in Amsterdam is a feast of light and heat, capable of infecting
the moods of its dwellers, who, fully enjoying the season, never manage

to completely forget that the good fortune is temporary, between two long, snowy winters whipped by blizzards and all too frequent rains, which drove humidity deep into everyone's bones. The light, always filtered by the steam of so much water, became dense, nearly compact, but shone for many hours of the day of that northern territory. Elias Ambrosius, also moved by the euphoria of the season, lived those days in a fit of pleasure and satisfaction, which were none too pleasant for Mariam Roca, who had to stoically withstand the physical and mental absences of her lover, who, when he was finally at her side, would get lost in digressions about the quality of the light or how quickly certain pigments dried (fast in the case of Cassel earth pigment, slow in the case of bitumen of Judea, capricious in the case of Naples yellow) and experienced sudden mood changes.

It is true that the Maestro had begun the process of working with one of his usual bitter rants, more frequent and expected when he had just taken a nap or when his teeth ached: Elias was forced to cover up his own first attempt to declare and practice artistic independence with a gray layer of primer, since the work that was in the Maestro's mind was *the* one he needed and not the first one that came to an apprentice's mind. He wanted, needed, sought out, very convincing expressions of the face of Elias-Christ that would breathe humanity, the simple humanity of a man, despite that man's lineage and mission on earth, even despite having been resurrected and finding himself once more in the tremendous position of being among mortals and sinners. That same afternoon, in his notebook—alongside the folder of drawings and the file of works he had been hiding at the Maestro's house for a few months— Elias tried to reproduce the man's words, obsessive and vehement: "It cannot be the Christ by Leonardo, humble and removed, too saintly, too much of a god in relation to the disciples . . . Even though we're going to put him in the red tunic from *The Last Supper*. Nor is he the one from Caravaggio's first *Emmaus Supper*: too beautiful and theatrical, almost feminine . . . Also with his red tunic. It should look more like Caravaggio's second picture, more man, more human, although it ended up being rather dramatic and perfect, as couldn't help happening when it's Caravaggio. My Christ has to be a man who, in front of other men, reveals his essence through a gesture we make every day, but that in him turned into the symbol of the Eucharist. The bread will be the most normal bread, and common as well will be the act of breaking it in pieces before initiating the supper . . . Without mysticism, without theatrics . . . Humanity, that is what I want, humanity," he emphasized, nearly livid, and added: "And you have to deliver that face to me and we have to capture it *au naturel.*"

The Maestro's idea of having two versions was that Elias would work on the panel, more malleable with the pigments, and offer him a face of Christ with a slight profile of his head tilting softly, creating a line of movement coming from the chin, running over the nose and, through the part of his hair, reaching the right upward-most angle of the surface. In that way, he aimed to make visible the entire cheek closest to the spectator and the complete contour of the interior one, at the same time that he marked a departure toward the infinite based on that daily gesture. In that pose, the gaze, tilting somewhat downward, should express introspection. The lights had to be uniform, full, and for that reason he had lifted the curtains, in search of the free movement of the thick summer light toward the studio's interior: his interest, at that moment, was the face and only the face of a man. And so that his purpose would be executed in the best possible way, the Maestro made lines on the primed and re-covered (with the same matte gray) panel the shape of a head and the placement of the shoulders to which the hair fell. Meanwhile, his own *tronie* of Elias-Christ—which he would execute on the canvas—would face forward and, as he worked, he would decide on the level of his gaze, although he already assumed it would have a different orientation but should also be facing something beyond the earthly. He would seek out the gaze of someone who, from his humanity, was already seeing the announced glory that was taken away from him during the thirty-three years in which he had to suffer, as a man, all sorrows and frustrations, including betrayal, humiliation, and death. "As a man . . . The man who on the cross asked his father why he needed to go through those difficulties."

Elias, conscious of how much was at play, set himself to the task. Following the Maestro's guidelines, he finished outlining the face, the hair, and the downward curve of the shoulders, leaving the space for the features in reserve. He then worked on what would be the background, filling in the matte red-orange with hints of ocher that had so intrigued him, since the Maestro did not tend to use it for that purpose. Elias at last discovered the painter's purpose: to take depth away from the piece, to give it its own light without working on sources of light and helping to highlight what would be the face. Beyond making it stand out, making it look out toward the spectator.

While the Maestro advanced in his experiments, frequently demanding that his model look him in the eyes, with his chin straight or raised, Elias barely advanced with his own creation. The hair would be the most difficult to get down. From there, he went down to the lower corner where the bust would go, covered with the earthen red tunic, marked by some deep brown folds. "Close the collar of the shirt," the Maestro said to him at some point. "Don't move the attention to other places: the face is the objective."

"Can I see your painting, Maestro?"

"No, not yet. I am the one who wants to see yours finished. Let's go."

The day on which he focused at last on depicting the face the Maestro wanted to see, Elias understood how much he had learned and how much he still had left to learn. He had to achieve the face of a man illuminated by the interior light of his divine condition. He worked on the beard, outlined the chin, and concentrated on the mouth. Over the upper lip he met the challenge of the mustache, sparse but visible. His own nose then revealed itself to be unknown to him, as if he were looking for the first time at that protuberance that had always accompanied him, so often sketched but suddenly declaring itself foreign. He looked at the Maestro's nose, flattened, increasingly fleshier, and wanted to have one like that. The one the mirror handed him seemed too anonymous, vulgarly perfect, definitively Jewish. Delicately and painstakingly, he brought to the panel the image delivered to him by the mirror and was almost satisfied. The forehead and arch of the eyes, crowned by the eyebrows, were less problematic for him, and he was able to work them out after a few consultations with the Maestro. And he assumed that he had arrived at the great challenge, the eyes and the gaze.

By that point, the Maestro had already finished the bulk of his work, which he decided to leave aside before making any final touches, for which he did not require Elias: only the demands of his art, his interior vision of the model, and his own processing of the Christ pursued through the living face of the young man. Elias could at last see the small canvas worked on by the painter and was shocked: that face was his, or not, in reality it ended up being more than his, and, for this reason, at the same time it was not. The gaze tilted upward set him to examining nowhere in particular, or perhaps somewhere that for the rest of men could be nowhere, and for that reason offered a powerful feeling of transcendence, of breaking with human limits, to glimpse the infinite and unknown. Without a doubt, it was he himself, Elias Ambrosius Montalbo de Ávila, but reborn, made divine in life, one would say, thanks to the Maestro's paintbrush.

Ashamed, he looked at his other face, pictured on the wood but still lacking eyes, and told himself that he would never reach the celestial heights through which the Maestro's artistic creation moved. Although he immediately reproached himself for his exaggerated vanity: very few men in the world had reached those heights, and that had not kept Veronese, Leonardo, Titian, Raphael, Tintoretto, Caravaggio, Rubens, and Velázquez from painting, each at his own level, but with care and beauty. Right there, in Amsterdam, hundreds of men dipped their paintbrushes every day, wondering whether or not to compete with the drama and force of that genius or with the sweetness and delicacy of Vermeer of Delft or the detailed exquisiteness of Frans Hals—but these men were committed to their art.

"I'll leave you so you don't get distracted," the Maestro said to him, on an afternoon at the end of August, as he removed his apron. "You're doing well. Now, work until you're exhausted. When you can't keep going, give a shout and I will help you. But before that, I should tell you two things: first, I don't want the gaze of a God; second, we are searching for what no one has found: a living God . . . And, incidentally, I also wanted to tell you that you are already a painter and I am proud of you." And without giving the young man time to react, he threw his apron in a corner and left the studio.

———

When the Maestro focused on making the final touches to the panel and canvas, they reached their definitive pictorial perfection, having attained a tangible warmth and a quality that was simultaneously unsettlingly earthly and transcendental. The two Christs, different but united by a clear family resemblance, at last exuded the desired humanity following the exercise of plucking them from reality with that corporeal condition intact. In the final phase, the painter had insisted on his purpose of conferring on them the exact balance, known only to him, that their gazes should offer: Elias's Christ looked inward, in contemplation of his own unfathomable world, while the Maestro's was looking outward, searching for the infinite and unreachable. It did not surprise Elias that, once the pieces were finished, the Maestro decided not to use either of the two heads as a reference for the image of Christ that, behind a table, would break bread before the pilgrims at Emmaus. "I have something different in mind," he said, as if that were perfectly normal. But, to feed the incommensurate joy amid which the young man was living, the Maestro made a decision capable of surpassing Elias's expectations: according to the workshop's custom, whenever warranted by the work of the student, he would sign the Christ created by Elias as his and, at some point, offer it for sale. By contrast, on the version he had sketched on the canvas, he would always place the initials of his name, and would present it as a gift to the apprentice, as recompense for his efforts in that search, but, above all, as recognition for the achievements of the young Jew who had arrived at his house four years prior, armed only with enthusiasm, a painter capable of going to the market with the work bearing the signature of the Maestro.

Elias, surprised and moved by that recognition and the Maestro's seldom seen gesture of gifting an apprentice a work of his, patiently waited until the end of the day, devoted to collecting and washing paintbrushes, placing easels, making space to accommodate the linen that, the following day, he himself would begin to prime in the company of the German Christoph Paudiss, at that moment the most outstanding of the students welcomed in the workshop. It would be the linen on which the Maestro would begin to work on his new version of *Pilgrims at Emmaus*, with which, for some reason he would not confess, he had been so obsessed for several months (almost as obsessed as he was with the young Hendrickje Stoffels, who day by day was taking over areas previously reigned over by Mme. Dircx).

As soon as the Maestro declared the day's work finished, Elias went running out to Jodenbreestraat and up Sint Antoniesbreestraat, passing proudly in front of the houses where other painters had lived (Pieter Lastman, Paulus Potter)—more famous, but painters *like him*—and the building where the merchant Hendrick Uylenburgh lived (at some point, he should speak with him), in the direction of De Waag and, from there, the house of Mariam Roca. In his hand, rolled up, he was carrying the small linen signed with a long *R* and a very small *v*, the linen that, after so much anxiety, had turned into the laurel wreath of his success and, very soon, would turn into the source of infinite disgrace.

As he walked with his fiancée around the Spui Square, in the direction of the banks of the Singel and the fresh air that always ran over that canal, Elias told her of the latest events, so transcendent for him. Mariam, more worried than happy, listened to him in silence, weighing perhaps the dimensions of the responsibilities and actions in which the young man had entangled himself. When they were seated on one of the wooden trunks that would soon be moved toward the Dam Square to be used in some of the construction being carried out there in a rush, Elias Ambrosius, taking advantage of the last light of that August afternoon, could not resist the push of his pride and vanity any longer and dared to unfold, in the middle of the street, the small linen that was his greatest treasure.

When Mariam Roca saw the face of her lover copied on the canvas, she had a small shock: that figure was *her* Elias Ambrosius, but it was also, without any doubt, the face established by the Christians as the man they considered the Messiah.

"It's very beautiful, Elias," she said. "But it's a heresy," she added, and asked him to roll it up again. "What are you going to do with that?"

"For now, hide it away."

"Well, make sure you do a good job of it . . . Haven't you gone too far, Elias?"

"It's a portrait, Mariam," he said, trying to downplay the significance of it, and he added, "A portrait made by the Maestro, like the ones belonging to Hakham ben Israel, or Dr. Bueno, who is such good friends with your father."

She moved her head, denying something.

"You know it's not. This is much more . . . So what are you going to do now?"

Elias looked at the pleasant current of the canal's dark waters, over which was falling the last light of that afternoon in Amsterdam, the good place, the home of freedom.

"I don't know. From now on, I don't know how long the Maestro will continue accepting me as a student . . . But I can't imagine my life as a simple printshop worker, or even as the owner of the printshop. Although I make a living moving presses and packing flyers, I won't be able to help being a painter."

"For how long, Elias? Or do you think your secret is invulnerable? Don't you know that people talk about you because of your close relationship with the Maestro?"

"And don't they talk about Ben Israel and the other Jews who are his friends and drink wine and smoke leaves of tobacco with him?"

"Of course they talk . . . But they say other things. I only want to tell you to be careful. You spoke to me of a line . . . But you left that behind long ago . . . Now let's go, they're waiting for me at home for dinner."

When Elias went to take her hand, Mariam withdrew it. In silence, they returned to the young girl's dwelling and Elias Ambrosius understood how far he had crossed the line behind which his religion and his time had confined him.

———

Elias, dressed in a gray tunic, his hair falling over his shoulders, was watching the Maestro work from his position, behind a table. The young Jew and Paudiss the German apprentice had dedicated two weeks to the work of priming the canvas and, later, to filling in the spaces signaled by the Maestro, applying a greenish ocher and a chestnut color that darkened the main part to black, then working with a matte gray on the columns, the walls, and the arch that would occupy the background of the piece, also delineated by the painter. In the assistants' work, the entire center and lower part of the space remained intact, in reserve, in which the Maestro now placed the figure of the young man behind the supper table that would reproduce the episode at Emmaus.

Although the relationship with Mariam had returned to its usual state of warmth, in those days Elias Ambrosius had devoted more time than ever in his life to thinking not about the act he wanted to carry out but rather the ways of practicing his vocation and preserving the balance, precarious but pleasant, in which his life had passed, thanks to the secret in which he had managed to preserve his audacity. It was only in those days that he'd had the true notion of how an adventure that in its origins had had much capriciousness and curiosity, of risky games and innocent tastes, had with time reached a temperature that was becoming more dangerous in the midst of an atmosphere definitively altered by the always more alarming news of the wanderings through Palestine of Sabbatai Zevi, a heretic to many, a lunatic to others, and the Messiah to a growing quantity of hope-filled Jews around the world, who talked of the advent, the return to the Holy Land, and the imminent apocalypse.

Amsterdam's rabbinical council lived in a constant state of meetings

and tense differences of opinion. The exaltation of rabbis and community leaders reflected the danger in which Zevi and his successful
campaign had placed the advantageous state of those welcomed in
Amsterdam. Like one thousand six hundred years before, the arrival of
a supposed Messiah was viewed with apprehension by the authorities—
Jewish, Catholic, Calvinist, Muslim; kings, princes, emirs, and sultans—
since the preacher's messages implied upsetting the order, a break with
the status quo, revolution, chaos. The members of the Mahamad summarized the two tendencies running through the community: those who
asked for sanity and the preservation of the well-being they had reached,
and those who were inclined to abandon it all to put themselves at the
command of the Savior. Perhaps, with the exception of the stubborn
Ben Israel, who declared left and right the falseness of that possessed
demon being sent to exterminate Judaism, all housed the unsettling fear
of the inscrutable possibility: What if Zevi was really the anointed and
they ignored him as, centuries before, they had ignored the Nazarene?
That dramatic internal tension had exploded from the conclaves of the
council, and Sabbatai's defenders and detractors alike expressed their
frustration by punishing anyone within their reach. The *niddui* and the
cherem had started to rain down on Amsterdam, distributing excom-
munications, civil death, a diversity of punishments, and penance for
any act challenging orthodoxy. The writings of the young Baruch, son of
Miguel de Espinoza, were shredded apart by scholars, and they were already talking about making an example by punishing the heretical writer
who questioned even the most sacred principles of Jewish faith and the
divine origins of the Book. And in the midst of that explosion of fury,
intransigence, fear, and insecurity, the revelation of Elias Ambrosius's
actions could be low-lying fruit. Nearly a temptation.

Lost in those worries, the young man came back to the reality of the
workshop when he heard knocking at the door. His deep knowledge of
the customs of the house warned him that it could only be one of a few
intimates (or favorites: the boy Titus, the diligent Hendrickje Stoffels) to
whom he had conferred the privilege of being able to interrupt him as
he worked. That is why he was not surprised when the door opened and
he saw the entrance of, hat in hand and a glass of wine in the other, a
sword at his waist, a paper folder under his arm, the very elegant gentleman Jan Six, one of the chosen ones. But he felt his heart somersault

when, behind the magistrate and poet's figure, the face became visible of the person he least imagined to find in that place: that of Davide da Mantova.

The Italian Jew's departure to his country had greatly contributed to relieving the fascination that this man had prompted in Elias. Convinced besides that approaching that man who was also known as Salom Italia could be deeply unwise, bordering on insolent and, at the same time, hardly beneficial given the convictions that he already possessed, his desire to know the man's motivations had weakened. And now, like an apparition from the great beyond, the painter was entering the realm where Elias was posing in the role of the Christ of Emmaus.

The second feeling that overcame the young man in Salom Italia's presence was rage and frustration when he saw how the Maestro, after greeting Jan Six with the same affection as always, shook the other artist's hand, smiling at having him in the city again, revealing the existence of previous familiarity, perhaps even intimacy. The third reaction was entirely shock.

"Davide," the Maestro said as he finished wiping his hands on his apron, "I would like to introduce you to your compatriot and colleague Elias Ambrosius Montalbo . . . And be careful, since he could become your competitor."

Not even the compliment received, the first public recognition of his work, served to calm Elias's spirits. But he immediately understood that there was no reason to be worried and many reasons for their meeting to be beneficial. If the Maestro knew Salom Italia before (did he know him when he took him to see Isaac Pinto's scroll, two, three years before?) and had not even revealed to him the man's identity, wrapped in the same secret, Elias could have the peace of knowing that his secret was safe in the hands of the Maestro: to everyone, he would still be a servant, one of the many Jews with whom the painter had a relationship.

Jan Six opened the carafe and Elias diligently obeyed his master's order to find four clean glasses. "The Venetian ones," he added as Elias withdrew. But only when he returned to the workshop with four glasses of etched crystal did he understand that his remaining in that place had already been decided by the Maestro. Elias placed the goblets on the low table where the carafe rested (Tuscan wine, from the best vineyards of Artemino, Davide da Mantova informed) and tried to pick up the thread of the conversation, which involved possible subjects for the etching that the Maestro had promised his friend Six, whose play *Medea* was ready to be handed in at the printers. Salom Italia, mundane, elegant, relaxed, was proposing ideas that could be productive for the solicited work and offered to bring the Maestro engravings, recently acquired in Venice, with re-creations of classic pictures.

Standing, Elias Ambrosius could not take his eyes off of that Jew who seemed to enjoy the talk and the wine without a care in the world. At a given point, it was inevitable that the conversation turned to the Maestro's work in progress, visible on the easel, and the painter explained to the Italian man what his purposes were with that revisitation to a subject that he had worked on at other times.

"But I have already introduced you to this colleague of yours," the Maestro then said. "I want to show you what he is capable of doing . . . So that you don't think you're the only Jew who can do this well." He kept talking as he went to the back of the room and, after removing the stained cloth that covered it, was carrying the panel painted by Elias. The young man who couldn't help but be shocked by that unveiling for which he had not given permission, anxiously awaited the other painter's judgment, although first he had to hear Six's.

"Your student has talent . . ." he said, and then turned toward the Italian man to await his judgment.

"Talent and testicles," he declared, and for the first time addressed Elias. "It's a beautiful piece, but very compromising."

"As much as an illustrated scroll of Queen Esther," Elias countered, with a daring and quickness that surprised even himself. The Italian man smiled. Jan Six nodded. The Maestro, against his habit in such situations, remained silent, seemingly willing to enjoy the Israelite controversy.

"Even heresy has degrees, my friend," Salom Italia began. "Mine is daring, yours is frontal: you can say all you want that it is a self-portrait, but our wise compatriots will say that you have painted an idol that is adored in Catholic churches—the most prohibited of all."

"And I would ask them, upon hearing that judgment, who among them saw that heretic, which of them could confirm what the false Messiah was like . . . And if he had any similarity to the face painted on the panel, it was because he was Jewish, like me," and he turned his face toward the Maestro, before concluding, "and no one doubts he was a Jew."

Salom Italia raised his glass toward Elias and he clinked his glass against it with all of the delicacy demanded by those expensive Venetian crystals (a gift from Davide da Mantova to the Maestro?), and drank. "I don't know if you know that there are several *conversos* here in Amsterdam devoted to art," Salom Italia continued, "and there is also another Jew, although it appears that he is so infamous as a painter that not even he takes himself seriously."

"I know about the *conversos* but not about that other Jew . . . But, even if he isn't good, it is important to me that he paints . . . And that you also do so."

"I am only an aficionado . . . And seeing your work, I have to take off my hat to you . . . Do you know how many painters in the city would give their right hand to have a work of theirs worthy of being signed by your Maestro? I would be the first . . . If I wanted to be a painter. But that is where your biggest problem lies, my friend: if this"—and he pointed at the panel with Elias's face—"if this is not just one of those miracles that happens sometimes and you manage to paint other works as well, it's going to be impossible for you to remain in the shadows. Somebody will expose you, or your vanity will be stronger than your fears and you will expose yourself." Elias looked at the Maestro, in search of a measure against which to calibrate those words charged with the unmistakable feeling of truth.

"You can paint much more," the Maestro declared, and Elias felt free; he didn't know from what at that moment, but free.

"Is it possible to see some of these pieces?" Jan Six interrupted.

"Not right now," Elias responded, as he regretted the decision to have returned the sketchbooks to his house, along with his small canvases and his notebooks, now hidden in the locked tower of the study he inherited from his grandfather.

"So what would you do, Mr. da Mantova?" the Maestro continued, and Elias refocused his attention on the dialogue. He noticed that this time the Italian man, who up to that point was so sure of himself and so sarcastic, did not smile. He left his cup half full of the aristocratic wine of Artimino (whose vines, he had said at some point, fed the same cellars as the Roman pontiff) and at last responded:

"Would that a talent like that accompany me, but I do not have it, and that greatly changes my perspective . . . But if the Blessed One had bathed me in that light, I would not renounce it. If I do not renounce a dimmer one, do you think I would close the doors to that splendor? My friend," he said, focusing his attention on Elias, "men will not forgive you. Because history has shown us that men enjoy punishing more than accepting, wounding more than alleviating the pains of others, accusing more than understanding . . . And more so if they have some power. But God is something else: He embodies mercy. And your problem, like mine, is with God and not with the rabbis . . . And God, remember, is also within us; above all, within us," he emphasized and continued: "For that reason, I have closed my businesses in Amsterdam and taken my wife with me. Because perhaps the Messiah has arrived. I am not sure, no one can be sure, despite the many signs confirming it. But, in doubt, I vote for the Messiah, and I'm going to place my fortune and my intelligence at his service. If I am mistaken and he turns out to be a fake, then the Holiest One who is within me, blessed may He be, will know that I did it with an open heart, as He asked us to receive His envoy. And if he is the true Messiah, my place has to be at his side. I believe the sons of Israel cannot run the risk of being mistaken and rejecting the one who could be our Savior."

———

As the days passed, the commotion grew, threatening to explode. What had begun as a curiosity was starting to take on alarming proportions, and in just a few months, Amsterdam's Jewish community was living as if it were in a state of war. Several of the richest members of the Nação, led by the affluent Abraham Pereira, decided to close up their businesses, as Davide da Mantova had done, to journey as pilgrims through the Palestinian deserts behind the presumed Messiah. The ones most exalted with the Coming dedicated hours to praying in the synagogue, to purifying themselves with ritual baths, to submitting themselves to long fasts not prescribed by the calendars, and some even handed themselves over to acts of contrition such as lying naked on that year's much anticipated snows (another sign of the end of time, they said) and, to the horror of men like Menasseh ben Israel, even self-flagellation, in a disproportionate display of Jewish faith.

Within the Montalbo de Ávila house, two factions in critical contention had been created: on one side was the young Amos, who said he was about to march to Palestine with a group of Eastern Jews led by the Polish rabbi Breslau, and ran around the city proclaiming the imminent end of time; on the other side was Abraham Montalbo, the father, who recommended prudence, since the information that had arrived and kept arriving about Sabbatai Zevi's sermons and actions seemed, rather than an envoy from the Holiest come to earth, more like those of an insane person: from the most predictable actions, such as declaring that, in one of his many dialogues with Yahweh, God had proclaimed him King of the Jews and had given him the power to forgive all sins, to the most outrageous ones, like his vow to seize the Turkish crown after gathering the tribes for the purpose of getting married, on the banks of the Sambatyon River, to Rebecca, daughter of Moses, who died at the age of thirteen, and whom he had resurrected. Elias, meanwhile, was full of hesitations, but, at least in his house, he tried to maintain a cautious distance from the debates, while he missed the presence of Grandfather Benjamin, the most solid equilibrium the family had had, and whose well-reasoned advice would have helped so much in that dramatic circumstance in which the fate of so many souls could be at play.

The November afternoon on which the first ship chartered by Jews left Amsterdam, loaded with more than a hundred people headed toward Palestine's ports, the young Elias had approached the wharf in the company of his former Hakham. It was a scandal in the Nação that Ben Israel, rising as Zevi's most heated critic, in recent weeks had advanced significantly in his conversations with the English authorities with whom he soon proposed to discuss in London the readmission of Jews to the island, absent from there since their distant expulsion, three and a half centuries before.

The port of Amsterdam, always ruled by a frenzied rhythm, on that autumn day seemed definitively crazed. The ordinary traffic of stevedores, sailors, merchants, prostitutes, customs officials, beggars, buyers and sellers of bills of exchange, pickpockets, and traffickers of cheap and especially fake tobacco joined the masses—more motley than usual—of Jews leaving toward Palestine (many of them dressed as if they were already in the land of Canaan); the carriers of trunks, luggage, and packages that would accompany them; and the men and women, the elderly and the children rushing to say goodbye to them; plus the same curious bystanders as always, multiplied by the notoriety of the spectacle, which had been spoken of so much ever since the sale was announced of places on the Genovese brigantine willing to lead them to the self-proclaimed Messiah.

Hakham ben Israel and his former student, resting on some recently arrived shipments from Indonesia, heard the bell announcing the brigantine's imminent departure and watched the acceleration of movement in that human ant colony. "Not even in my worst nightmares, and I've had many of them, could I have dreamed of something like this," the teacher said and added: "So much fighting to get to Amsterdam and make a space for ourselves here, so that these fanatics can toss it all aside. The need to believe is one of the seeds of disgrace. And this is going to be a big one . . . Look, there goes Abraham Pereira with his family. Luckily, his brother Moshe is staying and will keep the academy open . . . Until Abraham confirms he should depart." Elias watched the procession formed by the numerous offspring of the rich businessman, one of the men who had brought about the miracle of Sephardic opulence in Amsterdam.

"So what are you going to do if they close the academy, Hakham?"

"I'm not going to wait for them to close it . . . In two weeks, I leave for London. That is my mission before the Holiest, blessed may He be, and before Israel: to open the door through which the true Messiah will come and not a charlatan and heretic like that Zevi."

As soon as the bell rang, signaling the departure, the two men distanced themselves from the port and walked toward the area of De Waag, where they took a table at the Oudezijds Voorburgwal, the same place where a few years before, Elias had seen the Hakham meet with the Maestro and had the certainty that Ben Israel could be his passport to the painter's workshop. Taking refuge behind large, thick green glass goblets weighed down with a tremendous Portuguese red wine, Elias at last had the occasion to relay the concerns plaguing him to his advisor. The previous week, when the Maestro deemed the work on *Pilgrims at Emmaus* finished, the painter had touched on a subject that had been worrying Elias Ambrosius: that of his remaining in the workshop. The Maestro's financial situation was fraught once again, with unpaid debts on his mortgage and with the compensation he owed Mme. Dircx, whose services he had decided to dispense with and who was going around the city accusing the Maestro of having violated a marriage proposal. The Maestro could not allow the privileged position of the young Jew in his workshop to jeopardize the source of guaranteed income that the students represented. Besides, Elias already possessed the necessary skills to start on his own path if, as the painter recommended to him, he obtained the approval of the Guild of St. Luke, crucial to selling his own work. Elias understood the Maestro's motives, but the Maestro, in his desperation and enthusiasm, seemed to have forgotten those of the young man, who found it impossible to leave behind the secrecy surrounding his art—even more impossible in those turbulent times within the Sephardic community.

"I already have the rank of master printer," Elias continued, speaking with his former teacher, "and although I do not earn very much, I could continue working with my father, or even look for another patron. With these salaries, I could marry Mariam, since it is about time."

"I should say so," the Hakham reaffirmed as he asked for his glass to be refilled.

"But is that the life I want?"

"I imagine it isn't, judging by the way in which you ask me, or ask yourself. But your life is yours, as I have always told you."

"Only you can help me, Hakham. Or at least listen . . . Think with me, please. Let's see, think whether after having lived for years alongside the Maestro, of being present so many times for the miracle of seeing him reach a nearly divine perfection, of listening to him speak with you, with Anslo, with Jan Six, with Pinto, with Hendrick Uylenburg the merchant, with Steen the painter, and Vingboons the architect, many of the most educated and ingenious men in the city; after having had the privilege of learning with students who have already embarked on such successful careers; after knowing the secrets of Raphael and Leonardo, the tricks of the Flemish Rubens, the ways in which Caravaggio expresses greatness; after having suffered my own ignorance, of having lived on the edge of destitution in order to be able to hand over the florins that the Maestro demanded of me every month, but also of having lived the grace and the privilege of listening to him speak of art, of life, of freedom, of power and money, of having felt how my hand and the paintbrush grew in their understanding, of discovering that everything is in the eyes, at times beyond the eyes, and of being capable of inferring that mystery that others don't even intuit . . . My Hakham, after having entered the fantastic world of being able to create . . . And then, you know a lot about this, after having lived with a secret and many fears, to one day be able to work alongside the Maestro and earn the invaluable prize that that same Maestro considers me a painter . . . After all of that, Hakham, am I going to renounce that marvelous experience and grow old behind some presses, printing flyers or receipts, like a decent man supporting a family through his labor, but who feels abandoned in his dreams of carrying out the work that—forgive me, Hakham, for what is surely my vanity—the work for which the Blessed One has brought me to the world?"

The former rabbi drank to the bottom of his glass and looked out onto the street, as if expecting the entrance, like that of the always-awaited prophet Elias, of the answer that his unruly former student demanded of him with his impassioned speech. The thoughts, nonetheless, did not appear to arrive from anywhere, and the man extracted his oak pipe from the New World in which he liked to burn and absorb his tobacco leaves. Only then did he dare attempt a response.

"You want me to tell you what *you* want to hear, as I can deduce from that passion . . . As such, there's not much I will be able to tell you, my son . . . I can only remind you that in the whole range of human history, the Jewish maxim is to practice self-control and temperance, more than abstinence. And to achieve that would be a lot for you . . . For more than three thousand years, we Jews have been asking ourselves the same question you now ask yourself . . . What are we on this earth for? And we have given ourselves many responses. The idea that we are made in the image and likeness of God conferred to us the privilege of becoming individuals and, thanks to Isaiah and especially to Ezekiel, we received the idea that individual responsibility is the essence of our religion, of our relationship with the Holiest, blessed may He be . . . It was one of our ancestors who wrote the book of Job, a transcendentalist treaty about evil, so mysterious and visceral that not even the Greek tragedians and philosophers could conceive of something even close to it . . . Job expresses another variant of your question, much more painful, more overwhelming, when a man of solid faith is the one who interrogates the heavens aiming to know why God is capable of doing the most terrible things to us. He, who is kindness . . . And Job had his answer: 'Behold, fear of the Lord, that is wisdom; and to depart from evil is understanding.' Do you recall it?" The scholar placed his pipe on the table and locked eyes with the young man: "Take this verse as a response. Everything is there: Maintain your wisdom and always depart from evil. Your life is your life . . . And to not live it is to die in life, to anticipate death."

———

Always in search of the dubious shelter offered by the eaves and walls of the lock house on Sint Antoniesbreestraat, again withstanding, his feet sunk in snow, the blades of damp air cutting the skin of his cheeks and lips as they ran over the Zwanenburgwal and sought out the North Sea, bearing the invincible stench that the breeze ripped from the canal's dark waters, Elias Ambrosius was thinking of the future. As it had five years before, without ceasing to contemplate for an instant the house rising on the other side of Jodenbreestraat, Jewish Broad Street, his gaze focused on the green-painted wooden door that he had passed through so many times since the day on which he managed to soften the Maestro's heart and entered, through a small crack, that world capable of changing his life.

A feeling of satisfaction and painful nostalgia were with him on this occasion, since for the first time he would cross that threshold not as a suitor, or as a servant or even as a student, but rather as someone close to the Maestro. As a remembrance of his former condition, in one of his pockets he carried three and a half florins that he had owed the painter since the previous month, an outrageous amount for his finances, but that, in light of what he had achieved, now seemed petty and ridiculous to him.

When he at last crossed the street, it was the restless Hendrickje Stoffels, owner and lady of the house and of the Maestro's passions, who opened the door with the pleasant smile she always gave Elias, given the young student's familiarity with the Maestro and with his boy Titus, whom he had seen grow from the time he took his first steps. Once in the kitchen, as he drank a steaming infusion, habit forced Elias to look at the peat and firewood pile and he offered to notify the Nieuwemarkt supplier.

With the woman's authorization, Elias went up the steps leading to the Maestro's studio, and, with a melancholy capable of imposing itself over familiarity, looked at the paintings, busts, and objects gathered in the dwelling. As in the days in which he ran around the house carrying a broom and mop, Elias knocked at the studio door three times, and heard the response that had become habitual. "Come in, kid," the Maestro said, as he had said hundreds of times in those years of service, apprenticeship, and proximity.

The painter was seated in front of the panel on which he had begun to work a few weeks prior, and to his right rested the canvas of *Pilgrims at Emmaus*, awaiting the final touches to come after it dried and before the layer of varnish that he had decided to apply this time. The new panel, whose priming and preparation Elias had not participated in, would be a re-creation of the bath of Susanna at the moment in which the biblical heroine was being harassed by two elders ready to accuse her of adultery if the young woman did not grant them sexual favors. The characters, still sketched, made a spot of light falling from the upper right angle toward the bottom edge of the space, whose center would be the figure of Susanna. The background, already worked, offered a cavernous darkness in which deep brown carefully opened toward a greenish gray that, in the upper left corner, incorporated a robust architectural element, covered by a dome, more phantasmagoric than real.

Elias said hello and the Maestro muttered something as he added some more stains of red that, the young man assumed, would be the outfit Susanna was wearing before disrobing.

"Do you think Susanna should be nude, or do I cover her with a piece of cloth?" the Maestro asked, still without turning around and after spitting the hard candy he had in his mouth into a corner. Elias thought about his answer for a moment.

"It's better to cover her. There are two men in the scene," he said, just as the Maestro was placing his brush over the palette and putting it on the nearby table where the colors were laid out.

"You are right. Hendrickje thinks the same thing . . . But sit down, for God's sake."

Elias settled down on one of the stools without daring to move it from its place. He knew that even when the Maestro allowed him to enter the studio, the time he would devote to him would be minimal.

"I came to bring you the money I owe you, Maestro," he said and began to dig around in his pocket. The painter smiled.

"Stop looking, you don't owe me anything . . . Consider it payment for modeling for *Pilgrims* or an award for resistance . . . For everything you had to put up with these years."

"Don't say that, Maestro. I will never be able to repay you—"

"It's okay like that," the painter interrupted him, "forget about the damned money."

"Thank you, Maestro."

"Kid, my problems cannot be solved with three florins. That's why I'm painting Susanna, who already has a buyer, and I've left *Pilgrims* here, which still doesn't have any suitors; two possible customers have told me that the Messiah is too earthly. Both of them Catholic, of course."

"So they saw what you wanted to show them."

"Yes, but what I don't see are the florins I have to pay for the debt on the house. How long will I have to work under this pressure, by God? It's lucky that Jan Six loaned me some money to give me breathing room. An advance for the etching with which the printing of his *Medea* will be illustrated."

"It is lucky to have friends like that."

"Yes, it is . . . So, what are you going to do, finally? Are you going to Palestine with the Messiah, like Salom Italia?" he asked with a sarcastic smile.

"No, I'm not going, but I've been thinking and thinking and I don't know what to do, Maestro."

The painter, now serious, moved his body until he was in front of Elias.

"You know something? Sometimes I think I should have never accepted you in the workshop. You were too young to know what you were doing, but I was conscious of the problems this would bring you. Perhaps because of that, I did a lot to dissuade you, to make you think of the risks to which you were exposing yourself . . . But you put up with everything, because you have a strong will, like your deceased grandfather Benjamin. So much so that you have learned to paint as I never imagined was possible when I saw your initial sketches. Now there's no helping it: you are infected to the bone, and it's an illness without a cure. Well, yes, there is one: painting."

"You changed my life, Maestro. And not only because you taught me to paint. My grandfather, Hakham ben Israel, and you have been the best things that have happened to me, because the three of you, each one in your way, have taught me that to be a free man is more than just living in a place that declares freedom. You taught me that being free is a war that must be fought every day, against all powers, against all fears. That is what I was referring to when I wanted to thank you for what you have done for me in these years."

The painter, perhaps surprised by the young man's speech, listened to him in silence, the work he had been doing seemingly forgotten. But Elias rose to his feet and the painter made a gesture as if he had come back to reality.

"You have work, Maestro. Do you know what the only thing I regret is? That I do not know if I will ever work with you again. The rest is profit. Goodbye. One of these days, I will come to visit you and put coal in the stoves."

Then the Maestro stood up from his stool and, with his right hand, patted the young man's cheek twice.

"Go with God, kid. May you have luck."

The snow, which had been lying in wait for the city since daybreak, had started to fall when Elias went out to Jodenbreestraat, which, like other times, looked like a white carpet laid out at his feet. He walked along Sint Antoniesbreestraat, crossed before the Zuiderkerk, with its battery of bells in frozen silence, and headed toward the great esplanade of De Waag, where the most persistent or desperate merchants were withstanding the rain of white flakes behind their stalls. The young man's mind, relieved by the conversation maintained with the Maestro, had at last found some of the answers pursued with special insistence in recent weeks, although engraved on his consciousness for several years. And the decisions taken, so essential for his life, demanded Mariam Roca's understanding or denial, since they could affect her greatly if she decided to stay at his side in the midst of that war for which he would continue brandishing his weapons.

In front of the promised door, Elias again asked himself if what he was proposing to himself was fair. To drag others along with his decisions could be an egotistical act. But, what would love be about if not submission and understanding, commitment and complicity? In any event, the only choice was to show his cards and let Mariam, freely, as freely as possible, make her decision. Of that mind-set, he finally knocked on the door with the bronze knocker. He did not have to wait long for Mariam herself to open the door and for Elias Ambrosius to find himself looking at her upset face, which he would soon learn was from fear, as she delivered the news that would twist the young Jew's fate: "By God, Elias, run to your house . . . Your brother Amos found your paintings and has denounced you as a heretic before the Mahamad."

———

When some had forgotten what fear was like, how deeply it affected the essence of man, fear returned, like a giant avalanche, willing to cover everything. There had been many centuries of tense yet possible harmony, and the sons of Israel believed they had found in Sepharad—cohabitating with the caliphs of al-Ándalus and the fierce Iberian princes—the closest thing to paradise that one could aspire to on earth. Spanish cities and communities had become filled with famous doctors, philosophers, Kabbalists, prosperous silversmiths, businessmen, and, of course, wise rabbis. But with so much notoriety and success, they had at last brought about the cause of their perdition: they had become wealthy. And power never finds that the money it possesses is enough. Thus, fear returned with Catholic supremacy and, alongside it, to make it complete and irreversible, torture and death or a foggy exodus, which they could only undertake with the clothes on their backs.

For many years before the royal and Catholic solution was applied and the Jews' expulsion from Sepharad was decreed, they had lived in tense times, with a more than justified fear of the processes of the Inquisition unleashed in a Spain that was almost entirely recaptured by the Catholic faith. Grandfather Benjamin used to tell Elias that in the first eight years alone of the functioning of that tribunal, more than seven hundred Jews, including his two grandfathers—before they were grandfathers—had been sentenced to die in the bonfire. (Whenever he heard him speak of that torment, the young man recalled the words of Hakham ben Israel, witness to several of those macabre spectacles during which, Elias could not shake the image, the blood of the condemned boiled for several minutes before he lost consciousness and died, suffocated by the smoke.) He also told him that, after the expulsion was decreed in 1492 ("And all of our goods were confiscated," the elderly man stressed), many thousands of *conversos*, real and fake, had received all kinds of sentences. Any accusation before the Tribunal of the Holy Office or by the Holy Office itself was valid, so that an auto-da-fé would take place and the selected punishment be carried out in a public square. The most frequent charge tended to be, of all things, that of secretly practicing Judaism, but it could go all the way to having sacrificed Christian children to carry out certain Jewish cultural rites. For those condemned to the bonfire, if they recognized their sins and published their repentance and immediate adherence to the faith of Jesus, the Catholic clergy allowed them a generous relief: to die by the club instead of suffering the torments of the pyre. With those horrors, the invincible fear had been revived and had latched on to the memory of the Sephardic Jews like that miasma that, according to the wise inquisitors, emanated from the bodies of all Jews—a smell that disappeared with the act of Christian baptism. Fear had led them to take refuge in any place in Europe, Asia, or Africa where they were admitted, and although they were confined to ghettos, at least they weren't threatened with being burned to death. Fear had made them end up in Calvinist Amsterdam, where it turned out that they were not only welcomed but where the miracle had also occurred that allowed the Jews to proclaim their faith without fear of reprisals from the believers in Christ. But fear, in reality, had followed them. Transfigured, transmuted, crouching in wait, but alive and present.

Very soon, the rabbis began to dedicate hours of their prayers on Saturday—the day on which each Jew should enjoy Freedom as a right and benefit of being created in the image and likeness of the Lord—to warn the flocks about the ways in which the faithful should understand and practice that freedom. Willing to control the acts of licentiousness that propitiated heresy, including the actions or simple thoughts that went beyond the freedom conceded by the Law and administered by its vigilantes, the rabbis and leaders of the community, gathered in the Mahamad, encouraged fear. Trials followed and sentences were applied, from the lightest *niddui* to the terrible *cherem*. As had always been and would always be in human history, someone decided what freedom was and how much of it corresponded to the individuals whom that power repressed or guarded. Even in the lands of freedom.

By decree of the rabbinical council, the trial for the possible excommunion of Elias Ambrosius Montalbo de Ávila had been set to take place on the second Wednesday in January of 1648, in the Spanish synagogue, and the Mahamad urged the entire Jewish community of the city of Amsterdam to attend its sessions.

———

After hearing Mariam's words, Elias Ambrosius had run to his house to find out what had happened. When he arrived, the first thing he saw was his father's crestfallen face, which combined fury, fear, and indignation. Also, his mother's face, weeping, crumpled into itself like a scared animal. Without stopping to ask for a report or giving explanations, the young man went to the small corner where Grandfather Benjamin's desk had always been and looked at the catastrophe: the lock had been broken by force. A piece of wood from the furniture's beautiful frame had been splintered, and all of its contents had been removed. On the floor, ripped from the files, were the drawings and linens painted by Elias (the portrait of Mariam Roca!) and by other students, like his good friend Keil the Dane—some marked by dirty boot prints. Before even beginning to rescue the salvageable, Elias noticed that there were two notable absences: his notebook and the canvas on which the Maestro had portrayed him. Without a doubt, those had been considered the greatest evidence against him.

Pained by the shame to which he would subject his parents, Elias Ambrosius returned to the living room to face them. His mother, her eyes swollen with tears, lowered her head when she saw him enter, and remained silent like the good Jewish wife she always was. His father, by contrast, dared to ask him if he had any idea what awaited him. Elias nodded and asked him, please, to tell him what had happened. Abraham Montalbo, after taking a few deep breaths, summarized the acts: after forcing the locked compartment of the desk, Amos had gone running out of the house to return, shortly after, with Rabbis Breslau and Montera. His father paused. "They were inside for more than an hour, and, when they left, they told me I had a heretic son of the worst kind. They carried some notebooks in their hands, and they showed me that portrait of yours in which you look like . . ." The man went silent again. "They're going to open a case against you, Elias . . . But, how could you do what you have done?"

Elias thought of various responses—his responses—although he immediately understood that none of them would be good enough for his father.

"I don't know, Father. But if you can, forgive me for making you suffer . . . And if it is not too much to ask, let me stay in the house for a few more days until I find some solution. Then, I will leave," Elias said, and only at that moment did Abraham Montalbo de Ávila seem to grasp the true notion of what was coming for him and his family—that they would never again be the same family (a heretic son, another who was an informant, and what was he himself to blame for?)—and he, too, began to weep.

With the roll of canvases and posters under his arm, Elias Ambrosius had gone out to the street. As on other occasions on which he needed to think, he went to the area around the port. The premature winter night was coming quickly, and from the sea a frozen breeze was rising. Seeking out the poor shelter of the warehouses managed by the powerful East

India Company, who governed commerce with the ports of those remote confines of the world to which Elias had once dreamed of traveling, he spent several hours weighing his possibilities. The absence of his former teacher, Hakham ben Israel, who days before had traveled to England, left him without the only person whose advice, at that crossroads, could clarify the situation for him, and without the only man in the Sephardic community who, perhaps—only perhaps—would dare to overcome fear and raise his voice in his defense. Elias knew that in all certainty what awaited him was a noisy trial in which he would be accused of idolatry, the gravest of all sins, and at the end, his excommunion would be decided and a *cherem* for life would be prescribed, similar to the one applied to Uriel da Costa or the one pending against the head of Baruch, the son of Miguel de Espinoza . . . Although the portrait that the Maestro made of him would be the most resounding proof, he had well-thought-out reasons to refute that charge. But his notebooks, where for years he had revealed his thoughts, doubts, fears, and decisions, and besides, relayed his experiences at the workshop, would not allow him any margin for defense: in the eyes of his judges, those papers were the insurmountable self-accusation of a heretic who violated the second commandment of the Law. All doors were closed to him and there was little he could do to open them . . . But, he then thought: Even if he convinced the Mahamad that he had not committed an unpardonable sin, what would his life be like from that moment on? What would he be willing to do to live as a forgiven man within the community? Would he disown what he thought, what he believed was fair, what he wanted to be, every day, in order to obtain a forgiveness that was always conditional and guarded? Was it worth kneeling this once, a submission that in reality equaled kneeling forever, to continue living among his people and in the place where he had been born, where his beloved were buried and where his parents, his friends, and teachers, the woman whom he loved resided? What freedom would he enjoy as a forgiven one in the lands of freedom? With those questions, he became enraged: he had not committed any crime so cruel as to be condemned, and he was not an idolater, but rather a Jew who had practiced his free will. What human being could grant himself the power of seizing everything that belonged to him merely because he had dared to think differently regarding a law—even if that law had been dictated by God? And what if he didn't ask forgiveness? Would he have the courage to live forever like a pariah to everyone of his same origin? With some answers to his questions, he returned to his father's house and, against expectations, as soon as he lay down in his bed (Amos's bed, as in recent months, remained empty, and with more reason now given the repulsion that proximity to a heretic would cause him), Elias Ambrosius Montalbo de Ávila fell into the arms of sleep. In the face of what was imminent, for the first time in many months, he felt free of fear.

The following morning, again carrying his sketches and paintings, the young Jew headed to the only place that, he thought, he would be received and heard. He crossed De Waag without looking at the merchants or even at the sellers of paintings, sketches, and engravings that occupied the corner of the square where Sint Antoniesbreestraat begins, and on which he walked, as he had hundreds of times in those years, toward the house with the green door, marked with a number 4 on Jewish Broad Street.

Hendrickje Stoffels opened the door to him. The girl looked into his eyes and, without Elias having any time to react, caressed his cheek with her hand and then told him that the Maestro was waiting for him. Elias Ambrosius, moved by Hendrickje's gesture of solidarity, went up the stairs, knocked on the studio door, and waited until he heard the painter's voice: "Come in, kid."

Elias found him standing before the canvas focusing on the story of Susanna, as he wiped his hands on the stained apron.

"Last night, Isaac Pinto came to see me. I already know that there's to be a trial against you," the man said, and pointed at a stool as he settled into the other one. "What are you going to do?"

"I still do not know, Maestro. I want to leave the city."

"Leave? To where?" the painter asked, as if a decision of this kind were inconceivable.

"I don't know. Nor do I know how. Maybe I should go to Palestine, with Zevi. Perhaps Salom Italia is right and it is worth finding out if he is or is not the Messiah."

The Maestro was shaking his head no, as if he could not admit something.

"I should not have accepted you in the workshop. I feel guilty."

"Don't, Maestro. It was my decision and I knew what the consequences could be."

"So when does that useless Ben Israel come back? Something has to be done!" the man yelled.

"That's precisely why I came, Maestro, because I dare to ask you to do something: Please, recover my portrait. The rabbis took it. But if you demand it, they have to return it to you. They are capable of destroying it."

The man began to take off his apron.

"Who took it? Where do they have it?"

"Montera and Breslau took it, they have it at the synagogue."

"I'm going to get Jan Six, he has to come with me."

"Maestro . . ." Elias hesitated, but he thought he had nothing to lose. "They also took my notebooks. They are like your *tafelet*. Please, see . . ." he added, when the painter, already wearing his hat, was yelling to Hendrickje Stoffels to bring him his coat and his boots on his way out to the street.

———

Very delicately, Elias caressed the surface of the canvas recovered from the jaws of intolerance, and received in the palm of his hand the pleasant rough cut of the oil applied by the Maestro's art. He looked at his face impressed upon the canvas, the gaze a bit above his own gaze. The beauty that invaded him convinced him that it had been worth it. With four small nails, he affixed the canvas to the wall of the attic he had moved into—the same one in which Keil the Dane had lived for three years—whose rent was now being paid by Jan Six at the Maestro's insistence.

Two days before, he had left his parents' house. As he gathered his most valuable belongings—two outfits, some sheets and toiletries, and the books that had belonged to his grandfather Benjamin—he had had a conversation with his father, during which, both of them more calm, he had explained the origins and motives of his supposed heresy. His father had asked him to remain in the house, but Elias did not wish to submit them to the reality that he himself was living: that of being marginalized. Even when there were still several more days before the trial against him would take place, the majority of the city's Jews, aware of what had occurred, already considered him convicted and were already jumping ahead to condemning him to ostracism, exile, and contempt.

Elias was not surprised to find the doors to Dr. Roca's house closed to him and that Mariam herself, who knew all of his secrets and had even participated in them, refused to speak with him, fearful perhaps of her own implication in the heresy, a participation that in some way, or for some reason, had been left unaired. (Perhaps Amos and the rabbis had not identified Mariam Roca as the girl he portrayed in the small canvas? Was Elias such a bad portraitist? Or had the powerful hand of Dr. Bueno intervened to prevent mixing up the daughter of his colleague and assistant in the case?) Abraham Montalbo had not insisted on changing his son's opinion, but before the young man left, he gifted him with precious certainty: "These days, I have been happy that your grandfather is dead. The old man would have been capable of killing Amos. He was always a fighter, a pious man, and what he most admired were fidelity and reason."

"Yes," Elias said, "and what he most hated was submission."

In those days—during the Christian holiday of Christmas and the Jewish delight in the celebration of the eight days of Hanukkah—as he walked joylessly and aimlessly around the city, killing time and unease, Elias Ambrosius had acquired the feeling of being confined in a strange place. The many sites in Amsterdam holding meanings, evocations, complicities, now seemed distant to him, as if he were listening to declarations of war in a foreign language. But the certainty of that distance was multiplied when he ran into any of the Jews who knew him and these passed him by as if the young man had lost all physical form. Elias knew that many were reacting that way out of conviction, but others responded in that manner under the petty pressure of fear. In that hostile environment charged with ill humor, everything that for twenty-one years had belonged to him was beginning to run away from him, until it painfully pushed him from its heart. He then understood in all of its dimensions what Uriel da Costa had suffered when he was anathematized and turned into someone who was as good as dead to his brothers in race, culture, and religion. That state of invisibility in which he had been thrown, the condition of not being, of having disappeared to those who once loved him, differentiated him, accepted him, turned out to be the most painful of sentences to which a man can be subjected. He now even understood why Uriel da Costa had ended up giving in and had asked forgiveness, only to take his life a few weeks later: out of fear and out of shame, consecutively. But he, as Baruch Spinoza was doing, would not commit suicide or admit any blame, nor would he give them the pleasure of seeing him suffer no matter how much he suffered in reality, since the profit of freedom signified by living without fear was recompense for all of it. He would not submit, would not humiliate himself.

The decision that had been hazy at the beginning of leaving Amsterdam was becoming firm in his mind, and now he had only to find the way of concretizing the path by which he would depart, to anywhere. Because there were several things with which Elias Ambrosius Montalbo de Ávila had been born, raised, lived, and which he would not renounce, no matter how much the community's powerful leaders pressured him. The first of those was his dignity; then, his decision to paint what his eyes and his sensibility demanded he paint; and, above all, because it equally implied his dignity and his vocation, he would not hand over his freedom, the highest condition the Creator had conceded him and the most valuable currency with which his grandfather had prized him even when he was so far from becoming his grandfather, or the grandfather of his brother Amos. That glorious possibility of exercising his freedom that Benjamin Montalbo had stoked in him during the twenty years in which they shared a part of their respective stays on earth.

———

The days went by, cloudy and windy although without snow, bringing the dates of the trial. Elias had discovered that deciding to go anywhere, far from Amsterdam, could be much more challenging than he had imagined. The greatest difficulty, he would painfully confirm, came from his complicated situation as a Jew in the process of being excommunicated, since some doors were closed that looked down on his condition as a Jew, and others were sealed off by Jews themselves.

Among the possible destinations, Jerusalem was one that did not cease to tempt him. Although Elias continued holding many doubts about Sabbatai Zevi's messianic qualities, at times, perhaps moved by the same circumstance that he existed in vis-à-vis his community, the act of joining a messianic pilgrimage, of placing his faith and his will in a presumed Anointed One, of becoming a militant of the latest hope or getting lost with it, seemed almost appropriate. However, although the departure of a second boat chartered by the members of the Nação bound for the land of Israel was announced for the first days of the Christian new year, the simple possibility of boarding it, even if he had had the necessary funds to cover the ticket and the expenses of the journey, was unthinkable: those feverish members of the community would not admit him aboard.

The other path capable of seducing him was the one leading to any of the lively cities in the north of Italy, where he could perhaps live at the margins of the community and, even, as Davide da Mantova did in his day, devote himself with greater freedom to exercising his passion for painting. But in reality, the young man had weighed all the options, including that of signing up as a sailor on any of the merchant vessels that left daily for the West and East Indies, and found that a market filled with experienced men willing to set sail would cause the immediate rejection by ship owners and captains of a young man without the least expertise in tasks relating to the sea. Meanwhile, the shorter journeys to Spain, Portugal, and England, so traveled in those times, remained outside the possibilities of a normal Jew, unless, before he attempted it, he exchanged his condition for a certificate of Catholic baptism, something he did not intend to do. Journeys by land, meanwhile, were impractical at a time when the country's borders were on maximum alert: the imminent cementing of the awaited peace treaty with Spain, which would perhaps be signed in some German city, had turned those paths into military encampments weighed down by tension and nervousness, and by all appearances, it turned out to be less drastic to be considered a heretic by the Jews in Amsterdam than a traitor or a spy by those exasperated troops, often inebriated with the most ferocious alcohol consumed thirstily by some due to their certainty of victory, and by others due to their indignation over defeat.

The snow, as couldn't fail to happen, had returned for Christmas. The festive atmosphere of the celebrations, multiplied by the announcement of the end of the century of wars against Spain, had taken over the city, and its inhabitants were putting wine, beer, and hot beverages distilled in the sugar refineries in danger of extinction. Elias Ambrosius's solitude, by contrast, became more compact during prolonged stays in the attic that now seemed like a cell and where he couldn't even count on a menorah to place eight candles and enjoy the celebration of one of the great landmarks in the history of the people who, as Hakham ben Israel insisted so much in his lessons (evoking the warrior David, the invincible Joshua, the bellicose Hasmonaeans), had once been combative and rebellious, more than contaminated by fear and addicted to submission.

Three days before New Year's Eve on Christian calendars, some knocking at the door alarmed the young man. Like a hope that he could not give up, he dreamed that, at any moment, his beloved Mariam Roca would appear before him. Elias knew well of the girl's skills in slipping out, so many times put in practice during the many clandestine meetings they maintained in their years of amorous and carnal relations. He knew, besides—or at least he thought he knew—that Mariam would never be among those who would condemn him for his actions. He knew well the young girl's way of thinking, but at the same time, with each passing day, he was getting a better notion, through the girl's attitudes, of how paralyzing fear can be. Moved by the hope of seeing his beloved, he opened the door to see whether it was Mariam: in front of him were the flattened nose, the eagle eyes, and the cavity-ridden teeth of the Maestro. And he immediately had one certainty: at last, some door had opened.

The Maestro had in his hands a bottle of wine and on his body, several more. Perhaps because of that, the greeting was so effusive: a hug, two kisses on the cheeks, and a Christmas wish like the one believers in Christ usually exchange. But even so, it did not weaken the certainty in Elias that the man was bringing a solution.

With two glasses served of the rough and dark wine that the Maestro could afford, they sat down to talk. The painter, in fact, was bringing him good news: his friend Jan Six would hire Elias to go to one of the ports in the north of Poland on a merchant ship already under contract. There he should close the purchase of a large shipment of wheat that, for decades, the Dutch were importing from those regions. Since that deal required presenting bills of exchange for thousands of florins, Six and his associates preferred to deposit that fortune in the hands of the young Jew before giving it to the ship's captain, about whose honesty they had begun to hold serious doubts. Once the deal was carried out with the Dutch agents in that port and with the Polish providers, Elias would hand over the papers of the already completed purchase and the shipping guides to the captain and then he could do whatever he liked, whether that be stay in Poland, Germany, or somewhere else in the north, or return to Amsterdam, where perhaps things would have calmed down.

As he listened to the details of that commission capable of opening an unexpected and strange escape route, the young man started feeling an unforeseen anxiety over the evidence that, yes, he would leave, perhaps for always, his city and his world. And he understood that, instead of an escape, his departure would be a self-expulsion. Nonetheless, he knew well that it was his only viable choice, and he thanked the Maestro for his interest and help.

"Don't thank me for anything," the painter then said, and left his glass of wine on the floor. Only at that moment did Elias notice that the man had not tasted the drink. "What has happened to you can only be seen as a defeat . . . And the worst thing is that no one can be blamed. Not you for having dared to defy certain laws, not your brother Amos and the rabbis for wanting to judge you and condemn you: each one is doing what he thinks he should do, and has many reasons to back up his decisions. And that's the worst thing: that something horrible seems normal to some . . . What makes me saddest is confirming that stories like yours have to happen, or that regrettable withdrawals like that of Salom Italia do, so that we men finally learn how faith in God, in a prince, in a country—obedience to mandates supposedly created for their own good—can turn into a jail for the substance that differentiates us: our free will and our intelligence as human beings. It's the opposite of freedom and—" He cut off his sentence because, with the vehemence that had been taking him over, one of his feet knocked the glass over and spilled wine on the wooden floor.

"Don't worry, Maestro," Elias said, and leaned over to pick up the glass.

"No, I don't worry over something so trivial, of course not . . . What the hell can a little bit of lost wine and another little bit of dirt accumulated matter to us now . . . ? You don't know how I would like for our friend Ben Israel to be here now so that he, so knowledgeable about sacred things, could try to explain to me how God can understand and explain what is happening to you. I'm sure he would speak of Job and mysterious designs, he would tell us that the laws are written in our bodies and would show us the perfection of the Creator telling us that if in the Torah there exist two hundred and forty-eight positive prescriptions and three hundred and sixty-five negative ones, which add up to six hundred and thirteen, it is because we men have two hundred and forty-eight bones and three hundred and sixty-five tendons, and the sum of all of them, which again is six hundred and thirteen, is the figure symbolizing the parts of the universe . . . I would let him finish and then I would ask him: Menasseh, in all of these shitty stories, where would you put the individual owning those bones and tendons, the concrete man of which you like to speak so much?" The Maestro turned the palms of his hands up, to demonstrate the void. But Elias did not see the void: on the contrary, there was, on those hands, fullness. Because those were the hands of a man who had exhausted himself creating beauty, even from the confirmation of misery, all that age, pain, and ugliness, the hands through which so many times the sacred had manifested itself and become concrete. The hands of a man who had fought against all powers in order to hammer the armor of his freedom . . .

"And when does Six's boat leave?" was, nonetheless, what Elias had to ask. The Maestro, surprised, had to think before responding.

"On January fourth, in a week, I believe . . . Six will explain everything to you . . . I hope he pays you well."

"The sooner it sets sail, the better . . ." Elias said as the Maestro stood up, stumbled, and gave him a stained smile by way of goodbye.

"There's nothing more to say," he muttered, "one defeat, another defeat," he said, and left the attic. This time, the void was created. Elias Ambrosius felt that a part of his soul had just left him. Perhaps the best part.

After thinking about it a lot, he decided that he would go to say goodbye to his parents. At the end of the day, they did not deserve another punishment. But he postponed it until the day before the departure, when he already had in his hands all of Jan Six's instructions, the documents for the business, and the monies for his own pay, remunerated with an excess of generosity, certainly due to the Maestro's pressure.

When he left his father's house, after having again placed in the old desk almost all of the books that had belonged to his grandfather Benjamin—he decided to only take with him a volume by Maimonides, his copy of *De Termino Vitae*, his Hakham's work, and the strange adventure of a Castilian hidalgo who goes crazy from reading novels and believes himself to be an errant knight—he stopped by the attic and picked up his sketches and paintings and those that his colleagues had presented him, all of them displayed in an album he himself had bound. Outside of that book he left with only the linen on which the Maestro had portrayed him, the last and best portrait that he himself had made of Mariam, and a sketch of his grandfather in watery gray lines, besides a small landscape that his good friend and confidant, the blond Keil, had given him: those four pieces were too significant to leave behind, and he rolled them up and placed them inside a small wooden chest he had bought for that purpose at the market. With the rest of the works, including several oil portraits of Mariam, all placed in the album, he again went to house number 4 on Jewish Broad Street and knocked at the door painted green, convinced that he was doing so for the last time in his life. When Hendrickje Stoffels opened, Elias asked to see the Maestro: he wanted to give him a New Year's gift, as proof of his infinite gratitude. Hendrickje Stoffels smiled and told him to come back later: the Maestro was sleeping off the first drunkenness of the year of the Lord 1648. Elias smiled. "It doesn't matter," he said, and held out the notebook. "Give this to him when he comes to. Explain to him that it is a gift . . . That he can do whatever seems best with it. And tell him that I wish him, you, and Titus that the Holiest, blessed may He be, give you all much health, for many years." Hendrickje Stoffels smiled again as she placed the file the young man gave her against her chest and asked him: "Which God, Elias?"

"Any one of them . . . All of them," he said, after thinking for a brief moment, and added: "May I?" And with the palm of his hand, he caressed the ruddy and smooth cheek of the girl whom his Maestro had sketched so many times. Elias Ambrosius went down the steps toward the street, clean and brilliant as a carpet laid out by the recently fallen snow. He was again a man who wept.

Book of Judith

1

Havana, June 2008

From his grandfather Rufino, Mario Conde should have learned: curiosity killed the cat. But, like many other times, the former policeman, stirred in his softest parts, was incapable on that occasion of following the advice of the old man who had made such vain efforts to shape Conde's sentimental education.

That torrid and sticky June afternoon, as he was entering his house hugging two bottles of recently acquired rum, what Mario Conde wanted least was a visitor, any visitor, particularly a visitor capable of altering his plan to spend an hour in the shower, another having a nap, and then to while the night away at his friend Carlos's house, allowing the rum to dissolve all their tensions. Furthest from his imagination was that his unexpected visitor, who came with a disquieting and insistent knock at the door, would be Dr. Ricardo Kaminsky's granddaughter, Yadine the Goth (loaded down with piercings), whom he had met several months before and who (at the very dawn of the ensuing discussion through which she ensnared the man, and after which, his curiosity piqued, he would be dragged into complicating his own life and proving, once more, that parallel lines always end up crossing) started by making things quite clear. "You are completely wrong. I am not a goth or a freak. I'm emo."

"Emo?"

Beginning in the early morning, Conde had experienced one of his typical, tense days as a delicate negotiation unfolded that, should it succeed, would yield some juicy gains for all involved. Three weeks before, his partner, Yoyi the Pigeon, had received an order he couldn't pass up. "The Diplomat" was one of Yoyi's regulars who, unsatisfied with his salary as a First World public servant, moonlighted as the courier of literary gems for collectors and sellers in his European country, specialists with bookstores and Internet sites who knew that, with patience, good maps, and some luck, they could still hunt down certain marvels in some of the private Cuban libraries that had survived the cataclysms of the most difficult years and even the blandest aftershocks of the interminable Crisis, throughout which many people had to sell even their souls in order to stay alive.

The list that Yoyi received this time was of the kind that took your breath away. It began with nothing less than a request for two volumes of the *Comedias de don Pedro Calderón de la Barca*, in a very rare and coveted 1839 Havana edition, illustrated by the master engravers Alejandro Moreau and Federico Mialhe, and whose price outside of Cuba could reach one thousand dollars. The interested buyer continued his demands with three books by the always indispensable Jacobo de la Pezuela: the *Diccionario geográfico, estadístico, histórico de la Isla de Cuba*, in four volumes, edited in Madrid in 1863, and of which Yoyi had already sold one copy to the Diplomat for five hundred dollars; the four-volume *Historia de la Isla de Cuba*, also edited in Madrid, printed between 1868 and 1878, which could fetch a similar price or more; and his *Crónica de las Antillas*, the 1871 Madrid edition, which could be viably resold for three hundred dollars. But without a doubt, the crowning jewel on the list was the problematic *Historia física, política y natural de la Isla de Cuba*, compiled in thirteen volumes by the versatile Ramón de la Sagra and printed in Paris between 1842 and 1861 (with the addition of 281 engravings of which 158 had been colored *au naturel*) and whose price on the island's domestic market could reach seven or eight thousand dollars.

To successfully deal in rare books, Yoyi and Conde had to tiptoe around narrow and already overexploited paths. For starters, they had to figure out where to set their sights, without causing too many waves. Then, if they got a productive lead, they needed the patience and dexterity of professional excavators, since the majority of those who still owned these kinds of books claimed some knowledge of their value and thus always aimed too high, clamoring for irrational prices, convinced that they were holding something akin to Gutenberg's Bible. Secondly, the partners had to appear to be simultaneously very interested and not at all desperate, since, in general, these people didn't tend to be in a rush and, even with reasonable expectations, were in a position of power. In cases like these, the best course of action (according to Yoyi's business genius) was to present themselves as what they really were—mere intermediaries between someone who possessed a valuable book and the presumed and anxious buyer, an individual who was nearly impossible for the former to find due to the nature and price of the product. The cost of fomenting an agreement between both parties had been fixed at a (nonnegotiable) twenty-five percent of the sum of the sale (fifteen for Yoyi, ten for Conde), starting with a gesture of faith in the seriousness and trustworthiness of the respected middlemen. Although this arrangement didn't always work out, when it did, it ended up being most satisfactory for all of the parties involved, and Yoyi neatly complied with each particular term of the negotiation. But if the seller turned out to be stubborn and mistrustful, he would have only one option: the book (usually tracked down by Conde) would be bought by Yoyi (who possessed capital). Mid-sale, Yoyi would pull on his pirate costume (eye patch, wooden leg, hook, and all) and make sure to bring the seller's expectations down to reality.

Since they'd received that fabulous request, Conde had spent several hours of each day of the previous three weeks trying to track down the books, desperately digging in terrain that was more and more sterile. Just two days before the appearance of Yadine the Emo (not a freak or a goth), when he was on the verge of giving up, the former policeman had found the clue that would steer him to that old political leader from the early days of the Revolution who (who would have thought!) was willing to talk about some of the gems found in the library he had appropriated during the Revolution.

Because of his preeminent political background, shortly after the triumph of the 1959 Revolution, the leader had been assigned a splendid house, until shortly before then the property of a certain bourgeois family, one of the many who had left the island in those turbulent years with just two suitcases full of clothing. The owners had had to leave behind, among other goods, a well-stocked library in which, with the exception of Calderón's comedies, existed still (among hundreds of other appetizing treasures) the rest of the books requested by the Diplomat. The old *compañero* of political ambitions, despite having been discreetly removed from the spheres of power years before (after having destroyed several economic plans, businesses, and institutions with reliable ineptitude), had managed to maintain his lifestyle thanks to the conversion of his enormous, luxurious, formerly bourgeois dwelling into a small hostel where, under his beloved oldest daughter's management, rooms were rented out to bourgeois foreigners. But the recent decision of his also beloved grandchildren to depart for other lands in the world where one didn't have to live withstanding such heat and uncertainty had made him determined to sell part of the library. Thus he was an excellent candidate for closing a lucrative sale of the books, a sale that would help his grandchildren (were they also New Men?) achieve geographic resettlement in lands that were, of course, bourgeois.

The previous afternoon, the preliminary conversations between Conde and the former political leader, geared to the purchase of those specific books, had reached the culminating point of talking real prices (without agreeing to that final figure between what was possible for the buyer and dreamed of by the seller). As such, it required the presence of Yoyi the Pigeon, who, that morning, had joined the mission, determined to lay his cards on the table: it was either a sale with fixed commissions based on mutual trust in the good faith of those involved, or, in the absence of that credence, a straight-out purchase that the Pigeon, indignant over the presumed lack of trust by the owner, would carry out as ethically as a pirate. At the end of an afternoon of a tense negotiation, the options had been left in suspense and Yoyi had decided to withdraw as if he were doing so definitively, although he was already more than convinced, as he would tell Conde while he gave him a lift to his house, that the former leader, so frenzied and fundamentalist in his previous position of power, so affectionate with his beloved grandchildren, and in his present fall from grace, so in need of cash, would contact them shortly, willing to negotiate the sale of the clamored-for gems and, if the occasion presented itself, the rest of the treasure as well. Thus would the old man drop into their hands like a ripe mango.

"Look, man, either way, take this so you can get a leg up." Behind the wheel of the 1957 Chevy Bel Air, the young man counted several bills he had withdrawn from his pocket and gave a thousand pesos to his partner, who accepted them with the same shame and anxiety as always. "A little advance."

In reality, Conde wasn't at all sure that they had broken the seller's will, and the feared prospect of losing that gold mine pushed him into a sadness and depression aroused by continued poverty from accumulated monetary and spiritual debts. But, he thought, he wasn't going to feel much more miserable for having accepted the Pigeon's thousand pesos, and less still now, when he could see terra firma on the horizon. So, to avoid the slightest hint of dignity, he stopped at the Bar of the Hopeless and left weighed down by two bottles of that cheap, devastating, and even nameless rum that, for a few months already, Conde and his friends had been calling the Haitian.

———

He recognized her at first glance. Although it had been almost a year since their fleeting and only meeting, Yadine's peculiar face, still presumably goth, had remained intact in his memory. The lips, nails, and blackened eye sockets, the silver hoops in the visible ear and in her nose, the rigid hair falling like the wing of an ominous bird over half her face made her countenance something that was truly unforgettable, at least to a Neanderthal like Conde.

"I want to talk to you, Detective" were the first words the young girl said, when he had barely opened the door.

Even a former cop could be surprised by that sort of Chandlerian speak and Conde didn't dare wonder what Ricardo Kaminsky's granddaughter was looking for, although he had a bad feeling. His immediate concern was over where to hold that conversation. Inside the house, alone with that girl in the prime of her youth, no way; on the porch . . . what would the neighbors say if they saw him with a goth girl? *To hell with what they think,* he told himself, and after asking Yadine to hold on a moment, he fetched the keys to the lock that held together his uncomfortable iron chairs.

"If I'm not mistaken, I never said at your house that I was a detective . . ." Conde began to speak while he set up the chairs for their conversation, as he had done months before for the painter Elias Kaminsky, who was the girl's cousin, more or less.

"But you look for people, yes or no?"

"That depends on who, why, and for what," the man said as he settled in, his curiosity piqued already. "What's going on with you? Is there some problem at home?"

"No, not at home . . . What I want is for you to look for someone," the girl exclaimed, and Conde smiled. Between her belief that he was a private detective who dedicated himself to finding lost people, and the relaxed innocence (dressed up as seriousness or concern) on the face of the goth girl, whose beauty could be sensed beneath her exultant grooming, the situation was starting to seem halfway between hilarious and novel-like. But he chose to maintain distance, hoping for a quick end to the dialogue, although his curiosity had not completely diminished.

"If someone has really been lost, it's the police who should be doing the search."

"But the police don't want to keep searching and *she* has been missing for ten days," she said with fury and anguish.

Conde took a deep breath. That was the moment at which a drink of rum would do him good, but he pushed the idea aside immediately. He chose to light a cigarette.

"Let's see, who is this *she* who is lost?"

At that moment, Yadine took a cell phone out of the pocket of her studded black shirt, touched some buttons, and looked at the screen for a few seconds. Then she held out the device to Conde, who could see Yadine on the screen, alongside another young girl, dressed and made up in a very similar way. Only then, with her only visible eye fixed on Conde, did the girl reply with the greatest conviction, "This is the *she*. My friend Judy."

Conde returned the phone to her and Yadine put it back in the pocket of her shirt.

"So what happened to her, your friend Judy?" Conde avoided interjecting a "dammit" in his question and decided to do whatever he could to move forward a little more. "Because what I see is a freak goth like you . . ."

Then the clarification arose that would serve definitively to bait Conde's curiosity.

"No, you're wrong. I'm not a goth or a freak. I'm emo."

"Emo?"

"Yes, emo."

"And what's being emo, if I may ask? Excuse my ignorance . . ."

"You're excused . . . Or not. I forgive you if you help me look for her. *She* is my best friend," she clarified, always emphasizing the pronoun.

"I don't know if you'll be able to forgive me, because I can't promise you anything . . . But now tell me what being emo is . . ."

Yadine arranged her hair again and Conde discovered in that sole eye something that seemed like frustration or sadness.

"You see, now we could use Judy . . . *She* explains it better than *anyone*."

"About being emo?"

"Yes, and other things. Judy is off the charts . . ." she stated, and touched her temple to indicate that she was referring to her friend's intelligence.

"Well, tell me something about emos . . ."

"We're emos and those others aren't. Look, there are freaks, Rastas, rockers, Mikis, *reparteros*, gamers, punks, skaters, metalheads . . . and us, we're emos."

"Uh-huh," Conde said, as if he understood something. "And?"

"We, the emos, don't believe in anything. Or in almost nothing," she corrected herself. "We dress like this, in black or in pink, and we think the world is fucked."

"And you're emos because you like it?"

"You're emo because you're emo. Because it hurts us to live in a rotten world and we don't want to have *anything* to do with it."

"Well, on this last point, you all are not too original, shall we say," Conde had to tell her. He felt like he was treading water and tried to lead the conversation to an end. "So what happened to *her*, your friend Judy?"

"She got lost about ten days ago." Yadine seemed more at ease although sadder at that point in the conversation. "She disappeared like that, suddenly, without telling anyone, not me, or the other emos, or even her grandmother . . . And that's *very* strange," she emphasized again. "The police say that she hasn't shown up because she must have tried to leave on a balsa raft and drowned in the sea. But I know that she didn't go anywhere. First of all, because *she* didn't want to leave; second, because if she'd wanted to leave, I would have known, and her grandmother, too . . . or her sister who lives in Miami and who didn't know *anything*, either . . ."

Conde couldn't help his former profession taking over his mind.

"Doesn't Judy have parents?"

"Yes, of course she does . . ."

"But you only mentioned her grandmother. And now the sister . . ."

"Because *she* doesn't get along with her parents. Especially with her father, who was—no, not was, who is—a disgusting pig and didn't want her to be emo . . ."

Conde thought about her possible father. Although he still wasn't quite sure what an emo was, and despite not sharing the traumatic experience of having a child, he felt a slight solidarity with this parent and thus decided not to delve any deeper into the subject.

"Look, Yadine." He began to prepare his withdrawal by trying to be nice to the young girl, who seemed really affected by her best friend's disappearance. "I don't have any way to investigate a disappeared person, that's the police . . ."

"But they're not looking for her, dammit!" The girl's reaction was visceral. "And maybe she has been kidnapped . . ."

At that moment, Conde felt sorry for Yadine. Did the unbelieving emos watch soap operas? Episodes of *Without a Trace*? This kidnapping thing sounded like *Criminal Minds*. Who in the hell was going to want to kidnap an emo? Dracula? Batman? Harry Potter?

"Let's see, let's see, tell me a couple of things . . . Besides being emo, what did your friend do?"

"She's in high school, the same one as me. She's a genius," she said, and touched the same temple as before. "And tests start next week, and if she doesn't show up . . ."

"So she's your fellow student. Was Judy doing anything dangerous?" Conde tried to find the best way to put it, but there was just one option: to call a spade a spade. "Was Judy taking drugs?"

For the third time, Yadine moved her hair over her face. Conde wished at that moment to be able to see her full expression.

"Some pills . . . but nothing beyond that. I'm sure of it."

"And did she hang out with strange people?"

"We emos are not *strange*. We love getting depressed, some like to hurt themselves, but we're not *strange*," she concluded, emphatic once again.

Conde noticed that he was on delicate ground. They "loved" getting depressed? His curiosity took flight again. And to top it all off, they weren't *strange*?

"What's this about hurting themselves?"

"Cutting ourselves a little bit, feeling pain . . . to free us," Yadine said after a moment, and ran her fingers over her forearms covered with two tubes of striped fabric and her thighs ensconced in a dark pair of pants.

Conde thought that he didn't understand a damned thing. He could allow for those young people not believing in anything, even allow that they fill themselves with holes from which to hang hoops, but slashing themselves? Getting depressed for the pleasure of getting depressed to thus free themselves? From what? No, he didn't understand it. And since he knew that he would perhaps never understand it, he decided not to ask any more questions and to put an end right there to that absurd story of an emo who was lost and maybe even kidnapped.

"Well, well . . . as a favor to you, I'm going to see what I can do . . . Look." He carefully weighed his options and picked with utmost care the most noncommittal proposal that would allow for a quick escape. "I'm going to talk to a friend of mine who is a police chief and see what he says . . . And then I'm going to talk to Judy's parents, to see what they think of—"

"No, *not* to her parents. To Alma, the grandmother."

"Okay, to the grandmother," he agreed without arguing, and took out a piece of paper he had in his pants pocket and the pen hanging from his shirt. "Give me Judy's grandmother's address and telephone number . . . But bear in mind that I'm not committing myself to anything. If I learn something, I'll call you in a couple of days, okay?"

The girl took the piece of paper and wrote. But when she returned it to Conde, she let out her last request, while simultaneously lifting the hair that fell over half of her face, allowing him to see the true beauty and tangible agony that defined her seventeen-year-old face.

"Find her. Come on . . . Listen, this whole Judy thing has me depressed for *real*."

———

Skinny and Rabbit, like two of Columbus's lookouts, were watching over the horizon from the porch of Carlos's house. As soon as they saw him come around the corner, carrying a bag whose contents weren't at all difficult to imagine, Carlos put his automatic wheelchair in motion and yelled, "Damn! You're really full of yourself!"

"Who's thirsty around here?"

"Have you seen what time it is, beast?" Skinny admonished him as he snatched the bag away from him and rummaged inside it, making clear that there was enough thirst there to go around.

Conde patted Carlos's head and gave Rabbit a high-five.

"You're fucking kidding me, beast, it's not even nine o'clock. Wassup, Rabbit?"

"Skinny told me you were coming early, that you had money and had bought rum and . . . I'm . . . I'm fine, but could be better," his friend said, and accepted the bag Carlos was holding out to him before going inside.

"Where's your mother?"

"She's making something."

The mere knowledge of that promising information made Conde's insides rebel against the solitude to which they'd been subjected.

"Give me the lowdown," he demanded of his disabled friend.

"My old lady says she wasn't up for making more work for herself . . . Runny corn *tamal en cazuela* . . . with lots of bits of pork inside . . . And Rabbit brought some beer to wash everything down. With this heat . . ."

"The night's coming together," Conde admitted as Rabbit returned with glasses full of rum and ice. Once distributed, they drank the first drink and felt their worries losing traction.

"Really, Conde, why were you so late? Didn't you finish up early with Yoyi?"

Conde smiled and took another swig before responding.

"The craziest thing in the world . . . Let's see, who of the two of you knows what emos are?"

Carlos didn't even have the chance to raise his shoulders in confirmation of his ignorance.

"They're one of the urban tribes that has shown up in recent times. They wear black or pink, they comb their hair over their faces, and they like to walk around depressed."

Conde and Carlos looked at Rabbit, dumbstruck, as he displayed his knowledge. They were used to hearing him talk about the use of metals in Babylon, about Sumerian cooking or Sioux funeral rites, but his erudite lecture on emos surprised them.

"Well, yes," Conde affirmed. "Those are the emos . . . And I was late coming here because, until just a while ago, I was talking to one."

"An 'emette'?" Carlos played with words.

"The granddaughter of the Cuban Kaminsky, the doctor."

"So what did you talk about? Depression?"

"Just about . . ." Conde said, and he relayed the girl's unexpected request based on her mistakenly considering him some kind of tropical private detective.

"So what the hell are you going to do?" Carlos wanted to know.

"Nothing . . . I'm going to call Manolo to see what he knows and, if I have time, maybe I'll talk to the grandmother, to calm down Yadine, because I feel sorry for her. But where am I going to find that girl, who must be doing God knows what out there?"

"So what if she was really kidnapped?" asked Rabbit, who watched the most soap operas of their group.

"Well, then we wait for them to ask for a ransom . . . 'Give me a freak or I eat the emo!' As far as I'm concerned, right now, I'll take the *tamal en cazuela*, because I'm starving to death, dammit," Conde proclaimed, determined to free himself of that story, which sounded more and more outrageous to him.

They ate like Bedouins who had just emerged from a long time in the desert: two bowls of ground grains that Josefina had deftly turned into delicate ambrosia. On the side, they had a tomato and pepper salad and a large plate of fried sweet plantains. They doused it all in beer and stamped out any remaining hunger with a bowl of sweet coconut and cream cheese.

Around midnight, while heading to Tamara's house, Conde was certain that he was forgetting something important. He didn't know what. Or where. Just that it was important . . .

He entered the house and, after undressing and brushing his teeth, he tiptoed toward the bedroom, like the classic husband who has come home too late. In the darkness, he heard Tamara's light snoring, always wet and high-pitched. With extreme care, he settled into his side of the bed, fully conscious that he preferred the other side. But from the beginning, Tamara had been inflexible on what belonged to her: if you want to sleep with me, this is my side, always, here and wherever, she warned just once, patting the left side of the mattress. With everything Conde received from that woman, it wasn't worth fighting over spatial trifles. Although he preferred the other side.

The man placed his head on the pillow and felt his exhaustion—accumulated during a tense and hectic day—relax his muscles. The pleasure of the meal and the effects of the beer and rum propelled his relaxation toward sleep. In that journey, without him willing it, arose the image of Yadine, the Kaminsky emo. The girl, with her piercings and her sad gaze, managed to place herself above any known and even sensed worries, to accompany him as he glided toward unconsciousness.

2

As soon as he set foot in the entrance of the criminal investigations headquarters, Conde felt the desire to turn around and run away. Although it had been twenty years since he had run from (or even visited) that site, the memory of his tormented, decade-long stay in the police world always churned his insides with reliable pain. As he looked at the new furniture, the heavy curtains caressed by air-conditioning, the freshly painted walls, he asked himself if that sterile-looking place was the same one where he had worked as a policeman and if that experience had occurred in the same life he was living now and not in a parallel life or one that had ended long before. *How in the hell did you stand being a policeman for ten years, Mario Conde?*

He didn't recognize any of the uniformed people he passed and none of them recognized him—or at least, so it seemed, to his relief. Of the investigators of his time, only the youngest ones must have survived, like then sergeant Manuel Palacios, his trusty assistant investigator, who, after making him wait twenty minutes, at last came out of the elevator and approached him. Manolo was uniformed, the way he liked to be, and had major's bars on his shoulders.

"Let's go talk outside," he told him as he shook his hand and almost pulled on Conde to bring him out of the refrigerated atmosphere toward the indecent steam of the June morning.

"Why in the hell can't we talk in there, man?"

Manolo donned some mysterious glasses behind which he sought to hide, at minimum, the wrinkles and dark circles around his eyes. Manolo was no longer the thin man he had once been, either, although you couldn't exactly say he was fat, even if he seemed so. Conde studied him carefully: the body of his former colleague looked like that of a poorly inflated doll. The years of poisonous air had collected in his now-sagging abdomen and face, but his arms, chest, and legs remained dry and lifeless. *Holy shit, this bastard is doing worse than I am,* he thought.

Below the same Mexican bay leaf tree that twenty-some years prior Conde used to see from the window of his cubicle, the men sat themselves down on a wall, each with a cigarette in hand.

"What's going on now, brother? Let's see if the sparrows shit all over us here." Major Manuel Palacios was smoking, looking left and right, as if he were being followed. "On top of everything else, now you can't smoke in there . . . I'm telling you, Conde, things are at the point that no one can stand it . . ."

"When haven't they been?"

Manolo tried to smile.

"You don't know the half of it! The smoking thing is the least of my worries . . . Go figure that, now, all of a sudden, they noticed that if the ones lower down the totem pole were stealing, it's because the ones above them were giving them the keys and even opening the doors for them . . . There are a ton of higher-ups in prison or on their way . . . Really big fish . . . Ministers, deputy ministers, business leaders . . ."

"They finally shook the tree. But it took a lot of work . . ."

"Well, it's not avocados that are falling to the ground. It's big turds . . . and we're running after them." Manolo mimed hunting free-falling, rotten avocados. "The embezzlement and illegal businesses are worth millions . . . No one knows how much has been stolen, skimmed, given away, and squandered in fifty years."

"And here you were, putting away those little old sellers of plastic bags, ice pops, and clothespins . . ."

"Now we're going after the big fish. But besides, in the *Sábado Gigante* operation, we're looking for those who capture satellite signals from Miami and distribute cables so people can watch Miami channels . . . There are thousands upon thousands of them . . . Also, bringing down the brothels and sex clubs, of which there are a ton. That blew up because they killed a girl with some drug they put in her and then threw the corpse in a garbage dump. There are even some Italian pimps mixed up in that and—"

"How nice, right? The best of all possible worlds . . . and now, suddenly, they discover that this world is full of corruption, whores, drug addicts, perverts who prostitute young girls, and the pigs who looked like saints because they were always yes-men."

"And amid all this shit, how do you expect the bosses to ask us to investigate a missing crazy girl who surely met her maker on a balsa raft trying to get to Miami? Come on, tell me?"

"Her friend says that her parents and grandmother swear on all that is holy that the girl didn't leave Cuba . . . She didn't even get in touch with a sister she has in Miami."

Manolo took a loud breath.

"This morning, when you called, the first thing I did was look for her file . . . The girl was emo and those people, most of them, have a lock of hair over one eye and a sneaker practically hanging around their necks. But not just any sneaker, Converse, the kind that cost a hundred dollars and—"

"A hundred dollars for sneakers?"

"What world are you living in, man? Look, to be emo, you have to have sneakers like that and some other brand I can't remember, and a cell phone, but not just one for talking and sending short messages; rather, the kind that has a camera and can play music and videos. You have to wear black clothing, better if it's by Dolce & Gabbana, either authentic or made in Ecuador; it doesn't matter. You have to wear bracelets, those covers that they put on their arms as if they were sleeves, gloves that are also black—in this fucking heat—and you have to treat your hair with some kind of chemical that leaves it straight and stiff so you can wear it as if the wing of a vulture were hanging in your face . . . Do you know what they call that strand of hair? The curtain . . ."

"The curtain? Curtain? What's that, man?"

"Stop being cute and do the math: you need at least five hundred dollars just to become emo . . . What I earn in two years."

"And how do you police get on with the emos?"

"Let's see . . . on Calle G, all those characters get together: the emos, but also the rockers, the freaks, the Rastas, the metalheads, hip-hoppers . . . ah, and the Mikis."

"There are more every day . . . What is this? *Star Wars*?"

"They're all more or less the same, although they're not the same. The Mikis, for example, are the ones with the most cash because their parents are well connected in one way or another . . . We try not to mess with any of them since all they do is drink rum, play music, piss on the street, shit on the porches of houses in the area, fuck each other in any dark corner . . ."

It was Conde's turn to laugh.

"How you've all changed! When I was in high school, you got carried off to jail for wearing shorts in public . . . So what's the deal with drugs with these kids?"

"That's the real problem, drugs. When it comes to that, we do get fierce. The thing is that on weekends, a whole mess of them get together and that makes things difficult for us. What we do is look for the seller through the buyer and every once in a while, we land a big fish."

"So how do you do it?"

"For fuck's sake, Conde, what the hell do you think informants are for? We have a Miki policeman, a metalhead policeman, and a vamp policeman—there are also vampires on Calle G."

Conde nodded as if what he were listening to was the most natural thing in the world. And, it appeared, it already was. Either way, Manolo was giving him another reason to be glad that he was watching that show as a spectator and not as a working policeman charged, perhaps, with carrying out a vampire hunt. Had the country gone crazy? Was Yadine wearing sneakers that cost a hundred dollars?

"So you can't do anything to find the girl?"

"She's not a girl, Conde, she's eighteen years old. She's a little too old to be messing around with that emo nonsense or whatever it is, to be getting depressed just because, and to be cutting herself to feel pain and . . . And they say they're not masochists."

"Shit, Manolo, I feel like I'm about to turn a hundred. I don't understand jack. They fucked up our lives so much with everything about sacrifice, the future, historical predestination, and one pair of pants per year, to get to this? Vampires, depressives, and proud masochists? In this heat?"

"That's why I'm telling you that if she didn't just get the hell out of here, surely she's having a great time out there, enjoying some foreigner's money God knows where, taking whatever drug they're taking these days. Or cutting herself up into little pieces . . . All I can ask of those in charge of the case is that they not put it at the bottom of a drawer. But I'm sure that they themselves are too overwhelmed looking for pimps, whores, traffickers, con men, corrupt officials, and all kinds of sons of bitches to spend any more time on the emo who got lost because she wanted to. Besides, I don't have to tell you, after seventy-two hours, a person who disappeared doesn't usually reappear." Manolo smiled at his own verbal genius, and added, "At least, not alive."

Conde lit another cigarette and passed the pack to Manolo, who shook his head no.

"On what day did she supposedly get lost?"

Manolo took out a beat-up notebook from the pocket of his standard-issue pants.

"May thirtieth . . . eleven days ago," he read, did the math, and added, "Three days later, her mother filed a missing persons report. She said that sometimes Judy would get lost for one or two days, but not three. For an investigation, that lost time is fatal, you know that."

"And is there anything interesting in the file?"

Manolo thought for a few seconds. He had put his glasses back on so Conde could no longer enjoy the drama of his intermittent blinking.

"Did you already talk to her parents?"

"No, not yet."

"Her parents even sent a picture of their daughter to a TV show . . . But it took a lot of work for them to say that their girl had been seeing an Italian guy for a while . . . a certain . . ." Manolo went back to searching the notebook, which looked like it had come out of a garbage dump. "Paolo Ricotti . . . The name jumped out at me because we've had an eye on that guy, for being a pimp, maybe even a corruptor of minors, but they haven't been able to catch him in the act."

"And what's that character doing in Cuba?"

"Businessman . . . friend of Cuba . . . the kind who makes donations in solidarity . . . But what I don't understand now is why you've gotten involved in this whole thing with the emo, huh, Conde?"

Conde looked at the building where he had worked for ten years. He searched out the window of what had once been his cubicle and, despite himself, couldn't avoid feeling a wave of unhealthy nostalgia.

"I think it's because I'd like to talk to this Judy . . . To truly understand what being emo is . . ."

Manolo smiled and stood up. He was familiar with those evasive responses from Conde and decided to get straight to the matter.

"Or is it that you're feeling antsy because you still think like a cop?"

"Like my grandfather used to say: May God free us of this illness, if we haven't already gotten it . . . Thanks, Manolo."

Conde held out his right hand and Manolo, beyond shaking it, held on to it.

"Listen, compadre, aren't you interested in the father?"

A spark ignited in the former policeman's mind.

"Yes, of course . . ."

"The guy is in deep. He was one of the heads of Cuban cooperation in Venezuela. There's a shit-ton of imports on the left . . ."

"And?"

"And that's all I know . . . But I also got a bee in my bonnet and I'm going to find out more."

"I'm interested in whatever you find out. Even if it doesn't have to do with his daughter. Disgraces never travel alone . . ." he stated and, mechanically, patted himself below his left nipple, the place in which his premonitions (usually painfully) awakened.

"Oh, no, Conde, don't start talking about your premonitions . . . And look, put some cow shit on your head. They say that works . . . Because you're going bald like nobody's business . . ."

———

After several days of threatening to do so, the sky reared up and opened the floodgates: lightning, thunder, and rain flooded the afternoon, as if the end of the world had arrived. When it rained so apocalyptically and the heat receded, Conde knew an unbeatable method to await the passing of the summer storm: he filled his belly with the first thing he happened upon, let himself fall on the bed, opened a slow-paced novel by a Cuban poet always at hand for those circumstances, read a page without understanding a damned thing, and when he received that kick to his brain, wrapped in the sound of the rain, he fell asleep—and so he slept that afternoon—like a freshly nursed baby.

When he awoke, two hours later, he felt damp and heavy. The heaviness was due to sleep; the dampness, to Garbage II, who, in need of a refuge to spend the summer gale, had found his master in his glory and, fur still wet, was sleeping cheek to cheek with Conde. The man thought he should take advantage of the dog's sleep to kill him at that very moment: it was what that tamed son of a bitch deserved. But when he saw him sleeping with the tip of his tongue showing between his teeth as he emitted light little grunts of pleasure caused by some pleasant dog dream, he felt disarmed and got up as delicately as possible so as not to interrupt the siesta of . . . that bastard who deserved to be killed for having drenched the bed.

The rain had stopped, but clouds still covered the sun. As he made his coffee, despite himself, Conde thought about his conversation with Manolo. Could there be some connection between what Judy's father was doing in Venezuela and the girl's disappearance? Logic warned that there should be no link, but logic also tended to be quite fickle, he told himself.

After drinking his coffee and smoking a cigarette, he resolved to start the engine and called Yoyi the Pigeon.

"Talk to me. Have we heard from the seller?"

"Not yet," the Pigeon said. "Give him time, two or three days. Or do you not trust my Spidey sense anymore?"

"More than ever . . . Listen, Yoyi, are you busy tonight or can you come with me to see something I'm interested in but that doesn't make a lick of sense to me?"

"Is there money involved?" he asked, since he couldn't *not* ask, that Yoyi the Pigeon.

"Not a dime. But I could use your help . . . I want to see if I can find a woman."

"For yourself?"

"Not exactly. Too young: she's eighteen years old . . . An emo."

"An eighteen-year-old emo? I'm in."

Two hours later, Yoyi was swinging by to pick him up in his Bel Air. Since Conde had found out that the best time to see those characters was after ten at night, his partner had invited him to kill time by satisfying their hunger, and they carried this out at El Templete, the old port diner reborn as the city's most expensive restaurant, whose clientele, 99.99 percent of the time, consisted of people born or living abroad, or who were a new breed of Cuban entrepreneurs, the only ones in any position to overcome the price barrier of the establishment's delicacies. But Conde wasn't surprised to see how, from the parking attendants to the chef, everyone greeted Yoyi (a street rat like no other) with a reverence usually reserved for Arab sheiks.

Once they had eaten like princes and had their fill of drink—two bottles of a Ribera del Duero reserve red—they left the Chevy at the house of a friend of Yoyi's, who would be sure to guard it as if it were his unsullied virgin daughter, and walked along Calle 17 in search of Calle

G, formerly Avenida de los Presidentes. A couple of years before, on the avenue's central path, Havana's urban tribes, as those rough inhabitants of the night—among whom, it happened, there were even tropical vampires—had given to calling themselves, had staked their claim.

On several occasions, from inside a car or bus, Conde had noticed—always with great disinterest—the concentration of kids who, especially on weekends, had taken over Calle G's nights. From the start, they had seemed like a curious spectacle to him, scarcely understandable and rather singular. According to what he knew, everything had begun with a street gathering of rock fans who had nowhere else to go and, shortly after, turned into a massive concentration of bored kids and noncon-formists. They were self-excluded as opposed to marginalized, determined to waste time, immersed in chatting and drinking, and at the close of the night had a sexual plug-in through any of the available outlets. But he knew little more about that world, so distant and different from his own.

While they were eating, Yoyi had explained a little bit to him.

"Let's see if you understand."

"I'm not going to understand, but go ahead . . ." Conde agreed.

"All these kids want is to be left alone and talk shit without anyone bothering them. The subject of conversation varies according to the tribe. The rockers talk about rock; the Rastas, about how to dreadlock their hair; the freaks, about how to dress more extravagantly; the Mikis, about cell phones and clothing brands . . ."

"Intellectual matters . . . What about the emos?"

"Those are really tough, man. They don't talk much, because what they like is being depressed."

"Everyone mentions the depression to me . . . They really like it? It's not a pose? I'm intrigued by that . . ."

"To be emo, you have to be depressive and think about suicide a lot."

"I told you I wasn't going to understand."

Yoyi, who usually avoided sweets, scarfed down a plate of shrimp in garlic that he had insisted on as dessert, took a drink of wine, and sought a way to open up Conde's understanding.

"The deal with all of those kids is that they don't want to seem like people like you, Conde. Or even like people like me. They try to be differ-ent, but, above all, they want to be what they decide to be and not who they are told they have to be, as has been happening for a while in this country where people are continually ordered around. They were born when everything was the most fucked-up and they don't believe any tall tales and don't have the slightest intention of being obedient . . . Their goal is to be on the outside . . ."

"Now I'm liking this more. That I understand . . ."

"Right, man. They belong to a tribe because they don't want to belong to the masses. Because the tribe is theirs and not affiliated with those who organize and plan everything." And Yoyi pointed up high.

"I'm understanding . . . but not the main thing. So how do you know all of this?"

Yoyi smiled as he patted his pigeon chest.

"Because back in the day, I was a rocker . . . Nuts about Metallica."

"Well, look at that . . . I never got past Creedence . . ."

"But in my time, it was like a game. When I talk to today's rockers, things are more complicated." Yoyi touched his head to indicate the location of the complication. "And it's all serious. At least, that's what they think."

That night, cooled off by the evening rain, the street was overflowing with young people. At first glance, Conde confirmed that the majority of them were adolescents, almost prepubescent, who all seemed to have dressed up for a futuristic carnival. There were human circles around some who were focused on playing their guitars; kids who walked on one side or the other of the avenue's main corridor looking for something they weren't finding or perhaps not looking for anything; others were sitting on the ground, surely damp due to the afternoon's shower, passing around a two-liter plastic bottle with a dirty dark liquid, seemingly high-octane. Some were wearing tight clothing, others baggy pants; the latter had crests of gelled hair on their heads, medieval executioner's bracelets on their wrists, chains with locks around their necks; and others had hoops in their ears, painted lips, and pink clothing. Fed up with and alienated from an oppressive hierarchy, bored with everything, self-selected for marginalization, anatomically and musically obsessed with asexuality, candid, irritated, active tribal militants, anarchists without a flag, seekers of freedom. Rather than a Havana street, Conde felt like he was walking around Marsport, of course without Hilda. But that was Havana: a city that finally distanced itself from its past and, amid physical and moral ruins, foreshadowed an unforeseeable future.

Perhaps because he needed to remind himself what planet he was on, Conde couldn't help but recall that in the same city where the ten lost tribes had now to come to be, a few years before, when he himself was a teenager, certain dark warlocks of limitless powers had come out to the streets to hunt any young person who displayed hair a little bit longer or pants a little bit tighter than what they, those warlocks, considered admissible or deemed appropriate for the hair and extremities of a young person immersed in a revolutionary process determined, with those and other methods, to create the New Man. The weapon of mass destruction most wielded by the Red Guard had been scissors: to cut hair and cloth. Thousands of young people, judged merely by their capillary, musical, or religious preferences—or by sexual or sartorial matters—as social scourges who were unacceptable in the parameters of the new society being built, had not just been sheared and had their clothing redesigned. Many of them even ended up as recruits in work camps where, through difficult agricultural tasks under military regime, they were supposed to be reeducated for their own good and for the good of society. Being considered a troublemaker, showing hippie inclinations, believing in some god or having a nice, lively ass constituted an ideological sin, and the hordes of revolutionary purity, tasked with weeding the moral and ideological path to a better future, had a very productive harvest with those presumed perverts in need of correction or elimination. (Meanwhile, the real harvest, the sugar one, the development and subdevelopment one, wasn't getting good results.) And, as he recalled all of that, Mario Conde couldn't help ask himself if all of that pain and repression against those who were different, merely for being so, if that mutilation of freedom in the land of promised freedom, had been worth anything; at least, based on what he saw now, no. And that made him happy. Very, very happy. But . . . had the warlocks really disappeared or had they just gone underground, awaiting their time, even when life had taken from them the possibility of more time? Nonetheless, of the motley, undone world through which he moved now like a blind man without his cane, all that kept buzzing in his ears like a bothersome noise was the certainty that some of those young people enjoyed depression and practiced self-mutilation, even a culture of death, attitudes that the former policeman considered unnatural, further still, un-Cuban. The certainty was growing more and more in him that that incomprehensible attitude had been the push that had led him to this point.

"Yoyi, in this circus, how do you know which ones the emos are?"

"For fuck's sake, man, by the clothes and the 'curtain' . . . Let's look for them . . ."

"Listen, tell me if you see the vampires. Although I'm sure I'll know them by the fangs and because, instead of rum and Coke, they'll be drinking Bloody Marys."

Yoyi approached a group while Conde, who didn't stop thinking about what he was learning, explained to himself that world of ironic codes in order to protect himself from his perplexity, and watched from one of the passage's corners those New Men of the future, which was already the present. When Yoyi returned, the young man was smiling.

"They're down there, before getting to G and 15 . . ."

They crossed Calle 17 then, and just behind one of the new and ever more horrible statues of Latin American forefathers (that had been erected to fill the spaces left by the vanished effigies of Cuban presidents from the time of the Republic) they saw the inhabitants of the small but sovereign nation of Emolandia. The hairstyles with the straight lock of hair flattened over half their faces, the black and pink outfits, those striped sleeves like zebra skins, the metal hoops in various parts of their anatomy, and their darkened lips, eyes, and nails were the signs that distinguished them from the rest of the natives seen prior to this moment. Conde, unable to deny that he still thought like a policeman deep down inside, stopped the Pigeon in order to try to locate Yadine in the group, but didn't find her. He then took the time to observe and get his first image of this group. While the other tribes had sung, talked, or kissed each other, the young emos remained silent, seated on the damp grass that must have been soaking their asses through, their gazes fixed on anything or nothing at all. The circular structure of the group favored the movement of a plastic bottle going counterclockwise, as if journeying on an impossible time travel toward nothing. Watching them, Conde thought that perhaps he was beginning to understand the incomprehensible: these adolescents were tired of their surroundings. Nonetheless, they didn't seem determined to do anything to solve that state of profound fatigue beyond decorating themselves, getting drunk, and marginalizing themselves every night, without worrying too much about finding a way out . . . besides self-alienation. As Yadine's basic philosophy had suggested to him, they only aimed to be and to seem. Emos were the grandchildren of an overwhelming historical exhaustion and the children of decades of consciously distributed poverty; beings stripped of the possibility to believe in anything, solely determined to escape to a corner of their own creation, perhaps even inaccessible to all who fell outside of that mental and physical circle that, without further contemplation, the former policeman decided to breach. Heeding an impertinent and unstoppable impulse, Conde took the three most agile strides he'd made in recent years, walked toward the group, and sat down between an emo and an emette, or however they called themselves.

"Would you give me a drink?"

The kids had no option but to return to filthy-real reality; an extraterrestrial turned out to be something too out of the ordinary to just be ignored. And besides, the shameless and insolent alien was asking them for a drink.

"No," said the emo in front of him, clutching the bottle. Conde looked at the young blond kid, who was so white he was nearly transparent, with his hair falling over his right eye, his lips painted deep purple, one sole fake sleeve and a shiny ox hoop in his nose. He was so androgynous that he would require close observation under a microscope and only then could one aim to determine his gender identity.

"Okay. After all, it must taste like shit," Conde defended himself, moving a bit toward the emette sitting to his right and calling over to his friend, "Come, Yoyi, cram yourself in here, we're going to get a little depressed . . ."

Yoyi, who had watched Conde's absolutely odd actions with surprise, approached slowly. Even to a former rocker turned everyday warrior, Conde's approach seemed out of control. That's why he murmured, "Excuse me" before sitting down in the spot offered by his friend. Besides, it was obvious that Yoyi found no charm in sticking the seat of his Armani jeans on the ground.

"What the fuck!" The blond Pale Face recovered his testosterone and began to protest. The others were going to join in when Conde cut them right off.

"I came to find something out: Is Judy dead or alive?"

The bomb set off by the former policeman's malice left them mute. But their faces spoke volumes.

"Necessary clarification . . ." Conde said, lifting his index finger. "We are not policemen. We want to know what happened to her, to tell her grandmother," he chose to say, since he didn't know whether he should mention Yadine's participation or not. "The real police say someone mentioned that Judy wanted to leave Cuba and that maybe she boarded a balsa raft and . . . Forgive my impertinence and allow me to introduce myself: Mario Conde, it's a pleasure."

The kids listened to the unwelcome personage and exchanged looks while some searched out Pale Face, who was doubtless some kind of leader. Beneath their masks, Conde guessed they were between fourteen and eighteen years old and confirmed that his speech had had some effect and if he wanted to get something out of that buzz among the emos, he should act quickly.

"They told me that emos love balsa rafts and—"

Pale Face started speaking.

"Judy was always talking about doing things she later never did . . . She had told me about leaving on a balsa raft . . ."

The only black emo in the group cleared his throat. He had the advantage, Conde thought, of saving himself lipstick, but must have spent great effort and a number of chemicals to manage the straight-haired curtain across his face.

"I don't believe that," the kid said and looked at the leader.

"Well, she just repeated that to me the other day," Pale Face reacted, as if he were annoyed. "Whether she did it or not is another thing. But let's hope she got the hell out of here . . ." He whispered the last words as he fiddled with the striped sleeve covering his left arm from the wrist to his biceps. Who did that almost transparent kid look like to him? Conde again asked himself. Trying to stay ahead of the growing silence, he searched for a way to keep the young people talking.

"Is it fun to be emo?" he asked, trying to rile them up.

"You're emo because you're emo, not to have fun," the emo girl sitting next to him said. "Because it hurts us to live in a shitty world and we want nothing to do with it."

Condo made a mental note of that phrase, which was almost identical to the one said by Yadine the previous afternoon. Could it be the tribal motto, lines from its emotional anthem?

"And what do your parents have to say about that?"

"I don't know and I don't care," she said, and immediately proclaimed, in more than perfect English, "It's better to burn out than to fade away, as Kurt Cobain said."

A couple of "Yeah, yeah"s, flat but approving, followed the emette's speech and Conde asked himself who that poet or philosopher mentioned by the pyromaniac in the making could be. Cobain? Wasn't Billy Wilder the author of that phrase? Then he recalled the occasion on which he, still a policeman, had had a conversation with a group of freaks from that long-ago time: the freaks wanted to be free and distanced themselves from oppressive society to breathe in their freedom and fuck like the damned. If these emos didn't want anything but to display themselves as asexual phenomenon, and besides were the kind who would rather burn themselves just to enjoy the immolation, things were getting worse.

"Have any of you seen the photo of Judy that her mother sent to that TV program where they talk about lost people and dogs?" He tried to sound casual.

"Yes, I saw it! It didn't look like her, her hair all done up," said another emo girl, farther away and even smiling, to corroborate Conde's suspicion.

"So is it true that Judy had an Italian boyfriend?"

The black emo began to shake his head no, without letting the curtain come off of his face.

"I'm a friend of Judy's . . . from school," the kid said. "The Italian guy wasn't her boyfriend. How could he be when he was an old man of about forty . . ."

Conde looked at Yoyi: What the hell would he be, at over fifty? And why hadn't Yadine touched on the specific point of that Italian guy?

"So then?"

"She said he was her friend. That she liked to talk to him, that he really understood her . . . He used to give her books, he would buy them in Spain . . ."

"Listen to that!" protested the pale emo, who for some reason was bothered by the dark emo's opinions.

Conde looked at Yoyi again: that story about the kind old Italian man was fishy. He stayed focused on the black emo.

"So you say that she didn't talk about leaving Cuba?"

The kid thought about his response.

"Well, one time . . . but after that, she never talked about it to me again. Everyone talks about leaving, and a bunch do go, but Judy was doing something here that she liked a lot: fucking over her dad."

"Well, that's normal . . . Can I have a drink now?" He addressed Pale Face, who was still holding on to the bottle while operating the keys of his cell phone and looking at something on the screen, as if the talk had ceased to interest him. Grudgingly, the kid held the bottle out to him. Conde smelled it; he'd swallowed worse than this, he told himself, and threw a stream of it down his throat. He swallowed, snorted, and offered the jug to Yoyi. The Pigeon, of course, rejected the offer. "One last thing I'd like to know . . . for today . . . Why do emos have to be depressed for the pleasure of being depressed? Aren't there enough things out there to truly depress someone? Isn't it too hot in Cuba to get depressed just because?"

Pale Face looked at him with hate, as if Conde was profaning sacred dogmas. Yes, yes, the kid reminded him of someone. After thinking about his question, the emo answered him. "It's been a long time since I saw a guy as idiotic as you. And I could give a shit whether you're a cop or not." The anger overtaking him forced him to pause. Conde, willing to accept it all as long as he found out more, noted the glee in the faces of the other presumed depressives. "The only thing we really want is to not have a shitty life like you had and have. I'm so sure you're bitter because you never did what you wanted to. You lapped up all the stories they fed you . . . Because you're a coward and an idiot. And in the end, for what? What did you gain with them?"

The emo paused, and Conde thought he was waiting for a response, which he agreed to give him.

"I gained nothing at all. If anything, I lost . . . because I'm an idiot."

"Did you hear that?" Pale Face said, triumphant, addressing his brethren. Then he turned back to Conde, who had managed to maintain the stupid smile he considered imperative at that moment. "At least we don't allow ourselves to be led like lambs. We're going to lead the lives we want and we aren't going to pay tribute to anyone, man or god. We don't believe in anything, we don't want to believe . . ."

"Unbelievers or heretics?" Conde needed clarification, without knowing why, or perhaps because that last phrase, that proclaimed willful absence of faith, had touched off something in his memory.

"It's all the same. What matters is not believing," Pale Face continued, displaying his obvious leadership and releasing pent-up rage. "That's why we don't want them to give us shit, so that they can't come back later and say they gave us something. We don't talk about freedom, because that word was taken by sons of bitches for themselves and they wasted it: we don't even want that from all of you . . . We grab what belongs to us and that's it . . . And if we can, then we get away from here, it doesn't matter where, Madagascar or Burundi . . . So now go fuck off, because the mere sight of guys like you makes me even more depressed."

As the transparent kid went on with his emo pride speech, Yoyi had started standing up, as if lifted by a jack. He let him finish his rant and then exploded, "Okay, you little shit, I'm just going to ask you one thing: Where in the fuck do you get the money to walk around with those Converse you have on and with that BlackBerry that doesn't do shit here in Cuba?"

"Hey, listen, I—"

"Either answer me or shut up. I already let you speak, and in democratic Emolandia, everyone gets his turn . . ." Yoyi thundered, causing the young people from adjacent tribes to turn and stare. "Do you know what I have to do to have a cell phone? Well, run all kinds of risks with the real police every day, because they exist and in spades . . . God knows where your father, your mother, or the guy who gives it to you up the ass gets the money to support you, dress you, and pay for your whims. So stop being an ass and making yourself out to be so pure and such a heretic. And if you really want to get depressed, listen to what I'm going to tell you now: that Dolce & Gabbana sweatshirt you're wearing is faker than a three-dollar bill! Do you want more reasons to be depressed? Then listen up: you'll never be free! And do you know why? Easy-peasy: because you don't get freedom if you hide in a corner. You have to earn it, asshole! And because imbeciles like you are the ones enriching the makers of Converses, BlackBerrys, and of MP4 players, which are, incidentally, complete and utter shit . . ." Yoyi took a breath and looked at Conde. "I'm getting the hell out of here, man, I can't take this. And you," he addressed the albino emo, "if you don't like what I said to you and you want to work out some aggression, come with me and you'll be really depressed when I'm done . . ."

Conde, still sitting, felt the dampness concentrated on his ass and how numb it was getting. He looked at the emos, furious or surprised by Yoyi's explosion, and watched the transparent leader sputtering, but without moving from his spot. He noticed that, at that point in the debate, the only one who seemed depressed was the black emo. Fighting his own muscles, he managed to stand and put on his best smile.

"Forgive my friend . . . He's like that, impulsive. He was a rocker, you know. I was . . . I played ball." And he made a gesture signaling goodbye, as if announcing his definitive withdrawal from the playing field.

3

Back when Mario Conde was a baseball player (or, to be precise: tried to be one), and an avid consumer of the Beatles, Creedence Clearwater Revival, and Blood Sweat & Tears, he had also been a victim of depression, but for more concrete reasons. He was living the final days of an adolescence experienced without any grace and without having ever worn on his feet (or on any other part of his body) anything coming close to resembling some Converse or Dolce & Gabbana article, even a fake one. It was then that he arrived at high school in La Víbora and, in the same natural way that the acne faded from his face, he started acquiring some of the things that would round out his life: some friends—Skinny Carlos, who really was skinny then—Rabbit, Andrés, and Candito the Red; his enjoyment of literature, complicated by the alarming desire to write like some of the authors he read, like that son of a bitch Hemingway or that asshole Salinger, who hadn't published anything else in forty years; and the first, most painful and constant love of his life: Tamara Valdemira, Aymara's twin sister. And it was Tamara who was the reason for his first depression. (Hemingway would depress him later, when that author made a deeper impression on him. Salinger would simply disappoint him with his insistence on not publishing again.)

Although the twins were alike in all the ways that a human being could resemble another, so much so that to facilitate their identification, their parents decided that Tamara's color would be blue and Aymara's mauve (for hair ribbons, socks, bracelets), ever since he saw them, despite their uniforms and identical faces, Conde fell definitively, unmistakably, monumentally in love with Tamara. The young man's furious shyness, the young woman's alarming beauty, and the fact that Tamara came from a world so different from his (she was the granddaughter of a famous lawyer and daughter of a diplomat, while he was descended from a cockfighting breeder and a bus driver) made Conde suffer his passion in silence, until the ever expansive Rafael Morín showed up, led the cat into the bag, and, incidentally, smothered the hopes of Mario Conde. He endured an unhealthy but very justifiable adolescent malaise for many months—impossible to alleviate even through frequent masturbation, an art in which he came to consider himself a specialist and even an innovator.

Almost twenty years later, that bitter story from the spring of his youth had segued into chapter two in an unforeseeable and explosive way. Rafael Morín disappeared and fate wanted Lieutenant Mario Conde to be burdened with searching for the unblemished leader who, by poking around in all the right places, was quickly revealed to be anything but unblemished and only reappeared to be deposited six feet under, covered besides in the disgrace of his fraudulent businesses. Since then, Tamara and Conde (who was going through a rather traumatic separation and divorce) had maintained a pleasant and placid relationship in which each one gave the other their best selves without giving up what was left of their personal space. Conde even thought that the health of their relationship was perhaps founded on the fact that neither one of them, even when they had thought of it now and then, had dared pronounce any intention to see it through to the cursed word: "matrimony." Although the fact of not invoking it did not imply, either, that the word and all it signified was not circling around them, like a vulture and its prey.

Whenever Conde woke up at Tamara's house, he was seized by a warm feeling of estrangement and even, on occasion, an unforeseeable desire to get married. The first reason for that reaction had visual origins: since he tended to wake before the woman, the man enjoyed the privilege of spending several minutes in bed admiring the miracle of his luck and asking himself—the same question, again and again, during those fortunate, at least in that specific sense, twenty years—how it was possible that the previous night he had been intimate with a woman so beautiful, capable of bringing class even to the reflexive act of snoring as if playing an *oboe d'amore* typical of Bach's cantatas? Tamara, who was just two years younger than Conde, had passed fifty with surprising dignity: tits, ass, abdomen, and face retained much of their original smoothness, despite the fullness of certain of those attributes, like the breast that, escaped from her slip, was calling Conde's attention that morning. Tamara battled the collateral damage of age carefully: daily exercise, covering impertinent grays with a medium brown L'Oréal dye, a strict diet, through which—Conde guessed when he saw his own deterioration and counted his own excesses—she would soon appear to be his daughter. The second cause for his reaction brought with it a more conceptual character: How was it possible for Tamara to put up with him for so many years? To not think of that question, the most difficult one, on mornings like that, Conde usually left the bed like a fugitive and went to the kitchen to make himself the necessary eye-opening coffee. Although that day, instead of a painful premonition, this question lit a fire in his memory and kept him by the bed for a few minutes, looking at the naked nipple and the shine of saliva at the corner of the mouth of that sleeping beauty who . . . in two days would turn fifty-two.

Smoking the day's first cigarette, Conde saw through the open window how light was rising over what promised to be another infernal June day. He knew well that Tamara was no fan of birthday celebrations, less still since passing half a century, and perhaps because of that, it had taken him so long to remember. But now, the presence in Cuba of Aymara, who had lived in Italy for a long time, and who not coincidentally had the same birthday as her twin sister, created a more than propitious situation to have a celebration. And if he needed reinforcement and justification, there was Dulcita, Tamara's best friend, who was also visiting the island then. Yes, the party was ready . . . The only problem being that, with the two or three hundred wrinkled pesos in his pockets, Conde did not have enough to even buy a birthday cake.

As he got dressed, Conde smiled malevolently: yes, there was a reason Skinny Carlos was in the world.

———

As he distanced himself from Tamara's house with his compass set on the home of the missing Judy's family, Conde had no choice but to accept the dwelling's locale as a (not fortuitous in the least) coincidence whose significance he wasn't able to discover, although it did not cease to unnerve him: Judy had lived just a block and a half away from the house occupied for several years by Daniel Kaminsky and his wife, Marta Arnáez.

Once he was standing before the address indicated by Yadine, Conde thought that in times past that palazzo on Calle Mayía Rodríguez must have belonged to some family with less funds than necessary to erect a mansion on Miramar's Quinta Avenida, like the Cuban sugar and live-stock magnates, but with enough to build that construction in an up-wardly mobile middle-class neighborhood, as Santos Suárez had been in the 1940s and '50s. Two floors, cathedral ceilings, solid and beautifully wrought-iron fences, an art deco air, and a surrounding porch crowned by a gallery of Spanish arches still in fashion at that time, all of it having received the reviving benefit of some coats of brightly colored paint. Ac-cording to the information he'd been able to obtain that very morning from Manuel Palacios, this Alcides Torres, Judy's father, had managed to acquire the attractive property at the beginning of the 1980s, when the straggling owners of the house set sail for Miami and, somehow, *compañero* Torres, brandishing his claims and political power, had used all of his contacts to establish his royal seat as a rising leader there.

Conde delicately pressed the doorbell placed alongside the door. The woman he assumed to be Judy's grandmother opened it. She was a woman in her sixties who looked very good for her age, but had the signs of deep grief on her face, angst that seemed to predate the disappear-ance of her granddaughter. Conde, who often tended toward wandering ideas, asked himself upon seeing her how a painter would capture and translate to canvas that vague but simultaneously obvious feeling: a woman's sadness. If he knew how to paint, he would have liked to try.

As soon as he introduced himself, his hostess realized who he was.

"Yadine's detective friend who is not a detective but was a policeman . . ."

"That's one way to put it . . . And you are Judy's grandmother, right?" The woman nodded. "May I come in?"

"Of course," she said, and Conde entered the living room, very well ventilated by two large gated windows, a space where plants, decora-tions, framed pictures, and high-quality wooden furniture essayed to note the owners' financial prosperity, Conde thought, as he accepted the hostess's offer and sat down in one of the rattan chairs placed next to a window.

"Thank you, madame . . ."

"Alma. Alma Turró, grandmother of—" And she interrupted herself, overcome by a fit of sudden sadness.

Conde chose to look elsewhere, waiting for the woman to recover. In his other life, as a policeman, he had learned how uncertainty over the fate of a loved one tended to have a more piercing effect than a painful definitive truth, many times processed with relief. But the game of deceptions and hopes to which the spirits of a person awaiting confirmation about a missing person are submitted always dragged along a pernicious and exhausting component. Suddenly, the woman stood.

"I'm going to make you some coffee," she said, obviously in need of a dignified escape.

Conde took that time to study at his leisure those surroundings where the resounding falseness of some magnificent reproductions hanging on the walls stood out: Vermeer's *View of Delft*, Emanuel de Witte's well-known church interior, and a winter landscape, with a windmill in it, whose original artist he couldn't place, although without a doubt, it was Dutch, like the other two masters. Why did they insist on crossing his path, anywhere he went, these damned Dutch painters? Nevertheless, on the best wall, the most visible, there was no work of art: like a declaration of principles, there reigned a gigantic photo of the Maximum Leader, smiling over the slogan WHEREVER, HOWEVER, FOR WHATEVER, COMMANDER IN CHIEF, WE'RE AT YOUR SERVICE! He continued his visual exam and noticed, on a small table, a frame that enclosed the image of two girls, about ten and four years old, their cheeks together, smiling: Judy and her sister who lived in Miami, he assumed . . . He tried to imagine a young emo, depressed and unsatisfied in that place, with all of its inhabitants standing strong, at the ready (at least that's what they tried to make others believe), to do whatever might be asked of them. He didn't manage it. Without a doubt, for that family, the girl's attitude must have been as heretical as the enraged emo had mentioned the previous night, and he thought that in that house could lie the reasons for her disappearance, whether it was voluntary or caused by external forces.

Alma Turró returned with two cups and a glass of water on a silver platter. She placed it all on a table, next to Conde, and asked him to serve himself.

"May I smoke?" he asked.

"Of course. I also smoke a few cigarettes every day. A little more now that my nerves are . . ."

They drank the coffee and lit their cigarettes. Only then did Conde jump in.

"You already know that Yadine came to see me. I explained to her that I am not a detective or anything of the sort and that I don't know if I will be able to help you find Judy. But I'm going to try—"

"Why?" the woman interrupted him.

Conde took a couple of drags to give himself time to think. *Because I'm curious and I have nothing better to do* was a possible response, although too strong. *Because I'm an idiot and I allow myself to get involved in these messes* seemed better.

"The truth is that I'm not quite sure myself . . . I think mainly because of something Yadine said to me about emos and depression . . ." The woman nodded silently and Conde got back on track. "The problem is that it has been twelve days already without any news of her, and that complicates things. I talked to a former colleague and I know that the police are rather lost." The woman nodded again, still without saying a word, and Conde decided to go in by the most traditional and simultaneously necessary way. "I'd like to know if Judy did or said anything unusual before disappearing, anything that would indicate her intentions . . ."

The woman left the cigarette in the ashtray for a second, then immediately took it up again, as if she were making an important decision regarding the act of smoking. But she didn't bring it to her lips.

"Everything seems to indicate that I was the last known person to see her. That day . . ." She paused, as if she needed to breathe in more oxygen, and again left the cigarette. "Well, that day, she came home from school at the same time she always did, nibbled at a little bit of food, said she wasn't very hungry, and went up to her room. Looking at that in and of itself, she didn't do anything strange. From the perspective I have now, she seemed more focused or even depressed, at least quieter than at other times, but perhaps I'm imagining things . . . You didn't know anymore whether she was truly depressed or depressed for fun and out of habit . . . What nonsense . . ."

"And then?"

"She spent a while in her room, came out to shower around three . . . At four thirty, she came down, said goodbye to me, and left."

"She only said goodbye to you? What did she say?"

"Her mother had gone to the market, her father was fixing a spigot in the yard, but Judy didn't ask about them. She said goodbye like always, told me she was leaving, that she didn't know what time she would be back, and gave me a kiss."

"She didn't call anyone on the phone?"

"Not that I know of."

"She didn't eat anything before leaving?"

"She didn't even stop by the kitchen."

"Maybe she thought she'd eat something out, right?"

"I'm not so sure. Sometimes, she would spend almost all day without eating. Other times, she would eat like a lion. I always told her that that wasn't healthy or normal . . ."

"What was she wearing? Did she have a purse, a backpack?"

"No, she didn't take anything. She was dressed as she always was when she went to Calle G. In black, with pink sleeves. Very made-up with dark colors. For her lips and eyes . . . With metal and leather brace-lets . . . Well, she did take something: a book."

Conde felt that in that apparent normality there was something revealing, but where it came from and what it revealed escaped him. It became evident that in order to try to trace Judy's steps, first he had to do whatever was possible to get to know her.

"That was all on a Monday, right? And she said she was going to Calle G?"

"Yes, Monday, May thirtieth, but . . ." Alma stopped in her reasoning, alarmed by something that had just become obvious to her. "No, I already told you that she didn't say anything about where she was going. We all assumed she was going to get together with her friends . . . Although it was still early, and on Mondays they almost never go to Calle G."

"But she was dressed as if she were going there . . ."

"No, you're not understanding me. When she went out to meet up with her friends, she always dressed like that. She didn't only go to Calle G. I don't know why I thought and told the other policeman who asked that she had gone there. It was an automatic response . . . Some-times they got together at one of their houses."

Conde nodded, but mentally noted his question. *"If you didn't go to Calle G, where in the hell did you go, Judy? To see one of your friends? To meet up with the Italian?"*

"Are Judy and Yadine very close friends?"

"I wouldn't say very . . . Judy is a bit of a leader and Yadine followed her around like a little dog, always imitating her in every respect . . ." The woman paused and dared to say, "As if she were in love with Judy . . . But Yadine is a very good girl."

Conde made another mental note, and followed it with several question marks.

"Alma, I need you to tell me about Judy. I want to understand her. Two days ago, I talked to Yadine and, yesterday, I was with her friends on Calle G, and I'm more confused than anything else . . ."

The woman took two drags and crushed her half-smoked cigarette.

"Let's see . . . I think that Judy was always a singular girl. I'm not saying that as an impassioned grandmother, but I have to tell you that she was more mature than she should have been every step of the way, and too intelligent. She read a lot, ever since she was eight, nine years old, but not books for children, rather, novels, history books, and I, who was the one who practically raised her, encouraged those interests . . . Perhaps she matured too quickly, skipping phases. At fifteen, she spoke and thought like an adult. That was when my daughter and my son-in-law, Alcides, were sent to work in Venezuela and took her with them. From that point on, everything got complicated. If you spoke with your police friends, I'm sure you already know that Alcides was stripped of his post for something that he did or didn't do in Caracas and that he's being investigated . . . Well, that's neither here nor there. When they made them come back from Venezuela, the school year was about to end and Judy lost that year of her studies. But she also lost other things. It was almost as if they had exchanged her for another person: the prodigious girl who left was very different from the strange young woman who returned. She barely spoke to her parents; she talked to me, more or less, but didn't open up, didn't open up . . . It was as if she had returned to adolescence. With Frederic, a high school classmate of hers, she began to get together with those kids who call themselves emos, she got into wearing black and pink, and she herself became an emo. Luckily, she didn't leave school, and sometimes I got the feeling that she was living as two people, one who was a student and one who refused everything, rejected everything. The one who was a student continued to be my hope that someday she would get over that sickness and return to being just Judy . . . I was even afraid that she had some kind of illness, schizophrenia or one of those bipolarities that show up around that age, and I took her to see some doctor friends of mine. On the one hand, they calmed me down, and on the other, worried me: there were no traces of bipolarity or anything of the sort, but she did have a great attachment to nonconformity, especially an obvious rejection of her parents, and that could be the origins of a depressive tendency, a sadness that could end up being dangerous . . . And wasn't an emo pose."

"Forgive me for interrupting you." Conde scratched his head and leaned forward in his seat to speak. "And for asking something, but . . . Did Judy used to harm herself?"

Alma Turró made as if to grab the cigarettes, but stopped herself. Conde knew he had hit a sore spot. The woman delayed in responding.

"Not too much . . . Psychologically, she did . . ."

"Can you explain?"

"I've read about some young people, especially the ones who call themselves punks, but also about emos, who cut themselves, mutilate themselves, tattoo themselves. They express their hate against society with hate toward the body. That's how Judy would put it, just as it sounds . . . I don't think Judy had reached those extremes, but she did pierce her ears, her nose, her navel, and used those hoops, and she got a tattoo on her back . . ."

"All of that after she returned from Venezuela?"

"Yes, after . . ."

"Do the police know about that tattoo? What did she have tattooed?"

"A salamander . . . Small, like that . . . And of course, the police know . . . To identify her if . . ."

Conde took a deep breath. He had always been the kind of man who, if he had to have blood tests, closed his eyes when he saw the nurse and asked for a piece of alcohol-soaked cotton ball to avoid passing out. His visceral rejection of pain, blood, any aggressive offense to the body, didn't allow him to conceive of those self-harming philosophies. He only smoked (always Cuban tobacco) and ate and drank (everything that came his way, regardless of the national origin), trusting in the goodness of his lungs, liver, and stomach.

"And you said that psychologically . . ."

"Judy has gone about creating her world, a world that has less and less to do with this one that is ours. It's not just how she dresses or does her hair, but also how she thinks. She eats vegetables, never meat; she doesn't use deodorants or creams, but after her shower she rubs herself with cologne until she's purple; she reads very complicated books and was obsessed with some Japanese comics, the ones they call 'manga.' And"—Alma Turró lowered her voice—"she would proclaim anywhere that all governments are gangs of repressors . . . All of them," she restated, to calm herself down.

As he received this information, Conde had the feeling that Alma Turró was not a reliable source. There was something more than non-conformity and adolescent angst in the girl's attitude, as enumerated by her grandmother. Something more that might relate to her disappearance. Although she believed she knew her well, Conde was starting to think that the grandmother, despite having raised her, didn't know Judy, either. Or only knew one of the two Judys well. What about the other one?

"Alma, that classmate of Judy's, Frederic?" She nodded. "What's he like?"

"He's black, rather tall, very intelligent . . . Judy and he have been friends since early high school. That one really is a friend of hers, more than Yadine. Well, he was the one who got her interested in becoming an emo."

"It wasn't Yadine?"

"No." Alma moved her head. "From what I heard one day, Yadine was goth or punk . . . but not emo. Until she met Judy . . ."

Conde nodded. Frederic had to be the black emo with whom he had spoken the previous night and Yadine was another multilayered onion, he concluded.

"Why did you go to the TV station with a photo of Judy without . . . in which she doesn't look emo?"

"I said the same thing myself . . . It was Alcides's decision. He didn't want anyone to see what his daughter was really like . . ."

"What about school?"

"Yes, she maintained her interest in school and got good grades, as always. That's why one of the things that makes me fear for the worst is that in a few weeks exams begin, and if she doesn't show up . . ." The sob was now deeper, raw, and Conde again offered her the kindness of shifting his gaze. But this last fact confirmed his idea that the grandmother's narrative about Judy was lacking some component that, already, he intuited was linked not only to her public attitudes, but also to her mysterious evaporation.

"Does she want to go on to study at the university?" he asked when the woman had recovered her calm.

"Yes . . . but she doesn't know what."

"That's more normal," Conde said with certain relief, and received a brief smile from the grandmother as recompense. "So why do you say that your son-in-law's problems in Venezuela don't have anything to do with Judy?"

"Nothing that Alcides did has any relation to Judy. Besides, Judy didn't have much to do with her father, since a long time ago . . . He spent his days criticizing her, for anything. And look at what he was up to."

"What was he up to?" Conde decided to explore that breach.

"Some men who worked with him would 'save' for themselves the pounds of luggage that Cubans who were going to work in Venezuela couldn't use or didn't want. I don't know how things worked, but when there was a good amount of pounds accumulated, they would send a container with things that were then sold here. The two men involved in this mess were subordinates of Alcides and are in jail, because they were the ones signing for those deliveries . . . He swears he didn't know what his people were doing."

"And do you believe him?"

Alma took a deep breath.

"We were talking about Judy," the woman evaded him. Of course she didn't believe him.

Despite the fact that it was not the most appropriate reaction for that moment, Conde had to smile. Alma imitated him conspiratorially.

"Alma, why is almost everyone so sure that Judy didn't try to leave Cuba?"

The woman stopped smiling. Her seriousness became deep. She looked at the photo of the two smiling girls.

"She wouldn't have gotten herself into that without saying anything to her sister María José, who is in Miami . . ."

"María José?" Such a Castilian name surprised Conde, who was already used to hearing the most nonsensical names for the offspring of his generation: from Yadine and Yovany to Leidiana and Usnavy.

"Yes. María José left on a balsa raft and was on the brink of death . . . No, I am sure that Judy would have asked for my help to do something like that . . . Despite her character, or her act . . . No, she wouldn't have dared . . ."

Conde nodded. It wasn't worth reminding the grandmother that her granddaughter had many faces, as she herself had suggested, and that there were more than enough young people in this country who wanted to get far away. But for the time being that path was blocked, he thought. He needed to find a shortcut to the "other Judy," perhaps the truer one.

"Alma, would you let me see Judy's room?"

———

In the shadows, Kurt Cobain looked into his eyes, defiant, with the insolence that only those who believe themselves unassailable are capable. However, verifying that Cobain was a musician brought him certain comfort, since the incendiary phrase he'd heard the previous night, and that he had managed to translate for himself, turned out to be more pleasant if it came accompanied by some melody. Below Cobain's blond image, the poster announced his affiliation: Nirvana. Conde barely knew it was an alternative rock band, and he had not a single image or note in his mind, like a good Neanderthal clinging to the pure sound of the Beatles and Creedence Clearwater Revival's black melodies. But, hadn't that singer committed suicide? He should find out.

The room, on the palazzo's second floor, was wide but cavelike. The windows were covered with a dark fabric, barely pierced through by the ruthless summer sun. When he found the light switch and had a better view of the place, Conde verified that under the Cobain poster was the bed, made up with a purple-colored blanket, which served as confirmation of its owner's taste for gloom. On other walls were posters for musical groups also unknown to Conde—a certain Radiohead and Thirty Seconds to Mars—but the real encounter with something very twisted came when, as he closed the bedroom door, the former policeman saw the poster reigning there. Below some dripping letters in scarlet (yes, he thought of the word "scarlet," a strange color in the palette of his vocabulary) that warned DEATH NOTE was an image of a girl, without a doubt, Japanese, with a ferocious expression, rigid mouth, clenched fists ready to fight, and a strip of black hair over her right eye: a curtain, a screen? But the girl seemed covered by the strange and grotesque figure of an indefinable animal, with vampire-like wings, hair shooting up all over the place, and an enormous black-lined mouth—a clown ejected from the heavens or come out of the inferno. A Satanic image. Surely, this image must belong to one of the manga consumed by Judy. Going to bed

every night and falling asleep while seeing that visage of fury and horror couldn't be healthy at all. Or was the girl burning slowly with her
individual fires?

He found a couple of school uniform items hanging in the closet,
while the rest of the wardrobe was made up of a collection of emo designs.
Black clothing dotted with shining studs, platform boots, and some
Converse, apparently useless already due to how worn-down the soles
were, portable sleeves (some pink ones, others that were black-and-
white-striped), and some gloves designed to leave the fingers uncovered.
According to Alma Turró, the afternoon on which she went out to not
return, Judy was adorned in her emo attire. But there was the girl's other
battle gear, which added alarming ingredients to her disappearance,
since a planned escape would have surely implied a selection of at least
some of those clothes that were so specific.

On a small bookcase, he encountered what he expected and more.
Amid the predictable tomes were several of Anne Rice's vampire novels;
five books by Tolkien, including his classics—*The Hobbit* and *Lord of
the Rings*; a novel and a book of stories by a certain Murakami, obviously
Japanese; Saint-Exupéry's *The Little Prince*; a very, very worn-out copy of
Kundera's *The Unbearable Lightness of Being*; and . . . *The Catcher in the
Rye*, by that son of the bitchiest bitch Salinger!—we already know his
sins . . . But he also found more incendiary texts: a study on Buddhism,
and *Ecce Homo* and *Thus Spake Zarathustra* by Nietzsche, books capable
of putting much more than vampires, sprites, and alienated or immoral
characters in the mind of a young person who seemed too precocious
and impressionable, with an immense desire to separate herself from
the flock. Inside Nietzsche's *Zarathustra*, Conde found a rectangular
card, handwritten perhaps by Judy herself, and what he read confirmed
his first conclusion and explained the speech about disbelief by the previous night's transparent emo: "The death of God supposes the moment
in which man has reached the necessary maturity to dispense with a
god who establishes guidelines and limits on human nature, rather, morality. *Morality is inextricably related to the irrational* [the copier had underlined this several times], to unfounded beliefs, in other words, to
God, in the sense that morality emanates from religiosity, from axiom-
atic faith and, as such, *from the collective loss of critical judgment which
serves the interests of the powerful and the fanaticism of the masses.*" Had
Nietzsche written that? Had Judy copied and processed that? The un-

derlined idea at the end of the citation indicated a predictable feature in the developing picture of the girl as antiestablishment and determined in her pursuit of the uniqueness that freed her from the influence of power as much it freed her from belonging to the "fanatical masses." But why had she been drawn to that first underlined phrase in which morality and irrationality were connected? What had led a girl so young to worry about ethics and faith?

As he asked himself what the police in charge of finding Judy could have thought about that room and its revelations, Conde scanned his surroundings looking for something he couldn't specify, with the certainty that his discovery would help him understand the nature of and perhaps even the motives for Judy's voluntary or forced disappearance. Without his noticing, the former policeman was again thinking like a policeman, or, at least, like the policeman he had once been. He again opened the closet, looked in the drawers, and flipped through the pages of books without finding what he was looking for. Amid the boxes of dozens of DVDs, he read a title he hadn't noticed in his previous search and that enticed him: *Blade Runner*. He had seen that movie no less than five times, but it had been a while since the last occasion. He took the box and opened it to verify whether it was an original copy. It was. To find out, he had to lift the white card on top of the disc, which ended up having writing on the reverse side, in the same hand as the notes found in the Nietzsche book, although in more compact handwriting, almost miniature, forcing him to squint so he could better focus and read: "The soul has fallen into the body, in which it loses itself. Man's flesh is the damned part, destined to age, die, degrade. The body is the endemic illness of the spirit." Conde read those words twice. As far as he knew (and it wasn't like he knew too much about those matters), it didn't sound like Nietzsche, although he thought he recalled that through the mouth of Zarathustra the philosopher had talked about the soul's feeling of contempt for the body. Was what was written a conclusion of Judy's, a speech from *Blade Runner*, or a citation taken from some other author with those concepts meant to reflect utter contempt for the human body? Whatever its origin, it sounded unnerving, much more so given the specific circumstances of a disappearance that was perhaps voluntary, and clearly announced why Yadine had said that there was no one better than Judy to explain what it was to be emo.

Conde kept the card, put it in his pocket, and decided to go downstairs

with the DVD to ask Alma Turró if he could borrow it: he should sit
through *Blade Runner* again if he wanted to verify whether it was a forgotten speech from the movie. Either way, that combination of musical
and philosophical Nirvanas, of ferocious emos and ultra-postmodern
monsters, of vampires, elves, and supermen freed from bondage thanks
to the death of God, all topped with contemptuous concepts of the body,
could result in a complex mental state. The possibility of suicide grew in
that light. He already knew, through Alma Turró's words, that Judy had
created her own world and built her own house in it. But now that he
had some idea of the strange inhabitants of that universe (there were
as many sharpened swords as in a manga), Mario Conde had acquired
the certainty that the girl was much more than a girl who was lost,
misplaced, or hidden of her own volition: she seemed to be a dramatic
warning sign of the dangers of contemporary alienation. And a self-
inflicted death had perhaps presented itself as the shortest and quickest
path to that same longed-for freedom from the body and of the sickening sadness caused by what an emo had called "the environment."

———

At the mere sight of the reverberating asphalt esplanade of the so-called
Red Square, the hieratic bust of the Forefather, the flagpole without a flag,
the old *majaguas* in bloom, the short steps and the tall columns supporting
the building's portico, Conde felt how the story of Judy's disappearance
was becoming his. For men like Conde and Skinny Carlos, everything
that had to do with that profane sanctuary of what had once been and
was again now La Víbora High School evoked a special connotation for
those who refused to discard what remained of the most luminous moments of the past, fearful of a loss that could tear apart their memory
and leave them abandoned to a present in which, many times, he felt the
impossibility of finding his way. On that black esplanade, seated in
the path of the stairway and the desks sheltered by the building that rose
up behind the columns, Mario Conde had traversed three years with
which he still lived, rather, with the consequences of which he still lived,
as he was able to verify every morning and every night.

When the tide of warm nostalgia had settled in his spirit, Conde,
beneath the poplar where he had taken refuge from the beating of the
cruel midday sun, decided to take advantage of the wait and used the reno-
vated phone booth nearby . . . First, he called Carlos to delegate the

organization of a birthday party for the twins; he had to go through the whole playbook and do everything from invitations to the complex assignment of what each invitee should bring, conveniently divided between beverages and edibles. Then he called Yoyi to find out if he'd heard from the former leader who loved his grandchildren (and perhaps his dogs as well—he had to look into that), but the young man was still sleeping off the hangover of warlike rage that had exploded the night before during his close encounter with Emo World.

Past noon, a noisy flock of uniformed students came down the front steps on their way to the street. Hiding his body behind the coarse trunk of the poplar, he saw Yadine pass by and go off alone toward the Calzada. Watching her, Conde felt hit by nostalgia and disappointment. How many dreams of the future had he and his friends caressed as they walked down that same street, only to have them dashed to pieces in the brutal clash with the reality in which they lived? Too many . . . Yadine, at least, didn't believe in anything, or didn't have anything in which she wished to believe. Perhaps it was better that way, he told himself.

A few minutes later, when he had lost almost all hope, Conde saw Frederic Esquivel leave the building; he managed to identify the young black man he had met as an emophile practitioner the night before and who, according to Alma Turró, had induced Judy into embracing that world. From where Conde stood, he saw Frederic go to the right, accompanied by two girls, and he decided to follow him to try to approach him at the most propitious moment.

From his prudent distance, the pursuer tried to guess what the black emo had done about the hair that had been covering his face the night before and didn't find an answer to his curiosity since, following school regulations, the kid had moved aside the fallen piece of hair to leave his entire face visible. One of his companions split off in search of Calzada del 10 de Octubre and Frederic continued walking with the other one, surely to the also nearby Avenida de Acosta. Luckily for Conde, it was the girl (a rather well-developed blonde, nearly stunning) who dropped anchor at the Route 74 bus stop, where she said goodbye to Frederic with a long, sustained, lewd, wet kiss accompanied by mutual ass-grabbing, very easy in Frederic's case, since his fallen pants displayed, in the rear, more than half his underwear. As soon as they separated, the young man repositioned his member, excited by all the kissing, and continued on his way, as if he had just had a glass of water. About one hundred feet farther on, he crossed the avenue to turn at the first corner, toward the neighborhood of El Sevillano.

"Frederic!" The kid looked surprised when he turned around and recognized the man. Conde tried to smile as he approached him, thinking that if anything remained of the erection, he was responsible for making it disappear. "It was hard for me to recognize you . . . Can we talk for a minute? I just wanted to apologize for what happened yesterday, what my friend said and what I did. We were very impertinent with all of you. Do you have a minute for me?"

The hibernating emo kept silent. His black skin was shiny with sweat and suspicion. Now he seemed less androgynous than the night before. Conde pointed at a low wall, with the benefit of the shade from a tree, while he explained that it had been Judy's grandmother who told him his name and where to find him. Just in case, he again swore to him that he wasn't a policeman.

"Look, the truth is that I used to be, but in another life, about a thousand years ago . . . And before that, I went to the same high school as you . . . Well, that doesn't matter . . . Let's see: right now I'm coming from Judy's house and her grandmother spoke to me of you. Alma asked me to help them find out what happened to Judy, and I think your friend deserves that. If Judy tried to leave on a balsa raft—"

"She didn't try to leave on any balsa raft, I already told you," Frederic interrupted him, almost annoyed.

"So then surely she's alive. But if she's not showing up, there must be something . . ."

"Because of her father. That guy has always been a son of a bitch. She can't stand the sight of him, even in a picture."

"Why do you say that? What did he do to Judy?"

Conde shook at the mere thought of the source of the disappearance being mixed up in an act of paternal violence.

"He tried to kick her out of the house when she became emo. But Judy's grandmother said that if her granddaughter left, she would also leave. It was all complicated, her father would say that we emos are counterrevolutionaries and I don't know what other bullshit . . . He even came to my house one day to accuse me of steering his daughter off course . . ."

"So this Alcides Torres is into this line of bullshit?"

Frederic smiled.

"Worse than that . . . That guy is so afraid that he's shitting himself . . ."

"Because of what he did in Venezuela?"

"Maybe," he said, thought for a moment, and added, "I think so. It appears that he went too far and they gave him a good smacking."

The young man smiled again, without much conviction. He may have been sad, but not depressed, thought Conde, who still didn't understand anything: sad after kissing that blossoming blonde? At Frederic's age, and at every other age he had been through, he would have been dancing a jig.

"The girl you left at the bus stop, is that your girlfriend?"

"Nah . . . a friend."

"What a good friend," Conde muttered, envious of the kid's youth and of the warmth of relations he maintained with his friends, and went back to the point. "Look, if Judy didn't try to leave on a balsa raft and doesn't show up, there are three possibilities that I can think of as being the most probable. Two are very bad . . . The first, that something happened to her, an accident, I don't know, and that she's dead. The second, that someone is holding her against her will, God knows why. The third possibility is that she's hiding, and she would have reason to. If it's the latter and you help me find her, and I see that she's okay, doing what she's doing because she wants to, I'll forget it all and we'll let her go on as is. But in order to dismiss the fucked-up possibilities, I have to see if it's the third one. Do you get it?"

Frederic was looking at him very seriously.

"I'm emo, not an idiot . . . Of course I understand."

"So . . . ?"

Frederic lowered his gaze to his Converse sneakers, abused as they were. He did so with such intensity that Conde thought that at any moment the shoes would speak, perhaps like Zarathustra.

"Judy's Italian friend isn't in Cuba, so she couldn't have left with him . . . Our other friends from the group are out and about, so I don't think she is hiding at any of their houses. The last ones to leave on a balsa raft were rockers, not our guys; I don't think she even knew them. I don't know why Yovany was talking about that and then mixed up one thing and another . . . I've thought a lot about all of this and I really don't know where she could be. I think that one of the bad things you say happened—"

"Yovany is . . . ?"

"Yes, the one from last night's argument."

Conde nodded and lit a cigarette. He understood he'd been rude and offered the pack to Frederic.

"No, I don't smoke. I don't drink, either . . ."

The model emo, Conde thought. *He even speaks to me with respect.* And he decided that if Frederic was leaning toward the worst fate for Judy, then he should start to play the trickiest notes of that tune.

"Again, I swear on my mother that I'm not a policeman anymore and that I'm not going to discuss this with the police . . . What kind of drugs did Judy take?"

Frederic again looked at his disintegrating Converse, and this time Conde discovered three things: that the sneakers didn't speak, that the kid's silence was more eloquent than the most explicit response, and that Frederic's head was a work of art on which the hairs that had been straightened made layers on his scalp that ended up looking like cabbage, with superimposed leaves. Conde persevered. "If she's lost . . . could it have something to do with drugs?"

"I don't know," the kid said at last. "I don't take any of that . . . I'm emo because I like the group, but I don't do what the others do. I don't drink, I don't do drugs, I don't cut myself . . ."

Conde picked up the detail about what "others do" in reference to drugs and decided to keep going, making him out to be dense.

"Cut what?"

"The body . . . arms, legs . . . to suffer."

To prove it, Frederic showed him his arms, free of scars. Despite already knowing about those practices, Conde couldn't help but feel a stabbing pain. But he feigned surprise.

"It can't be—"

"It's a way of understanding the pain of the world: feeling it in your own flesh."

"And here I was, thinking you were all crazy. You really are crazy, dammit!"

"Judy cuts herself and does drugs. As far as I know, just pills. Pills and alcohol make you fly."

"So are there others who take drugs besides pills?"

Frederic smiled.

"I'm emo, not—"

"Okay . . . Her grandmother says Judy had piercings everywhere, but that she didn't hurt herself."

"Her grandmother doesn't know anything . . ."

"So what do you know that could help me?"

Frederic lifted his gaze and locked eyes with Conde.

"Judy is very complicated, more than the average girl. She takes things seriously."

"Because of what she reads and all of that?"

"Also because of that. I couldn't imagine that everything about being emo was going to hit her so hard . . . She started looking for books and knew one by heart by Nietzsche, the one about the supermen, and she started saying God had died . . . But at the same time, she believes in Buddhism, in Nirvana, in reincarnation, and in karma." Conde preferred not to interrupt him, let the enumeration go on, perhaps until a revealing point. "She said she was living life number twenty-one. Before, she had been a Roman soldier, a sailor, a Jewish girl in Amsterdam, a Mayan princess . . . and that if she died young, she would come back with a better fate," Frederic said, and again interrogated his Converse.

"She talked about dying? About suicide?"

"Of course. There's a reason she became emo, isn't there?"

"Do you talk about that?"

Frederic smiled ironically.

"Yes, just like the others . . ."

"But you don't believe in that. What about the others?"

"Yovany and Judy talked about those things a lot. I already told you, they take everything seriously. He also cuts himself. Right now, he has a real gash on one arm."

"I didn't see it."

"He had the sleeve on."

Conde recalled the tube of fabric covering the arm of Yovany, the pale emo who incessantly reminded him of someone. He concluded that, based on what he had seen until that moment, despite his appearance, Frederic didn't mesh with the attitude of someone worried by suicide and possible reincarnation. He then took out the card he was carrying in his pocket and read the text to the kid.

"What can you tell me about this?"

"Judy read things by a certain Cioran. She had found him on the Internet when she was in Venezuela. I think this is by Cioran," he said, and started looking in one of his notebooks as he spoke. "She likes to talk about what she's reading, to pass on quotes to us, she wants to educate us, I'd say . . . Look, she wrote this in my notebook," he said when he finally found what he was looking for, and read: "'Stripping pain of all meaning means leaving the human being without resources, making him vulnerable. Although it may seem the strangest event to man, the most opposed to his consciousness, the one that along with death appears to be the most irreducible, pain is nothing more than a sign of his humanity. Abolishing the ability to suffer would be abolishing his human condition.'"

As he listened to Frederic, Conde started noting how that story became complicated at each new attempt to peer into Judy's mind, and, especially, how he was heading into a territory that was, to him, impenetrable and unknown: a field crossed with opposite paths marked by incomprehensible signs. And the girl could have gone down any one of them, since, if he understood anything in that mess, the quote Frederic had read appeared to point in another direction. How in the hell had he allowed himself to get caught up in this story?

"She enjoyed and valued suffering, but held contempt for the body and, besides, took drugs to live in another world and didn't believe in God, but did believe in karma and reincarnation and in the humanity of pain, besides?"

"Before going to Venezuela, she still wasn't really emo-emo, and I think she didn't take drugs. When she came back from there, she had already tried them, although it didn't seem to me that she was addicted: it was like an experience, or at least, that's what she said. Although, in Venezuela, more things happened to her, and she didn't want to talk about that, or about what her father had done, although she said he was a big fake . . . What I do know is that there, since she could get online, she discovered several emo and punk websites where they talked a lot about these matters of the body and physical suffering, and she chatted with them. When she came back, she had become more emo than me, more than anyone, and started to get piercings, then a tattoo, and anytime she could, she talked about these things, about marks, about pain . . ."

Conde assumed that Judy's emo-masochist militancy could have encouraged a voluntary flight, but to carry it out, she would have needed some support. Especially depending on the place she aimed to go. And if she was alive and in Cuba, where in the hell could she be hiding?

"If she had wanted to go somewhere, or hide . . . Did she have access to any money?"

"She always had something, five, ten bucks, but no more. I imagine that, little by little, she would steal from her father, I'd say . . ."

Conde noted the detail and continued.

"What about the Italian? Tell me something about that story. Did he have anything to do with drugs? Did he give her money?"

"It was a strange thing, because Judy doesn't like men and . . ."

Conde couldn't help it. "Hang on! Are you telling me that Judy is also a lesbian?"

Frederic couldn't help it, either. He smiled again.

"Well, what the hell have Judy's parents and grandmother told you? They didn't tell you that she's gay, that she cuts herself, and that she's going to be reincarnated? And they still expect you to find her? That seems very fucked up . . ."

Conde felt the essence of what a fool he was, or, more clearly, the role of the idiot that he was playing in front of the kid. And he convinced himself that the operation to get to Judy's core wasn't going to be easy. With the image of Yadine in mind, he shot out his question. "Did she have any serious relationship, a girlfriend or something like that?"

Frederic again interrogated his Converse.

"Yes. But I can't tell you who it was."

"Fuck that!" Conde exploded at hearing the kid's response and took the opportunity to clean up his image by acting offended. "What the hell is this? Everyone here has to give an air of mystery, say just a little piece about things, offer nothing more than whatever the fuck they feel like?"

If he had still been a policeman, Conde would have had other methods to shake down Frederic. Fear tends to bring down mountains, as Buddha, Siddhartha Gautama—perhaps a friend of Judy in one of her last twenty lives—could have said. But, for this very reason, among many others, Conde had ceased to be a policeman. He lit another cigarette and looked at Frederic. He was certain that, at least at that moment, that oracle had closed. Nonetheless, he decided to play a surprise hand when he asked, "Was Judy Yadine's girlfriend, or did she have something going on with her?"

Frederic smiled.

"Yadine is a fool who wants to be emo and the truth is that she's not anything . . . But she's in love with Judy up to here . . ."

Frederic held his hand up to his chin and Conde nodded. He looked at the young man and pleaded: "So then, you don't have any idea where in the hell she could be, what happened to her or what didn't happen to her?"

Frederic pondered this for a few seconds.

"There was another Italian. I saw him once. I don't know if anyone else from the group met him. She called him 'Bocelli,' because he looked like the blind singer. And the other thing I know is that Judy wanted to get out of being emo. About a month ago, she told me we were too old for this, we should do other things, but she didn't know what . . ."

Conde took a drag and crushed his cigarette on the sidewalk. That last revelation sounded promising.

"The super-emo wanted to leave the tribe? So what was she going to get into then?"

"The truth is, I don't know . . ."

The man looked at the kid and understood that the dialogue was coming to an end. But he needed to know two more things. He tried it.

"Help me understand something, kid . . . Do you really, really think that Judy wanted to commit suicide, or is that all a character she created?"

Frederic thought about it and smiled at last.

"Judy didn't create a character. She was the most authentic girl in the group. She dressed like an emo, talked like an emo, but she thought a lot . . . That's why it doesn't seem to me like she wanted to commit suicide . . . Although if she wanted to, she would also do that. Judy is capable of doing anything . . . But no, I don't think so . . ."

"Shit, Frederic, keep helping me understand . . . Tell me, why does a kid like you become emo?"

The young man moved his head, negating something, and caused one of the leaves of his cabbage bouffant to come out of place and fall, defeated, over his face.

"Because I'm tired of being told what I have to do and how I have to be. Only because of that. I think it's enough, right? And because it makes me seem more mysterious, and that helps you get more girls."

"Now I understand you . . . I already saw some of the results. So what about Bocelli? What's that guy like?"

"I don't know, I only know him by what Judy would say about him . . . And he did take drugs."

Your life has gotten complicated, Mario Conde, he thought, and felt exhausted, with as much desire to abandon the story as to find meaning to it.

"Thank you very much for what you've told me. If Judy doesn't show up, I might come back to see you," Conde said, and held out his hand. He shook the kid's hand and, before releasing it, wished him luck on his journey through the Nirvana of Emolandia.

4

"Of course it's me . . . Wassup?"

"Get over here now, the leader has collapsed like socialism in the country of the Soviets . . ."

Very much despite what Nietzsche stated and what he himself had thought for years, in recent times, Conde was ready to believe in the existence of God. It didn't matter which one, since at the end of the day, they were all more or less the same, and at times, even the same, despite people, with different understandings of God, falling on top of each other, kicking and fighting (at best) every once in a while. Now it seemed evident that some god must have peered out of that sky and, in a moment of boredom, exercised divine will. That god, taking his role very seriously, appeared to have decided: *I'm going to throw some rope down to that unlucky idiot who's always broke and doesn't even have one peso to give his girlfriend a nice gift for her birthday . . .* On the bus, as he traveled toward Yoyi's house, Conde started to calculate, without much success, what he would make from the percentage distribution of the book deal, and from there, he went on to the very difficult deliberation of what would be the most appropriate thing to give Tamara for her birthday . . . now that he would have money. In that process, anytime some scruple over the fate of the books tried to come up, Conde would give a mental push, trying to remove it from his conscience. And, to be on the best terms with himself, he would raise the Pigeon's most pragmatic reasoning: if they didn't do it, someone else would. In that case, better them than those other guys, the sons of bitches who were never in short supply and among whom must be the invisible kidnappers of several of the bibliographic gems of the marvelous library discovered by Conde a few years before and that, because of those same scruples, he had refused to negotiate so as not to participate in their irreparable exit from Cuba . . . which in the end, "the others" had carried out in order to grow fat with the proceeds and feel as happy as clams.

Almost without his noticing, in a sibylline way, Conde's theological and literary reflections as well as his birthday party plans were driven out of his mind by the emo mystery novel into which, with the disinterested solidarity of his uncontrollable curiosity, Yadine Kaminsky had thrust him. Something always escaped him every time he tried to imagine a definition as a starting point: Who was Judith Torres? Without the answer, it seemed impossible to find out the cause of her disappearance. The fact that she was emo could be essential, but perhaps it would only end up being a secondary component in the configuration of her character. At least one certainty existed: Judy was not the simple (for lack of a better word, in a terrain in which simplicity did not exist) rebellious adolescent and black sheep of the family. What most besieged the former policeman's thinking lay in Judy's relationship with herself: her reading, her musical tastes, her perception of a world that, according to her grandmother, was a universe created by her, herself. All of these ended up being more intricate connections than they usually were at the young woman's age. There was something much more inaccessible inside the girl, as the four personae he'd managed to put together for her indicated: the sketch handed over by a lovesick Yadine, that one drawn by her grandmother, the one that Frederic and perhaps other emo friends knew, and the one that Conde himself had outlined as he searched around in the girl's room and got closer to some of her more difficult obsessions. Her certainty that God had died (something that at that precise moment, Conde the atheist refused to accept just like that) turned out to be more complicated than an inability to believe in divine plans, or different than a lack of faith in otherworldly lives and powers. Judy appeared to have elaborated an entire philosophy, capable of including a credence in the existence of an immortal soul but simultaneously in the free will to guide it and, further still, in the need for that free will as the only path to individual self-fulfillment, without interference from the castrating religious or mundane powers, the keepers of faith and established morality.

The discovery of the young woman's lesbianism had, to some degree, come to alter the perspectives from which Conde had started to contemplate her. If she identified as a lesbian, why would a girl like Judy, who idolized freedom, decide to shroud the identity of her partner in secrecy? Something wasn't right about that . . . To make the picture more complicated, there was her close relationship with the two Italians, the good one and the bad one, which even opened a pathway to drugs, among other thorny possibilities. And what about the mystery of what had happened in Venezuela? Was it an experience capable of personally affecting Judy or was it the result of the shadowy business that cost her father his removal and the hounding of an ongoing investigation? Was it only because of her cyberspace encounters with emophile philosophers, tribal theorists of the painful, physical practices such as punishment of the body and the search for humanity? Conde knew that he was amassing too many questions for a policeman who was no longer a policeman and whose only tools were his tongue, his eyes, and his mind. And Judith Torres was evading him every time he tried to corner her . . .

Yoyi, recently showered and wearing a fair dose of cologne, still shirtless, was waiting for him on the porch of his house, engaged in the obsession he had for sucking the medallion over his plucked pigeon's chest.

"What a break, man," he said, all of his enthusiasm unbridled, when his business partner approached. "If we sell it for what I anticipate, do you know how much you get?"

"I've been trying to do the math for two days, but no . . . Four hundred dollars?" He dared to pronounce the alarming figure.

Yoyi had put on his linen shirt, fresh and unblemished. With the key to his Chevy in one hand and his best smile on his lips, he grabbed Conde's ear with the other hand to better whisper to him.

"That's why you failed math . . . You get almost a thousand bucks, man . . . One-zero-zero-zero!"

Conde felt his legs go weak, his stomach leapt, his heart stopped. A thousand dollars! He had to keep himself from kissing the Pigeon.

"Yoyi, Yoyi, remember that I'm an old person, my health . . . You're going to give me a heart attack, dammit!"

"The former leader called me and says that, since we're serious people, he accepts the sale by percentages. But he wants discretion and prefers that we do the transaction outside his house. And since we're so serious, he asked me, as a sign of good faith, to leave him two thousand big ones on deposit." And he smacked his pocket, where the evidence of a bulge announced the excellent health of the young man's businesses. "What a character!"

When they were getting into the Bel Air, Conde looked at the June sky and lifted his index finger up high, in his best sports stance, and communicated his conviction to whoever was lingering in the celestial sphere. Some god had definitely survived and was hanging around up there.

"Nietzsche was an idiot," he said.

"And now you realize that?" Yoyi smiled as he pressed the accelerator.

"I owe you one, friend. That money is saving my life . . . The thing is . . . Let's see," he finally dared. "If Tamara were your girlfriend, what would you give her for her birthday?"

Yoyi thought very seriously.

"An engagement ring . . ."

"An engagement—? But I don't want to get married . . . for now."

"And you don't have to get married. But a ring is perfect . . . White gold, with some nice semiprecious stones . . . I myself can sell it to you, man. A really pretty one, and with a friends and family discount!"

———

Added to the atmospheric heat of June in Cuba was now an interior combustion caused by the noisy entrance of the devil into his body. The proposal dropped by Yoyi regarding the engagement ring had had an unexpectedly deep impact on Mario Conde's consciousness. The idea of commemorating Tamara's birthday with that gift which, in all certainty, would be appreciated by the woman, so taken with courtesies, formalities, and old habits, was tempting. But, in equal measure, it was dangerous, since if there was one thing Conde and Tamara had discussed little and poorly throughout those twenty years of intimacy, it had been the possibility of getting married. Would Tamara take that gift as an obligation? Should he ask her before giving it to her and annihilate any surprise effect? Did he really want to get married? And what about her, did she? Did they ever have to get married? Did giving a ring imply *having to get married*? How had Yoyi guessed that lately, that possibility had been going around in his head?

After satisfying his hunger with the food that Josefina had saved for him just in case—and it was almost always the case—Conde and Carlos went to the porch in search of the relief of a breeze. But while Carlos explained to him the organizing strategy for the party they would have in two days, for which he had already distributed verbal invitations and inalienable responsibilities to guarantee a sufficient amount of edibles and beverages, Conde couldn't stop thinking about the damned ring.

"So there will be nine of us: Rabbit, Aymara, Dulcita, Yoyi, Luisa, Tamara's ugly dentist friend, you, Candito, the birthday girl, and a waiter."

"Candito is coming?"

"And how! He told me that that night he's closing the church because he can't miss this party. Old Josefina is going to make us some filling things to eat with supplies that Dulcita and Yoyi are bringing, since they offered, also voluntarily and in advance, to make that contribution . . . What do you think?"

"Since when does Yoyi know about the party?"

"I talked to him a little while after you called me."

Conde estimated: Yoyi had had several hours to think about the subject of the ring. That time turned his proposal into a premeditated and treacherous act.

"What did you say I'm responsible for?" Conde asked, trying to get back to the reality of the moment. To facilitate the process, he took a long swig of rum.

"The cake, the flowers, and two or three bottles of rum. And rum is rum, real, with a label, not that one they sell at the Bar of the Hopeless . . ."

Conde put his hand in his pocket and removed a bill worth fifty *pesos convertibles.*

"Yoyi gave me an advance until they pay us for the books we're negotiating. I need you and Candito, who knows about flowers, to take care of my share. You buy the rum . . . I've gotten tangled up in the story of that damned emo and—"

"Tell me a little about it. Do you have any idea yet where in the hell she went?" Carlos imitated Conde and took a drink.

"I have thousands of ideas, but about where that girl could be, none. I've made things hard for myself, Skinny. Now it turns out that I'm the one who is most worried about where she could be or what could have happened to her . . . It's not every day that someone gets lost who was out there warning that God is dead and philosophizing about the freedom of the individual. Tomorrow, I want to see if I can talk to Candito. He's the one out of all of us who knows the most about God . . ."

"There's a reason he's an emergency pastor, right?"

Conde nodded, again valuing the persistent presence of a god in the story of a missing girl. Yes, perhaps his friend Candito the Red, who had turned into some kind of makeshift evangelical pastor, could help him understand the knot of acceptances and denials of the transcendental in which the young girl had pushed him. But Conde sensed, without knowing the exact reason for that feeling, that in Judy's life and disappearance, there were other shadowy things that he hadn't even brushed upon yet, and that it wasn't by crossing the paths to heaven that he was going to arrive at the darkness enveloping Judy. Yes, he had to understand other things. Who could help him?

"Wait, let me call Rabbit. I thought of something that maybe he could give me a hand with."

Conde picked up the cordless telephone that was on the porch's little table. The device was also a gift from Dulcita, who was more and more generous and attentive to Carlos's needs. He dialed Rabbit's number, and when his friend answered the phone, he explained the reason for his call: he needed Rabbit to give him advice about who he could speak with to understand something about the subject of young people who harm and scar themselves. And if that person existed and Rabbit could try to get him an appointment, the sooner it could be done, the better. His friend agreed to find out.

"This whole matter is really heretical, beast," said Carlos. "I can't believe that they enjoy suffering and getting depressed, I swear on my mother, I can't—"

"The world is crazy, Skinny . . . And I am, too," he admitted, drank what remained in the glass, and stood up. "Although not so much: Judy knows what she wants, or at least, what she doesn't want, and I know that you have to give me what money is left over from what I gave you . . . Now I'm leaving, I want to talk to Tamara about something."

Carlos looked at the bottle of rum brought by Conde. Half of its contents still remained. Something much more serious than a lost emo must be tormenting his friend's mind for him to ask for his money and leave mid-game when the best was yet to come.

"Conde . . . Are you going to tell me what in the hell is going on with you now? You arrived here looking down in the dumps and now you're up to your neck in garbage. For fuck's sake, today you did a deal that's going to rake it in, you're doing what you most liked doing when you were a policeman and you can do it without being a policeman, and in two days, we're going to have a big party for Tamara's birthday and, except for Andrés, all of us survivors are going to be here . . . What more could you want, beast? Tell me, what's there to complain about, Dick Head?"

Conde smiled at Carlos's final words, which went back to the joke about the redskinned warrior named Dick Head, who expresses to the great chief Eagle Head, son of the legendary Bull Head and brother of the brave Horse Head, the disagreeable side effects of his appellation. And he concluded that Carlos was right: *What's there to complain about, Dick Head?* It seemed obvious: he couldn't help himself. His capacity for suffering as a result of anything that came his way made him, in a way, a precursor of the emo philosophy. But he didn't open the floodgates. The matter that was needling him was not something he could talk about with Carlos before having solved it with Tamara, because it concerned her as much as it did his own doubts.

"I'm not complaining, beast, I'm just being an idiot . . . If Rabbit calls, he can find me at Tamara's." Conde got closer to Carlos and leaned over his spilling-over anatomy, barely contained by the arms of the wheelchair, and couldn't resist the wave of tenderness that pushed him to hug the damp, sweaty body of his invalid friend. If Skinny needed additional proof of Conde's pitiful state, the latter was giving it away with that hug, free of alcoholic impulses. It was obvious that he was hurt. Carlos, contrary to habit, this time preferred to stay silent as he returned the sign of affection.

Conde decided to travel the distance to Tamara's house by foot. He wanted to give himself more time to meditate on a way to solve his new conflict. What bothered him most about that situation was its vulgar financial origins, since if he didn't have the thousand dollars on the horizon promised by Yoyi, then nothing of the sort could be happening. And they say that the rich don't have problems! *But,* he asked himself, philosophically, *was the problem the ring in and of itself, or its implications?*

Tamara, recently showered and wearing a nightgown, was on the sofa watching one of those documentaries about animals that those responsible for the nation's TV programming liked so much. Just at the sight of her, in those familiar daily, routine surroundings, Conde felt a stab of anguish. Did he really want to get married forever? But as he leaned over her generous cleavage to give her a kiss and inhaled the clean scent that Tamara's skin gifted him, his anguish was displaced by a pleasant feeling of belonging. This made him start to come up with immediate plans.

"You keep watching that. I'm going to take a quick shower," Conde said, and went to the bathroom.

As he washed off layers of filth and heat and handed himself over to imagining a satisfying sexual end to the day, Mario Conde thought that, truth be told, he could consider himself a very fortunate being: he was lacking thousands of things, he'd had hundreds stolen from him, he'd been tricked and manipulated, the whole world was going to hell in a handbasket, but he still possessed four treasures that, in magnificent conjunction, he could consider life's best rewards. He had good books to read; he had a crazy son-of-a-bitch dog to take care of; he had friends to screw around with, hug, and with whom he could get drunk and recall, without inhibition, times past that, with charitable distance, seemed better; and he had a woman whom he loved and, if he wasn't too mistaken, who loved him. He enjoyed all of that—and even money now—in a country where many people had barely anything or were losing what little they had left. Too many people he ran into while out and about on the street, who would sell him their books in the hopes of saving their stomachs, had already lost their dreams.

Like a long-term bachelor, Conde hung his recently washed underwear on the tub and recovered the pair he had left there the night before. He went to the bedroom and looked for the hole-ridden and gigantic shirt he usually slept in. As he heard the TV voice narrating the story of a hermaphrodite elephant, a friend to the birds and a fan of eating yellow flowers (maybe he was simply just a gay elephant?), he prepped the small coffee pot and brewed some coffee. At that hour, Tamara wouldn't join in, so he served his portion in a cup and, with a cigarette in hand, went to the TV room with a resounding decision in his mind: the hell with it, he would ask Tamara if she wanted to marry him. *After all,* he thought, *if I already want to give her a ring, why not throw myself in headfirst once and for all?*

When he entered the living room, he found Tamara asleep on the sofa. To not wake her, he took a seat in the leather armchair purchased many years prior by Tamara's father in London, when he served as ambassador to the United Kingdom. With the remote control, he turned off the television set: he didn't have the energy for stories about elephants with sexual trauma. He drank his coffee and lit his cigarette. And he understood that that was the best time to launch his proposal: "Tamara," he whispered and dared to continue, "what do you think about us getting married?"

The woman's first snore was the only response to his big question.

5

The esplanade, baptized many years before as Red Square by some stunned and enthusiastic promoter of the indestructible Cuban-Soviet friendship, radiated from the blackness of its paving. They left their car on a side street and, as soon as they took refuge under the kind shade of a tree, Conde and Manolo, as they couldn't help but do, handed themselves over to evoking the grotesque episode of the death of a young chemistry professor who, twenty years before, had forced them to go back and forth across Red Square to La Víbora High School. Thanks to that investigation, they ended up finding a mountain of shit—moral double standards, opportunism, social climbing, sexual, academic, and ideological deviances—and, the icing on the cake, a killer that neither one of them would have wanted to find.

Early in the morning, Conde had tracked down Major Manuel Palacios before he left his house (he now lived with his eighth wife) for work at investigation headquarters. Manolo protested as much as he could, but in the end agreed to see him around eleven and later accompany him on that trip to a present plagued by connections to the past. Since Tamara had gone out at dawn (it was the day that they did surgeries with the maxillofacial surgeons), Conde dared to leave her a note on the dining room table. He would try to return early to talk to her about something important, he wrote. He knew that he had conceived of that note with the worst of intentions: to not leave himself any margin for escape. Then he went to his house to change and feed Garbage II, who received him with a growl of reproach for subjecting him to abandonment. What if he got married and went to live at Tamara's house, which was much more comfortable than his own? What would he do with his crazy dog, a fan of sleeping on beds and sofas after spending the day on the street rolling around with other dogs and even with hermaphrodite elephants (if any pachyderms with those qualities showed up)? If he took him with him, the most likely thing would be that, one week in, Garbage II and his owner would be declared undesirables and kicked out, both of them (the elephant, too, if it went with them), from a house where one lived in accordance to certain rules of etiquette that those riotous savages were surely unaware of. Admitted cause for divorce: the unbearable ungovernability of a man and his dog.

At headquarters, Conde explained to his former subordinate the steps he had taken in his search for the emo and the reason for his request for help: he needed to identify and, if they managed to do so, locate the Italian whom Judy had nicknamed "Bocelli." To calm down Manolo, who was always anxious, he had brought up the subject by telling him that it was about a man who would be interesting for him and his policemen, since according to what he had found out, it seemed very possible that he had something to do with drug consumption and sales in the city. He needed Manolo's support, since the only tangible way to identify Bocelli implied asking Immigration for details on Italians under the age of forty, frequent visitors to the country who had entered the island in the last two months. They must use that information to confront Frederic, from whom Major Palacios, in his condition as a real policeman (the kind who can interrogate and imprison you), also had to get the identity of Judy's mysterious girlfriend, as tempting as an unexplored island. Somewhere between the Italian and the hidden girlfriend could lie the reasons for the emo's disappearance, forced or voluntary.

As he waited for the information about the Italians, Conde nonchalantly tried to introduce the other subject with which his former subordinate could help: Alcides Torres's Venezuelan story, which showed up again and again as the background to the daughter's rebellions. To his surprise, that day Manolo reacted as if he'd been wounded: regarding that investigation, they, the same detectives as always, didn't know anything. With the argument that they weren't dealing simply with common criminals, the investigation had been handed over to a special corps that was tracking Torres and other similar cases. But what was clear to the "same detectives as always," like Manolo himself, was that it had to

do with corruption, pure and simple. If Alcides Torres was still out there
looking for his daughter and driving his Toyota, it was solely due to the
fact that they hadn't been able to implicate him directly in those shadowy dealings with the containers loaded down with flat-screen television sets, computers, and other technological delicacies purchased
in Venezuela, later resold in Cuba. But, in Major Palacios's opinion,
when two of your subordinates have cake, they let you try the icing at
least, right?

With the photos of thirty-two Italians who met the required parameters, Conde and Manolo were waiting for the students to come out. As
usually happened in similar circumstances, Conde felt the heartache
caused by his opportunistic decision to place Frederic in the position of
revealing a secret the boy had committed to maintaining. He had done
something similar in the case of the murdered professor when he practically forced a student from that institute to reveal information capable
of placing the kid in the none-too-pleasant position of rat. Why in the
hell had he agreed to get involved in this story? The former policeman
was reproaching himself when they heard the bell that put an end to the
high school's morning session.

Like the day before, Yadine was one of the first to leave the building,
and, alone as always, quickly, as if intent on something, she took the hill
toward la Calzada. Minutes later, Frederic came out sporting his student look. Instead of two, today there were three girls accompanying
him, including the spectacular blonde he'd been kissing as a good friend
the day before. With the established routine, the first of the young
women left the group toward her destination, and a few minutes later, it
was the blonde who—after a kiss that was lighter but involved tongue—
separated from Frederic and the other young woman. The pursuers had
to walk for several blocks behind the couple who, as soon as they freed
themselves of their companions, had started to engage in a frenetic kissing in the streets that forced them to stop every few feet and made
Conde consider his inability to understand anything. When they got to
Parque de los Chivos and sat down on a bench, the intensity and depth
of their caresses reached higher levels. Their tongues went crazy, the
young people's hands acting like snakes trained in the art of sliding under
clothing, and they insisted on sinking their teeth into nerve points, causing convulsive muscular disturbances in their respective bodies. Conde
and Manolo, at a prudent distance, had to resign themselves to smoking,

sweating, and evoking past times and loves, trusting that the kids wouldn't throw themselves on the grass and go further (the girl already had her hand inside Frederic's pants and the latter had one under his friend's skirt, who at one point arched so far backward that Conde feared she would break in two). Perhaps the heat would exhaust their out-of-control ardor quite quickly. At one point Conde moved his vision away from the show and looked at his former colleague; he discovered that Manolo's eyes had reached an extreme state of being crossed, attracted for too long by the fully clothed porno happening in the park.

Twenty minutes later, after a very long kiss, the young people separated themselves—although not without effort. The girl (this one had dark hair, was tall, thin, and well-proportioned) crossed the park with a convalescent's gait, and Frederic, after readjusting his member so he could walk without breaking it, walked down the slope that led to Avenida de Acosta. Manolo, who already deemed he'd invested too much time in that voyeuristic pursuit that seemingly altered his hormones, decided not to wait anymore and hurried his pace to catch up to the kid.

"Frederic, wait there," he yelled, and took advantage of the slope's momentum to accelerate his stride. Conde, trailing behind him, couldn't help but smile. Neither he nor Manolo were in a condition anymore to carry out street chases.

The young man had turned around and his face clearly expressed his feelings when he saw Conde in the company of a uniformed policeman who, on top of it, had bars.

"What do you want now?"

Conde tried to maintain his smile.

"Your pants are stained . . . We need a little more help . . . Not for us, but for your friend."

The opening phrase hit its target and Frederic lowered his defenses and his gaze to see the proportions of the effusion. Conde knew that noting that evidence made him more vulnerable.

"What do you want?" he whispered as he used his backpack to hide the stain on his inner thigh.

"Look, Major Palacios"—Conde pointed at Manolo—"is also interested in finding Judy."

"And we need to see if you can identify the Italian she used to call Bocelli," the major took over. "I have some pictures here. Come see if it's any of these men . . ."

Frederic looked at Manolo, then Conde, and took the folder where the pictures were. Slowly, he flipped through the pages without any expression taking over his face. At the fifteenth image, he reacted and said, "It's this one. I'm sure. I only saw him once, but it's this one . . . Don't you see that he looks exactly like the singer?"

Conde took the folder and looked at the picture: a man of about thirty-five, lots of hair, and olive-colored skin. He turned the card over and read the details: Marco Camilleri, twelfth visit to Cuba; had entered the country last on May 9 and had left on the 31st, three weeks later . . . The day after Judy left her house with an unknown destination.

"He was in Cuba when Judy got lost, but . . ." Conde muttered as he tried to imagine what that coincidence could mean. And he was only able to wager the worst.

"But what?" Frederic wanted to know.

"If Judy is in Cuba, she can't be hiding with him . . . But if before leaving Cuba, this Bocelli . . ." Conde's mind was thinking what his mouth refused to say: that Judy had not disappeared due to a specific reason, but that her absence was as irreversible as death. Had Bocelli concluded his stay in Cuba or had he interrupted it for one of the reasons that Conde was guessing? In an almost automatic way, he looked at Major Palacios, who made a slight affirmative motion. He was thinking the same thing. "Maybe this man could have done something very bad to Judy."

"He killed her?" Frederic's question was almost a yell.

"We can't know right now," Conde stated, and decided in that instant to take advantage of the young man's altered state. "But the person who is surely still here is Judy's girlfriend, and we need you to tell us who she is."

"No idea," the young man began, ready to leave.

Manolo, with his senses on high alert, chose to get right to it.

"Look, Frederic, this isn't a game. In case you don't know, it's called a criminal investigation . . . Judy has been lost for thirteen days, and is probably dead. We're talking here on the street because my friend says you're a good kid, but I don't want to waste my time. So, either you tell us right now who in the hell Judy's girlfriend is or we continue this conversation in a much less pleasant place, and I swear to you, you will tell us there. You can't imagine how convincing we . . ."

"Ana María, the Lit teacher," Frederic said and, without waiting for any commentary, started running down the hill.

Conde saw him go and felt more pity than relief.

———

She must have been twenty-seven, twenty-eight years old and was stunningly beautiful. Intensely black hair, tragic eyes that were jungle green, crowned by full eyebrows raised in slight surprise, lips as if silicone filled but in reality fattened merely by the nature of ephemeral ethnic mixtures. Conde saw himself threatened by small breasts pointing skyward like surface-to-air missiles, and perceived the woman's hips either as an oasis of peace or as a battlefield. Her skin shone thanks to a smoothness reached at the point of her maximum splendor, tinged with that color made by a few drops of coffee in milk. Angelina Jolie? Conde's male chauvinism—which could not be helped—forced him to consider that sexy woman who loved other women as a painful waste of evolution.

Ever since Frederic had given them the information, Conde had thought that that conversation should occur with a certain semblance of intimacy. Fortunately for him, it wasn't hard to get rid of Manolo. The policeman, also alarmed by the proximity of dates between Judy's disappearance and the departure of Marco Camilleri, aka "Bocelli," had decided that the investigators should follow that lead, looking around in the records and simultaneously pulling the strings of the networks of informants capable of knowing something about the hot points that beat most insistently in that drama: Italians, drugs, and young girls. And he had gone to put that machinery in motion, with the promise of getting in touch with his former colleague if some revealing detail appeared.

When he returned to the school and found the teacher Ana María, Conde felt his pulse racing before the show of high aesthetic value offered by that beauty, capable of destroying all of his imaginings and prejudices that he was searching for a butch (for God's sake, she was hotter than Angelina Jolie!). To his surprise, Conde barely mentioned the motive for his visit, and the woman agreed to leave with him to talk privately.

Thanks to the *pesos convertibles* remaining in his pockets, Conde was able to invite her to have a soda at a newly opened café, generally deserted and luckily air-conditioned. As they walked the streets of La Víbora in search of the proposed site, the man chose to keep their talk in the neutral and pleasant territory of his memories of the days in which he had studied at the institute where Ana María now taught, evocations that went back to a time before the teacher was even born.

In reality, Conde's body craved a beer. But his professional sense made him settle for a soda, like the woman, after asking that the sticky table be cleaned for them. Knowing that it was an attack against his health and his principles, he took a drink of the dark, sugary liquid that tasted like syrup as he explained to Ana María the details of his interest in Judy and, without beating around the bush too much, the motive for which he had requested they speak: he had been told that she and the young emo had a close relationship—although he didn't qualify it, neither the quality nor the closeness. (What a waste, dear God!) Ana María listened to him speak, taking sips from the plastic glass in which she had poured her soda, and Conde paused silently when he saw a pair of huge tears spring up from the green fountain of her eyes and run down the teacher's smooth face. Like a good gentleman, he waited for the woman to recover, after drying her tears with a feminine gesture that allowed him to see, on the inside of her forearm, a very small tattoo of a salamander with its tail gathered up in the shape of a hook.

"I'm going to assume that you're really not a policeman and that you wouldn't be enough of a bastard to record this conversation," the teacher began with authority and a regained control of self. "I'm going to believe you that, in reality, you're interested in finding Judy for the good of Judy herself and for her grandmother's peace of mind. And I'm going to ask you, of course, that if you get anything from this conversation that you only use it to recover Judy but without revealing where you learned it. This last thing is for three reasons that you will understand: because I am a lesbian and I like being so, but we live in a country where my sexual preference is still considered a disgrace; because I'm a teacher and I like being so; and, above all, because a teacher should not have an intimate relationship with a student and I was having one—or, more precisely, I had one—with Judy. If you reveal the existence of this relationship, I'm going to deny it. But although I could continue working as a teacher, it would do me irreparable harm. Do you understand what I'm saying?"

"Of course. You have my word that if something you tell me helps me find out where Judy could be, I am only going to use it to find her and tell her family. Although I should also warn you that I can forget about pedagogical or romantic indiscretions, but I wouldn't be able to hide a crime should I find out that you are in any way implicated in this, and if the story of Judy's disappearance becomes complicated."

"What do you mean by this last part?"

Conde weighed his words, but decided on the most direct and re-sounding.

"If she has been kidnapped or if something worse has happened to her and you have any link to it."

"Then we can talk," she concluded authoritatively, and added, "But don't have any false expectations: no matter how much I think about it, I don't have the slightest idea of where Judy could be and less still of whether something happened to her. A few days before"—she hesitated, looking for the most appropriate word—"she left, she and I had broken up and the only place we talked was in the classroom, as teacher and student.

"Judy made her way into my life through a crack in my defenses: the one that goes straight to the heart. It sounds horrible, cheesy, but that's how it is . . . It's been six years since I've been teaching with my degree, nine that I've been at the front of a classroom, and never, not even when I was still a student teacher, had I even had the temptation to start an affair with a student, much less a sustained relationship. Perhaps because until just under a year ago, I had a steady partner, a deeply satisfying relationship that lasted twelve years . . . Perhaps because I am a teacher by vocation—not out of obligation or compulsion, like many others—and respect, or respected, to speak formally, the academic and ethical codes of the profession, which seem sacred to me, do you understand?

"When Judy became part of my classroom, recently arrived from Venezuela, I noticed that she was a very special young person, in her virtues and in her problems. She had an intelligence that was above average, she had read things the rest of the students would never read, in quantity and depth, and she could simultaneously be so mature and so childish that she seemed to be two people in one. Except that the mature Judy and the childish Judy wanted the same thing, although of course from different perspectives: not to act like a regular person, to be as free as someone her age could be, especially in this country where you can't do what is forbidden . . . and to be willing to fight for that freedom. Her way. The mature one battled with her mind, and had her reasons; the childish one was on a stage wearing a costume, I'd say, playing a role. But both of them were searching for the same thing: for authenticity, a way of freely practicing what she wanted to practice.

"You already know that Judy is emo. She is so by choice, I would say also by conviction, not as a passing fad or in imitation, like the majority

of kids involved in these things, do you understand me? Being emo allowed her to think like an emo and also act like an emo, with all of those
accessories on display . . . According to what I know, since before leaving Venezuela, Judy was carrying within her the seeds of her rebellion,
or of her nonconformity. She had seen too much fakeness, heard too
many lies, learned of her father's maneuverings and those of other characters like him. But she was still too young to understand the proportions
of those opportunistic schemes. It's obvious that she matured over there
very quickly and discovered two things: that her father and other men
like her father did not in reality practice what they stood for in their
speeches. In short, they were a group of scoundrels of the worst kind,
socialist solidarity scoundrels, to call them something, or the worst thing.
And that caused a great feeling of rejection in her, of disgust, of hate . . .
Then she discovered the other thing that changed her: the virtual world
in which emos moved, in which some young people spoke with a lot of
freedom about their cultural, mystical, and even physiological experiences, insistent on the search for their individuality. And she was able to
see how beneath it all there was a philosophy, more complicated than
appears at first glance, since it's related to the freedom of the individual,
which begins with the social and goes on to the desire to free oneself
from the ultimate bind, that of the body. But, careful, don't be confused.
That freedom does not have a direct connection with any suicidal attitude,
but rather with physical and spiritual will. Do you understand me? Judy
isn't lost because she committed suicide, I am more than certain of that.
Or rather certain. Because, besides, she had decided to stop being emo . . .

"In any event, as soon as she came to my class, she turned into my
star pupil, academically speaking. But in a strange way: she was as likely
to read a work on the lesson plan in depth as she was to decide not to finish reading another one and expounded on the reasons for her attitude
right in the middle of class, and they were never the banal reasons of the
book being boring or her not liking it. That would put me in a real bind,
a good bind, I think. As you can imagine, in reality Judy turned into a
challenge. Yes, a challenge more than a star student. On all levels, understand me? And as a challenge, she dared me one day. It was about six
months ago, we had stayed alone in the classroom, talking about Calderón's *Life Is a Dream*. She was interested in the relationship between real
life and dream life, the role of fate or the predestination of the individual,
all of that about every human being marked by karma, and at one point

she told me she dreamed about having sex with me and . . . other things that I'm not going to repeat to you now, of course. How had she discovered that I'm a lesbian and, further still, that I was so attracted to her? I found that disconcerting, since I have never taken my sexuality or my attractions to the classroom. Then I asked her how she dared to say that to me, to her teacher . . . And she said that I was so transparent, that she could see me inside and out, and that she liked everything about me and . . . She spoke like a fifty-year-old woman.

"We began seeing each other, although before that, I demanded the most absolute discretion from her. Something that, I see now, she didn't fulfill, since you have come to see me because someone told you, and the original source can only have been Judy herself. Perhaps her childish side . . . Despite that, we had a mature relationship. Until she suddenly decided to end it . . .

"Judy needed to free herself or she was going to explode. She had freed herself of God, she wanted to free herself of her family. She freed herself of me, she was going to leave the emos. She was trying to cut off all commitments . . . She dragged her dissatisfaction with everything surrounding her everywhere, with the lies amid which she'd grown up. Everything she read, listened to, saw, deepened that feeling of having to rid herself of any burden in her search for total freedom, although she didn't know too well how to carry it out . . . Look I have an example here. She wrote this in a reading exercise . . ."

The teacher took an envelope from her folder and removed several handwritten sheets. She went through them and, when she found the one she was looking for, read: "'Literature serves to show us ideas and characters like this one:

"'. . . he remained imprisoned with an entire city, with an entire country, as his jail . . . The only door was the sea, and that door was closed with huge paper keys, which were the worst ones. He was watching, at this time, a multiplication, a universal proliferation of papers, covered in stamps, seals, signatures and counter-signatures, whose names exhausted the synonyms for "permit," "safe conduct," "passport," and however many terms could signify an authorization to move from one country to another, from one region to another, at times, from one city to another. The tax gatherers, collectors of the tithe, toll-collectors, revenue officers and customs officers of other times remained only as a picturesque warning of the police-like and political armed retinue that now applied itself, in all parts (some out of*

*fear of the Revolution, others out of fear of the counterrevolution), to re-
strict man's freedom, as pertains to his primordial, fecund, creative possibility of moving across the surface of the planet they had been blessed with
the fate of inhabiting . . . He felt exasperated, kicked in rage, when he
thought that the human being, denied an ancestral nomadism, had to submit his sovereign will of moving to a piece of paper . . .'*

"What do you think?"

"Amazing," Conde admitted. "It sounds familiar . . . Who wrote it?"

"Guess . . ."

"Right now . . . I recognize it, but no, I don't know." Conde felt out-
classed.

"Carpentier. *Explosion in a Cathedral.* Published in 1962 . . ."

"It feels as if it were written for right now."

"It's written for always. Also for right now. Judy knew what literature
is for . . . Because she added this," she said, and again started to read. *"If
a country or system doesn't allow you to choose where you want to be and
live, it is because it has failed. Faithfulness by force is a failure.'"*

"More amazing still," Conde admitted. "At that age, I was a moron . . .
Well, more than now . . ."

"I didn't discuss that with anyone, either." The teacher moved the
paper, then placed it back in the folder, and smiled lightly. "Imagine the
commotion that would have happened . . . Well, the fact is that things
started to get more serious ever since she met Paolo Ricotti, a dirty old
man who tried to court her with stories of his trips to Venice, Rome,
Florence, the museums, the Roman ruins, the Renaissance. Above all,
they talked about Ricotti's specialty, Baroque painting . . . She loved
talking to him and dreaming about what he promised . . . But without
going any further, very aware of what he was up to. And then a friend of
Paolo's showed up, Marco Camilleri, the guy who, according to her, looked
like Andrea Bocelli, and things became even more complicated, since
this guy took I don't know what drugs and she, who was desperate to try
them, well . . . It's hard for me to talk about this, I lose all perspective, I get
jealous, these things make me angry. Although I know that that whole
relationship with the two Italians didn't involve sex, they were friendships
too dangerous for a girl who in reality is only eighteen years old, no matter
how liberal she is or how mature she seems.

"I don't know if it was because of my jealousy or because of something happening inside of Judy—the fact is that she decided to end the

relationship. I don't know if it was out of spite or rationality, but without thinking twice about it I said yes, that was best. Although I knew well how much it would hurt, I preferred to end something as soon as possible that was going to end anyway, and better still to do so without any complications. That was why it was only at the school that I found out no one knew where Judy was and, the truth is, at the beginning, it didn't seem too strange to me, because I thought, and I still think, that she must be primarily responsible for her own disappearance. Surely she was all caught up in something; that was the real reason she wanted to end things with me and even with the emos, and, in four or five days, she would be running around here again, without any explanation and pleased with herself, as always when she did something capable of breaking with the norm . . . From the beginning I rejected the police's idea that her grandmother told me about when I went to see her, since I know that Judy wasn't going to get on a balsa raft with some group of kids. That didn't interest her, nor had it gone through her head, nor is she one of those young people who do things out of peer pressure or enthusiasm . . . Well, you've seen how she thinks." She took a breath and touched the folder. "So if she hadn't tried to leave, and she wasn't with the Italians, and she didn't commit suicide and hadn't been kidnapped . . . Then, she was hiding. I only thought it was strange that she wouldn't have said anything to her grandmother or to me if she was thinking about hiding. Although that would imply that her childish side had too much influence, something utterly irresponsible. But with Judy, anything is possible. As you can imagine, with the days going by without any word from her, I started to think of other things, bad things, I don't know . . . Do you understand me? No, surely you don't understand me."

Conde stood up and asked for some napkins from the café's server, who gave him two, counted out grudgingly. The napkins made up part of the server's implicit perks. Conde placed them in the teacher's hands and saw how, even crying, that woman was alarmingly beautiful. Perhaps more so. *Do you understand me?* Conde understood, and very well. He even felt it: like agony in his genitals, unbecoming of his age. And he also understood that for the second time someone very close to Judy was telling him about a double personality or capability of splitting in two, of a capacity for alternating masks that made that irreverent and daring young girl more unfathomable.

When Ana María calmed down, Conde thanked her for her honesty and told her that her words were helping him very much to understand (the damned word so repeated by the teacher had rubbed off on him) Judy and, perhaps, to find the path by which she'd gone off.

"I only want to ask you two or three more things . . . I just don't understand very well," he added, to satisfy the teacher's pet phrase, and he succeeded.

"Go ahead . . ."

"What's this story about Judy wanting to stop being emo? You can join and leave like that: to be or not to be?"

"That's the good thing about voluntary militancy. When you don't want to do it anymore, you give it up and that's it . . . As far as I know, because with Judy nothing is simple, she became emo searching for her own free space. And she found it, but she exhausted its possibilities. Freedom turned into rhetoric for her, and she needed something much more real."

"But what about all of that talk about God being dead, that she was going to be reincarnated, that the body is a prison?"

"She kept thinking it, of course she kept thinking it. But she needed more. I don't know what, but she needed more."

"And what you read me by Carpentier, doesn't that have to do with leaving? She wasn't interested in that text because of that?"

"No, you're mistaken . . . Leaving or staying is not what's decisive. What matters is the freedom of people to leave or stay. Or the lack of that freedom . . . And others. Do you understand me?"

Conde nodded as if he understood, although he was back to square one. Or not; in truth, he knew more and, despite her contradictions, Judy was becoming more and more attractive to him. It was worth finding her, he told himself, and launched the next question.

"Did Judy tell you anything about what happened in Venezuela that affected her so much?"

The teacher took a sip of her soda, perhaps to give herself time to think about a response.

"I already told you: she got to know emo philosophy better, and also her father . . ." Ana María hesitated for a moment and continued. "Judy knew that her father was getting ready to do something that would make him lots of money . . ."

"The things that he and his subordinates were bringing to Cuba?"

"No, those were trifles and he had almost nothing to do with that business. It was something else, something he took out of Cuba."

Conde felt a shiver of alarm.

"Something he took out of Cuba that would make him lots of money? Did Judy tell you what it could be?"

"No . . . But she talked about a lot of dollars."

Conde closed his eyes and pressed his index finger and thumb on his lids. He wanted to look inside himself: How much was a lot of dollars?

"Judy didn't give you any indication of what—?"

"No, nor did I ask her. I didn't and don't want to know about those things. They make me nervous . . ."

"Yes, of course," Conde said, and decided to postpone reflecting on that alarming detail that altered some of his perceptions. So he preferred to move in another direction. "What about Yadine, Judy's friend, is she a student of yours?"

"No, she is a year below Judy."

"What do you know about her?"

Ana María tried to smile.

"That she was in love with Judy . . . She was falling all over herself for Judy," she capped it, almost with satisfaction, perhaps because she felt victorious over that rival. But the more than trustworthy confirmation of the real nature of Yadine's feelings for Judy and the unveiling of the deep causes of the sadness that dragged the girl along could indicate something revealing, perhaps unseemly, that Conde still couldn't specify. Although this time, he didn't veer off the path.

"The salamander tattooed on your arm . . . ?"

"Something silly. Let's say proof of love. Judy had it on her left shoulder, on the part below her shoulder blade . . ."

"Of course," the man said, and took a few seconds for himself. He wasn't sure how to approach that other subject, and again chose to be direct. "How do you know that Judy wasn't sleeping with either of those Italians she talked to and, seemingly, even did drugs with?"

For the first time, Ana María smiled strikingly, before giving in to another wave of tears. Despite the crying, the teacher was able to say, "Because she doesn't like men and because I know that Judy is a virgin. Do you understand me?"

Conde, who had elegantly handled the other blows of information, felt surprised by that direct blow to the chin. Spread out on the floor, he heard the referee count to one hundred, or more. Now he didn't understand a damned thing.

———

"Tell me something, so I have it all clear . . . God forgives everyone?"

"All who repent and approach Him with humility."

"Does He even forgive the most son-of-a-bitch sons of bitches?"

"He doesn't make those distinctions."

"Distinctions . . . ? Now, you always have to talk like that, with words like that?"

"Bite me, Conde."

Conde smiled. He had taken his friend Candito the Red as far as he wanted to: more or less where he was when he had met him and Candito was a budding criminal. Although, Conde knew well, the journey achieved had ended up being only transitory, since the group's mystic had years ago found in religious faith a permanent relief to the torments and doubts of a life that had seemed to fully satisfy him. And Conde was happy for him, keeping in mind something that was quite clear: better a Christian Candito than an imprisoned Red.

In the last two years, increasingly more caught up in matters of faith, Candito had turned into something like a "pinch-hitting" preacher, the kind that go to bat when the game is really heated. The growth of the flock (that word also belonged to the white-haired *mulato*, who had once had bushy and saffron-colored wiry hair) had forced the official pastors to train various enthusiasts so they could work in some of the so-called houses of worship, where many, increasingly more, went for help, desperate and desperately in search of solutions, tangible or intangible, to an existence that had turned to shit in their hands. Perhaps for that reason, not only were the Protestant houses of worship and temples full, but also the Catholic churches, the waiting rooms of *santeros*, spiritists, *babalaos*, and *paleros*, even the mosques and synagogues in an inhospitable desert without Arabs or Jews. All of them full in the country in which atheism was imposed, and in the end, what was harvested was a mistrust and anxiety about comforts that reality did not provide.

One of those emergency almost-pastors was Candito, who, while he didn't possess a gift for oratory, had fireproof faith. For those willing to believe, the *mulato* could prove to be a convincing voice and even an example. His capacity to believe was so visceral and sincere that Conde had come to say that if Candito could guarantee for him the existence of a miracle, he would accept it. But, to admit that any son of a bitch (such as, for example, that Alcides Torres), also deserved divine forgiveness? No, Conde couldn't believe that coming from the Red or even from God himself should He come down to confirm it.

"Red, how much is *a lot* of dollars?"

"What are you talking about, Conde?"

"Let's see, if I tell you that I'm going to earn *a lot* of dollars, how much would you guess?"

"A hundred," Candito said, convinced.

Conde smiled.

"And if I tell you that a guy who runs businesses is going to earn a lot of dollars?"

The other man reflected for a moment.

"I would think of millions, right? It's all relative. Except for God."

The men had settled into the chairs that took up almost all of the space in the small cubicle turned living room. Behind a partition were the kitchen and the bathroom, while the opening made through the wall led to the bedroom that, in reality, had been another of the rooms of the cramped tenement until Candito's father had managed to appropriate the neighboring living space. The two friends kept each other in balance, talking about *a lot* of dollars and even drinking the cold guava juice the host's wife had served them. Conde had told him he would be visiting much earlier than he did, but, despite his tardiness, Candito had waited for him, with that capacity for patience that, thank God (Candito would say), he had developed.

Perhaps due to the unbearable heat, the mixed-company tenement where Red had been born and still lived was displaying at that moment its calmest face: the inhabitants of several of the dwellings distributed along the hallway of what had once been the interior courtyard of a bourgeois house remained immobile, like desert lizards awaiting the setting of the sun to start moving. Nevertheless, radios and CD players, like inventions with minds of their own, competed in an eternal musical battle with which those piled-up beings with troubled pasts, facing a difficult present and an unclear future, knocked themselves out to spend their lives without recognizing pain. The volume of noise they consumed made conversation so difficult that Candito had to close the door and set a fan on high.

"This flock is really something. How can you stand it?"

"With many years of training and with God's help."

"At least He throws you some rope . . ."

After bringing him up to speed on the details of his solo investigation (due to his unforgivable curiosity), Conde explained to his friend what he needed from him. Things had changed so much in Candito's life that, instead of information about criminals, Conde now was asking for opinions about the missing girl's strange relationship with God, a mystical sphere outside of his dominion.

"That girl seems too smart. But she has a lot of confusion in her mind," Candito said at last, and Conde lifted his hand, asking him to contain himself.

"Red, you're not leading a church service."

Candito looked at him intently. Some flickering remains of the indomitable and aggressive man he had been could still shine in his also-red eyes, generally veiled by an expression of spiritual peace.

"Are you going to let me talk or—?"

"Okay, okay, talk . . ."

"Does the girl have a few screws loose or not?"

"Yes," Conde admitted. He didn't dare say it, but he preferred that his old friend talk about screws being loose than about mental confusion.

"Your guava juice is going to get warm," the *mulato* warned him, pointing at the half-empty glass.

"It's okay. I just had half a soda. I don't want to risk an overdose . . ."

"True," Candito conceded. "Well, getting back to the subject at hand . . . I'm not gonna tell you that the loose screws in her head are the work of the devil, although it could be . . . Instead I'll tell you it's the result of how we've been living, of what we've been living, Conde. That girl is desperate to believe, but she doesn't want to believe like everyone else, because she rejects the establishment, and she has been inventing her own faith: she likes the idea that God is dead but believes in reincarnation, she disdains the body but tries to save the soul, she attacks herself in any way she can, and is a lesbian although she maintains her virginity, she can't stand her father's falseness and, simultaneously, is the friend of some Italians whose sliminess can be sensed from afar . . . And all of this so she wouldn't be like anyone else, or, better still, to be different from everyone else, because she got tired of the story that we're all alike, when she sees that we're nothing alike."

"So you don't think her problem is with God?"

"No. She uses God to seem more different . . . Don't go down that path. Her problem has to do with things down here, I'm sure of it. Note that it's not that she doesn't believe in God: it's that it seems more startling to say that He is dead. It's not the same thing to be an atheist as to believe that God is already dead and is powerless . . . Or having lost the capacity to believe in something, as has happened to so many people we know. That's very fucked-up, Conde, but it's what we're living now. I'm telling you . . . A girl like this one doesn't just come up through spontaneous generation, she needs some fertilizer to grow, and that fertilizer is in her environment. If not, look around: How many kids her age are leaving and going anywhere they can? How many are near criminals or complete criminals, how many have become whores and how many are their pimps? How many spend their days looking up at the clouds without caring about anything? How many are more interested in having a cell phone or an MP-I-don't-know-what-number than in working, because they know that by working, you don't get to have an MP whatever or a cell phone . . . ? Something very fucked-up is happening in Denmark. And, according to you, Shakespeare said that."

Conde agreed. The panorama could be even more dismal than it appeared. Calle G with its urban tribes was, in reality, just the tip of the iceberg . . . But was the inability to believe directed at him? Fuck it, he told himself. He wasn't what was important here. Because, at that pivotal moment in the conversation, he could obtain what Candito was truly capable of offering him: a confirmation to a question he'd been stuck on since visiting Judy's room and that had driven the recently maintained conversation plagued by the teacher's disquieting revelations.

"Red, you talk to a lot of people in crisis who are looking for a way out, do you think that somebody like Judy could end up committing suicide? That's what most worries me now . . . The teacher thinks no . . ."

Candito left the glass from which he was drinking on the small wooden table.

"I can't tell you one way or another, absolutely, because each person is a world unto herself . . . But I wouldn't find it strange if she is not showing up because she committed suicide or that, if she is alive, she would try to do so. So, if she still hasn't done it, the best thing would be to find her, because she is capable . . ."

"And if she shows up, do we perform an exorcism?" Conde couldn't let the chance to ask go by.

"For this girl in particular, it would be better to send her straight to a psychiatrist," Candito said, and the other man felt how his friend exceeded him with elegance. "I already told you that her problem is not with God, or even with the devil . . . She's fighting everything."

Conde agreed, disheartened.

"And where does that 'a lot of dollars' fit into all of this?" his host asked him.

The other man scratched his head.

"Well, I don't know . . . But it's better if I don't even think about that because then *I'm* going to suffer from loose screws in the head . . . Let's see, tell me, Why do I have to find myself these messes, huh, Red?"

Candito smiled with the most beatific and pastor-like of his expressions.

"Because although you say and are even convinced that you don't believe in God, at the end of the day, you are a believer. And, above all, you are a good man."

"I'm a good man?" Conde tried to lace the question with sarcasm.

"Yes. And because of that, despite everything, I am still your friend . . ."

"But although I'm good and a friend of yours, I'm not going to be saved, because I haven't humbly approached God. And if another bastard humbly approaches Him, he is going to receive redemption. Do you think that makes sense?"

"It's divine justice."

"Then, with your pardon, I have to say: what shitty justice . . ."

Candito smiled without any beatific expression: he truly smiled.

"There's nothing to be done for you, my friend . . . You're going straight to hell . . ."

Conde looked at Red. Ever since he had married for the second time and stopped smoking and drinking alcohol, Candito had gained about twenty pounds. Despite the gray hairs that had substituted his red corkscrew curls, in reality he seemed healthier and even fresher compared to the Candito of the past, a sinner and businessman, a troublemaker and violent man.

"And if I married Tamara, do I have more chances for salvation?"

The question hit a nerve of surprise in Candito. Through Skinny

Carlos, he knew about the birthday party being planned and had confirmed his non-alcoholic presence. But, there was a wedding and everything . . . ?

"Are you serious or fucking around?"

"I think I'm serious." Conde regretted having to admit it, although he clarified: "But it's only an idea . . ."

Candito leaned back in the chair and, with his hand, wiped the sweat that, despite the fan, was starting to run down his face.

"Conde, my brother, you do whatever you want. But think of just one thing: it's better to let sleeping dogs lie, to leave well enough alone . . ."

"With an exception, right?"

Candito, at the end of the day, was still Candito.

"Well, if you wake the right dog . . . But then it has to come to an end, right?"

———

From the only surviving bench (although it was already missing a board) in the Parque de Reyes, as he was hit by blasts of the foul smell coming from a pipe expelling refuse onto the street, Conde saw Yadine's figure get larger, halfway dressed as emo, with her hair falling over her face.

To avoid the family hearing his adult and masculine voice, half an hour before, Conde had asked Candito's wife to telephone the girl's house and make an appointment that, for the former policeman, had become urgent.

"You hadn't called me . . . Yesterday I went to your house and you weren't there . . . Tell me, what do you know about Judy?" the girl reproached him when she was a few feet away from the presumed detective, her face without the black makeup was equally sad and anxious.

"Come, sit down." Conde tried to calm her down as he patted the seat that held up his own ass poorly.

"So, what do you know?" Yadine's anxiety was definitely greater.

"Nothing and a lot . . . I don't know where she is or what could've happened to her, but I know other things," he said, and got straight to the matter. "Why didn't you tell me what your real interest was in my looking for Judy? Don't make things up, I already know the truth about that subject . . ."

Yadine had beautiful, deep eyes. All of the intensity of her gaze was better revealed that way, without the black circles with which she made herself up.

"The truth is terribly simple . . . People *don't* like us lesbians. But what matters is finding out about Judy, not what I feel for her . . ."

Conde had several responses to the statements, but he decided that he shouldn't attack the young girl with his irony.

"Did she break off her previous relationship to be with you?"

Yadine lost her anxiety and only a sign of sadness remained on her face.

"No . . . I was the one who took advantage of that and worked so hard so I could finally be with her. The thing is, Judy drives me *craaazy* . . ." she emphasized, and drew out the loss of sanity.

Those revelations always alarmed Conde, a heterosexual Cuban *machista* from a militant, although tolerant, line. But hearing two lesbian confessions on the same day, made by two young, beautiful women, exceeded his capacity for understanding. Nevertheless he had to contain himself, he thought.

"How long had you had that more intimate relationship?"

"Only once. The day before Judy got lost . . . But it was the best thing that has ever happened in my life."

Conde thought about asking for details, but understood that it wasn't the most appropriate.

"But you had been in love with her for a long time, right? Did you become emo because of her?"

"Yes, I was kind of emo, but I became emo-emo because of Judy. And I've liked her ever since I met her. No, not like her, she drives me *crazy, crazy* . . ."

Conde would have liked to know the difference between being emo and being emo-emo, but he didn't get off track.

"And you really don't have any idea where she could be, or why she's lost?"

"Of course not . . . Why do you think I came looking for you? It's not easy to go around out there telling people what you are and what you like. But I was desperate . . . That Monday, Judy said she would call me so we could see each other. Around seven, I was the one who called her house and Alma told me she'd gone out a while before. She thought she went to Calle G, but, on Mondays, almost no one goes there. All the same,

I went to look for her, but there were few people, no emos, and she wasn't there, either. Then I called some people . . ."

"Who?"

"First Frederic, who was at his house with another chick from school. Then Yovany, but he didn't pick up his cell . . . Then . . . Then her old girlfriend . . ."

"The teacher."

Yadine lifted an eyebrow, then nodded.

"She hadn't seen her, according to what she told me."

"And what do you know about the Italians? About Bocelli, for example?"

"That's one of Judy's crazy things. She knew what those old guys wanted, but she played with them. I warned her that that could be *verrry dangerous.*"

"Because of the drugs?"

"Because of everything. Bocelli is a son-of-a-bitch drug addict who's pretty *craaazy.*"

Conde thought about it for moment.

"Judy must have found something different in that man, don't you think? Or are you jealous of him?"

Yadine took a deep breath, again very sad.

"Yes, I am *very* jealous . . . She liked to talk to Bocelli and said that one day she would go visit him in Italy. Judy was a *real* dreamer . . ."

"Let's see, Yadine . . . And tell me the truth, was Judy in love with you or did she have sex with you just because?"

The girl smiled at last.

"Judy didn't do anything just because . . . But no, she wasn't in love with me, at least not how I was with her. She had sex with me because she was more depressed than usual and needed someone to listen to her, and I was *dying* to listen to her. Judy wanted to stop being emo, she started to tell me that someday she was going to Italy with Bocelli, that her life was a disgusting mess and she had to do something to change it."

"Why was her life a disgusting mess?"

"Thousands of reasons . . . Because of the world, because of her father . . ."

"Did she tell you anything about her father in Venezuela? About a really big deal?"

"She told me he did things . . . Many things. But I don't know what *things*."

Conde thought the time had come and he let out the question: "Did she talk about suicide as a way out?"

Yadine reacted immediately.

"No, Judy could *not* have committed suicide."

"Why are you so sure?"

The girl smiled, this time more widely. And with conviction.

"Because Judy wanted to change her life, but not lose it. I already told you that Judy didn't do anything just because . . . She had a reason for everything. And she had more than enough reasons to keep living. She had a ton . . ."

Conde nodded, satisfied. Why did the people who had talked to him about Yadine consider her a little stupid? Or was it that Yadine, besides the emo mask, also knew how to use other faces?

"One more thing," Conde said, lifting his ass from the torture of an incomplete bench. "How many books by Salinger have you read?"

Yadine seemed pleasantly surprised. She smiled. Without a doubt she was *very* beautiful.

"All of them, *alllll*."

"I was starting to imagine why you talk like that. It's extremely easy to know . . . I've also devoured *alllll* of them. A *bunch* of times. With love and squalor . . ."

6

When he was under the hot tin roof of the Bar of the Hopeless, Conde, awash in juices, sodas, birthday plans, and complicated revelations (including two lesbian confessions, which he battled against heroically to not allow his imagination color in), looked with the affection of the prodigal son at the modest simplicity of the cheap bottles of rum and the packs of infamous cigarettes placed on the table. He finally felt closer to territory that was more undemanding and comprehensible, where things were what they were, even what they seemed to be, without any further complication. But that afternoon, the spell of Conde's stable sense of self was nearly broken by a sign displayed on the table where Gandinga—the black server known as Gandi by certain customers—rested one of his flabby ass cheeks: "Esteemed customer: Pay BEFORE being served! THE ADMIN."

"What's that about, Gandi?" Conde asked him, pointing at the strict administrative guidelines. "Isn't there any trust anymore in the esteemed customers?"

"Tell me about it, Conde . . . Yesterday, I gave two bottles to a guy and the real son of a bitch ran away. He really fucking fucked me up."

"Dammmmmn! The hopeless break out of their chains" was the first thing to come out of his mouth. "Well, give me a double and a pack of cigarettes," Conde requested.

"Do you know how to read or not . . . ? Come on, fifteen big ones, pay first," the barkeeper said, and without moving his heavy ass cheek, he waited for his esteemed customer to put his money on the counter. Only after taking it, counting it, and distributing the bills in the old cash register did he throw him a pack of cigarettes and start to serve the drink in a glass whose cleanliness Conde doubted more than a committed Marxist, who theoretically doubted everything, or rather, everyone.

When he was ready to taste the rum that his soul asked for so vehemently, he felt a foul-smelling presence to his right. He turned his head and found one eye watching him and, very close to the alert eye, a fallen lid, defeated beyond any help. The man hadn't shaved for several days and, incidentally, seemed to be on bad terms with the shower. His sleepless eye, reddened, was studying Conde, until he seemed to find what he was looking for.

"Did you see this, Gandi?" the man said to the barkeep. "A clean guy . . . That deserves a drink. I mean, two." And he raised his voice toward the barkeep: "Gandinga, one for the clean guy and another for me."

Conde thought that, even though he showered every day, he would never have classified himself as an especially clean guy. And less still after having spent the whole day on the streets, suffering the sweltering June heat.

"And who's paying?" Gandinga asked, per his trade.

"The clean guy, of course . . ."

"No, my friend, thank you," Conde said. He didn't want to talk, only to drink. And not to drink to think, but rather, to forget.

"Don't fuck around. You're not gonna buy me a shot?" And he not only looked at him with his good eye, but his fallen lid also shook, as if carrying out a major effort to revive itself. The Cyclops had the breath of a vulture.

"Okay, okay, but on one, no two conditions . . ."

"Come on, shoot, here I am."

"If I pay for your drink, will you then leave me alone?"

"Done. Go on . . ."

"Right, the second one: just one drink . . ."

"Done, done . . . Come on, Gandi, pour one out generously," One Eye ordered.

Conde placed the money on the bar and Gandinga, after taking it, served the man a drink. One Eye took it right away and had a small sip, with a heightened sense of economy, and only then did he turn toward Conde. Where had that scarecrow come from?

"Meh, I don't want to talk to you, either . . . You look like you're a real asshole . . . Because you are a policeman."

When he heard One Eye's first reason, Conde felt the desire to kick his ass, but he received his final conclusion like an electric shock. Once on alert, he again looked at the man and tried to place what could be left of that semblance in the archive of faces he had met over the course of the now-distant ten years in which he had worked as a policeman and rolled around in shit. With difficulty—not only due to his memory—he discovered that those human remains were none other than Lieutenant Fabricio, dismissed for corruption, and with whom he had had all possible differences, including a fistfight right in the middle of the street.

Regretting his fate, Conde threw the portion of his rum still in the glass on the street, intent on leaving the place. Fabricio, or what survived of him, was still repellent. "Listen, Gandi," Conde said as he gave the glass back to the barkeeper. "Don't have mercy on this guy. He was, is, and will be a real son of a bitch. And there's no salvation for this one, no matter what he does." And he went out into what was, for him, a benevolent and same old dog day of June.

———

The meeting with Fabricio did not end up being a favorable prologue to the scene that Conde needed to prepare for at that moment: a conversation with Alcides Torres, Judy's father. Speaking with two sons of bitches of that caliber in the same day—worse still, on the same afternoon—seemed like an abuse of his stomach's fortitude. And, more so since Ana María the teacher had mentioned a certain business involving millions and, to top it off, Candito informing him about the potential for redemption of that type of character. But the urgency enveloping him to find some clue capable of leading him to Judy and, in passing, to be able to distance himself as soon as possible from any connection with that overly murky and simultaneously intriguing episode, was stronger and he decided to face the risk of an overdose of dialogues with certified sons of bitches.

They had agreed to meet at seven, in Alcides's palazzo, but when Conde arrived, the man had not shown up yet. Alma Turró was the one who greeted him, offered him a seat, good ventilation, coffee, and conversation.

"Please, tell me something about my granddaughter," the woman asked after placing the tray with coffee within reach of the recently arrived man.

As he drank the beverage, Conde thought about his response, since there wasn't much he could say to the woman. Even in what he could reveal, there existed a part that was too alarming, and he preferred not to touch upon that with her.

"Alma . . . I still don't have the faintest idea of where she could be or what could have happened to her. The police feel the same. They don't even have a clue, a suspicion, nothing. Neither they nor I know what to do . . . When someone gets lost like this, there are generally two possibilities: either something very serious has happened or she herself has done everything possible to disappear without a trace . . ."

Alma listened to him silently. She had her hands on her lap and was rubbing them as if they burned.

"Are you going to stop looking for her?"

"No . . . Now I'm going to talk to your son-in-law, because, to keep going, I need to know certain things . . . And tomorrow I have an appointment with a person who has spent a lot of time studying young people like Judy—emos, freaks. Especially people who tattoo themselves, get piercings or hurt themselves . . . And after that, I don't know, truly, I don't know. Judy appears to be a labyrinth, and the worst is that I don't have any idea of how or where I'm going to find a way out because I haven't even been able to enter it."

The woman rested her chin on her open hand and her elbow on the arm of the chair. She was looking out to the garden, barely visible in the light coming from the porch.

"Did you already talk to her literature teacher?"

"Yes," Conde said, and remained expectant.

"The two of them had . . . something more."

"I don't know."

"I'm telling you. They were . . . girlfriends. Or once had been . . ."

Conde remained silent. Until he surrendered.

"She doesn't have any idea, either, of what could've happened to her."

The woman looked at Conde.

"What did she say to you?"

Conde thought about what would be appropriate to reveal to the grandmother.

"Something that surprised me," he said, taking advantage of the most tempting path. "Judy wanted to stop being emo. Did you know?"

Alma nodded, but said: "No, I didn't know. Although it's to be expected. Judy is too smart . . ."

"But all of her emo fundamentalism . . . By the way, there's a kid from Judy's group called Yovany. Do you know how I can get in touch with him?"

"She had a little book with telephone numbers and addresses. Let me see . . . The police were going through Judy's things and, incidentally, they haven't returned her computer to us."

Alma stood up and went up toward the second-floor rooms, and Conde at last could light the cigarette demanded by the taste of coffee. Since talking to Yadine, meeting the albino emo again seemed interesting to him. His gaze, nonetheless, concentrated on the magnificent reproductions of Dutch paintings hanging in the living room. Vermeer of Delft, De Witte, and getting closer to the landscape, he read the copied signature: Jacob van Ruysdael. The fact that a few months before, a Rembrandt had come into his life and that he now had allowed a girl to enter his life in whose house existed a marked interest in Dutch painting seemed to him a circumstance that must respond to one of those works of a cosmic nature that the Pole Daniel Kaminsky had spoken of to his son Elias so many times. So, did those things happen just because, or due to some inscrutable will?

A few minutes later, the woman returned with a piece of paper in her hand.

"Alma," Conde asked her, still standing before Ruysdael's winter landscape, "why do you have these reproductions of Dutch paintings?"

The woman also looked at the landscape for a response.

"They're first-class reproductions, made in Holland by painting students as academic exercises. Coralia, Alcides's mother, bought them in Amsterdam for almost nothing, back around 1950. That was before she had the accident that left her an invalid. And he inherited them when she died, about four years ago. Coralia lived in her wheelchair until the age of ninety-six, and never wanted to get rid of her fake paintings. But they're pretty, right? Especially this landscape . . . I would say that today, these reproductions would be worth quite a few dollars . . ."

Conde looked at the copies a little bit more, and couldn't help his mind returning to the story of the fake Matisse that seemed authentic and that had stoked the ambitions of various people. And to the Cuban fate, still unknown, of the portrait of the young Jew executed by Rembrandt whose ownership was being challenged by Elias Kaminsky. Could one of those reproductions be worth *a lot* of dollars? No, at the levels at which Alcides Torres moved, it couldn't be *a lot* of dollars.

Alma Turró finally handed the piece of paper to Conde.

"Look, this must be Yovany . . . Here you have the address and telephone number."

When he went to put the paper in his pocket, Conde understood that something wasn't quite right.

"Was the address book in Judy's room?"

"No, I have it in my room . . . The thing is, I called everyone she wrote down there. To see if anyone knew anything about her."

"And what did you find out?"

"Nothing that would help me to find her." The woman took a deep breath as she sat down again and focused on Conde. "Look, if you stop looking for her, it's going to be as if she were lost forever. Don't you understand that? You give me hope that—"

"The police will keep going. It's an open case."

"Don't try to fool me . . ."

"I'm going to continue . . . But, I'm telling you, I've run out of leads. Or, someone is blocking me. Maybe even Judy herself," said Conde, who, upon seeing himself on a road that had reached its end, had the sudden premonition that in reality someone was cutting him off. At that moment, Alma raised her chin and made a canine gesture, with results capable of surprising Conde.

"There are Karla and Alcides," she announced, stood up and picked up the tray to enter the kitchen. Before leaving, she added: "I'm going to give you Judy's address book. Maybe it will help you somehow."

"Of course. Thank you . . ."

Alcides Torres came in, falling over himself with excuses, a last-minute phone call, traffic. Karla, his wife, held out her hand and sat down in the chair her mother had been sitting in previously. Karla was forty-some years old, which looked good on her from the nose down and from the forehead up. Her eyes were a well of pain, sadness, and insomnia. Alcides, who was perhaps a few years older than Conde, at last settled into a rigid armchair and let out a sigh of exhaustion. Just behind him was the sign in which the Maximum Leader was asked to command however and for whatever purpose.

"Conde, right? Alma told us about you, and I appreciate, we appreciate, your interest . . ."

"There's not a lot I can do . . ."

"So you don't know anything?" Alcides asked him.

"I know many things, but not what happened to Judy."

"So what do you need to know to continue?" Karla interrupted, anxious.

Conde thought for a few moments and finally spoke.

"May I speak to Alcides alone?"

The woman's response was an arrow that went straight through him and nailed him against the chair.

"No. Speak to both of us." And she maintained her gaze fixed on the former policeman, without looking at her husband. "About anything. It's my daughter . . ."

Conde wasn't expecting that precise circumstance to tell and ask Alcides Torres what he needed to, but if they gave him no other choice . . . He dove in.

"Well . . . I don't have any proof to support it, but it seems that right now there are only three possibilities: the best is that Judy left because she wanted to leave, and she's somewhere where she does not want anyone to find her, especially you; the other, that something very serious happened to her . . . But it would be really strange for there not to be any trace whatsoever. The worst is that she may have done something to harm herself."

"No, my daughter is not suicidal. She may be as strange as she is, but she is not suicidal. Let's think of the best," Karla proposed as she swallowed what Conde deemed to be a bitter pill. "What can be done?"

"Wait. Keep looking for her . . ." Conde enumerated, and decided to continue on the path they had opened for him. "Or, if you're so sure that she wouldn't harm herself, leave her alone. Because whatever may have happened, something is sure: Judy didn't want to live with you, with your rules. That's why she created her own world and threw herself into it headfirst. A world of emos, German philosophers, Buddhas, of anything that could be very far from you, of what you defend or aim to defend. She wanted to feel free of that burden and, at the same time, more at ease with herself . . ." he said, and looked straight at Alcides Torres. Conde felt the push of his conscience and Judy's ideas, and he couldn't contain himself anymore. "Because what you were doing, Alcides, was disgusting to her. What Judy saw in Venezuela and what cost you your position blew the lid off of things . . . Your daughter discovered your worst side and couldn't and didn't want to be near you."

Alcides Torres was looking at and listening to Conde with submissive attention, as if he didn't understand or as if the discussion was about someone foreign to him. That unforeseen torrent of Judy's disapproval, which emerged like vomit from the former policeman's soul, seemed to have surprised him to the point of freezing him. His wife, from her spot, had lowered her gaze and was moving the tip of her right foot, tracing small circles, without daring to speak, perhaps wounded by her own feelings of guilt or some trace of shame. Was she part of her husband's corruption schemes? Conde, already immersed in the depths of his unveiled hostility, continued firing.

"The worst part is that, in order to *not* reach that conclusion, Judy went through her own hell. But when you went to Venezuela and she saw what she saw, she couldn't take it anymore. And you know what? I don't doubt that she herself may have denounced you . . ." The blood that had been rising to Alcides Torres's face seemed to disappear, leaving a sickly lightness in his skin, and Conde went for the kill. "Later, Judy mistreated her body and her mind, she got involved with emos, she did drugs, she became friends with some sinister people who helped her escape herself, she began an intimate relationship that distanced her from you and all of the shit that you did to steal whatever came your way and to get involved in a deal that could yield you lots and lots of dollars . . ."

Alcides Torres stood up, propelled by the last springs of a battered dignity or by the mainspring of his surprise, and lifted his right arm, ready to strike. Conde, prepared for a reaction like that, pushed the chair back and dodged the reach of his fist, which Alcides left suspended in the air, perhaps due to Alma Turró's shrieking, "Alcides! What in the hell is wrong with you . . . ! Can't handle the truth?"

With his arm still up in the air, Alcides Torres was looking at Conde, who pronounced a phrase that hadn't passed his lips for many years but that, at the critical moment, Conde enjoyed letting loose.

"If you touch me, I'll rip your arm off . . ."

Conde, who had never ripped a leg off of a cockroach, took another step backward, free already of the burden of rancor and frustration, more willing to avoid than to provoke: after all, he had said what, for many, many years, he had wanted to say to guys like Alcides Torres. Just when he was going to continue his retreat, Alcides's voice stopped him.

"Forgive me," he said as he lowered his arm and turned toward his mother-in-law. "Alma, I love my daughter, I want her to return, I want to ask her forgiveness . . . Everything I have done—"

Alcides cut short his apology and left the living room to go upstairs to the second-floor rooms.

Karla, still sitting in her chair, had not stopped looking at Mario Conde, and he discovered that her gaze had recovered part of its lost vitality.

"At some point, somebody else had to say it to him," she spoke at last. "Judy was the first, about three or four months ago . . . Alcides came to tell her that the way in which she was living and acting was harmful to him, that he wasn't going to allow her exhibitionism or her speeches about freedom, that having a daughter who lived in Miami was already problem enough . . . And Judy exploded. She let out everything she thought about him, even worse than what you have said, especially because his daughter was saying them to him . . . Ever since then, she stopped talking to him."

Conde felt his heart rate normalizing.

"What she saw in Venezuela affected Judy very much," Conde said, and put a cigarette to his lips, although he did not light it. "This is important, Karla. How much money could Judy have left with?"

It was obvious that the woman was not expecting that question.

"I don't know." She tried to be evasive.

"The thing is, having or not having money can be the difference between having disappeared or being hidden . . ."

Karla took a deep breath and looked at her mother before turning her attention back to the former policeman.

"She stole five hundred dollars from her grandmother that my daughter Marijó—María José—sent her from Miami . . ."

Conde thought: Five hundred dollars was not much to buy a seat on a launch leaving Cuba, although it was *a lot* for someone who needs to buy very little to get by. But, at the same time, for five hundred dollars in Cuba, there could be people willing to do *a lot* of things, bad things. In that story in which he only heard half-truths, all of this new information, more than certainty, brought other questions. And brought with it that fucked-up notion of what constituted *a lot* . . .

Karla again moved her foot, when she demanded Conde's attention.

"I'm going to ask you something, a favor: if you can find Judy, or if you have any idea of who could know where she is, I want her to know that her grandmother and I love her very much, that despite everything, her father also loves her, and we can't forgive ourselves for what we have done to her. We already have a daughter who decided to go live far away from us, so we can understand if Judy prefers to do the same. But she should know that whatever she does and wherever she is, we're going to keep loving her."

———

Conde walked along the battered sidewalk of Calle Mayía Rodríguez and smelled in the air a stench of scrap metal, burnt gas, and dog shit. The shit was sticking to the soles of his shoes, the stink of scrap metal and gas came from a 1952 Chrysler that two black men, their color deepened by the grease and soot covering them, were trying to revive. They were the real smells, of everyday life, to which he so desired to return.

Karla's request, made with Alma Turró's visual consent, was again pushing him toward the path that he would have preferred to abandon. But the feeling of freedom brought by his conversation with Alcides Torres still surprised him. He had, looking for information, ended up exorcising old rancors, frustrations, and deep hatreds for characters like that Alcides Torres who so reminded him of Rafael Morín, Tamara's deceased husband. In reality, had he said to Alcides what he would have wanted to yell at Rafael? He would have to ask when he saw some psychologist friends.

That afternoon, before leaving his house, the former policeman had dared to reread the prologue to *Thus Spake Zarathustra*, trying to reflect the mirror of Judy against that transcendental and mystifying spiel of Nietzsche—an author who, on the same lamentable level as Harold Bloom, Noam Chomsky, and André Breton, among others, channeled an illuminated prophet who hit him with a one-two punch and kicked him in the most vulnerable parts of his anatomy. As he was reading, he tried making the effort, just the effort, to understand the sympathetic relationship that, across a hundred years, an eighteen-year-old Cuban emo could establish with the German who had clamored for a New Man divested of the burden of God and all of the submissions demanded by Him. And that was when he started to focus more on the emo-fundamentalist expressions of Yovany, the boy who was so capable of disturbing Yoyi. As he digested Nietzsche with difficulty, he convinced himself that perhaps the young man was the person most suited to explain Judy's mental confusion, as Candito had classified them with such benevolence. When he had nearly finished reading the prologue, he received a call from Yoyi, who was always able to bring him back to the reality of his own life: the next day, the Pigeon explained, the Diplomat would settle his debt with them, and afterward they had to visit the former political leader to pay him his part and, of course, distribute the earnings.

"And do you still have the ring?" he had asked him, trying to sound casual.

Yoyi laughed heartily.

"So you finally want it?"

"I was thinking . . . I don't know what in the hell I was thinking," he said, since it was the truth.

"Look, if I were you, I would think it's a good birthday present and—"

"I already thought that, my friend," Conde interrupted him.

"Then it's yours, man . . . I'll give you a very special price. But on one condition."

"Don't start fucking around, Yoyi. This is already complicated enough without you making conditions and—"

"Look, man, the discount comes with this condition, or there's no discount," the other man continued. "It's easy: I want you to let me hand it over to Tamara, of course, on your behalf . . . And if you get married, that you let me be the godfather of the wedding."

"Hey, you, no one's going to get married."

"I said *if* . . ."

"If it's *if*, Skinny isn't going to forgive me if I take away the pleasure of him fucking me over again. He's the godfather of my weddings and divorces *ad vitam*."

"No one says there can't be two, three godfathers for a wedding, or as many as you feel like."

"*If* . . . Tomorrow I have something at eleven."

"I'll pick you up at nine, and in an hour we close the deal. I'll see you, godson."

"Stop screwing around, Yoyi . . ." Conde had said before hanging up the device.

Now, in front of Tamara's house, looking at the concrete sculptures inspired by Picasso's and Lam's figures that covered the front of the building and made it stand out, Conde concluded that his grace period had ended and he should fulfill the promise in the note he left for Tamara that morning. Before entering, he made sure his shoes were clean. He couldn't talk about those matters while stinking of shit. Or was it better to let sleeping dogs lie?

Since she was expecting him, Tamara, who was not terribly fond of cooking, was making the effort to prepare something edible: rice, onion omelettes, and a tomato salad. A shameful menu. If old Josefina saw that, she would have a stroke. *So this is the woman you're thinking about marrying, just like that, just because you like her, and now you decided that maybe you want to get married?* Conde toasted some bread crusts, improved them with the olive oil brought by Aymara from Italy, and turned them into a delicacy with some leaves of Italian basil planted in the garden and a sprinkling of grated Parmesan that he tossed on top.

Half an hour later, when they had already exhausted the subject of preparations for the following day's party and were drinking the coffee Conde had brewed, the man told himself that he couldn't keep dragging this out.

"Tamara, for days I . . ."

She looked at him and smiled.

"Go on, I'm listening. Give me a little drag," she asked, after drinking just a few drops of coffee, to get the flavor. She smoked from Conde's cigarette twice and returned it to him, then immediately pressed him: "So for days, what . . . ?"

Conde sensed the trap: his dusted-off policeman's instinct was warning him of danger.

"Do you know about this thing?"

"Me?! This thing? What thing?"

The exaggerated surprise gave her away.

"Skinny, Dulcita, Yoyi . . . Who has loose lips?"

Tamara let out a hearty laugh. When she laughed, she was more beautiful.

"Since it's your birthday and all of those sons of bitches are going to be here, well, I thought . . ."

The woman couldn't keep it going. She was too soft with Conde and making him suffer that way, although amusing, seemed cruel to her.

"Last night, when you talked to me about 'the thing,' I wasn't sleeping. I pretended I was, then I heard you . . . I even snored a little."

"So . . ."

"And today, Yoyi came by the clinic with the ring to see if he had to make any adjustment for my finger. It fit me perfectly. And it's beautiful."

"But, how could he dare . . . ? So . . . ?"

"Well, if you ask me, I will officially become your girlfriend. And if you ask me later, I will think about whether it's worth it to get married or not. But first, boyfriend and girlfriend, as it should be. I have to think about the rest . . . A lot. It's not just any 'thing'."

Conde smiled, stood up, and placed himself behind Tamara, who was still seated. Delicately, he lifted her chin and kissed her: her saliva tasted like olive oil, Parmesan, and basil, with a hint of coffee and to-bacco. Tamara tasted like real things and the best in life. The man felt another "thing" stretching out, despite the exhaustion and the mental confusion accumulated in a day that had been too long and hot.

From the table they went straight to the bedroom, where the future boyfriend and girlfriend handed themselves over to their respective knowledge of each other's needs in order to enjoy a calm and deep round of mature sex, which was, as such, sweeter and juicier. Conde, through whose perverse mind at some points had passed the created images of Ana María, Yadine, and Judy, rebellious, fresh, handed over to their feminine games, thought at the end of the process that this was the last time he would make love with a Tamara who was fifty-one years old, single, and free of commitments. The next time, it would be with a very similar woman, but at the same time different.

7

Conde was imagining Garbage II running around the grassy yard that could be seen through the window of Tamara's kitchen. In his dream, he was horrified (in reality, it was the kind of thing that made him laugh) to see the dog digging in the earth, tearing apart the grass, ripping apart shrubs and flowers with his teeth, shitting on the plastic chairs placed below the trellis. That would be his way of expressing that living confined, even in a golden cage, was not his definition of the good life. Freedom, for him, was freedom, without much philosophical thought—and as the dog's owner, Conde had always accepted it—and Garbage II enjoyed wandering the streets of his neighborhood, following dogs in heat. That way of life, chosen of his own will, was, for the animal, more important than two meals a day and anti-tick baths.

The smell of the coffee that was starting to percolate took him out of his problematic zoological digression. He waited for it to rise, added sugar to the coffee, and, as he was about to drink his first sip, the phone rang. *Whoever it is can wait,* Conde thought, drinking the resuscitating infusion and, at last, around the tenth ring, lifted the receiver.

"Yes?"

"Conde?" the voice asked. It was familiar, but he didn't identify it right away.

"Yes . . ."

"Listen, it's me, Elias Kaminsky," said the far-off voice, and then he greeted him with true affection as he sat down in the living room's armchair. "I called your house before, but—"

"What happened? Is there news?"

"Yes, very good news . . . A legal case is going to be opened claiming the painting for the Kaminsky family. I managed to have it heard in New York's civil court and have already hired some lawyers who specialize in recovering works of art. These lawyers have even managed to return to Jewish families works that were seized by the Nazis. So I have a lot of hope."

"They must be expensive as hell," Conde commented, unable to imagine how that world of first-world lawyers and judges worked.

"That Rembrandt is worth it," Elias confirmed. "I called you because I want you to do me the favor of talking to Ricardito . . ."

"Why don't you talk to him yourself?"

"The thing is, I'm embarrassed to tell him that if I recover the painting, I'm going to give him half of the money . . . I'm afraid that he won't want to accept it . . ."

"Well, you can give it to me and that solves everything . . . Let's see, let's see, what do you want me to tell your relatives?"

"The thing is that news of the trial could reach him and I don't want him to feel pushed aside, or to think that I'm doing things with the Rembrandt behind his back . . . Just tell him that this case is being opened, that it's sure to last years, and that there's no certainty that we will win, although I hope that, yes, we do win . . . And if we win—"

"When you say years . . . How many years do you think?"

"Nobody knows, everything is complicated and slow . . . Sometimes more than ten years. Tell Ricardito."

"Holy shit, ten years . . . ! Okay, I'll tell him . . ." Only at that moment did Conde recall his personal dealings with Yadine and look for a way out. "Elias, can I wait a few days to talk to Ricardo?"

"Yes," the other man said. "But why?"

"Nothing . . . Complications I have." Conde chose not to mix the stories together and looked for a way to distance himself from the required explanation. "So when are you thinking of coming to Cuba again?"

"Right now, I don't know, but soon. Remember that you owe me a meal at Josefina's house, with your friends . . . Oh, shit, so are you going to marry Tamara after all?"

The question surprised Conde, who took a few seconds to discover the origins of that rumor: Andrés, via Carlos.

"Well, I don't know. I'm not sure that she wants to marry me . . ."

"Congratulations, in any event."

"Congratulations to you about the trial . . . And don't worry, I'll see Ricardo."

"Thank you, Conde. I owe you a day's pay."

"Put it down as volunteer work so I can win the socialist medal . . ."

"Noted. Thank you, and I send you a hug. Well . . ."

"Hold on a moment," Conde stopped him, pushed by the force of an irrepressible doubt.

"Talk to me . . ."

"Your father, Daniel, he really never again believed in God?"

Elias Kaminsky took a few seconds to respond.

"I don't think so . . ."

"Okay . . . That's what I thought. Well, I'll take care of talking to Ricardito, don't worry."

"I hadn't told you that about my father? Why are you asking?"

This time, it was Conde who had to think about a response.

"I don't really know . . . Because in the past few days some things have happened that made me think it's easier to believe in God than to not believe . . . Look, if God doesn't exist, any god, and men have been hating each other and killing each other over their gods and for the promise of a better great beyond . . . But if in truth there is no God or a great beyond or anything . . . Forget it, Elias, I'm really fucked-up right now, and I start thinking about this shit . . ."

"It's not shit, but I just noticed that, yes, you are fucked-up . . ."

"Yes, but I'm not the only one . . ."

Elias Kaminsky was silent on the other end of the line, and Conde regretted having conveyed that feeling to him, so he decided to say goodbye.

"Well, don't worry, I'll talk to Ricardito . . . And when you find out anything new, call me . . . To let me know . . ."

"Of course I'll call you . . ." Elias began, and stopped. "Conde, I want to thank you again."

"Why? With what you paid me—"

"For what you made me think . . . Forget it. I'll call you any day now." He said goodbye and dropped the call.

Conde put the receiver in its place and realized that after the coffee he had not had a cigarette. He lit one and smoked it. He had the certainty that that conversation was altering something in his mind. Something indefinable, crouching in a dark corner, but there regardless.

"Fuck me," he protested as he crushed the butt. "As if I didn't have enough already . . ."

———

"Nietzsche, *Death Note*, Nirvana and Kurt Cobain, a little bit of Buddhism," the recounting began, and gained momentum for the ascent. "*Blade Runner* with its replicants, piercings, tattoos, cuts on arms and legs, a little bit or a lot of drugs, online chats with groups of fundamentalist emos, and she was leader of the tribe in Cuba, but she had decided to stop being emo and leader. A lesbian and virgin besides, disgusted by what her corrupt (and, according to you, typical, certified son-of-a-bitch) father was doing. A true believer that God is dead and that dying was the best thing He could do to free people from His dictatorship . . . That girl is just a ticking bomb!" Thus concluded Dr. Cañizares as she reviewed her notes after Conde gave her details about the young disappeared girl's personality and her vital and existential circumstances. Conde had tried to be as explicit as possible for the sake of clarity, and for that reason the only thing he had hidden was the fact that Judy's most sustained gay relationship had been carried out with a teacher from her high school, since it appeared episodic to him and dangerous to reveal.

Dr. Eugenia Cañizares was considered the foremost Cuban authority on the subject of the body issues of young people addicted to punk, emo, Rastafarian, and freak philosophies. She had devoted years to living with the anxieties and anguish of those kids and to exchanging notes with specialists like the Frenchman David Le Breton, who was, according to her, a charming guy and the most coherent of those who studied the subject. Cañizares's book about the history and the present practice of tattooing in Cuba was one of the results of that contact.

The woman, who was somewhere in her early sixties, bore the marks of the influence that her objects of study exercised over her. In each ear she wore four hoops, on her hand she had a small tattoo of a butterfly, and she wore a load of bracelets and necklaces in all colors and materials imaginable, more colors and materials than she could pull off without bordering on ridiculous at her age. In a way, with that load of cheap jewelry and her aggressively green eyes, she looked more like one of the witches from *Macbeth* than a sociologist, according to Conde's schematic criteria.

"In the background of this behavior there always exists great dissatisfaction, many times with the family. But that circle expands outward to include society—also oppressive—which they try to break with, or at least distance themselves from, to find other family and social alternatives: hence belonging to the tribe. The tribe is usually democratic, nobody forces you to belong or to stay, but as a whole, it fuels the feeling of voluntary choice, and with it, that of freedom, which is the ultimate aim of this searching. Freedom at any price and zero family or social or religious pressures. And forget about discussing politics . . . But it's not just the freedom of the mind with respect to the ideas imposed by a system of old-fashioned relationships, but also the freedom of the mind from the body it inhabits. As you can imagine, aiming for all of this in a socialist, planned, and vertical country . . . is playing with fire!

"Note that, from the times of the Gnostics—as Nietzsche would take up again, and now the post-evolutionists—the body is considered a poor container for the soul. Because of that, an important basis for the development of those philosophies, processed by those young people, is that man will not be completely free until any concern regarding the body has disappeared from him. And to begin to distance themselves from the body, they accentuate its ugliness, its darkness. They harm it, they mark it, dirty it, although many times they also drug it to get rid of it without getting rid of it."

As he listened, Conde tried to follow her along that flow of revelations that could bring him face-to-face with a concept of the search for freedom that, in the end, didn't do anything more than lead to its denial, since it opened the gates of other prisons, as far as he understood—he, the militant agnostic and, with all certainty, pre-evolutionist. The most corrosive thing was the fact that, for the past few years, he had lived in the same city with those young people but had barely stopped to look at them, since he considered them a class of postmodern clowns determined to set themselves apart from social codes by making themselves *notably* different. He had never granted them depth of thought and libertarian objectives (libertarian more than liberators, he stood by this idea, based on the anarchy of their searches) despite the shackles they placed on themselves. But they were their shackles, and that piece marked the difference. The difference that Candito would talk to him about. The difference that Judy seemed to be in search of. The difference in a country that pretended to have erased them all, and that in its everyday reality was

being filled up by strata, groups, plans, dynasties that destroyed the presumed homogeneity conceived of by political decree and by philosophical mandates.

"The Gnostics, who mixed Christianity and Judaism to aim to arrive
at knowledge of the intangible, are in the origins of all of these juvenile
philosophies, although its practitioners almost never have the slightest
idea of it . . . Those who think about it a bit consider that the soul is
captive in a body subject to a fixed duration, to death, to a material and,
as such, dark, universe. That is why they have taken hate for the body to
the extreme of considering it an indignity without remedy. That process
is called ensomatosis, because the soul has fallen into the unsatisfactory
and perishable body in which it is lost. Man's flesh constitutes the damned
part, condemned to death, aging, illness. To reach the intangible, it is
necessary to liberate the soul: always liberation, always freedom, as you
can see . . . But all of this thinking, poorly anchored and even more
poorly woven together, functions in very different ways in the minds
of these kids. Because, while they disdain the body, they also often fear
death. And they insist on correcting the body, in surpassing what Kundera (why do you think Judy reads him?) called the unbearable lightness
of being. Do you remember *Blade Runner* and its creatures who are
physically perfect but also condemned to death . . . ? These young people
congratulate themselves for living in what Marabe calls post-biological
time, and what Stelare refers to as post-evolutionist, although the truth
is that the majority of them don't have any idea of these syntheses, but
rather of their consequences, sometimes only of their fanfare . . . But,
whatever the case may be, they participate in the certainty of living in
the time of the end of the body, that regrettable artifact of human history
that now genetics, robotics, or computers can and should reform or
eliminate . . ."

"So are we going to end up having a big head and thin arms, or strong
arms and an empty head? Because the replicants in *Blade Runner* are big
and athletic . . ." And he stopped in his foolish diatribe when he was about
to give his male chauvinist evaluation of the female replicants, who, as
he recalled, were hot.

"What I want to tell you is that overdosing on all of those concepts
can have very bad results. The search for depression opens the doors to
real depression, anxiety for freedom can lead to freedom but also to licentiousness, which is a poor use of freedom, and the rejection of the body

often leads to more shadowy depths than some holes in the ears, clitoris, or penis, or some cuts on the arms. The nonexistence of God can lead to the loss of the fear of God . . . You have to find this girl, because someone like that is capable of doing anything. Even against herself."

Shit! Conde thought, already feeling fatigued by the new information.

"The worst thing," Cañizares continued ceaselessly down the hill of her theories and obsessions, "the terrible thing, is that although they seem to be a small group, those young people are expressing a feeling that is rather pervasive in their generation. They are the result of a loss of values and categories, of the exhaustion of believable paradigms and expectations of the future that run across all of society, or almost all of it . . . Or another part of it that says and does more or less what it really thinks. The margin between political discourse and reality has become too wide, each is going on its own way, without interfacing, although the discourse should be the one following reality and redefining itself . . ."

"Can you put that another way, Doctor?" Conde begged her. "The thing is, I'm getting old and stupid . . ."

The woman made her bracelets jingle and smiled.

"My friend, the thing is that those kids don't believe in anything because they're not finding anything to believe in. That whole story about working for a better future that has never arrived, they could care less either way, because for them, it's not even a story anymore . . . It's a lie. Here, the ones who don't work do a little better than the ones who do work and study; the ones who graduate from the university later find it damn hard to be allowed to leave the country if they wish to leave; the ones who sacrificed themselves for years are today barely scraping by with pensions that aren't enough to even buy avocados. So then they don't even try to make it work: some go wherever they can, others want to do so, others live however they can, others become anything that will make them money: whores, taxi drivers, pimps . . . And others still become freaks, rockers, and emos. If you add all of those others together, you'll see that it's a hell of a lot, there are so many of them. That's what there is. Don't think about it anymore. That's what we've come to after the same old song with the fraternal dispute to win the flag of the collective national vanguard in the socialists' emulation and the condition of the exemplary worker."

"Shit!" said Conde, now overwhelmed. Or, as he always preferred to say, *ano-nadado*: he was in it up to his ass.

———

"Are you post-biological or post-evolutionist?"

Yovany's epidermic pallor almost immediately took on a pink tone, as if the boy were coming back to life.

"You know about that?" he asked him by way of reply, incapable at that moment of conceiving of that insistent, prehistoric character and former policeman being up on his possible post-anything militancies . . . And then a light went off in Conde's head: Yes, shit, that nearly transparent boy reminded him of Abilio the Crow, his elementary school classmate! Abilio was so white, almost ghostly, that, for some reason forgotten by Conde, they had nicknamed him after that black bird that was also considered a bird of bad omens. What could have happened to that sullen and mysterious guy who raised his eyebrows just like Yovany, when asked about something he didn't believe? Years without seeing the Crow or even remembering him and suddenly . . .

After the mental blow delivered by Dr. Cañizares, capable of placing his presumptions on a scientific plane, Conde headed toward Yovany's house, without much hope of finding him. What had pushed him in that direction, in the El Vedado neighborhood, was the conviction of Judy's clear danger to herself and his desire to knock on the last possible door on his horizon, perhaps the very one that would lead him through the labyrinth of the missing emo. And if he didn't find anything beyond that threshold, then the best thing would be to tell it all to go to hell at last and continue on with his usual life, with more gusto now that he had a thousand dollars.

Once he was standing before the opulent mansion, with a fresher coat of paint and even better maintained than Alcides Torres's house, Conde started to make his conjectures about the origins and possibilities of young Pale Face, the bearer of Converse shoes, MP4 players, and a BlackBerry. Looking at the huge house with its very high mainstay, a garden looked after with Japanese care, its wide porches, delicate and artistic wrought-iron gates and wood shining from a recent varnishing, the man had had two certainties: that the original owners of this dwelling must have belonged to some bigwig in the pre-revolutionary Cuban bourgeoisie, and that the current inhabitants were certified members of that crop of post-revolutionary nouveau riche that had arisen in recent years like a re-emergent illness, considered eradicated for decades by egalitarian and poor socialist planning, but ready to flourish. Official discourse on one side and reality on the other?

After pressing the intercom embedded in the exterior wall and asking the electronic voice if Yovany was home, and even explaining that he was coming to see the boy since he was a friend of the father of one of Yovany's friends (he didn't hesitate to lie), the palace's gates opened for him with a dramatic screech and, immediately, he was met by the typical woman who "helps in cleaning the house," as socialist good taste had baptized the previously known maids or servants. The woman, white, robust, with an air of German governess about her (Federal or Democratic? Conde couldn't help asking himself, always so focused on history), took him to a receiving room as large as a tennis court and ordered him to take a seat in the exact same electronic voice that Conde had attributed to the intercom.

"Would the gentleman prefer coffee, Indian black tea, or Chinese green tea? Soda, juice, beer, or mineral water, sparkling or flat?"

"Bubbly water and coffee, thank you," Conde muttered, almost convinced that the woman was a new replicant model, purchased perhaps in the same store where Yovany's BlackBerry had come from.

Abandoned to the immensity of the living room with its spotless checkerboard marble-tiled floor and ceiling of plaster arabesques with a fleet of ceiling fans determined to keep the air cool, Conde felt the palpable evidence of his smallness and devoted himself to proving anew the existing distance between Judy's house with its hastily made wealth, reproductions, and political posters and this overwhelming, pretentious mansion: on the walls shone original paintings by the most coveted Cuban painters of the last fifty years. A nude and well-endowed ephebe by Servando Cabrera Moreno, a dark city by Milián, a woman with disproportionate eyes by Portocarrero, a reclining mermaid by Fabelo, a disjointed doll by Pedro Pablo Oliva, a perfect landscape by Tomás Sánchez, a mango by Montoto—he counted and stopped when Frau Bertha (that had to be her name) returned with the coffee tray set with porcelain cups, silver spoons, the options of white, brown, and artificial (Splenda) sugar, some little chocolates, a glass of bubbling water, and a cloth napkin. As he drank the strong coffee, made perhaps in an espresso machine with grounds purchased in Italy, he again looked at all the artwork and guessed at the dozens of thousands, hundreds of thousands, of dollars hanging there. So many dollars that they were capable of laughing in the face of that small fortune of a thousand dollars that had made Conde feel so power-ful. Those were really adding up to be *a lot* of dollars.

Amid that luxury of paintings, porcelain, wood carvings, Tiffany lamps, sculpted bronze, and fashionable furniture, the face of the recently ar-rived Yovany looked like that of a tick on a pedigree terrier. The boy, with his hair dripping down both sides of his colorless face, tattered pants and shirt with holes, sat down in front of Conde without greeting him, looking at him with a corrosive intensity that the former policeman, trained in those arts, disarmed with his question to the boy (who had at last reminded him of Abilio the Crow) about his "post-" affiliation.

"I know more than you imagine . . . I was once even postmodern, now I'm post-police . . . Nonetheless, I don't know who your parents are . . ." he said, and waved his hand around, as if caressing from afar the objects and paintings.

"*My father* took off when I was a kid. During a layover in Canada, he went running off his plane from Russia and didn't stop until he got to Chile . . . *My mother*, who is slightly smarter than a cockroach and harder to kill than Bruce Willis, then got together with a stupid old Spaniard who looks like he escaped from a nursing home, but has some crane businesses and shit like that here and is filthy rich . . . As you can see."

"And the Spaniard buys you those Converse?"

The boy smiled. He had recovered his vampire-like paleness.

"Why do you think the old man is rich? He's cheaper than his fuck-ing mother. The things I have, the other guy sends me from Chile. Just to fuck with *my mother* . . .

Conde also smiled, but not because he was getting to know the pal-ace dwellers, but because the words popped into his head from that ver-sion of "A Whiter Shade of Pale" by Procol Harum, sung in Spanish by Cristina y los Stop, about a loved one who, dead and buried, appears to the singer with a "white paleness" that to Conde had always seemed dis-gusting and necrophilic. A paleness like that of that boy whom Yoyi had called "bottle o' milk." A whiteness on which the reddish scar four inches long, which Conde had managed to see on the inside of Yovany's left fore-arm, stood out like a scream.

"Okay, okay," Conde said, trying to find a way to focus on what, at the end of the day, he was interested in. "That scar on your arm . . ."

Yovany's reaction was electric. He hid his arm behind his back, like a child surprised with forbidden candy.

"That's my problem . . . What do you want? I'm not up for speeches . . ."

Conde supposed he'd touched a nerve in the boy and decided to change the direction of his questions.

"You know that Judy still hasn't shown up. And I found out something that I'd like to confirm."

"What's that?" Yovany still had his arm protected by his body.

"I've been told that she wanted to stop being emo . . ."

"That's a lie! A lie!"

The reaction this time, more than electric, ended up being explosive, as if instead of touching a sore spot Conde had wounded him, plunging a scalpel into him.

"She was the most emo of all of us!" Yovany continued, still shaken up. "Who in the hell could say that? That black idiot Frederic?"

"No, it was Judy's grandmother."

"That old lady doesn't know nothin' . . . Judy wasn't going to leave us. Judy was a brain, the one who knew the most about emo things, the one who always talked about freedom and not letting us be lied to by anyone—by anyone."

"How long have you known her?"

"Since she showed up on Calle G. I was half emo, half Miki, half rocker, but one day I talked to her and, whoa . . . complete emo," he said, and, apparently unconsciously, he displayed his arms so that his emo-belonging could be better appreciated. And Conde again saw the scar, recent, vertical, typically suicidal. Except that real suicides slashed both forearms. And died, right?

"How did she convince you?"

"Talking about the heresy that exists in the practice of freedom."

"Is that how she said it?"

"Yes. And she lent me some books so that I could learn. Books that aren't published in Cuba, because here the thought police don't want us to know these things. Books where they explain that God is dead, but the dead god is not only the one in heaven: it's the god that wants to rule over us here. Books about the reincarnation that we are all going to go through. And she talked a lot about what you can do with the only thing that truly belongs to you, your mind. Because even the body, she would say, could belong to them: they could beat it, put it in jail. But they couldn't do that with your thoughts, if you were sure of what you wanted to think. That's why we had to be ourselves, be different, and not let ourselves be ruled by anyone, by no bastard, neither here"—he pointed at the floor—"nor there," he signaled the ceiling, where the fans were still turning. "And never, never listen to the sons of bitches who talk to you about freedom, because what they want is to keep it for themselves and fuck you over . . ."

Conde felt an increasingly unmistakable desire to speak with Judy. Her ideas about freedom and tribal belonging, even after crossing the steppe of the brain of that dysfunctional kid, seemed challenging, more intricate than the reactions of a postadolescent rebellion. The former policeman recalled the Pole Daniel Kaminsky and his search for spaces of freedom to redefine himself. Another strange convergence, he thought.

"When was the last time you saw her?"

"I don't know, about two weeks ago. She came to get me and we went over to the Malecón, before going to Calle G."

"What did you talk about?"

Yovany thought for a moment, perhaps too long, before responding.

"I'm not sure. About music, about manga . . . Oh, about *Blade Runner*. She was *crazy* about that movie and had seen it again."

"And did she or didn't she talk about leaving?"

"I don't think so. She talked about that every once in a while, about getting the hell away, on a balsa raft or however. But no, that day I don't think so. I don't remember . . ."

"The other night you told me that she had mentioned the subject recently."

"Oh, I don't know what I said the other day," he protested, and made a circular gesture with his finger by his right temple. He had been flying high. Perhaps to catch God in the act of hanging up His saber.

"Tell me something about the Italians . . . Was she very good friends with Bocelli?"

Yovany looked at Conde as if he were a smear on the slide of a microscope. For someone who was no longer a cop, he knew a lot and was a real pain in the ass, he tried to say with his scientific glare.

"I don't know anything about that Bocelli you mention, and I also don't know how a girl as cool as Judy could get together with those disgusting and shameless guys."

"Why disgusting and shameless? You didn't even know them . . ."

"But I know that the only thing they wanted was a piece of her ass.

What else could they want, huh? Listen, listen, look . . . Those guys, maybe they, I don't know, even raped and killed her . . ."

"Do you think they could have done that?"

"More than that, too."

Conde thought the same thing. He then hesitated about his next question, but dove in.

"Do you think that Judy isn't showing up because she committed suicide?"

The word "suicide" had the effect of another electric shock on the boy, who moved his left arm even farther back. If there was something he didn't doubt anymore, Conde thought, it was the origin of that wound: Yovany was not looking for emo suffering, but rather, he had tried to kill himself. But, had his wound been stitched? His doubts were piling up. It seemed to Conde that the scar did not have the typical marks of stitches. Then, it had been so superficial that he had been able to staunch the bleeding with a rag. What kind of suicide attempt had that been? A test run?

"Maybe . . ." Yovany at last whispered, paler than in his natural state. "She also talked a lot about that. She liked to cut herself, taste the pain, talk about suicide. How can you think someone like that is going to stop being emo from one day to the next because of some drooling old Italian or any old thing? No, Judy couldn't leave us," he insisted, with the vehemence capable of revealing to Conde the degree of Yovany's mental dependence on Judy's daring and dangerous philosophy.

"And did she ever talk to you about her father's business dealings?" Conde tried his luck with that dark point that had come up so often regarding the girl's social and family rebellion.

"She said something . . . But I can't really remember. Some deal with lots of money . . ."

"That's it, without specifics?"

"That's it, and nothin' else . . ."

Conde took a deep breath, frustrated.

"One last thing, Yovany, and I'm leaving . . . Where's your mother?"

"In Spain, and England, and France, around . . . Enjoying the ride and spending all this dumb-ass Spaniard's money. *My mother* is thirty-eight years old, and the old man is two thousand . . ."

Conde nodded and stood up. He didn't know if he should hold out his hand to Yovany to say goodbye with a certain formality. What he did know was that he should shoot him the next question point-blank.

"That wound you're hiding . . . Did you try to commit suicide?"

Yovany looked at him with hate. Pure, hard hate.

"Get the fuck out of here! You're making me sick!" he yelled, and left Conde in the empty living room, with his last question on the tip of his tongue: *By any chance, was your father named Abilio González and did they call him the Crow . . . ?* The abandonment only lasted a few seconds. Like an overweight ghost, there appeared the image of Frau Bertha, who moved toward the front door and opened it. All she needed was the flaming sword to point out the path by which those expelled from the earthly paradise should exit.

———

One of the walks that most pleased Conde was the one that allowed him to wander in and out of the tree-lined streets of what had been in earlier times the majestic neighborhood of El Vedado. Between the house where Yovany lived and the site where he could pick up a shared taxi headed toward his rough and dusty neighborhood was precisely that magnetic landscape where, a few years before, he had discovered the most fabulous of the private libraries that he could've imagined and, in it, the traces of the most melodramatic bolero that real lives could turn into.

Now he didn't have the eyes or the will to enjoy that decadent and pleasant panorama, or barely enough presence to feel the stifling heat of June, mitigated by the poplars, Mexican bay leaves, flamboyant flowering trees, and acacias flanking the street. In his brain, two unrelenting concerns alternated, battled each other neck and neck, capable of blinding him, and both carried the names of women: Judith and Tamara.

That morning, after speaking with Elias Kaminsky, he had escaped from the house of his nearly betrothed before she woke up. Tamara had made the necessary arrangements to take two days off, which, along with Sunday, made a long and relaxing weekend that her body, fifty-two years old already, was screaming for. The woman, as opposed to Conde, had the enviable capacity of being able to sleep all morning when nothing required her to rise early. Because of that, her body's sexual appetite satisfied and her soul's expectations met, she had ordered her mind to sleep as much as possible so that all of them, body, soul, and mind, would be in the best condition to face a day that would surely be emotionally charged.

Conde thought of what his life would be like from that specific day on. When that night, he and Tamara made public—to the only public who would be interested—their intention to begin to think about the possibility of getting married (that was more or less the plan), something would begin to be different. Or wouldn't it? At their respective ages and after so much time in the relationship and sharing their lives, nothing had to change: only settle. Because they were fine as they were and the best thing, of course, was to let sleeping dogs lie. But, Conde told himself, with a desire for adventure and a talent for self-deception capable of surprising even himself, at the end of the day it all came down to a formality, to the two of them, and to the years they had left to live. Tamara and Rafael's son was a distant presence, he was already twenty-six years old and, like so many young people in his generation, had decided to try his luck outside of the island. For years he had lived in Italy, first under the wing of his aunt Aymara and her Italian husband; now, independently, as a marketing specialist for Emporio Armani. He only materialized in the occasional telephone call, some photos sent by e-mail, and, very infrequently, the delivery of a suitcase full of clothing for his mother (but not even a single piece of Armani underwear for Conde) and two or three hundred euros. Mario Conde's remaining human interests were made up of the fate of Garbage II (golden cage or street sloth?) and the lives of his friends who would celebrate with them that night.

Of that tribe of the faithful, the most vulnerable member was Skinny Carlos, whose heart, liver, or stomach could (even all at once) burst at any moment, although, in recent times, their owner seemed to walk with a more measured and pleasant rhythm. He even smoked less and ate with a certain discretion. Because, following Dulcita's widowhood, what the woman and Carlos tried to maintain in secret, with adolescent strategies, was no mystery to any of their other friends. Despite Skinny's physical limitations, it was obvious that, however and whenever they could, they had to be desperately rolling around together again, following the habit they acquired when they were studying at the ever recurring high school of La Víbora.

So what was worrying him? That the country was falling apart in plain sight and accelerating its evolution into another country, more similar than ever to the cockfighting ring to which his grandfather Rufino tended to compare the world? Concerning that, there was nothing he could do; worse still, there was nothing he was allowed to do. Did it worry him that he and all his friends were getting old and continued with nothing in hand, same as ever, or with less than they had had since they had lost even their dreams, much of the hope promised for years, and, needless to say, their youth? In truth, they were already used to those circumstances, capable of branding them as a generation that was more hidden than lost, more silenced than mute. Was it that the book business was getting increasingly precarious every day? Well, it sometimes yielded unexpected and very advantageous dividends. Could it even be that the national baseball team never won international tournaments anymore? There was a lot that could be done in this realm: for starters, tell everyone who fucked up a national brand as sacred to the Cubans as baseball, which had always been more visceral than mere entertainment, to go to hell. So what if they decided to get married and the routine of married life revealed to him that, in the end, he had the right conditions to cease procrastinating with a thousand reasons and excuses, and compelled him to sit down at last and write that squalid and moving novel he had dreamed of for years and years? Well, maybe he should just write it and be done with it.

Without his wanting to, Judy's indomitable story pushed those digressions aside and came to the surface. In reality, each step Conde took toward the girl resulted in a newer and greater distance, as if veils were falling over her face, insistent on hiding and even blurring her. Candito's ideas and those of Dr. Cañizares, in addition to the elaboration of her thinking as relayed by Yovany, had reinforced a more urgent concern in Mario Conde's former policeman's spirit. If at the beginning he was convinced that Judy was hiding of her own free will, determined to live on a planet where she found the freedom she wanted so badly, that certainty had now been consciously removed. The complexity existing in the girl's mind could be, in fact was, charged with explosive components. Might she have truly committed suicide? Was the hate toward her father merely an ethical reaction? Had she willingly entered the jaws of an Italian wolf, as Yovany had suggested? He hoped he was wrong, but he had a bad feeling about each of his questions.

Now it seemed interesting to Conde that his association of Judy and Daniel Kaminsky's heresies, fueled by that insistent presence of some copies of great Dutch painters and encouraged by Elias's reappearance, would have reminded him that the Jewish Pole's sister had the same name as the missing young emo. The image that Elias Kaminsky had given him of the other Judith, a vision created by the grief-stricken mind of his father Daniel and simultaneously related in turn to the biblical Judith, had begun to move through Conde with a chiaroscuro and drama made tangible by Artemisia Gentileschi: Judith as Holofernes's executioner, at the precise moment in which she slashed the neck of the Babylonian general and preserved the freedom of the kingdom. Conde thought he liked the image, but the fusion of the biblical heroine with the Polish girl wiped out in the Holocaust seen through a famous seventeenth-century painting could help him very little in resolving the mystery of a Judith lost in the torrid, chaotic, and Cuban present, because he couldn't imagine the emo as anyone's executioner . . . Except her own. Or was there some other connection between the Polish girl and the young Cuban girl who shared a biblical name? Why did he think this? No, he didn't know . . . But he sensed that there was some reason for it.

The problem for the private detective and, he supposed, for the professional policeman who was increasingly and with greater intensity engaging in the hunt for the missing girl was the lack of the most minimal trace capable of guiding them. The path marked by the Italians seemed to be the most promising, although the absence of those characters had blocked him from exploring that possibility. Because of that, he was even more frustrated by the lack of evidence and by having to shed certain assumptions after the conversations with other emos and with Judy's teacher-lover.

What Mario Conde did know, something he sensed before and now had been able to reliably prove, was that Judy and her friends were the most visible and most remarkable tip of the iceberg of a generation of certified heretics. Those young people had been born just in the most arduous days of the Crisis, when there was more talk of Option Zero, which, at the height of the disaster, could have sent Cubans to live in the fields and mountains like indigenous hunter-gatherers of the Neolithic island in the digital and space age. Those kids had been born and raised without anything, in a country that was starting to distance itself from itself in order to turn into another place in which the old slogans sounded more and more empty and undone, while daily life was emptied of promises and filled with new demands: having dollars regardless of how they were obtained, making a living on your own, not aiming to participate in public life, looking at the world beyond the island's reach as if it were a piece of candy and aspiring to leap toward it. And they made that leap without any romanticism or fairy tales. As Dr. Cañizares told him in her way, for those young people the lack of faith and trust in collective projects had generated the need to create their own intentions and the only visible path for them to arrive at those intentions had been freedom from all burdens. Not believing in anything but themselves and in the demands of their own lives, personal, unique, and volatile: after all, God was dead—but not just the god in heaven—ideologies are not to be consumed, commitments tie you down. The depth and breadth of that philosophy had managed to show Conde the most painful framework of that world that, he intuited thus, his eyes had barely been able to examine. It was true that many times Yoyi the Pigeon had insisted on showing him that reality by way of a pragmatic cynicism and absence of faith. And that somebody like Yovany's mother, fighting aggressively to get ahead, had reached the heaven of the good life without feeling nauseated by the past-its-shelf-life mouthful she needed to swallow. But the few years separating Yoyi's generation and the mother of the pale emo from that of young people like Judy seemed to be centuries, one could almost say millennia. The disasters that these kids had witnessed and been victims of had generated individuals determined to distance themselves from any commitment and to create their own communities, reduced spaces in which they could find themselves far, very far, from the rhetoric of triumphs, sacrifices, and new planned beginnings (always directed at triumph, always demanding sacrifices), of course, without consulting them. The terrible thing was that those narrow paths appeared to be flanked by bottomless precipices, often fatal. An antinatural component even powered the searches of some of these young people: self-harm by way of drugs, marks on their bodies, pretensions of depression and rejection; a break with the traditional ethical limits concerning the practice of promiscuous, alternate, empty, and dangerous sex, often devoid of emotion and feeling—and even devoid of condoms, in times of unaffected depression.

If that was the path to freedom, without a doubt, it was a painful way, like many of the roads that have aimed to lead to redemption, either earthly or transcendental. But, despite his many prejudices and his pre-revolutionary morals, now that he knew more about that emancipating effort, Conde couldn't help but feel a warm admiration for some young people who, like Judy the philosopher and leader, felt capable of throwing it all to the flames—"It's better to burn out than to fade away," Cobain *dixit*—including their bodies. Because their souls were already incombustible, further still, unimprisonable. At least for now.

Bothered by everything because he'd had to acquire that knowledge that was so unpleasant, he placed the coin in the telephone and dialed the direct number to Manolo's office. He was going to tell him to tell the special—or were they spatial?—investigators the detail about the deal involving a lot of dollars in which Alcides Torres appeared to be involved, but, above all, to demand a new effort by the criminal investigators to find Judy, if she was still findable. Anything possible to find her quickly and alive. Because, based on the accumulated evidence and despite her dangerous friendships, Judy could be the greatest danger to Judy herself.

Instead of a secretary, like in old times, it was a machine that answered with its eternal "at your service!" Major Palacios was not available. If he pressed one, he could leave a message. Two, and he would be connected to an operator. Three, four . . . As he was about to hang up, he pressed one. "Leave your message," he was encouraged.

"Manolo, are you cross-eyed or what?" he said, hung up, and told it all to go to hell. Even Judy. He had enough with his own problems.

"What would you like to listen to?"

"The Beatles?"

"Chicago?"

"Fórmula V?"

"Los Pasos?"

"Creedence?"

"Yeah, Creedence" was the agreement again. For a thousand years now, he liked to listen to John Fogerty's compact voice and the primitive guitars of Creedence Clearwater Revival.

"This is still the best version of 'Proud Mary.'"

"That's not up for discussion."

"He sings as if he were black. No, he sings as if he were God. What the hell . . . That's why he never got married."

Conde looked at Carlos, but Skinny, as if he hadn't said anything, focused on the act of placing the compact disc in the exact slot, pressing the button that would swallow it, and later the one aimed at making the music play.

It had been Dulcita's idea: they would celebrate a classic birthday, in the best "chichi" style, very cultivated in Miami, according to her. With the exception of the guests of honor and Conde, the rest of them, including old Josefina, would all arrive together, some aboard a car she had rented, others in Yoyi's convertible Bel Air, beeping their horns. They would enter the house with balloons in their hands, birthday hats on their heads, a bouquet of flowers, and a cake crowned by fifty-two can-

dles, already lit. And they would do so singing "Happy Birthday to you."
The birthday cake had been designed in two halves: one covered with blue
meringue for Tamara and the other with violet-colored cream for Aymara. White letters spelled out the indispensable "Happy Birthday," but
this time with the two on the end, the number charged with squaring
the greeting.

Candito, Rabbit, and Yoyi, under the watchful eye of Josefina—also
sporting a birthday hat and a whistle hanging around her neck—had
been in charge of taking out the rest of the provisions prepared by the
old woman: a leg of roast pig, a pot of black beans and rice shining with
the perfumed oil of Tuscan olives, the perverse yuccas, split open like
desire, their insides moist with a dressing of sour orange, garlic, and onion, and the brightly colored blooming salad. They left for last the bottles
of red wine, the beer, the rum, and even a bottle of soda—just one,
lemon, the kind Josefina liked—since it wasn't the day for geriatric idio-
cies, as Skinny warned.

The table set, Dulcita gave Rabbit and Luisa the order to serve the
plates, without anyone tasting anything, since it was time to make a
toast. She then removed from her purse two incredible bottles of Dom
Pérignon and searched through Tamara's crystalware, a family heirloom,
for the Baccarat glasses most suitable for champagne. Even Candito, now
absolutely abstemious, accepted the glass brimming over with efferves-
cent liquid, since he knew that he would be the witness to a great event.
Almost a miracle.

When each person had a glass in hand, Carlos tapped on his with a
fork to demand silence, followed by all. Then he asked that another glass
be filled and placed it on the table. Only when he had the glass in front
of him, from the wheelchair that had made him misspend the last twenty
years of his life, did he begin his speech:

"In September of 1971, six of those present here, in addition to an
absent one whose glass is served"—and he pointed at the fine receptacle
placed on the table—"we began to walk down an unpredictable path, full
of potholes and even cliffs, the most beautiful one that can be traversed by
human beings: the path of friendship and love. Thirty-seven years later,
the physical remains but indestructible souls of those seven magnificent
beings gather here to celebrate the perseverance of love and friendship.
We have been through many things in these years. One of us is looking
at us and listening to us from a distance, but he does look at us and he

does listen to us, I know it. The other six, some more fucked-up than others, are here (although sometimes we wander over there). Some of us have become what we dreamed of being, others have become what life and time have forced us to be. Since we are sectarian, but with democratic tendencies, we have even grudgingly accepted, but accepted nonetheless, subsequent additions that enrich us. That is why, with us here today, sharing our story, our nostalgias, and our happiness, are friends like Luisa and Yoyi, already indispensable although condemned to the eternal rank of soldiers without any possibility for promotion . . . I'm sorry . . . And out of recognition for the amount of hunger she has satisfied in us and all that she has put up with, my mother is also here . . ."

Whistles, applause, and spontaneous cries of "*¡Viva!*" for Josefina. A renewed demand for attention by Carlos.

"As I was saying: we have the great fortune of being able to get together today to celebrate, eat, drink, and confirm that we were not mistaken when we chose each other, decided to love each other and submit ourselves to the tests of friendship. But today is a special day, and that is why this toast is also special, with some Dom Pérignon that even Candito is going to drink, that even the absent Andrés must drink . . . And will drink, with his soul. Because today, when we celebrate the twins' birthday, today my soul's brother, Mario Conde, is going to say the words that thirty-seven years ago he dreamt of saying and that, fortunately, all of us still on this side are going to hear . . ."

At that moment, the telephone rang and Carlos asked Rabbit to pick it up. Rabbit asked who it was and, smiling, put it on speaker.

"So what the hell is Conde going to say?" Andrés's voice over the telephone made Tamara cry. "He has to say it quickly, I still haven't wished the twins a happy birthday or said anything to Josefina about some medicines I'm sending her . . ."

"Conde," Carlos invited him.

Mario Conde looked at each one of the members there listening, even the telephone. He placed his glass on the table and got close to Tamara. With his two hands, he took one of the woman's hands and, in the least ridiculous way he could, pronounced the phrase:

"Tamara, would you dare marry me?"

Tamara looked at him and remained silent.

"*¡Ay, mi madre!*" Josefina, who was the most excited by the telenovela-esque scene, couldn't keep from exclaiming.

"What's going on, what's going on?" Andrés's voice demanded over the telephone.

"Tamara's thinking," Rabbit yelled. "Anyone would take their time to think about it."

The woman smiled and was finally ready to speak.

"Mario, the truth is that I don't want to marry anyone . . ." Tamara's words surprised the others, who remained tense, waiting for some explanation or for disaster. "But, since you bring it up, I think that if I ever got married again to anyone, it would be you."

A commotion of hoorays, bravos, yells of *Damn, Tamara is really brutal*. While the engaged couple kissed, relieved by the way they had come through that tight spot, others lifted their glasses and Carlos, anticipating what could or perhaps would never come to be, was throwing fistfuls of rice from his wheelchair.

"Happy birthday, Tamara. Happy birthday, Aymara," they managed to hear Andrés's voice over the telephone, who added: "Jose, I'm about to send you some new medicines for your circulation that are really good. I'll explain how to take them on a little piece of paper . . ."

"Thank you, *mi'jo*," Josefina yelled toward the phone.

"Conde," Andrés continued, "Elias Kaminsky says he'll call you soon."

"He already called me," Conde yelled. "And some gossip told him about what's happening here right now . . ."

"Really? You don't think that I . . . ?" Andrés laughed. "After all, Conde . . . Well, I'm going, big hugsssss." Their far-off friend said goodbye and a click could be heard that cut off the line and the flow of spent dollars with it.

Yoyi then approached Tamara.

"An engagement like that"—and he put his hand in his pocket, from which he withdrew a small box—"deserves a ring like this . . . This is my wedding present."

And he gave the stone-studded ring to the bride, who looked at him in confusion, as if she had never seen it before. Then she showed it to the other women, with the most feminine of pre-matrimonial pride. A typical scene of the very refined and classic chichi aesthetic.

"Is this really crazy, ridiculous shit truly happening to me?" Conde asked Candito, observing the scene of the women with the birthday hats, the glasses of champagne, the ring, the congratulations.

"Well, it seems like it to me . . . And you know what the worst part is?"

"There's something worse? Tamara didn't even say she was going to marry me . . ."

"She did say it . . . In her own way. The worst thing, Condemned, is that this has the looks of being irreversible. You didn't let sleeping dogs lie, and now, bro, there's no way to stop it . . ."

———

Waking up was just as terrible as Conde deserved: his temples throbbed, the back of his head was on fire, his skull treacherously pressed into his mushy brain. He didn't dare pat the area around his liver out of fear of discovering that the organ had escaped, fed up with the abuse. When he was able to open his eyes, challenging the anguish, he confirmed that he had gone to sleep with all of his clothes on, even one shoe. Tamara, on the other side of the bed, with the ring on her finger, looked dead. She wasn't even snoring. The explosive mix of champagne, wine, rum, and Irish cream had created an atomic reaction in their respective senses of ridiculousness and caused devastating internal combustion. Now, the newly engaged couple was paying the price of the excesses committed the night before.

Like someone out of a bad gangster movie wounded by bullets, Conde managed to reach the bathroom by leaning on the walls. He took the bottle of aspirin out of the medicine cabinet. He tossed two in his mouth, and drank water from the washbasin tap. He undressed however he could and got under the shower's cold jet of water, holding himself up on the built-in soap dish. For ten minutes, the water tried to clean his body and the washable parts of his spirit.

Carefully, he dried his head and then rummaged in the pocket of his discarded pants, from which he withdrew the small jar of Chinese ointment and slathered it on his temples, his forehead, the base of his skull. The balm's heat began to penetrate through him as, a towel on his shoulders and his nuts in the air, he went to the kitchen to make the coffee. He had to sit down to wait for the infusion to percolate, although he knew that the army called upon to relieve his cephalea was already en route. When he drank the coffee, the improvement became obvious, but the cigarette caused a hacking cough, and in order to avoid shaking his head, he chose to put it out. "I'm getting old," he regretted in a whisper, and to prove it, he had only to look at his hanging scrotum dotted with gray hairs.

Only then did he have a notion of the domestic disaster that had occurred the previous night. Putting that kitchen and dining room back together would be a mission for the Titans. Had nine or ninety people eaten and drunk there? His first and logical reaction was to go back to the bathroom, get dressed, and escape as soon as possible. But a strange and unprecedented feeling of responsibility prevented him from doing so. Despite the poor state of his brain, he managed to reach the understanding of that unforeseen attitude and was horrified. Could it be possible that he had turned into a different person from one day to the next? Or was he still experiencing the worst drunkenness of his life? Could these perhaps be the most alarming symptoms of entering his years as a senior citizen? Any response seemed worse. As always, Candito was right.

He peeked into the room and confirmed that Tamara was as still as the dead, although she was now snoring. With another cup of coffee in his hand, he tried again with the cigarette that his body demanded. This time, he managed to smoke without the cough bothering him and felt himself becoming a person again. In reality, another person. Because he put on Tamara's apron and, with his ass uncovered, began to wash the dishes with the same gusto that some believers practice their penitence: conscious that they do it to screw themselves, sully themselves, punish themselves. *Through my fault, through my fault, through my most grievous fault . . .* And he kept washing.

Two hours later, a resurrected Tamara marveled at her would-be husband's attitude, kissed him, and, after giving him chills when she caressed his uncovered ass cheeks, told him that she would take care of putting away the plates, the crystalware, and the newly shining silverware. Conde, shocked at himself, returned to the bathroom in search of his clothing, but first stopped before the mirror to look at himself with the apron on and his ass in the air. *Pathetic and irreversible* was his conclusion.

Whatever force was responsible for his patheticness now compelled him to go straight to the TV room and place in the DVD player the copy of *Blade Runner* taken from Judy's room a few days before. Amid his own tribulations, he had completely forgotten about the young disappeared emo and his intentions of calling Manolo, but the unexpected demand to take in that dark and rainy movie again had revealed to him that his concern was only submerged and a deep claim was bringing it back to the surface. The idea that he was out of ideas, the certainty of not knowing which door to knock on to get closer to the girl, jabbed at him with an unhealthy persistence as he watched the story of the hunt for some replicants (very well done, incidentally, he told himself, surprised by the beauty of Sean Young and Daryl Hannah) who become conscious of their condition as live beings and, along with it, the desire to keep that extraordinary quality that, nonetheless, their creator has denied them. Toward the end, when the last of the replicants pronounces his farewell to the world, Conde felt how that speech in the movie, which his memory had taken hold of, gave him at that moment a strange resonance, capable of stirring him like one of his painful premonitions: "I've seen things you people wouldn't believe. Attack ships on fire off the shoulder of Orion; I watched C-beams glitter in the dark near the Tannhauser Gate. All those moments will be lost in time, like tears in rain. Time to die."

With the uncomfortable feeling that that lament was the bearer of a dismal resonance capable of reaching all the way to him, Mario Conde went out to the yard of the house that would probably soon be his house as well and, below the avocado tree weighed down by green fruit with its shining skin, promising the basic delicacy of its matter, he sat down to smoke and to wait. This time, he didn't think about Garbage II destroying the surroundings . . . Because his premonitions never failed him, he was sure that that was going to happen. That was why, when Tamara leaned out and yelled that Manolo was calling him, the former policeman knew the time had come. *It's time to die.*

9

Leaning out the window, Conde lit his cigarette and concentrated on observing the panorama that seemed sterile from the perspective of distance and height. He saw the green blanket made by the foliage of the Mexican bay leaf and the sparrows that, in groups or alone, came and went between the leaves. He looked in the distance, beyond the houses and buildings crowned by antennae, pigeon lofts, and laundry lines with sheets so worn they were nearly transparent. Like years before, he had a glimpse of the sea, in all certainty, reverberating and magnetic below the June sun. Although the picture that could be contemplated from the window had barely changed, Conde knew that this was a deceptive perception. Everything moved. Sometimes toward a cliff: because that would also be lost in time, like tears in the rain.

Manolo returned to the office with a folder in his hand and a shadow of visceral exhaustion across his face.

"Put out the damned cigarette, you already know you can't smoke here."

"Go to hell, Manolo. I'm going to keep smoking," Conde said. "And if you want, put me in jail."

Manolo shook his head and took the chair behind the desk. He opened the folder and took out a photo that he handed to Conde.

Next to the coarse trunk of a tree, on the grass, rolled up any which way, were the black pants and blouse and, next to them, what Conde thought could be the tubes of striped fabric that emos usually wore as sleeves, and on which it was possible to make out some darker stains. Scarlet?

"Give me the others," Conde demanded.

Manolo gave him the two sensitive photos. In the first one, you could barely see a coarse field of weeds that sank and darkened into what ended up being the opening of a well. In the other, on top of that same field of scrub, placed on a plastic sheet, putrefied, swollen, eaten away by ants and other insects, lay the body of the person who had been Judith Torres. After looking, in silence, at that image of death for a few minutes, Conde let the three photos fall on the table. He felt useless and frustrated.

"She really hadn't gone anywhere . . . Or she had. Fucking hell! Tell me about it," he then demanded of Major Palacios.

"A few days ago, a man who has some crops in that area was seeing some vultures. He searched several times to see what it could be, but not too much, thinking it must be some dead animal, but he didn't find anything."

"Where is that?"

"Coming out of the Cotorro, about a mile along the Carretera Central. There are hardly any people living in that area . . ."

"How in the hell did that girl get all the way there? Did you notice that she was naked but wearing her Converse?"

Manolo nodded and moved his hand across the table to take a cigarette out of Conde's pack. He looked at it, decided not to light it, and returned it to its case.

"Yesterday afternoon, when he returned from work, the man searched again, because he was curious. Then he says he remembered that there was a well on the property. When he approached it, he got a whiff of rotten flesh . . . And he found the clothing. The well is about thirty feet deep. It appears that they covered it many years ago . . ."

"What does the autopsy say? Did they find any traces of drugs?"

"They're still working on her, look at the state of the corpse." Manolo made a decision and lit the cigarette with the lighter hidden in a drawer of his desk. "But they already know that she died due to a massive loss of blood."

"Because of the fall?"

"Yes and no. When her body fell in the well, the girl was still alive. But it appears that she had already lost a lot of blood. She had two vertical wounds, one on each arm. The kind that real suicidals make. And a very strong contusion at the base of her skull, perhaps caused by the fall in the well. Although it could have been premortem."

"How long had she been dead?"

"Between twelve and fifteen days. It's not going to be easy to be more specific. In recent days, it has been very hot, it has rained several times, the temperature at the bottom of the well goes up and down more slowly than on the surface, the humidity level . . ."

"There's something that doesn't make sense," Conde muttered, lamenting the poor physical state of his brain. "She cut herself and then threw herself headfirst into that well?"

"Could be. But now, they're analyzing everything they found. Because on Judy's clothing there are two blood types."

"What the fuck, Manolo?" Conde protested when he heard the information capable of moving the pieces he had been placing in his mind.

"I'm telling you, old man! One thing at a time . . ."

"One is her blood. And the other one?"

"Somebody who maybe was with her, I'd say. But God knows how that blood got on her clothes. Because it still looks more like a suicide."

"But she was naked. Why? What did she cut her arms with?"

"With a scalpel . . . They looked for it all the way at the bottom of the well and finally found it near her clothes. It has remains of blood, but no fingerprints. If it had any, the rain washed them away."

Conde's brain screeched as it tried to place each piece of evidence in reasonable slots.

"What else did they find?"

"This piece of paper."

Manolo opened the folder and removed the clear bag that held half a sheet of white paper, no longer very white. He held it out to Conde, who read: "'Once the soul looked contemptuously on the body, and then that contempt was the supreme thing. The soul wished the body meager, ghastly, and famished. Thus he thought to escape from the body and the earth.'"

"*Thus Spake Zarathustra* . . . But I don't know that it's a suicide note . . . She often wrote things like that, she copied them from books."

"It was in in her pants pocket, along with her ID card and a plastic baggie. But there wasn't any money or anything else . . ."

"There wasn't money?"

"No, I'm sure. Since the man who found the clothing saw it was stained with blood, he didn't touch it."

"She had stolen some money from her grandmother. About five hundred dollars."

"The investigators don't know that. Nobody told them anything . . ."

"Well, it's a clue."

"Yes, the money." Manolo was writing something down in his battered notebook. Conde, meanwhile, was trying to process that information and marry it to what he had already amassed.

"How much time does the lab need to do a DNA test?"

"Five days."

"What the fuck do you mean five days, Manolo?"

"Listen, this isn't *CSI*, this is Cuba and this is reality . . . Besides, when you were a policeman, DNA tests didn't even exist and cases were also solved. While we wait for the results, they're going to keep working . . . But there are no DNA banks here, so proof of the other blood type isn't going to do much for us. Unless we compare it to some suspect and it matches."

Conde nodded ill-humoredly.

"Isn't it possible to find fingerprints or footprints or traces of blood?"

"I already told you that it has been too many days and the heavy rainfalls took everything away. We can't even determine how long she has been dead."

Conde took back the pack of cigarettes, lit another smoke, and looked out the window again.

"I wish she had gotten on a balsa raft . . . Maybe she wouldn't be dead . . . But there's something fishy in all of this."

"You think that somebody cut her arms, then undressed her and threw her in the well? That that same person took the money, if she had it with her that day, but left the stained clothing, perhaps even stained with their own blood, and left Judy's ID?"

"It's something I am thinking, yes."

"But who could put that whole thing together and at the same time commit the idiocy of not taking the clothing, the ID, the scalpel?"

"Somebody who nearly went crazy when what happened happened. Somebody who maybe didn't want to kill her, but killed her . . . I don't know . . . We need the forensics to verify whether Judy was really a virgin or if she had had sexual relations . . . if she had them shortly before dying."

Manolo took a deep breath. Forcefully, using his nails, he rubbed his head.

"Conde . . . don't put more noise in the system. The forensics know what to do . . ."

"I'm thinking about Bocelli, the Italian . . . I can't imagine a character like that playing the platonic little friend of an eighteen-year-old girl . . ."

"Me neither, but . . ." Manolo was speaking in his firmest tone. "Look, I called to tell you that Judith Torres showed up dead." He paused, looked toward the window, and made a decision. "Give me a cigarette."

Conde handed over the pack. Manolo lit the cigarette and exhaled the smoke.

"I called to tell you that we're investigating all evidence . . . But also to warn you about something. Please listen closely to me." Manolo put his two index fingers to his ears, to emphasize his demand. "From now on, you can't get involved in this story. It's no longer a missing, hidden, or whatever girl. Now it's a dead person, and until it's proven that it was a suicide, there's a criminal investigation in process. And any interference can fuck up the case, and you know that better than anyone. Her friend asked you to help find her and the family thought it was fine that you do so . . . Well, you've done what you could, and if you couldn't do any more, it's because she had already been dead awhile . . . From this point on, keep yourself far from the investigation, for the good of the investigation itself and that of the truth. We have to move very carefully now . . . You know what I am asking you and you also know that you can't do any more on your own."

Conde had been moving until he was in front of the window again, his back to Major Palacios. Through his own experience as an investigator, he knew no reasons existed to refute the other man's demand. But that bothered him.

"If anything else shows up," Manolo continued, "if we find any clue, or we declare it murder or suicide, whatever, I'll call you and tell you. Besides, you know that if you get involved in this investigation and they find out, the first person they're going to come asking is me, and then the one they are going to kick in the ass is me. Is that clear? The private detective game is over . . ."

Conde turned around and looked at his former subordinate.

"Who's going to tell her parents?"

"Chief of headquarters and the captain leading the investigation. They are already on their way over there."

Conde thought of Yadine, Frederic, Yovany, Ana María the teacher. But no, he wouldn't tell them what had happened. In his time as a policeman, he had never liked that difficulty.

"Am I going to be questioned?"

"Certainly. Her father, her mother, or grandmother are going to talk about you. And what you know could help the investigator."

"What about Frederic? Yovany? The teacher? . . . Yadine? Are they all going to be questioned?"

"Yes. They have to do it. And they're going to tighten the screws . . ."

"It's all so shitty, isn't it?"

Manolo smoked his cigarette.

"As shitty as can be," the policeman agreed.

———

Garbage II was quite disgusted by the abandonment to which Conde had subjected him in recent days. To relieve that feeling, the man merely said a few words, excused himself, and served him a plate brimming over with the luxurious leftovers from the previous night. The dog, beyond hungry, turned his back to his owner and concentrated on what mattered.

The headache was again tormenting Conde, although he was well aware that it was not due to the effects of the hangover. Despite having gone past lunchtime, he hadn't felt any desire to eat. He decided to send another aspirin to his devastated stomach, rubbed his temples and his forehead abundantly with Chinese ointment, and, after turning on the fan, let himself fall on the bed, which looked more like an abandoned nest. He didn't even look at the soporific, asthmatic novel that helped him sleep.

He felt a deep exhaustion in his arms, shoulders, legs. Also an emptiness in his chest, an inability to move, or to even think. Feelings of guilt hounded him over not having been able to find the way that would have led him to Judy, and even the certainty of knowing that when Yadine had asked for help it was already impossible to help the young girl brought him no relief. But it still seemed like a macabre game to him that while he was thinking about books, money, rings, weddings, birthdays, and lost

Rembrandts, the body of that girl who had dreamed of so many free-doms and who had searched for them via so many paths could be rotting in a dry well, after having watched the earth swallow up her blood and the eighteen years she'd been alive. Was this her own choice?

It had always been difficult for Conde to conceive of a young person making an attempt on her own life, even when he knew that those atti-tudes were very common. But if Judy had killed herself, which was in-conceivable, in her case, it reached tragic proportions: so much thinking about death, playing with it, contempt for life and the one thing that kept her going—her body—had perhaps been the one to lead her down that absurd path. Could the girl truthfully have believed in her future reincarnation? Did she really think that solutions could be found with an exit? Perhaps even that by ceasing to be, she would be free? Hadn't she understood that not even the replicants wanted to die after they tasted the miracle of being alive, the ephemeral but enormous privilege of thinking, hating, loving? No. Judy, as Frederic said about himself, could be emo but not such a moron. Or could she? If she had killed herself, she would have some reason, and it would be an important one: much more important than fading emo militancy or flirtations with a self-destructive philosophy. But if someone had taken her to that end, none of what was known would end up mattering: only her killer's hidden reasons. But, who could want Judy dead badly enough to risk acting on it? Why make the effort to hide the body but leave the bloodstained clothing strewn where they were bound to be found and, further still, be incriminating, or, at least, leave the door open to other searches? If Bocelli was behind that act, why disguise it as a suicide . . . ? What about the money, did Judy have it with her that day? As he thought more with his poor and aching brain, Conde started understanding that some piece still didn't fit in the puzzle that he had managed, with so much effort, to build based on the different faces of Judy obtained in his research . . . By her own choice or by a killer's hand, Judy was dead and her exit from this world should have been related to the way in which she aimed to live in it: free. That certainty was the only thing Conde had. And for Judy, per-haps, it had been the only thing that mattered. Finding the guilty party would not bring her back to life, back to her family, back to her disquiet-ing reading and her passionate militancies. Nothing anymore would bring her back from her dreamed-of Nirvana. At least until her reincarnation. Or, in the end, would she now in reality be more free?

At some point in the afternoon, the physical and mental fatigue overcame Conde. Like so many other times, he felt himself gliding through sleepiness until he found himself in the dream that returned to him the image of his grandfather Rufino. This time, the old man appeared clearly and convincingly, as if he were alive and it were not a dream. Because he had come to take him out of his unhealthy state of mind with the persistent recourse of reminding his favorite grandson that the world, at the end of the day, had always been and would always be a cockfighting ring.

———

As he got older, with terrifying inexorability and speed, Mario Conde had had countless occasions to confirm, thanks to dreams like that afternoon's, and to many other examples encountered in the starkest reality, the fact that, in truth, he had learned almost nothing from his grandfather. And he couldn't blame that pedagogic waste on Rufino el Conde, who had been prodigious in his advice, his practical demonstrations, and attempts at imparting lessons that were even metaphysical at times, focused on training his grandson in the very complex art of living life. The old man had started to undertake that careful instruction, almost Socratic, as far back as Conde could remember, when the old man started taking him with him to the cockfighting pens where he raised and trained his animals, and to the official rings, at first, and later clandestine ones, after the revolutionary and socialist prohibition on cockfights; those circular enclosures, like copies of Roman circuses, in which the ferocious disciples were made to fight until the death and where bets were placed.

Looking at and listening to his grandfather, trying to respond to his constant questions, he would have had the enviable opportunity to become the owner of a sharp practical philosophy that the by-then ancient Rufino el Conde had cultivated in each circumstance. The grandfather adorned his lessons with such glorious maxims as the one that went "Curiosity killed the cat" (as his grandson had just felt, in his own flesh and that of another) or "All I know is that you should play when you're sure you're going to win, and if not, it's better not to play," a sentence that was generally flaunted minutes before the start of a fight of dubious prognosis. Almost always, as his grandfather gave that advice, he was placing, on the most inconceivable sites of his body or his outfit, the drops of Vaseline heavily loaded with mild or hot pepper of which, like a magician of indecipherable skills, he would spread a practically undetectable but sufficient amount on the feathers of his cock just before the fight started, to suffocate and debilitate his opponent. Playing to win.

"But that additional help has to be used as a very last resort, you know?" he declared from his stool, leaning against a post, that son of a Canary Island–born fugitive who reached port in Cuba back in what was still called "the time of Spain." "What matters is that you yourself have stacked the deck in your favor, the way you prepare a cock: from the time you pick the parents until you train it to turn it into a perfect machine. That means that you teach it not to let it be fucked up by the other cock . . . Do you understand me, my child? I'm asking you if you understand because it's important for you to learn this: in life one has to see himself as if he were a cock . . . I bet you don't know why?" He would insist at this point in his speech so that his interlocutor, even when he understood him perfectly and knew the answer due to having heard it hundreds of times, would raise his shoulders and shake his head no, ready for the surprise and revelation. "Because the world is a damned cockfighting ring in which you go in to annihilate your opponent and only one of the two comes out with all of his feathers intact: the one who doesn't let himself get fucked up by the other one," Rufina would conclude and finish off with "Everything else is just filler."

As a gamecock, Mario Conde would have been considered a failure. Perhaps because, despite the grandfather and great-grandfather he'd had, he turned out to be dragged down by defective genes. For starters, he was lacking spurs and he was too soft, as a woman would once tell him, rightly so, many years before. Then, he didn't know how to use his beak or his wings, since he was just a sentimental piece of crap, as he would tell himself with good reason. Not due to coincidence or bad luck, but because of his glaring inabilities, he had received so many spur marks, pecks, and kicks in the ass over the course of his years that they were branded on his soul. So many that, had his grandfather Rufino el Conde seen them, he would have withdrawn his last name and perhaps even twisted his neck like those chickens that he preferred to put in the cooking pot before letting them loose within the confines of a cockfighting ring, since just by looking at them, he knew that they would be a lost cause in life's battles.

In a country that was turning into a high-walled cockfighting ring by the day, in which the strange custom was practiced of having many cocks fighting among themselves, each trying to take something from another one and not have anything taken from him, Conde felt like a puppet that, with great difficulty, avoided the blows, looking for a tiny space to survive. The most terrible thing turned out to be knowing that nothing could be done about his defects: in life's cockfighting ring, his manifest destiny would always place him on the receiving end of pecks that weren't even meant for him.

If in the reality of his day or in the flexible universe of his dreams, he would have known how to pray, Conde would have liked to pray for the immortal soul of Judith Torres. But, in the face of his devotional inabilities, he had to resign himself to wishing her luck in the journey toward her next earthly stop. Perhaps she could land in a place and a time at which life wasn't confined to the oppressive limits of a cockfighting ring.

10

Havana, July 2008

The invincible vocation for nostalgia had been what decreed the choice: almost without thinking about it, he had chosen the point where Paseo del Prado comes undone, like a wilting flower, following its meeting with el Malecón's always aggressive exposure. Twenty years before, Mario Conde, still a lieutenant investigator, had arranged a meeting at that cross-roads with the theater producer Alberto Marqués to begin an amazing journey through Havana's homosexual nightlife, a nocturnal round over-flowing with revelations about the survival strategies and reaffirmation of those ignored, further still, marginalized individuals, who were at times even condemned. That outing had made an indelible mark on his memory that, by spontaneous generation, had moved him to choose the spot for this new encounter.

As he waited for Major Manuel Palacios's arrival, Conde forced himself to not get caught up in digressions. The fact that, after five days of silence, his former colleague had called him and proposed having a beer could be due to too many reasons for him to get entangled in trying to predict them. In any event, what was clear in the telephone conversation main-tained a few hours before was that, six days after having found the corpse of Judith Torres, the police were still incapable of giving any definitive answer regarding the circumstances in which the girl had died.

Over the course of those same days, Conde's spirits had managed to recover, more or less. The police order to keep himself at the margins of Judith Torres's case, in addition to his personal decision to try to forget that regrettable story, had combined with the favorable circumstances that, instead of taking his planned vacation (which in his case consisted of the most compact *dolce far niente* possible), he had seen himself forced to work and concentrate on less painful matters. Because Yoyi's diplomat friend, made aware of the library of the former leader that still retained some juicy marvels, had asked for a list of works that the old man would be willing to sell and of the going prices. As could be expected, Yoyi had charged him with that tedious but saving mission, which had required that he keep his five senses on alert. Besides, Conde had definitively forbidden himself from giving in to other unhealthy desires that went through his head: that of attending Judy's funeral or of holding a final conversation with the sure-to-be-inconsolable Yadine. And for that reason he had even decided to indefinitely postpone the moment for passing on to Ricardo Kaminsky the message from his relative Elias about the litigation involving the painting.

In an effort to maintain the purpose of not trying to guess what he would find out (or not) anyway thanks to the conversation with Manolo, Conde focused on looking at the surroundings and trying to establish, on that return, how much the panorama had changed since that far-off night of learning about gays. The remains of the old Basque façade had disappeared and in its place, the hotel promised for years by an ad had not been erected; the small plaza of the old La Punta fortress, placed at the entrance of the bay, had been restored and now seemed to be occupied by a statue of Francisco de Miranda. On the ground floor of the triangular building on the corner of Prado and the abominable Calzada de San Lázaro someone had opened a bar that Conde, thanks to the dollars he had earned in recent days, had his eye on. The rest of the components remained stuck in time, with their dramatic warnings: there was the same class of little gay trolls in search of victims—who didn't even look at Conde—the Mexican bay leaf trees marked by salt spray and sea wind survived, the buildings that were definitively deceased or in their death throes, the remains of the old Havana jail, and the unsolvable enigma of the bust dedicated to poet Juan Clemente Zenea, on whose bronze face his maker had tried to express the inescapable tragedy of the bard capable of making himself the repository for all hate. Accused of being a traitor, by Cuban independence activists as well as by colonial Spanish authorities, that ethereal being had confused his possibilities, daring to play his cards in the realm of politics, to end up executed in the trenches of La Cabaña fortress, visible on the other side of the bay.

The sun was beginning its final descent when Major Palacios got out of his car and approached Conde. Already in the mind-set of the invitation to drink some beers, Manolo had unburdened himself of his uniform jacket and was wearing a sleeveless shirt, very worn, that made him look like the physical monstrosity that he was.

"Wassup, my friend?" was his greeting, with his hand held out.

"Poor guy," Conde said, pointing at the bust of Zenea. "He believed that he could think with his own head and that poets can play politics. It cost him very dearly. They said horrible things about him and later dedicated a bust to him. What a shitty country . . ."

"Well, I see that today you're feeling happy and even patriotic."

"Yes, luckily . . . When I'm feeling down, I think that this country is a real shithole and a half. Come on, let's go sit over there."

They took the most distant table, in a wing of the porch overlooking the Prado, through which the scarce breeze coming from the sea ran more freely. They asked for beers and, as a snack, some croquettes allegedly made of chicken, which, at least, ended up being edible.

"I can tell you have some cash . . ." Manolo said as he refilled his glass with the blond beer.

"Not much," Conde said, who was embarrassed by the fact of having money almost as much as he was of the more frequent situation of not having any.

"Just in case, don't erase me from your will."

"No, I would never." Conde smiled and drank from his glass in order to immediately push Manolo. "So?"

Manolo took a deep breath.

"The forensics discovered that Judy had had sexual relations, perhaps shortly before dying. In her vagina, there were remains of the lubricant on the one type of condom currently sold in Cuba."

"And what else?"

"Well, nothing else. There are no signs of violence, it's as if it were consensual . . . At the end of the day, we're in the same place . . ."

"And you called to tell me this?"

Manolo looked at the bust of Zenea as if he were deciding whether to speak or not.

"Well, not really in the same place . . . Bocelli returned to Cuba three days ago . . ."

"What are you saying?" Conde's surprise was resounding.

"He was going to Mexico for some business and he returned . . . They held him at the airport when he arrived." Manolo paused and drank to the bottom of his beer, more out of thirst than the desire to savor it. With a gesture, he requested another. "You can imagine the shit show that took place. Ambassador, Italian consul, and fucking everybody involved . . . But the guy agreed to a DNA test . . ."

"So he was clean?" Conde asked, guessing the predictable answer.

"The lab results arrived just now. The blood that was on Judy's clothing was not his . . . It appears that the guy is clean."

"But that doesn't mean that he wasn't the one who had sex with her." Conde tried to find his way in the dark.

"We don't have any way to prove that. Remember that they used a condom. Forget it, we had to let him go. Tomorrow he's leaving Cuba . . . They say he's not coming back."

"That's better," Conde said. "I don't think we're going to miss him too much."

Conde looked at the street, where, in one fell swoop, night had established itself. The cancellation of that possible clue didn't even leave the investigation in the same place, but rather, more behind. Everything related to Judy was definitely turning out to be complicated.

"There's more . . . The lab finally established that one of the substances Judy had in her body was a hallucinogenic."

"What drug was it?"

"That's the problem . . . They don't know for sure. It's a strange substance, not a common drug around here."

"What the hell are you talking about?"

"What you're hearing: she had taken a drug similar to ecstasy, but that isn't common among those who take those things here in Cuba. It's like ecstasy squared, with more chemical shit."

"That son of a bitch . . ."

Conde scratched his arms as if he himself were suffering from classic withdrawal symptoms.

"And the latest: yesterday, they put the girl's father in jail, your friend Alcides Torres," Manolo dropped as if he were talking about the summer heat.

"Shit, Manolo! Why don't you just say everything at once, dammit?"

"Because I can't . . . I only have one mouth. And they're going to sew it shut if they find out that I've told you all of this . . ."

"What happened to the guy?"

"He's being investigated. I'm sure he's in so deep that he's even got shit in his hair . . ."

Conde did not feel petty: he was truly and deeply happy with that act of historic justice. For once, a son of a bitch was paying for his faults. And he tried to imagine what Judy's reaction would have been if she had been able to learn of the foreseeable end of her father's career.

"Judy knew that Alcides was involved in some deal that could make him a lot of dollars."

"With what they were sending from Venezuela, I don't think they could become millionaires," Manolo assured him, his forehead wrinkled and as cross-eyed as ever. "But they got a nice kickback from it . . ."

"Well, then the guy was dealing in something else and not in the businesses you imagined . . . And something else that would yield him a lot of dollars."

"What the hell could it be?" Manolo had taken the bait out of curiosity. "How much is 'a lot of dollars'?"

"That's the problem . . . How much is *a lot*? More than I have, that's for sure . . . Say something to your friends, see if they can find out," Conde said, satisfied at having added more fuel to the fire that was already heating up under Alcides Torres. "So what comes now?"

"Well, nothing else. Now there really is no more news."

"What about the investigation into Judy's death?"

Manolo shrugged his shoulders, as if he wanted to reach his major's bars and wasn't finding them.

"It's going to remain open, but . . ."

"There are no more leads?"

"No. The DNA says that the blood on Judy's clothing belongs to a man, under the age of fifty, white . . . With that, we can't get very far."

"Unless you know where to go."

Manolo stopped the motion of tossing a croquette in his mouth in midair and looked at Conde. Again his eyes looked for the best way to anchor themselves on either side of his nose.

"What are you talking about, Conde?"

"Nothing. About searching . . ."

Manolo swallowed the croquette almost without chewing it.

"Look, what I told you the other day still stands. You cannot get involved in this. If I decided to tell you about Bocelli and the drug and the other things and even about Alcides Torres, it's because I think I owed it to you, do you know why?"

Conde looked at him.

"Because you're my friend? Because years ago I was your boss? Because I'm more intelligent than you?"

"No . . . Because you've behaved. It's like a reward for good behavior."

Conde shook his head.

"Manolo, Judy's case is more dead than she is. What in the hell could it matter to you if I investigate a little bit on my own?"

Now it was Manolo who shook his head no.

"With Alcides Torres under investigation by a special team, things change. A lot. These stories are being looked at by the very top." And he pointed to the top floor of the building, although both knew that Manolo meant a much more elevated point. "So it would be best for you to stay quiet. What if there's some kind of relation between what the father's doing and the girl's death?"

This time, Conde nodded. After a pause, he dove in.

"A few days ago, I was remembering Major Rangel," he started, as if distracted. "I think I withstood working as a policeman for ten years because we had a boss like him. With old Rangel, with Captain Jorrín, even with that corrupt son of a bitch Contreras, I learned some things . . . One is that being a policeman is a shitty job. And although you are still a policeman, I imagine that you agree with that, right? Another, that that shit is sadly necessary. Especially when things like the death of Judy Torres happen . . . Because if I'm sure of anything, it's that in the story about that girl, there's something fishy. And surely you also agree, right?" Manolo didn't confirm or deny, and Conde continued. "A policeman like Major Rangel or like Jorrín, or like Fat Contreras would never have underestimated his sense of smell. What did you learn from those people, Manolo?"

————

When he said goodbye to Manolo, instead of heading toward any of his usual spots, Mario Conde felt pushed to wander aimlessly, which, he was well aware, had a set destination. He started walking along el Malecón, in the direction of El Vedado, as he allowed his brain to get wrapped up in the digressions that he had avoided before. Now, knowing that Bocelli, his most tenacious suspect with any murky connection to Judy, did not seem to have any link to the girl's final fate, he was insistent on reorganizing the few surviving pieces on his mental chessboard as he aimed again and, despite Manolo's repeated warnings, to delineate a possible path toward the knowledge of what happened on the farm on the outskirts of the city where they found Judy's sexed, drugged, mutilated, and dead body.

The now-proven fact that the young girl had lost her virginity, apparently just a few hours before dying, the certainty that on her clothing was the blood of a young white man, the evidence that she had taken drugs that were not usually available on the island, the macabre evidence that she had languished at the bottom of the well, in addition to the impossibility of determining if the contusion discovered on her head had occurred with the fall or before it, gave shape to a premonition that was pounding all the more forcefully in the former policeman's chest: somebody had helped Judy die. He was sure. But, and there was the question: Who? Why?

The distance between where Prado and Malecón crossed and the beginning of Avenida de los Presidentes had disappeared beneath his feet thanks to Conde's pondering of those realities and possibilities. Something seemed to be increasingly incontrovertible: Judy had gone of her own will to that remote place where she was found. Unless the drugs she took had left her defenseless. This last possibility would imply the existence of a car and, perhaps, of two people to carry her from the road up to the well. But that premeditation did not square away with the criminal idiocy of leaving the bloody clothing there—as it was almost logical to conclude—by the person or the people who had led her to that resting spot. Or was he forcing, out of pure stubbornness, information that only pointed toward the act of suicide? Hadn't he been convinced that Judy had all of the mental attributes capable of feeding that possibility? Drugged to her eyeballs, couldn't she have undressed herself, allowed the penetration of her vagina, and then cut her arms and jumped into the well? Had the loss of her virginity acted as a catalyst for her attitude? Couldn't the note found in her clothing be read as a statement of principle, or rather, of the end?

When he left the Malecón and turned down Calle G, Conde started to run into the nightlife of young, withdrawn explorers toward those dark corners, more fitting for the sexual games they handed themselves over to with Pantagruel-like appetites. When he crossed Línea and entered the sites of greater tribal concentration, he asked himself what it was that he was really looking for there. Or what he aimed to find. And he couldn't answer himself, because another cunning question surprised him: Why had Manolo, after having forbidden him before and now again forbidding any intervention, thrown those bits of information to him? There was something suspicious in that change of policy that was never announced as such.

The heat and the darkness seemed to have come together that night to bring to the surface and make visible hundreds of those young people who displayed themselves like catalog models. Conde felt compelled to remember the carnivals of his childhood, still authentic, for which people voluntarily and joyously selected ridiculous costumes, bought grotesque masks, and made up their faces exaggeratedly. But while the consumption ended along with the party in the case of the carnivals, this juvenile street masquerade party of the new era implied a deeper transfiguration that went from the surface down to the mental depths of those young people determined in their singular pursuit. That spectacle was reality. The attitudes of those young people represented the present, further still, the glorious oft-promised future, which had ended up turning into a carnival with too many masks and no party. A sad future, like an emo convinced of his militancy.

With his doubts and conclusions on his back, he continued along the climb up one of the avenue's side streets and, from the corner of Calle 17, where Emolandia tended to take residence, he tried to find some recognizable face below the capillary curtains, under the black outfits, hidden by dark lipstick and makeup. He didn't make out Yadine, who was surely mourning the death of the woman who made her *craaazy*; Frederic couldn't be seen around, either, perhaps because he was giving in to his sexual urges somewhere less visible; he didn't even find Yovany, the superwhite emo, perhaps because he was wandering those indigenous lands in search of lost brothers. But, there were still two, three dozen adolescents there, emo-outfitted to the nines, enjoying their pretend depression, dreaming about musical Nirvanas and religious Nirvanas, displaying their mercilessly but enthusiastically hole-ridden bodies, feeling part of something in which they believed and that made them feel free . . . And he didn't understand how it was possible that Judy had considered leaving the group and, less still, did he understand how he, Mario Conde, had accepted the demand to keep himself at the margins. Judy was a loud scream clamoring for him from the bottom of a dry well.

11

They had had breakfast sitting across the table from each other. For Tamara, it was a café con leche in which she was dipping some crackers smeared with butter; Conde, a piece of toast baptized with olive oil over which he had sprinkled salt and crushed a garlic clove. (The milk was a luxury that Tamara could permit herself thanks to the euros that her son sent her; the olive oil, an unthinkable eccentricity on the island, a privilege that Conde had access to by means of his near sister-in-law Aymara, who resided in Italy.) Then, to round out the feeling of a comfortable routine, they both drank another coffee, recently brewed (uncut coffee—or with less additives—than other ignoble grounds, purchased thanks to the dealer in valuable books' most recent commercial transactions). But both knew that routines like that were unattainable for so many, too many, of the island's inhabitants.

"You taste like a vampire," Tamara said to him as she tasted the hint of garlic when she kissed him goodbye.

"And you smell like freshly cut grass . . ."

"Yves Saint Laurent . . . A gift from a patient. Are you jealous? I've got to run . . ."

Conde watched her leave and felt the weight of Tamara's absence in an unearthly way. Something had to be going very poorly within him for as confirmed a hermit as he was to suffer the wing beat of solitude for such a mundane reason and, at the same time, to not feel any distress from the act of starting a new ritual, a pleasant one, but a ritual nonetheless, embellished with talk of jealousy, to boot. The former policeman didn't have to think too long to understand the reason for his numbness: the mystery of life, but, above all, the mystery of the death of Judy Torres.

A half an hour later, when he was getting ready to go out, the sound of the telephone ringing pulled him out of his thoughts.

"Conde, it's me, Elias Kaminsky . . ."

Conde greeted him with the warmth he felt for the behemoth.

"I called your house but . . ." the painter continued. "Are you living at Tamara's house already?"

"No, I'm still there, here, I don't even know, my friend . . . Well, what's new?"

"Something interesting. Or at least, that seems interesting to me . . . The lawyers discovered that the painting hadn't come from Los Angeles but rather Miami."

"That makes more sense."

"But why make that move and hide the origins?" Elias Kaminsky asked, and Conde agreed with him. Why the concealment?

"And were they able to find out who had it? Was it a relative of Román Mejías's?"

"Well, we don't know if it was anyone from that man's family," Elias continued, informing him, "but it's a young woman, Cuban, and the weird thing is that she arrived in the United States about four years ago on a balsa raft. Perhaps she brought it with her, or rather, that it was always in Cuba until—"

An electric charge ran through Conde's brain when he heard the words "balsa raft." Two wires were activated that had been far apart until that moment, now brushed against each other, allowing the charge stirring around them to go on. But he thought, no, what his mind was formulating wasn't possible.

"Shit, Elias! Shit, shit . . ." Conde interrupted Elias's reflections, but got stuck, because his thoughts were moving over a surface that couldn't find a focal point.

"Hey, what's going on with you?" Elias seemed alarmed.

Conde hit his forehead three, four times, and took a few seconds to gather his ideas and find the ability to speak.

"Do you know the name of that Cuban woman?" And then he closed his eyes, as if he did not want to see the avalanche headed toward him, ready to crush him.

"The last name is Rodríguez," Elias said. "Her married name . . ."

Without lifting his eyelids, Conde took in all the air around him and asked, "And is her name María José?"

The silence on the other end of the line, 1,800 miles away, announced to Conde that his declaration had hit the painter Elias Kaminsky in the face. He himself, with the receiver stuck to his ear, could feel at that moment how his hands were sweating and his heart was beating.

"How do you know that name?" Elias's words came at last, weighed down with the incapacity to understand what was happening.

"I know because . . ." he began, then stopped. "First, tell me something. You told me that your father told you that, besides the Rembrandt, Mejías had other reproductions by Dutch painters, right?"

"Yes, others . . ." Elias must have been searching his memory to be able to respond to a question without knowing where it was going. "A church by De Witte—"

"A landscape by Ruysdael and Vermeer's *View of Delft*," Conde interrupted him, and continued. "And he had a sister who had become wheelchair-bound after an accident?"

"But what in the hell . . . ?"

"The thing is, I know the man who kept the painting, Elias . . . He's the father of a girl who . . . Well, he's the father of María José and I'm sure that he's the nephew of Román Mejías. I was at his house. I am now nearly convinced that the authentic Rembrandt never left Cuba until he could get it out, I think by way of Venezuela, and from there he was able to send it to his daughter who was in Miami so she could sell it . . . And that man was hoping to earn *a lot* of dollars, truly a lot. Shit, now I know how much a lot of dollars are: more than a million . . ."

On both sides of the line, there was a silence for a while that seemed infinite, until Elias reacted.

"But how is it possible that you—?"

"It's possible because Yadine, Ricardito's granddaughter, set me on that path, without her imagining where it would go . . . Not her, not I . . ."

As best as he could, Conde relayed the story that Yadine Kaminsky had thrown him into and that, by way of Judy's disappearance and her death, connected, in the worst way, a remote past and the families of the two young emos through a tragedy that reached into the cabin of a passenger ship anchored in the port of Havana in 1939.

"Elias, this has to be one of those cosmic circumstances of which your father used to speak . . ." Conde concluded, and added, "Do you see how it's easier to believe that God does exist?"

"Conde," Elias Kaminsky said at last, obviously moved by the story. "Is there any way to prove that that Alcides took the painting out of Cuba?"

"I think only if he confesses it . . . And I don't think he'll do it, because there must not be proof that he took it out. There might not even be proof that he ever had it . . . And because there's a lot of money at stake. If Alcides waited for your mother to die to take it out and try to sell it . . . No, without any other proof, I don't think he'll confess anything."

"It doesn't matter," Elias accepted. "In any event, I'm going to mention it to the lawyers."

"Yes." Conde was still thinking about what could have caused that unexpected revelation. "But I'm not going to tell Ricardito. His granddaughter is involved . . ."

"That's okay. Did you already tell him about the litigation and about the money? And that things are going to take a good long while? You don't have to tell him anything else."

"No, forgive me, I still haven't said anything to him . . . But today I'm going to go see him to tell him about the litigation . . . And, of course, there's no need . . ."

After another long and heavy silence, Elias asked, "What are you going to do?"

"Well, I don't know . . . The truth is, I don't know."

"Don't worry. Since the painting left Cuba, it doesn't change things too much . . . Although knowing for sure could help . . ."

"Yes, it's always better to know . . ."

"Yes, to know . . ."

The silence returned and Conde felt exhausted. In reality, disappointed. Because even knowing the truth, without being able to prove it, he couldn't guarantee that justice would be served.

"Forget it, Elias, call me whenever you want . . . And say hello to Andrés for me."

"Thank you, Conde. I don't know how to thank you for what you've told me . . ."

Conde thought for a few moments before saying, "Today, I would've preferred that you didn't have to thank me for anything. That would have meant that perhaps Judy would still be alive . . ."

Again, silence took over the conversation. Conde realized that he had spoken of Judy and that perhaps Elias would've assumed he meant Judith Kaminsky, the girl who never got to be his aunt, lost in the Holocaust.

"Goodbye," Elias said, and Conde hurried to hang up and finish that conversation that fueled his unease with the world and some of its inhabitants. More than was healthy.

He returned to the kitchen and drank the rest of the cold coffee. He didn't feel better after discovering the path taken by the Rembrandt painting Joseph Kaminsky had thought he had destroyed and that the heirs of the infamous Román Mejías had kept hidden for almost half a century, perhaps knowing the way in which Mejías had become its owner. Or not knowing. But dreaming of getting *a lot* of dollars from it.

As he got farther away from Tamara's house, feeling the collision of ideas that kept arising inside his poor head, Conde seriously considered whether it would be best to just take that whole story about the Rembrandt painting and some white, black, and *mulato* Jews, tell it all to go to hell, and drink until he passed out.

———

It was easier for Mario Conde to omit the recent revelations and explain to Ricardo Kaminsky only what he had to tell him about the possible, although quite drawn-out, recovery of the Rembrandt painting and the future intentions of his cousin Elias than to hold the dialogue he'd put off for days with his granddaughter Yadine.

Just when her grandfather Ricardo was again telling Conde that he didn't have any property rights regarding the painting and, as such, he didn't feel he had the right, either, to accept any money sent by Elias Kaminsky, the girl came out onto the porch and, after coldly greeting him, threw a coded message into the air, in the best Kaminsky style.

"Grandpa, I'm going to Parque de Reyes for a while."

And she headed toward the place where she had last met up with the would-be detective. Conde reconfirmed for himself the difficulty of that conversation when he saw the young girl walk away, now without her emo clothes and with her hair in a ponytail that fell over the back of her neck.

"We're really worried about that girl," Ricardo Kaminsky said when she couldn't hear him anymore.

"Kids these days . . ." Conde commented noncommittally.

"For days, she has barely eaten anything and hasn't dressed up as emo . . . I think she is depressed for real."

"What a shame . . ."

When he arrived at the park, Conde found her sitting on the same dilapidated bench where they had spoken a few days prior. Au naturel, Yadine was a girl of real beauty, in whom the contributions of the mixed heritage running through her veins had obtained the best balance. But her overflowing sadness ruined that intense beauty.

"Aren't you emo anymore?" was Conde's greeting as he waited to see the best path to take.

"If Judy wanted to stop being emo, why should I be?"

"Are you sure she was going to get out?"

"Yes, she told *everyone* . . ."

"So then, what was she going to be?"

"That, she didn't tell *anyone*. Judy could be tremendously *mysterious* . . . When she wanted to."

Then, Yadine fell apart. She started to cry with some deep, choking sobs as her tears made two mighty streams.

"I can believe that. More mysterious than usual," the former policeman, who was capable of coming out with any nonsense when he felt disarmed, dared to say. Did Judy know anything about the source from which her father expected a lot of dollars to come? He asked himself again, motivated by his intention to ask Yadine, but decided not to do so: in any event, what Judy knew didn't decide anything, and he wasn't going to mention the details of that other sordid story to Yadine. Besides, the girl's weeping was affecting him so much that he felt the possibility that he himself would join her to make up a strange chorus of the plaintive.

Conde lit a cigarette to calm himself and to give the young girl time to recover herself.

"You didn't look for her enough . . ." she accused him, still between sobs, as she wiped her face with her hands.

"I did what I could," he defended himself, although without presenting his best reason: Judy was already dead when he started asking about her.

"But they killed her, man, they killed her . . ."

And she began to sob again.

"The police don't know . . ."

"The police don't know anything . . . She did not commit suicide, I'm sure she didn't."

Conde hesitated between trying to console the girl and explaining to her what he himself thought, telling her what he knew and believed about her friend's death, because if there is anything he was convinced of, it was that Yadine must be the person who most felt affected by Judy's death. Because not only did she love her and have the occasion to physically express that love: Yadine idolized Judy. And in that weeping, Conde knew well, there was not a single trace of guilt. It was just pain, pure and raw.

"Are you going to school?" He found himself a chink through which to escape.

The girl was putting herself back together and nodded.

"Yes, next week, exams start . . ."

"Your grandfather says you're barely eating."

She raised her shoulders and sobbed mutely. The man felt the girl transferring her sadness to him.

"I'm sorry, Yadine," he said, after throwing the end of his cigarette far away. "I have to leave, because . . ."

Yadine looked at him with her reddened and sadder-still eyes.

"Everyone leaves . . . It doesn't matter to anyone . . . They killed her and it doesn't matter to anyone," she said, and started to sob again, to make more tears, as she stood up and looked at Conde with clearly ac-cusatory intent. "It doesn't matter to anyone," she said again, and started running to her house, on Calle Zapotes, the same house where, fifty years prior, her great-grandparents Caridad Sotolongo and Joseph Ka-minsky arrived in the company of teenage Ricardito, who was already the owner of a Jewish Polish last name.

As he watched her get farther away, Conde felt himself gasping for air, a knot rising in his throat and tears blurring his vision. Although it was not his fault, he felt the weight of fault, his share of what was in the air surrounding him. *Just what I needed*, he thought as he started to feel his ass cramping due to the lack of support caused by the broken plank of the only surviving bench in Parque de Reyes. Then he thought that Yadine and Judy's love had been born marked by the most classic and tangible tragedy: that of being the descendants of Montagues and Capulets.

⸻

Conde definitely knew a better method than reflection when he needed to clear his thinking and free himself of heavy spiritual burdens. The formula was simple and had demonstrated its efficiency many times: two bottles of rum, the right mouths and ears, and an abundance of conversation. A few years before dying, his old friend, *el chino* Juan Chión, had taught him that, in the sensible Tao philosophy, those spiritual jolts were usually called cleaning the *tsin*.

Before handing himself over to the necessary Asian ablution, Conde decided to fulfill one last obligation: he called Major Manuel Palacios and told him what he knew of the possible exit route of a Rembrandt painting from Cuba, perhaps exported by Alcides Torres. If the super policeman in charge of the former leader's case managed to get anything out of Alcides, all the better. And if they didn't, fuck them. And he went out to the street.

Of course, the porch of Skinny Carlos's house, like nearly always, ended up being the best place for the foreseen cleaning of the *tsin*. Although Conde arrived with a bit of a delay, since, unexpectedly, the Bar of the Hopeless had closed that afternoon FOR EXTERMINATION!, according to the markered sign in Gandinga's hand, always a fan of love letters. Conde imagined that if the chemical product sprayed on the place turned out to be truly efficient, the following morning it would be possible to find the bodies even of species considered long ago extinct. *Megatherium*, for example! Tyrannosaurus, for sure! And in the surrounding areas, as collateral damage, several of the neighborhood drunks on the verge of dying of dehydration.

That night, Carlos and Rabbit appeared thirsty, since they asked Conde to quickly serve them the first liter of the top-shelf white rum acquired in convertible pesos. Candito accepted the can of TropiCola that his friend had brought him by virtue of his ethylic retirement.

As they warmed up their engines with the right fuel, they talked about Elias Kaminsky's phone call, although Conde preferred to not yet reveal the extraordinary connection he had discovered. After the first drinks, Conde at last focused on his true purpose and narrated, with interruptions caused by Carlos's questions, the last known details about the disappearance and fatal reappearance of Judy Torres, which was the matter most poking at his conscience.

As expected, the news that the girl's father was under police investigation garnered most of the interest of those present, who passionately hated that type of shadowy character, representative of a resistant and endemic national plague. And that was without knowing the best part of the story!

Candito the Red, more grounded than the rest of them, still thought that the girl had committed suicide: he had thought so ever since he learned of the mental confusions that she possessed so forcefully, and the entire ritual preceding her death confirmed it for him. Carlos, meanwhile, went back and forth between the death being a suicide and it being a crime, and he supposed that Judy's loss of virginity had a lot to do with either of these two options. Rabbit, on the contrary, was more supportive of Conde and Yadine's suspicions of murder, although he also thought that Judy had gone of her own will to that remote place where they had found her: there, she had drugged herself with her companion and, voluntarily or involuntarily (voluntarily, Conde reminded him), had had sexual relations with him, and then . . . Had she cut her arms or were they cut? And why was there other blood on her clothing? And where had those strange drugs come from? And what about the damned missing money?

Close to midnight, Conde got on his way toward Tamara's house. Despite the fact that he had barely had anything to drink, he felt drunk and frustrated, since instead of certainties capable of generating solutions, he had become weighed down with new doubts. The conversation with Manolo and the ones held that day with Elias and Yadine had made the confusing story of Judy's death come back with overwhelming pressure, definitely unbearable, and Conde had the conviction that that obsessive insistence would only be relieved with a categorical response. *But where in the hell and how in the hell will I find it*, he said to himself and, thanks to the fact that his judgment was impaired by the alcohol, the kick he aimed at the granite block serving as a street sign failed and he fell on his ass on the sidewalk, from where he discovered, joyous, the moon's enormity.

Like a thief entering the house of the woman whom he aimed to marry someday, and, to not disrupt her sleep, he decided to lie down on the sofa in the living room. He undressed and, as soon as he laid his body down horizontally, a sudden and surprising dizziness forced him to stand up. Alarmed by that reaction, he tried to think: *How is it possible that I am so drunk with so little rum? Am I getting that old? Might it be true that I'm an alcoholic? No, no* . . . When his brain stopped going around in circles, he went to the bathroom and put his head under the spray of the shower and, having turned a towel into the turban of an Indian aspiring to blessed Nirvana, he walked to the kitchen, where he placed the coffeepot on the burner.

With a half cup of coffee, he returned to the living room. As he drank the beverage, he felt sleepiness leaving him and the fog in his mind was starting to lift, like the sky after the rain. *Was I drunk and now I'm not?* He lit a cigarette and, when he was looking for an ashtray, he saw it. There, amid other discs, was the DVD copy of *Blade Runner* that had belonged to Judy. Since he had nothing better to do, he turned on the player and inserted the disc, and then turned on the television.

Sitting in his favorite armchair, he started to watch the movie without watching. As the plot unfolded and his brain settled down, he focused on the story again. That futuristic fable was communicating something remote, further still, something intimate. His sympathy for the replicants and for their desperate demand to have the right to live turned out to be more dramatic and visceral this time, perhaps due to the remaining effects of the alcohol, or perhaps merely because that drama was preparing him to communicate something that could still not be pinpointed. Toward the end of the film, when the replicant hunter and the last model of those condemned creatures have their agonizing and bloodied duel, Conde felt himself on the verge of tears. Did everything make him want to cry now? That epic figure with the very white skin of the humanoid mutant, so perfect and powerful, became for him a familiar image, almost known, while the replicant ran out of the final seconds of its vital mechanisms, maliciously programmed by its creator.

Five hours later, just as it was starting to get light out, Conde opened his eyes and, from the sofa where he had fallen deeply asleep, fixed them on the living room ceiling. The explosive force of a conviction, born in some wakeful corner of his brain, had taken him out of sleep with a large push and even a few kicks. Now Mario Conde knew where to look for the mystery of Judith Torres's death. And he knew, besides, that his premonitions had inopportunely changed their way of manifesting themselves: instead of a pain in his chest, just below his left nipple, now they showed up like a dizziness similar to one that could be caused by common drunkenness. Nothing changes for the better, he thought.

———

He pressed the intercom button and turned to look at the expression on his former colleague Manuel Palacios's face. The policeman was looking, enthralled, at the mansion, to which a few thousand well-placed dollars had returned it to what must have been its original splendor. Through every one of the agent's pores, instead of sweat extracted by the July heat, rose liquid envy before the magnificence and the sensation of peace and well-being the dwelling exuded, in the middle of a city that was dirtier and noisier every day.

For Conde, it had been difficult to make Manolo listen to him but, later, very easy to get him to go over there with him. First thing in the morning, when he showed up at investigations headquarters and asked for Major Palacios, Manolo told him over the internal telephone that he was in a meeting and couldn't see him. Conde lowered his voice and, to avoid revealing too much to the sergeant who sometimes worked as receptionist on the line, told him to stop fucking around and come down for a couple of minutes: if he wasn't interested in what he was going to tell him, then he, Mario Conde, would forget about it all and would get the hell out of there forever. Manolo, after a pause, asked him to wait below the bay leaf tree on the street. He would be down in ten minutes.

The policeman was wearing his uniform with bars and displaying the stressed face that went nearly everywhere with him in recent years.

"What?" Conde attacked him. "You don't want them inside to see you talking to me?"

"Go to hell, Conde. I don't have time to be—"

"Then find time," Conde interrupted him. "Because I am more than sure that I know who was with Judy on the day she died . . . Or was killed."

Manolo was looking at his former colleague with his usual intensity and cross-eyed-ness. He knew Conde too well to know that he didn't play with things that really mattered to him.

"What are you talking about?" Manolo started to get soft. "Does it have something to do with the Rembrandt painting that you told me about yesterday?"

"No, I don't think that one thing has anything to do with the other . . . But before going on, I want to tell you something . . . Manolo, you are a cross-eyed son of a bitch. You called me two days ago and told me what was and wasn't happening in Judy's case to—"

"So you would get involved in it without my telling you to get involved.

And you got involved . . . Well, yes, I'm a little bit of a son of a bitch. And since you asked me the other day, I want to tell you that that was one of the things I learned to do with you . . . Was it worth something?"

"I believe so," Conde admitted, and told him about his premonition.

After that moment, the easy part began. And because of that, an hour later, a sweaty Manuel Palacios was alongside Conde when the intercom's metallic voice asked for the visitor to identify himself. It was Manolo who responded.

"It's the police. Open up . . ."

The words worked like a magic spell, and the electric sound of the lock opened by remote control almost overlapped with Manolo's final demand. Meanwhile, on the porch, the figure of Frau Bertha was visible next to the solid wood door of the dazzling mansion.

Manolo, determined to take control, approached the woman and showed her his badge.

"Hello. We came to speak with Yovany González."

The woman's Germanic face turned almost red.

"What did he do now?"

"We're looking into that," Manolo limited himself to saying.

"And is this gentleman a policeman or is he not a policeman?" the luxury maid asked, referring to Conde.

"No, Frau Bertha . . . I was, I already told you," Conde reminded her.

"Frau Bertha?" The woman didn't understand anything, but she preferred not to attempt comprehension. "That kid is always getting into trouble . . . I'll go find him. Sit down."

If the outside of the dwelling had made Major Palacios sweat, the interior, despite the cyclonic insistence of the ceiling fans, had him on the verge of melting.

"How much money is there on these walls, Conde?" he asked, looking at the works of art surrounding him.

"Hundreds of thousands, I'd say . . . Less than *a lot* . . ." he added.

"And you really think that this kid . . . ? Living in this house? What could he need . . . ?"

"The mysteries of the human soul, Manolo. Incidentally, let me be the one to try to reveal them . . ."

Manolo, who loved interrogating suspects, reluctantly agreed, perhaps convinced that he didn't have enough of a grasp of the territory in which that conversation would move.

Yovany, with his light-haired curtain falling over his right eye, looked at them from the entrance to the dining room. He was barefoot and wearing flowered shorts and a mauve-colored T-shirt. Around his neck, like some kind of postmodern torture gadget, he had some headphones with padded earflaps. The presence of a uniformed police officer with bars contributed to accentuating his paleness, if that chromatic degradation was possible. *He looks like a damned replicant,* Conde thought, and waited for him to get closer.

"We have to speak with you, Yovany . . . And if your mother isn't here, we prefer that this woman be present," he said, and pointed to a seat for Frau Bertha, who was looking at them from a respectful but interested distance.

"What happened now?" the boy asked.

Conde waited for the maid, without a doubt violating orders by the owners, to take a seat in the living room.

"Let's make it clear that this is just a conversation, eh . . . ? Well, there's something I've been wanting to ask you for days," Conde began. "Is your father's name Abilio González?"

When they heard the question, the faces and colors of Yovany and the presumed German governess recovered their altered balance.

"Is that why you came to see me? What happened to the dude?" Yovany asked with a small smile already on his lips.

"You didn't answer me . . . Is his name Abilio González Mastreta?"

"Yes . . . That's his name. Did he die?"

"I knew it, dammit! Now, what's this about him dying?!" Conde exclaimed, with the joy of victory. Yovany smiled, relaxed, Frau Bertha settled into the forbidden armchair and Manolo looked at Conde the way one looks at a crazy person or a child, and even crossed his eyes more when Conde addressed him, exulted. "Every day I prove it, dammit: it's a small world! Yovany is the son of Abilio the Crow!" And, addressing the boy, "Your father was a classmate of mine in elementary school . . . We called him the Crow, because he was so white and so tiresome . . . Wait until Rabbit finds out, he's not going to believe this."

They all smiled, even Major Palacios, accustomed to being witness to the methods of the man who had helped him so much to understand what he had shortly before qualified as "the mysteries of the human soul."

"Well, Yovany." Conde started speaking again, without ceasing to smile. "The best part of the party is over. Now we're going to clean up the shit . . ."

His tone changed imperceptibly when he asked, "Why don't you tell us now about what happened on that farm in el Cotorro the night that Judy Torres died?"

Frau Bertha raised her eyebrows and Yovany recovered his maximum paleness. Nearly the funerary white paleness that Cristina y los Stops sang about.

Conde, without asking permission, took out a cigarette and lit it. He seemed relaxed.

"Let's see, to help you think and decide . . . We have the DNA of some blood that was on Judy's clothing. If we test you, in four hours—" He looked at Manolo, who interrupted.

"In one hour . . ." the man in uniform corrected him, lying shamelessly.

"In one hour, we can find out if that blood is yours . . . So . . . Can we keep things moving here and you'll tell us?"

Mechanically, Yovany removed the headphones from his neck and placed them next to him on the sofa. His hands were shaking when he tried to place the curtain of hair falling over his face behind his ear.

"Doesn't Yovany's mother have to be here . . . ?" Frau Bertha started to ask, but Conde didn't let her finish.

"That would be fine . . . But about two months ago Yovany turned eighteen . . . He's already a man, responsible in the eyes of the law. What do you have to say to us, Yovany?"

The boy looked at Conde with an unexpected challenging attitude.

"I don't know what you're talking about . . ."

Conde listened to him and felt a wave of fear. Had he been mistaken in his conjectures? Wasn't the thing about DNA proof enough? There was only one way to know. By tightening the screws.

"You know it pretty damned well, kid . . . That scar you have on your left arm and that you tried to hide from me the other day . . . I'm sure that that's where the blood on Judy's clothing came from . . ." Conde said and could read on the young man's face that he had touched a nerve. He decided to throw himself into the void, confident he would land on his feet. "And I'm sure that with the money you steal from your mother and that your father sends you every once in a while, you bought the drug that you and Judy took that night, the drug that made you crazy, the one that first led you to rape Judy and, when you realized the mess you'd gotten yourself in, or she made you realize, you proposed that you both cut your arms to seal some kind of emo pact or I-don't-fucking-know-what, it's all the same, and you cut yourself first, but knowing full well what you were doing, because you had already done it other times. And then you cut her. But you cut her for real, opening her veins . . . And when you thought that she was about to die, you threw her in the well that, coincidentally, was there. Or not coincidentally, as you're going to explain when you yourself tell us the story and say why you went to that place, although I can already imagine . . . You went all the way there because you were really, really pissed off at Judy, because Judy, none other than Judy, the one who made you emo and put all those ideas in your head about Nirvanas, pain, hate for the body, freedom at any cost, that same Judy . . . Wanted to stop being emo."

Frau Bertha had begun to slide across the genuine leather armchair, with the risk that, at any moment, she could fall on her ass on the spotless marble-tiled floor. Yovany, meanwhile, seemed to have been consumed in just a few minutes, after having been stripped of his arrogance and self-assuredness. Conde looked at him and, without being able to help it, felt how the usual unease was beginning to creep over him as usually happened in these cases. That kid, who had had every opportunity and then some, who had enjoyed in his youth privileges and luxuries that the majority of people his age didn't even know existed—and that Conde and his own father, Abilio the Crow, could have never even dreamed of in their school days of being condemned to dragging along one lone pair of shoes for a whole year—that kid enmeshed in a libertarian tribal crusade, had fucked up his life. Forever. *The paths of redemption and freedom tend to be arduous like that,* Conde thought.

"I threw her in the well . . . But she cut herself on her own. And I didn't rape her, we slept together just because, because it happened . . ."

Manolo, who had placed himself on the edge of his seat, decided that his turn had come.

"But you gave her the drug . . ."

"That wasn't me, either . . . That Italian friend of hers had sold it to her . . . Bocelli . . . It was Judy's idea that we go to that farm. She had been there once, on one of those kids' scouting outings, and had found the well . . . She liked that place, I don't know why, since it was just pasture like any other. One of those Judy things . . . When we were there, we took those pills and . . . That's where everything got fucked-up. We lost control, we were way out of it . . . We slept together, we talked about cutting ourselves, about other lives and all that shit. Then she told me she was going to leave the emos because she had discovered another spirituality. She had discovered that God was not dead, or that He was resurrected, I'm not sure, but that He existed. That God existed . . . ! And as proof, she dared me to cut my arm. She had the scalpel, she carried it around with her . . . I was so high on the pills that I cut myself any which way . . . But she cut herself for real, she opened her veins up and down. Judy was crazy, she wanted to kill herself, she wanted to see God . . . That was her way of ceasing to be emo . . ."

"But when you threw her in the well, she was alive . . ."

"I believed she was dead, I swear to you . . . She was bleeding like crazy, she wasn't moving . . . So what was I to do? Leave her there, for the dogs and vultures to eat her?"

"What in the hell do you use your cell phone for? You could have called the police. It would've been easier to believe you then than now."

"But you have to believe me, dammit! In that shitty field, there's no cell phone coverage! Judy was crazy, completely out there with the drug, she cut herself! I don't know if she went too far or if she really wanted to fuck herself up . . ."

Yovany was shouting and crying.

"I'd like to believe you, but, man, I can't," Manolo said in a low voice, as if he were talking about inconsequential matters. "I believe that, in addition, you stole Judy's five hundred dollars. Didn't you kill her because of that?"

"No, I'm telling you no . . . She had three hundred and forty left, the rest she had spent on the drugs. I have them saved upstairs, I haven't even touched it. I put it inside the book she had with her."

Conde remembered that lost detail . . . Alma had told him that when she said goodbye to her, the last day she saw her, Judy had a book.

"What book was it?" he wanted to know, perhaps to close the circle of understanding Judy Torres.

"Dante's *Purgatory*."

Conde thought for a moment: not even that post-evolutionist Cioran, or the readings of Buddha or less still Nietzsche. Nor was it *The Inferno* or *Paradise*, but rather *Purgatory*, perhaps because that was where she thought of heading. No, it wasn't possible to close the circle around Judy: she always escaped through some crack. But Yovany would not slip away from Manolo.

"You weren't that crazy if you took the money, and if to have sex with her you put the condom on before—"

"I always put it on! Always! Even if I'm drunk or high, I put it on! You have to believe me! Upstairs, I have all of the money!"

Manolo was shaking his head. Conde was about to believe him. But that story, which he had caught when it appeared to be evaporating, had flown out of his hands. So much thinking, searching, dreaming about freedom for one to end up in jail and the other bled to death at the bottom of a well and wandering through Purgatory in search of God. What a disaster.

"Yovany." Conde returned to the conversation. "Did Judy talk to you about a big deal that her father wanted to do?"

"Yes . . . In Venezuela."

"And did she know what he would be dealing in?"

"With television sets and computers and stuff like that, right?"

"She never talked to you about a very valuable painting?"

Yovany pouted, no longer able to hold back the flood of tears.

"No, no, she didn't talk to me about any painting and I didn't cut her, I didn't cut her . . ."

Yovany had started to cry, like the boy he still really was. More than a woman's weeping, the former policeman was affected by the tears and sobs of a man. He imagined Yovany in jail. The pigs would have a feast with that pale flower. Then he noticed that he felt sick, trapped by a nauseating vertigo, as if the drunkenness of the previous night's premonition had returned to his head and his stomach to make him pay for his infinite excesses. The vomit of coffee, alcohol, and sadness made a dark and irregular star over the floor of shining marble tiles.

12

Havana, August 2008

Cuban summer, during the month of August, can become exasperating. The relentless heat, the sticky humidity that fuels perspiration and rank odors, the rains that evaporate and turn oxygen into a gas on the verge of combusting, attack and make everything worse: allergies, skin, glances, and especially moods.

Conde knew that that predatory meteorological environment was not the best to make certain decisions. But, for too many days, he had been dragging along that demand and, as he covered the well-worn path between Skinny Carlos's house and Tamara's, he made the decision: he would speak.

He had spent the first part of the evening in conversation with Carlos and Rabbit, by the shade of a bottle of rum. It ended up being a dull exchange, more weighed down by nostalgia than was healthy, as if none of the friends wanted to exit the pleasant caves of memory and face the blinding light of an aged present without much hope, now dominated by that infernal heat, to boot. At some point in the conversation, as the sweat ran down to his eyes, Conde had felt, moved by an unknown source, that his spirit couldn't keep carrying the weight he placed on it. Then he had fallen into a prolonged muteness.

Carlos, who knew him better than anyone and, besides, couldn't control his need to try to solve his friend's personal conflicts, took it upon himself to break through to him in the most subtle way he knew.

"What the hell is wrong with you, beast? Why are you so quiet, huh?"

Despite the fact that he showered three or four times a day, sprin-

kling himself with water from the yard's hose, Skinny exuded a penetrating acidic smell caused by the ignition of his corporeal mass. Conde
looked at him and felt devastated. But he did not harbor the least desire
to open the floodgates, even when he knew his friend would not give up
easily. Either he said something to him or he killed him. He looked for
an in-between solution, with the hope of escaping.

"I'm in a bad state . . . It must be because of this shitty heat . . ."

"Yes, the heat is unbearable this year," Rabbit, the most sober of the
three, backed him up. "Global warming . . . The world is getting fucked-
up, fucked-up . . ."

"But there's something else going on with you . . ." Carlos opined,
cutting off the possibility of a retreat through the apocalyptic gap Rabbit
had opened up for him.

Conde took a sip of his drink. That infamous rum really must have
been Haitian.

"It's about my marrying Tamara . . ."

Carlos looked at Rabbit with a face that said, *Where did this come
from?*

"Did she say something to you?" he asked.

"No, she hasn't said anything . . ."

"Then what?" Carlos expressed his inability to understand.

Ever since Conde discussed the subject of matrimony with Tamara,
and what had always been a dream, a possibility, a more or less predictable
end, had turned into an express plan thanks to that impulse, a feeling
of suffocation had started to prey on him, and, lately, his stomach was in
such knots that it made it difficult to breathe. The main problem lay in
the fact that even he himself didn't clearly understand the reason he was
reacting that way. Because he didn't know for sure, either, why he'd had
to knock on that door. And now, he knew less still if he should enter or
turn around and walk away. His constant desire to continue sharing his
life with that woman was still unaltered and decisive. He knew perfectly
well, besides, that getting married would only be a legal or social formality; it was all the same, as easy to enter as it was to dissolve, at least at a
given time and place. Why then that deep, petty, insidious fear? Conde
had, for himself and for the world, just one response: because, whether
he wanted to get married or not, whether he more or less accepted the
challenges of cohabitation and even trusted that Tamara would admit
him with all of his burdens (even the canine burden, made tangible by

Garbage II), once the woman became his wife, the relationship would weaken one of the few things that still belonged to him: his freedom. That of getting drunk or not, sharing his bed with a street dog, of buying or not buying books, of starving or eating, of not deciding to write, of living like a pariah, of becoming melancholy without the need to explain it to anyone . . . Even investing his time searching for an emo who in turn was in search of a resurrected God and, seemingly, harbored the hope of finding Him. The problem got complicated when Conde considered those possible losses against what could be the woman's aspirations to enjoy the calm life she always sought and that, he knew well, she would never want to give up. What about love? Might the story about love conquering all be true? Is it even capable of overcoming routines? Conde didn't believe it. Why in the hell couldn't he have let sleeping dogs lie?

"Then nothing, Skinny . . . I don't want to get married, but I don't want to lose Tamara. And if I tell her that deep down I don't want to get married, that I'm scared to try it again, maybe . . ."

Carlos finished his drink. He looked at Rabbit and then at Conde.

"Can I tell you something?"

"No," Conde said immediately.

"Well, I'm going to tell you: you got yourself into this mess . . . Now, you're fucked. But try not to be too fucked-up, my brother. We're all fucked-up enough without getting any worse . . ."

An hour later, standing in front of Tamara's house, as he looked at the concrete figures stolen from the imaginations of Picasso and Lam, capable of exerting a permanent attraction over his spirit, Conde thought through his strategy. It remained to be seen whether he didn't fuck himself up too badly.

Tamara was in the studio that had belonged to her father and later her first husband, the deceased Rafael Morín. The place where, he assumed, Conde could have the necessary comfort and privacy to undertake his always postponed literary projects: to write squalid and moving stories, like that son of a bitch Salinger who . . . The air-conditioning took the temperature down ten degrees and improved his spirits.

The woman was filling out some forms that she had to take to the dental clinic the next day.

"Let's see if they fix the dental chairs, if they put in the lights that we need, if they give us soap to wash our hands and towels to dry them, if there's always water, if they give us full sets of instruments, if the gloves arrive . . ."

"So how in the hell do you remove molars? With little pieces of string, as if they were baby teeth?" Conde didn't understand.

"Almost," Tamara admitted.

Conde took a deep breath and dove in without more delay.

"Look, I wanted to ask you something . . . I'm afraid, but I don't have any choice, because . . . Tamara, do you really want to get married *a lot*?"

Conde placed emphasis on the adverbial quantity that had been maliciously pursuing him recently. How much is wanting to get married *a lot*? The woman dropped her pen and took off her reading glasses to better concentrate. He, of course, felt a chill go through him. Of fear.

"Why do you ask?"

"Don't start, Tamara. Answer me . . ."

Now she was the one who took a deep breath.

"The truth is that it's all the same to me . . . To me, it was as if we were already married. Almost . . . But you are the one who wants to sign papers . . . And because of that, before screwing up what we have, then I'd marry you if you ask me to, if it's important to you . . ."

The feeling of relief washed through Conde's body like new blood. He felt on the verge of happiness.

"Well, Tamara, I propose the following: if we're fine like this, isn't it better to let sleeping dogs lie?"

"What about the ring?" she said, alarmed.

"It's yours. Keep using it."

"What about morning coffee?"

"That will still be up to me."

Tamara smiled.

"What about everything else?"

"The rest is all yours . . . But whenever you want, we can use it."

Tamara stood up.

"Why are you so soft and so complicated, Mario Conde?"

"Because I'm a moron," he said, and kissed her. It was a long kiss, wet, exciting more due to the mental relief than to the hormonal convergence. And at that moment, Conde even felt like he wanted to marry that woman whom the most pleasant of cosmic plans had placed in his path, *a lot.* But, for the moment, he kicked aside that desire and concentrated on his remaining desires.

Outside, the heat was burning the city, its streets, its houses. It was even burning its people and the few dreams that they could still have.

————

With asphalt separating them, from that corner of Calle Mayía Rodríguez he could look at, in just one glance, the two-story building in which, until just a few weeks prior, Judy Torres had lived and, in the distance, the ruinous project that the house had become where Daniel Kaminsky had lived the happiest years of his life, and where he had also recovered the feeling of fear. After several years without feeling compelled to dig around in anyone's life, in the span of just a few months, two stories of death had come out to meet him, moved by the same spring: the one that had released a Jewish Pole who had ceased to believe in God, and taken it upon himself to be Cuban who, at the most arduous crossroad of his life, believed himself to have the sufficient strength to kill a man who had held his parents' and his sister's lives in his hands. And those stories, seemingly remote, had had one of their points of visible convergence at precisely that Havana corner, a physical space that Conde now devoted himself to looking up as he wiped his face dampened by the sweat being pulled from his deepest insides by the shameless heat of August, and asked himself about the ways in which the life paths of different and distant people were created, progressed, twisted, and even converged. The most disturbing thing however was not the casual proximity of the two buildings or the connection that, without meaning to, young Yadine had fostered, or even the recurring presence of a work painted by Rembrandt three centuries before. What most alarmed him was the coincidence of motivations revealed by the knowledge that he now possessed of the lives and hopes of Daniel Kaminsky and Judith Torres, those two beings' insistence—each one in their own way and within its possibilities—on finding their own territory, chosen with sovereignty, a refuge in which they could feel like the owners of themselves, without external pressures. And the consequences, at times so painful, that such yearnings for freedom could cause.

The feeling of disapproval, of himself and the whole world, caused by the discovery of the final truths about Judy had not left him for several weeks, although it had begun to recede with time, as could be expected. To accelerate the process and finish ripping that grimy burden from his soul, Conde had decided to distance himself from the only material evidence that connected him to the young girl, and resolved to return to Alma Turró, the dead girl's grandmother, Judy's address book and the copy of *Blade Runner* that, by almost poetic association, had opened the path to the truth. Because of that, from the corner, he was looking at the two houses, with the address book and the plastic DVD case in his hands, focused on thinking, without daring to act.

If he entered that house and spoke with Alma Turró, what could he say to her? Judy was dead, in part through her own will, in part because of the libertarian fundamentalism that she was capable of awakening in others, but dead and buried, and her grandmother already knew the details of the denouement. And any consolation, as far as Conde knew, had never brought anyone back to life. The house's inhabitants, who could have been an ordinary family, had turned into victims of dispersion. One was dead, another was in Miami, another was in jail accused of a long list of crimes of corruption. Alma and her daughter were damaged, surely depressed, and with reason. Celestial vengeance for sins committed in the past and continued in the present? The satanic price that deceit and ambition must or should pay? Divine punishment for Judy's insistence that God was dead and buried and finally recycled . . . ? The atheist that, despite everything, Conde carried inside of him was not willing to admit transcendental Olympic organizations but rather strings of cause and effect that were much more pedestrian. You can't play with what doesn't belong to you: not with money and less still with the hopes and souls of others. If you do so, always, at some point (sometimes very delayed, it's true), the arrow of punishment will be released, he concluded philosophically.

He then opted for one of his furtive hunter exits. He entered the porch, walked to the main door of the house trying not to make any noise, and deposited the plastic case and the small book against the white-painted wood. And he fled like a fugitive. He needed to run, distance himself as much as possible from that regrettable story.

He lit a cigarette and quickened his pace along the slope of Mayía Rodríguez toward the house of Tamara, who was again simply his girlfriend, feeling himself freed of all burdens. When he arrived, out of breath and damp, he greeted the concrete sculptures and opened the door. Just by putting one foot over the threshold, he had to recognize that, at least for him, that small territory was the best of all possible worlds. *What are you complaining about . . . ? About life: I have to complain about something,* he told himself, and closed the door behind him.

Genesis

Havana, April 2009

In his fifty-five years, Mario Conde had never been to Amsterdam (nor anywhere else outside the four walls of his island). The strangest thing was that, throughout what was turning out to be a drawn-out existence, he had never even considered it in a more or less serious or possible way. As a boy, it is true, he had dreamed of traveling to Alaska. Yes, Alaska, with a party of gold-seekers. As an adult, a reader, and would-be writer, he thought that sometimes he would like to visit Paris, but, above all, to travel around Italy, as his deceased friend Iván had also dreamed. But they were always just dreams, unattainable with his means and as a citizen of a country whose borders were practically closed off by walls of decrees and prohibitions, as Judy would remind him. And, he knew, dreams themselves are only dreams. Because of that, like other immobile travelers, he devoted himself to journeying the world through books, and felt satisfied.

But the letter he had just read had stirred some unexpected desires to get to know Amsterdam, a city riddled with past and present myths where, they said, an unusual atmosphere of freedom had been established at one point and this place still prided itself on its pleasant tolerance of faces and virtues, beliefs and disbeliefs. This was the city where the rebellious Rembrandt had displayed his pride, his fame, his irascible nature, and always his marginalization and final poverty, perhaps conscious, nonetheless, that one day he would return triumphant and even in a position to return to the house from which his creditors had expelled him. Because that building from which he had to depart defeated, with his head down, could not be anything but Rembrandt's house. Fate's dirty tricks and reparations always arrived with delay.

Mario Conde, although he had never reached the rank of colonel, was also one of those people to whom no one wrote. Because of that, it had been a hundred years since he received a *real* letter. Not a telephone bill or a note like the one sent by Andrés nearly two years before. No. A *real* letter: with an envelope, stamps and postmarks, an address and return address, and of course with written pages inside the envelope and . . . delivered by a mailman.

The return address on the yellow envelope, medium-sized, belonged to none other than Elias Kaminsky, under whose name appeared the address of the Seven Bridges hotel in Amsterdam, Kingdom of the Netherlands. Without opening the sheath that the mailman placed in his grateful hands, Conde had gone to the kitchen of the house, prepared his coffeepot, and looked for his pack of cigarettes. He was so intrigued by the matter of the letter hidden by that manila envelope that, quite on purpose, he prolonged the anxiety of learning its contents, to better enjoy such a rare feeling. Since his departure from Cuba, the painter had called him several times. First to thank him for his help during his stay in Havana that had freed him of so many burdens; then to tell him that he had begun a legal process to recover the Rembrandt painting; later to fill him in on some of the turns of events of the litigation, which had gained new momentum with the information regarding the possible route that the damned painting had taken on its journey from Havana to a British auction house.

His coffee served, Conde carefully slit open the envelope and withdrew a tourist postcard and a wad of sheets, some handwritten on both sides. He spent several minutes looking at the printed card with a photo of the house where Rembrandt had lived for years, on the street then known as Jewish Broad Street, long ago turned into a museum. And he felt the first hint of what could cause him to feel the desire for more intimate knowledge of the sanctuary where that disconcerting painter had created so many works, including the head of the young Jew too similar to the Christian image of Jesus of Nazareth, which, without Conde having asked for it, had gotten stuck in his own head. His mood, perhaps softened by that feeling of closeness, led to his spirit—a few minutes later, as he was reading the pages of the letter and almost without his noticing— flying after the words, until he felt how they surrounded him and were dragging him through some remote worlds that Conde only knew by name and through his readings. *Incidentally,* he would think a little later, *now I have to reread* Red Cavalry. *Wasn't Isaac Babel also Jewish?*

———

Spring in Amsterdam hands itself over like a gift from the Creator. The city is revived, shaking itself from the slumber of ice and cold winter winds that, for months, beat down on the city and oppress its inhabitants, its animals, its flowers. Although temperatures were still significantly low, the shining April sun occupied many hours of the day and the feeling of rebirth became tangible, widespread. Elias Kaminsky, since he already knew and had enjoyed that epiphany that nature tends to gift, had decided to wait until the season's arrival to travel to the city where everything had begun, before the seventeenth century had reached its midpoint and when Amsterdam was forging the glorious moments of the golden age of Dutch painting.

Elias Kaminsky thought and wrote that perhaps because of one of those many cosmic plans that had appeared throughout Jewish history—and in the drama in which he himself had been caught up and had even tangled up Conde—he had organized his visit to the city precisely when an incredible event was being revealed. Just next to the house where Rembrandt had lived, in the Zwanenburgwal flea market selling old tin pitchers, candelabras missing an arm, bronze lamp stands, and sets of glasses and dinnerware as ancient as they were incomplete, an old document collector had purchased, just a few months prior and for a ridiculous price, a *tafelet* or sketchbook belonging to a presumed seventeenth-century student of painting, judging by the quality of the sketches and the dominant style. On the book's leather cover, ill-preserved by time, appeared the engraved letters *E.A.*

That *tafelet* contained several studies of the head of a bearded elderly man, obviously Jewish, since in several of the nib-pen or pencil sketches, he was crowned by a kippah or basking in the light of a menorah. In order of quantity, in various states of completion, there appeared a young woman, about twenty years old, portrayed from several angles but with the harmony of her features always standing out with an insistence on contouring her eyes and gaze. The notebook also contained several landscapes—rather, sketches of a muddy countryside, perhaps close to Amsterdam—that much recalled the style of some of Rembrandt's sketches and engravings with that subject matter. But what would inspire the buyer's greatest interest and later that of classic Dutch painting specialists to whom the antiquarian had immediately handed over the sketchbook to be studied and analyzed were the nine portraits of a young man, of markedly Hebrew characteristics, whose features offered an unsettling likeness to that of the anonymous model Rembrandt used for a series of *tronies* of Christ or portraits of a young Jew, as they have been equally called. Could it be possible that it was the same model, used by both Rembrandt and the apprentice? The question appeared and immediately grew to unexpected proportions. And the existence of the strange sketchbook, bearer of other secrets and mysteries, reached the ears of Elias Kaminsky almost at the same moment he arrived in the city.

Since the *tafelet* was taken apart to submit it to a variety of laboratory tests by the specialists at the Rijksmuseum, a secret door was opened: beneath one of the battered leather covers, several handwritten pages were found. It was undoubtedly a letter, whose first part was missing, although the entire second part was intact. The text, written with exquisite calligraphy, in seventeenth-century Dutch, was signed by the same E.A. to whom, based on the cover, the *tafelet* must have belonged, and narrated an episode of a pogrom in Poland between the years 1648 and 1653, of which E.A. had been a witness and, for some reason, aimed to involve his "Maestro," as he called the addressee of that missive. Elias Kaminsky, sharing his speculations and conclusions with Conde, at that point of his narration, transcribed a fragment of the letter found in the *tafelet*, according to the translation made by a specialist in seventeenth-century Dutch Sephardic culture . . . And he asked forgiveness for what he would make him read. More intrigued by that request for mercy, Conde began reading the fragment of the found letter, but without being able to glimpse the darkness of the human condition that he would be forced to stare down into from the first to the last lines of what was written.

. . . I cannot stop hearing the cries of panic of some men driven insane by fear, pushed to undertake a desperate flight. Beings driven away by the vision of the most atrocious torture to which a human being can subject another, warned of their fate by the stench of charred human flesh, blood, and carrion that has taken over that unfortunate country. You will soon understand the reasons for which they flee, but know that not even my greatest efforts will be capable of expressing what these men have lived, nor of drawing the images that their stories have hung in my soul. Not even the great Dürer, who alarmed us so with his infernal visits, considered by many to be the by-products of a sick mind, would have had sufficient mastery to portray what has happened and is happening in these lands. No imagination would be able to journey as deeply into horror as what has occurred here in reality.

Like them, I will also depart, as soon as possible, but in the opposite direction, in search of an improbable breach that will perhaps lead me to atone for all of my mistakes and perhaps even witness the greatest of miracles. Or which will lead me to death.

But first allow me to put things in context. Due to the conversations I had during the first weeks of my stay in this country, I managed to learn something of the customs of the Israelites who live in great quantities in this kingdom. It surprised me greatly when I learned of the very advantageous situation that they have enjoyed in these lands for years, the reason for which numerous Ashkenazi Jews coming from territories in the East, including the Russia of the czars, had come to settle in its cities, many having seemed to amass notable fortunes. Among them, a curious maxim went around which, they maintained, reflected their position very well: Poland, they said, was the paradise of the Jews, the inferno of the country folk, and the purgatory of the commoners . . . All controlled from above by the nobles, the so-called princes, lords of the land and of souls. According to what I learned, the belief that that Jewish paradise existed was based on the confirmation of a political statute much more benevolent than any which could exist in another country in Europe. In this kingdom, the sons of Israel enjoyed a very notable freedom of religious practice, led by countless rabbis, learned men deeply familiar with the Torah and commentators on the Kabbalah, considered community leaders. However, in contrast to what happens in Amsterdam, there existed for these Jews, as much by Byzantine Christians, the so-called Orthodox ones (they tend to be the poorest Poles), as by Roman Christians, a hostility that has its origins in the fact that the best-known work of these Ashkenazi Jews has been that of serving as money lenders to the princes' class and, at the same time, of tax and payment collectors to the country folk. The method applied is very simple and petty: the nobles take money from the Hebrews and then pay them with the debts from the people who work in their lands, leaving the management of getting paid in the hands of the Hebrews. As you can imagine, with the Jews as the collectors of some onerous dues, in the minds of the country folk, they are the oppressors, and not the princes, who are Polish, noble, and believe in Christ, although they pay for their luxuries and eccentricities with money borrowed from the sons of Israel.

The recent death of the country's monarch, King Wladyslaw IV, of the royal house of Vasa, had already awakened the concern of those Ashkenazi Jews. The king, who was on the throne for more than fifty years, maintained a policy of tolerance toward the Jews. When he died, he was the Monarch of the so-called Polish-Lithuanian Commonwealth, placed as king of Sweden and at one point in the past even came to be the czar of Russia. The Poles say that his death left them like a flock without a shepherd, since until the pivotal problems of succession are resolved, the country has been left without a head and internally, the scepter is held by the Catholic cardinal Casimir, whom my brothers in faith have always considered a wise and pious man.

When winter began to recede, I at last began my delayed voyage to the South. Still riding over snow, I had some Ashkenazi Jews as guides who were traveling toward the kingdom's capital. After a couple days' rest in the city of Warsaw, I returned to the road, always in the direction that would best lead me to the region of Crimea, bathed by what is called here the Black Sea, from where I would try to fulfill my dream of reaching Italy.

Two weeks I spent getting to the city where I find myself today, called Zamość, and to which I arrived on the eve of the holiday of Purim, whose celebration was prepared for with great joy by the very considerable Jewish community in this village. But I had just arrived when alarming news came fast at my heels: the so-called Cossacks from the south had rebelled against the Polish princes and, with the help of a mob of Crimean Tartars, had sent the royal army's border detachments running. For me, at that moment, the enormous concern caused by that news was a great surprise, as much among Poles as among Hebrews. Today, I now know that, because it dealt with those so-called Cossacks, the consequences of the revolt could be much more complicated.

Sir, these so-called Cossacks are like centaurs of war. They say their origins as a military power are due to King Sigismund, who governed over Poland about a hundred years ago. Knowing that the border with the country of the Tartars had always been a problem for the kingdom, the monarch had thirty thousand serfs chosen from that region and made an army: that of the Cossacks. For their services, those men received the privileges of not paying tribute to the king or the princes. But it was precisely the concession of those privileges that became the cause for the Cossacks very quickly beginning to lead revolts in which they claimed equal rights for other men to join their parties.

The current rebellion began developing a few years ago due to disputes between Prince Choraczy, general of the Polish army, and a military chief, the ataman, as the Cossacks call them, a certain Bogdan Chmielnicki. This man, also known as Chmiel, communicates, like almost all countryfolk, with the Byzantine church, despite having studied with the Jesuits and, they say, he speaks Polish, Russian, Ukrainian, and Latin, and came to become Ataman thanks to his raids and ferocity as well as for the immensity of his possessions. His prosperity was such that he ended up inspiring the prince's envy, who resolved to eliminate him. Because of that, Choraczy confiscated half of Chmiel's livestock and the Cossack did not protest, but swore to take revenge. The Jews of Zamość say that the ataman's tactic was to go to the South and alert the Crimean Tartars about the secret intentions of the Polish general, who, he told them, soon aimed to wage war against them. With the Tartars placed on a war footing, Choraczy had to flee, since his forces were very inferior compared to those of his neighbors.

Apprised of the move, the prince put Chmiel in jail and ordered his decapitation for acts of treason. But the Cossacks decided to rescue the ataman. Then Chmiel declared himself in rebellion and, with his pals, organized a great band of poor country folk, more than twenty thousand men, under the banner of a battle against the despotism of the princes and the abuses of their Jewish allies, who had become rich off the work of the country-folk of the Orthodox faith.

Before throwing themselves into combat against the princes' armies, Chemiel made an alliance with the king of the Tartars—the khan, they called him—thanks to which they raised a legion of sixty thousand men between them with whom they began their rebellion attacking the army summoned by Choraczy, whom they disbanded. As could be expected, the victors, drunk with success, then unleashed their cruelty against their opponents and carried out a great quantity of decapitations, kidnappings, rapes, and confiscations of goods, from Catholics as well as Jews. To stop the killing, several princes from small Russia decided to make a pact with Chmiel, and came to swear fidelity to the ataman as they had previously sworn to the king.

You can imagine, Maestro, the tension among the people of that city when that news arrived, and more so, when a few days after Purim, Chmiel and his Cossacks began what some of them called a holy war, which, as Chmiel announced, will not abate until they put an end to the exploitation by the parasitic princes and their Jewish front men.

All of the information that I have accumulated since then I have heard in person from some Jews who managed to escape from the cities of Nemirov, Tulczyn, or Polanów and found refuge in Zamosc, where I see myself trapped by the events. At the beginning, as I listened to them, I refused to accept that the barbarities they relayed were real and not a nightmare forged by the confusions of miscommunication . . . Because the horror that was unleashed at last past 20th of Adar, Shabbat, when Cossacks and Tartars, in numbers surpassing a hundred thousand, approached the city of Nemirov, where they have told me that, in a climate of prosperity, there used to live (and it is not by coincidence that I use the past tense) a very rich and large Jewish community, adorned with the presence of important scholars and scribes. When these Jews learned that an army, larger than they had ever seen, was approaching the city, even when they were unaware of whether they were dealing with Polish troops or mobs of Cossacks and Tartars, they chose to take refuge with their families and wealth in the fortified citadel. Other Jews, less confident, preferred to leave their homes and many of their goods behind to await the development of events far away.

Only when they no longer had any salvation did the Jews of Nemirov come to know that, while they and the princes were confining themselves in the citadel, the ataman Chmiel had sent a group of men to the city to ask the citizens for their help against the Jews responsible for all of their misfortunes. That alliance concluded, the Cossacks, raising Polish flags, approached the walls disguising themselves as men from the king's army, while the city's inhabitants announced that those arriving were Polish soldiers and they opened the gates to the citadel.

It was then that, all at once, the Cossacks, the Tartars, and Nemirov's inhabitants unleashed their hate and thirst for loot and entered in pursuit of the Jews with all possible weapons. They immediately massacred a great number of Hebrew men and raped the women, regardless of age. They say that many young girls, to avoid dishonor, leapt into the cistern providing water to the citadel and drowned to death there. But, when the attackers took over the square, so many men dead already and women raped, that was when the true horror began: the cold and perverse horror of a crime without humanity . . . Drunk on hate, alcohol, and the desire for revenge, the Cossacks then handed themselves over to carry out the most incredible ways of causing suffering and death. They ripped the skin off of some men and threw the flesh to the dogs; they cut the hands and feet off of others and threw their bodies in the path to the citadel so that the horses would stomp on them until they died; and still more were forced to dig graves, then thrown alive into them and beaten with shovels until they issued their last groan of pain; some others were quartered alive, or slit open like fish and hung in the sun . . . But every rung on the ladder of cruelty had not yet been covered: they opened the bellies of any women who were pregnant and removed the fetuses; they cut the bellies of others and put cats inside, although, before this, they took the precaution of cutting off their hands so that they could not take out the animals stirring inside of them. Some children were beaten to death or thrown against walls and then roasted in the fire and brought to their mothers to force them to eat them, while their executioners announced, "It's kosher meat, it's kosher meat, we bled them first . . ." According to the rabbi who brought the news to Zamość, there was no way to bring about death that was not used against them. More than six thousand sons of Israel were killed in Nemirov during that bestial orgy of sadism practiced in the name of faith and justice. The most terrible thing is that they were massacred without any one of them offering resistance, since they considered their fall into disgrace a celestial decision.

Many women were taken captive by the Tartars, who take them to their lands as servants, or as wives and concubines, announcing that they can be freed if someone pays a ransom . . . But while some Cossacks and Tartars participate in executions or rapes, others occupy themselves in seizing the scrolls of the Torah, which were broken apart, to make bags and socks with them. They rolled up the threads of the phylactery in their feet, like trophies. They used the holy books to make walkways on the roads.

As we listened to Samuel's story, that is the name of the surviving rabbi who arrived in Zamość, the worst is that all of us knew that that massacre, which took place in the holy community of Nemirov, represented just the beginning of a slaughter without any foreseeable end, since the strength of the Cossacks and Tartars could only be stopped by the most impregnable walls and, a long time off, by the presence of a Polish army whose arrival to these lands had not yet been spied. And because I must tell you now that the tragic fate of Nemirov, as we foretold, turns out to be just the prologue of a horror story whose next chapter took place in the city of Tulczyn.

At the same time that Chemiel, whom they have started to call "The Pursuer," focused on destroying small communities on the banks of the Dnieper River, one of his representatives, known as Divonov, went to Tulczyn with the mission of taking it. When they found out Divonov's purpose, the two thousand Jews taking refuge in Tulczyn and the Polish princes banded together to fight them, after swearing not to betray one another. They fortified the citadel and with their weapons they took their posts at the walls, at the same time that the Orthodox joined the ranks of the invaders. The Cossacks, meanwhile, loaded up on battering rams: they say it was like a sea of men, thousands upon thousands, who advanced uttering extraordinary shrieks, capable in and of themselves of intimidating the most courageous. But those who were defending the walls of Tulczyn, since they were fighting for their lives, managed to repel them.

In the face of that unexpected resistance, Divonov decided to change tactics. The crafty Cossacks proposed peace to the princes, promising them not only their lives but also that they could keep the Jewish loot. Seeing that the situation was not sustainable for long, the princes accepted the treaty, under the condition that the lives of the Jews would also be administered by them. The Jews, who soon realized the betrayal of which they were the object, decided to resist by force, but the leader of the community gathered them and told them that if the taking of the city was a decision by the Holiest, they had to accept it with resignation: they were not worth more than their brothers in Nemirov, who died as martyrs . . . Thus, compelled by the rabbi to accept their destiny, or crushed by the evidence that their fate had been decreed by the impossibility of escape, the Jews handed over all of their goods. The princes, satisfied with their earnings, at last opened the doors of the fortress to the Cossacks. The duke who served as the chief of the nobles, a man so fat that he could barely move, told the victors: here you have the city; here is our payment. Immediately, the princes took what was due to them from the arrangement and put the Jews in jail, they said to better protect them.

Three days later, the Cossacks demanded that the princes hand over the prisoners to them and, without thinking much about it, they agreed, since they did not want to make enemies of the invaders. The Cossacks took the Jews to a walled garden and left them there for a while. Among the prisoners, there were several eminent teachers, who exhorted the people to sanctify His name and not change religion under any circumstance, reminding them that the end of time was coming and the salvation of their souls was in their hands. Why did they not incite them to fight for their lives, with sticks, with stones, with their hands? Why the resignation, submission before insurrection? The Cossacks, who knew those sermons, decided to test the Israelites' moral fortitude and told them that whoever changed their religion would be saved, and the rest would die tortured beyond words. They even announced it three times, but none of those Jews, who had not rebelled, agreed to deny their God. The Cossacks, irritated, entered the garden and, without further delay, began the killing of the defenseless . . . In just a few hours, they annihilated about one thousand five hundred people, massacring them in the most incredible ways which I will omit mentioning since they are known and the very act of writing them is so painful. Thanks to the intervention of the Tartars, Cossacks left ten rabbis alive and withdrew from the city with the young women, the rabbis, and a part of the booty, mainly the gold and pearls the Israelites had amassed. A few days later, it became known that those rabbis had been saved thanks to a very high ransom that arrived from the rich community of Polanów.

But the Cossacks were annoyed, since, apart from the blood that they so love to see run, they received barely any benefit from taking that city. For it, they broke the pact with the princes, willing to recover the loot. To begin their macabre diversions, they lit the fortress on fire, then took the Jewish loot hoarded by the Catholics and left the torture of the princes for the end. As they so enjoyed, Divonov and his men were merciless with some of them, especially the duke of the city, the same one who had opened the doors to them. They raped the nobleman's wife and two daughters in front of him, and then amused themselves dishonoring him, until a miller of the Orthodox faith took things into his own hands and, after reminding them of the state of slavery to which he had subjected the poor people of the region, exhibited him nude throughout the city, like a fattened pig, and after flogging him endlessly and sodomizing him with a stick, they decapitated him with a sword right in the middle of the street.

We had just received the news of this massacre when several Jews arrived in Zamość who had escaped from the Cossacks' incursions on the other side of the Dnieper River, where the events of Nemirov and Tulczyn had repeated themselves. According to those survivors, Chmiel the Pursuer already had an army of five hundred thousand souls and, in fact, controlled all of Little Russia, and at this pace, like the tenth plague, he not only killed Jews but also destroyed churches and tortured the priests. This last piece of news sounded like the trilling of birds in the ears of the Jews, since, when they learned it, the princes decided not to believe again in Chmiel's pleas for peace, and not to repeat the mistake of Tulczyn that led them to hand over the Jews to their mutual enemy.

After listening to the news coming from the Polish side, I was able to understand in all of its dimensions why the country's inhabitants were crying over the death of King Wladyslaw IV and felt that the kingdom was like a flock without a shepherd. Perhaps the misfortunes that took place these weeks had to occur for Cardinal Casimir to decide on the intervention by the kingdom's army and give the order to all the princes to prepare their men and get ready for war, under threat of losing their condition and goods if they refused. The fate of the murdered noblemen of Nemirov and Tulczyn and of the fathers of the Church influenced greatly in taking that position, but I estimate that a reality has also weighed into that as well, as has happened in other known countries, and has brought such evil to the sons of Israel: being the moneylenders to the kingdom. Because, if the Cossacks and the Tartars run away with all of the Jews' money, this country will be ruined. It is clear that the deaths and fleeing of the Hebrews, in addition to the raids of their goods, would greatly affect life in the kingdom and especially its noblemen and leaders. Would that that money serve as the source of our salvation today rather than the basis of our perdition, as happened to us in Spain.

A few days ago, after we found out about the fate of Tulczyn and other cities on the eastern shore of the Dnieper, the surviving rabbi from Nemirov, who responds to the name of Rabbi Samuel, allowed me to have a talk with him. We sat close to some watchtowers, in the high part of the city. The landscape at our feet seemed to be of insulting beauty to me, so calm in the middle of the panorama of pain this country is experiencing. Summer has arrived with all of its splendor to this region of Little Russia, a territory of immense plains and mighty rivers, where riches sprout from the earth prodigiously, but where injustice, misery, and hunger have been capable of generating hate, fanaticism, and the desire for the cruelest revenge among men.

I conversed with Rabbi Samuel for hours. Ever since I heard him speak at the synagogue, he seemed like a pious man to me. He is a man who feels guilty for having managed to escape with his life while his family was devoured by the fury that destroyed

Nemirov. For those reasons, as I spoke to him, I reaffirmed myself in the idea that he could be the suitable person to fulfill a need that had become urgent for me: to confess to someone the true reasons for which I have come to be in these lands from where, I feel it more every day, I will never be able to leave. Unless the Holiest has another plan and allows me to carry out what, learning what I have learned, is now my only purpose: joining the troops of Sabbatai Zevi. Maestro: the barbarism and horror unleashed here have persuaded me that, as certain Kabbalists announce, the end of time could be near and Sabbatai could well be the Anointed, arrived on earth when it moans in pain, like a mother who sees her child die . . . It is only thus that I can explain to myself that the God of Israel, all-powerful, can allow His children to be the objects of the most inconceivable cruelty. Only if the punishment is part of a cosmic plan that leads to redemption . . . Isn't it thus, Lord?

When I set off on my story, the rabbi listened to me silently and finally told me he regretted what had happened to me and that I so easily—according to him—could have avoided it by accepting my mistakes and making a public petition for forgiveness for my confused interpretations of the Law. When I thought of rebutting him, the kindness I had thought I saw in him came to the surface, since he told me that, in his opinion, the mentioned possibility of joining Zevi's followers, in Palestine, seemed the most pertinent: my personal problems with God could be overcome with that proof of faith. And, to leave me without any options for controversy, he added: after what he had seen in Nemirov, what had happened in the communities along the Dnieper and in Tulczyn, my heresies seemed like such a minor shortcoming that no one should have even noticed them and, in contrast, they should think more about the reasons for which humans are so given to devouring one another.

When the rabbi confided to me that he had chosen to continue his voyage to the North, I asked if he could do me the favor of taking from Zamość and safely delivering a letter that I wanted to reach my Maestro. Then the rabbi asked me something that seemed to make him doubt: "Why do you write all of that to your Maestro and not to your teacher Ben Israel or one of the rabbis in your city? They would better understand what is happening here and could turn it into a lesson for the community." At first I thought he was right, I even concluded that in truth, I didn't have a very clear idea of why I wanted to write that letter and, besides, I had chosen you and not, for example, my own father or my beloved Mariam, much less my Hakham. It was at that juncture that I dared to take a further step and removed from the saddlebags with which I carry the ark where I keep your painting, the landscape Keil the Dane gave me, and a pair of my works that I decided to maintain with me because they are especially beloved. Showing him the portraits you made of me, I responded, "Because the Maestro is a man who is capable of painting something like this." The rabbi took the linen and fell into contemplating it. His silence was so prolonged that I had time to conceive of too many insane notions, the first, that that man was going to accuse me of idolatry for having allowed myself to serve as the model for that painting, and, above all, for preserving it with me. But the response he gave me was an enigmatic relief: "I now understand you," and he returned the linen to me, to then ask me to show him my own works. Very ashamed, although at the same time with pride, I unfolded the paper on which I had sketched my grandfather and the canvas with Mariam's face, conscious that I was submitting myself to an inevitable comparison that I would never dare to carry out. With the sketch in which I drew my grandfather in his hands, he asked me about him and I told him a little bit about his life. Lastly, he contemplated the portrait of Mariam Roca, and when he noticed my mood, he told me that he already knew who that young woman was, and began to collect the linens and papers, as he recommended to me that I not be exhibiting them, less still in those times.

Two days later, after the morning Shabbat prayers, Rabbi Samuel asked me if we could talk for a while and we went to a small square in the city in the middle of which there is a great stone cross. We sat down on some steps and his initial phrase caused me some surprise logically: "Would you let me see the painting by your Maestro again?" Without imagining the meaning of that demand, I took out the ark and unrolled the linen to hand it to him. "I have been thinking a lot about what you told me regarding your dream of becoming a painter," he said to me, after looking at the linen for a moment. "And what have you been thinking?" I wanted to know. "I have been thinking about how many things we sons of Israel should change to achieve a happier life in our transit on earth . . . If my rabbi colleagues in Nemirov heard me say this, they would think I am crazy or that I have become a heretic. But I myself think like this: we men cannot live condemning one another merely because some think one way and others, a different way. There are inviolable Commandments relating to good and evil, but there is also a lot of space in life that should be only a question of the individual. And it would be worth it for man to manage it freely, according to his will, just as it is: a question between him and God . . ." he said and devoted several minutes to contemplating the painting until he spoke again: "I do not know much about this art. I have never heard of your Maestro. From what I see, I understand that he is a famous man, that kings and rich men pay for his work . . . And now I also understand why you want to make him the repository of your thoughts and experiences of these terrible days . . . Ever since you showed me this painting, you insist that it is nothing but the image of your Jewish head. But, as I contemplate it again, I have discovered that it is much more, because before it one becomes full of strange feelings. Yes, this could be the image that your Maestro has in mind of the person who, to him, was the Messiah. Since I think differently than he does, I see something else and that is what attracts me to this image . . . There is something intimate and mysterious, an unsettling layer below the surface that comes from that face and from that gaze. It is a combination of humanity and transcendence. It is obvious, your Maestro has a power. He achieved so much with so little that I have no doubt that behind his hand there must lie the will of the Creator. It is not strange to me that you would have wanted to imitate him. The attraction that the human being feels before the infinite beauty of the sacred must be unbearable. Because this is the sacred," the rabbi concluded, and caressed the linen.

Dear Maestro: this wise man confirmed for me at that moment the answer that I have sought for years. For him, seeing your work, there was something that was obvious: art is power.

Only that, or especially that: power. Not to control countries and change societies, to cause revolutions or oppress others. It is the power to touch the souls of men and, incidentally, place there the seeds of their improvement and happiness . . . Because of that, ever since I heard Rabbi Samuel speak of your work, I was convinced that there cannot be a better man in the world to take this letter out of Zamość. I have asked him that, with it, he remit to you the painting that belongs to you. With my poor works, which I will also hand over to him, I have told him that he can do what he feels best, to which he responded: "Keep them until we see each other again. In this world or the next, if in fact we are called . . ."

Yesterday, Rabbi Samuel said goodbye to the sons of Israel who remain in Zamość with a prayer in the synagogue of the high city. He urged all of us to escape from the city and it appears that many will follow his advice. The events that we have received news of in recent days warn with too much clarity that remaining in these lands constitutes a suicide act, because just a few days ago, as we recently learned, it fell upon the holy community of Polanów to be tortured, where about twelve thousand Jews, along with two thousand men of the Polish princes, decided to resist the attack of the Cossack and Tartar forces. They trusted in the double line of walls and the water moats that, they said, made the city impregnable. But the prince's serfs, of the Orthodox religion, facilitated the entry to the besiegers. They say that ten thousand Jews died in one day alone . . .

When they learned of Polanów's fate and the defeat that the Polish Army immediately suffered, the Jews living in the nearby town of Zaslav decided to flee. The majority of them went to Ostrog, the stronghold and metropolis of Little Russia, and others ended up in Zamość, bearing this discouraging news and a new one, which reaffirms the messianic and apocalyptic warnings: the outbreak of a plague epidemic, blooming in the unburied human flesh and now latching onto live flesh.

The recently arrived say that the Jews of Zaslav fled in a stampede. Those who could left by horse and wagon, the poorest ones by foot, with their wives and children. As is already occurring in Zamość, they left in the city many of their belongings, everything they had amassed in their lives of work and observance of the

Law. And as they fled, the most irrational panic spread when someone said that their executioners were coming behind them. Desperate to advance more quickly, they threw to the fields golden cups, silver adornments, clothing, without any of the Jews coming behind them stopping to pick anything up . . . But, no matter how quickly they ran, the moment came in which they felt on the verge of being reached by the Cossacks and to save themselves they stampeded through the woods, leaving behind even their wives and children, since they could only think about not falling into the hands of their pursuers. Except that the fetid breath of the most horrible of deaths felt at the backs of their heads ended up being just a part of what these Jews today consider divine punishment: because it had all been the product of a wave of panic, and the much-feared enemies in reality were not coming behind them. Yet.

Maestro, as soon as I finish this narration to which I have devoted myself for the last two days, I will hand it to Rabbi Samuel, along with your painting and some of the others I brought with me. I have made a leather case to better preserve them. I trust that this holy and wise man will save his life and, with it, the treasures I have handed to him. As far as I'm concerned, after today, I do not know what my luck holds for me. I hope that the Holiest, blessed may He be, allows me to cross the masses of barbarism and arrive at my destination. Knowing that my finances are agonizing in the midst of a stay in this country that has been prolonged over what was foreseen, Rabbi Samuel has given me a significant amount of money so that I can maintain myself and even purchase a passage on one of the ships traveling toward the country of the Ottoman Turks, from where I hope to take the path to meet up with the followers of Sabbatai Zevi, over in Palestine. May God will that I can traverse the inferno and set foot on the land promised by the Creator to the sons of Israel, to there join the troops of the Messiah and announce the renewal of the world with him. In this adventure, I know that my faith accompanies me, never diminished, and the will and ambition to reach the goals that I was taught to have by my unforgettable grandfather Benjamin, from whom I also learned that God more joyously helps the fighter than the inert . . . What my regrettable personal pettiness still will not allow me is to stop thinking about what could have been of my life, perhaps even what should have been, if after having the luck of seeing the light in what my brothers in faith considered to be *Makom*, the good place, I had also found there my space for freedom. If I had been able to place my life on the path there that the best of my soul demanded. Was what I asked for so terrible? I only trust, in the notions my mind is given to as I listen to the laments of those who flee, that my personal destiny was written long ago. Also, the announcement of the coming of the end of the world that the Anointed will bring will at least serve to make men more tolerant with the desires of other men and their freedom of choice, as long as they do not hurt their fellow man, which should be the foremost principle of the human race. And if none of my desires come true, at least I will feel consolation, as I write to you, that perhaps these words will reach your hands, and the beings of today and tomorrow will be able to have a first-person testimony of the suffering of some men and of the extremes reached by the cruelty of other men. If that knowledge arrives by some path, I will feel rewarded and know that my life has had meaning, very different from the one I thought it would have when I dreamt of paintbrushes and oils. A necessary and useful meaning, perhaps, for revealing the depths of the human condition that I've had to witness . . .

Maestro, this very day I leave for the South in search of the Messiah. I pray for the Blessed one to be with you, young Titus, and the pleasant Hendrickje, that you may always enjoy the happiness and health you deserve, as I have requested so many times in my prayers, since you are part of the dearest memories I treasure from a life that was mine and from which I now feel separated from not only by the sea . . .

Eternally indebted to you,

E.A.

His heart cringing and a feeling of unease running through his body, Conde maintained his vision fixed on those two letters finishing off the missive: *E.A.* The initials of a name. A name that identified a man, he thought. A man who had gone down to the inferno and, from there, sent his message of alarm.

The former policeman had to give himself a few minutes to continue reading that letter, which included such an extraordinary tale.

Because Elias Kaminsky then began his announced digressions and conclusions: as far as he could read, he wrote, this E.A. had been a Sephardic Jew who, fleeing Amsterdam, had ended up in Polish territories in 1648, just when it was being devastated by Cossacks and Tartars and, as he confirmed, was determined to continue his journey to the South to join the hordes of followers of that Sabbatai Zevi who, shortly after, would reveal the imposture of a mentally unstable fraud when, to save his neck, he would end up converting to Islam after having tried to overthrow the sultan of Turkey. The sultan, the story went, after imprisoning him, had known how to most easily resolve the enigma of whether Sabbatai was or was not the Messiah when he offered him two choices: "Muslim or the gallows?" To which Zevi immediately responded: "Muslim."

But the questions that the notebook had prompted among historians and art historians of Dutch painting were infinite, as one could presume. The first of these referred to the identity of that E.A., in whom converged the difficult conditions of being a Sephardic Jew and a painter, when art was anathema for the Jews. The second, of course, had to do with the origins and later fate of that *tafelet* turned junk sold at a flea market. The question followed of why only a fragment of the letter survived, addressed without any doubt to Rembrandt, as the mention of his son Titus and his then lover, Hendrickje, Hendrickje Stoffels, confirmed. And, amid many other question marks, the one that beat most loudly was the group of sketched faces in the notebook, so similar to the head of a Jew that had served as a model for Rembrandt for his studies of the heads of Christ. Studies and pieces that, just around then (coincidence or cosmic plan?), were for the first time in history being displayed together, thanks to an exhibit organized by the Louvre . . . From which the piece held in London and under litigation was missing.

Ever since Conde began to read Elias Kaminsky's missive, and more intensely after going over E.A.'s letter, the feeling of an important mystery had begun to take him over, growing as he read the last part of the text and immediately taking root in his spirit inquisitively, forcing him to read Elias Kaminsky's words over and over again, destined to show an enigmatic panorama for which, he already sensed it, it would be impossible to establish a definitive map. The image that Conde had in his head of that street market of worthless junk, open alongside a canal in Amsterdam as the city enjoyed the privilege of its spring, pushed an unforeseen desire in the man to wander around that magical place where one could find, just like that, in the middle of the street, traces of remote mysteries, no matter if they were solvable or unsolvable.

In the last part of his letter, Elias Kaminsky (perhaps pulling at his ponytail, Conde thought) fully entered speculation based on what was known and what was possible. The most striking thing for him was proof of the real existence of the Dutch Sephardic Jew E.A., who wandered around Poland in the time of the massacre of Jews, and had a relationship with painting. How many Dutch Sephardic Jews who were painting aficionados could have been in Poland at that time? Almost without a doubt, Elias stated, E.A. had been, *he had to have been*, the enigmatic character who gave three paintings and some letters to the rabbi infected with the plague and dead in Kraków, in the arms of his ancestor Moshe Kaminsky. If E.A. was that man and his "Maestro" had been Rembrandt, then that explained the fact that E.A. was in possession of the head of Christ or the portrait of a young Jew (seemingly, E.A. himself), painted and signed by Rembrandt, one of the oil paintings that Dr. Kaminsky received from the hands of the dying rabbi.

Knowing that story didn't prove anything that could help in the painting's possible recovery, Elias Kaminsky noted. But, at the same time, it proved everything and the New York lawyers would take advantage of it. And if at the end of the day it did not serve to help him recover the Rembrandt painting, it gave the ponytailed behemoth the certainty of its origins and authenticity, and ratified that the family story was true about the bizarre way that the painting had come to be the property of the Kaminskys of Kraków, three and a half centuries ago.

The other outstanding question was the existence and tribulations, nearly impossible to trace, of the *tafelet* capable of causing all of those unexpected revelations. Where had it come from, where had that notebook in which the flea market vendor had acquired with a lot of old objects left by the heirs of an old woman without the slightest interest in keeping some dusty ruins? Elias Kaminsky had a tempting response: it could have come from the boxes of Rembrandt's objects auctioned at the end of 1657, when the artist had declared bankruptcy and lost his house and almost all of his material goods. The rest of the many possible questions (who was E.A.? What had been his final fate? Why did his notebook end up, as it appeared, in Rembrandt's seized files?) would perhaps never have an answer.

Nonetheless, Elias Kaminsky had already given *his* answer to some of those questions: the young Jew too similar to the image of the Christian Jesus *had to be* E.A., he insisted, and in that way, his face, always nameless, had been the one to accompany the members of his lineage for three hundred years. Because of that, he promised, or Elias Kaminsky promised himself, he would do everything possible to recover that image, since it was the moral and blood right of his family . . . But, when the probable recovery would occur (a decision that could be influenced by Conde's discovery concerning the identity of María José Rodríguez, who had placed the painting for sale, and her relationship as the great-niece of Román Mejías), Elias would hand over the piece to a museum dedicated to the Holocaust. He simply could not and did not want to do anything else, he said, because if Ricardo Kaminsky didn't want anything to do with money coming from a possible sale, neither did he. That painting, in reality, had never served his family at all, and, just when it could have had a concrete use, it turned into the motive for a tragedy that marked the lives of his uncle Joseph and his father Daniel. "Do you think I'm a real moron for having made this decision?" Elias asked him in the final lines of his letter, to then give a quick answer: "Perhaps I am. But I am sure that, in my shoes, you would do the same, Conde. I owe it to that painting and to its real owner, E.A., dead perhaps in the lands of Poland during one of history's many anti-Semitic rages . . ." And he signed off, promising new letters, new news, and, of course, a sure return to Havana in the nearby future.

Only when he finished reading the letter for the second time did Conde return the papers to the yellow envelope. He served himself a new cup of coffee, lit another cigarette, and watched Garbage II, who had entered the house as he read, sleep peacefully. When he finished the cigarette, he stood up and went to the bookcase in the living room and took out the Rembrandt volume published several years before by Ediciones Nauta. He flipped through the pages of the book until he reached the section of illustrations and stopped on the one he was looking for. There it was, with a red shirt, brown hair close to his head, the curly beard, and the gaze fixed on the infinite, a real man portrayed by Rembrandt. For several minutes, he looked at the reproduction of the work, a close relative of the one he'd seen in the picture of Daniel Kaminsky and his mother Esther, taken in the house in Kraków before the beginning of the misadventures of that family exterminated by a hate crueler than that of the Cossacks and Tartars. As he contemplated the face of the young Jew who could now, at least, be identified by some initials and some twists in his life history, Conde felt surrounded by the greatness and the invincible influence of a creator and by the atmosphere of a mysticism that men, since the beginning of time, had needed to live. And he perceived that the miracle of that fascination capable of flying across centuries was in the eyes of that character, fixed for eternity by the invincible power of art. *Yes, everything is in the eyes,* he thought. Or perhaps in the unfathomable that lies behind the eyes?

The man dragged that question to the rooftop of his house. Like every night that season, the warm and aggressive Lenten winds marking Cuban spring had abated, as if withdrawing, in order to regain strength and pick up their exasperating battle with the arrival of the following dawn. The city, more dismal than it was tempting, extended itself toward a sea made invisible by distance and night. Behind Mario Conde's eyes, in his mind, he was seeing through the eyes of the young Jew E.A., a painter's apprentice, who died three and a half centuries before, possibly following, like so many men in so many places throughout the centuries, the trail of another self-proclaimed Messiah and Savior, capable of promising everything, only to end up revealing himself as a fraud, sick with the thirst for power, with the overwhelming passion to control other men and their minds. That story sounded too close and familiar to Conde. And he thought that perhaps, in her libertarian searches, at some point Judy Torres had been closer than many people to a devastating truth: there is no longer anything in which to believe, no Messiah to follow. It is only worth being a part of the tribe that you yourself have freely chosen. Because if there is a possibility that, had he existed, even God was dead, and the certainty that so many messiahs had ended up turning into manipulators, the only thing you have left, the only thing that really belongs to you, is your freedom of choice. To sell a painting or donate it to museum. To belong or stop belonging. To believe or not believe. Even to live or to die.

Mantilla, November 2009–March 2013

Acknowledgments

Like all my novels, this is a work to which other eyes, other intellects, many other sensibilities and assistance have decisively contributed.

As in previous years, three faithful and demanding readers have participated in the review of the different versions of the novel. Vivian Lechuga, here in Havana; Elena Zayas in Toulouse; and Lourdes Gómez, in Madrid, have made their time and energy as critics available to me, and I took full advantage of them. Likewise, my brother Alex Fleites saw himself forced to swallow many pages of the book.

During the variety of research projects carried out on the ground, and in the search for exact dates, I have found indispensable the collaboration, in Amsterdam, of my friends Sergio Acosta, Ricardo Cuadros, and Heleen Sittig, without whom I would not have had the understanding of this marvelous city; in Miami, meanwhile, my colleague Wilfredo Cancio and my old friend Miguel Vasallo, with whom I shared dreams of playing major league baseball, were my guides around Miami Beach, in search of Daniel Kaminsky's footprints, and through Miami's cemeteries, to find José Manuel Bermúdez's tombstone.

An essential and invaluable contribution to understanding the ins and outs of Jewish customs and history was provided to me by Professor Maritza Corrales, the expert on Cuba's old Jewish community; Marcos Kerbel, a Cuban Jew living in the United States, who drew for me the best map of Cuban-Jewish Miami Beach; my colleague Frank Sevilla, whose practical experience and intellectual knowledge of Judaism were critical to me; my dear Joseph Schribman, alias "Pepe," a university professor in Saint Louis, Missouri, who frequently recalled for me his childhood and adolescent experiences in Havana's Jewish community; and my old and good friend Jaime Sarusky, who was one of the engines who set this machine in motion. As for my dear fellow Stanilav Vierbov, he was the one responsible for placing in my hands the most complete and select bibliography that would allow me to understand what I could from a practical standpoint.

As on prior occasions, the reading and work discussions with my Spanish editors, Beatriz de Moura and Juan Cerezo, turned out to be saving and fortuitous, as much as their moral support, which was so necessary in the face of my hesitations. Likewise, the reading and opinions of Madame Anne Marie Métailié were decisively encouraging.

Finally, as is my habit, I would like to publicly thank Lucía López Coll, my wife, for her energies as a critic and her ability to withstand so much. Without her readings, opinions, lunches, and dinners, this book would not exist. And I don't think that I would, either.

L.P.